# ØÜR
# £ÅÐ¥

# ØÜR £ÅÐ¥

## Dale Gershwin

Mosaic Press
TORONTO PARIS NEW YORK

Canadian Cataloguing in Publication Data

Gershwin, Dale, 1950-
    Our Lady

ISBN 0-88962-692-8 (bound)    ISBN 0-88962-693-6(pbk.)

I. Title.

PS3557.E78O97 1999        813'.54    C99-9314432

No part of this book may be reproduced or transmitted in any form, by any means, electronic or mechanical, including photocopying and recording information storage and retrival systems, without permission in writing from the publisher, except by a reviewer who may quote brief passages in a review.

Published by MOSAIC PRESS, P.O. Box 1032, Oakville, Ontario, L6J 5E9, Canada. Offices and warehouse at 1252 Speers Road, Units #1&2, Oakville, Ontario, L6L 5N9, Canada and Mosaic Press, 85 River Rock Drive, Suite 202, Buffalo, N.Y., 14207, USA.

Mosaic Press acknowledges the assistance of the Canada Council, the Ontario Arts Council and the Dept. of Canadian Heritage, Government of Canada, for their support of our publishing programme.

Copyright © Dale Gershwin, 1999

Book Design by Amy Land
Cover Design by Lindsay Burger
Cover Painting by Ralph Petty
Printed and bound in Canada
ISBN 0-88962-693-6

**In Canada:**
MOSAIC PRESS, 1252 Speers Road, Units #1&2, Oakville, Ontario, L6L 5N9, Canada. P.O. Box 1032, Oakville, Ontario, L6L 5N9

**In the United States:**
MOSAIC PRESS, 85 River Rock Drive, Suite 202, Buffalo, N.Y., 14207

*To my Ira.*
*May the little blue record-player spin forever…*

# Table of Contents

• • • •

| | | |
|---|---|---|
| I. | The Lion and the Pussy | 1 |
| II. | Plato's Television Set | 17 |
| III. | Napoleon's Anchovy | 37 |
| IV. | The Japanese Monk With the Pot on His Wall | 57 |
| V. | His Majesty's Basketball Team | 72 |
| VI. | The Stars on the Ceiling | 97 |
| VII. | Kilometer Zero | 129 |
| VIII. | A Wailing, Howling Belch Begging for Relief in the Ice-White Insulated Death-Silent Dawn | 162 |
| IX. | Little Crystal Old Ladies With Gift-Wrapped Pastries in Their Hands | 187 |
| X. | The Toaster-Oven | 198 |
| XI. | The Shiitake Mushrooms | 240 |
| XII. | Screaming-Chartreuse-Matthew June | 264 |
| XIII. | The Belle Epoque Curlicue Metal *Métro* Sign | 301 |
| XIV. | The Eunuch-Sorcerer | 315 |
| XV. | The Boat-Ghosts | 339 |
| XVI. | "Thank you, Chan. That will be all." | 367 |
| XVII. | The Seven Deadly Goldfish | 383 |
| XVIII. | 1193.66 Kilometers Per Word (Or 1074.30, Depending on How You Count) | 406 |
| XIX. | The Waistband of Martin's Undershorts | 431 |
| XX. | "SSSHHHH! "SSHH!" "Sh!-sh!-sh!-sh!" | 452 |
| XXI. | The Moon Walk | 456 |

# I
# The £ion And The Pussy

A young woman in a navy-blue business suit and white silk blouse, with a handbag and weathered leather satchel slung over her shoulder and a *pain au chocolat* in her hand, enters her car then her compartment, immediately closing the sliding glass door. She lowers it's shade to the floor, as if being pursued and needing to prevent everyone passing through the corridor from seeing in. From coming in. From even knowing there's a compartment there not to see or enter.

After taking her notebook, Walkman and cassettes out of the satchel she heaves it onto the overhead rack. She leaves her medium-heeled navy pumps on the charcoal-gray carpet and lies along the red-velvet *banquette*, her head against the window, her *pain au chocolat* in its napkin by her knee. She looks at her watch ("six thirty-nine") and at the covered compartment door. Props her handbag as a pillow, shifts down the seat to lie flatter. Closes her eyes. If there is no one in the compartment when she shows up, chances are she can hold on to it, keep the neighbors out through a force field forged from ritual and pieces of thought.

She folds her hands on her stomach, focusing on the fact that the only way she's going to get to Paris is to live in total isolation for the next one hundred ninety minutes. Total isolation will deliver her as through a chute as through a pourspout as through a birth canal to her apartment door. She translates her awareness of the train into an awareness of a birth canal with it's multichannel trainbeat with its multitracked heartbeat and the protective rhythmic rocking which will pulse her through, and out the other end. Then she concentrates on all the people passing in the corridor and actively avoiding entering her compartment—all the train personnel all the passengers who have reservation cards bearing everything other than the numbers on any of the seats in proximity to hers all the sobbing retinue of Gallic weekenders returning to post-mussels-n-fries reality.

But she admits that total isolation is nowhere near sufficient. It is selfish and small, she should know better! On total isolation she might barely make it out of Brussels, up the path, to the yard with the yellow and slate-gray graffiti on the high walls near the junk. Then the force field will lose power unless all of civilization is interlinked by traintracks and goes to Paris in total isolation with her. She engages and empowers every being one by one with the wisdom of a train and rests them each, eyes closed, totally isolated, in a compartment of their own. The compartment where she lies fills with the total isolation of the billions of compartments where each aloneness takes a voyager to an end. Then she concentrates on all the people passing in the corridor and actively avoiding entering her space. She hears the presence of decisions not to enter. She hears the feet and the voices, shoulders, hands which cannot pierce the force field. The will which will not pierce the force field. She inhales slowly and deeply, her hands riding the gentle rise of her stomach, and exhales in increments, guiding the air out through pursed lips.

Now she takes her force field away with her, magnifies her force field and spreads it, to put every passenger onto every train and protect them in their single spaces at that spark of instant everywhere. She crosses continents with her force field, she carries vegetables and bandages, words, livestock, labor, hugs, electoral college votes, escaped prisoners, heat, tools, pilgrims, each unit sealed inside an inviolate privacy which she replicates from her own compartment here and now. And now she concentrates on all the people passing in the corridor and actively avoiding entering her privacy and all the people who have reservations for the very seats across which she is lying and the very seats facing those seats but who at this second are stopping for the redlight the phonecall the emergency up in the third-floor fuse box which will be responsible for their missing the train. She is lying in a compartment with five people who have missed the train.

Finally she empties her head. Packs up her pieces of thought and throws them through the window onto the welcoming track. She has instructed the images which now must work for her. On her red-velvet *banquette* she allows the details of the day to return, like members of an audience filing into a theater, taking one seat after another until the hall is filled. She feels her thigh pressing against the Walkman and thinks about doing some Doors. She hears a train straining in, remembers the *pain au chocolat*, doesn't want it now. Opens her eyes. Looks around the compartment. Closes them. Opens her eyes. Looks at her watch. ("seven minutes to lift-off")

Sitting up, her legs still stretched along the *banquette*, she wedges herself into the corner by the wood-framed window, excited by the race that's pitting her, and the potence of the force field and the authority of the emergency up in the third-floor fuse box, against the unconditionality of time. Through the window she watches the platform, as if the battle is being played out right there on top of the huge blue metal luggage-dolly. Time won't ("fuck around! It'll either let the unwashed jokers in") or it won't. In ("fouourrr minutes we place our flag on the moon! fouourrr... three and three qu.....ohh frchri shihihttttt!"). The compartment door ("I lost!") opens. At least it (" 's a guy...... Shii-IITT!") In abrupt bits of movement she snatches the Walkman from the middle of the *banquette*. Shakes ("at least it's *one* guy") a tape out of its case. Hurls the case onto the floor near her shoes. Shoves the tape into the player. Slaps the headset into her ("three hours and ten fucking m ") ears. The train begins to buck and hum. She turns to the luggage dolly. It's not there any more. Looks at her watch. There's one minute left for him to slap his palm against his forehead and remember he left the cover off the fuse box. Jim Morrison is trying to take her to Texas. The train bucks and lurches out of its Virginia swamp and throws her and Jim off balance as they get ("a-gain!") up to close the compartment (" damage down to a goddamn minimum's all we can do n ") door. ("frchrii-iisayyyyykes!")

"*Ce train*," the walls announce, "*à destination de Paris,* will serve the following stations:" She wonders why they always wait until it's way too late for you to—she decides not to make eyecontact ever with whoever's attached to the brown laceup shoes and jeans-coated knees on the *banquette* across the compartment she hears a newspaper open "*et la Gare du Nord à Paris.*" Just about to tell the loudspeaker how much its information has meant to her, she reasons that if the shoes and jeans don't hear her voice they won't know she's there. Instead she reaches for the napkin, breaks open the *pain au chocolat*, starts picking the *chocolat* from the *pain*. The train is inching past the tops of fleamarket stalls at the southern end of the city. The Royal Palace looks like a paper-maché movie set. Morrison is alone on stage in the dust of a spotlight-she hears the newspaper-he is whispering poetry in an open shirt-and people softly laughing as they walk past in the corridor she stiffens until they go away-into a microphone squeezed in his hand and stuffed in his mouth she scoops a chocolate filament from the flaky dough and slowly lifts it into her mouth keeping her index finger between her lips between her teeth between her lips ingesting Jim sucking her finger, "Come live with us in forests of azure," the maidens say to Morrison, rocking with the tracks, feeding on the *chocolat*, rocking with the tracks, her head lifts, she flashes on an armrest, she's looking across the compartment, she hears the newspaper, focuses, she is looking into the eyes of the guy on the *banquette* opposite hers.

She snaps away. And stares out the window where the foliage has changed from pipes and bricks and wrinkled train cars making Christmas decorations in a nursing home to tall graceful grass bending back toward Brussels. They've been pulling strugglingly out of the station since pulling strugglingly out of the station. Swallowing the last of the dough, she grabs her day-old *Herald Tribune*—lifts her eyes—he's looking at her. ("Olympicsr gonna be great this y ") Mary Blume's article about the demise of the Paris cafe. The napkin slides off her thighs onto the floor she stops herself from following it with her gaze. He'd had *Le Monde* ("Socialist pi ")—up in front of his chest but not of his eyes. He was wearing a denim shirt and a dark sportcoat—not sure what color, maybe some kind of brown, maybe tweed, maybe brown—she peers across the top of her page—he has relaxed into the back of his *banquette*—legs crossed—open—his hands are resting one atop the other on his groin—he's looking at her—he's not reading his paper.

Strategy all wrong. If you think about getting sick you get sick. If you think about flunking the law boards you flunk the law boards, if you think you're ("disturbed because some good-looking asshole's polluting your space you wind up disturbed all") the way to Paris. In a—she glances over—his jacket is a brown/rust tweed—he has alot of hair— dark hair—it's not unruly—his eyes have not moved from her—he looks calm—couple minutes he's going to get up, go out for a beer and never come back. He never will have been here. She takes off her earphones and lays the Walkman by the tape case on the floor. Finds a pen in her handbag, reaches down the *banquette* ("late forties") for her notebook ("just celebrated his fiftieth birthday"). He didn't come in with ("luggage did he? had to shave again before going out to the party it was at the *Opéra*")—he looks like he's never been to an opera in his life— he looks ("leathery. Leather-y.")—he's looking at her.

She bends her knees to her chest, fanning a puff of air between her legs, and sets the notebook before her. Presses her thighs together, tightens-relaxes her vaginal lips while making a l—corner of her eye— he's kept his right hand on his thigh and moved his left arm up across the seat back—both feet on the floor now—legs open—head slightly back—he has thick dark hair—she feels like there are handfuls of fingertips tapping lightly along her upper body and inner thighs—he's looking at her—his face is relaxed—his face is rough—making a list of what she has to do for the NATO event. She makes no list yanks the page out begins writing again writing anything ("Jeezzuss took mah hayund ayund moooved it acrawst the payuhge!"). She listens to her breaths, writes, turns her head they stop hold each other's eyes, fit into each other's eyes with a locking click..........................................................
..................................................................................................
..................................................................................................

..................................................................................................
..............................They are looking at each other numbly—even he is taken by surprise. What do we do now? Their bodies are floating out of the compartment into the southern suburbs of Brussels, across Europe, through Russia Asia the layers of space, flapping out wildly, decomposing, reconstructing, taking the shape of every object in their paths. But their eyes are fixed along a stiff cable of electric attention and are bracing their senses in place.

She thinks she sees him barely move—or—feels him barely move—across the current carried by the eyelink. He may be adjusting a bit on his seat. He lifts his pelvis so slowly and so slightly, she's sure he's not lifting it at all—maybe it's her own pelvis that's lifting, maybe that's what she's seeing ("feeling"). She feels herself getting wet against the lining of her skirt. She hasn't moved her body but to breathe. They are pushing insistently into each other's eyes. He rocks forward and stands up. She gasps. She watches him walk to the door of the compartment...........................He.........................locks it....................And comes back to his seat.

In slow floaty movements, keeping her head turned toward him and her eyes clasped into his eyes, she sets her notebook and pen onto the red velvet. He is big, solid in his stone-still silence. There is an extra-beat second which will never be counted in the passing of time when together they stop breathing. Then her breaths sneak out on the cusps of little uneven sighs. The pulsing between her legs ripples back to her buttocks and she squirms on the *banquette*, looks away for the first time since they locked in, glances at the door. Turns back to him. He nods once, lowering his eyes to his groin. Then raises and tunnels them back into hers. With one smooth sweep she swings her feet off the seat and drops to her knees between his thighs.

She holds her head downward, sitting on her heels, placing a hand on each of his calves. The denim draws her in she smells his spice for the first time. Facing the floor she gradually passes both hands in unison up his lower legs, around to the insides of his knees, out across the tops of his thighs, in again to meet at their juncture, to meet where his thighs meet. Her fingers spread and wrap around his hips, thumbs touch and press up into his crotch. Her head is still bowed she ("AHHCHCH") feels his hands on hers. Hot on her hands on his hips. Still does not look into his face. He presses down onto the span of her hands, covers, obliterates them, bores them into his body, moves them around to the front and slides them up over his cock. She looks like she's kneeling, praying, at an ancient sacred stone. Held above her head, her arms force her shoulders forward. She is oozing, heaving. He bursts bigger and harder in his jeans. She shudders—her breaths are pelting out like little stones—lifts her head. Enters his eyes. Rocks up off her heels full onto her knees. His smell is in her brain her thighs are weighted and soaked. She opens his zipper. Takes him out with both hands, he is thick, wraps both hands around him, one below the other, lowers her head, packs him into her mouth into her throat he slaps his palms onto the back of her head, rhythms his pelvis to meet her. The grunts from his guts from his throat from his groin heat her movements heat her guts she keeps him in her right hand, backs her mouth up to the head, closes her lips around the head and encircles it with her tongue and runs her tongue over its top and encircles again, in the other direction, while her voice rumbles in her chest, while she lowers her left hand to her skirt under her skirt presses caresses penetr

He pushes her away by her shoulder and forehead..........Stands, zips his pants. Weaves his fingers through her fingers, almost daintily, politely, and pulls her to her feet. She is limp, energized, limp. Energized. He is taller than she is and broad, his clean sweaty spice moving through the air as he moves through the air. Her head is raised to him. He grasps both sides of her collar and flicks it back, sending her jacket spilling down her silky blouse. She breathes before him and flashes on violence in her overheated brain, submission in her elastic body. With his left hand he catches the jacket and tosses it behind him onto the seat while his right arm wraps around her waist, turns her, directs her across the gray carpet several steps to her *banquette*. She kneels onto the red velvet, facing the mirrored wall, and raises her arms above her head to wrap her fingers into the rungs of the rack. She pays attention to fastening herself around the metal rod, bringing each finger down joint by joint hand by hand only after the last has been secured. When she looks up to check her bonds she meets her flooded face in the mirror and in the mirror sees him behind her, standing back, standing still, breathing still, watching her, his thumbs hooked into his belt..................................................................................
................................................................................
...........He bends forward—doesn't move his feet—to tap the insides of her knees with the backs of both hands. She realizes they haven't said a word, now she doesn't want them to, the silence spikes their senses and she's afraid even to think. This is the last thought she'll ("ever have. Ever in my life.") She spreads her thighs as far as her short skirt will allow.

Here he is flush behind her, his—she feels his open mouth at her neck—hands up over hers then tracing down along her arms—at her curls trussed in white satin ribbon—on top of her shoulders around her neck down her back across her sides into her waist over her hips, grazing her buttocks on the way to the hem of her skirt. He touches the hem of her skirt. Joins his hands at the front of her hem and caresses it full around to the back. Lets the fabric lightly lie between his fingers she chokes the luggagerack and pumps her pelvis back and forth foraging for contact trying to attract a touch into her heaving, to smother her heaving when no touch comes, to swallow her sounds, and the unsatisfied catlike whimpers and the satisfied rolling moans spurt out anyway, she can even hear her wetness, she c

He stops everything.

Steps completely back, waits for her to calm.

She is angrily impatient and needs to turn around to look at him direct and doesn't dare. She stares and breathes into her own fiery-pale eyes in the mirror. The coffee cart rattles outside the compartment door. The coffee man knocks. She wants him to know why there is no answer. She wants him to live and die knowing. The coffee cart rolls on and the man in the compartment has a hand on either side of her hem.

His feet on the floor and his bent knees resting on the edge of her *banquette*, between her spread thighs, he starts to lift her skirt. By millimeters, avoiding contact with her skin, by punishing millimeters he takes it up. When she reacts in the slightest—jerks her buttocks back, rolls her hip out, shakes her head, tenses a muscle in her neck, whimpers gasps shudders—he stops where he is until she is still and quiet again. Each time he stops where he is until she is still and quiet.

Now she channels all response into her labia, contractingcontracting releasingreleasing contractingreleasing contractingreleasing in pace with her bloodbeats, concentrating the intense buzzing of her network of nerves, cramming all awareness of life into the lubricated little machine she's set in motion. She wants to bring her arms down from the rungs overhead but gets the message mixed up. She holds on even tighter suddenly smells her perfume.

He lifts the skirt, uncovers the tops of her stockings fixed in clasps behind tiny navy satin bows. Taking slightly deeper breaths he nods in a slow single dip of his head. Then moves on. To where the heights of her thighs are striped by her garter belt's long elastic navy lace.

She bites her bottom lip bites and stops only when her mirrorimage floats out at her and shows her what she's contractingreleasing contractingreleasing doing she's cool at the moisture between her thighs she's flaming where he's working and at the tips of her breasts and under her knees on the velvet.

A millimeter and he allows her body to be touched. He holds the hem taut and guides it into the seam between her thighs and buttocks, sliding it back and forth, curving and pushing it progressively up so that it hints at grazing the fleshy beginnings of her cheeks. He does not know she's not wearing panties. She twitches and yelps and releases the rungs and bounces her bottom onto her heels and off and grabs on overhead again and this time he does not stop and wait he pulls the skirt back out away from her skin and continues to lift.

She thinks the compartment has shrunken. Thinks it is now the size of the space inside her head. And then she thinks it's not there anymore at all. There is only his breathing.

He lifts the skirt. He peels it back and begins the baring of her buttocks. He is moving yet more slowly than before and when he realizes she is wearing no panties, when he sees how her dark garters hug the outsides of her cheeks and, with the tops of her navy stockings and the raised hem of her navy skirt, present her white bottom to him in a frame, he controls his movement even further. She looks beyond her wild head in the mirror through to the mirror on the opposite wall, above the *banquette* where he'd sat, and watches her muscles tense and twitch and sweat as he offers her flesh to the dense compartment air, until she can watch no longer and shakes her hair like a horse and thrusts her body back begging contact with her skirttip with his body with her heels she needs to impact something her nerves are shooting up straining out sucking in anything that can touch against them and absorb the shock of their urgency then return it to its source. He takes no account of her bucking, and busies himself securing the fabric into her waistband.

Then he steps back.

She thinks he's waiting again for her to quiet. She breathes in and straightens up, brings her knees almost together then parts them once more, stretches her fingers open between the rungs above and wraps them afresh around the metal. They're stopped at a station. She rubs her head against her arm to brush some soaked hair from her face. She has no idea how long they've ("been here Holy Shit! There's no ") curtain on the window. People can see in from acro ("Holy Shit What

If Someone Has A *Seat* In Here!"). She whips her eyes away from the window, won't even glance toward the door, expects he'll start in again any second now. Her cheeks squeeze together by reflex, reminding her she's totally ("where is")............................................
..................................................................................................
.....................................................................She looks in the mirror.

He is standing before his *banquette*, the backs of his legs at the edge of the seat. Arms crossed in front of his chest, left leg slightly bent, right hip thrust out. He seems to be breathing calmly, normally. His head is tilted as if he's admiring a painting. No. As if he's analyzing a p—not exactly.............As if he's viewing a painting. As if he's viewing a painting of the buttocks which he's just exposed.

She closes her eyes to try to put out the fire. ("hssssssssss") A lion leaps across her brain and into the compartment and straight hot up between her legs. She squeezes the lion into her lips, catching it, trapping it as it fades into a million maned molecules back into her head. She needs desperately to be touched, or to be covered ("where *IS* he?!")—to be touched violently, to be brutalized, or to be covered tenderly, to be held. She doesn't want to be here anymore it isn't comfortable anymore she's too overheated she's too bare the timing's all wrong she's cooling down she can cool down she can come down she thinks of her arms above her head and her hands around the rungs and begins to—"I'm going," he informs her in a gutty exhaled French whisper close into her right ear—she starts and gasps, stiffens—"out to the corridor for a smoke." Some seconds pass, the lips and breath still on her.

"It might not be a bad idea"............his voice grows softer as his movements had grown slower. She feels exhausted from the fevered effort of hearing him............................"if I found you in this same position when I got back." She jerks in waves and cries out as if he's just hurt her, struck her—a whiny groan dispatched along the wire binding suffering to pleasure. He moves to the compartment door and turns the lock. She hears him leave. He's at her neck again,

"I'd also keep my fingers away from my pussy if I were you." breathing close. Waiting. "I'll know," he tells her, cutting the edge of his left hand along her slit from front to back, and is gone.

The young woman kneels brutalized and the young woman kneels held. She does not know how long it has been since he bared her and left the compartment but she does know she can stop this at any time, she *can* stop this. She is not attached to the rack overhead yet she has been holding on as if she were. For that very reason. She is attached by her freedom to be mastered, by whatever control she knows she has over the controller. At this moment breaking the scene is the release of a finger away. And it is not an option. And that is why he left her alone. And that is why she loves to think about all this but thinking about all this at this very time will tame the lion in the pussy she's been told not to touch. So she looks in the mirror instead and stares at the state of her sweet submission.

She does not know how long it has been since he bared her and left the compartment but she does know he'll be back. It is with her certainty of that, and with her certainty of that part of herself which calls him back, that she has bought her ticket for this visit to the other side. When he does come back he smells of smoke and his eyes are gray and burning and he leaves the compartment door open long enough for an elderly couple to pass in the corridor and wonder whether what they think they just saw was what they just saw. He removes his jacket and hangs it by the collar from the lock. She giggles, realizing the door was unlocked while he was out, then imagines the compartment packed with elderly couples, packed, vacuum-packed, elderly matched-set couples filling the field of the compartment to the scientifically maximum degree, replacing every possible pocket of air with a withering anatomical part, fitting themselves into each other's creaky contours, so that the space becomes a solid impenetrable block of elderly-couple bodies, with just a narrow margin, a selvage, left in front of her *banquette,* like the beginning of that piece of ocean around a country that doesn't belong to the country or any country but to, what is it?, international waters or something like that, she imagines them stopping their expansion in a geometrically perfect elderly-couple wall just at that self-sovereign selvage around

"AAHHCHCH!!"

he's clutching her hips his knees are on the *banquette* between hers the tips of his feet are on the floor he's ramming her grunting into her hair. She slams to him, shifts her pelvis back and up in a down and dirty angle that gets him in as deep as he can go. They're screaming together she's holding onto the rods above for both of them he rips her blouse out of her waistband and presses at her breasts under her camisole shoving along her wetness to the wall of her he slaps his lips onto her neck she shoots her shoulder up in reflex and holds his head there the salt-smell of his skin is on her skin he breaks free she throws her hair tosses it what's left of her ribbon takes off across the compartment. He's stabbing through her, rasping her ass with his bleujeaned belly, he's stabbing through her "Giveitittomegiveitomegiveittomegiveittomegiveittomegiveittomegive ittomegiveittomebabygiveittomebabydoitdoitdoitdoitdoitdoitdoitdoit yeaahhyeaahhIloveitdoitdoitIloveitttttttttttttttttttttttyeahhohhhhhhhoh ohohohohohoooooooooooooooooooooooooooooooooooooooooooooooooooo ooooooooooooooooooooooooooooooooooooooooooooooooooooooooooooooooo ooooooooooooooooooooooooooooooooooooooooooooooooooo............................................"

Sitting on her heels, her head weighted forward, she is almost totally covered, hidden, by the cocoon of his arms and shoulders. He has lain the right side of his face on her rounded back and rounded his own back so as to enwrap her even further and tighter. In the hot, airless compartment, they are breathing and perspiring into each other's vapor and pores and denim and silk. Like a modern dancer he slowly unfolds and stands, reaching again to the front of her and unbuttoning her soaked blouse. While he hangs the blouse from a hook on the opposite wall, she shoots her arms up, as a child being undressed for bedtime, so that he can slide her white satin camisole over her head. She steps off the *banquette* and out of her skirt, leaving it just where it's fallen. Just where it's fallen, in front of her, he drops to his knees. Caresses her right thigh with both hands, unfastens her stocking, slinks it down and off then holds it for some seconds up to the daylight, finally tying it in a bow around her right ankle. She smiles with puzzled amusement ("attack-dog with a sense of humor") and, answering the challenge, removes her other stocking and ties it in a bow around his neck. Naked except for her watch which she refuses to look at ("ever again"), her empty garter belt and the stocking-bow at her foot, she lies on her back along the red velvet ("zee sceeene of zee craheem") seat.

"You sure you got the right compartment?" she asks in French as he sits, facing the window, on the floor in front of her berth. He starts to stroke her cool, sweat-beady body.

"What's your name?"

"Getn a little personal there, aren'tyuh, rock n rollers? I don't go around givin my name tevery Joe I meet on a train frchrissakes!"

Ensuring that her intergalactic search for a creature whose cock and brain are of equal relative dimension will not end on this vehicle, he looks at her blankly.

"*Tu es américaine, n'est-ce pas?*"

"Was it the Herald Tribune or the Giveittomegiveittomegiveittome which gaveittoyougaveit toyougaveittoyou?"

"*Les cris du coeur viennent toujours dans la langue maternelle.*"

"What dyuh think othem Phillies?"

"What?"

"What's *your* name?"

"Xavier."

"Xavier."

"Xavier."

"Xavier?"

"Xavier!"

"Gimme A Break! No one's named Xavier! What's your name?"

"Xavier. What's the ma "

"Jeez if I'da known that, I don't know if any of this woulda "

Xavier, who's been tracing lacy little sweaty swirls across the young woman's stomach, stops abruptly and looks up. "I've never met anyone li "
"Count your blessings, Xavier! Can you imagine if you hadda go through this every time you got on a train! You'd wind up like—you know those people you read about who haven't left their who have this fear of leaving their house and haven't walked outside for like fifteen years they have groceries and everything delivered, toilet paper and pizza? It has a some kinda phobia name—Parisphobia I think

is what it is. You got a last name? Maybe there's still hope."

"Roque."

"RRRROQQQUE! I...LOVE...ITT! There *is* hope!" She pops up, kisses him on the nose then deepens her voice "Roque. Rrroqqque!" and squints under narrowing eyebrows. "ROQUE! You don't mind if I call you.....Roque...do you?" she rasps through what she thinks is a squared jaw.

Roque lays his right palm between her breasts, heel first, slowly and meticulously as if trying to match it to an outline of a palm already there. With the concentration and solemnity of a tribal healer transferring energies, of a magician smoothing the way for the workings of a spell, he grazes his big hand over her chest as he raises the other to his face and reads from the passport he's just lifted from her handbag. "Brittain. Leslie Marsha. Born in nineteen fifty n "

Leslie whips up and snatches " The Fuck Are You Doing?" the passport away from him, pitching it and the handbag down the *banquette* toward her feet. "No One Does That To Me Whatrya Some Kinda Con?"

"No," he says calmly, trying to nudge her back to where she was lying. He resumes the corporal conjury where he left off. "I'm some kinda cop."

"Oh-ho-oh, Hel-*lo* Of-fi-*cer*! You got one helluva interrogation technique there, sports fan. You oughta offer it at the Academy, enrolment'd go through the r—now I see why you have such an overdevelopped sense of huMAAAAAACH!" Moving on to his pulling-the-tablecloth-out-from-under-the-dishes number, the magician has stood up, placed both forearms under Leslie and rolled her onto her stomach, partly to stop her flying arms from flailing further in his face. Partly so he can caress her ("zee sceeene of zee craheem") buttocks. She lays her head on her folded hands for an instant then bounces up onto an elbow, grabbing Roque's wrist from behind her and zooming into his dark face. "No.One.Does.That.To.Me. You.Got.It?"

With his free hand, Roque continues to caress. They both look toward the rattling on the other side of the door. Then back at each other.

"S a n d w i c h - m a n!"

they declare in unison.
"S a n d w i c h - p e r s o n!"

"Want something?" Roque asks, jumping to his feet and reaching into his pocket.

"What I want, you don't find in an SNCF snack-cart." Leslie glances at her watch by reflex and remembers "SHIT!" that she doesn't want to glance at her watch. "I'll take a fake chocolate chip fake cookie and hot—that's hot—that's.....how do I put thisss..............OK! I have it! Here it is—you ready?: hot—tea with milk. Tell the guy if it's not hot you'll arrest him. Or you can ask him in and I'll tell him."

"You're kidding. Right?" He points both index fingers at her.

"Yeah. What I meant was, or I can go *out* ntell him."

Roque squeezes discretely through the inched-open door ("prude!") and comes back with "a whole lotta food goin on there, Roque—what, dya wanna impress me with your purchase powOhh-hoo Nohh-hoo!" Leslie starts snickering, jabbing her index finger toward his throat.

"I'm hungry, what dyou w"

Like a mother whose kid just said the wrong line during the school Christmas play, she covers her eyes and shakes her head. "You know *what*?"

He drops two croissants two *pains aux raisins* tea coffee four packs of cookies two napkins four packs of sugar four creamers two stirrers four apples and four oranges at his little homestead by the *banquette*..........looking at Leslie..........after each item..........hits the ground ..........waiting..........for her to tell him.........."WHATT, for the love oGod?"..........as she slips off the seat..........onto her toes..........putting her hands at his shoulders..........and her lips to his ear..................................................................................................."You still have my stocking tied around your neck. Cop!AACHSHIT!" He ducks the flail, bends her at the waist, "AHWAITSHITT!" delivers a run of ringing smacks to her "WAITWAIT! WAIT!—WE GOTTA CALL THE OLD COUPLE BACK IN HEEERESHITT, RO-OQUE!" bottom.

"*Bon appétit!*" he wishes as he sits cross-legged amidst the litter of their snack.

Leslie sits cross-legged on the *banquette* and reaches down for her cup. "So where do you do your cop-biz? This tea "

"It's as hot as it's going to get, Leslie."
"The tea or the cop-biz?"

"Quai des Orfèvres."

"*Ooohh-ooh*, Pee Dee Aitch Cue! I run past there every morning! You one othe guys in the guardbooth? I know you're not one othe *gals* in the guardbooth."

"You run?"

"Yeah, practicing for my big get-away. So which one oyou guys is in bed with the terrorist gang?" The napkin Roque hands Leslie falls to the floor before she can take it.

"You live in Paris, Leslie?"

"Actually, I live in San Francisco," she says, picking up the napkin and spreading it with mock prissiness across her pussy. "But I come to Paris every morning to run. So which one of you guys is in bed with the terrorist gang?"

"Now I *know* you're kidding."

"You're right. San Francisco would be a ridiculous place to live if I wanted to come to Paris every morning to run. Bangladesh. Bangladesh is the real answer. Many more direct flights. What kinda cookiesdjyuh get? More leg-room, too."

"Chocolate-chip and butter. When can I see you again?"

"I think retaining our status as nameless faceless strangers in the train car carries with it a lot of real advantages. So which one oyou guys is in bed with the terrorist gang?"
"We're not nameless or faceless anymore. I want to see you again. In Paris."
"That's not my real passport. That's a decoy I keep in my handbag for the odd post-seduction-scene-in-the-train chatter. I'll tell you what—it's—lemme see your watch—almost nine—God it took a long time to play our game, didn't it?—we have a little over sixty quality minutes left together—which is about twenty times what most golden-anniversary celebrants can boast for their entire life on Earth with

each other. Let's make every minute count, Roque..." She leans down to stroke his hair gently. Softening her voice and eyes, she coos "...and talk about which one oyou guys is in bed with the terrorist gang."

"There's an investigation........t's all I kncan tell you." Roque rises to his knees, grabs the back of Leslie's neck and kisses hard and long into her mouth. He holds her head lightly between his hands, looking at her with caution, almost despondency, as if she's already loved-and-left him................*"Leslie!"*

*"Yes,,,,,! Xavier?????!"* she exhales like an escapee from daytime television, her soap-operatic eyes wide and batting.

"Where will you be tomor—toda—for the rest of today?"

"We can tell our grandchildren we met on a train where you did glorious things to my body."

"Leslie for the love of God get serious!"

"Well You're The Cop Frchrissake! You An Investigator? Investigate! If You Wanna Find Me Badly Enough You'll Find Me!"

## II

# Plato's Television Set

("woman...LA woman.....LA woman Sunday aftern") "Ohh ma petita colomba!" Leslie's compact Italian *concierge* is leaning out the window of his spartan *loge*, stretching his torso and open arms as far as possible into the passageway without having to follow them headfirst onto the concrete. He has it down to a science, starting his incantations, as if on an electric timer, just as Leslie rounds into view, his annoying Italo-Anglo-French jumble wholly unintelligible to most native speakers of any of the three. Seen from up at the large avenue at one end, or the hustling market-stalls street at the other, he looks almost charming—as if about to break into a serenade. Which serenade will cause all the surrounding shutters to fly open. Through which shutters all the neighbors, in colorful nightwear, will thrust their beaming heads and join him in glorious refrain. Which glory will lead to a general stoppage of commercial, scholastic and administrative activity in the *passage*. Which general stoppage will spread through the *quartier*. Then through the *arrondissement*. Then through the Rive Gauche. Then the city, the suburbs, the country, the continent, the planet, so that the entire global count of living things, in colorful nightwear and loden-green wool tweed caps—replicas of the one Umberto Darotto has not removed since it replaced his helmet at the end of World War II—can devote themselves to experiencing the festival.

But it only takes a couple more yards for reality to kick in.

"Ma petita colomba! How bella she eesa, my piccola colomba! Ohoo-ooo-ooo! Tu es inna sécurité! Petita colomba, ohoo-ooo-ooo, tu es inna vita! Ce matin whenna je no see youa, je was inquiet. Tu wanna Umberto hellpa con le sac? Ohoo, tu es inna vita, colomba! How eesa il papa? Il cumma encore per Noël?"

(".....drive through your suburrrrbs...into your")"bloo-oozz...into your bl*Noël*'s eight months away, Il Duce, get real! We don't even have the plastic grass all put away yet!" Leslie chooses the comfortable familiarity of English as the vehicle for her parallel monologues with Mr. Darotto.

"Colomba Mia!" As she enters the building, Mr. D. disappears from the window facing the *passage* and

"This just in from the front, Duce: I'm on the clock here."

pops out of the *loge* door opposite the mailboxes in the hallway. "Il cumma encore per Noël, colomba?"     Just in time.

A tall emaciated old man in pajamas wanders out of his apartment and asks if today is Sunday.

"You know I can't come out n play when I'm in a hurry, donchya Dooch?" Leslie breezes past, head straight front as if talking to herself.

"Je makea souppa, je makea souppa per ma petita c "

"If I stop and talk to you when I'm outa here," she says to the heavy wine-wooden door as she strides through to the courtyard, "I'll catch high-tension wires and die and you won't be able to talk to me anymore when I come in from "

"Listen ignore him." Italian as well, and half a body taller than her husband, Mrs. D. is moving methodically among little grouping of different-sized terra cotta pots along the courtyard walls.  The plants look like they're at a cocktail party, a chic clique at the bottom of the stairs huddling together, catching up on news-n-views, eyeing that new stubby crowd standing over by the drain grate near the door. With a huge red plastic watering can, Mrs. Darotto goes around freshening drinks. Every several spoutfuls she takes a small white towel from the pocket of her flowered-cotton housedress and dabs around the rim of the pots, as if sopping applesauce from a toddler's chin.

In France, Mrs. Darotto holds her conversations in French.

"...or is it tell-tale dandruff? I always get them confused. You know I try to be polite to him but it's just "

"Sh! - sh! - sh! - sh!" Mrs. D. jabs the side of her index finger against her pursed lips and whisks Leslie over to the staircase. "Listen if he knows y're still down here we'll never get r "

"Are we rid of him now?" From her satchel Leslie fishes a gold-wrapped box of Belgian chocolates and presents it with outstretched arms and a schoolgirl smile. "Thanks for forwarding the faxes. Maybe he can put a couple pieces in his soup—I'm told the pralines go especially well with leek."

Mrs. Darotto looks at the gift tag. "Now he'll know where ywere."

"Why? Where dhe think I was?"

"Listen I told him you were on a special government mission in Washington."

"And you and James Baker were the only ones on Earth who knew. You *know* he didn't even know I was away!"

"That's cause he thought I was lying to him."

"You *were*."

"Listen how was the trip? Did yget rich? Did ymeet anyone on the train? Why's your suit so creased?"

"No rain after all—just like you said! How do you do it?"

"Ain't me. Horoscope. Listen what'r'yuh stoppin and talkin when y're in a hurry for? Get upstairs!"

"You should go on television with that shit!"

"Y're outa fax paper."

"Course you'd hafta lose a coupllluhhh..." Patting herself on the hips, Leslie starts up the steps.
"Listen You're Outa Fax Paper!"............................................
...................................................................................................
.........................................................."FEEL FREE "
"OOOOOH-MAMM!" Mrs. D. jumps, and waters her shoes, as Leslie suddenly reappears in the courtyard.
" to stop up any time othe day or night to check if I'm outa fax paper or not, OK?"

As soon as Leslie slides paper in ("I see your hair is burr-rnin..."), the machine on the dresser starts its secretions ("hills are filled with fi-ire...."), not stopping until she's put water up to boil ("Drivin down your free-eeways...."), changed into a big gray Euro-Disney Mickey sweatshirt and white shiny tights, and brought her Prague Marathon mug of Earl Gray tea/cream/honey from the kitchenette past the dinette table in the living room into the bedroom-alcove. Kicking the little photosensitive scrolls out from underfoot, she sits on the edge of the bed ("LA woman Sunday afternooooon......") and pounds the playback button on her answering machine.

"HELLO! LESLIE! THIS IS JACK KOTE! MONDAY, MAY ELEVEN! SEVEN NINE AM! I'M CALLING FROM MY CAR ON THE WAY TO THE AIRPORT! WHAT, Y'OUT RUNNING ALREADY IN THE MEAN-STREETS OF PARIS? LOOK! IF YOU CAN BE IN LONDON NEXT MONDAY—MAY EIGHTEEN—I HAVE A GREAT JOB FOR YOU! IT'S PERFECT FOR YOU! SOME BANK PEOPLE WANT TO DO THIS BIG THING—THIS HUGE...AWARDS DINNER OR SOMETHING—BE HELD AT ONE OF MY PROPERTIES—I SAID MY LORD, I HAVE THE PERFECT GIRL! THEY WANT TV—THEY GOTTA HAVE TV! YOU BE HERE ON EIGHTEEN YOU GET THE WHOLE PARTY! I'LL BE IN MARBELLA TONIGHT BEFORE I LEAVE FOR THE ORIENT—BACK SUNDAY—CALL ME OR CALL CHARLOTTE SHE'LL BRIEF YOU SHE'LL FAX YOU! I'LL TALK TO YOU! BY THE WAY, WHAT'S THAT ON YOUR MESSAGE, THE DOORS? MY LORD!" *BeeeeeeeeeeeeeP*****BeeeeeeeeeeeeeP*****

"STILL IN MY CAR! SEVEN SEVENTEEN! AT THIS MEETING—IT'S AT NAT WEST HQ—CHARLOTTE WILL TELL YOU—I'D KEEP A LID ON YOUR SMART-ASS REMARKS. THESE GUYS ARE—WELL NOT EVERYONE THINKS YOU'RE FUNNY, LESLIE! I'LL TALK TO YOU!" *BeeeeeeeeeeeeeP* ("Well *I* don't think *they're* funny, either!) *BeeeeeeeeeeeeeP* (" 'll show them funny....wear my *ben-wa* balls frchrissakes!") *BeeeeeeeeeeeeeP* "Excuse me, Ms. Brittain? Ms. Brittain?" Leslie says in a boardroom voice. "Someone just asked you a question. / Oh pardon me, sir," she answers herself sweetly, "I must've been busy contracting my vaginal walls so my ben-wa balls could "

"HELLO LESLIE, DEAR! I CAN'T SLEEP SO I THOUGHT I'D CALL TO SAY HELLO. YOU MUST BE JOGGING, DEAR. I HOPE YOU'RE WATCHING OUT FOR CARS. DID YOU GET MY PACKAGE? I HOPE YOU GOT MY PACKAGE. I HEARD ON THE NEWS TONIGHT THEY FINALLY CAUGHT THOSE BOYS WHO KEEP SETTING THOSE BOMBS OVER THERE AND LOCKED THEM UP! I DO WISH YOU'D COME TO YOUR SEN " *BeeeeeeeeeeeeeP*****BeeeeeeeeeeeeeP*****

("never saw a womannn so alo-one...so alone, yeh..........so alo-one...............")

```
DATE: Sun May 10, 1992 9:49 pm
FROM: Danney-the Great-Brittain / uk@netcom.com
TO:   L.M. Brittain * International Relations
Inc. / iri@mail.fr
SUBJECT: Sahara you?
MESSAGE:  Well that's it!  Can't back out now!
Consider it announced! On Fri's show all I had
to say was: "June twenty-sixth—my sister Leslie
will fly in di-rect from Paris France expressly
to do the Doubly-Great-Brittains-in-the-Morn-
ing-Show right here on WDVQ FM" & them fones
started ringin off the console.  The station's
even cutting a promo—it's big shit around here—
can't back out now!  Sent a new tape shipment
today—all last mo's shows. Hey—Chris Eton wants
to kno if it's against the law there to listen
to an *American* radio show on a *Japanese*
Walkman when running on *French* soil. Catchyuh
later!  Cosmological love!
```

```
DATE: Mon May 11, 1992    11:16 am
FROM: L.M. Brittain * International Relations
Inc. / iri@mail.fr
TO: Danney—the Great—Brittain / uk@netcom.com
REPLY TO: Sahara you?
MESSAGE: Scared this morning! No e-mail at 5a.m.
when I checked from the hotel!  Then here it
miraculously is.  But markd w/last nite's time/
date—should've been there all along.  Wierd shit!
& in-box said I had 1.  Anyway, great re phones
& promo! One of my greatest runs yesterday be-
fore leaving for Brussels—there's a light that
shines over Paris & particularly the 6th
arrondissement that shines over nowhere else on
Earth.  Tell Chris my Walkperson's made in Ger-
many so it's ok.   Later.  CosmoLove!
```

    Leslie jumps into red cotton shorts to match Mickey's and Nike 180s too ragged to run in. Freeing her huge shoulder-length auburn curls from their rubberband as she shoots down the courtyard stairs ("on through to the other side break on through to the other side break on thr"), she has just enough time to snatch the mail and paper, hook a right through the open front door, sprint past an idling black Peugeot 405 to the market end of the *passage* and slip into her booth at Chez Georges—before her perfume makes it from the hallway through the olfactory war-zone in Mr. Darotto's kitchen into his nose all the way to his mouth via his diminutive brain:

"Petita colomba?.........."

"Is today Friday?"

"Thursday!"

*"Un - Thé - Au - Lait?"* Georges bellows from behind his brass bar while setting a draft beer on a cardboard coaster in front of a workman. Leslie always thinks Georges should be out either plowing in some Steinbeckian field or fucking in some D.H. Lawrencian barn. All this glassware and mirrored shine will bring shame upon his earthy head some day.

*"Un - Thé - Au - Lait!"* She matches his cadence and pitch and opens an envelope. When she doesn't hear the hiss of steamy water and the rattle of a tiny teapot-lid she looks up. Georges is moving his bulk out around the bar and over to her booth with the grim, deliberate focus of an arms negotiator on his way to averting an international catastrophe.

"*Mademoiselle* Lessslieeee.....whenn eess eet zat...?"

"It's OK, Georges. You can speak French."

His thick left thigh presses against the table while his heavy hands roll a big rancid dishcloth into and out of a ball. " whenn eess eet zat...?"

"You can speak French, Georges." Leslie rips the envelope and its contents in half and starts in on another.

"Whenn eess eet zat *Mademoiselle* Lessslieeee comme ssee mee upp zee staihrs?"

"When was the last time you got laid, Georges? Can I have my breakfast?" She reaches over, plucks a pen from his shirtpocket and starts filling out a questionnaire she's just opened. Georges bellows Leslie's order back to a woman buttering *baguette* halves at the end of the bar closest to the kitchen. "And a napkin. Please."

*"EH MAUDE! ET UNE SERVIETTE, HEH? FAIT VITE!"*

"Bonjour, madame! Georges here was just telling me how attractive he still finds you after all these years." Maude wipes her painfully plain face with the greasy towel attached to her apron. Her face looks like it was created as a place to temporarily store a couple eyes, a nose and a mouth until they could be delivered to the various people for whom they were originally made. A kind of surrogate face, with no biological or even emotional connection to the features it carries around on it. She bolts back to her *baguettes*. "You got a real jewel there, Georges. Take care of that woman!"

"*Mademoiselle* Leslieeee.....Forh whaht you nott comme ssee mee?"

"Georges.....sit down." Georges works his thigh deeper into the tablemolecules, staring down at Leslie as she finishes the questionnaire and opens her paper to the sports page. "Sit down, Georges. Olympicsr gonna be great this year, huh?" Sliding the top sliver of his bloated buttocks along the maroon-vinyl *banquette*, he wedges himself into the booth, the rest of the entire lower half of his body dangling forward almost to the floor. Like a schoolboy about to hear a marvelous tale, he leans over his crossed arms on the table.

"Just checking, Georges: this the first time you ever asked me that question?" Georges shakes his head with seriousness bordering on fear. The place is packed and smoky and noisy now and Maude the jewel is trying to be out taking care of the clientele and back crouching into her corner at the same time. "I'd like some more tea, please."

*"EH MAUDE! ENCORE DU THE!"*

"Well here's the answer anywMY-YY GAH-AHDDD!" The stream of Georges's marvelous tale is shattered by the sound of Maude, pressured by the exigiencies of her tea-bringing duties, transforming her burden into hundreds of tiny porcelain pieces on the black-and-white-tiled floor. "Forget the tea, Georges." Leslie hands his pen back.

*"EH MAUDE! LAISSE TOMBER!"*

"I gotta go, anyway." She sips what's left in her cup and starts gathering her things. "Why I don't come see you, Georges—and by that I take you to mean why I don't come *fuck* you?" Georges looks like a cardboard replica of himself—the kind you get photographed with on the Boardwalk so the folks back home think you've spent the afternoon with Ronald Reagan or Elvis Presley—staring straight ahead with a smile laser-printed onto his laminated face. Leslie looks at her watch. "Sport-fucking, Georges—gotta be careful not to fall for the guy.....too messy, yknow what I mean? Risk's too high with you and me. I'll take my check now."

"*EH MAUDE! L'ADDITION! VITE-VITE!*"

Whistling while she works, Leslie rips an article out of her paper.

## TERRORIST GANG SUSPECTS ARRESTED IN PARIS AFTER VIOLENT SHOOT-OUT
Police officer and 3 youths die, many hospitalized
Investigation into police force
accomplices intensifies

Maude sends the folded check over in a saucer with a potato-delivery boy on his way out. Georges goes to reach for it. Leslie slaps down a 50-franc bill. Pinning and squeezing his fleshy fingers, she leans forward into his space, whispers "Buy Maude a new apron...or combs for her hair—I always get them confused." then slips out of the booth. He removes and replaces the cap of the pen with quick little stingy stabs.

"THIS JUST IN FROM THE FRONT, DOOCH: DON'T EVEN THINK ABOUT IT!......................................................................................
..................................................................THURSDAY!"

"BONJOUR, PRINCESSE! C'EST GILLES. I WON'T BE ABLE TO COME OVER TONIGHT AFTER ALL BECAUSE ROSALIE WOKE UP WITH A COLD AND" She recites along in a sing-song. "MADAME SAUSSON IS IN LILLE VISITING HER SISTER AND NATHALIE HAS TO GO TO HER AEROBICS CLASS
    **"Madame Sausson is in Lille visiting her sister and Nathalie has to go to her aerobics class**
AND THERE'S NO ONE TO STAY WITH THE LITTLE ONE. LET'S COUNT ON

TOMORROW. I'LL CALL **and there's no one to stay with the little fucker."** YOU LATER. BIG KISS." \*BeeeeeeeeeeeeeP\*\*\*\*\*BeeeeeeeeeeeeeP\*\*\*\*\*

"LESLIE! NAN FROM THE AMERICAN BUSINESS CLUB! HEY YOU CHANGED THE MUSIC ON YOUR TAPE—LET ME SLEEP ALL NIGHT IN *YOUR* SOUL KITCHEN, TOO! HEY THERE'S THIS CUTE KID WHO'S LOOKING FOR AN INTERNSHIP—WANT IM? WE DON'T HAVE ROOM FOR IM. HE'S CUTE NAME'S PATRICK TRUCORE AND I THINK HE HA—A LITTLE SHY BUT I THINK HE HAS HALF A BRAIN (NOT LIKE YOU KNOW WHO—WANNA TRADE?). LEMME KNOW. HE'S IN PARIS TIL JULY. MAYBE I'LL FAX YOU HIS RESUME. SEE YON THE TWENTY-FIRST! BYE! NO! AM I ON JUPITER OR WHAT?—I'LL SEE YAT THE BARBARA FRANKLIN LUNCHEON TODAY—SCREW IT I'LL FAX IT ANYWAY BYE!"
\*BeeeeeeeeeeeP\*\*\*\*BeeeeeeeeeeeP\*\*\*\*

"IT'S JUST ME, CALLING UP FOR A LITTLE PHONE-SEX…WELL…I'LL SEE YOU AT THE FRANKLIN L "

"HI YEAH I'M HERE I'm Here no you won't!"

"You know what happens to naughty little girls who screen their calls?"
"Yeah, their conversations-with-jerks quotient hits an all-time low am *I* glad you called I was just literally this instant just gonna call y "

"I won't what?"

"See me at the Franklin lunch."

"You're not going?"

"*You're* not going."

"Well, thank God you called, Leslie, here all along I thought I was going—then I would've shown up and found out I wasn't there."
"I didn't call—*you* called—I was *gonna* call. Here's the scoop: We hang up, you put all your magazines and videos back in their brown-paper wrappers, we disguise ourselves like business-humanoids, meet at the Intercontinental, *make like* we're going to the lunch— you know, have a drink, ask a couple people if they gotta loada that article today in the Trib about those nasty GATT-talks—we won't even stand next to each other, we'll work different ends othe room—

then, when everyone's filing the fuck in to sit at their little round tables of eight and look like they wouldn't rather be in some high-walled garden somewhere debauching their asses off—just before hosts of nameless, faceless, disembodied white gloves start insidiously inserting smoked salmon into our lives—we slip out and walk over to the Ritz and sit by Hemingway's bust in the bar and you tell me about the shoot-out. K? Good! We're doin this thing! Seeyuh there! Bye!"

"LESLIEISWEARTOGODYOUHANGUPNOWANDI "

"And you what?"

"I *gotta* go to that lunch, I *paid* for it."

"If you ever drop out of consulting, Martin, you can give seminars on priority setting."
"You're a Board member, you think you could get me my money back? "

"High-level seminars."

"If you want to know about the sh "

"To an elite group of hand-chosen vict "

" shoot-out the last thing you want to do is not go—everyone there'll be talking about it!"
"You know about *hand*-choosing, donchya, Martin?.....Martin!.....I don't want.....*everyone*..... I want.....*you*!"
"Don't You Wish! You know, this conversation wouldn't even be taking place if you "
"If you took the time to read the articles and interviews instead of just looking at the pictures—you'd never've even picked up the phone frchrissakes you'd still be on the first p "

"If you had a television."

"What does that have to do with *anything*, Martin?"

"How can someone who does what you do not have a television? How the fuck do you know what's going on?"
"That's why God invented my pal Martin Finger for! Besides,

Thomas Jefferson seems to have pulled through pretty OK without a television. He, like I, had better things to do with his disposable hours tha "

"Like fuck the Camerounian maintenance-man in the sauna at the gym."

"And Plato."

"You fucked Plato?"

"No—Thomas Jefferson fucked Plato. And Christ. No one's public relations skills were more in demand than Christ's—Christ!, he opened up branches all over the goddamn globe!"

"Cumawn if he was alive today he'd have his own network!"

"He already does, Martin, cumawwn, gimme a break, will ya? we're doin this thing, right?"
"You know, with a television, one can take advantage of all the fine offerings of life. Like ballets and old farces and documentaries about the mating habits of all kinds of different creatures."

"You can do that just by takin a walk on the Rue St-Denis."

"At least you could last time you checked."

"What, dyhave stock in Motorola?"

"It's wearin real thin real fast, Leslie!"

"See you're not the only one with good ideas in this family, huh? Gladjyuh like it—see yin a bit!"
"Hey, Leslie! Wanna hear about the shoot-out? I'll start right now: Bout half a year ago the immigrant kids and kids of immigrants in the housing projects—northern and eastern suburbs, mostly—finally got a little "
"Shit I thought you'd never ask! Wait a minute—I'm trying to decide—I really wanted to go to that luncheon...I'm a Board member, you kn "

"Sh! - sh! - sh! - sh! - sh! - sh!" When she hears Leslie come down a little past noon—half-humming/half-singing ("a whole lot")"ta shootin go"("in on") to the tune of A Whole Lotta Shakin', etc.—Mrs. Darotto hurls her broom at the mailboxes and lurches into the courtyard, jabbing the side of her index finger against her pursed lips.

"I thought he was at the doctor's," Leslie tells her.

"Listen it went away."

"It was never there!...Did *you* ever see it?"

"Why would I want to see something like *that*?"

"Well it was never there, believe me."

"How do *you* know, did *you* see it?"

"Why would I want to see something like *that* frchri—Oh! I can't get through to Moe the Magician I wrote out a fax the number's on it would you try? it's on the table."

"Listen where ygoin?" The good woman straightens the gold safety-pin brooch on the lapel of Leslie's navy pin-striped suit

"To the Hotel Interc "

then gets behind her "I mean Moe." and reties the wide white satin bow bunching her curls.

"He has to rub his lamp nget me tickets tLondon on Monday.....don't look now..."

"No, Monsieur Fontaine," Mrs. Darotto says, straightening the ribbon ends while she peeks around to the right of Leslie's head. "It's Thursday. Wednesday was yesterday."

Leslie nods to her watch. "All right let's do it."

Mrs. D. winks and tears through the corridor to her *loge*, obliterating its doorway with her broad frame. "Listen What Kind Of Onions Are These? You Call These Onions? What, You Were Raised In Downtown Rome? You Call Yourself A Boy Of The Earth? These Are Cat Turds Not Onions! Listen I Wouldn't Put Cat Turds Like These In A Soup If I Had One Foot In The Grave! That's What It Meant, The Horoscope! Water Trouble Today! Cat-Turd Water It Meant, The Horoscope!"

Scurrying past her *"Merci bien!"* out of the building, Leslie hears Mrs. D. start to inform her husband that she's too busy to be squabbling over the size of his onions. The good woman turns around to the mailboxes and picks up her broom.

" too bored and too unemployed and too angry for anyone's own good," Martin continues as he and Leslie ride the hotel's glowing glass and brass revolving door out onto the Rue de Castiglione. The driver of a double-parked black Peugeot 405 mock-salutes to the doorman.

"Martin what is this, James Michener? Why don't you start with the first amoeba that ever crawled on its stomach across the ocean floor and DON'T tell me amoebas don't have stomachs! Tell me about the guns, were there guns?" They turn left down the long, grandly arcaded block toward the Place Vendôme.

"No but there were rabbits."

"I Know! I Know!" Leslie slams one index fingertip onto her nose and shoots the other straight ahead, jumping up and down as she walks. "A Grapes Of Wrath Reference I Got It I *Won*!"

"The kids organize and for about two months, take out their frustration on their own communities—vandalize housing projects, playgrounds—if you can call them that—hit mom n pop stores, spray graffiti, set a couple fires, slash a couple tires."

"Sounds like a rap tune, Martin, if yever drop outa priority-setting-seminar giving, you can—" she spins around, hunches over, snaps her fingers, chants "Trou - ble - with - a -T- and - that - rhymes - with - P - and - that - stands - for - hou - sing - pro - jects," and regales the Hotel Lotti doorman with a finale consisting of a one-foot-landed leap, outstretched arms and a spread-lipped, fluttered-lashed Baby Jane face.

"Meanwhile, while all this is going on "

"Mar-tin, frchrissake!"

"I remember him—the P.R. expert!"

"Martin to the rescue with some comic relief! Martin to the rescue with some comic relief!" Leslie makes the sound of a siren and twirls her hand in the air like a flashing light. They wait in front of Godiva BRUXELLES - LONDON - NEW YORK to cross the Rue St-Honoré. NOUVEAU! LA COLLECTION FRUITEE DE GODIVA.

"Thankyou, thankyou," Martin acknowledges in the middle of the street, nodding his pudgy head, bowing left right left right, looking, as always, like a short middle-aged fairytale creature in a suit.

"Hey Martin!"

"Yeah?"
"Tell me about the shoot-out!"

"Ohhh the *shoot*-out, it's the *shoot*-out you want me to tell you about, and here all along I was wasting your precious time telling you about the shoo "
"This Is Ancient History You're Recounting Here, you're reading from papyrus scrolls, we're wearing clubs and carrying loincloths here, what, you think I don't know all this already?"
Martin grabs at one of Leslie's flailing arms. "Oh. Well I wasn't sure. News travels slowly in saunas."
"Yeahit does but we hire someone tstand there n read us headlines while we're doin it."

"Oh........doesn't the paper get soggy?"

"That'd be the steamroom, not the sauna, this is the sauna."

"Oh."
Leslie hitches her elbow around Martin's, although she almost has to stoop to keep hooked and moving at the same time. "Do you think they know who we are!" she whispers, pointing to a Japanese couple in front of Cartier.

"Hope not!" Martin answers.

The Place Vendôme looks like a giant spindle—the kind that used to be on a little round metal or marble base near the cash register in old grocery stores and diners, the kind where a white-haired man with garters on his shirtsleeves and a visor, or a cinch-waisted maiden-lady with a neat chignon, would impale the bill after you paid it— impale it with deliberateness and finality, like putting a period on a sentence. Like stamping the bill **PAID**. So that by closing time the spindle had collected the traces of the entire day's transactions. It was all there. Only, the spindle that's the Place Vendôme—the cloudward greened-bronze deeply-textured column with Napoleon far up there at its peak and the world's jeweler-elite around its vast pearl-gray-*place* base—collects the traces of the entire day's Paris sky. The Paris sky floats in flakes, flies in sheets, in from outside the field of the *place*, and skewers overflowing onto Napoleon's head. By closing time it's all there. To be read, reviewed, to be tallied: this sky was from a generous Paris, a free-spending Paris. This from one who came in quickly, picked up something simple and left. This sky's Paris made a fuss—I remember this one. Not like the one under here—bright and calm, stayed a long time, bought a round for everyone. Made everyone feel good. It's all on the spindle.

"If I ever kill myself I'm gonna do it at the Ritz!" Leslie announces as they pass the permanent pack of dark-suited phone-draped men in various stages of bringing around/leaning on/escorting into/helping out of/driving away their dark-windowed cars at the edge of the hotel's red-carpeted entrance-portico. Pass them without really seeing them, subliminally reassured that they're there. A low-grade, ongoing, swarming, rumbling perpetual background motion this.....thissss.....car business. Crucial to the picture but never to be highlighted as part thereof.

Like extras in a movie.

"Or you can become a scandal-driven rock star," Martin says, "and be in a constant state of sneaking out the back door while you send the chambermaid disguised as you out onto the Place Vendôme to the cries of the "

"jerkfaces"

" waiting for you."

"You know what happens to naughty little Ritz chambermaids who don't correctly "

"Don't you wish."

"YeahIdo!"

In front of Leslie the waiter sets a filled teapot, a cruet of hot water, a creamer, a sugar bowl with silver tongs, a cup and saucer, a silver strainer and a saucer for the silver strainer. He serves Martin his scotch. When he reaches to replace their half-finished dish of fruit-and-nut mix with a fresh supply, Leslie doesn't let him take the old and gladly accepts the new. "I know his lover," she whispers as he walks away. "Works out at my gym."

"Must get pretty crowded in that steamroom."

"That'd be the sauna. Not the steamroom. The steamroom is for when we read the paper."

"So meanwhile, the cop at the door pulls "

"How the hell do you know all this?"

"How can you not have a television?"

"Let's talk about something else," Leslie snaps, looking at her watch. "I gotta get back soon."
"I gotta eat something........You sure you can't get me my money back?"
"Does your next meal depend on it, you know, Hemingway woulda loved and hated it at the same time."

"Getting me my money back?"

"Yeah, that too. This bust. He woulda loved it cause he was an egomaniacal prick but he woulda thought it was commercial bullshit."
"Maybe they should've stopped messing around and just stuck him on top of that pillar out there in the *place*. He hated women, you know. I don't know how he can be your hero if he hated women."
Leslie serves more tea through the strainer then fills the empty pot with the water from the cruet. "Let's talk about something else. The teapot is the most perfect shape created by humanoid." Posing her right hand on her right hip to form a handle, and extending her other arm sideways into a spout, she tilts in one piece to the left and pours herself. "When I'm rich and famous I'm gonna collect teapots. But not those revolting gimmicky teapots like in the shape of kitchen sinks and pussycats and gas stations—I'm talking fine beautiful teapots—like this one. You know once I saw a teapot in the shape of a woman in a garterbelt sitting in an armchair with a riding crop in her hand frchrissake!"

"Did you knock anything over when you came?"

"I like my riding crops on flesh. Martin." Leslie leans over to Martin's face and fixes her eyes into his. "Flesh.....Not on porcelain."

"I always get those two mixed up, don't I?"

"That's why it's so good you can buy all those magazines and videos—to remind you which is which. Doesn't matter who's arrested.....they'll hit again."

"I thought you didn't want to talk about it any more."

"Let's go you ready?"

"No, but I'll go anyway, won't I?"

"I don't know, will you?"
Martin throws a 100-franc bill on the table and they get up. Leslie looks at her watch.

"How the hell do you know all this?"

"I don't have a television. Leaves a lotta dull hours to develop your powers of figuring things out. Whereyuh parked?"

"Rue du Mont-Thabor, near the hotel."

"Who djyuh have to sleep with for *that* spot?"

"Chief of Police."

"Don't you wish!"

"Don't *you* wish!"

"YeahIdo!"


"BONJOUR, PRINCESSE! C'EST GILLES. I JUST FOUND OUT FIVE MINUTES AGO I HAVE TO BE IN MARSEILLE TOMORROW TO LOOK AT A NEW SITE FOR A " \*BeeeeeeeeeeeeP\*\*\*\*\*BeeeeeeeeeeeeP\*\*\*\*\*

"LESLIE! IT'S ME! YOU WILL NOT—YOU WILL YOU GOTTA YOU JUST GOTT TOOO CALLLL MEEE! I HAVE SUCH FILTH I HAVE TO TOUCH IT WITH RUBBER GLOVES! I CAN'T SAY ANY MORE; WE LIVE TOO CLOSE TO THE CHINESE EMBASSY HERE I'M ALWAYS AFRAID OF THE PHONES. IF I CAN'T TALK WHEN YOU CALL YOU'LL KNOW YOU-KNOW-WHO IS HOME. LESLIE! OH, GOD! WAIT—I CAN AT LEAST TELL YOU IT HAS TO DO WITH SOMEONE IN...GE-NEEEE-VA!" *BeeeeeeeeeeeP*****BeeeeeeeeeeeP*****

"HELLO, MS. BRITTAIN? GUILLAUME. MR. GLASS WANTS TO KNOW IF IT'S OK FOR ME TO DROP OFF THAT MOCK-UP INST—THE INVITATION—INSTEAD OF FAXING IT. OUR MACHINE'S NOT W—IF IT'S OK COULD I DO IT TONIGHT ON THE WAY HOME? I'M JUST UP THE STREET FROM YOU—WHERE THAT BLACK PEUGEOT'S ALWAYS PARKED. IF IT'S OK COULD YOU " *BeeeeeeeeeeeP*****BeeeeeeeeeeeP*****

"THIS IS A CALL FOR MS. LESLIE BRITTAIN. I GOT YOUR NAME FROM PATTY ARON-GARTHE WHO SAID YOU MIGHT BE AVAILABLE TO HELP US PUT AN EVENT TOGETHER. OH!—THIS IS I'M ON THE EXECUTIVE COMMITTEE OF THE AMERICAN LIBRARY MY NAME IS LEE ANN WALTON THIS IS FOR OUR ANNIVERSARY GALA IN OCTOBER? WELL, WE'D LIKE IT TO BE IN OCTOBER. YOU CAN REACH ME ANY DAY AT THE LIBRARY. OR YOU CAN FAX ME AT MY HUSBAND'S OFFICE" ("wifeoid!") "AT FOURTY-TWO.FIFTY-SIX.THIRTY-THREE HUNDRED. HOPE TO HEAR FROM YOU SOON. THANK-YOU. GOOD-BYE." *BeeeeeeeeeeeP*****BeeeeeeeeeeeP*****

"LEAVE-ME-A-LONE!" Leslie screams, ripping off her suit "myy-huzz-binnd myy-huzz-binnd myy-huzz-binnd myy-huzz-binnd", jumping into her shorts and Mickey "myy-*HUZ*-binnd *MYY*-huz-binnd myy-huz-*BINND* ", throwing Soft Parade into the tape player on the livingroom-kitchenette partition. "myymyymyymyymyy huzzhuzzhuzzhuzz" She dials the number on the fax which arrived while she was out. "huzz binndbinndbinHello, is this the famous Patrick Trucock?"

"Y-y-well......it's Tru-c-*core*. Actually. Wh—Imean—wh-who's...this?"

"Of the Trucock *family* of the United States?"

"It's Tr—wh-who *is* this?"

"Of America?"

"Is this R-Rebecca?"

"Does the name...Nan...mean anything to you?"

"....."

"Hello?"

"Wh-what—Imean—dyou w "

"Now is that any way to speak to your future internship-supervisor?"

"Are y.....a-are you M-Ms.......Br-Brittain?"

"I am Ms. Brittain."

"You got—Imean—b-back to me...well...f-fast. Fast. Actually."

"I need you, Patrick. I have a mission for you."

"Dyou—what d—dyou mind if I a-ask what I—Imean—what I have t-to...well "

"You meet me."

"Where?"

"At Jim Morrison's."

"Who's J-Jim M-Morrison?"

"PATRICK! You Shame Yourself!"

"You don't—well—m-mean J-Ji "

"Yes, Patrick."

"But he's "

"Dead, Patrick. But lucky for us, he's buried in Paris. At the Père Lachaise Cemetery in the twentieth *arrondissement*. And that's where you're going to meet me."

"Dyou mind if I if I ask—Imean—if th-this is.....is this s-some kinda j-j "

"Tomorrow OK for you?"

"....."

"Patrick? Stay *with* me, Patrick."

"Yeah."

"Shall we sayyyy..........two thirty? PM? Although come to think of it AM would be more appropriate in this case, wouldn't it?"

"Y "

"You can get a map of the cemetery at the entrance. Jim's in division six—not too far from Francis Poulenc, who's in division five, and basically on the same latitude as Chopin, though Chopin's in a whole different sector. You'll find him—I have all the faith in the world in you. A dry run between now and then might not be a bad idea. If you have any problem—did Nan give you my numbers?

"Yeah."

"So if you have a problem, leave a message or send a fax. If not—dress casually but solemnly, by the way—see you tomorrow, OK, Patrick?"

"H-how w—dyou mind if I—h-how'll we—well— "

"I'll be carrying a copy of War and Peace. Have a nice day."

"Yeah."

# III
# ÑAPOLËON'S ÅNCHOVY

On her way in from the American Library "I know I told you it was Thursday, Monsieur Fontaine, but that was before the Earth revolved around the sun", Leslie picks up her mail and paper and unwedges a huge padded envelope from the communal box, below the others, for cumbersome packages. Before she can get her jacket off upstairs ("or was it—shit—the sun around the Earth?—I always get those two conf") there's the tapping at the door. She lets Mrs. Darotto in and checks her machine.

"BONJOUR, PRINCESSE! C'EST GILLES. WAS IT MAY TWENTY-EIGHT OR TWENTY-NINE THAT YOU HAVE TICKETS TO ELEKTRA? I FORGET. SOMETHING HORRIBLE'S JUST HAPPENED. I HOPE IT'S TWENTY-EIGHT SEE ON THE TWENTY-NINTH NATHALIE'S AUNT PAULINE IS COMING IN FROM LYON SHE'S NEVER SEEN THE TWINS........ARE YOU GETTING MY MESSAGES? IS YOUR MACHINE WORKING? YOU HAVEN'T CALLED LIKE I'VE ASKED FOR DAYS N "

"Ooh-ooh là listen when did *this* come?" Mrs. D. takes the big padded envelope from the dinette table and weighs it in her hands.

"I dnknow, you tell *me*. You're the one who puts the packages in the box."

"Well I didn't put this one in! Horoscope said surprise before dinner."

"They make movies about things showing up in mailboxes through forces other than postal."

"Go ahead go ahead go ahead open it!

"You usually only get ben-wa balls once in your life. We better prepare ourselves for a let-down."

While, like a giddy teenager, Mrs. Darotto bounces her heels on the floor and her fists against her hips, Leslie pulls the quick-open tab and "I don't got a lotta time here!" removes four packages, each wrapped in a sheet from the *Herald Tribune* "ofvvvvvv...........yessterr-dayy—hmmmm—whadya make othis, Watson?", and tied with a narrow white satin ribbon. "I really gotta change and get outahere! Wanna save em for when I get back?" Mrs. D. looks destroyed. "Well

Which One Should We Open First Frchrissake? I don't have a lotta time!" Mrs. Darotto points to the bulkiest of the four. "Why did I know y—didn't you ever hear what they say about small packages?"

Leslie rips into the sports page ("no less") and uncovers a round metal English Breakfast tea canister decorated with a train-station scene. "English *Brreakfassstt*. Hmmm—as opposed to English Middle-of-the-Day tea. Whoever sent this, Wats, "

Mrs. Darotto has no patience for forensics. Too excited to speak, she thrusts the smallest of the packages under Leslie's nose. "Closing stocks," Leslie notes as she unties the bow. "Maybe this one comes from the Chairman of the Federal Reserve. You know I can use these, actually." She picks up both ribbons and takes them through the alcove arch toward the dresser.

Mrs. D. grabs the package from her and unwraps the financial page with application and respect, as if defusing a bomb. "AOOHHLALALA MAMMMMMMA MIIIIIIAAAAAA AOOHLA" Leslie comes rushing back. One by one, with the tips of her fingers, Mrs. Darotto lifts a white silk-and-lace garterbelt, white silk stockings and a white silk-and-lace camisole.

"Oh-oh My Goh-ohd They're Exquisite!" Leslie takes the camisole and grazes it against her cheek. "Oh-oh My Goh-ohd!" She looks at the labels. "Christian DHoly Shit! La Nuit Satinée, ParHoly Shit!" Looks at Mrs. Darotto. Looks at the labels. ("can't be Jack...not anymore...n he'd have it wrapped in gold-leaf and delivered by Air Force One.......cop's life savings") "Here!" She jams the square parcel into Mrs. D.'s stomach, takes the long one, they both get to work.

"Listen ygot somethin you want to tell me?" Mrs. Darotto asks, tugging furiously at the knot with her teeth. A fax starts pouring out of the machine.

"Save the ribbon!" Leslie answers.

Out of the Op-Ed page Mrs. D. removes a box containing a battery-powered water-heating coil. "For hot beverages at home or office," she reads.

"Or train compartment," Leslie adds, backing up through the alcove arch and tossing her package onto the bed.

"Listen what's in yours?" Mrs. D. wants to know.

"I'll show you later, OK? Really—gotta get outa here—have a date with a dead rock-star." She grabs the woman's shoulders, turns her around and prods her bulk out the door. "Tell him there's a sale on coriander at Franprix!" she shouts after her into the hallway.

"Listen ywon't forget to show me "

"We'll catch up later. And eggs!" Leslie ducks into the apartment. Slams the door. Falls back against it, breathing audibly, unevenly, looking off into some distant thought-space. She walks tentatively back into the bedroom, as if bracing for danger, and finishes unwrapping the comics from around the riding crop. Moving with uncustomary slowness, and awe, she lifts the instrument and draws the length of it between her index and middle fingers, straightening it where it had been bent to fit into the envelope, then tapping the tip lightly against her palm. One strong stroke through the air. Lightly again. One str—she slumps onto her bed as if the matter has just been drained from her through pinholes in her feet. She's thinking flash

ing flashing the train the package she's sixteen years old his thighs the Quai des Orfèvres a Valentine card cop-movies that book that book in the basement Jack Kote a cop in her bed a cop in her head nobody likes a smart-ass there's a fax doittome doittome giveittohergood yeahah! sheneedsitgoodbad cop in the innercourtyard of the cell where her psyche sits and plays all alone Leslie feels like layers of skin have been removed—from the inside—collapsing her closer to her core. And farther from the air outside her. She stands up too quickly and her head floats as she senses the sudden stillness in the room. On the dinette table she gently poses the tight braid of rust leather atop the lace and silk, itself resting on the raw smudgy fibers used to line birdcages and tell of death by famine and wrap dead fish.

"OHH KAYY, SPORTSS FANNSS! UP N ATEMM, ATOM ANTT!" she screams to the ceiling, suddenly ripping off her library clothes and replacing them with a black lace teddy, black leather jeans, a black silk t-shirt and a wide black leather belt with a big handcrafted silver buckle in the shape of a dove. She pins her gold safety pin to her collar band then

"Yo Leslo! You don't remember me but "
*BeeeeeeeeeeeeeP*****BeeeeeeeeeeeeeP*****

fastforwards through the rest of her messages

"Hi! Bet you've wondered where I've been for the past eighteen hours! Ge-nee-vah, Ge-nee-vah, it's my kinda t "
*BeeeeeeeeeeeeeP*****BeeeeeeeeeeeeeP*****

       while she laces into short black boots

"Ms. Brittain, it's Elizabeth Townsby from NATO. Oh, there's a change already, don't you know! General Kunz can't give the speech because he dropped d—excuse me, Ms. Brittain—passed away of a heart attack in his bath this morning. But everything else is the same so you just keep organizing and we'll look for another general. You can call me when you g "
*BeeeeeeeeeeeeeP*****BeeeeeeeeeeeeeP*****

       and gathers her curls into a medium-wide hot-pink satin ribbon.

"H-hello, M-Ms. B-Brittain? It's Patrick T-Trucore. Actually. Remember—Imean—me? J-just, I thought…well…..I if you don't mind I th-thought I'd j-just—well Imean—ch-check to see if our if we're s-still…..well…meeting meeting. I g-guess so. Well if not it's it's OK. Actually. M-Ms. Brittain. Well—I got a m-map t-to the—Imean—m-map to the c-cemetery. Well that's—I got it in a in a fl-flower shop just at the e-entrance. L-like you said. Actually. Ms. Br-Brittain. Well that's…..all. I g-guess. I'll—Imean—h-hang up…..now. Ms. Br-Brittain. Brittain."
*BeeeeeeeeeeeeeP*****BeeeeeeeeeeeeeP*****

"Good morning, Mrs. Brittain. You don't know me but my husband and I were given your name by the Amer "
*BeeeeeeeeeeeeeP*****BeeeeeeeeeeeeeP*****

("*Missus* Brittain, give me a ro-yal br ") Leslie grabs her mail and the fax that just came in, ("You don't know me and MYY HUZZ-BANND") rushes out, "but MYY HUZZ-BANND and I just went to the bathroom together because" locks the door, "MYY HUZZ-BANND And I Are Velcroed To Each OTHER'S *HIPP*!" unlocks the door, rushes in, snatches one of the package ribbons, stuffs it in her back pocket, leaves again. Tip-toeing like a cartoon character past the *loge*, she sees Mr. Darotto, his back thank Providence to the entrance, laboring at separating all the milk-chocolate Belgian bon bons from all their dark-chocolate co-habitants, apportioning them into little regional masses sharing life-space with celery stalks and lentils on the checkered oil-cloth of his wooden table. He looks so touchingly at play, so purely absorbed, that Leslie is tempted to stop and watch for awh ("are you—get *out* of here!").

Where the river threads through its monuments like a silk cord through precious stones, the 69 bus cuts northeastward across Paris. Leslie studies her mail in her favorite single-seater behind the driver, looking up every several blocks to see the next jewel added to the necklace.

The bus hits the Place Gambetta at 2:12. Leslie enters the cemetery through the Porte de la Dhuys, walks first past Oscar Wilde. The Avenue Carette takes her left along one of the cross-avenues all the way over to Edith Piaf, from whom she doubles back to the Colombarium to visit Maria Callas and Max Ernst and absorb Isadora Duncan's blessed message. A turn past Apollinaire toward Balzac allows a quick call on Gustave Doré, Corot, Ingres, Molière, Bellini, Chopin, Rossini and Colette. From Colette Leslie heads up the Avenue du Puits, which becomes the long Avenue Casimir-Perier, and into a side lane where first an occasional then almost every headstone bears assurance in chalk or paint or blood or wine that if this is where you want to be, this is where you are: we love you Jim    Morrison is still alive    come back to us Jim    it's over there    let it roll roll roll let it thrill your soul    take your hat off! Morrison Hotel this way    And then on some graves, lyrics to entire Doors works or original poems of homage and adoration written in laborious precision and obviously written over in places where twenty years of weather and worship have not shown due respect for the deified.

There has been a twenty-four-hour vigil at Jim Morrison's tomb every twenty-four-hour period since his twenty-eight-year-old body lost its battle with his millennia-old mind's death-wish in 1971. Of all the titans of human accomplishment and human promise buried at Père Lachaise, of all the billions of humanity-altering words and notes and brushstrokes represented by its pensioners, Jim Morrison draws the crowds. And keeps them. Jim Morrison, still in the dust of a spotlight. Young adults—children—who were not yet alive by the time Jim was dead make it their business to replenish the flowers and beer bottles, candles, scribbled notes, the revelatory graffiti and handmade Jim-likenesses which have become his sepulcher. Weathered eye-witnesses to the lighting of the Lizard King's fire are relentlessly here to revere the ashes. Why does Jim Morrison's gate beat out Chopin's, or even Honoré de Balzac's and Edith Piaf's in their home town? What truths did he hold out to his disciples—create for them—hold back from them—that Pissaro the impressionist or Jane Avril the dance-hall muse could not? Is it because his body waited to give out until he got to Paris? Is it because he touched his cock on stage that there is always life at Jim Morrison's tomb? Crawly, life-affirming-activity life, like an Escher drawing. The swooshing of interknotted swatches of textured fir-green and burgundy velvet, grazing the grave-grazers draped in massive amber beads hung from the blackened silver of ancient chains. Layers and depths of amoebic pure movement shaping itself into sitting into meeting into touching into looking into singing into reading into reading to each other into praying then just as quickly transmuting into amoebic pure movement again. Jim Morrison's is the only grave in Père Lachaise Cemetery's 110 acres of 100,000 tombs (featuring 200 superstars for your otherworldly pleasure) where a paid guard stands to persuade peace among the pilgrims.

Leslie sees the back of a shaggy blond head darting and disappearing between the tomb and a brick ledge behind it. It pops up again at a low stone slab near the grave guard's boots. She squeezes between Morrison and his neighbor, moving, over the moist uneven ground, around a cluster of very young girls with whitened cheeks and darkened eyesockets. Short black fishnet gloves. The guard is swatting into the air, screaming to a middle-aged German couple trying to stage a photo that it is forbidden to climb upon the shrine. Plopping onto the slab, Leslie inches over to a kid in jeans, white dress shirt, wrinkled navy cotton sportcoat, mud-brown crocheted tie who looks like he took a wrong turn on his way to buy a Bible.

They sit in silence for awhile, staring straight on. Out of the corner of her eye she sees him tilt his head to peek at her then whip it self-consciously back to where it was. He looks at his shoes then up at the sky. "Eet eez ironique, n'est-ce pas?" Leslie asks in a French-accented near-voiceless lifetime-chain-smoker wheeze. "Weess zee darhkness ehnd ow cloze zee grhaves arh ehnd all zatt, you forhget zere eez ehneessing abuff all zosse trheez." The kid scoots a couple inches down the slab, away from Leslie. Then, trying to smile and failing, he relaxes his shoulders slightly and half-turns toward her, as if attracted by the prospect of a conversation with the living. "Aye mean, zesse guyss—zatt eez whatt zay arh all doink," Leslie continues, flicking the kid on the shoulder with her left hand while pointing overhead with her right. "Zeir mattehr eez shootink arhound upp zere—rhight upp zere. Ehnd *wee* forhgett to look upp, zere eez so mahch to ssee down eerh."

"Yeah."

"All zeess, eet eez jahst to gett you een zee storhe." She waves her right arm in a large arc "Like parfum-bohttle rheppink. Zee rheel sseeng, eet eez" then raises her chin skyward. The kid looks up, more out of need to please than interest or even understanding. "Ydon't find this shit down at the strip-mall in Lincoln, do yuh?" Leslie asks him in her natural voice.

He bounds off the slab and springs backward.

"You better watch it. You'll wind up in Auguste Comte's lap."

"N-no!"

"Well, I guess you're right—Auguste *is* a little down the road apiece for that. You'd have tbe a pretty good jumper. And even at that, what with the backward spin and all th "

"No! N-no!"

"Yes, Patrick. Yes."

"M-Ms. B-Br ?"

"Patrick Trucock?"

"C-core."

"Core what?"

"Tr-Trucore. Imean—well........Tru-c-*core*.....N-not Truc "

"Not what, Patrick?" Leslie's voice is soft and calm.

"What you.....s-said. Actually."

"Trucock. That's what I said. Patrick Trucock."

"M-Ms. Br-Brittain....." His phone-message delivery aside, Leslie is not sure whether Patrick usually speaks this haltingly or whether this is merely the breathtaking effect of spending an afternoon in such close proximity to Héloïse and Abélard. "I h-had—well—Imean—if you don't m-mind—no—well—i-idea....." The boy is staring out at Leslie but not focusing on her. "Imean Imean I exp-expected.....well—"

"*What* did you expect, Patrick?"

"Well Imean "

"Did You Think I Would Desecrate Jim Morrison's Eternal Resting Place By Showing Up In A *Business* Suit Frchissake? Patrick! Use that London School of Economics brain I've heard so much about!"

"Ohyeah. I...I b-brought it. M-Ms. Brittain."

"Your brain? I do hope so!"

"No not m—Imean—n-no, Ms. Br-Brittain. I m-mean my my resume. Actually." Stooping beside the slab, Patrick unbuckles a maroon canvas backpack and digs out some crumpled pages. He presents them to Leslie who ignores the gesture completely

"Cumawn!" and throws her head in the direction of the main gate. "Let's get outa here!" she commands, forging a *"Pardon!"* path through the "Scuse me." pilgrims "Thanks. *Pardon!*".

Patrick grabs his bag and follows in an awkward trot, his resume dangling from his hand as he tries to catch up. After some silence he renews the "M-Ms. Br-Brittain?" offer.

"Patrick," Leslie says indulgently, slowing her steps. "Resumes are for Personnel Directors. Resumes are so file-cabinet makers can send their revolting little progeny to Harvard where they will learn to ask prospective interns for their resumes. Your resume ooh look! Wanna see what Molière's up to?" She hooks her arm into Patrick's and guides him over to a grave.

"There's a—Imean—isn't there—Imean—a m-metro s-stop.....n-named after "

"Yes, that *was* his claim to fame. He was an exceedingly renowned seventeenth-century *métro*-engineer who met a tragic death-by-electrocution trying to help an imaginary invalid save a miser from committing suicide next to a misanthrope on the northbound line."

"Yeah."

Leslie disengages from Patrick's arm and they continue walking. "Your resume says that when some total stranger tells you to show up for a potentially career-rocking interview at the tombstone of a counter-cultural icon who had just doped and fucked himself to very premature death at about the time you were asking the incubator nurse for some more intravenous, you show up frchrissake! That's the only paragraph in your resume that interests me, Patrick. You win! You get the job! Nan did tell you it was an unpaid situation, didn't she? Patrick?"

Patrick is not focusing again. Or he's focusing, but on something infinitesimally small and close—like a single space between two silk fibers on Leslie's t-shirt. Or on something unfathomably large and far—like the launch pad where a certain star's light is beginning it's thirty-seven-year voyage to our eyeballs. In any case, he's not focusing on Leslie. "Patrick," Leslie whispers reverentially. "Sarah Bernhardt." She bends forward to read the inscription on the tomb and asks, "Nan did tell you it was an unpaid situation, didn't she?"

"Yeah."

They take the Avenue des Combattants-Etrangers toward the exit. "But you can help yourself to what'sever in the refrigerator."

"Th-thanks. Thanks," Patrick says with only half his vocal chords. As Leslie heads straight through the gate for the Place Gambetta, he stops and points left. "N—M-Ms. Br-Brittain? Th—well—th—if ydon't m—this way. M-my bike's over.....there."

"Your bike."

He nods to the bottom button on his jacket.

"As in...Daisy, Daisy?"

"As in—Imean—P-Peter Fonda and and Dennis H-Hopper. Hopper."

"Keeping the late-night video-delivery service hoppering, I see! You have...a Harley."

"Well I ha—I have—well—a.....Y-Y-Yamaha. Anyway. Actually," he tells the layer of oxygen just above the sidewalk.

"Just like I said, Daisy, Daisy."

Patrick's shoulders look lopsided—one up one down—as if he can't decide whether to feel cocky or crushed.

"I know I trifle with you, Patrick." They start walking along the outside of the cemetery wall. "Don't take it personally. I trifle with everyone. For two good reasons. One, because mostly everyone merits being trifled with. And two, it's a very convenient flaw because in a job interview when some constipated corporate drone who hasn't fucked his own wife in ten years asks me what my weaknesses are I have one ready-made, which impresses the shit out of em since they expect you to have to go think about that one. Patrick?" when they reach a section of sidewalk where a number of two-wheeled vehicles are parked, Leslie puts a hand on his shoulder—the higher one. He begins opening the luggage compartment of his motorcycle. "I have just read page two of your resume!"

Patrick suddenly seems taller, more mature. A war-wounded whose member has been miraculously sewn back on. He grins at Leslie almost condescendingly, as if saying We are on equal ground now—your mouth and my bike. Pleased with the new improved Patrick, Leslie notes, "It all comes down to the size of one's cock, doesn't it, Patrick?"

"M-Ms. Br-Brittain?"

Leslie's mouth wins this round.

Patrick removes two helmets from the luggage compartment and gives one to Leslie as she tosses her handbag and mail into the well in exchange. He throws his bag in and secures the lock. "Good job I didn't wear a business suit, huh, Patrick? I would've had to take my skirt off for the ride."

"Where to?" Patrick asks, climbing on and starting the engine.

"I'll show you the office—which is also the apartment—we'll have to get you a key." Leslie mounts and clasps her arms around his midsection. "Seventh *arrondissement*—Ecole Militaire—Hello, Soldier!—I'll scream directions into the deafening wind as we go."

"M-Ms. Brittain?" Patrick turns his head around and focuses on the middle of Leslie's chinstrap snap. "I still don't kn-know what I'll—Imean—be doing....w-working for.......you. Actually."

"You're doing it!" Leslie tells him.

And off they are.

Up on the large avenue at the mouth of the *passage*, Leslie's ribbon falls to the ground when she removes the helmet. She shakes her head to fluff out her curls then dives to save the satin from being savaged by a passing black Peugeot 405. As they walk deeper into the inevitability of a bilateral Darotto onslaught, she asks Patrick, "How well do you speak French? Or actually Italian?.....Or actually English?.....Or actually.....?"
"Oohhoohhoohh sono jealousso!! Sono jealousso!! Ah mamma, qui est ce younga uomo con ma petita colomba? Oohh la bella colomba she"   "Listen this isn't the one who sent you the"   "quitte Umberto per un younga"   "sexy underwear, is it?"   "uomo! Ahhhh!"
"Madame Darrrottttohohoh, Monsieur Darrrottttohohoh," Leslie the Ringmaster trumpets at the door to the *loge*, waving her top-hat and whip to the throngs.   "May I Pre-sent To Youououououou................Fresh From The Homogeneity Of Middle America, Byy Wayy Of The London Stool Of Wreckonomics Annnndd—Just This Very Dayyy—The Sacred Sepulcher Of The Lizard Kinnnnnngg....................PAT-RI-ICKK TRUUU-COCK!"
"*c-core*," Patrick whispers, otherwise understanding not a word of her French and wondering how small he'd have to be to crawl into a mailbox. Leslie draws three huge loops in the air with her left forearm and stops a fourth, halfway around, in front of Patrick's chest, her fingers gracefully indicating his blanched presence in the building's entrance.
"Patrick was found—mercifully—on the doorstep of the London Stool of Wreckonomics "

"Oohhoo" "Ahhh"

"just—Hey you guys'd be super at a *Rocky Horror Show* screening—just about—JUHUHSSSTT ABOUOUOUOUTT" Leslie whips around into Patrick's face "to become a........" then spins back to the Darottos who are standing side-by-side at attention next to Mr. D.'s wooden table. Leslie gasps. The Darottos gasp. Almost involuntarily. "........member of the............ have-a-nice-weekend-see-ya-Monday crowd." Leslie sees she's losing her audience. "AND SO!" She stomps her feet. Right Left. The crowd snaps back. She cracks her imaginary whip. They're hers. "in an act of benevolent rehabilitation, Patrick Tru" she looks Patrick straight in the eyes "cock" then at the Darottos "will be assigned to two months of total-submersion in how to keep the public out of public relations and the relations in! ANNNNND NOWWWW BEFORRRE THE ACTIONNN BEEEGINNNSS," The Darottos are facing each other like a set of unmatched bookends, bobbing, babbling in Italian. Patrick, realizing this isn't gonna go away, has settled in against the front-door frame and is focusing on the top-hat Leslie isn't holding in the same hand where she isn't holding the whip. "I bid you, Madame Darotto, Monsieur Darotto," Switching to English and her normal voice, Leslie starts "let's not make a collective big fucking deal about this, OK?" walking toward to the courtyard, turns, smiles, beckons Patrick with her head and they go for the stairs.

Halfway up she realizes Patrick is no longer behind her. When she gets back down he rushes over and grabs her arm "M-Ms. Br-Brittain!", leading her urgently back to the mailboxes. His face is flushed, his eyes furiously shifting focus from the clasp of her handbag to the space between her left eye and ear. "Ms. Br-Brittain I d-don't kn-know wh—th-this man—I don't—well........u-unders "

"It's still Friday, Monsieur Fontaine...Cumawn Patrick!" She flicks Patrick on the shoulder then gets behind him and pushes him all the way up to the apartment. "That," she explains, jiggling her key in the lock, "was risk management. They don't know exactly what went on with Brittain Brothers Barnum n Bailey down there but they know enough tgo find something in her horoscope warning them not to mess with what walked into my building with m "

"Y-you—Imean—ride...h-horses! Actually." Patrick has preceded Leslie into the apartment.

"Nohh-oohh, wha—ohh!"("shihtt!") In one motion she rushes past him to the table, scoops up the riding crop and underwear, "Actually, I do steeple chases in a garter belt and one othem velvet caps." whips into the bedroom-alcove, shoves them randomly into a dresser drawer "Cute, huh?" and floats back to the livingroom to take his backpack with a welcoming smile. She hangs it on the coat-rack in the entrance and asks if he wants to take off his jacket.

"D-dyou mind if I—well—k-keep it.....on? On? Dyou mind if I a-ask you if you if you live al—Imean—alone?"

"I mind if you ask me if I mind. Just me and my riding buddies." Patrick looks like he's believed her. "Yes. Alone. Patrick. Alone."

"Well—w-why—well—dyou m—are there there are s-six p-pairs

of r-running...I mean—shoes?"

Leslie hooks her arm into Patrick's and walks him back to the entrance, pointing pair-by-pair: "Concrete dry, concrete rain, soil, treadmill, going-to-pick-up-dry-cleaning, shoulda-been-thrown-away-four-months-ago-but-can't-bring-myself-to. Well this is the last time you'll be a guest in my space so you better take advantage of it—want some tea?"

Patrick stares at Leslie's left hip. "Bu-but I th-th-thought—aren't I—w-we're not "

"Patrick, if we're gonna work together you're gonna hafta.....do you want some tea?" Patrick nods to his shoe. "This is the last time you're going to be a *guest*. Next time," Leslie proceeds patiently, "either we each make our own tea whenever the fuck we want some or in the best of all options you make tea for both of us. Now! Here's the scoop! Sit down!"

One atop the other, at Patrick's spot on the dinette table, Leslie drops the operating manuals for the fax machine, the answering machine, the computer, the software, the modem, the e-mail service, the small photocopier and the stove "the most important one and it's in French so if you ever wanna eat again you're gonna hafta learn how to swim. For industrial-strength photocopying, by the way, we go to the *papeterie* downstairs on the Avenue Bosquet so that the owner's wife doesn't have to be jealous of the dry-cleaner's wife whose full-length ermine coat I've also financed." Patrick opens his mouth to ask a question but shuts it as Leslie arrives from the bookcase with "Here." a huge pressbook and three giant looseleaf binders. "Clippings from events in here. The white one has files worth keeping of past jobs, the red is what we're working on now and the black is prospects. Reverse superstition. What y—anyway, they get married in black in Japan and buried in white, and we say we don't have alot to learn from those guys!—what you'll be doing—besides the basics like taking rides with me, discussing art, truth, beauty and the meaning of life and going to the opera—we have tickets to Elektra on May twenty-ninth—is everything from stuffing envelopes to more routine tasks like lunching with Barbara Bush." She opens the pressbook and points to a picture of herself and several other people at a round table with Barbara. "What do you want in your tea?"

Patrick fingers the unwieldy plastic page while not looking at it. He glances around the room, at the pressbook, around the room, then at the dishtowel on a hook next to Leslie's head in the kitchenette. "C-c-may I h-have.....sugar? Actually...P-please. Who's—dyou mind if I a-ask you wh-who...n-next to.....this m-man n-next to.....to M-

Mrs. B ?"

"I don't have sugar and I'm outa honey. I mind if you ask if I mind. Want cream?"

"Yeah. P-please. M-Ms. Brittain."

"The Ambassador to the US mission at the OECD. Do you want the Snoopy mug or the one with erotic Picasso drawings?"

"....."

"Don't expect to learn everything—or anything for that matter—first time around," Leslie says, pushing the books away from Patrick to make room for the Picasso mug. Never ever be afraid to ask a question—no such thing as a stupid question—what's stupid is being afraid to ask a question. And what's stupid*est* is fucking up where you wouldn't've if you'd've only asked the fucking question! What's stupid?" Patrick squints, not sure she really wants an answer. Leslie leans close.

"N-not-as-king-a-qu-qu-ques-tion. Ms. Br-Brittain," he answers in a monotone, his blue eyes focusing on her left cheekbone as soon as she smiles. He looks like he's about to both hug her and run out the door.

"Except if I mind! If I mind! That's the only question that's stupid but that's not really a question, is it, that's just a manifestation of criminally poor parenting. And here come the most important thing I'll ever tell you about all this—in fact, it's the only thing you'll ever need to know about making a living anywhere in any field and I wish you'd've come to me before spending all that time and money on the London School of Economics where I'm sure you never dared wear that tie:"

A fax comes rolling in. Leslie gets up to boil more water. "Want more tea?"

"A f—M-Ms. Br-Brittain, a f-fax.....just came...in. Actually."

"I'm in Rio for the evening. You getting hungry? I'm getting hungry. I'm gonna order a pizza. Want a pizza? Want more tea?"

"Yeah. P-please. You—dyou—well—want me to s-see what—Imean—that.....f-fax "

"The most important thing I'll ever tell you about all this," Leslie continues from the kitchenette, peeking under the teapot-lid, "is to always start each project asking yourself what's the most ruinous disaster that could possibly befall and then knowing beyond question that worse than that's gonna happen. You book a name for an event? His sister eats it at the age of twenty-six in a hit-n-run that morning and he's on a plane for Texas. You're doing a live international charity-broadcast? Every satellite on earth gets swallowed five minutes before air-time by giant space-snakes who metabolize metal. You're giving a press conference at noon to launch synthetic coffee? The President of France is discovered in the generator room of the Elysée Palace at eleven-thirty with his mouth on the other end of his chauffeur's cock. DON'T UNFOCUS ON ME PATRICK THESE THINGS HAPPEN! Well, maybe the example about the President of France *is* a bit overdone *quand même*. It would most likely be the other way around, wouldn't it? It would be *he* who was getting serviced and the *chauffeur* who was doing the servicing. But you get my drift. Now I need four things from you:"

Leslie sets the tea on the table and takes her seat again. Patrick looks much paler than he did in the murky dankness of the cemetery. "C-M-may I use the...m-men's room? P-please."

"VERY GOOD QUESTION!" Leslie booms, pounding her palm on the table. Patrick looks terror-stricken. "No—I don't mean it's a good question whether you're *permitted* to use the bathroom frchrissake Patrick! Or whether you're *capable* of using the—of course you can use the bathroom! I mean it's a good question because—next to the stove—it's the most essential part of the apartment to get acquainted with. Through there—after the coat-rack."

While Patrick is making friends with the lavatory Leslie transfers her new underwear from it's temporary refuge into its proper place among fellow fine fabrics. She notices that she has four messages and picks up the fax, which is from Gilles, telling her that since her answering machine is broken he's writing to let her know he can make the twenty-ninth after all as Aunt Pauline decided to wait a week until her friend Marie-Josette can come with her because she's afraid of taking the train alone. "And well she should be!"

"What w-was—dyou m—w-were you s-saying....." Patrick asks, emerging from the encounter.

"I was reminding you to set a week from Friday aside—May twenty-ninth—for the opera..... whatr you doing?"

"You have—well—f-four messages. Actually."

"From Rio I took a dinner-cruise cargo-ship to Kowloon. Patrick? How anxious do I look to get to my messages at this particular moment? Sit down. These are the four things I need to know from you:

an address and phone number where I can reach you—that's one question, two parts—how much time you can give me and when—that's also one question, two parts—what you want on the pizza and if you have any questions other than if I mind anything." Leslie walks through the alcove arch to the phone on the dresser "Or statements." and dials. *"Oui, bonsoir, je voudrais commander une pizza...Brittain...client numéro cent trente-cinq.* You're On, Patrick! We've gotten to the point in the interchange where like it or not we're obliged to divulge just what kind of pizza it is that we had in mind...*un moment, s'il vous plaît"*

"C-M-May I h-have anything—well—b-but.....a-anchovies? P-please. Ms. Br-Brittain."

"Shit, Patrick! That's the only thing I like on my pizza—no cheese, no *Un Moment, S'il Vous Plaît!* sauce, just dough and anchovies *un m* all right, we're gonna have to deal with this *donnez-moi du fromage, des olives, des oignons, des poivrons et un anchois...Oui, c'est cela— Un Seul Anchois...Oui oui, ça m'est tout à fait égal combien ça coûte, je.....*OK OK, fuck-face, *je sais bien,* ybetter get off the line—your wife might have a minute between tricks and be tryin tget through, *à tout à l'heure,* OK?! THE CUSS—ANND I DOO MEEANN CUSSSS—TOM-ER IS NEH-VERR— ANND I DOO MEEANN NEH-VERR— FUCKINNGG RIIGHTTT—ANND I DOO MEEANN FFUH- KKKINNNNNGGG" Leslie is twirling in place in the middle of the livingroom, arms stretched toward the ceiling, head dangling backwards. "Yseedat Sign On The Computer? Lookadat Sign On The Computer! Yseedat? Whadoes It Say?"

"Trust-no-dog," Patrick answers in a monotone, reading one of two little word-processed slivers taped to the top of the screen.

"N—the *other* one frchrissakes!"

"The-cus-tom-er-is-nev-er-right."

"Did you understand anything that went on over there?"

"Y-your name. Actually. Ms. Br-Brittain."

"Great! I asked for all kindsa shit on the pizza and one anchovy. Just one—kinda as a joke for you but not really 'cause I wanted at least one fucking anchovy on my pizza! Well since when Josephine screamed over to Napoleon from the phone what he wanted on his pizza and he didn't say *un seul anchois, ma Reine* then Leslie Brittain can't order one fucking anchovy on hers! The sub-minimum-wage jerkhead on the other end of the phone just used one of the three magic words in the French motto!"

"L-Liberty.....E-e "

"IMPOSSIBLE, FORBIDDEN AND INEXISTANT!" Leslie bellows to the ceiling, shaking her arms in a high evocatory Elmer Gantry V. She comes back to the table *"Impossible"* and calmly takes her seat. "was his word of choice in this particular case.............Fuck-face—in case you didn't catch that either—was mine."

"H-here. M-Ms. Brittain." While Leslie was exorcising her pizza-devils, Patrick took a small spiral-bound notebook from his backpack and in tiny, meticulous, self-effacive characters printed his address and phone number. He then wrote: OPEN ALL YEAR. ROUND-THE-CLOCK SERVICE.

"Maybe we should communicate by note, Patrick. You have a personality on paper. And to thank you for your dedication and loyalty I won't even comment about there being one ell too many in the next-to-last word." Patrick slowly takes the notebook from Leslie and finds the object of her thoughtfulness, immediately focusing on the little dancey lines around Snoopy's left foot on the mug. "The only way we can do this is on a day-to-day basis cause not only do I rarely know what my schedule's gonna be past a week from any given Thursday, I don't wanna know. The day I look forward to any predictable regularity in anything but my period, I w—and my running—I want you to—ysee that rock over there?" Leslie points to the bookcase. "It comes from the beaches of the Aegean where bones of brave Phoenician sailors still wash up—I want you to tie that rock around my left ankle and throw me in the Seine........ Ms. Brittain?" she asks in a deep, self-important interviewer-voice, ripping out Patrick's note and scrutinizing it as if it were a resume, "Where do you see yourself in five years?" She puts the resume down and folds her hands in her lap. "In the Seine, sir," she says sweetly. "OH KAY, ROCK N ROLLERS! Tomorrow w—by the way, if you have to throw me in it's gotta be from the Pont Alexandre Trois, OK?

The phone rings, Patrick jumps, Leslie puts her hand on his shoulder and holds him down.

"So tomorrow we're gonna pretend to be working onnn..." She

unearths the red looseleaf book from the pile on the table and opens to the NATO papers from the Brussels meeting "...this. Come at noon—first I'll send you out to get keys made—and then we'll go over all this other insanity and then decipher the rest of the Dead Sea Scrolls we couldn't get to last Monday. I still need to know if you have any questions or—let the machine pick up—statements. And if you promise it'll be the Pont Alexandre Trois."

"OK OK OK LESLIE, SHIT! WHERE THE—I HOPE YOU'RE NOT THERE FUCKING YOUR BRAINS OUT NOT PICKING UP I DON'T CARE WHO HE IS! LESLIE ARE YOU THERE? GOD, LESLIE! HE **"Pay no attention to the man behind the curtain, Patrick."** FOUND OUT! FOUND I TELL YOU OUT! SENT A PRIVATE FUCKING DETECTIVE TO GENEVA! WON'T BUY ME A BIRTHDAY PRESENT—BIRTHDAY PRESENT?—I SHOULD BE LUCKY ENOUGH TO SEE GROCERIES WALKING IN HERE!—WON'T PAY THE GODDAMN PHONE BILL BUT HAS ENOUGH MONEY TO SEND SOME SLEEZEBALL DICK TO SIT IN THE LOBBY ALL FUCKING NIGHT! LESLIE I DON'T CARE WHAT TIME IT IS YOU GOTTA—OH GOD!    HE    JUST    WALKED    IN    BYE!"
*BeeeeeeeeeeeeeP*****BeeeeeeeeeeeeeP*****BeeeeeeeeeeeeeP*

"Certainly paid the phone bill this month, didn't he Roz? Or statements," she smiles to Patrick.

"If you d—dyou m—m-mind I h-have a...qu-question....and a and a—well—s-statement. Actually." Patrick waits for a go-ahead. Leslie waits for Patrick to figure out there will be none. "The qu—well—the qu-question is...well—do you h-have.....E-Excel? I think I can—Imean—if you don't m-mind I think I can d—well—h-help you—well—d-do your b-budgets...a little.....b-better."

"Patrick, Where Has Your Left Brain Been All My Life? Yes! Take my budgets! Make women and men out of them! It's in there!" Leslie bangs on the computer with the back of her fingers. "I just never used it." She leans toward him, resting her chin in her hand and her elbow on the table. "I was waiting for *you*, Patrick!" she croons. Sitting up taller, he focuses sharply, "And the statement?—tough act to follow, huh?"  then pales, looks around the room, slumps back in his chair.

"I-I h-have to g-go n-now." Patrick says abruptly. He stands, and replaces his chair neatly at the table, adjusting it several times as if preparing for a home-arts magazine photo shoot.

"What about the pizza? Patrick I just got myself written onto the *Assemblée Nationale*'s list of Unfrench Activities by ordering a non-Napoleonic topping and you're gonna leave me alone with my anchovy?"

"They...s—if you don't m—s-said they they couldn't do—Imean—one...a-anchovy. Actually."

"This your idea of round-the-cee ell oh cee kay service? OK! Good! More *Fromage*, *Olives*" Leslie shoots up and flails into Patrick's face. "*Oignons* And...WhatTheHellWasTheOthOhYeah Peppers For Me!..........And the statement?"

Patrick goes over to the entranceway. He takes his backpack from the coat-rack antler and unbolts the front door. As he inches it open, Leslie approaches. She leans against the frame, watching him walk down the corridor.

"Ms. Br-Brittain?" Halfway to the staircase he stops and turns.

"Patrick, just how big a problem does calling me Leslie present for you?"

"....."

"OK, Patrick. I can still call you Patrick, can't I? I don't have to call you Mr. Trucock?"

"co " Patrick stops mid-syllable. He tries to smile and walks back toward the apartment. "M-Ms. Brittain?"

"Yes, Patrick? Wanna come back in?"

"N-no th-this—Imean—is.....OK. Actually. Well—Imean.....t-ten years ago—exactly ten years ago this month—when I was thirteen and my father died, my uncle took me out for the day." Like a stutterer who breaks into perfectly enunciated song, or a phobic speechmaker sounding self-assured when reading from prepared text, Patrick begins his story with smooth sentences confidently delivered in a relaxed voice. "*He* had the bike then and yes, it was a Harley. We went away for the whole day and it was the first time I was ever that far from the house. I don't know where we went—I'll never know cause he's gone too now." It is as if the story is so much a part of him that he need not fret, or think, about producing its syllables. "But I remember there were two kinds of sounds—there was the sound of the wind in the fields so strong that my uncle said it contained all the sounds of the world and there was the sound of no one around at all—a sound of being alone together that we created that day." Or as if the story is so removed from him that recounting it is no different than singing lyrics written by a total stranger. "So we could say—and scream—anything we wanted and no one would hear us. You see, Ms. Brittain, it came to the same thing. Those two sounds." Patrick takes his backpack off and sets it at his feet. "And because there was no sound at all and all the sound in the world at the same time, whatever we said there would be accepted. Okay. Would be okay.

"We talked about girls that day. We talked about motorcycles and girls. We even had lunch with this girl we met on the road and I was sure she thought I was just as old as my uncle cause when she talked she looked at us both talked to us both. Then we just paid the bill and went off again. I had a feeling that day I never had again. Sorta like the sound—there were two parts to it. I felt like a kid. My uncle knew all the things to say and he'd been far away from home tons of times and I knew he wouldn't let anything hurt me. But I felt like a grown-up too because for the first time in my life I could say whatever I wanted to and whatever I said would be accepted. And cause we went out on the motorcycle and went to lunch with that girl.

"When I told my mother all we did that day she of course told me I could never see my uncle again. That it was just that kind of acting up that killed my father. The next time I saw him was five years later—in his casket. For a long time afterward I was sure that was why I thought that day—that day we went out together—was the best day of my life—because my mother took it away from me. But last year in England I—I don't know why—I realized—finally.....realized—I don't know why—but I did—why it was." Leslie reaches out and puts her hand lightly on his shoulder. She wants to take him in her arms.

"That day was the best day in my life because it was the only time when the same person who was making me take risks was the person who was there to protect me from risks. At the same time. Wh-while the risk was going on................Wh-what I wanted—well—to...s-say back there...........M-Ms. Br-Brittain.....w-was that..........was that..........w-what I w-wanted—Imean—t-to s-say back...there w-was that I.....h-had that had that f-feeling todagain today. Actually. M-Ms. Br-Brittain........................Th-thanks for the p-pizza. Anyway. Th-that's dumb. Dumb. J-just thanks. S-see you—well.....t-tomorrow. Actually."

Patrick and the pizza-delivery boy pass each other on the staircase.

# IV
## THE JAPANESE MONK WITH THE POT ON HIS WALL

A hefty man in his early sixties, dressed in khaki pants and a navy cotton pullover, rips the end off a *baguette* at a large lacquered oak table. He pitches the bread downward then swirls it around in his plate where it's landed, launching little splashes of gravy, like flying fishes, above the meatchunks he's attempting to shovel onto his fork with it. Totally absorbed in study, he analyzes the configuration of his dinner, occasionally experimenting with the effect different fork-beef-bread placements have on the navigational capacity of the potatoes within their viscous brown sauce. Having finally cornered a particularly recalcitrant nugget of potroast between his soggy-crust-reinforced fist and the silverware, he moves in for the jab, rushing his prey past a full graying mustache to his mouth like a youth trying to hide a stolen penny by quickly swallowing it.

His three guests look at him as they enjoy their meals, ready to hear what he was about to say before he turned his attention to culinary tectonics.

The man chews. Stares into his plate. Chews and nods, seeming to be carrying on a conversation in food language with the esteemed assemblage before him. While he makes eye contact with a potato cube, a lethargic woman who looks several years his senior lugs a pained smile and a huge silver tray of seconds into the wood-beamed diningroom, only to be shooed away by his wagging hand which then abruptly changes direction, waves her back in and points to the table. From which he has not moved his eyes. As soon as she finds a place for the tray between the bread basket and two nearly empty bottles of wine, the impatient disembodied wrist wipes her out again.

The three silent colleagues are still turned attentively toward their host, as if he's been speaking all along and has just stopped for an instant to take a bite of food.

He takes a bite of food. "Won't work," he says to the cooked carrot-cube cruising around with his potato pal.

"Yeahit'll work," answers Xavier Roque.

The man of the house grabs a bottle of wine around the neck like Bluto used to grab Popeye just before attempting to strangle him to death. He holds it up to his guests, all of whom nod, and empties it into the half-filled glass before a thin sandy-haired kid wearing jeans, an Eric Clapton t-shirt and a blue-madras sportcoat. Grunting into an armoire "Won't work." behind him, the man produces two more bottles of Burgundy.

"It'll work, Marcel. It's working now." Roque laughs nervously and glances quickly at the others.

Marcel serves Roque the rest of the second open bottle and flaps his hand across the table at a man in a brown suit, about Roque's age, who slides the corkscrew over. Marcel shakes his head, pierces the cork. "Nah!.......It don't feel good no more."

"Maybe we can get a new girl," the man in the suit suggests in a slow twangy voice. "Someone less......endearing." Roque jerks his head and starts to say something. "More...business as usual," the twang interrupts. "Someone who "

"runs in front othe station every day?" Marcel snaps, his outsized eyes seeming to work independently of each other. "Who's run in front othe station every day at the same second for so long no one even notices her no more? Gimme your fuckin glass, old man!" The kid in the t-shirt titters as Marcel pours. "Broad's a fuckin piece oparkin lot!"

"You g "

"No matter" he cuts Roque off. "what the fuck the—I got officers won't go out in weather that babe runs in."

The kid says, "Maybe we can get a new guy."

"*You* wanna fuck er?" Marcel snarls into his face.

The kid smiles, his voice stretching into a high-pitched warble. "Yyy...yeaahh!" He looks around the table and puffs out his chest. "Yyyeaahh! Why not?" Marcel and the guy in the suit laugh along with him. Roque shoots up and pounds his fist so hard into the tabletop that everything on it bounces and skids, bringing the lethargic woman padding in from the kitchen. "I'LL TELL YOU WHY THE FUCK NOT YOU FUCKING HOGS I'LL TELL YOU WHY NBECAUSE IT'S WORKING JUST FINE AND YOU'RE GONNA KEEP YOUR FILTH OUT OF IT, OUTA MY LIFE AND HER "

" running shorts," the kid says.

The guy in the suit flies from his chair at Roque. The kid rushes over to the guy.

Struggling to his feet, Marcel "Will You Just Look At Yourself For The Love OGod!" kicks his chair back, "Isn't This What The Fuck I Mean?" slams both palms onto the table, "You Ridiculous Love-Sick Asshole!" leans forward into Roque's space, "You're Making A Mockery It, Of Us, And Most Of All" then, his thick neck expanding and contracting in spurts, grunts his way back into his seat. "of yourself........You're not too far gone to at least see that.....Are you Xavier?...Yet? Bring The Cheese!" He waves his hand at the lethargic woman when he realizes she's standing in the doorway.

While the band sits listening to each other's agitated breathing, the lethargic woman clears the table and lopes back in with small plates, another *baguette* and a large round wooden board which she holds out before Marcel's chest. He points a stubby finger to the brie, the chèvre, the roquefort and the butter, dispatching her to serve the others once he's gotten what he wants. Roque smiles at the woman and shakes his head. "Jacques?" she offers, in the agreeable, undisturbed voice of a woman who either is used to such outbursts in her diningroom or has been successfully trained to pretend they haven't happened. The man in the suit doesn't want any. "Thierry?"

"*Merci, Madame*, the kid says. He nods to the chèvre. "Don't you worry about what the ol—madame—hears around here?" he asks Marcel through ventriloquist teeth as the lethargic woman, her smile so artificial it begs to be replaced by a frown, shuffles away with the ch

"Leave The Cheese!" Marcel barks, guillotining another slab of butter before *madame* can get the board onto the table. "*Non!*" he barks in response to Thierry.

"I'm not too far gone to see that," Roque answers calmly. "I'm not too far gone to see anything. I'm not too far gone. We're not gonna get another girl, another cop, another plan, we're gonna stop wasting everyone's time and doing everyone else's job," He fills Marcel's glass. "and you jealous, rarely fucked sonsobitches are gonna stop trying to get a second-hand hard-on on my back." He relaxes into his chair and raises his glass to his colleagues. Thierry laughs. Marcel drinks. "To Your Loves!" Roque declares.

"I don't have a problem with it," the kid tells his partners as Jacques pours him a refill.

Jacques says, "Marcel doesn't like the way Xavier looks—he's not suffering enough." He kicks Roque's chair a little harder than a friendly ribbing would require.

"I don't like the way Marcel looks." Roque fills his host's glass and nods to the armoire. "He's suffering too much!" The man of the house hauls out a couple more bottles and hands one and the corkscrew to Jacques who first pours Roque the rest of what's left on the table. "So how did you know?" Roque asks the kid.

"Was I right, Xavier?"

"Dosnee He Look Like You Were Fuckin Right For The Love OGod?" Marcel growls.
Thierry punches his fist into his palm and jumps out of the chair. "I Was Right! *Pu-tain!*"
"You're too smart to be a cop, kid," Roque says, pointing both index fingers. "How did you know?"

"Ain't me who's smart, old man, tsuh machine. Here goes— "

"And then you'll tell me why it was such a fuckin national security secret" Roque looks at Marcel. "how you found out."

"International," Jacques sniffs.

" Here goes—once Jacques had her followed and we knew her address I ran a check on everyone who lives in her building and she was the only one who met the description. Jacques's assholes—excuse me—" The kid grins at Jacques. "that's not the most respectful way of putting it, is it? The assholes who Jacques supervises asked some questions, hung around, and we were sure as we were gonna be she was who she is—I mean—not like, not like just goin there every day after her run to polish someone's silver."

"Or get tied to someone's bed."

Roque starts toward Jacques and Marcel waves him back to his chair.

Then I went shopping. Tapped into her credit card records and got lists got a good half-dozen years' worth olists oshit. Back teighty-six."
"But the kid coulda gone back bef "

Thierry smiles at Marcel. "I coulda gone back to when her mother charged her diapers!"

"They didn't have computers then," Jacques says between his teeth.

"So with I had these lists so I started grouping first the types of purchases. Plane tickets, hotels, restaurants, sporting goods, books, tapes, clothes, shoes, software, cosm—hardware, cosmetics, "

"We Get It!" Marcel flaps his hand.

" monthly métro pass, opera tickets, "

"ExxxCuu-uuzzze Uh-Uhsssss"

"Why, the guys you date don't go to the opera?" Roque asks Jacques, who starts toward him until Marcel waves him back to his chair.
" meheh-ehehnnnnn's wea-earrrrr. She buy ya present, Xavier? Ywant some more?"
"I don't think so," Marcel tells the kid.

"Magazine subscriptions, memberships, groceries, stationery, knitting needles, "
"You're joking!" Roque squawks.

"She knit, old man?" Thierry asks.

"Notice there's no yarn. Just..." Marcel's brows arch over his independently active eyes. "...needles."
Jacques takes his hands out of his jacket pockets and lights a cigarette.

"Keep going," Roque says, moving his chair closer to Thierry's.

"Just what I did. I took first I looked to see if any of the categories themselves could tell us something—like if she had a history of shopping in....in nautical-supply stores or if she "
"Then you woulda hadda fuck er on a *boat*!" Marcel blasts, motioning for the corkscrew while he works himself up into a laughing wheeze.
"Or if she eats out every meal," Thierry continues. He reaches around and pounds on Marcel's back to calm him down. "Yknow she drinks alotta a real lotta tea this real expensive t "
"Of course I know she drinks tea I'm supposed to keep track of

her!"

"The kid's toys are supposed to keep track of her," Jacques tells Roque. "You're supposed to fuck her."

"Nothin there. So then I start lookin inside each category—OK, plane tickets, but is it always Air Iraq? Does she drag her ass all the way out to Versailles to buy her running shoes when the best store in town's a block from her place?"

"I Want Dessert!" Marcel announces.

"Letim finish, old man! You hear this before?" Roque asks Jacques.

"All except the "

" opera tickets. I want to know why *I* never heard it bef "
" and the knittin needles I Want Des "
Into the diningroom shuffles a huge refrigerated grin under which rigid dishtowel-draped arms present a handsome homemade hot apple pie. "Don't you worry," Thierry asks again, "about wh "

"*Non!* I gotta piss!"

"We'll miss yold man!" Roque leans over and puts a hand on Marcel's arm. Marcel brushes it off as if it were pigeon shit and extracts his lumpy legs from under the table. "*Merci, Madame!*" Roque says. He makes a place for the plate by serving Thierry the remainder of a bottle and handing it to the lethargic woman. "We'll take care of it."

"DON'T YOU COCK-SUCKERS CUT INTO THAT WITHOUT ME!" Marcel bellows through the half-open john-door in the corridor, competing with his urine stream to be heard.

*Madame* removes the cheese service and brings in antique dessert plates, each bearing a different sketch of Notre Dame. "Voudriez-vous du café?" she permits herself to whisper through tight pale lips to her husband's friends.

"*S'il vous plaît, Madame,*" Roque tells her, heading down the corridor after he hears the toilet flush.

"*Merci, Madame.*" The kid gets up to look at the finely framed engravings of Notre Dame on the walls.

Jacques stuffs his cigarette between his teeth and his hands in his jacket pockets.

"Kid spent weeks!" Marcel says proudly as Roque takes his seat.

Thierry comes back to the table. "There were two Visas in France, one Visa in the States, an American Express, a—this new American Express thing you can stretch out payments, and a Galeries Lafayette card. So for each—and a Hôtel de Ville Hardware—I gotta know what her apartment looks like, ol man, she do creative shit with plumbing apparatus?—so for "

"Smart girl—she got back-ups in case the main pipe don't work any more."

"You bet, Jacques." Roque points both index fingers at him. "Man speaks from experience."

" so for each card there were six years of lists and more if that wouldn'ta done it and needless to say I wasn't gonna be workin on this at my little toy terminal next to Marie-Laure the department chief's whore."

Marcel pulls the pie over to himself. "Kid spent weeks!"

"What's the rest of us gonna eat, old man?" Jacques asks.

"My Ass!" Marcel beams and starts slicing.

"I'll have an extra-big piece, please," Thierry says. "And some pie, too! So about middle othe second week—thanks, boss!—on one of her French Visas I discover a charge shows up like every month, coupla months, a couple hundred francs at a store in the sixth I never heard of. I put it to one side with all the other shit I gotta check out "

"This shit really gets you off, doesn't it?"

"Yeah but not as much as takin out my wang in trains," the kid tells Roque. "Most of it I could do in the machine—she charged a college course once and I got into the school's system—nothin weird—something like Rock Music And Its Effect on Marketing Trends or—thanks "

"No that's not weird," Jacques twangs, trading the lethargic woman his full ashtray for a coffee.

"The rest I did in person, so I go like a week later to this place—it's called The" Thierry waits until *madame* leaves the room. "The Goldenrod."

"A garden-supply store? I ask the kid when he first tells me."

"A garden-supply store? the old man asks when I first tell him."

Thierry reaches around and pounds the breath back into Marcel's laugh. "No. And she wasn't makin donations to save the biosphere either or buyin rags in a boutique with a cutesy name.....This is a bookstore, Xavier.......A bookstore...Whose name can be separated into two words." Thierry pulls a pack of cigarettes from his jacket and offers it around the table "If you're so inclined.", his gaze fixed on Roque. Roque takes one and the kid lights for them both. "BING-FUCKING-O I tell myself when I—I hadn't even walked in yet—all you gotta do is look in the window!"

"Golden...Rod" Roque recites slowly, aloud to himself, nodding then shaking his head. "Amazing. A-*ma*-zing! Incredible work!" he says to the kid. "Amazing fucking job!"

"Comic books and story books and magazines, CDs, audiocassettes, videos I guess you can't really just call it a bookstore photos and catalogues, novels, fucking coffeetable books fucking serious like works of art more like a I'd say like a full-service one-stop greeting cards postcards for th—little these like little figurine things—for those who share an interest in.....in what, Xavier?" Roque squints through his smoke. "In relationships. Right, Xavier? And the potentials to be explored in the balance of power inherent therein."

Marcel and Jacques applaud.

Jacques says, "I think the kid means S n M."

"And in French—get this—English, German, fucking Dutch what else, I don't know, a half-dozen languages this like Oriental language. Deliveries—cartons oshit comin in thdoor all the time, woman gift-wrapping this real expensive-looking lithograph thing. We're in the wrong business, old men."

"We're workin on gettin in the right business real fast here!" Marcel says. "She looks like such a...healthy little babe runnin past every mornin—hair in a ponytail, Mickey fuckin Mouse sweatshirts, "

"That's just the type you gotta watch out for," Jacques says in the back of his throat. "They don't all go around wearing leather masks." He kicks Roque's chair. "Right, old man?"

"She's not—I don't think she's.....she just plays with it. She "

"Plays with it enough to want more. Can't be your charm, old man!" Marcel starts sputtering between roars but holds his hand up to stop Thierry from coming around to pound on his back.

"Ahhh, you're gonna hurt Xavier's feelings, old man. It's not that it's not his charm. It's just that we didn't want to be dumb enough to *count* on it being his charm."

Roque points both index fingers at Jacques.

"I left. Went back home, got the store up on the screen and matched her dates and times of purchase to their inventory records and came up with what she bought. Then I went back and bought what she bought. Books—I asked this...you OK, old man?"
Marcel can reach the brandy from his chair but the glasses are too far back on the armoire shelf. Grunting, he presses onto the armrests and heaves himself up "Wait!" then splats back down. Turns around. Counts heads with his stubby cheese-choosing finger. Begins the heaving process anew.
"I take it back," Roque says, getting out of his seat. "I think you two should switch jobs." He leans against the wall by the armoire and looks at his cigarette. "I think the old man should handle all calculations and the kid should mastermind the bombing."

"But you still keep the pussy," Jacques sneers.

"Got that right, old man! Good stuff."

The three men watch while Marcel sets the glasses in a neat row then meticulously measures the drops so that all the lustrous little liquid horizons match, seeming to connect to each other despite their crystal barriers.
"I asked this sweet old lady knitting at the cash register for the serial numbers from the inventory l "
"See I" Marcel pounds the table and "Did I" swigs his brandy. "What I Tell You About The Fuckin" Flaps his hand. "Knittin" Swigs again. "Needles!"
"Bought every one they had that she got—they didn't have em all I wound up with six—expensive sons obitches—and here comes, old man—" The kid looks Roque in the eye. "in one of em there's this story about this American student and a young Italian soldier in uniform alone on this night train and you can im "
"*Hoh la vache!*" Roque wipes his face with his hand and shakes his head, looks at his brandy. Doesn't want it sips it anyway.
"Student a girl, was it?"
"Last time I looked, old man," Roque answers Jacques before

Thierry can. "Not the soldier, though. Soldier was a boy. Do I got that right, kid?"

Reaching back without turning around, Marcel lifts a mahogany box of Havana cigars from an armoire drawer. "You know, old man," the kid tells him, digging a joint out of his cigarette pack, "—no, thanks! I saw this picture once of this Japanese monk who lived in a little cell so small he could touch the four walls. Put everything he had on shelves around him and sat on his mat and no matter what he needed in the whole world all he had to do was stretch his arm out.........just a little bit....." Thierry demonstrates by reaching across Jacques's nose ".....see?" Jacques whacks him away. "And there it was. Kinda looked like you, too, boss. Had a....." He traces the outline of a big belly onto Jacques's midsection. Jacques whacks him away.

"I Gotta Go Piss!" Marcel announces.

"Did he have a john on his wall?" Jacques wants to know.

"A pot."

"Kid says he had a pot," Jacques tells Marcel in case he didn't hear.

"What were the other ones?" Roque asks Thierry. "I'm gonna open a window."

"It's Open!" Marcel growls as he lugs out of the room.

"The other what?"

Roque is feeling like a wad of raw cotton standing on the edge of a very sharp blade. He's fascinated by what he's hearing, excited by it, he feels manipulated and indignant, proud, possessive. He misses Leslie. Wants to get back to her. "It's open," he notices at the window.

"The other what?" the kid repeats.

"The other stories—in the books—the other.....stories."

"Not as easy to pull off. Rich bitch kidnapped n tamed by her own butler, reform school scene, after-hours spanking at the gym, fantastic slave societies."

"Usual stuff," Jacques says, running his cigar under his nose.

"It was too perfect," Thierry goes on. "The messages come in about the meeting in Brussels an "
"T's why we let yrot in ignorance, old man! First thing outa your fuckin mouth woulda been" Marcel returns with a laugh that's too tame to worry the kid. "hey babe read any good books lately about "
"pree-verts in trains?" Jacques says.
Thierry takes a drag and holds the joint up to his pals. "Good!" he strains out through blocked lungs "More for me!" when they turn him down. "So the soldier's sittn there it's the middle othe "

"I gotta see the kid's set-up."

"Chez moi," Thierry tells Roque, "you don't get no antique plates and potroast, ol man. Pizza n pot. Jimi Hendrix posters, none othisssuhhh" He runs over to a wall and reads from an engraving in a mock-scholarly voice. "External Buttresses of the Notre Dame Nave collection shit. So they're sittn "
"Kid's place.....kid's place," Marcel tells Roque, "looks like a fuckin intensive care unit, for the love oGod! Cept it's for keepin track oyour girlfriend insteada fuckin around with someone's guts."

"Same thing," Jacque spits through a crooked mouth.

A laugh starts in Marcel's jowls and implodes through his throat, burrowing back into his intestines, reverberating off their walls, becoming more shrill and breathy the deeper it drills. "Lights and cables computers phones fuckinnn...fuckin screens. These screens—" He giggles into his hand like a child. "when they're not doin—when they're not givin us her her uhh "

"seat reservation number," the kid offers.

" you know what they got? YOU KNOW WHAT THEY FUCKIN GOT?" Marcel's red face turns redder and his voice sharpens and thins so that it's difficult to tell whether he's laughing or weeping. The men wait for him to come back to them. "THEY GOT FLYIN FUCKING TOASTERS FOR THE LOVE OGOD TOASTERS WITH—MOVIN TOASTERS WITH FUCKIN WINGS!" Thierry gets up and pounds on Marcel's back when he starts to "INhhhuuhh....Ccc-hhh-olor!" choke.

"Pssssst! Xavier!" Jacques whispers. "Kid wants to show you his flying toasters." Roque looks out the window. Jacques kicks Roques chair.

"So they're sittn there," the kid continues, rubbing tight circles with the heel of his hand below Marcel's shoulderblades, "and the girl's just nodding off, like propped up against the seat, and the soldier-boy takes his dick out n starts playin with it—'crisp dress uniform' it said in the book—real slow like, reaeal slow." He rubs one last time and looks around into Marcel's face before going back to the table. "She's sittin there across from him "

"That what you did, old man?" Jacques asks.

Roque slides his chair along the polished parquet floor. He puts his arm around Jacques's shoulders and looks him in the eyes. "You can tell me, old man........Just how long's it been, old m "
"MAYBE XAVIER WANTS TO GIVE US A DEMONSTRATION!" Jacques yells, kicking Roque's chair away.
"MAYBE I DO!" Roque yells back, shooting up and grabbing at his zipper. "YOU TELL ME YOU GOT PROBLEMS WITH *ME*! YOU TELL ME YOU GOT PROBLEMS WITH *ME*! We Gotta Get This Guy Laid. Laid" He peers down at Jacques "Or Wasted!" then yanks his zipper up and takes his seat. "Or the only thing gonna be blowin up is our asses!"
"Good idea, Xavier, what's Mademoiselle Leslie Brittain doing this evening?"
"YOU WANT ER FUCKIN NUMBER? ASK THE WUNDERKIND!" He throws his jaw at Thierry. "BUT GUESS WHAT—SHE'S THE WRONG SEX!"
With nervous eyes Thierry follows his host's hand as it flaps the lethargic woman out of the doorway then plants its cigar in a big glass ashtray near the pie plate. "Nothin tworry bout now," Marcel tells him. "Save it for when they *stop* goin at each other. I didn't pick you fuckers to love each other. I didn't pick you to not love each other. I picked you to get me into the Cathedral." Suddenly there's no more wheeze and no more red face. "I think I picked the best. We got work. That you guys don't even know about. And if we can just keep Xavier Roque's pecker from gettin so big it works its way up and wraps itself around what's left of his brain—and I'm not totally convinced othat yet—" Marcel looks at Roque Roque looks out the window. "then we're good as halfway through the tunnel. When we

meet at the kid's—I'll let you know—I'm—couple days—soon—I'm bringin the cop who'll be goin in with me—DON'T SAY IT!" He points at Thierry. "I'll know by then. Down to two possible. Then we'll lay it out for im."

"And for ourselves," Jacques twangs, jamming his hands into his jacket pockets. "Not a bad idea to go over it another couple hundred times."

"Not before. I won't paint no pictures til you get a feel for im."

"What's their names?" Roque asks. "Do we know them?"

Marcel flaps his hand. The group falls silent. Thierry jerks his chair back - stands - bends his knees - squints - raises his right arm - steadies his right elbow in his left hand - aims - launches his roach. Objective: floor-to-ceiling window across the room. Jacques makes dive-bomber noises through puffed cheeks as the missile aborts. In the post-mission silence, the kid stands facing the window for a couple minutes then turns and addresses the table as if orating from a podium. "The old man.....thinks—here—the old man here—Marcel—thinks......that when we get the wall of the station down there's gonna be a chauffeured BMW waiting on the other side. And him and this new guy thisss........new guy.....are gonna get in, pour themselves a couple whiskies, watch a little video—maybe a little.....S n M video...maybe not...maybe a rerun othe World Cup.....more like it—or just admire the fine tilework on the walls of the tunnel which we hope hasn't disappeared in the past half-millennium if it was ever there in the first place, and a couple minutes later, when they get to the notorious secret hiding place that Lord help us better not've moved in the past half-dozen-hundred years if it was ever there at all, a grinning helpful fellow in a porter's uniform'll hold the car door for him—as well as the several purchases he made at the fine boutiques along the way—so he and his coal-mining pal can go in and receive his priceless ancient document which someone at the other end will've already gotten outa the wall for them and put in a little plastic bag with handles for him—and which we hope hasn't been removed—or fuckin disintegrated—in the past five hundred years if it was ever there at all—and they'll get back in the car and be back at his desk in time to answer questions from his press pals about why those bad Arab kids would set a bomb off at the Quai des Orfèvres and how in his high opinion they were able to pull it off!"

"And was it an inside job," Jacques snickers.

"Old man," Thierry sits down and wraps his hands around his Marcel's forearm. "stay the fuck outa the hole. You know what they built those tunnels for, old man. Bettern all of us. Hot little nuns to slither through on their pregnant bellies on their way to the other end of a cock. They built em to bury babies in. They built em to kick rats down."

"They Built Em" Marcel flaps his free hand at the kid and reaches for the ashtray. "So *You'll* Never Have To Look At A Fuckin Price Tag Again For The Rest O Your Wasted Life!"

"Yeah, kid, think of all those Jimi Hendrix concerts you can go to."

"He's been dead for twenty-five y "

"My point exactly," Jacques says.

"You guys think those nuns went in with overnight bags the size othe old man's here?" Roque asks as he stands, sweeping his sportcoat from the back of his chair. On his way out he strolls around the table to drum on Marcel's stomach with his fingertips. "The rats maybe. Maybe the rats did—thanks for dinner, old man—but those are the ones you'll be trippin over." He points both index fingers. "The others made it out. Thank *madame* for me, willyuh? Good meal. See you guys tomo—well, all except Jacques...Word has it" Already out in the hallway, Roque shouts through the entrance as he closes the door. "That He'll Be On A Job.....Hot Pursuit.....Somethin About Flying Little Boys And Their Kitchen Appliances........Kick My Chair For Me, Willyuh, Jacques?" Marcel flaps his hand.

Roque takes the Rue de Turenne to a cafe off the Place des Vosges. He feels like a receptacle for blood and adrenaline, can almost sense them crashing and curling up against each other within the walls of his skin and organs, like the ocean waves in a Hiroshige painting. He orders a double-espresso and asks where the phone is, decides to leave the car under Marcel's building and send one of his guys for it in the morning. Whenever that is. His coffee ain't talkin but while it gets cold on the counter he keeps it company anyway, then walks once around the *place*, stopping for a smoke in front of Victor Hugo's House, moving out from under the arcade to look at the points of light shining through where someone pierced pinholes in the black-blue sky. They don't know either. So he goes back and orders another

*"Double?"*

*"Non."*

on his way downstairs. Phone's still there when he comes out of the men's room. He turns around halfway up the staircase and goes down again.

"WELCOME TO INTERNATIONAL RELATIONS! PLEASE LEAVE A MESSAGE AFTER THE TONE OR FAX OR EMAIL US AT THE FOLLOWI"BEEEEEEEEEEEEEEEEEE

## V
## HIS MAJESTY'S BASKETBALL TEAM

    *and she's the laydee who way-ayts Since her mind left schoo-ool it nehvah—he-si-tay-ayts She Won't Waste Time *"ON" *E-Le-Men-Tree Taw-awk caussse* "SHE'S" *—twen-ti-eth-cen-tur-y foh-ox She's a—twen-ti-eth-cen-tur-y- foh-ox*
                           "SHE'S A—TWEN-TI-ETH-CEN-TUR-Y-FOH-OX"

  Leslie and Jim Morrison are chasing the drizzle down the Boulevard St-Michel.

  *She's a—twen-ti-eth-cen-tur-y-foh-ox*
                           "SHE'S A—TWEN-TI-ETH-CEN-TUR-Y-FOH-OX"
  *Got the wor-rld—lohohked up—insi-ide—a pla-a-astic boh-ox*
                         "GOT THE WOR-RLD LOHOHKED UP—INSI-IDE—A PLA-A-ASTIC BOH-OX"
  *She's a twentiethcenturyfox huhyeh*
                           "SHE'S A TWENTIETHCENTURYFOX HUHYEH"
  *twentiethcenturyfox uhbayb twentiethcenturyfox huh*
          "TWENTIETHCENTURYFOX UHBAYB TWENTIETHCENTURYFOX HUH"
  *She's a Twen-Ti-Eth-Cen-Tur-Y Foh-oh-Ox-oxxxxx*
          "FOHHHHH-OHHHHH-OXXXXX-OXXXXX!"

  "YEAHHH! Monnndayeee mawrrniiinn DOORSzzzzz-ffiiiiixxxxx forrr Lessslieee, Remindin you that mahah sister Leslie will be sharing this very air-chair with me here on June twenty-sixth for the Doubly-Great-Brittains-in-the-Morning Show right here on WDVQ FM eighty-eight six, Cheshire County, New Jersey, *thee-ee finest* listener-supported community radio station in thiss heere nation. Six"

At the bottom of the boulevard, **"Twenty-nine in-your-mornin here. Gonna take care of a few pieces of biz"** traffic is blocked on both sides of the river, from the Place St-Michel ("Holy Shit Martin was right!") clear over the bridge to ("pee dee aitch cue") on the Quai des Orfèvres. (" ly Shit") Leslie **"an beee—as per usual—riiight"** turns off the tape to try and hear what the driver of a black Peugeot 405 is shouting to one of the city cops directing soundtrucks and camera crews through the barricades and past the end-to-end national guard transport vehicles which now outline the *quartier* as with bold green marker strokes on a map.

("Jeezuss you were right, Mar-tin") had rung after Patrick left—just as Leslie was explaining to a member of the scooter-pizza fleet the relationship between coming prepared with change to a customer's house and walking away with "more of a tip than you would when you make it your business to purposely show up with no change at all just so you can satisfy your uncontrollable need to inflict on others the type of negativity with which your pitiful little daily struggle is remarkably overflowing." For which the poor thing gave her an extra packet of hot-sauce. Much too drained from Patrick-in-the-hallway to call Martin back, Leslie took as playful provocation his message about avoiding the Quai des Orfèvres on her run tomorrow. "They're transferring your favorite vandals to a max security," he breathed into the phone, trying to sound like a handkerchief-filtered informant. "There are bomb threats every time the Chief of Police goes to piss ("there a connection?") and they're running into each other like Keystone Kops ("Kocks") in there, trying to smell out their own garbage. It's gonna be war-torn *premier arrondissement*, Leslie, starting at they say four a.m. Go run in the gym. You can do some Camerounian maintenance in the sauna. (*"Vas t'en faire foutre, Martin!"*) You'd know all this if you had a television. Call me." \*BeeeeeeeeeeeeeP\*\*\*\*\*BeeeeeeeeeeeeeP\*\*\*\*\*

**"back." "Hello, this is Brooke Shields. June is National Domestic Violence Awareness Month and across the country millions"** ("of civic-minded women will generously get themselves beaten bloody so that you can be made aware of this age-old modern plague.") Disappearing into the arithmetic and geography and topography of getting her route and timing back on track, Leslie doesn't realize the end of Brooke's soliloquy has done come and gone—the part about how **"YOU CAN HELP"**—until in the Tuileries Gardens she revives from her left-brain daze and finds herself running in time to a big-band finale-drum-solo. And thinking **"YEAHH, DON'T GET MUCH BETTER N THAT AROUND HERE! BIG BAND-IN-THE-MORNIN RIGHT HERE ON THE** about **DANNEY BRITTAIN—DANNY-THE GREAT-BRITTAIN—"** Roque. **"SHOW."**

Roque was the other four calls—the ones Patrick had been so anxious about getting to. When Leslie heard the first word of the first message and knew it was him she immediately stopped the machine, sat down at the dinette table and ate most of the pizza ("not a fucking not even a little piece of anchovy shit. They're too dumb to even be good scum! If I'd'a gotten my call I'd'a sent it with enough anchovy droppings tha—You want anchovies, lady? Surrre, noh-ohh prohh-blemmm! You want a little pizza with that, too?"), sticking the rest in the refrigerator before changing into an oversized Cannes Film Festival 1990 t-shirt then straightening the apartment, e-mailing to Danney and making a list of what she had to do the next day and the next week, what Patrick had to do the next day and the next week, what she and Patrick had to work on together right away and the trouble they needed to get into between now and July, at which time, she told herself, he'll be either too happy or too terrified to abandon her. Once the Picasso mug of double Earl Gray and milk was in place on the nighttable, the huge red-ink note saying HOW MANY MORE DAYS ARE YOU GONNA FORGET TO BUY HONEY, HONEY? was taped to the inside of the front door and all the lights in the apartment were turned off, Leslie lit the silver-glitter Mercedes candle idling behind her tea (a gift from Jack Kote: "The grossest thing, Leslie, I've seen in a long time. Thought of you. Here. With my compliments." "You think that's gonna make me not take it, doncha, Jack. Thanks! I'll cherish it forever."), rewound the answering machine, set it to play and dove into bed like someone who's just put the camera on delay-automatic and needs to scurry in front of the lens for a picture with her beau.

Propped on pillows, she felt as if she were about to listen in on someone else's life.

*"BONJOUR, LESLIE! C'EST XAVIER—ENFIN, C'EST ROQUE. JE*

T'APPELLE PLUS TARD. A TOUT À L'HEURE."
*BeeeeeeeeeeeeP*****BeeeeeeeeeeeeP*****BeeeeeeeeeeeeP*

"BONSOIR, LESLIE! C'EST MOI DE NOUVEAU. I WANT TO TALK TO YOU. DID YOU GET TH—DID YOU FIND THE PACKAGE?..........IF YOU WANT TO CALL ME TONIGHT IT'S FORTY-EIGHT NINETY-TWO NINETY SEVENTY-FIVE. CALL—I—CALL LATE...I HAVE A.......MEETING."*BeeeeeeeeeeeeeP*****BeeeeeeeeeeeeP*****

"LESLIE!" ("CHILL, ROQUE, I AIN'T GOIN NOWHERE!") "IF YOU CAN'T CALL ME TONIGHT CALL TOMORROW MORNING! FORTY-TWO SIXTY-SIX TWELVE THIRTY-FOUR. LESLIE! I WANT TO TALK TO YOU I HAVE TO TALK TO YOU I HAVE TO SEE YOU. I HAVE TO SEE YOU IN........DID YOU TRY THEM ON? DID YOU" *BeeeeeeeeeeeeeP*****BeeeeeeeeeeeeP*****

"DID YOU TOUCH YOURSELF IN THEM? I CAN BE THERE AT EIGHT TOMORROW EVENING. ANYTHING YOU WANT TO DO. ANYWHERE YOU WANT T.....LESLIE! FORTY-TWO SIXTY-SIX TWELVE THIRTY-FOUR. I'M IN AT EIGHT TOMORROW. LESLIE, I'M GOING TO TOUCH YOU IN IT. I'LL TOUCH YOU *WITH* IT, LESLIE." *BeeeeeeeeeeeeeP*****BeeeeeeeeeeeeP*****

Leslie runs around some refuse workers watching a National Guardsman bomb-proof a wastecan by sealing its lid. Danney is **"EXPLORING THE MUSICAL UNIVERSE WITH THE ENSEMBLE NIPPONIA—TRADITIONAL JAPANESE MUSIC—UNDER ME HERE. BUT WAIT!.....WHAT IS THIS?.....WHAT *COULD* THIS BE?.....DOES THIS SOUND LIKE THE BLUES, BABY?.....I THINK"** in a dripping dawn-garden. Cool and clouded and empty, with Leslie and the trashmen. **"THIS SOUNDS LIKE DA"** Thinking about Roque. Leslie and the trashmen thinking about Roque. Everything she passes thinking about Roque. Everything she passes steps on slips through ducks under avoids runs into thinking about thinking about and the deeper Danney's dirty beat bores dark into her layers....the more it becomes a heavy primal heart-pump...the stronger it drives her feet and her pulse to channel the feeling of the sounds through her skin, the deeper the more the stronger she runs with the need to have **BLOOOOOOOOZZZZZZ!** Roque again. Thinking about Roque Thinking.........................................
..............................Thinking.......................about........................
..........................................................................................
Roque..........................................................Thinking about She emerges from the verdance onto the Place de la Concorde and Paris

seems like it's moving backward in its day. Going to sleep under the grayened ceiling of rain. Smashing its newborn sun into bits of yellow headlights. The *place* is stifled and confused, trying to do its *place* work in a morning-dusk, where the monuments and hotels and official buildings demarking its vastness don't know the difference between one daybreak and the next and have turned off their lights despite the dark dampness damp darkness.

Into the damp darkness Leslie is absorbed, drawn to the narrow *quai* constricted by its ill-tempered river and uncomfortable trees. She turns off the tape because the thumping of the blues in the thumping of her pussy is making her want to stop and she can't let herself stop running and she looks around into the shadows knowing that if this were a sunny life-affirming morning, if she were running through heat and light and color and listening to Ethel Merman, she would be in touch right now with a healthy need for an ordered, clean day, lived above the surface, and maybe she'd call Roque back today and maybe she wouldn't get to it, and either way it would be fun. But she is driven home in this mist soaked with a healthy need for a lawless, entangled day, lived dense below her surface, and she will call Roque and it will be dangerous.

She prepares for the call all morning by pretending there is none to make, helping herself to little servings of dialogue and monologue which she knows won't spoil the main meal. "Sorry you don't like semi-sweet, Dooch! Next time I'll bring back escarole." "Georges, I know it must be huge. It must be even bigger than you yourself are describing, since we never really see ourselves as others do, do we? You know who I think would probably be able to give us an accurate, reliable reading on this, Georges? Maude. Maude—that's who. Don't you think?" "Frchrissakes, Martin, what kinda pal are you, why didn't you warn me about the fucking blockade? I hadda do every cop in a four-block radius tget em tlet me through!"

"DON'T YOU WISH!" *BeeeeeeeeeeeeeP*****BeeeeeeeeeeeeeP*****

"BONJOUR, PRINCESSE! C'EST GILLES. I'VE COME TO A DECISION THAT WILL BE VERY UPSETTING TO YOU, PRINCESSE, BUT I HAVE MY FAMILY TO THINK OF. WHAT I WANT TO SAY IS I THINK IT BEST IF WE STOP SEEING EACH OTHER.....FOR AWHILE. I KNOW HOW THIS WILL CRUSH YOU, PRINCESSE, BUT YOU KNOW, LA FRANCE WAS BUILT ON SACRIFICE! AND I AM NOW CALLED UPON TO MAKE MINE! AU REVOIR." *BeeeeeeeeeeeeeP*****BeeeeeeeeeeeeeP*****

"Bonjour, Princesse! C'est Gilles. I'm also sending this by courier in case your machine's still broken." *BeeeeeeeeeeeeeP*****BeeeeeeeeeeeeeP*****

"Bonjour, Princesse! C'est Gilles. You can call me if you want to discuss this." *BeeeeeeeeeeeeeP*****BeeeeeeeeeeeeeP*****

"I got your name from—this is—excuse me—this is Mrs. John Moore of the American School of Nice, I got your name f " *BeeeeeeeeeeeeeP*****BeeeeeeeeeeeeeP*****

("Heyyy, Missusjohn! Howydoin, babe?") A bit before noon, when she's had her fill of verbal snacking, she coats her body with white—white lacy anklets, whiter lace teddy, whitest cotton roll-up-cuff shorts, weathered and relentlessly rewashed but still white t-shirt—and ties her hair back in a wide black satin ribbon. Sitting on the edge of the bed, she dials 42.66.12.34.
"*Allo!*"
("Cave-dwellers!") "Is this the Préfecture de Police?"
"Of Course It's The Préfecture De Police!"
"I certainly could tell from the way you answered the phone. Although I must admit that for a minute there I couldn't help but thinking it was my Aunt Simone sitting there with the cat in her lap. That's exactly the way she answers the phone, believe it or n " The nice lady at the Police Department hangs up. Leslie dials 42.66.12.34.
"*Allo!*"
"*Monsieur Xavier Roque, s'il vous pl* " Put brutally on hold to a tape about what *not* to call the Police Department for, she continues to warble into the receiver, stretching a lippy smile. "Thank you. You have a nice day, as well. And please—do give my regards to your lovel "
"INSPECTOR ROQUE'S OFFICE!" a throaty Marseille accent croaks, and Leslie smiles for real as hot little bubbles crash into each other in her chest.
"Is the Inspector there, please?"
"WHO WANTS TO KNOW!" spits the throat from Marseille.
"You must know the nice lady at Central Switchboard! Went to public relations school togethD-D-Don't Don't Hang Up Don't Hang Up Dtell him it's it'sss....("ohshit").... National Velvet!"
A muffled gurgle upchucks something like "*Jpas! Alvelve ou quelquechose jpas!*"

He doesn't have time for this shit, Leslie hears Roque grunt as he rips the phone away..............
............He sure is wired today, she hears his subordinate grunt back.
" e Fuck Is This?" Roque wants to know.
"Ih-ihnspeh-ehcc-tor-Roque!" Leslie singsongs in mock awe.
"*L E S L I E!*" He tenses then deflates then tenses,
"Ih-ihnspeh-ehcc-tor-Roque!"

whacking his palm over the mouthpiece. "Gtthe Fuck Outa My Office!"
"But I'm not the fuck in your office, Roque."
"Not you, for the love of—Excuse me, Leslie. I was addressing myself to my colleague here."
"Miss Manners? Roque! What's this Inspector shit? I thought you gave out parking tickets. Directed traffic. Saved women from being accosted on trains.......Guarded rock concerts from terrorist attacks."
"That's not funny, Leslie."
"I know. It's not meant to be. Everyone's guilty until proven innocent. You can whip me for my smart mouth later tonight."
"I intend to."
"I know. Shall we say eight, then?"
"*LESLIE!*" Roque sounds plaintive, nearly desperate. His voice reminds Leslie of the look on Omar Sharif's face in the bus scene at the end of Dr. Zhivago ("or was it a train....?").
"Not necessarily eight for the whipping," she continues, stepping lightly between his breaths. "Eight for at least the hysterical reunion scene. We can have maybe a nice pre-abuse dinner—I have some dead pizza somewhere around the apartment but going out might be pleasant."
"*LESLIE!*"
"Well, eight it is! You know, Roque—now you're even. The Inspector more than makes up for the Xavier. God if I'da known that Monday I'da been on my knees way sooWUH-UHNNN MIH-IH-NIH-IHTT," she screams to Patrick. "Seey'at eight," she sings in English to Roque, "and don't be *en retard* !"


"It d-didn't w—dyou mind if I—M-Ms. Brittain, it didn't—well.....w-work! Actually." Patrick focuses on his right hand and hangs his backpack over a coat-rack antler,
"Good! Be angry, Patrick! It's good for you!"

keeping his navy-cotton sportcoat

on when Leslie gestures to take it. "The ci—Imean—ci-circus act........It d-didn't—well—it d-didn't "

"Whadjya do with the real Patrick, Patrick? The one who used to make sense? Dyou have him bound and gagged in some closet?"

"Y-you know—dyou m—well—y-you know what I what I m-mean. Y-your—th-that little g-guy.....downstairs downstairs. Pr-preventitive m-maintenance or—w-what you.......you c-called " Leslie suddenly looks deadly serious. "M-Ms. Br-Brittain?" She shoves her feet into a pair of running shoes in abrupt broken pokes, forgetting to tie the laces. "G-going-to-p-pick-up-dry-dry-cleaning. Actually.....R-right?" Patrick says, beaming down at the shoes as if he's just identified a rare-vintage wine through his advanced sense of smell.

"What" Leslie "Did" tugs "He" at "Say" the "To" apartment "You?" door. "WHAT DID HE SAY TO YOU?" she screams from halfway down the corridor, marching backwards, her shoelaces whipping at her ankles.

"Y-you sure—well—dyou mind—well—y-you sure are—Imean—w-wired wired today. M-Ms. Br-Brittain. Actually." Standing in the doorway, in Paris, Patrick is focusing on a cigarette wrapper lying on the hallway carpet, in Peru.

"WHAAATT DIDD HEEE*FUCKKK*!" In the middle of one of her most intricate flails—kind of like a double-gainer of the forearm—Leslie cracks her right hand into the wall. She immediately socks it into her left hand and brings them both up to her mouth to try to squeeze the pain away with her lips. "I'm overreacting. Aren't I? Patrick." she whispers, her hands still pressing against her face. "Maybe we should get the fuck to work, huh?" She walks back home. "It's OK, Patrick! You can laugh! I see you holding it in! Holding it is isn't good for you, Patrick! Holding most things in is no" Patrick closes the door behind her. "good for you. And anyway, they come out anyway. Sooner than later. And they come out even worse! Want some tea? No—you don't get any—I mean—you make it yourself—God, Patrick, I'm beginning to sound like you frchrissakes it should be the other way around! What I meant to say is, I am making myself some tea, and should you wish to do the same, you are more than welcome to help yourself to the electricity. They come out in strokes and cancer and alcoholism and wife-beating and lack of ability to masturbate. So if you ever want to masturbate again, Patrick, let that laugh out and let's frchrissakes get the computer turned on!"

"D-do you w-want some—well—ice.....f-for your.....Imean...h-hand?" Patrick asks the fold in the *Herald Tribune* on the table.

"That's sweet of you. That's really sweet of you. If I can't stand a little idiocy-generated pain, how am I gonna be able to go out into the real world and buy honey? Which is exactly what" She puts her individual-serving teapot on to boil and points her upturned palm toward the burner. "your turn! I'm going to do and leave you alone with the entire future of my planetary enterprise on your head. Here's the scoop:" Piling pages of lists at his place at the table, Leslie leaves just enough instructions to keep him from washing up on shore with a tangle of seaweed in his mouth. "And if I'm not back after you've done all that, you can walk around in the computer and try t "

"But but M-Ms. Br-Brittain bwhat if........well.....y-you know."

"You already know where it is—remember? The good question?" She pounds on the table in a reenactment.

"No! Imean—ex-excuse me—Imean n-no, Ms. Br-Brittain. If I make a say s-something—well........w-wrong. Wrong. On the on the.....ph-phone or "

"Then there will still be children dying of starvation all over the globe tomorrow!" Leslie's out the door, the BUY HONEY! sign scotchtaped to her t-shirt. A second later she's back in. "And if it's really wrong we'll be forced to abandon it all and run away to Tahiti in shame—I'm gonna—topless—I'm gonna get your keys made while I'm out and when the phone rings don't—that's: don't—as in: don't—pick up until they say who it is and until I tell you who we never pick up for ever, just let the messages come in." She leaves. She comes back. "Your anchovy pizza's in the refrigerator—heat it up. It's always better the second day when the cheese molecules have had a chance to commune with each other. Bye." Leslie's out the door

and stays away for several hours, wanting Patrick to establish his turf and his rhythm, looking to create a break between the space where she will have spent that healthy ordered day and the space where she will be spending that healthy lawless night. Seeking to be alone with the tens then hundreds then thousands then millions of herself who keep boarding her, as if she were a *métro* car, crushing in closer and closer in their rush with her to the extreme ends of her line, while each hour of anticipation isolates more exquisitely the need ("Did I invent him?") for what she does with Roque.

At the front gate to the Luxembourg Gardens she buys a little bag of peanuts and a narrow tube of nougat from the round ruddy candy-lady whose band of assiduous young helpers combines the enchantment of the Nutcracker with the street wisdom of Al Capone. The lady herself, the original—and unsung—android, way pre-dating even the most elementary forays into Stepford Wifery or either-gender bionics, enjoys many of the advantages of her species: pastel-flowered cotton dress worn crisp and uncovered year-round, bib apron in continuous state of starched brilliant whiteness, immutable optimism-fostering facial expression. Her candies are androids, too, which is why, whatever the weather, she never has to adjust the parasol over the wide wooden table where the tiny bins of colored treats are displayed. The only thing that through the years has made Leslie suspect the Luxembourg candy-lady may be made of flesh, is that each autumn she's a little rounder and ruddier than the autumn before. Leslie hopes that the day the Luxembourg candy-lady gets so round and ruddy she turns into a huge Thanksgiving Day Parade float and explodes over the sixth *arrondissement*, she won't just have finished ingesting too many tiny binsfull of her own colored treats.

She's a nursery rhyme. For a good time go see the Luxembourg candy-lady. A guy in a brown suit gets out of a black Peugeot 405 at the curb, goes and sees the Luxembourg candy-lady, gets back into the car with his licorice-squiggles, pulls away.

In the back of the park, beyond the bandstand, past the statues and flower-ringed fountain and the palace, Leslie lifts a green metal chair from an outdoor refreshment area and carries it a couple yards to a concrete oblong. Here at all hours of the day, tall black American students play basketball with short pale French guys who stand around and watch the tall black American students play basketball. Leslie is always proud of the sacred violence with which the Americans move across that court, colonizing their territory between the drippy *politesse* of a neighboring tennis match and the impotent correctness of perfect French families sitting and sipping at the litterless ("not even one fucking styrofoam-atom frchrissakes!") refreshment area. She is content to think that every "Heyit was your fuckin ball, asshole!" floats up into the trees with each "Oui et mon husband has a very important position which requires that he stay at the office very late—even on weekends—in fact, especially on weekends—and even holidays." and gets absorbed and scrambled by the branches and that one day in the far future alien tree-readers will come to the Luxembourg and take back word that Parisian females with their young used to stroll here on warm spring afternoons saying "Hey on holiday weekends it was your fuckin husband, ballass!" to each other.

"You gonna get them nice white shorts oyours all fulla park dirt, aren'tchya, miss?"

"How nice oyou to be concerned, man! Whadyuh propose we do

about that? Want a nougat?"

"Thanks." The kid bends over and sticks two long fingers down into the plastic tube resting in Leslie's lap.

"Cn these guys play basketball?" she asks, tossing her chin toward the short pale ones. Her new pal twitches in a single-breath laugh to himself. "Gives painful new meaning to the term only game in town, doesn't it? What'ryuh studyin?"

He squats beside her chair "You." and flicks at the gold safety pin on her t-shirt.

"Bachelor's, Master's or Ph.D.?" Leslie wants to know, looking him in the eyes while she squeezes his sweaty forearm. "And you better get it right." She squeezes again.

"Ba-chelorrr's?" he tries tentatively.

"Actually makes no difference to me. But you'd make a goodOOPP!" An out-of-bounds ball comes at her. She pops up, flicks it onto the court "Master. 's candidate." and heads for the rear gate.

Telescoping to six feet seven inches, the kid shouts, "CnI Getn Touch Wichyuh?"

Leslie trots back and places the plastic tube with one remaining nougat chunk at the toe of his left shoe. "The candy-lady'll be our contact!" she whispers up the tower, then straightens "You know what they say about the size othe foot." and walks away again.

"I Thought It Was The Thumb!"
"You Must Know More About It ThAN ME! IT'S YOUR..........THUMB."


"Did you get my plane ticket?"
"....."
"The plane ticket—you know! I can finally have my dream and run away to the jungles of Brazil! You don't need me anymore frchrissakes! You have things much more under control than I ever did! Look at this place—I didn't take you on to do my *ménage*! So when's your lunch with Barbara? Didjeat?"

Patrick unfocuses.

"Housework," Leslie defines as she strings his keys onto a paper-clip. "Did you eat?"

"D-don't you want to ch—well—Imean—ch-check—Imean—if I d-did what........what y-you—well—if I didn't m-make a—well—if I m-made a "

"You know how I'll know if you made a mistake, Patrick? You know how I'll know if you made a mistake? If we show up at the NATO event and there's no little silver wire baskets on the tables with assorted nuts in them or if we show up at the American Embassy thing and all the guests are wearing bullet belts and have big mustaches and are ending their words with a lotta vowel sounds. Otherwise, as revolutionary as this might sound, I trust you."

Looking as if he didn't hear a word of what Leslie just said, Patrick asks "Dyou mind if I if I a-ask you wh-who........is...D-Danney Br-Brittain your d-your d-dad? M-Ms. Brittain."

"He call?"

"You have—well—three—well—e-mails. Actually. Fr-from......him."

"How djyou get in there I have a code what's next, the fucking Pentagon?"

"Dyou mind if I "

"YES! I MIND! JUST ASK IT!"

" if-if I a-ask who you g-got th-this—Imean—c-computer from?"

"Patrick you of all people should know that buying a used computer is as dangerous as—worse!—having sex with someone whose genital history you know nothing about. You don't know what torrid nights in some university broom-closet are lurking in the bloodstream of a used computer. I get my computers new, Patrick! Squeaky-clean new!"

"Well th—because—well—it looked to m-me like...maybe... someone's—well—been in h "

"Here, Mr. Vice-President of International Relations Incorporated," Leslie is standing with feet together, chest out, right arm stretched in front of her. "are your keys to the mildewed executive john. I wanted to get you a great key-chain but have to find one with life-rocking significance that you'll haul out of your backpack when you're eighty-four years old and tell sacred stories about to people trying to ignore you on the bus."

Patrick takes the keys and slides them into his pocket, pulls them out of his pocket and fingers them, as would a blind person, but with his eyes on them, slides them back into his pocket. "Y-dyou m—M-Ms. Brittain—y-you I b-bet—did you did you—you d-didn't—

Imean—eat.....either. I bet. Actually," he says to a pinhead-size oasis of clean in the veneer of dust coating the computer screen.

"Ah-hah! I knew it! *I*, on the other hand, had a nutritionally balanced fine luncheon sure to keep the cornstarch breeders eating fine luncheons for a long time. And I had it under the high patronage of the athletic elite of this nation and if you knew how lamentably true that was you'd take the next plane to the nearest Lakers game to stock up!"

"Wh-when can I—well—dyou w-want me to show you—Imean—th-the.....c-computer?"

"Tomorrow and maybe you can stay focused til then." Patrick unfocuses. "Right now I'm" Leslie looks at her watch. "holyshit it's not five forty already oh God! throwing you out I'll walk you down—here!—take 50 francs out of my bag and get yourself an anchovy sandwich—and then tomorrow you can come back at "

"N-nine.....I mean...well..........un-unless "

"Have mercy, Patrick. Eleven."

"T-ten........T-ten?"

"You're learning. That's good. Ten and pick up some honey." Patrick starts, then stops starting, to shake his head, focuses then unfocuses on the western sector of Leslie's neck. She takes the BUY HONEY! note from her shorts pocket and tries to make the tape stick to his mud-brown crocheted tie. "Look I can't remember everything frchrissakes!"

On the way back from seeing him off "Find Out How Much It'd Be To Rent a HarlEY INSTEAD....................Binn-goh, Monsieur Fontaine, that's *exactly* what day is it! Way to go, man!..........No listen you can't check faxes tonight I'm having a very very high-level meeting in the apartment with some very very scary men who told me they think it's best we check our own faxes for tonight I'll tell you all about it I promise.", Leslie designs her next two and a half hours, working backwards, so as to stay as calm and as excited as possible. She decides to function in total isolation, draw her circle around her as do actors before stepping on stage. Then she realizes that being in this particular circle for thirty-three years ("plus extra-credit for in-utero") is what got her to this point in the first place. ("Don't need any more time in the circle, thanks! Yup got enough circle stocked for the winter, thanks! Nope that's perfickly awright, maybe next time, thanks!")

"Roz-Roz Roz-Roz ROZ! I gotta go! I only called as preventive maintenance here ("or was that risk management?")..........No, nothing, forget it, look—I got Genevas of my own goin on here...no no nothing like that. Only a figure of speech, Roz. Roz? Ro-oz? If I woulda known, Rosalind, that I was buyin into the Book othe Month Club here—it keeps comin at you whether you want it to or not— bugs on the windshield, Rosalind—I'da been in the shower fifteen minutes ag......What are *you* doing this evening?.....No, what?...Good! Have a super time—stay til the very end of this one—great ending— surprise—like nothing you've ever seen!.........No I'm going to bed reaeally early tonight..........Yeah headache! Bad!.....Yeah I know— I'll cut it down to a kilometer starting manana important not to call tonight, Rosalind—really gotta getta *real* lotta sleep here............I know, sweetie, they're all garbage. Just some of em have more orange rinds thrown in. Gnii-iight!"

At seven thirty-eight Leslie is flying naked around her apartment— arms outstretched into wings, back flattened forward into fuselage— making engine noises and aerodynamically drying the drops of water lotion perfume on her body. "I Knew This Was Gonna Happenzhzhzhzhzh zhzhzhzh zhzhzhzhI Fucking Knew This Was Gonna Fucking Hapzhzhzh zhzhzh zhzh zhzhzh," she screams amid revs, lamenting her inability to time the final stretch tightly enough so as to squeeze out the luxury of having any minutes to spare on anxiety. She's suddenly ("sstarrr-vinnngg"). Waiting for clearance to approach her closet she eats up some seconds thinking about where they can go for dinner before th—"Clearance! Clearance To Approach Closet!"—cruise-speed—she slips on a sleeveless collarless black knit minitube. ("OK I'm ready now what? Now what? Where's the non-fucking Junior Guild when you need them?.....plan an event or two while I'm waiting...Hello, is this Constance Neverscrew? I'm Leslie Brittain, sitting")"here without undies on waiting to be ravaged by the cop of my darkest *fantasmes*. Now about that Cock. Tail. Party. If we served big thickAAAGGGHHHEEE "

Leslie's startled out of her ladies' tea. Roque is at the door.

(" shit I forgotta") She inches the door. ("change the sheets holysh ") Roque pushes it "Oohooh!" open. She opens her mouth to say somHe fills it with his tongue. He scoops her up  kicks the door closed behind him  carries her into the bedroom-alcove  drops her on her back on her bed. She goes to get up and he pins her wrists over her head with his hands and kisses her big and rolling and hot, pinning harder and kissing her again when she won't lie still she pushes against his grip he holds both her wrists with his left hand and slaps her across the face with his right. Leslie is stunned. ("You Don't Hit Me! This has never happened") to her before she smells Roque smells him all around her inside her head she thinks she sees he's in denim again denim again with brown leather in the blur of the burning he's brought in with him she wants not to want it to stop she is liquid spilling off the bed across the floor out the door running into every space she ever occupied black knit liquid and flesh swelling flowing pouring spouting jetting squirting gushing she is sailing her essential liquid back into her first spark of time.

Leslie shudders and watches Roque jerk open a dresser drawer. Slam it shut. Jerk open another. Slam it. Anoth—he freezes. Tugs his sportcoat off, throws it to the floor. Turns and faces her, his legs slightly apart, and unbuttons his denim-shirt cuffs.......rolls them halfway up his forearms.......Slowly.......Presses her down with his eyes. He turns back to the drawer. With delicate care, reverence, he pinches the white-silk stockings he gave her and plucks them out in his fingertips, one with each hand, holding them up to the light.

Leslie's eyes are huge hoops. Roque sits on the edge of the bed with the stockings in his left hand and bends forward, lightly kisses her forehead. She feels protected by her tense anticipation, comforted by her fear. Aggressive in her stunning need to submit. She feels like floating lead. Her weight reaches up-out to feel the weight of him, her lightness looks to meet and mix and swirl together with his lightness, like warm wind-currents, exchanging energies and essence.

As he strokes her face with the back of his right hand, she raises her shoulder, turns her cheek into the tenderness, purring the sound of a caressed child. Between his fingers he traces a thick loop of her hair on the pink pillow then fastens his eyes into her eyes—plaintiff little shudders squeeze out from her throat with every uneven breath—and holds them there locks them there while he slides a stocking under her left wrist, around her left wrist, while he threads it through a bar in the wooden headboard. And ties it into a knot.

Deep through the tunnel of his eyes Leslie watches herself watching Leslie sees herself binding herself to her bed. Deep from the tunnel of his eyes Roque slides a stocking under her right wrist, squeezing his stare tighter around hers, around her right wrist—Leslie warms with her submission—and jolts his whole body as he snaps the ends of the silk in his fists into a knot through the bar. Roque's shirt and face are wet. Only now.

Only now when she knows she is captured, only when getting free demands a struggle, does Leslie struggle to get free. While she plays at pulling her arms up and away as far as they will go, Roque straddles her calves on his knees. Leslie stops playing. He glides his thumbs beneath the bottom of her black knit tube and rides it up her flesh, bunching it over her thighs, her pussy, her hips, her tummy, her breasts, leaving it under her chin. Under his jeans her legs are hot, her torso is cool where the air licks her sweat.

With the gold safety pin plucked from her bodice he pins her hem to her neckband.

His hands on his hips, Roque sweeps a look up Leslie's body, stopping for study along the way, speaking for the first time this evening. "You are very exposed, young lady. You are very exposed to my view." Leslie looks away "Leslie." shrieks inside her skull whimpers into the pillow. The hot and cold touches and thoughtstreams bearing down against her skin collide with the hot and cold touches and thoughtstreams bubbling up beneath it and her body and head feel wrapped in a filmy membrane. She centers her head back to Roque. Very slowly, never turning his eyes from hers, he grasps the end of his wide brown belt and begins to pull it from the buckle. Leslie churns her pelvis "ah", flutters it in little waves, then "Mmhhmh" bangs her bottom down into the mattress and thrusts up "Mmh" between his "Mmhhmhmh" legs. Roque puts his hand back on his hip. Leslie bucks for some seconds then calms. She closes her eyes, inhales fully, exhales slowly. When her eyes are wide and round again, Roque finishes unfastening his belt. Lowers his zipper. Without waiting for the order from her brain Leslie's mouth opens. She's shivering-coughing out pieces of groans-Roque slides his knees up her thighs-she feels all the wetness in her pussy spurt up into her heart-starts caressing himself inches from her face-feels all the substance in her hot heart flood down into her pussy-smoothing his hand up and down himself "ROQUE!"-squeezing it swelling it "ROQUE!" thicker "giveittomeRoqueyougottagiveittomebaby"-brings his other hand from his hip and looks at his cock while he pumps with both fists and presents it to her breath-Leslie is trying to roll from side to side in the container of Roque's legs "I Can't Look Roque I Can't Look At It Anymore It's I Gotta I GottA I CAN'T I"-she pleads in English tears her upper body from the bedclothes "WANTYOU GOTTAGIVEITTOMEI CAN'T STAND IT" jerks her wrists against the knots in the stockings Roque reaches cups her head in both hands lifts her to him and guides his thick cock down her throat. Leslie and

Roque

    meet each other with savage strokes. She heats him in the back of her mouth, flicking her tongue at his taut flesh as he shoves in and out. Broken shrieks and yelps pelt up from far below her gut. He squeezes his knees tighter around her thighs when he feels her tilt her hips downward to try to touch her vulva to the bed, to the sweaty cotton comforter, rubbing, struggling for contact. Roque begins to grunt

    to stuff his grunts inside his rolling breaths before releasing them. He drops Leslie's head, falls forward against the headboard, bracing himself with his open palms against the bars, isolating liberating his pelvis to dip and grind in full waves and circles and jousts deeper and quicker into Leslie's mouth and Leslie's mist in Leslie's bed. Leslie feels him being pulled into orgasm she wants to grabs his ass dig each finger through the denim to the flesh she can't she tugs and breathes smells their wet skin opens her eyes full to his dark brown hair whipping into her headboard she bucks and rubs one last furied time before coming and screaming and laughing onto his relentless cock. Roque stops cold.

    Jumping off the bed, he tears his clothes to the floor. "Hoooohhh why don't you just stand out in" Dives down into his jeans for a pocketknife. "the hallway and stick it in" Leaps back across Leslie. "from there!" Grips her right wrist pulls it taught against her bond cuts the stocking follows with the left "God knows it'd reaeaeaaahheeeee" heaves her over onto her "aaACHCHch" stomach and slams inside and on top of her. Leslie's face is buried in the pillow. Her shoulders are weighted by Roque's. In slow controlled power he pushes through while he lowers his mouth to her ear and breathes, "Who do you belong to?"

    Leslie does not answer. He asks again. *"A qui tu appartiens, Leslie?"* When she whimpers a protest he raises his hips and crashes his cock against her inner "aaHH" wall "AAGH" almost as punishment for her silence. She meets his thrust, tightens her muscles around him and releases, tightens releases tightens and churns rises pumps they are both breathing through roaring open mouths the air is wet and white with their heat he screams it this time "LES-LIE! ckhaahh—ckhh—haackh WHO IS....YOUR MAhaahhh—hST " "I can't RoquehahhhI can't give you thaaahchAahthat oneIc "

When he feels ready to cross back in, Roque raises his head and bounces little open-lipped quasi-kisses across Leslie's neck and shoulders. Her voice says something in her throat without her lips' bothering to form the words as she reaches behind her to touch his buttocks. In a dialogue of movement he answers by rolling onto his back, adjusting her so that she lands on her right side, cradled in his left arm, her fingertips free to caress his chest and thighs. To trace the outline of his cock along his stomach, swirl in the veneer of wetness. His cooling skin smells spicy and hot where she goes down to lick and kiss him dry, smells of her perfume where she comes up pressing even closer into the shield of his big frame.

"Where is it?" he asks calmly, looking at the ceiling.

Leslie floods inside, splashes. Says nothing,

He turns to her with a clear, relaxed gaze, waiting for an answer.

opens her mouth, holds her breath. Shifts her eyes quickly right-left then back to Roque. "Where's what?...............Roque."

Roque smiles patiently, almost neutrally, as if transacting a newspaper purchase at the corner kiosk. He tilts onto his side, drawing his sound torso up before her, spilling her off his arm. His head propped peacefully on a pile of pink pillows, he looks at Leslie, waiting for an answer.

"Yeah hey I thought you said in your message you said we could go anywhere I wanted," she perks, flashing a face full of eyes and trying to touch his hip.
He stops her arm en route and folds it back onto the sheet.
"New and different experience for us, hey Roque?"
Nods.
"M-making love in a bed, hey Roque?"
Hints at a private smile.
Leslie giggles nervously into his tranquil face. "All those hot couples who spend good money on a train ticket when all they have to do is y-you're waiting for an answer."

"No I'm not."
"You're not?"

"I'm not."

"WHY? Don't you wanna know where it is I bet you wanna know where it is!" Roque shakes his head. "And here I totally misj—when they were giving out senses of humor you were actually camped out the night before—like a Who concert." She pushes to get up, expecting him to resist, and he sweeps aside, swinging his legs off the bed. "Are you—Not A Bad Idea Here Would Be Telling Me What's Going On!" Leslie snaps as she stands and pulls off what remains of the black knit tube. "Frchrissake!"

Roque bends to the floor for his clothing "Where shall we go for dinner, Leslie?",

"ROQUE! I Can't Bel—Don't You Want "

      puts his shirt on while Leslie flails. She hops from foot to foot. Her breasts bounce.

Right between the end of an old flail—dying as a spent firecracker—and the beginning of a new one—revving up as a freshly tuned go-cart—he catches her arms and guides her onto her stomach across the bed. His voice deepens the more slowly he speaks, and the more slowly he speaks, the more lightly he caresses her buttocks, occasionally running the edge of his hand between them and along the tops of her thighs. "Only, pretty little girl, after you've stopped playing with it and started acknowledging that you really need it," Leslie raises her hips into the touch and purrs. "will you have earned the luxury of pretending not"

"aaaaaahhhooo!"

    "to"

"aeeeiiiRoququququeshitt!"

    "want it."

"st-R-shittaaaoooowww!"


When Roque comes out of the bathroom Leslie is standing by the front door in jeans, a white cotton t-shirt with the gold safety pin on the neckband, and white Keds, ready to go. "Ready to go?" she smiles.

"Put on a skirt."

"Why do I do this, Roque?" she asks, working each tied sneaker off with the opposite foot.

"Why *do* you do it, Leslie?" He pulls a chair from under the dinette table and straddles it—its back to his front, Marlene Dietrich-style—so as to watch her through the bedroom-archway.

"Why do *you* do it, Roque........OK OK. I'll show you mine if you show me yours." She gets a denim mini-skirt out of her armoire. "Why do some people hSHIT! Who The Fuck Is That At A Quarter OTen! Let the machine get it!"

"LESLIE! YOU'RE PROBABLY SLEEPING BUT—YOU WERE RIGHT—GREAT FILM—THAT EN—WHAT

**"How well do you understand English, sweetie?"**

**"Not very."**

**"Good! Keep it that way!"**

KIND OF MIND WRITES AN ENDING LIKE THAT? LESLIE! CALL ME WHEN YOU GET UP—NO—*I'LL* BE SLEEPING—CALL ME TOMORROW AFTERNOON—I THINK I HAVE A PLAN. I WAS THINKING—I WAS ALL" Leslie glares at the machine "WRONG ABOUT HIM I MEAN EVEN IF HE DOES ONLY WANT A JEWISH GIRL I " then swoops down and pulls the phone and fax plugs out of the wall.

"Come On Sports Fan!" She flicks Roque on the shoulder and they head for the door. "Let's Do It!"

"Don't you want to hear your message?"

"Do you" She locks the door behind them. "have aHOLYSHIT turn around we gotta have a little strategy session here." Leslie pivots. "I didn't I gotta prepare you for "

Roque follows her back up the corridor. "Umberto? We're fast friends."

"Ro-oque?"

"He got weird on me when I walked in so I showed him my badge. Told him I was coming to investigate you on "

"Vice charges."

"How did you know?"

"Bonsoir, madame." A pasty little lady bundled in a long beige wool shawl shuffles through the hallway. "She's probably on her way back from cabling her asphyxiating nonagenarian mother in Rouen about the major police-raid on the building tonight!"

The sides of his mouth twitching into a pre-smile, Roque unhooks his thumbs from the waistband of his jeans and points both index fingers at Leslie. "That why—let's go" He anchors his arm around her waist and steers her toward the stairs. "—that why you run so early? Before the spies get up?"

"Just tr—you don't know how early I run—just try not tcuddle up too tight to Benito when you crawl into bed with him, OK?"

"Umberto."

"Benito. Use your brains—they were giving em out at the same time as senses of humor. Do you have a car?"

"Yeah, it's parked on the Av "

"Shhhh, gnight, Monsieur Fontaine, you're close—you just got two little hours to go. Don't ask. I wanna walk." They hear a toilet flush as they spurt past the open door of the *loge*. "Good! Let's do it!" Leslie takes Roque's hand, they squeeze left past a black Peugeot 405 cruising down the *passage* and they don't stop running until they're out the other end.

They head for "the sixth! I like there's a bistro along the Seine—facing, let me seeee, what landmark can I give yououou?.....the Police Headquarters for example! Noth—just a coincidence—I like the color of it's front." but they do not eat there and do not sit and eat anywhere but roam through traffic carrying people to their Wednesday nights and keep walking and walk all night and mostly Leslie talks and feels Roque has not gotten her deeper drift and mostly Roque listens with a stony face and occasionally points both index fingers at Leslie and there is rarely a moment when they are not touching in some way when they are not holding hands when Roque's arm is not rooted around Leslie's waist or sheltering her shoulder when he is not pinning her to a streetlight to kiss her when she is not standing on her toes to whisper something in his ear. She has the sense that he's trying hard at something he wants to be able to do naturally—like a person with very fat fingers attempting to sculpt a miniature scene he sees so clearly in his mind, or a storyteller who has the story but just does not have the words.

They walk through the mystic first streets of Paris, little and dark, dense and cobblestoned, the way all Paris was "before Haussmann's boulevards gave it a cardiovascular system but you know that, don't you, Roque?" Leslie leads Roque by the hand and shows him where

Picasso painted Guernica and took his coffee, shows him where Sibelius spent the night, where Benjamin Franklin signed the treaty of Franco-American "they called it Friendship I call it—you know that strained smile someone has when they need to be friendly to you but you know down deep—well, no—maybe they *were* really hot for each other then—before the invention of Americans trying to buy a stamp in a French post office." They read the side-by-side stone plaques in the Rue de l'Odéon marking the buildings where Thomas Paine wrote on human rights and Sylvia Beach published Ulysses for her friend James Joyce....stand before the apartment where Gertrude Stein coined the phrase Lost Generation....visit the *bouquinistes* on the riverbanks where Thomas Jefferson bought the basis of the Library of Congress. Touch the spot at the Closeries des Lilas bar where Hemingway lived his personal poetry. Leslie takes Roque by the hand each time as with a child to a shrine. And Roque each time "look what I'm showing you frchrissakes not at me—LOOK!—didn't you see enough of me when you were jerking off two inches from my face?—this is sacred stuff here!" watches Leslie go to pray, stroking her hair, imploding a smile, floating in and out of listening to her, in and out of looking enlivened and looking worried. He seems at times not to be able to get enough. At times to have had too much.

When they get hungry he buys them *crêpes* at an all-night stand at the Place St-Michel. "That's weird, Leslie! Tuna, banana and jam! Look—the guy doesn't even want to make it for you!"

"Doctor's orders," Leslie whispers, on tiptoes, into the stand. She nods gravely, squints, "Horrible condition—left my entire right breast in the most repulsive—" goes to lift her t-shirt "wanna see?.....No that's OK—one banana will suffice! Great perfect exactly the way I like it! The customer's never right! Thanks!" She peers into Roque's hand as they walk on. "Whadjyuh get?"

"Ham and cheese."

"That Crook! I thought you wanted ham, banana and strawberry jam!" he pushes at her shoulder then pulls her back to him.

When she gets cold he buys her a Sorbonne sweatshirt from a hawker in front of Notre Dame. "Extra large—I'll run in it."

"What color?"

"Oh God! How long do I have when do you close?"

"*A deux heures. Enfin, à peu près.*"

"Hmmm, that gives us a good hour—you wanna go see if you can get little Xavierella her braces while I stand here and decide, dear?.......OK OK RED! Theee colorrr ovvv myyy "

"How much do I owe you?"

"Hundred twenty-five."

" ASS!" Leslie screams as Roque drags her away by the waist then "WAIT!" as she stops between Polish tour-buses to put the sweatshirt on. "I love it! I'll run in it! It's so soft against my skin. You remember my skin, dontchya, Roque? Thanks, pal! Don't say you never gave me nothin. This makes up for the stockings you ruined."

"I'm afraid it's going to have to make up for more than that," Roque says, straightening the bottom of the sweatshirt below her hips. "You look like you're twelve years old."

"I *am* twelve years old! Everyone's twelve years old, Roque! You're twelve years old, that bum's twelve years old. Notre Dame's twelve years old. Notre Dame's more twelve years old than any of us! Afraid for you or for me?"

"Want to take a cab back?"

"Well there's my answer! No I wanna walk do you mind?" She throws her head westward and starts off "We can walk along my run route.", turning up the bottom of her sweatshirt to look at the lining.

"We might as well stay on the left bank. The Tuileries are closed this time of night anyway."

"Tsa shame it never stays so soft. You wash it once and it turns to flint against your nipples one great thing about that particular comment you just made, Roque, is I never told you I run through the Tuileries...............Roque?........I never told you I run through the Tuileries."

"On the train."

"How did you know I run through the Tuileries? I never told you where I run!"

Roque guides them back to the Place St-Michel. "You told me you run on the Quai des Orfèvres."

"GODDAMN HIM what the fuck—I-Kneww-Itt I-KnewItt I KnewItt—ELSE did he tell you? GODD—little soup-making fascist microbe!"

"Hey l—watch those arms—look over here!"

"I know! I love it! Don't you? Can we go in isn't it locked?"

With his knife Roque springs the padlock to an ancient iron gate at the far western end of the *place*, across a small street which separates the defining concrete expanse from the weighty gray buildings watching over it. Leslie waits for him in the black air at the bottom of some jagged stone steps while he closes the gate and puts the lock back in place. "I've always wanted to go in here! I've alll-wayyys—there's never been an instant since I've lived in Paris that I didn't actively apply myself to wanting to go in here!" Through huge stone archways, down more worn steps, they walk into a knot of three cobblestoned misty slivers whose tightness must be in constant battle with all invading light. "Does anyone *live* here I *knew* it'd look like this they sure didn't take em to the guillotine on *this* route is this the first street ever in Paris—like walking through Paris's inner ear—like we're worms crawling on our stomachs through original rock and don't tell me worms don't have stomachs—while the guys in ermine upstairs are busy figuring out where to put Notre Dame!"

Roque leads Leslie by the hand down one of the alleys then stops half-way and reverses their direction, winding up in the most cloistered of them all. "His Majesty's basketball team lived on this particular block," she whispers, pointing to the cul-de-sac with wooden doorways no higher than her chest. In the middle of the slender street they come to a pile of large white rocks. "A Roman well," Roque answers before she has the chance to ask. "Put your hands on it and bend over."

"Oh my God I'm soaked!"

He pushes Leslie's shoulders gently forward. She crosses her arms and rests her elbows on a wide flat stone, spreading her legs, thrusting her behind up and out. Wiggling it. Waiting for the show to begin. "Aren't you glad I had the good sense to wear a skOuoowww!" He bites her on the thigh then jerks her skirt up rips his zipper down seizes her hips pulls her toward him pushes himself into her crashes his thighs against her cool white buttocks in the close dark air digs his fingers into her haunches rams up rough and fast rougher and faster makes his gut-breath sounds in rhythm with her throat-breath sounds buries his face in her back Leslie throws her head Roque throws his head bends his knees to a final-angle stun stops battering for a second's breadth a second's breath then howls together with Leslie into the textured mouth of Paris-phantom time.

"I knew the bed thing wouldn't last. Can we stay here for the rest of our lives?...................Roque?" His arms clasped around Leslie's middle, Roque's body and breathing are heavy against her. She spreads her legs a little wider to let whatever air there is play up against the prickly wetness of her thighs.

"I almost" He shakes out his hair "fell asleep there do you believe it?" as he unfolds.

"I can image what you must be like when you're awake!" They slowly straighten their clothing "I want another crêpe." and start walking back toward the gate and the unreal world beyond. Roque closes the padlock.

A guy in a brown suit gets out of a black Peugeot 405 and orders a *crêpe* while, up on her toes, Leslie peers into the stand to see what kind of jam she's getting with her tuna and banana. Roque looks like he's about to say something very important. He stares at Leslie for some seconds, takes a step, stays, opens his mouth with a quick intake of breath, stares, then points both index fingers at her. "You want to take a cab now?"

"You want a crêpe?"
"No, I'm on duty."
"Nobody likes a smartass."

# VI

# The $tars øñ The ©eiling

At 9:57 on the morning after the romp at the Roman fountain there is an erratic sound at Leslie's door, as if someone can't decide whether they really want in. Or as if there are two people out there taking turns: one pounding with a determined fist, the other tickling with apprehensive fingers....................*/////*........*//../*.......*//////////////*......*/* *///////////////////./*....................................*////*..............*///./././././././*.....*/...* */////*.....*////////////*..........*/////////////////////*..*/////*..............*//* */////////////////* */////*Leslie and Roque bolt awake. Roque tears the comforter off. Slams both feet on the floor, ready to counterattack. Leslie scampers over. Grabs him from behind, locking both her arms around his waist before he's fully standing. The*/////*pounding*///////*gets*/////////* louder*///* *////////*Roque slaps his hands onto Leslie's arms. Rips them away. Just as quickly she rocks up onto her knees and encircles his "WaitWaitWaitWait" shoulders. He snaps his head around to look at her. "WUH-UHNNN MIH-IHNIH-IHTT" she sings, crooking her neck in the direction of the entranceway. "Patrick" she mouths to Roque then

"*Ah merde!*"

flies "HEE-EERE IEE-EE CUH-UHMM, Sweetie!" out of bed, knocking the side of her fist against the inside of the front door on her way into the bathroom to grab a kimono. "YOUOU'RRE AZZ GOOOD AZZ IH-IHNN!"

"*Sweettee!*" Roque grumbles as he picks through his clothes on the sofa and crams "*Swee*" his legs into his "*tteeee!*" jeans.

Tying her sash, Leslie dashes out of the bathroom, plugs the phone and fax back in while she checks to see how covered Roque is, puts her hand on the bolt, takes her hand off the bolt, zips over to give Roque a little kiss, zips back to the door by way of the fax machine to catch a message pouring out, opens the bolt, slaps a smile on her face, opens the door, sees Patrick focusing on a loop in his mud-brown crocheted tie, and exchanges the smile she slapped on her face for one which gets there all by itself, spreading out wide from a sharp point within her like fingers of fountain-pen ink on a paper napkin.

"M-Ms. Br-Brittain? I-is e-everything—well—all.....r-right?"

"Everything's wonderful, Patrick! Where are your vice-presidential keys?"

"The l-little—well—m-man s-said you were were h-home...home. Actually. Di-didn't—Imean—dyou m—you s-say.....t-ten? I mean—he also s-said you w-were—well—not..... Imean.....al "

"Sure did! Ten AM! And not a minute later! If you're not early you're late! is what I always say and imagine my luck to finally find some " Wearing only his jeans, Roque comes up close behind Leslie in the doorway, pressing his pelvis into her buttocks. His legs are slightly spread, his hands are on his hips, his full dark hair is dipping disarrayed across his forehead. " one who lives by that principal as well. Right, Roque?" She turns around and puts her hand on Roque's upper arm. "Patrick, this is Inspe—*Monsieur* Xavier Roque. *Je* t*e présente* Patrick Tru....core." Patrick releases his held breath. "There's a time and a place for everything, Patrick," Leslie says out of the corner of her forced smile. "My Assistant!" She flips her palm proudly toward Patrick's chest. Patrick focuses on the kimono sash and masks his terror and embarassement by thrusting out a hand seemingly unconnected to his body. Spreading his left shoulder and arm across Leslie's left side, Roque reaches around her right side to squeeze the young man's hand to the point of pain. While the bucks butt horns she reads the fax and stuffs it in her pocket.

"Well!" she declares in her best Lucy Ricardo. "The question now is do I move the shower and computer out into the hallway or do we all come into the apartment and have some tea." Roque goes back over to the sofa to finish dressing. "I vote for the tea but all colonies haven't been heard from yet. In the event of a tie we can ask the nice lady in the courtyard below my window who complains about the underthings I hang out to dry."

"I—M-Ms. Br-Brittain—th-think I b-better be I think—Imean—it's I b-better b-be g-g " Patrick's eyes are floating furiously from wall to wall in the corridor.

"You can't better be going! Get In Here Frchrissakes!" Leslie blares, causing Roque to reappear in the "Ooh!" entranceway, "Don't you want some tea, swee " snatch Leslie into his arms and kiss her deep long grinding, causing Patrick to want to run away despite the fact that his distressed brain and weighted feet don't appear to be on speaking terms at the moment.

When he's finished showing the chieftain from the other village all the land and cattle and precious metal he has, Roque says *"Sweetie!"* into Leslie's face *"Tout le monde est sweetie!"*, nods to Patrick and starts down the corridor.

"IF I *STOP* CALLING *YOU* SWEETIE IS THE ONLY THING THAT SHOULD BE OF CONCERN TO YOU!"

"I'LL CALL YOU LATER."

"WON'T BE HERE! PATRICK AND I ARE GOING TO SPAIN FOR A MEETING. BACK REAL LATE TONIGHT."

Patrick is unfocusing in the direction of his loafers, which have not shifted position on the hallway carpet by any unit of measurement since the painful handshake. "Patrick and I are going to Spain for a meeting," he mouths to his ankles, then raises his horrified eyes to Leslie. Eventually the rest of his face follows.

"OKAYEEE! UP 'N AT 'EM, ATOM ANT!" Leslie looks at her watchless wrist. "What the fuck time is it! we gotta get on it here! come in! grab a pen! here!" She wrenches Patrick's backpack from him  kicks the door shut  sticks a notepad in his hand  starts untying her sash  "While I'm in the shower I'm gonna tell you what needs to be done in the next forty-five minutes if we're gonna be on that plane!" rips her kimono off  shoots into the bathroom  turns on the water  begins her list. Patrick's loafers are doing the same non-moving as several minutes earlier, just on a different carpet. In the middle of a soapy sentence, realizing she's lost him—or never had him—Leslie runs out of the shower toward the livingroom, runs back to get a "fucking towel frchrissake!", runs back to the livingroom, screams "THEM SATURDAY NIGHTS AT THE VIDEO ARCADE IN DOWNTOWN LINCOLN SURE ARE BEGINNIN TO LOOK GOOD, AREN'T THEY PATRICK TRUCORE?" and whizzes back into the shower. Shocked into focus by the affront of her using his real name when it's just the two of them, Patrick brings himself to move a shoe.

"WHAT? I Can't Hear You! You're gonna have to speak louder or I'll have to open the curtain so I can "

"I-I SAID I'M...H-HERE. M-MS. BRITTAIN. H-HERE. AC-TUALLY."

"Number one: e-mail to Jack Kote in Marbella and tell him we're coming to the meeting. Type in j no space kote in small letters when it asks to who but if you don't treat him like a capital-letter guy when we're down there he'll have his bodyguards compress you into the size of a gold ingot and bury you in his nuclear-waste dump like they do in James Bond movies. Tell him Leslie's coming with her assistant and give your name: Patrick Trucock." Patrick feels redeemed. "Tell him to start without us but to make sure the cassette's running and that if that bitch from the Congress of Overseas Women—or, appropriately enough, *COW*—says don't bother, she'll take notes, then to make sure Frederico Fellini's there to *film* the fucking thing. Tell him that after we get there, Frederico can be excused. Ask him to e-mail back who else is coming—no! fuck it! we don't have time to get into that! Got that?"

"Yeah."

"Next call Moe the Magician at One World Travel—number's in the memory—punch eight—and tell im to have two return-trip business-class tickets to Malaga—birthplace of the Master—waiting for us at CDG, charged to my account. Confirm the time. It's around one. Then confirm it again. Then, what you might wanna do before going any further is the following: confirm the time. Book the return for as close to exactly four hours after we land as possible. If Moe's not there ask for Marylène or Katherine and speak to no one else—even if the Chairman of the Board of Air France gets on. Got that?"

"Yeah."

"Give your name....................Oh God Patrick!" Patrick sees the shower curtain move and lurches for the door. Leslie thrusts her lathered head out of a discrete opening she's managed to create by holding a loop of plastic away from the wall. "PATRICK!" Patrick seems too afraid to unfocus, afraid that any uncontrolled head motion might result in his eyes' landing on something his psyche really doesn't want to see. "Patrick?"

"M-Ms. Br-Brittain?"

"I want you to say the following words: I always carry my passport with me at absolutely all conceivable times."

"I d-don't. Actually."

"Oh." Leslie takes a deep breath and looks up to the ceiling. "We'll run the gate."

"B-but I d—well—d-did to-today cause I n-needed it to—well—r-rem—Imean—you a-asked me ab—well I n-needed it to ex...change the...Y-Yamaha. F-for the the H-Harley. Harley."

"AAHHIIEEEEEEEEEEEEEEEEEEEEEEEEEEEEEEEEEEEEE EEEEEEEEEEEEEEEEEEEEEEEEEEEEEEEEEEEEEEEEEEEWay! To! Go! We'll Take The Fucking Harley!"

"T-to Sp—to—M-Ms. Brittain t-to...well........Sp-Spain?"

"To the airport, microbe-brain! Patrick there's so much hope for you it's overflowing its borders." The water stops. "Quick! Go do what you gotta do cause the alternative is seeing this curtain o-o-o-o-oPEN!" Patrick's already at the computer. "CALL MOE FIRST!" Patrick leaves the computer and heads for the phone.

"One o f-five. Actually," Patrick, looking taller than during his shower-curtain days, reports from the computer as Leslie emerges semi-wrapped in a Dick Tracy towel some minutes later. She carries a dinette chair through to the bedroom-alcove and stands on it to fetch her satchel from the top of the armoire.

"Didjya send Jack's message?"

"I th-thought you—well you—Imean—s-said we'd be.....b-back. To-tonight. Actually," Patrick says to the right lace of the left running shoe just as it disappears into its special compartment in the satchel's peach-moiré lining.

"We most likely will, sports fan, but in case all the electronic aviational guidance systems in the world break down and we have to stay, I can run tomorrow. And every day until they come rescue us. What are *you* gonna do til they come rescue us? Who booked us, the Big Man himself?" Leslie puts on black jeans, the dove belt and short black boots,

"Wh-what if it if it r-rains and y-you've—well—only...dyou m—p-packed sh-shoes for dr-dr "

"You wanna get that?" she nods to Patrick as a fax drops.

her black silk t-shirt and a long bright-yellow linen jacket with huge shoulder pads. "Who is it?" From a cloth bag full of scarves hanging off the side of the dresser mirror she pulls a multicolored-and-black-striped raw-silk handkerchief and dunks it into her breastpocket. "Who booked us, Moe himself?" She ties her hair back with one of Roque's ribbons.

"The Women's Auxiliary of the Amer "

"File it!"

"I-is he a—well.....b-big man man?"

"He's four-foot-nine and shrinking! Annually. Huge for a magician—don't believe everything you see in Fantasia."
"Yeah. He s-said—th-this is what h-he s-said, he s-said bon voyage and thanks for the cartoon from the New Yorker. M-Ms. Br-Brittain." Patrick goes back to the computer and clicks away in little spurts of electronic lust. "Does anyone h-have your e-mail code?" he asks in a confident voice without taking his eyes off the monitor.

"Were Outa Here *Now*, Rock n Rollers!"

"WAIT!" Patrick shoves his hand between Leslie's finger and the keyboard. "Someone's b "
"I'll send yapost card, Patrick!" She blows him a kiss, scoops up her satchel and turns the bolt.
He focuses far into the screen "Someone's been in here!", sounding both fascinated and indignant, sitting straighter in his chair than he usually does.
Leslie opens the door. Patrick spits a series of technical terms under his breath which amount to a curse in computerspeak, closes down the machine, grabs his backpack, "Lock The Door With Your Keys!" locks the door with his keys and catches up to her in front of the "No time—we'll get it tonight!" mailboxes.
"Morrnninnggyou-have-the-right-to-remain-silent-you-have" she chants in English as they skim past the *loge* "the-right-to-an-attorney"

"COLOMBA!"

"smile-Patrick-and-keep-walking-anything-you-say-can-and-will-pretend-we're-in-the-jungles-of-Brazil-be-held-against-you-in-and-they're-two-innocent-exotic"

"COLOMBA!"

"a-court-of-law-birds where'd you park I'm paying the difference by the way for the rental."

"TU ABANDONNES UMBERTO"

"Makes you want to seriously think about knotted sheets from the courtyard window!"

"PER EVERRE!"

"Where'd you p " Leslie looks back at Patrick trying to keep up with her escape-pace down the *passage*. He points straight ahead while he focuses on the left taillight of a black Peugeot 405 next to his bike. "Aahhhhhhit's gorgeous I'm running to the bakery Here!" she blurts, throwing her satchel at him. "You want something?" He doesn't answer. She doesn't wait. The bakery's too crowded. She sprints ("people have nothing the fuck else to do but buy bread frchrissake!") down the block to Georges's, nicks two croissants from the silver basket on the end of the counter close to the door, tells him he shouldn't keep the silver basket on the end of the counter close to the door because people are "liable to come in and help themselves, Georges!" and gets back to the Harley just as Patrick is guiding its head into the street.

In the airport lot Patrick takes Leslie's helmet while she stoops to pick up her ribbon. They begin walking toward the terminal. "Good move, Patrick, bringing that bike into our life." Turning around for a last look, she puts her arm on his shoulder. "And Noah took them threes by threes" she begins to orate. They start moving again. "into the ark. Female birds, male birds, and" In the elevator, a tall man in a business suit and a turban is digging furiously in his briefcase. "Harley Davidson birds. Female sheep, male sheep, and Harley Davidson sheep. Male Vermont trout, female Vermont trout," The elevator stops and a young couple gets on. "and Harley Davidson Vermont trout. Harley Davidson cock" Leslie looks at Patrick. "er spaniels, female cocker spaniels, mwhat?" The doors open at the departure floor; Patrick has tapped Leslie on the shoulder.

Rising slightly onto his toes, he motions for her ear. "Dyou mind if I t—Imean—well—th-they didn't h-have.....Ver-Vermont tr-trout then. Actually."

"Oh!" Leslie looks pensive. She checks a directional sign and they turn left. "Female Boston trout, male Boston trout, and Harley Davidson Boston trout. And Noah, Patrick, And Leslie Thus Elevatedeth Harley Davidson," she declaims in English to the check-in woman, "To The Status Of: Gender." and hands her her passport.

"Gate 23, boarding in 20 minutes," the check-in woman says.

"Amen!" Leslie says.

"So you have a choice!" Leslie announces, waving the flight attendant away with his tray of champagne-filled glasses. "You can receive a pre-meeting briefing from me and be horrified or you can wait and see for yourself and be horrified."
"Br-briefing. If you d—p-please. M-Ms. Brittain." Patrick unwraps the little calculator from his Air France welcome-packet.
"Jack Kote............................................................................"
Patrick puts the little calculator back into its cellophane wrapping, back into his Air France welcome-packet, then into his backpack. He focuses on his knee. That's good enough for Leslie. "Jack Kote is an American businessman of Middle Eastern—Lebanese—parentage—Israeli—who lives part of the year in a hotel suite in Brussels, part of the year in the villa on the Costa del Sol where we'll be today, and part of the year several miles overhead with his private parts inside his private air personnel aboard his private jet. Unfocusing, Patrick, is certainly not going to make that—thank you" The flight attendant brings more mixed nuts when he sees that Leslie has already eaten hers and Patrick's. "reality go away. No one—at least no one I know who knows Jack—is sure just what it is that he actually does—except own every building and business on Earth—or even if that's his real name. But we know enough not to ask and to spell it with capital letters except in e-mail.
"Early this year during what when I think of it must've been a real slow news-day in Jackland—maybe a day when all his flight attendants were out getting their upper thighs waxed—Jack decided he'd build a chain of American-style universities in every major capital in the world. Legend has it he'd been thinking of throwing some money at the Mid-East peace thing—Egyptian parentage—instead, but because this guy who he met with about it was an industrial-strength anal aperture, Jack said he wasn't interested, and when the guy persisted, Jack had his bodyguard throw him out and it wasn't even Jack's

own office!"

Patrick mouths "BODYGUARD" to a fleck in the ceiling.

"So he had this idea to have a two-day Global Classroom Conference—his idea, my w—my very expensive words—and invite repressed frigid-wife-beaters disguised as high-placed officials from the fields of—well all the normal fields you'd think of for something like that—education, construction, finance, pizza-delivery—to brainstorm about brainstorming about brainstorming about brainstorming about some day founding a chain of American-style u's in every major capital in the world and don't ask me how major or capital is being defined in this particular case.

"I met Jack in Gstaad a half a dozen Christmases ago through a mutual friend with whom I went to watch other people ski. You OK with this so far?" Leslie tilts her head back to try to enlist the fleck as a communications clearinghouse between herself and Patrick.

Patrick tells the fleck to say, "M-Ms. Br-Brittain, d-did y-y n-neverm-mind."

Leslie tells the fleck to tell Patrick to just spit it out.

Patrick tells the fleck to ask Leslie if she minds if he doesn't continue with that particular question.

Leslie tells the fleck to tell Patrick that she minds if he asks if she minds and that if he had any brains he'd've immediately switched his original, uncomfortable question for any old other question and she'd've never known the difference but now that he's admitted it's a question he's having difficulty asking, she certainly is not going to let him off the hook!

" s-sleep w-with h-him dyoumindnowifIs-sayn-neverm-mind?"

"PATRICK! MY HEAVENS! WHAT KIND OF QUESTION IS THAT?" Leslie flails into a passing passenger, Patrick focuses on a fragment of the fleck. "Of *course* I slept with him! Well—I didn't actually sleep with him on the ski trip—at least when I first met him—I slept with my gentleman friend at the time, and Jack.....wasn't asked to leave the room."

"I don't.....dyou m—I mean..........don't l-like him. Actually. M-Ms. Br "

"You haven't met the man frchrissake Patrick!"

"N—Imean...n-no, Ms. Br-Brittain. N-not him. Your b—well—b-boyfriend. Actu "

"But you haven't met him ei—oh. Oh OK. Well givim time.

Roque grows on you."

"Dyou m—I mean—G....dyou m—G—get rid of h—M-Ms. Br-Brittain—Imean—h-he's gonna....................h-hurt y-you.............Dyou mind "

"Do I mind if he hurts me? That's a matter of interpretation. Do I mind getting rid of him? Probably not some day. Do I mind your telling me? No. Do I mind your asking me if I mind? Ordinarily I would, Patrick, but since this is the absolute last time in your days on Earth that you're going to ask if I mind your saying something because the time after the next time you'll be saying it on a postcard from the video arcade at the Lincoln Mall and if you think I'm kidding try me, then no, this time I don't mind."

Patrick wedges some minor focusing in between following the clouds and letting his eyes float freely within the cabin.

"So we had some brainstorming meetings at the beginning of the year to brainstorm about organizing this brainstorming Conference which by now has become a brain-major-alert-evacuate-the-entire-population-at-once-divine-revenge-tornadoing Conference, but everyone—shit there were people there from all over Europe, Israel, Thailand, Kuwait frchrissake, Brazil, Nairobi, incredible, Australia—but they all came to Spain each time thinking their world and their agendas were the most important things we had to talk and meet about when everyone really knows it's only *my* world and *my* agenda that matters, so after a brave attempt to altruistically get our thirty seconds on CNN we decided to postpone the Conference thus any more meetings until we could get our priorities straight and let some of the inter-ego bloodwounds heal, but everyone really knew that, one, that meant never have the Conference and, two, by the time any healing would get done Jack certainly would've found a toy to amuse himself with between business deals that wasn't such a pain in the ass and didn't leave his pool house as dirty when it was over."

"H-he has a...p-p "

"I never asked you this, Patrick—were you at the London School of Economics as a *student*?"

"Yeah."

"I thought so. Or at least I thought it was either as a student or a groundskeeper. Which often amounts to the same thing but I just wanted to—you want my sandwich?"

"Th-thank you. M-Ms. Brittain. Dy—w-what will y-you—Imean.....e-eat? W-why are we g—well—going? Going?"

"Patrick! You've come back to me! What was it like?"

"....."

"The other side—never mind—so this morning when I was running to open the door for you"

"W-with h-h-"

"No, Mr. Roque was not running to open the door along with me, it was only I who was running to open the door, Mr. Roque was putting his clothing on, a fax came in and it was Jack saying he'd just worked a deal at ten o'clock last night for us to have the Conference in the get this Patrick in the I can't get over this Olympic Fucking Village—see if there's not a *dea-uhl* involved J—a deal he needs to *brrieeff* you about—Jack gets real bored real fast. Has a real tough time staying focused. Kind of like you, Patrick—what kinda sandwich did I give you?—I don't know whether that's encouraging or not."

"S-smoked salmon salmon. Actually"

"CnI have a bite?"

"Ms. Br-Brittain it's *y-your* s-s—Imean"

"Thanks. It's incredibly delicious. Wonder why I didn't get one like that. And can I come to an emergency meeting he's calling for three-thirty this very pee em for anyone who can make it—including not coincidentally his friend Senator Nolan Dougherty of the Foreign Affairs Committee who's in town as part of a task force snooping not coincidentally around the Olympic Village and would be a key player at our event—which obviously leaves out the Americas and the Orient and cuts it close even for the Middle East but at least *we're* gonna be there, Patrick, and that's all that counts, right?" Leslie slaps her palm against her thigh.

"C-can I have a...nother.....C-Coke? P-please."

"I don't know, can you? I bet the flight attendant over there is better equipped to inform you of that than I. And while you're ordering, I'll have a glass of half-Perrier half-orange juice. Thanks, sweetie! I'm gonna go call Jack & tell him to send Raoul to the airport with the car—we shoulda thought othat when we were battling it out with the shower curtain. Will you still be here when I get back?"

"W-what if...Imean m-maybe he s-sent his car f-for s-someone—well.....else. Else."

"Then he'll send another one."


"The PR possibilities are breathtaking!" Leslie continues, plopping back into her seat. "The Willie Sutton school of press relations if there ever was one! And from what I can well imagine, Magic Johnson got up this very morning and said to Cookie, "Damn! I wish Jack Kote would get his act together and bring them American-type-university types down to hang with me in July........Patrick?.....Was the Coke good?"

"Yeah."

"I'm glad. I'm also glad you're spending some quality calculator-time right now because I always did wonder how much a hundred and twenty-five times ninety-three was."
"Eleven thousand six hundred twenty-five. M-Ms. Brittain," Patrick says without using the machine, an expression of surprise in his tone and on his face as if Leslie has just admitted to not knowing the words of the National Anthem.
Pointing an imaginary knife toward her midsection, she contracts her stomach like a Martha Graham dancer and pantomimes the puncture. She then lightly grabs his chin and, holding his head toward hers, tells him "You're a wondrous onion, Patrick Trucock." in a quiet, airy voice. "There are no coincidences in this world. There's only cosmic synchronicity." Patrick rides off on a coke bubble. "BUT!—that means as usual we gotta do more than six months' work in less than two, we put everything else on hold including NATO call them tomorrow and tell them—no! I'll tell Jack—remind me!—I'll tell Jack to tell them they can't have his room until the next month—good!—and you're not going back to the mall to file a report with friends and family who don't give a shit and you know it and who wouldn't believe how I spent my summer vacation by Patrick Trucock anyway!"

"B-but "
"I need you, Patrick Trucock!"

"B-b "

"Potential pizza-orderers in every major capital in the world need you. You'll go directly back to London from Paris this fall.....It says here-" Leslie plucks the safety instructions from the seat-pocket-in-front-of-her "-in your contract." and smacks the back of her hand next to the phrase about oxygen masks dropping down. "Patrick!" Patrick watches a lemon seed fall off an ice cube. "Magic and Cookie need you.....Well, OK. Magic. Cookie, frankly, stopped needing you a good couple weeks ago.....but keep that one in perspective when you're weighting your variables."

Patrick's eyes shift back and forth between Leslie's eyes and a hairline crack in his fold-down tray-table. "B-but—well—I c-can't ask for.....Imean.....if I don't go b...Imean—I c-can't ask for any more—well—m "

"You're Working For Me, I'll Pay You Frchrissake!"

"But-but s-summer in-internsh-ships—you're not you c-can't h-have to be...un—well—p-paid. Unpaid"

"HAH!" Leslie shouts, causing the woman in the seat in front of her to jump, and glare over her headrest. Leslie glares back. "HAH! THEY'LL NEVER KNOW!" She sounds like a combination of Boris Badinoff and the Wicked Witch of the West. "WILL THEY? HAH!— I didn't anticipate having this conversation so soon, Patrick. HAH! Gottem there!.....And if you don't want it I'll just give the money to the Harley and let you two fight it out." Patrick smiles at the flight attendant as he clears the lunch-droppings but Leslie knows it's for her. The pilot announces in French, Spanish and English that they'll be landing in fifteen minutes.

"Penis size."

"....."

"Penis size."

Patrick folds up his tray-table "....." and, with it, the hairline crack.

"Penis size," Leslie repeats, brushing crumbs off her lap. "The briefing, Patrick."

"Yeah."

"Around the table today there will be men and women of varying penis size ranging from where-did-I-put-it-I-know-it's-around-here-somewhere, as in the case of the nice gentleman from Berlin who represents the Association of International Educators, to organs which must be registered as lethal weapons just as boxers' hands are, such as in the case of the nice lady from London who's with American Express. You will have no difficulty whatsoever determining a delegate's penis size because this measurement is in direct inverse proportion to the number of times you'll hear the sound of their voice and, within that factor, to the intensity of their attempt to show that their penis is exactly the opposite size from what it in fact really is. I know you're following me, Patrick, because you're not focusing and that has I'm afraid to say become an excellent barometer for me to know whether or not I'm making my point.

"Now there's one nice gentl—actually he's neither nice nor a gentleman he's scum—there's one scum from Amsterdam—lawyer—whose penis must be, well, inexistent. Inexistent, Patrick, and you can unfocus all you want but the man, frankly, must have a sign—like in a Monty Python movie—with an arrow scotchtaped where his penis would have been had he had one, saying: penis. The way I know this is the obnoxia-level in the room rises so exponentially when he is occupying space therein, and his efforts to savage any work anybody does and replace it with his own impoverished attempts at accomplishment are so bludgeoning, that this, and the fact that he gets birthday cards with scenes of fishing and baseball players on them, must be the only means he has for reminding himself that he is of the male gender. Looking, in other words, in his pants, must obviously not do it." Patrick is peering intently at Leslie and she becomes worried. "You *are* still following me aren't you, Patrick?"

"Yeah."

"His name is Ronald Lightner. Sounds like a clown who works in a hair salon, I know, but that's the scum's name. Anyway, after the last run-in we had six weeks ago around the very table where we're going to be trying to make it through today, I told Jack to find another conference organizer and Jack promised me he'd have his" She deepens her voice into Jack range "people" then resumes in her own register. "take Ronald in the back room and beat some sense into him—or the administrative version thereof. Probably told him he'd take away his scotchtape and sign if he didn't back off. So there you have it, partner. You are now equipped to guffaw duly into your sangria for the next couple hours. I'll leave the rest an unintelligible muddle for now so as to pollute no further perceptions or conclusions. The tabula rasa school of meeting attendance—unless you have questions and I wouldn't waste our precious time, Patrick, asking me whether I slept with him."

"Wh-who's the M-Master?"

"Picasso."

"Wh-what's he a...m-magician of? of?"

"Art, truth, beauty, women and the meaning of life."

"NM-Moe. Moe."

"Oh. The world. Getting you there. Even if he has to reroute you through your mother's womb. Even if he has to reroute you through someone else's mother's womb. Even if you want to go to a country that doesn't exist. He'll found it, coronate its king, the king'll have the airport built and you're already there waiting for your bags to come off the belt!"

"C-CDG?"

"A famous French general named after an airport."

"Wh-what if if—Imean—the m-meeting i-isn't...over. By-by the t-time we h-have to—well—"

"Leave? Then we'll be in luck, won't we!"

Leslie and Florita, Jack's housekeeper and mama-in-residence, shriek and whoop and hug and yelp and kiss each other on both cheeks when Florita opens the door to the vast glass-walled main pool-house on the grounds of the bird sanctuary off the villa's East Wing. ("Florita looks like everyone's little round old Aunt Florita," Leslie told Patrick in the car, "but she was teaching economics at Yale—speaks English *muh-uhch* better then you and me—when Jack, whose housekeeper had just disappeared with one of the bodyguards, literally tripped over her in a lounge at Kennedy. There she was—stressed-out like a maniac—trapped inside a little fortress made of laptop, books—which *she'd* written—and papers, preparing for a seminar she was invited to give to the fucking Finance Minister's staff in Madrid. Jack said hey baby let me take you away from all this glitter and put an apron on you. She asked how much. He said he was kidding. She said she wasn't. She earns more in a month to make sure Jack has enough toilet paper in stock than she made in *a year* disguising herself as someone who gave a half-a-shit about supply and demand. She has all the supply and demand she'll ever need now—there's no toilet paper, there's demand; there's toilet paper, there's supply. *Twelve times her salary* and all the relentless greenery her baggy eyes can absorb! Economics at the service of waranteed sunshine," Leslie said, sweeping her arm out toward the horizon as Raoul opened her door. "If you like this sort of thing.")

Florita ("not her real name but I swear the reversed snobbery of it makes her come!") fluffs Leslie's curls and straightens her ribbon. "And who is this fine young gentleman?" she asks, liberating Patrick's crumpled sportcoat-lapels from under the straps of his backpack. Leslie says nothing. Focusing on a fistfight between two sunbeams raging above Florita's head, Patrick does his Roque-handshake thrust and says, "P-Patrick T-Tru" He looks at Leslie as if waiting for directions at a busy intersection. "c-core." Leslie throws her chin toward him as if to tell him the street you wanna take is over there. "Ms.-Ms. Br-Brittain's........assistant. Actually." He seems a bit taller than he did when the door opened. Florita wedges her happy hips between Leslie and Patrick, puts her arms around their waists and walks—almost pushes—them down a long bright golden-tiled corridor overcrowded with massive hand-painted earthen pots of spicy-smelling tropical flowers.

"What's Oz look like?"

"About half couldn't come. Even the senator. About eight here."

"Is "

"Including your friend."

"Damn! The guys must've dropped the piano from the wrong window again."

"Now, my dear, you know what they say about the mills of the gods."

"Fuck that, Flo! I don't want the crud ground I want him first granted eternal life then fastened in front of his mirror with his eyes tooth-picked open, in a head brace, bottom part of his body naked, forced to stare til the end of time as we know it at his crooked penis-sign hanging by a thread of scotch-tape. Don't you worry, Mr. Lightner, we'll do your" The trio turns a corner into an identical corridor. "laundry and feed you—in that order—your job is to live forever and stare at the pitiful invisibility of your sex organ!"

Florita looks at Patrick. "Do you know what she's talking about?"

"Yeah." His spine stretches.

"You know, Mr. Kote tried to get to you last night but nothing answered. That's why the others are here al "

"You don't call him Missster Kote when he's fucking you, do you, Flo?"

"ME?" Florita gurgles a rolling little giggle "Fucking ME?" that bubbles up from her belly and swells in volume and velocity as it bounces among the glass walls and ceramic floors of the corridor. "With these HIPS!" Flo is now shrieking in laughter. "Bes-sides," She chokes out the words as she calms "I think given a choice between the three of us....." and eyes Patrick.

"WELL HERE WE ARE AT THE CONFERENCE ROOM, RIGHT, ROCK N ROLLERS?" Leslie cuts in to the rescue, opening the door and shoving Patrick through. She winks "You figured it out all by yourself!" at Flo.

"Don't leave without saying good-bye!" Florita orders. Leslie follows Patrick in and closes the door behind her.

Impeccably dressed in a beige suit and an open-collared white shirt with no tie, a bald, massively overweight man of medium height rises with awesome agility from his chair at the head of the table. As he ambles over to greet "My Lord," Leslie, "you're here." the background conversation becomes a flattened chatter punctuated by shots back and forth across the room: "Whatdja do, run all the way from Paris, Leslie?" "Hey! My buddy Edwin Franklin! You didn't move back after all, frchrissake!" "Better watch it kid, you don't know what happened to the last so-called assistant she had!" "Djyuh get the article I faxed two weeks ago?" "I've been looking all over for a bag like that." "Hope you left all the terrorists back up in Fra "

"This," Leslie announces to Patrick, poking her elbow into Jack's enormous soft belly, "is The Living Legend himself! Jack Kote and company, this is my assistant, Patrick Trucock!" From the corner of his terrified eye, Patrick focuses on the cavern between two scintillas of gold in Leslie's safety-pin brooch. "This is the time and place I was talking about," she murmurs to him through one of her smiles.

"Trucock!" Jack puts his arm around Patrick's ossified shoulders and starts walking him to the table. "What an interesting name! Old English, isn't it, son?"

"Chaucerian." Leslie grins, looking around the room to see who's missing.

"Or maybe we're trying to tell me something." Jack peers into Patrick's face and tries to follow his eyes.

"He's not for sale, Jack!" Leslie rushes sing-songing up behind them, still smiling through still-clenched teeth.

"My Lord, everyone's for sale, Leslie!" Jack sing-songs back through clenched teeth of his own. "Why don't we just put Mr. Trucock next to his new friend Mr. Ko "

"Why don't we" Leslie grabs Patrick's elbow "just put Mr. Trucock next to his old internship supervisor Leslie!" and does not let go until they are both well installed several places from their host.

Pushing a little button under his armrest, their host asks Patrick what he wants to drink. "Half-half-P-Perrier h-half-orange....juice. Juice. P-Please," Patrick half-half-whispers half-aggresses. From the corner of his other terrified eye he focuses first on the question mark in Leslie's tilted head and crunched up face, then on his shoulder as he shrugs it. Florita appears instantaneously—almost as if there are two Floritas—one on the other end of whatever the little button under the armrest is hooked up to and one who appears instantaneously. She ceremoniously spreads an antique flowered-porcelain tea-service before Leslie and, setting a silver coaster at Patrick's spot on the gleaming rosewood table, serves his drink in a tall icy crystal goblet.

"Well!" Jack declares. "Why don't we all go around the table and introduce ourselves and our affiliations to Mr. Trucock." He beams at Patrick. Patrick writes PABLO P. with his fingertip in the condensation on the side of his glass.

"Why don't we not, Jack. All due respects," Leslie moves the tape recorder out of her line of vision. "it'll all run together after the second stand-up routine. As long as each person knows who they personally are in this life half the battle's won and we got a plane outa here in a couple hours. What've we missed? What's this?" She picks up her copy of the red-white-and-blue brochure mock-ups on the table in front of every attendee.

"Oh, I'muhh notuhh convinced of the usefulness ofuhhh going over territory we've already covered thisuhh morning," whines a spindly, ashen man, with a scraggly red Abe Lincoln beard, hunched over three geometrically perfect piles of paper across the table from Patrick. A woman next to him begins to explain the usefulness of going over territory we've already covered this morning, "especially for the conference organizer, Ron, and since Seiji couldn't be here we can just move his thing til nex "

"What did we miss? What's this?" Leslie repeats in the same tone as the first time she asked, not turning her head from Jack.

"Your brochure. Good job. Fine piece of work, isn't it?" He nods around the table. "Just need to fill in the particulars and it's "

" and make it a little more.....Olympic," says a woman scribbling on Embassy letterhead.

"and it's a print!" Jack extends his raised arms as if simultaneously bestowing a blessing and adjourning the meeting.

"No tsnot," Leslie answers.

"Fine piece of work. I'm stealing this cut-out idea for the new brochure for one of my companies, it's the mos "

"Tsnot my work, Jack." Leslie is speaking extremely softly, with a measured, sweet voice. As the other participants open their copies, Patrick reaches tentatively for his. "What's the scoop, sports fans?" The more impatient she becomes, the more charming becomes her smile, the calmer her bearing. "The least you coulda done is send it to me before the meeting. Frchr "

"My Lord, Leslie," Jack raises his arms again, his blessing converting to a commandment. "one of my people hand-delivered it to your building yesterday." Leslie looks at Patrick Patrick looks at Leslie's left shoulder-pad. "Says your concierge threw it into the back of his car—black Peugeot—" Leslie scowls at Ronald Lightner. "ran it right over to where you were working." Patrick focuses on the Embassy lady's wedding ring.

"Guess again, Jack—sure that wasn't black shopping cart?" Leslie flicks Patrick's thigh with the back of her hand. "Cumawn, P"

"Maybe I canuhh add someuhh clarification here," Ronald Lightner whines after clearing his throat. The whole table turns toward him. "I've haduhh some experience doing brochures myself and I you might say I took it upon myself to uhh draft someuhh—some needed modifications anduhh and fax them to the printer.....Uhh in the name of this committee of course and pending its final approval. It is my opinion thatuhh what is of primary importance here is"

Leslie flicks Patrick's thigh with the back of her hand.

"a document whereby if our names areuhh going to appear"

"Cumawn, Patrick," she says dryly. Patrick tries to sip from and look at the inside of his goblet at the same time.

"therein, it needs to reflect theuhh substantialuhh significance"

"Let's go." She pushes her chair back and stands up.

"of our ongoing personal" Jack plops forward onto the table, his mighty stomach spreading across the workspace of three people, and tries to grab Leslie's arm. "participation anduhh investment in and contributions to thisuhh project's uhh"

At the door Leslie stops, turns her head, raises her eyebrows and quietly says "Patrick." She nods then leaves the room, Patrick bounding from his chair and tripping out after her.

"life." Ronald looks at the door and smiles.


"WELL! HERE ARE OUR OPTIONS!" Leslie says, realizing neither how loudly she's speaking nor how quickly and violently she's walking as they retrace their route through the pool-house corridors. "WE CAN GO TO THE BEACH, GET NAKED AND EAT FRESH FIGS. THAt's" She calms a bit. "one whole package-option, not a set of three." Patrick is so worried about not keeping up with her that at times he trots out ahead. If not on her person, he is focusing on the sounds and pace of her reactions. "We can go to Madrid and look at dark paintings of dark skies in a dark museum.....And get naked and eat fresh figs. I'm trying to make these choices as attractive as possible, can you tell? We can rent a hotel suite in the jungles of Brazil and crash our guitars against the walls and do thousands of dollars of damage. Naked. Eating "

" f-fresh.....f-f-figs," Patrick tells the flowers.

The clean snap of Leslie's bootsteps stops on the polished patterned tile. She waves the arm not anchoring the satchel and looks up through the arched glass ceiling. "YOU DON'T NEED ME, PATRICK TRUCOCK! YOU HAVE ALL THE ANSWERS!" she bellows, then, eyes still skyward, starts walking again, crashing into Florita's "Ahooo! frchri" chin near the front entranceway. Florita has a cellular phone in her right hand and a fat envelope with the logo of one of Jack's companies in her left.

"I—we're "

"I know."

"He beeped you."

"Told me to order the car."

"Did he tell you why?"

"Does he have to?"

"Well why doesn't he do something about it! What does the scum have, naked pictures oyour boss or something? I thought this kinda shit was supposed to be resolved! Who Needs It! He can host the collective organs of the whole fucking Dream Team down his *own* throat now!" Florita hands Leslie "Thanks!" the envelope and Leslie hands it to Patrick. Patrick keeps it squeezed between his fingers, exactly where Leslie put it, like precious recess-money. "And he probably will! I don't need this shit—there's enough crazoids in Paris I don't have to come all the way down here to "

"He doesn't like conflict."

"But he's a fuckin mil—LOOK AT THIS!" Leslie flails toward

the scene on the other side of the glass wall. "What did he do with the conflicts when he was building all this—ram them up his little adolescents' asses and hope they'll go away?"

"C-can I use—well—th-the.....m-men's room? Room? P-please," Patrick asks Florita's phone antenna.

Flo smoothes his hair with her fingertips. "It's that orange door there."

"I Donknow *Can* You? Watch Out For Conflicts Peeking Over From The Next Stall!"

"Your flight's in an hour and a forty-five minutes," Florita says, then throws her head in the direction of Leslie's flails. "That's different—that's business. Business conflicts give him a hard-on. Your-little-circus-in-there conflicts make him head for the nearest "

"Women's underwear! Richard Burton was the same way."

"He wore women's underwear?"

"He said on a talk-show once how different—how little—he was offstage. In the privacy of his own pair of eyes staring at his own self in his own mirror. When he didn't have an audience of two thousand eight hundred people and a king with numbers after his name to hide behind. Physically *and* emotionally. Maybe Jack really looks like Ronald Lightner at the end othe day. Our flight's in an hour and forty-five minutes," Leslie tells Patrick when he reappears, the envelope still attached to his fingers. "Physically *and* emotionally. Maybe that's what the big attraction is. QUICK! GET ME A BUSINESS DEAL! QUICK!" Feigning breathlessness, she hugs Florita goodbye. "THE EIGHT PREGNANT WOMEN I CARRY STRAPPED TO MY WAIST ARE SHRINKING!" As Flo opens the sculpted blond-oak door, she holds out her hand and Patrick shakes it without any terror or embarrassment. "MY WORLD-CLASS AWARD-WINNING ROLEX IS SLIDING OFF MY OOZY WRIST!" Leslie and Patrick walk to the circular drive and disappear into the car. Lowering the tinted window, Leslie stretches her mock-trembling arm in mock desperation toward the pool-house entranceway, where Florita is gurgling a giggleand waving good-bye."B-B-BUYOUT.....MERGERRR.....THREAT OF L-L-LEGAL ACTION...I'LL SETTLE FOR A SIMPLE WIRETAP-SCANDALLL..." Raoul starts the engine. "SAAA-AAAVE MEEE-EEE FROM INTRIGUE-DEFICIENCY-INDUCED DEBILITY...TYCOONIAL-MALNUTRITION-BASED

INSINCERITYYYyyyy......AHHHHhhhhhhhhhhhhh..................."
Leslie does the Wizard of Oz witch-melt scene and they're outa there. With slow faint claps Patrick applauds, stopping himself just short of asking if she minds.
"Thank you, thank you," she acknowledges. He hands her the envelope. She hands it back.

"Wh-what.....is it? Actually."

"The Sunday-after-Thanksgiving New York Times. Shredded. Magazine section *and* book review included.....or maybe they didn't make the switch after all. If you can tell me you can keep it."
He meticulously unglues the flap. "Oh M-My G—Oh M-My G—W-W-What's It All F—well—F-For. M-Ms. Br "
Leslie removes one of the hundred-dollar bills while Patrick delicately cradles the envelope in both palms like a hand-grenade. "This" She holds it up, rotating her wrist back and forth. "is Jack standing up and saying to Ronald Lightner, now, Ronald, I thought we weren't going to be sticking our nose—which happens to be bigger than our sex organ in fullest erection—in other committee members' tasks." She lifts out another hundred-dollar bill. "This is Jack adding, especially Leslie's!" And another. "This is him and the eight pregnant women running—so to speak—down the corridor after us begging us to come back to the conference room to agonize over whether the National Association of University Trustees gets seats for ten of their own delegates or whether they have to share some of them with the *Inter*national Association of University Trustees. She puts the bills back. Patrick gives her the envelope. She gives it back to him. He lays it in her lap.
"Buy yourself some mall-stalking shoes and if you don't take the money I'm gonna throw it bill by bill Hansel and Gretel-style out the window starting" She opens her window as far as it will go. " now." Patrick pushes what he thinks is the button to open his, so he can study the response time of the mechanism, but what is instead the command which lowers the glass between the driver and the backseat. He quickly raises it, his eyes ricocheting around the inside of the car. In his rear-view mirror Raoul watches Leslie take one of the hundreds, hold her arm out, let the bill flap for some seconds and release. Patrick dives by reflex across her lap after the money........and watches it skip away on the wind. He gingerly picks himself and the envelope up from Leslie's knees.

"So whadjya learn at summer camp today?" she asks.

"Y-you c-could've—dyou m—you c. You c-could've g-given it to a—Imean—b-beggar. In the.....ai-airport. Actually."

"You couldn't be righter. That's certainly what I could have done. Whadjya learn?"

Patrick opens his backpack. He tucks the envelope way in at the bottom, focusing sharply on the bar in the middle of the buckle as he tightens the strap back through. Raoul answers the phone then stops the car to write something in a black leather-bound notebook kept between the front seats. Leslie is looking at Patrick. Patrick is looking straight ahead. The car starts moving again...............................

........"The p-price of.....f-fresh...f—well—f-figs. Figs," Patrick finally whispers to the control panel on his armrest.

"Good...Very good...Very very good, Patrick Trucock," Leslie tells him, brushing his cheek with the back of her hand. "That's exactly what you learned." Patrick's window slides down. "That's exactly what you learned."

"CnI borrow some money?" Leslie asks as Patrick returns from an airport-reconnaissance mission and sits at her little round table in the lounge. He stands up and looks at her boot. "Cabfare" she says. "From the airport."

"B-but "

"It's OK. It's safe. Sleeping in its little parking stall where we left it," She hands him his boarding pass. "the beauty. They didn't have any left for Paris so I took two to "

"R-Rio. Actually."

"That Does It, Patrick! You're history!" She slaps her hand against her thigh. "Once you're on to my lines your effective usefulness has been patently outlived." She half-rises from her chair and looks around the room. "Hmm-mmm—lemme seee-eee, are there any fresh new administrative interns out there who haven't a clue as to what I may be about to say next........"

"Y-you could—if you don't m—Imean—if you got—well—f-fresh n-new.....If you got f-fresh new l-lines you could could keep the.....o-one you—well—h-have. Actually. Intern. Actually."

"Nobody likes a smartass. The bomb only hit a major lavatory and grazed a giftshop." Patrick sits down again. "Parking lot OK but cordoned off until at least tomorrow and you shouldn't go without calling." He gets back to his feet. The waiter brings tea.

"*Señor?*"

"No time!" Leslie yelps, paying the waiter and waving him away. "You'll have a cashew on the plane. We gotta be at the gate in fifteen!"

"How-how d-did you.....f—M-Ms. Brittain—f-find "

"Nice check-in lady told me. And we're landing in Orly. No flights to the famous-French- general-named-after-an-airport until the Harley's been rescued."

"BOMB" Patrick mouths, his eyes seeming to try to focus on the inside of his own head.

"See why I brought my running stuff? If Paris only had one airport.........."


The cab driver stops as instructed behind a black Peugeot 405 in front of the gourmet take-out shop on the Avenue de la Motte-Picquet. "Want anything special I'm sssttaaarrrvviiinnngg!—here take my worldly goods I'll meet yupstairs."

Patrick catches the satchel and fishes for his keys in his backpack. "Wh-what are are—what are *y-you* g—well—g-going to h-h "

"Want anything special?"

"Can I—dyou m—c-can I a-ask for—well.....qu-quiche? P-please. Ms. Br-Brittain."

"I dunno can you? What kind?" As she studies the shop window Leslie realizes he's no longer standing next to her. "Hello, I'm Ms. Brittain—" she yells as he heads down the avenue, "And I'll Be Your

Waitress This Evening. Our Specials Today Are: SALMON/SPINACH." She yells louder. "OR MUSHROOM/LEEK." Patrick turns around for the smallest number of seconds needed to show her his crunched-up face. "SALMON/SPINACH!" she confirms and is up in the apartment "It's late, Monsieur Fontaine, *I* don't even know what day it—well we're in luck, aren't we, here comes Mr. Darotto,"
"COL "
"you can ask him!" fifteen minutes later with the newspaper; the mail; a big white envelope without postage; four slices of quiche: salmon/spinach, mushroom/leek, celery/roquefort, vegetable garden; three varieties of salad: seafood, *niçoise*, tomato-mozzarella; a *baguette de compagne*-and-a-half; three types of cheese: goat, brie, cantal; two masterpiece pastries: an *opéra* and a *sachertorte*; a bottle of Perrier; four huge day-glo oranges and a Mars-bar: hazelnut. "They were outa Havana cigars. We get any faxes?"

Patrick hands her five pages. "I don't wanna look at them!" She starts grabbing place-setting components from every cabinet, drawer and shelf. "The nice lady micro-waved the quiche for us how could we forget to eat? Jungles of Brazil'll do it to yevery time!" Patrick hands her five p"President of the United States been assassinated?" she asks, nodding to the faxes.

Patrick scans them. "N-No. They're j-just "
"Then file the fuckers and here—" She dumps dishes and silverware on the table for Patrick to arrange "use this for garbage." and hands him the big white envelope, with the Ronald Lightner brochure inside.

"Y-you have f-four messages. Actually."

Leslie looks instinctively through the bedroom-archway to the machine "I don't wanna Oooohhhh-Ooohhh, what'sss thi-issss?" then walks over to see what's lying on the bed. "Iiii Luhuhuhvve Ihhhtt! I LOVE it! I love IT!" She holds up an oversized white t-shirt with the silhouette of a runner exploding against a fiery red-and-yellow Barcelona Olympics logo. "Patrick! Don't say you never gave me anything, right? I love it! What Ay Trehhhhh-Zhurrrre!" Patrick slowly approaches the alcove, almost smiling, jabbing holes in a flowered paper napkin with the tines of a fork. "And just to show you how much I love it I'm gonna *warn* you that I'm about to rip all my clothes off and put it on rather than just insensitively ripping all my clothes off and putting it on without warning you!" He whips around and runs back to tend to his cutlery. "Works every time!" Leslie sneaks up behind him once it's safe and whispers "It's safe! It comes down almost to Ms. Brittain's knees!"

"W-which—well—qu-quiche dyou.....want? Quiche. Ms. Br-Brittain." Not reacting to Leslie's reactions, Patrick picks up the spatula.

"I really do love it. It's so soft! And I love it especially because it came from.....money that Jack Kote bought us off with! Do you have to focus on me like that when I speak to you, Patrick? What happened to the good old hours when I didn't know whether you were hearing me or receiving orders from your home asteroid through a little electronic implant in your ear? Thanks. Really. We'll split everything—except the mushroom/leek—that's all for yooohh-oohh—what's thi-is?"

Leslie reaches for two blue-and-yellow packets next to Patrick's plate. " 'Glows in the Dark'," she reads. " 'Big Luminous Stars' 'Astro-Magic' 'Glows in the Dark' 'Planets' 'Our Solar System' 'Astro-Magic' 'Adhesive, Luminous Stars and Heavenly Bodies' 'To sleep in outer-space, stick these decals on your walls and ceiling; expose them to light for several seconds and they will glow in the dark. Good night and bon interplanetary voyage!' Patrick this is the greatest thing! Is this not too amazing? Where did you—you got these in the airport? Patrick give me a break here! Will your landlord create an international incident if you put these up?"

"Yeah. L-look!" Patrick opens a flap in the dark-blue packet containing the planets and points to a paragraph of yellow letters.

Leslie reads. " 'Astro-Magic will shine in the dark for sixty minutes after being exposed to FIFTEEN SECONDS', " she emphasizes with surprise, " 'of light.' Holy shit!—it doesn't say holy shit here. 'Try it as often as you wish. This packet contains the sun and all the planets of our solar system'—Look Patrick! 'and Haley's' fucking 'Comet'—it doesn't say fucking either—with the tail look at the tail! and Saturn's rings and those gas those stripe things on Jupiter. I Cannn Nnnottt Standdd Ittt! 'Peel them from their backing, put them on your ceiling, walls, furniture. Astro-Magic: with your head on your pillow you can sleep under the right star. Have a good trip through outer space!' And these are" Opening the other packet she announces " 'THEE-EE TWENTYYY BRIGHTTESSST STARRRS' " in a Wellesian voice. "This is definitely worth having your passport confiscated by your landlord for. I think there are more than twenty here, Patrick, whad'you think? Way to go! Good day at the old airport magazine-kiosk! Where are these manufactured? I'm gonna reheat the rest of the quiche." She stands and reaches for the platter.

Sitting very straight and tall, Patrick asks "W-wanna...try one? O-on your ceiling. Imean."

Leslie slams the platter back down. "THE LADDER'S IN THE CLOSET BY THE FRONT DOOR! I'll close the curtains will my little lamp be enough?" While she pulls one of the yellow rubbery stars from its backing "I wouldn't dare waste Saturn. Or Haley. Who are these little guys?—maybe one of them's your home asteroid, Patrick!", Patrick secures the ladder as close to the bed as possible so as to be able to place the heavenly body directly above the point between the two pillows. She hands it up to him. He takes it from her with slow, surgical care "Frchrissakes you'd think it was a real star!" and respect.

"It *i-is* a r-a real st-star. M-Ms. Brittain." Patrick sounds surprised she didn't know that.

"Oh!.....You think my little nighttable lamp is enough?" Perfectly prone on her back, Leslie positions herself just right of center on the bed, looking straight up, her hand on the lampswitch. "There's anticipation in the air, Patrick Trucock!"

"Yeah." Patrick starts down the ladder. Leslie pats the comforter with her left palm, indicating his spot. "I can't stand it I can't stand it! SHINE SHINE!" she tells her lamp, drawing herself up on her right elbow to peer into the bulb. Patrick stands still on the lowest step, focusing on the blinking light in the answering machine on the dresser. "Patrick Trucock if you're gonna get nineteenth century on me now, now's not the time, Patrick, we are about to give birth to a star! It was your fucking idea to put it up there they're *your* I promise that any brutal sexual attacking I'm gonna do to you in this bed will be delayed until further notice will you just get here frchrissake! I know! I know what you're doing, you intelligent earthly body, you're stalling so our baby'll be able to soak up EVEN MORE light but the envelope said *fifteen seconds*. The fucking thing has enough light stored by now-WAIT!" She jumps up, scampers over to switch off the lamp in the livingroom, scampers back, dives into position in bed. "-to be able to guide Portuguese sailors from one end of the earth to the other. Take your shoes off before getting in."

Patrick lies down next to Leslie. Leslie turns off the lamp. "Ohh-hh Myee-eeee Gohoh-ohohdddd!" The star shines brilliantly on the blackness of her ceiling in the blackness of her bedroom. Patrick bolts out of bed. Leslie tries to grab him. "WAIT!" she cries.

"No! Wait!" he replies and runs over to the table for another star.

"What'rydoing?" He climbs up the ladder. "Don't waste them, they're yours, sweetie!"

"T-turn on the the lamp. Quick!" Patrick orders and leans over to stick a smaller star to the northeast of the first one. He scrambles down and flops into bed backwards. "GO!" he shouts. Leslie reaches for the lampswitch again. "WAIT!" he shouts. "A-another few seconds!...... NOW!" Leslie turns off the light. The big original star and its baby offshoot star spontaneously combust in the apartment sky. Leslie and Patrick study their heaven in silence—Leslie prays the phone won't ring, wants to get up and unplug it, stays to absorb the starlight—then stare at each other for some seconds, only their heads out of perfect alignment with the axis of their bodies flat against the bed. Their breathing falls into sync, their eyes are happy and quiet..................................................................................................
..................................................................................................
.........."I'm going to do it," Patrick says, his soft words flowing unbroken. Leslie squints and tilts her head. Outer space is silent again............ Then....."SATURN!" Patrick announces and— "AAAAAAAAH!" Leslie screams—flies over to pick his planet off its protective backing. "THE LIGHT!" Patrick demands. "THE LIGHT!" Leslie responds and the planet goes up and stars follow planets and planets surround stars and Patrick tries to get the Milky Way as accurate as possible, shuttling back and forth between the table and the ladder and up the ladder, with Leslie the "Vice-Intergalactic Chancellor in Charge of Lamp, OK, Patrick?", and every time he comes down from the sky they take their positions to make sure all is right with the universe and when "THE SUN!" goes up "THE SSUNN, PATRICK!" it's the most spectacular celebration of all with neither of them asking or even caring how the sun and the stars can be shining in the same couple square meters of firmament at the same time and they stare on their backs at Saturn's rings and Patrick decides to save Haley's Comet for last because he's gotten nuts about perfect placement, and though in the beginning every several celestial bodies Leslie wanted to know whether Patrick realized he was going to have no stars or planets left for his own ceiling "Don't you even want Jupiter? I hope you know what you're doing.", by the end of the packet of stars and the end of packet of solar system all Leslie's concerned with is doing a good job at her light-station and soon when the lamp is turned off again the ceiling in the bedroom-alcove "looks no different from heaven, Patrick" and Patrick is exhausted and they are lying on their backs on

the comforter getting a load of the miracle of matter.

There they lie, at once buoyant and anchored, each fitted into their own essential space like beings about to be kryogenically frozen and transported into the next wave of time. They say nothing because ("there is nothing to say. What is there to say? We just created a universe.") but absorb each other's light through the kind intervention of the stars and the planets which draw up the light from one, nourish and reinforce it, and dispatch it down into the other, exchanging it for the light the other is giving up to the same seamless process. After her light has stopped at every star and planet along the way to Patrick's light, Leslie slowly stands, leaving the form of her light behind her, beside Patrick on the bed, and goes over to the dinette table to have her dinner.

Patrick follows several minutes later, rising languidly, moving languidly, like someone who has just donated blood. Just donated energy to the source of energy. While he dishes himself some *salade niçoise*, Leslie strolls to the bookcase for a Stones cassette and tucks it into the machine on the partition and after tonight she and Patrick never speak about the stars and the planets on her ceiling again, just as people never speak about how the earth is revolving under their laundry room or about the oxygen they're breathing. Just as people during the Renaissance did not stop each other on the street in downtown Milan and say, "Hey, man! What's hapnin? T's the Renaissance today, man, cnyuh diggit?" One of the last times they visit their firmament with words is when Leslie, cutting some goat cheese, tells Patrick to get his resume out of his backpack and adds in magic-marker under "Professional Experience": *Created a Universe — Paris, 1992*

Then Mick and the boys start asking *Brown Sugahhhhh, How kum yuh dance so guh-uhd noww-uh,* which Leslie takes as her divine cue to cut the *opéra* and the *sachertorte* each in half and haul the pastry platter, two dessert plates *Juss like a young girl shou-ould-uh-huh-mah,* two dessert forks, two fresh napkins, two champagne glasses, what's left of the bottle of Perrier, and Patrick onto the bed. The big silver metal ladder is still wedged as far against the mattress as it will go, looking as if it's just landed and deployed its unloading platform, one empty *you shoulda heard im jusst arou-ounn midnigh-ight* blue-and-yellow cardboard Astro-Magic envelope draped across its top step, the other on the floor. *I said yeah-ehuh yeah-ehuh yeah-ehuh whooo-ooo how kum yuh how kum yuh* "dance so go-oodd whooooh!" Leslie sends Patrick into the livingroom to turn off the light and switches on the lamp *jusss like a* "jusss like a" *black gir-irl shou-ould* "yeah-eah-eah-uhhhhhhHHHHHHHHH!", knocking Tropic of Cancer off the nighttable with the end of the fork in her hand.

"There are no coincidences in this world, Patrick." She picks up the book and sets it, open, on her crossed legs, between the plate of pastries and her tummy. "What is there only?"

"I-I kn-know. Ms. Br-Brittain. What there......is. Actually."

"Ordinarily, you know, I wouldn't be so sure but after what you just manufactured up there I'd be a fool to doubt you," she tells him and starts reading: " 'But in Matisse, in the exploration of his brush, there is the trembling glitter of a world which demands only the presence of the female to crystallize the most fugitive aspirations. To come upon a woman offering herself outside a urinal, where there are advertised cigarette papers, rum, acrobats, horse races, where the heavy foliage of the trees breaks the heavy mass of walls and roofs, is an experience that begins where the boundaries of the known world leave off.....Even as the world falls apart the Paris that belongs to Matisse shudders with bright, gasping orgasms, the air itself is steady with a stagnant sperm, the trees tangled like hair.....The wheel is falling apart but the revolution is intact...'\* Page one sixty-eight. You're a virgin, aren't you, Patrick?"

Patrick bothers neither to focus nor to unfocus. He's too drained to do anything but let his eyes settle wherever they land and they land on Leslie's eyes. He doesn't bother to answer either. "Mick Jagger is in the tapeplayer, Henry Miller is in our genitals, the solar system is occurring overhead and you're a virgin." Leslie contemplates Patrick and nods, sets her plate of untouched dessert on a ladder step. Takes a swig of Perrier then offers the bottle.

" gin, too," Patrick mumbles, pushing her arm away.
"Huh?"
"Y-YOU'RE A—I s..........n-neverm-mind. M-Ms. Br "
"Huh?"
" a v-virgin.....too. Too. M-Ms. Br-Brittain. I s—th-that's whatI s........said. Actually."

"You're either trying out a new smartass routine on me before taking it on the road or you've gone back to your asteroid without kissing me good-bye. You're absolutely right, though. I'm a virgin, too. We're all virgins too and we're all brutally fucked on a daily basis. Daily virgins and daily fucked. I never want to know, Patrick, *why* you are a virgin at the age of twenty-whatever-the-fuck-you-are. It'd make me too angry. It'd make me too angry..........If you want my cake you can have it." Leslie turns off the lamp and they get into their kryogenic-freeze positions and look at the balls in space for a long time. *Leh-eht's do some lihihving* They both know that Patrick did a sensational job with the Milky Way and they both know not to say it.

"If you give me nothing else ever you will *after weeih die-ie* have brought astronomy into my bedroom." Staring straight up, Leslie is watching a brilliant sun keep *Wii-iild horses, couldn't drag me away Wii-iild wild horses we'll ride them someday* track of its responsibility on a darkened field. *Wii-iild horses, couldn't drag me away Wii-iild wild horses we'll ride them someday.....* "If I give you nothing else ever I will have punctured your senses and poured Henry Miller in." She switches the lamp on. "Listen to this: 'O Tania, where now is that warm cunt of yours, those fat, heavy garters, those soft, bulging thighs? There is a bone in' " The phone rings. Leslie rests the book on her thighs and looks at the machine:

"Bonsoir, ma belle! It's after twelve thirty. I know you're sleeping. I just wanted to hear your voice—well, your answering machine's voice. It's really that rock music I wanted to hear. No. I wanted to hear your voice.....Leslie........I'll call you in the morning...I wish—I wanted to t.......... Je t'embrasse, ma belle!" \*BeeeeeeeeeeeeeP\*\*\*\*\*BeeeeeeeeeeeeeP\*\*\*\*\*

\* Henry Miller, *Tropic of Cancer*, Grafton Books, 1965, page 168

# VII

## KILOMËTER ZËRO

Leslie crosses the small square uncovered cobblestone courtyard contained by tall green-trellised stone and stucco walls along which windowboxes are spilling gerania.

She opens the heavy wine-wooden door to the corridor, windowless and dark. At the other end, with the mailboxes on her left and the front door of the building before her, she stops and looks at her watch.

The digital dial shows: 5:58:11.

Moving her head almost imperceptibly, she beats the rhythm of each passing second as Monsieur Fontaine, in pajamas, slips from his rust-colored door and asks a question that she ignores. The watch is at 5:59:14. Still counting to herself, she raises her head toward the entranceway. At 5:59:30 she presses a silver button on the right-hand doorframe to release the latch with a soft silence-cutting *click*.

The front door groans as it opens to the street, the narrow passageway whose random dotting of little overhanging gardens courts wonder about why one window would merit flowers and another not. There are ancient emblems, left over from ancient trades, swinging from the high stone walls: a huge metal jailer's-key—what did they used to do in there?—a woodturner's shingle in wood. Covered at its mouth, about forty yards ahead, by a bridging building, the passage seems to constrict, to form a suction spout, just before it relaxes and rolls into the intersecting avenue. Paris smells of dew drying. It is purple outside—the color of the night ceding in defiant languor to the pre-openings of the day, with tinselstrands of light lacing randomly through the thick dawn.

Standing square, she shifts her weight from foot to foot. Watches a lone black Peugeot chase its own headlights through the shadow of the avenue. 5:59:50 and she slowly starts. Two ticks. Two steps. Pushes the on-button of the Walkman grasped in her right hand. 5:59:55...56...57...58...59...at 6:00 she thrusts down onto her right foot, spilling out of the passage under the blue-and-white regulation plaque

> 7ÉME ARRONDISSEMENT

affixed to a topmost stone, while The Star Spangled Banner blares into her headphones.

Up in the cool purplevelvet tinselmorning she runs left onto the *contre-allée* of the Avenue Bosquet, half a block to the Place de l'Ecole Militaire. ("Hello, Soldier!") **"WDVQ NOW BEGINS ITS BROADCAST DAY. WDVQ IS LICENCED TO THE PENSTAR EDUCATIONAL RADIO CORPORATION AND OPERATES ON AN ASSIGNED FREQUENCY OF EIGHTY-EIGHT POINT SIX MEGAHURTZ, WITH AN EFFECTIVE RADIATED POWER"** Left along the *place* and across the Avenue de Tourville, **"OF THREE THOUSAND WATTS VERTICAL AND FIVE WATTS HORIZONTAL"** then straight on the Avenue Duquesne **"POLARIZATION. WDVQ UTILIZES STL WLD TWO O NINE."** behind the rippling rearends of four out-lander matrons dragging valises to the Derby Hotel. ("t's see if they have enough brains tget outta thNOHHHHH *not* enough brains tget outta the wthe only exer")"Cise They've Ever Gotten In Their Life Is Chew-ing!" she screams back over her shoulder into their blank faces. **"OUR OFFICES AND STUDIOS ARE LOCATED IN ERMEDE, NEW JERSEY, AND OUR TRANSMITTER IS"** From here uphill for the first twenty minutes, heading for then through Montparnasse—boring into the burned-sugar beginning of the baker's day of smells, past the favorite cane chairs out this early at the little *tabac/café*, across the open, **"LOCATED IN LAFAYETTE TOWNSHIP, CHESHIRE COUNTY, NEW JERSEY. OUR MAILING ADDRESS IS POST OFFICE BOX TWO O TWO, ERMEDE, NEW JERSEY, O EIGHT O THREE FIVE."** broad Avenue de Ségur with on-strike nurses, in their uniforms, waking up under slogan-slathered tents to her right, and **"SOME OF THE PROGRAMS AIRED ON WDVQ ARE PRE-RECORDED. THE STAFF AND MANAGEMENT HOPE"** Napoléon, presumably in his, still sleeping under the gilt-touched Invalides dome to her left. The first lasting light of her morning always bounces down from the Emporer's roof. ("Hello, Officer! Hello, Officer!") **"YOU ENJOY OUR BROADCAST OFFERINGS FOR TODAY."** She runs across the Avenue de Breteuil at the Place El Salvador, curving and climbing with the rue d'Eblé past ("Hello, Officer!") the Racing Club de France as the spot for Charles A. Pratt & Son, Plumbing and Heating, **"NEIGHBORS SERVING NEIGHBORS"** follows the credits. By the time Danney's greeting eases in on top of a gurgly Brian Eno guitar she's on the other side of the Boulevard des Invalides, beating a black Peugeot 405 at the right turn.

"AAH-AAHND *THAT* WE ARE, NEIGHBORS SERVING NEIGHBORS! YOU—OUR NEIGHBORS—YES, YOU! YOU THERE WITH THE CEREAL BOWL! THAT'S RIGHT, DON'T LOOK AT ME LIKE THAT! YOUR DIAL'S TUNED TO THE *FINEST* LISTENER-SUPPORTED PUBLIC RADIO STATION *INNN THEEE* NATION, FM EIGHTY-EIGHT POINT SIX, WDVQ, BOWMAN TOWNSHIP, NEW JERSEY. VERY VERY PLEASANT GOOD MORNING! IT'S SIX O FOUR! IT'S A FRIDAY! IT'S APRIL TWENTY-FOURTH! ANNND MY NAME IS DANNEY BRITTAIN—DANNEY-THE GREAT-BRITTAIN—I AM HERE TOOOO-KEEEEP-YOUUUU-COMPANYYY TIL NINE O'CLOCK!" ("Fuh-uh-King D")"Get Yourself A Leash, Lady, And While You're At It Get One For Your Fucking" Streaming left on top of the Boulevard des Invalides "Dog!", she hooks the quick right across the Rue de Sèvres toward the long high passion of the Boulevard du Montparnasse. Towne Toyota's jingle transports her to the base of the boulevard and Danney over Coltrane takes up from "AWWWLLLL RIGHT" there. "SIX-O-EIGHT...INNN-THE-MORRNIN...HERE AT DVQ...IN THE MORNING...*DANNEY*-IN-THE-MORNING...DANNEY-THE GREAT-BRITTAIN SHOW...THE NAME OF THIS RECURRING"

Up from there the sidewalk steepens, "MONDAY AND FRIDAY MORNING EXTRAVAGANZA—KEEPIN YUH COMPANY TIL NINE O'CLOCK." fast past the pizza places and train-station cafes. The one-star hotels. Maybe exactly as much as the Boulevard St-Michel drops later on. "WE HAVE A GREAT SHOW PLANNED FOR YOU TODAY, Maybe not. LOTS TO TALK BOUT, SOME TOPICALITY AT THE SEVEN O'CLOCK STRIKE, SOME EXPLORATION OF THE MUSICAL UNIVERSE

**AS ONLY WE KNOW HOW, SOME MORE OF YOUR MUSICAL EDUCATION FOR YOU. I'M VERY TALKATIVE THIS MORNING, AREN'T I?...IT'S THE PURE UNBIASED LOVE I HAVE OF HEARING THE MODULATIONS OF *MY* VOICE IN THESE JOSEPH GRADO HEADPHONES...BUT I'M GONNA SHUT UP FOR AWHILE...LET YOU ENJOY SOME '*TRANE* ."**

As if opening a door Leslie stretches through the threshold where the Rue de Rennes rolls in from far down to the left, bringing with it taxis and trucks and first bus-runs to pour into the *place* dominated by the Montparnasse station and it's tallest office-tower in Europe. Amidst the multi-movietheatres and magazine kiosks she enters the magic oxygen that holds Hemingway's Select and Fitzgerald's Coupole and Joyce's Dome. A black Peugeot 405 is idling at the light in front of the Rotonde. **"LISTEN WITH ME, WON'T YOU?"** She runs across the Boulevard Raspail.

At the hour when the russet cane chairs rest bundled together against the building and the pinkclothed tables aren't out yet, she kicks left past a ("Hello, Officers!") clump of cops at the tree-heavy Closerie des Lilas. **"HAP'NIN' STUH-UHFFF, A LITTLE JOHN COL TRANE TO WAKE Y'UP ON A MONDAY MORNING, AT 6:18 ON DVQ,"** The leg of the angle becomes the Luxembourg Gardens, becomes both a solid wall of immediacy—a sudden cartoon-wall against which it's too late for the startled Road Runner to prevent impact—and a Renaissance carpet the rhythm of whose rolling out before her is paced by her progress along its fibers. **"COLABORATING ON THAT ONE WITH THE LIKES OF MCCOY TYNER, JIMMY GARRISON AND, OF COURSE,"** One morning, just out of the turn at the Closerie, she sighted the distant northern Basilica of Sacré Coeur **"GOD: ELVIN JONES."** seeming to sit tight atop the Gardens' regnant Medici Palace in an illusion **"WE HAVE SOME WEATHER WORDS FOR YOU—ALWAYS A FAVORITE MOMENT OF OURS HERE ON THE DANNEY-THE GREAT-BRITTAIN SHOW BECAUSE IT GIVES US A CHANCE TO HEAR ME READ MY OWN WRITING—BROUGHT TO YOU BY"** she knows looms for her passing only, and then only at the spark of second when the streetlights switch off with a city-wide click. **"THE NATIONAL WEATHER SERVICE AND WDVQ. AND THIS IS WHAT THEY WOULD HAVE US BELIEVE:"**

As the Gardens flow off in a northwest fork a man in a brown suit chucks a cigarette butt in her ("Hey! Watch")"It Jerkface!" path from the driver's window of a black Peugeot 405.  She speeds straight down past the sensual art-gallery posters (and one particularly sensual art-gallery poster offering a naked teenaged beauty atop an extravagant winding gold staircase owned surely by an aged business baron who has no end of ravaging her perfection) in the Boulevard St-Michel windows. Bookstore windows, travel and temp-help agency windows. Jazz-clubs whose opaque windows look like false facades and *crêpe* stalls that have no facades but all manner of signs and flyers and hand-lettered menus and price lists tacked and taped to their simple wooden structures. Windows which preview the presence of the Panthéon **"YUK! THAT'S WHAT THEY READ LIKE: YUK! THAT'S"** staring from the right down the Rue Soufflot to the main Gardens-entrance up ahead. **"ALL YOU NEED TO KNOW FOR TODAY: YUK! IT'S SO YUK THAT I FORGOT TO CUE UP MY ENVIRONMENT HERE—I'M NO GOOD FOR NO ONE DOIN' THE WEATHER"**

There are runners now—and a skinny guy on skates—coming up toward her along the boulevard, energizing and encircling the vast iron-post fencing, waiting for the Gardens gates to open at seven. **"WITHOUT MY RAIN FOREST UNDER ME. SH—BY THE WAY, IF THAT GUY WHO CALLED LAST WEEK TO TELL ME HE THINKS MY RAIN FOREST IS A TAPE—A *TAPE*, ARE YOU *INTO* THIS?—IF YOU WANNA HOP ON YOUR TRICYCLE AND COME DOWN AND HAVE A LOOK I'LL BE MORE THAN HAPPY TINTRODUCE YOU TMY CONURE PARROT UP THERE—IF YPROMISE TSTAY OUTA MY POND—SHUT-UP!, WILL YOU?"** ("Talk to your frog, Dan!") **"NOT YOU! MY FROG!"** The French runners don't say hello. Don't nod their heads to tell her they know how early she got up this morning and that she, too, must've run in that muddy rain yesterday. Don't register her passing smile in their eyes or their jaws or their "Yeah! That's Right! Hello! Supposed To Say Hello, Jerkface!" shoulders. A social implosiveness issued with every birth certificate. "What, are we out here doin errands here!" Louis and his viceroys didn't exchange high-fives jogging between bushes at Versailles. No reason to start any bad habits now. "Frchrissakes!"

The others make eyecontact in little squirts of cardiovascular bonding. " llo!"

And the French non-runners stare. All over the city. They stare. They have never seen a runner before. And have always known that day would come. And here it is. And she's it. And tomorrow when she passes they will never have seen a runner before again. They will always have known that day would come again. And here it will be again. They **"DANNEY-THE GREAT-BRITTAIN AND WDVQ KEEPING YOU INFORMED OF THE GOINGS-ON IN *YOUR* COMMUNITY BY MEANS OF THESE"** pierce her peace with dumbfounded dumb faces from which she at times abruptly turns her head and into which she at times "Pluto! Yep! Landed Just Seconds Ago, Lady!" rivets.

Going for the big corner.

Looking left to the yellow-and-green hand-painted promise on a small black enamel sign fixed to a fence post:

> LES MARIONNETTES
> DU
> THEATRE DU LUXEMBOURG
> *Amusent petits et grands*
> *Spectacles artistiques*
> ROBERT DESARTHIS-DIRECTEUR

Looking left into the layers of the Luxembourg. The orderly *allées* of erect guard-trees protecting the path to the Palace, and the massive white statues who relieve them at the flowered fountain further on. **"COMMUNITY BULLETIN BOARDS—CEE-BEE-BEES—CEE-BEE-SQUAREDS, AS MY BIG SISTER SAYS—CEE-BEE-TO-THE-TWO-POWER—AND SOME OF THEM** sound like this:" To the roof-geometry beyond the leaves, and out of the neighborhood to the sky. The sky which absorbs her salutations and sends patterns of once-lost light back to her. "The Glenview YMCA is sponsoring free bike-safety classes every Saturday from now until July third. Participants must be at least 10 years of age and bring a helmet. That's—*brinnngg ayyy helll- mettt!* For further information you may contact Kerry by mashing the numbers on your phone so designated: six o nine-eight three two-YMCA. And oh—I forgot to tell you—bring a helmet! And this: do you know what goes into the perfect hoagie? The Carnell Volunteer Fire company does and they'd like to show you! Stop by! hoagies"

Shifting her eyes from the red light to her watch ("Helloareallottaofficers!") while a packed police bus slithers past on the Rue Medici, Leslie trots in place at the five-point *place*. Crosses. Zig-zags to realign with the Boulevard St-Michel. Spans the Rue Monsieur le Prince, the summit of the slope. Begins her descent toward the Seine. "are yours for the asking—well, for the buying—at one dollar each or a dollar fifty for two, every Sunday afternoon at the firehouse on Quarry Street. A black Peugeot 405 begins its descent toward the Seine. All proceeds benefit"

In the little-lit dayrise when the sleepy bright-green-overalled thirdworld men spray Paris with their bright-green sidewalk-stalking scooter-hoses and sweep Paris with their plastic-straw bright-green brooms, in the little-lit dayrise when the overpriced jeans and cheap suits and martial arts regalia are not yet out on street-front racks and tables, when the near-bald cleaninglady in the same dull dress in the same gleaming *tabac* storms the manicured Montblancs with her dustrag, and the croissant-&-sandwich spots release their first student-trapping scents of the morning, she tracks "The" the Boulevard St-Michel to its "Carnell En Jay" source. "Volunteer Fire Company." How bizarre and uncomfortable the boulevard always looks to her at any later hour—with all signs of life and no bright-green broom-men, who are not signs of life at all but partners with her in the prehistory of each new day on the streets that together they at their hour own.

"EXPLORING THE MUSICAL UNIVERSE WITH YOU ON THE DANNEY BRITTAIN—DANNEY-THE GREAT-BRITTAIN—SHOW ON FRIDAY, APRIL TWENTY-FOURTH, A LITTLE WALK TO THE GALLOWS WITH HECTOR BERLIOZ THIS MORNING IN THE SYMPHONIE" ("Dthey change th—nfrchrissakes wmany more weeks are Three Student Nurses gonna have A Fire In Theiryou'd think they'd change th ") "FANTASTIQUE, LEONARD BERNSTEIN AND THE BOYS—AN EMI ("*COMING* Soon—cute!—yI'll *Suce* you til it *Fait Mal*, honey!") RELEASE TO GET YOU UP AN RUNNIN THIS MORNING—I KNOW SOMEONE WHO'S UP AND *REALLY* RUNNING THIS MORNING" In front of the Gibert Jeune textbook emporium next to Cinépornorama's decayed marquee she hurdles the arm of a yellow metal dolly, slowing for the long light at the Boulevard St-Germain. Paris smells of cigarette smoke. "POLICE BARRICADES, ANYONE?" A black Peugeot 405 runs the red. Then waits at the curb until it changes.

Café de Cluny on the other side, more student bookstores, record shops, what are the Doors still doing in the window!, Morrison Hotel, little cobbled cross-streets, she looks at her watch, Danny whispers over the drumroll "THE GREAT-BRITTAIN PHONELINES ARE ALWAYS OPEN AT SIX O NINE-FOUR TWO TWO-NINE TWO TWO TWO—NINE-TWO-CUBED—GIVE ME A CALL AND COMPLETE THE CIRCUIT THAT IS RAY-DEE-OH.", socks and t-shirts, cheapfood, currency exchange, she steps onto the start of the expanse of the Place St-Michel, the fountain and greencopper dragon, with a left-over prostitute, rolls into a quick Beatles before the bottom-of-the-hour, two Macdonald-carton escapees from the scooter-men, sees the Seine, Sainte-Chapelle is where Marie Antoinette waited for "MAXWELL'S SILVER HAMMER—THAT" the blade, makes the light, squeezes between the lightpost and a wrought-iron railing on the sidewalk at the corner, always between the lightpost and the railing, sees down to the Seine through the pinhole in the pavement at the beginning of the bridge, **"REMINDS ME—GET-WELL WISHES GO OUT TO BILL WYLIE OUR CHIEF"** glances at her ("good!") watch, looks **"ENGINEER,"** up and right to Notre Dame, **"RECOVERING FROM A PRETTY SERIOUS BACK OPERATION—THINKIN' ABOUT YMAN!"** does the Pont St-Michel to the Ile de la Cité, receives Notre Dame, the Seine sleeping at its feet, Danney does the station I.D. and the first of two spots, she looks left and down to the river, the river is different every morning from every different bridge and she waits every morning to see how different it will be.

At today's version of 6:30:23, the Pont St-Michel Seine is sleek charcoal with pink mist smoking up from its face and not letting go, playing with the water, teasing it, until a barge slides ripples into the smoothness, ripples brought from far before the bridge, moving the charcoal gloss out toward each stony bank, scaring away the pink. Chopping up the river. Heading west into town.

**"YEAHHHHH,"** Across the street at the end of the *pont*, left turn onto the Quai des Orfèvres. Danney's thrown on obscure jazz and she paces her progress ("Hello, Officer!") against the colorparade of shops dwellings bistros lining the left-bank frontage on the other side of the Seine, from where she just ("Hello, Officer! Hello, Officer! Hello Officer!") ran. ("Hello, Officer! Hello, Officer!") Here daily Leslie reclaims into her consciousness of Paris the metal piano-man shingle playing out his red/black/white puffery over his red/gold music-store door. The sweet yellow shutters of the slim blue juice-bar. Lapérouse's grand aged three-story burgundy wood facade through whose windows at night the diningroom chandeliers blaze. She knows that close up, they and their merchant neighbors and the somber *portes cochères* that separate them, the old bent trees that partially hide them, the fir-green *bouquiniste*-stalls along the river under their windows must be no more than wide brush-strokes of pigment, only giving the impression of substance to the facing shore. ("Hello, Officer! Hello, Officer! Hello, Officer!")

A man in workclothes and two graceless women—one swinging a cigarette like a majorette's baton by her hip—are marching to the Courthouse-Police Headquarters complex which fills and commands the Quai des Orfèvres. The *quai* of the goldsmiths, the embankment of the goldsmiths. As Leslie catches up, they all spring together off the sidewalk into the ample parking lot, where uniformed police officers materialize in clusters wherever she casts her eyes and an annotated white line divides the known cosmos down the middle

## PALAIS | POLICE
## DE JUSTICE

Plainclothes **"ALLLWAYS GOOD TO HEAR FROM MISTER CHRIS ETON, WHO WILL LIFT THAT BIG HEAVY LID OFF THE RECORD RACK THIS MONDAY—AS EVERY"** cops move from old-model cars ("Hello, Officer!") toward the mystery of the compound's cavernous courtyard-entrance while matched sets of blue-uniformed *flics* huddle around guardbooths **"MONDAY FROM NINE TO NOON, FOLLOWING THE DANNEY BRITTAIN—DANNEY-THE-GREAT-BRITTAIN—SHOW RIGHT HERE ON WDVQ FM EIGHTY-EIGHT POINT SIX, THE *FINEST* COMMUNITY-SUPPORTED PUBLIC RADIO STATION INNN-THISSS-NATIONNN. SOME FAHH-AHHHNNNNN LISTNIN *FOR* YUH"** and whisper into patrol-car windows. Populate the lot along the oak-shadowed Seine. **"ON"** In an exaggerated gesture of civil chivalry— **"DVQ FM EIGHTY-EIGHT POINT SIX —I JUST SAID THAT, DIDN'T I? SIX-THIRTY-FOUR IN THE MORNING. I BETTER FIGURE OUT WHAT PLANET I'M ON AND"** aimed more at impressing each other than at pleasing her—a trio near the electronic barrier manually raise the red arm to ease Leslie's exit she tries for a last glimpse into the entranceyard throws the cops a kiss the cops kiss back Danney **"THROW THIS FOR LESLIE."** throws Janis onto the ("OHHHHH, SHITTTTT, DAN!! YEAHOHHH *CUUHH-UUHH MMAWWNNN CUUHH-UUHH* MMAWWNNN *CUUHH-UUHHMM*") turntable and all up along the shaded cobblestoned slope to the Pont Neuf.

("AWWNNN CUUHH-UUHH MMAWWNNN, NOWTAAYYYYYYYK IHHHHHTTTTT, TAKE ANOTHER LITTLE PIECE OF MY HEART NOW

BAYYYBEEEEYEAHHHHHHUHHHUHHHEEEOHHHHHHBRBRBR BRRAAYYYYYYYYKIHHHHHTTTTT, BREAK ANOTHER—GOD, DAN!")

("You do it on") Danney does it on ("purpose!")—knows she's in-the-front-lot-of-police-HQ-and-the-supreme-courthouse-for-serious-international-peace-disturbers-every-morning-around-6:35-where-she-probably-shouldn't-be-running-in-the-first-place-and-especially-now-with-all-the-beefed-up-brigades-of-beefed-down-pale-policepeople-stalking-the-terrorists-stalking-the-populace-but-it's-been-so-many-years'-of-months'-of-mornings-through-that-lot-that-they-long-ago-began-to-depend-on-her-to-keep-the-astral-bodies-in-proper-alignment and every morning around 6:35 he slashes open her soul and stuffs one in that slithers about and makes her scream and makes "YOOOOO! KNOW! YOU! GOHHT! IT! IFFF! ITTT! *MAYYYYKKSSS* YOOO" her scream out beaming in a grunted foreign tongue in front of concentrations of "FFEEEEL G" *UUUU-UUUU* law enforcement personnel and draggy cleaningladies on their way into work whose history of contact with speeding Janis Joplin-imitators at dawn has got to be *UUUUD* "D*DD!*" limited.

Against the One Way arrow, a black Peugeot 405 cruises the shaded cobblestoned slope to the Pont Neuf. Leslie's secret passageway through the forest. A privileged peek into something she really shouldn't be seeing, or that doesn't truly exist, or that exists now but in such a different form that the original form has been put into a museum through which she—with Janis or Jimi or Smokey and the cleaningladies—runs before opening hours. It's finding far back on the closet ceiling the only slat of wood in the whole house that was never victimized by the renovator's brush. Seeing what color it all really once was. Darkened by dense Seine-side trees and tall Norman-stone buildings, by the pearled-slate sheen steaming up from the cobblestones which always seem moist, the western leg of the Quai des Orfèvres looks like a back alley with main-avenue architecture. It is unseeable from most neighboring vantage points and missable from the others. A thin single streak burned as with quick acid through the thick-layer Ile de la Cité grid after all else was set in place—or the absolute initial channel around which the entirety of Paris was carved.

A corridor through courthouse territory. Like so much in Paris in so many spheres, through root-source courthouse territory, first-ever conception of courthouse territory, where the solemnity of the structures is solemnity absorbed from two millennia of tribes and monarchy and Church.

It is the *Journal Officiel d'Annonces Légales* where Parisians with businesses to found or names to change or deaths to declare place their little requisite ad, and in the beige-curtained windows of whose storefront office, cracked yellowed framed front pages feature engravings of frockcoated men in vandykes striking each other with walking sticks to the horrified shrieks of bustled women. It is old eating-houses with older woodbeam ceilings and menus dictated by yet more ancient cultural rules and rites, frequented much later in the day by men, mostly, whose professional honorcodes go back even farther than that. It is concierge-eyes beading furtively through shutter slats in a sense of turf surpassing the requirements of the trade.

When **"AWAWRIIIGHTT—ONE OF LESLIE'S FAY-VOH-RITTS HERE ON THE DANNEY-THE GREAT-BRITTAIN SHOW"** she reaches the top of the slope, Paris becomes vast again.

**"AND WE DO SEND THAT OUT TO HER ON WDVQ EIGHTY-EIGHT POINT SIX FM AND ALL THE FINE MEMBERS OF THE LOCAL CONSTABULARY MAKING SURE THEM BOMBS ARE CONFINED ONLY TO THE CONCERTS OF DUDES I DON'T DIG—THANKS, GUYZZ! IT'S A FRDIAY! WE HAVE ACHIEVED WEEK-END *WWONCE* AGAIN! GOOD MORNING! APRIL TWENTY-FOURTH! SOME SPRING IN THE AIR AT SIX THIRTY-SEVEN. AND WE'LL BE BACK—YOU GUESSED IT—RIGHT AFTER THESE—LISTEN-UP!"**

**"THIS IS PAUL NEWMAN. WHEN YOU GIVE BLOOD,"**

As if shaking out a great pastel-patterned bedsheet whose tight little creases puff up and smooth out to reveal the whole intricate design all the way to the corners, the dawn-kindled city now spreads its fabric in waves, sending the: Pont Neuf's Napoléon III lamp-posts rippling into the stunning expanse of the bridge itself which bounces its equestrian Henri IV on top of a crest which indicates the scope of the silver sky which sweeps into the pinkened river below and beyond which rolls away west under the bridge that connects the Palais du Louvre to the house where Voltaire died which unfolds farther into the leaf-darkened Tuileries Gardens which draws the remote 16th *arrondissement* into view with it's own sky and Seine and threading of light whose source shines again on the lamp-posts before Leslie as she takes two quick rights and disappears into the tight protection of the Place Dauphine. A piano fills Paul Newman's every pause with a phrase from "Making Whoopee".

**"YOU GIVE ANOTHER BIRTHDAY.....ANOTHER DAY AT THE BEACH.....ANOTHER NIGHT UNDER THE STARS.....ANOTHER WALK WITH A FRIEND....."** Into the Place Dauphine's little insulated keyhole-shaped containment. To the **"ANOTHER HUG."** right of the clean central oval of greenery and benches separated from the sidewalk and shading buildings by a tiny cobblestoned ringlet. More courthouse accessories—lawbook stores—more wood-studded restaurants, the notoriosly inexpensive Hôtel Henry IV so out of place in the *place* where Yves Montand lived and died **"A MESSAGE FROM THE AMERICAN RED CROSS—GIVE BLOOD!"** and whose elegance is anchored by the majestic Pont Neuf at one end and the venerable Palais de Justice at the other.

**"ALLLWAYS GOOD TO HEAR FROM THE OWNER OF THE NEWMAN-HAAS RACING TEAM! NOT A BAD PERFORMANCE LAST WEEKEND AT LONG BEACH,"** Cutting left across the grass, Leslie trots between twin trees, nodding rpivots, cuts back across the grass to avoid a ("Fuh-uh-Ki-ing D ") "He wont hurt y " "Trust No Dog, Lady!", runs a little further up, cuts left across the grass, nodding rightward to the courthouse where it sits, as with arms crossed, beyond the head of the *place*, deciding whether to inhale the whole of the delicate space before it. **"OVERSHADOWED A BIT OF COURSE BY NIGEL MANSELL'S ANNOUNCEMENT—MORE ON THAT LATER—WE HAVE"**

Back toward the Pont Neuf along the opposite ("Hello, Officer!") sidewalk ("Hello, Officer!"). **"LOTTERY INFORMATION! I SHALL NOW RECITE TO YOU LAST NIGHT'S LOTTERY PICKS FOR YOUR LISTENING PLEASURE: THE PICK-THREE FOR LAST NIGHT WAS EIGHT FOUR O; THE PICK-FOUR FOR LAST NIGHT WAS SIX O TWO FIVE;"** The patrolman **"THE PICK-SIX WHICH HE SAID FIVE TIMES QUICKLY FOR LAST NIGHT WAS ELEVEN FIFTEEN EIGHTEEN FOURTEEN TWENTY AND TWENTY-SEVEN;"** shelters in a dark narrow doorway near **"AND THE BONUS-MILLION WAS TWO ONE FIVE FIVE NINE."** the base of the keyhole, the patrolman paces past the aged wood and aged stone of the rustic taverns and formal dwelling places.

It is hard to imagine people living here who see that it has finally stopped raining, cancel lunch at the club, grab a sweater and their sweetie and rush her somewhere far and forbidden to fuck her silly in a field, although sometimes there's a Harley parked near the first lawbook store or an artist at work up toward the bridge, facing the pastel sheet, or a well-fed restaurant owner dreaming in a deckchair in front of his shop while his scottie watches the sun appear and licks at the leash in his master's drooping hand. **"SO, IF I WAS AT ALL INSTRUMENTAL IN LETTING YOU KNOW THAT YOU HIT, THE GREAT-BRITTAIN PHONELINES ARE OPEN AT SIX O NINE-FOUR TWO TWO-NINE TWO TWO TWO—NINE-TWO-CUBED—GIVE ME A BUZZ HERE AND SHARE THE.....WELLLLL, SHARE THE.....NEWS...OH WHAT THE HECK, SHARE THE WEALTH!—AM I ALLOWED TO SAY THAT? WELL SHARE *SOMETHING* ! OR GIVE ME A CALL JUST TO SAY HEY!—OR TGET A MESSAGE TSOMEONE—OR TO SCREAM AT ME—TO USE ME AND ABUSE ME—EVEN IF YOU NEVER EVEN *PLAY* THE LOTTERY!"**

Yellow seedlights sparkle at the base of the median strip the length of the *pont*, electric breadcrumbs marking the way in the gray between both banks through the Ile de la Cité. Leslie exits the Place Dauphine ("Hello, Officer!"), cruises to the other side of the bridge, right and straight down its slope, catching the game along the way:

The Eiffel Tower, over her left shoulder, pitches a ball of light. Notre Dame, a ways to the right, hits a high-flyer to the salmon-colored fingers in the sky—bobbled—it drops into the stirrysteel Seine and splashes back toward the Tower in an arc. Running backwards, its dome high in the air, the Académie Française screams "I got it! I got it!".

Weather words with wildlife sounds, two Community Bulletin Boards **"Cee-Bee-Squareds"**, Stu Alberts's promo for his **"Starlight Ballroom—Wednesday nights, seven to ten—music from a time gone by"**. At the corner a jazzed-up screamy version of the **"Flintstones themesong—Dennis DeBlasio and the boys in his trio—some reaeaeall hapnin stuff for yat six fourty here on DVQ"** makes her smile as she tightens her left shoelace and keeps an eye on the light. People begin to break into the fortress of Leslie's morning. They crawl out of the Pont Neuf *métro* station, infiltrate her physical and spiritual space. Anger and fascinate her with their instinctive inability ("rooted in a national aversion to sweat") even to see her much less move aside ("If Napoleon didn't jog around Isola Bella with Jojo in tow there's no reason I can think of for you to use your brains in this particular situation.") and let her pass.

Like a dowager queen across the street the Samaritaine department store rules two full city blocks. Leslie runs between pregnant mannequins, laboring at promoting all sorts of passionless ("maternity-victims!") preoccupations, and cigarette-sucking drivers, hunching over newspapers at the wheel or drifting around the outside of their number-70 and number-58 buses, all waiting for the day's launch.

The Flintstones theme is a stitch—DeBlasio and the trumpet are screaming out the words and music like desperate breathless kids trying to prove a point to their emotionally distant father. She smiles at the surreal serious monotone they're making of a message born of counterpunctal cartoon ease and she smiles because she needs the hit of quick and fun at this point in the run. Up to the Rue de Rivoli, to the other side dodging stampeding delivery-trucks, Paris smells of diesel fuel, left, she checks her watch past popular shoestores jewelry shops clothing shops the reflection of a black Peugeot 405 in the window of a philately exchange upscale bath-products *crêpes*-&-sand-

wiches, across and right on the Rue du Louvre, the Louvre begins its westward sprawl behind her, across and left on the Rue St-Honoré. **"Start your weekend"**, a sweet female voice invites, **"with Danney-the great-Brittain!"**

**"Six-fourty-six. And a good mornin *tooo* yuh—It's Friday Mornin! the twenty-fourth! Of April! For this nineteen-ninety-two year boy the year is goin by fast already! t's pretty amazing! Danney-the great-Brittain *with* yuh! You are tuned to the *only* class-a fm in the area—the three *thousand*-watt beacon of Cheshire County, that is of course fm eighty-eight point six WDVQ Bowman *Towowown*ship, New Jersey."** Three minutes thirteen seconds **"Reminding you that the Friday-Morning Opinion with Rob Greenbaum, phoned in live! weekly! from Noo York Cit-tee!"** of boring open wide concrete along the part of the Rue St-Honoré which can't decide whether it wants to contract in classical cafe quiet or expand off the tip of a construction **"comes your way in just fifty-one minutes. Stay tuned for that."** crane... **"Ella. And Louis. Again. Volume two."**

...over the paving block from which, if she looks left into the courtyard across the Place du Palais Royal, she can see the Pyramide du Louvre gleaming like an enormous mutant diamond, waging light-war within its infinite-faceted field, the dimensions of its striking incongruity oozing out of the narrow ancient archway attempting to frame it... **"A Verve release."**

...to the back of the Comédie Française (<small>"Hello, Officer! Hello, Officer! Hello, Officer! Hello, Officer!"</small>) where she and Ms. Fitzgerald and Mr. Armstrong **"A Fine Romance, even!"** indent their route and trace the jagged outline of Molière's playground and its neighboring cafe. Under the arcade. Along the pillars. Past a gate a glimpse right of the Palais Royal gardens. Hurdling over (<small>"Hello, Officer!"</small>) pieces of cumbersome scenery stashed next to company vans. An old plump lady makes her ragged bed in a neat corner of the inlaid walkway behind a sheltering motorcycle. Around the corner. Out free from the arcade. Over the vast twin-fountained *place* as Danney's cassette flips automatically in the machine and a black Peugeot 405 stops to let a bus pass. Across the Avenue de l'Opéra. Right. On up to the superchaged jewel in its crown. On up to visit the Phantom.

"N*III*SSSTUFF, FOR A FRIDAY *MOR* -NIN. PROGRESSIN NICELY HERE AT SIX FIFTY ON WDVQ. DANNEY *WITH* YUH. THAT ONE OF COURSE OUT TO MY SWEETIE, DENISE. I DO SO LOVE IT! AND, UH, WHOLE BUNCH OF UH, INTERESTING THINGS THAT WE CAN THINK OF WHICH AS THE MORNING PROGRESSES WE'LL GET INTO. GONNA TAKE CARE OF A COUPLE OF ANNOUNCEMENTS AND WE'LL SEE YON THE OTHER S*III*DE..."

When she's out even earlier, when the dawn is even darker and the streets are yet more still, and the Opéra floats all the more hauntingly in its goldblue flood of light at the far elevated end of the wide approach, Leslie runs up the middle of its avenue. Up the middle. Like a zipper. Like a kite. Up the middle. Like she'd hidden in a dressingroom when Paris closed for the night and no one knew she was there and she was left alone with the City behind locked doors and went to the base of the Avenue de l'Opéra, near the Comédie Française, near the fountains, near the Palais Royal, and she shouldn't be there—nobody should be there—but there she is, alone with the goldblue Opéra blocks away before her in the morning, declaring her defiant homage by running up its gateway to its core.

Steve Allen: "HELLO, THIS IS STEVE ALLEN."
Danney (soft and mocking): "HELLO!"
Steve Allen: "HAVE YOU EVER WONDERED WHAT IT'S LIKE TO BE TOTALLY ALONE IN THE WORLD?"
Danney (soft and mocking): "NO! HAVE YOU?"
Steve Allen: "WELL, MILLIONS OF AMERICANS DON'T HAVE TO WONDER—"
Danney (soft and mocking): "HMMMH!"
Steve Allen: "THEY *KNOW!* "
Danney (soft and mocking): "AAHWHWH!"

Steve Allen: **"But thanks to USA—the United Students of America—"**
Danney (soft and mocking): "оннн?"
Steve Allen: **"These folks can put those lonely days behind them!"**
Danney (soft and mocking): "Yaayyy!"
Steve Allen: **"USA volunteers bring hope and joy to the lives of millions through letters, phone calls, visits."**
Danney (soft and mocking): "e-mail, satellite transmission, cb radio....."

But at this late early hour, the traffic already too thick and confusing, Leslie files on the sidewalk before a flipchart of///exotic promises and ethnic artifacts in an atlas of airline-window displays///perfumeries and pricey-French-clothing stores for Japanese tourists

Steve Allen: **"Become a USA volunteer! For more information call one-eight hundred-student."**
Danney (soft and mocking): *"What was that?"*
Steve Allen: **"That's: one-eight hundred-s-t-u-d-e-n-t."**

and Japanese giftshops for

**"And show you care!"**
Female voice: **"A message from the advertising council."**

the French///awnings of opera-name cafes///magazine stall at the light at the Rue des Pyramides///LE SOCIALISME DE L'AN 2000///1001 JOBS DANS L'INFORMATIQUE///TERRORIST GANG SUSPECTS ARRESTED IN PARIS AFTER VIOLENT SHOOTOUT///MAMAN EST SUPERMODEL!///magazine stall at the light on the other side///EXCLUSIF! JOHNNY HALLIDAY NOUS PARLE:"LES FEMMES DE MES VIES"///KOHL'S PLÄNE FÜR DIE ZUKUNFT///LE JARDIN DE VOS REVES EN PLEIN PARIS///OPERATION VIGIE-PIRATE POSTS THOUSANDS

OF POLICE ON PARIS STR///left-over pieces of Easter in Monoprix's windows and **"ANNNNND THE FOLKS AT WDVQ—*OUR* COMMUNITY RADIO—YOUR AND MY COMMUNITY RADIO!"** monster-egg chocolates next door/// Opéra closer///bank machines///bank walls///lifesize lit-up Lido-dancer ticket-agency cardboard///glass-and-brass windows telling lingerie stories in black and pink silk///porcelain eggs///Swiss army knives with little clocks in them///giant movie-ads on turning Napoléon III deep-green textured-metal kiosks at the curb///escargot dishes ("I need an escargot dish.") and flowered slotted-spoons///slivers of slanted cross-streets slicing into the aveneue///baseball books in Brentano's and rock bios///fat paper-maché clowns///even fatter paper-maché ("hee!") clowns///little Gault replicas of Paris buildings fusing into little Gault replicas of Paris neighborhoods///no traffic in the cross-streets, the Opéra within reach///massive doors, discreet brass plaques, gynocologists, publicists, Dr. Micheline Naboor • Dr. Nassar Naboor, Mme M-C Verney, design-house reps///knots of Oriental men with briefcases///*VISITEZ EURO-DISNEY RESORT*///men in shirtsleeves standing in open doorways pulling cigarettes out of their mouths, looking, looking out over the avenue (*"What are th "*)///three-women-six-ample-thighs-one-white-joggingsuit-with-pastel-stripes-and-matching-shoes-one-mint-green-joggingsuit-one-pair-of-jeans-that-must've-shrunk-overnight-in-the-suitcase-one-Galeries-Lafayette-Parismap-two-cameras///*Dégustation De Nos Huitres A Toute Heure*/// glass-and-mustard-yellow-metal busstop-shelters' poster-size route maps+schedule information+ dishwasher ads budding on every block now, last page of the flipchart, up the slight slope to the signpole at the corner, the Place de l'Opéra.

The Opéra is protected from invasion by a wide moat of complex traffic-pattern.

Around the pole\back down toward Monoprix\the imaging parading in reverse.

("Too many Officers! for me to say h ") A black Peugeot 405 makes an illegal U-turn at the Place de l'Opéra and cruises back down toward Monoprix.

"......AT MY NEIGHBORHOOD MECHANIC OF GILHAM, NEW JERSEY, WHERE YOU PUT YOUR CAR IN OUR CARE AND WE PUT OUR CARE IN YOUR CAR! NINE O EIGHT-FIVE SEVEN SIX-SEVEN FIVE TWO O. MY NEIGHBORHOOD MECHANIC OF GILHAM. ANOTHER FINE EXAMPLE OF NEIGHBORS SERVING NEIGHBORS."

("Aida extras. Hello, Aida Extras!")

"AAANND SOME WORDS OF WISDOM FROM THE F*III*HNN FOLKS WHO HELP KEEP THE REELS ROLLIN AND THE LIGHTS BURNIN AND THE TURNTABLES SPINNIN AND THE ELECTRIC COFFEPOT CORD ABOUT TO SHORT OUT THE WHOLE STUDIO HERE AT DVQ. AND WE *DO* THANK THEM *FOR THAT*. DANNEY-THE GREAT-BRITTAIN SHOW—SIX-FIFTY-FIVE ON A FRIDAY MORNING—THE TWENTY-FOURTH OF APRIL—" Danney points the needle and injects the first bead of warm Roadhouse Blues introbeat under the top tissuelayer of Leslie's skin *doo-doo doo-doo doo-doo dooo-ooo-ooo doo-doo doo-doo doo-doo dooo-ooo-ooo doo-doo doo-doo doo-doo dooo-ooo-ooo doo-doo doo-doo doo-doo doo-ooo-ooo* "HERE IN CHESHIRE COUNTY—AND MOST OF THE EAST COAST FOR THAT MATTER!" She's tired down the slope, aware of her heartbeat, aware that Danney's music is dosing in at the rhythm of her pulse the needle goes *doo-doo doo-doo doo-doo dooo-ooo-ooo doo-doo doo-doo doo-doo dooo-ooo-ooo* deeper Danny does the down and dirty drivetime voice "YYYEHEHAHAHUHUH" hits her systemic circuit releases Lesl "IEEE'S FRAHHHDAYEEE MAWRRNIIINN DOORSZZZZZ-FFIIIIIXXXXX" releases *deeeeeeeeeeeeeeeee-dee-dee-dee-duuh-duuuuh-duuuuh dee-dee-dee-dee-dee-dee-dee-duuh-duuh-duuh-duuh-duuuuuuuh-duuuuuuuuh* Ray Manzarek's electric organ's kicked in, the warmliquid soulworms are threading through her chambers with Morrison's song in streamers attached to strings in their mouths, *ddih ddoo-ddoo ddoo-ddoo ddih-ddih—dduh—dduh ddih ddoo-ddoo ddoo-ddoo ddih-ddih—dduh—dduh ddooooooooooooooooooo-ddeeeeeeeeeeeee eeeeee* looking for, finding the backdoors of her bloodvessels, busting out at the rims of her pores, forcing further each time they dig. She runs past Brentano's she forgets she's running past Brentano's she's not tired anymore she's not running anymore she runs past Brentano's *doo-doo*

*doo* and there's Morrison erupting at her from the cover of his biography ("DANNEY frchrissakes!"). Hendrix is propped on a metal stand on the shelf beside him. Michael Jackson.

At the Rue des Pyramides, sanitation green-men are sweeping a Monoprix sidewalk that's already spotless. *doo-doo doo-doo doo-doo dooo-ooo-ooo doo-* Jim instructs her to keep her eyes on the road and her hands upon the *whee—eeuhl* so she leaves the ladies in black and pastel mini-officesuits behind on the full-daylit corner and cuts to the right at the other side, grazing the bistro whose inert german shepherd keeps his eyes on the road and his hands upon the wheel. *you gotta roll roll roll gotta thrill mah soul, all rah-aht*

"YEAHHHSIX-FIFTY-EIGHT WITH LESLIE'S DOORS-FIX—WOULDN'T WANT YUH TO GO THROUGH WITHDRWAL, BABY, NOT ON *MY* SHOW!—HEARD MONDAY AND FRIDAY MORNINGS HERE—THE DANNEY BRITTAIN—DANNEY-THE GREAT-BRITTAIN—SHOW, REMINDING YOU LUCKY PEOPLE THAT TWO MONTHS—TWO SHORT MONTHS—FROM TODAY—JUNE TWENTY-SIXTH—MYYY SISTER LESLIE WILL FLY IN *DI*-RECT FROM PARIS FRANCE EX*PRESSLY* TO DO THE DOUBLY-GREAT-BRITTAINS-IN-THE-MORNING SHOW RIGHT HERE ON WDVQ FM EIGHTY-EIGHT SIX, *THE FINEST LISTENER-SUPPORTED COMMUNITY RADIO STATION IN THIS HERE NATION.* THAT'S—EX*PRESSLY* TO DO LESLIE-AND-DANNEY-ON-THE-RAY-DEE-OH. CHRIS ETON DOESN'T BELIEVE ME—HE THINKS SHE'S COMING IN TO VISIT FAMILY! OR TO ORGANIZE SOME GALA PR DEAL! WILL SHE BE VISTING FAMILY? IF SHE DOES, THAT'S *HER* PROBLEM! BUT THAT'S NOT WHY SHE'S COMIN IN. WILL SHE BE ON A HOT PR GIG? NO WAY FAYE! THAT'S NOT WHY SHE'S COMING IN, CHRISS-TOH-FFER! TUNE IN JUNE TWENTY-SIXTH. AND SEE. MEANWHILE, NOW THAT I'VE SUCCESSFULLY TALKED US *ALLL*MOST UP TO THE TOP OF THE HOUR...SEE YUH—THAT'S RI-IGHT—ON THE OTHER SIDE OF TH*EEEZZZ* ..."

Across the Rue St-Honoré, both sides of the Rue des Pyramides become covered arcades which lead up to then wrap around right angles at the Rue de Rivoli, streaming for blocks eastward—opposite the Louvre, to the Rue du Louvre—and westward—opposite the Tuileries Gardens, to the Place de la Concorde. Along the short Pyramides leg, the arcades' arched roofs, wide stone street-side pillars and polished marble-mosaic floors squeeze and focus all surrounding reality into the tight dark tunnels they create, and force all light out their far Seineward ends. All new vision and light which flow in through the arcades' St-Honoré side are aspirated, processed and ultimately thrust through the shadows, first across the Rue de Rivoli, then onto the Pont Royal, then over the river. Once finally across, this stream has accumulated and stocked enough vision velocity and light velocity that it crashes into the antiques-gallery facades lining the remote Left Bank and gilds them with its splattered stored shock. Leslie crosses the Rue St-Honoré, approaches the arcade, enters the arcade. The floodlit scene across the Seine seen through the cool compressed arched darkness looks like a miniature Italian Renaissance village viewed at the end of a long telescope. It is always unexpected. Each time it is unexpected; it alters her breathing each time.

As the covered corridors snake into quick symmetric **Ls** before turning their corners en route to their respective ends, *shoh-doh n sho-bee-doh* at the Place des Pyramides where a golden Joan of Arc from her golden warhorse defends the glory of the passing taxis, *shoh-doh n sho-bee-doh* Leslie follows left. Groupings of sightseers are already dividing into little national protectorates in front of the bus-tour agency with big pictures of big *shoh-doh n sho-bee-doh* can-can dancers (*"can-can* frchrissakes dancers") and perfect *châteaux* in its windows: *shoh-doh n sho-bee-doh* tight islands of Japanese, *Wohoh!-uh in the stillll* rolling fields of Americans, *shoh-doh n sho-bee-doh* busy cities of Italians. *of the nii-iight* While their coaches crouch at Joan's feet, *shoh-doh n sho-bee-doh* their tight-skirted tour guides flit in and out of the company's chestnut wood doors. *I-I-I held youu* Drivers, *shoh-doh n sho-bee-doh* pushing cigarettes into their mouths, *heh-ehld you tii-iight* stalk and slouch and spit. *shoh-doh n sho-bee-doh* An immediate right trace along the Hôtel Regina's gilded-dark-glass/stucco/wood-frame front. *Woh-oh! 'cause I luhuhuhv*

Every morning a strategy caucus is held on the sidewalk. *shoh-doh n sho-bee-doh* Under the arcade. In front of the *hôtel*'s revolving doors. *luh-uhv you soh-oh* Right on the very square of inlaid flooring where Leslie needs to place her feet. *shoh-doh n sho-bee-doh* Every morning the principals at this session include: *promise I'll neverrrr* a liveried doorman shuffling litters of luggage; *shoh-doh n sho-bee-doh* a garbage green-man examining his plastic green bins; *leh-eht you goh-oh* a bulky taxi-driver pacing around the other two, *shoh-doh n sho-bee-doh* keeping his pants above his gut and his cigarette butt balanced between his gums. *in the stillll* The distinguishing characteristic of this regularly scheduled session *I re-mem-ber* is the level of intensity evident in the collective decision not to get out of Leslie's way. *sho-bee Woh-oh! of the nii-ii-iight* Up at the Rue de Rivoli she checks her watch and reads the etched-marble plaque on the pillar by the light: *in the still of the niiiight* ("Here fell for France, at the age of nineteen, Jean-Paul Lambert, August twenty-fifth, ninetee ")

At the green *I rememmber* she races a black Peugeot 405 out of the starting block, *that night in Mayyyy* landing victorious *I re-mem-ber* at the Louvre side *the stahhrrz* while the car turns right onto Rivoli. *I re-* Leslie turns *were briiiight* right onto Rivoli, *mem-ber* adjusts the soaked sweatband on her slippery forehead, *ah-ah-ah buh-uh-uh-uhv* nods to the right *I re-mem-ber* at Saint Joan's gold across the *place*, *I-I'll hoh-ohp* strikes the opposite pavement, *I re-mem-ber* crooks left through the sloppy gauntlet of construction trailers *and I'll pray-ay* lining the aisle to the Seine. *I re-mem-ber*

This is a slow-motion sidewalk. *to-keep* Short North African laborers *doo doo* with big moutaches *your-pre* and jackets that smell of smoke *doo doo* look like they're trying to walk toward their trailers. *cious-luh-uh-uh-uh-uh-uhv* Short North African laborers *wheh-ehn we wah-ahlk* with big moustaches *shoh-doh n sho-bee-doh* and jackets that smell of smoke *ah-ah-ah-loh-oh-ohng* look like they're trying to walk away from their trailers. *shoh-doh n sho-bee-doh* Pedestrian commuters in trenchcoats, newly arrived from the across the bridge, *hold me ageh-ehn* look like they're trying to march past the worksite mess *shoh-doh n sho-bee-doh* to rush to their Right Bank business. *with all of your might* Lovers, married but not to each other, *shoh-doh* look like they're trying to hold each other's attention tightly enough to make up for the other fourteen hundred twenty-five minutes during which they won't have it today. *in the still* Hunched-over ladies *sho-bee Wohoh! of the niiiight* and bundled-up men *in the still of the niiiight* look like they're trying to give their raggedy dogs *doo-wah doo-wah* the morning-excrement experience of the season. *doo-wah doo-wah*

Leslie always has the feeling she's the only one cutting through the air. *doo-wah doo-wah* That the others are pushing up against it, with little success in penetrating its viscous body. *doo-wah* And she's pretty sure it has to do with the landing of the construction trailers on Tuileries soil. *doo-wah doo-wah* The way she figures, *doo-wah doo-wah* the trailers were always here—right here— *doo-wah doo-wah* even in Louis's time— *doo-wah* especially in Louis's time. *ohoh oh oh oh ohoh* They were the king's trailers. *so befaw-awr* And when they looked like they weren't here anymore, *shoh-doh n sho-bee-doh* it wasn't the space that had been altered—they were still occupying the space— *thuh-uh-uh lii-iight* but the time—the time during which they were present had been altered. *shoh-doh n sho-bee-doh* When the time no longer called for them, their time-existence, *hold me ageh-eh-ehn* not their space-existence, *shoh-doh n sho-bee-doh* had been removed. *with all of your mii-iight* So the fact that they're back now *shoh-doh n* means there's been a superimposition of the King's time-containment *in the stillll of the niiiight* onto today's space-containment, *in the still of the niiiiiiight* and the laborers, commuters, lovers and walk-doggers have been caught in the confluence. *in the still........of the........nii-ii-iiiight*

Leslie is caught in no such confluence. Because of the way she enters the space. *dohmn shoh-doh n sho-bee-doh* Slapping herself onto it each time, *ohhhhhh shoh-doh n sho-bee-doh* crashing through it as a racingcar through a sheet of shelfpaper, *whoooo-hoooo shoh-doh n sho-bee-doh* not staying long enough to participate in its molecular pull. *whoooo-hoooo-hoooo-hooo-hoooo-hoooo-hooo-shoh-doh n sho-bee-doh hoooo-hooo-hooo-hoooo-shoh-doh n sho-bee-doh* Escaping just as swiftly out the other end. *hoooo-hooo-oooo-oooo*

"Visiting our rock-n-roll past at seven o five on this April twenty-four with The Five Satins. In the Still of the Night. Danney-the great-Brittain Show, the name of this recurring

BROADCAST EXPERIENCE, MONDAY AND FRIDAY MORN-
INGS SIX TNINE. DANNEY-IN-THE-STILL-OF-THE-MORN-
ING HANGIN *WITH* YUH HERE ON CHESHIRE COUNTY'S
THREE *THOUSAND*-WATT SOUND OF WDVQ EIGHTY-
EIGHT SIX FM. SENDING THAT ONE OUT TO ALL THE
GUYS IN ARMOR MAKIN WHISKEY! UNDER ME,"

At the other end everything is white. Halfway to the Seine, as she turns right into the Gardens, Leslie winks back "CARL FILIPIAK" at the enormous mutant diamond flashing tranquil morning angles from beyond facets of construction rubble on "AND COMPADRES. TITLE TRACK FROM HIS BLUE ENTRANCE" her left. "LP." There is a little ante-garden and then a graceful black wrought-iron gate, opened just about the time she's circumnavigating the bulky taxi-driver, "ELECTRIC JAZZ—JUST LOVE THE SOUND OF HIS" and beyond the gate, at this moment of the morning, in this freshness of the sun, the brown ground of the Tuileries is powdered pearl. "GUITAR! YEEEAAAAHHHHH...I WAS WAITING FOR THAT LITTLE GLIS*SSANN*DOHHH THERE......ENJOY THE MUSIC...ENJOY THE FUN......" A sweet female voice reminds: "DANNEY!......IN-THE-MORN-ING!"

It's wondrous—who prepares it every day? ("the King's Vagabonds")—the private whiteness of a ground which is never white at any other hour, and certainly never when it welcomes more than the smallest number of people into its reach. Will the people bring the brown ground in with them later on? Who monitors the regularity with which every irregular surface is bleached—every pebble-surface, every earthclump-surface? Every footprint-surface in the space around the stone *banquettes* under the outlining trees. Around the great round centered fountain which seems flatter and more expansive and more exposed in the open air without children and tourists and members of the royal court pulling at it and making demands on its wealth.

Spreading out from the fountain to form the base of an I, the white soil fetches the cold correctitude of the Rue de Rivoli's somber buildings from the right, and the fancy grandeur of the Musée d'Orsay's radiant clocks from the left, bringing them through the side gates into the Gardens' awareness. Just ahead a workman and his three-wheeled trucklet of tools stirs up dusty puffs near the brilliant flowers planted in large symmetrical squares, and dustier puffs near the symmetrical statues who watch them grow.

("Hello, Officer!") The brown ground which is white at this moment, and which does not even shine under the clean morning sun because then it would be golden, darkens past the statues and their flowers where the running aisle narrows between thick tree-lanes into the stalk of the **I**. Dark white. Leslie lets Danney pace her as she feels her fatigue again, feels it most heavily since the distractions are few. Though it means slowing and widening her steps, she runs in time ("Hello, Officer! Hello, Officer! Hello, Offcier!") to the electric jazz ("Hello, Officer!"), the two-minute-eleven-second game taking the place of relationships with dogs and green-men, waves in the river, handbags in the window. When she awakens from her woods-riffs into the top of the **I** and its matching fountain and graceful black wrought-iron gate beyond, the open ground is no longer white.

But the Vagabonds are there.

Mobilized around a water spout to Leslie's left. An organized, civilized group of six who obviously spend their nights, locked into the Tuileries, among the trees near the fountain at the Concorde end. They are no doubt granted this exceptional privilege in return for the fine daily work they do in pearlizing the soil for Leslie's arrival. Neither their unthreatened campsite nor the state in which she finds the Gardens every day can be explained in any other way. Especially since the studied care with which they tend to their morning *toilette* at the slim brass spigot by the benches reflects a degree of discipline of which only the most accomplished soil-jewelers are capable. These are the King's Vagabonds, no doubt about it! **"THIS IS EEDEE JACKSON."** And since the Revolution was merely cosmetic, since two thousand years of old organization cannot **"COME HERE. YOU KNOW WHAT? LOVE IS HERE TO STAY!"** be undone by two hundred of new chaos, the place they hold along Leslie's route is a comfort **"WELL,"** to all concerned. **"AT LEAST ON SATURDAYS, FROM THREE TIL SIX. AND YOU CAN JOIN ME THEN TO SEE FOR YOURSELF! WE'LL HEAR ALL**

**YOUR FAVORITE LOVE SONGS.....FROM SINATRA TO MCCARTNEY...FROM PRINCE"**

Around the fountain - between twin **"TGERSHWIN."** statues - out the gate - past an idling black Peugeot 405 parked halfway on the sidewalk - confronted with the infinity of the Place de la Concorde.

Running **"AND WE'LL EVEN TAKE A REQUEST OR TWO—FOR MUSIC, THAT IS, HEH! SO TUNE IN! LOVE *IS* HERE TO STAY...HEY—** from the northeast quadrant of the Place de la Concorde southwest to the quais of the Seine is **THREE HOURS IS BETTERN NOTHIN, RIGHT? THAT'S SATURDAYS, FROM THREE UNTIL SIX, RIGHT HERE ON WDVQ, EIGHTY-EIGHT POINT** like going on a diet. Like redoing your resume, learning to let people finish **SIX FM, YOUR STATIONN.....FORR DIVERSIFICATION!"** their sentences. Like any life-changing exercise.

**"RECOMMENDED LISTENING FOR DANNEY-THE GREAT-BRITTAIN LISTENERS. THE LOVE IS HERE TO STAY PROGRAM SATURDAY AT THREE WITH EEDEE JACKSON, SOME HAPPPENNIN HAPPNIN STUUFFF. BEAUTIFUL BEAUTIFUL MUSIC THAT SHE PLAYS,"** Danney starts his rain forest. ***"SOME- OF- THEEE- VERY- BESSST* MUSIC EVER RECORDED. THAT OF COURSE ERIC CLAPTON, THE BED FOR THE SPOT.....AANNNDD AT SEVEN TEN I GOT THE WEATHER *WORDS* FOR YUH FROMM THEE NASHNUL WEATHER SERVICE AND DANNEY-THE GREAT-BRITTAIN: BECOMING MOSTLY SUNNY AND WARMER TODAY AFTER SOME EARLY-"**

Viewed in its big picture, it is overwhelming: there are all those tedious pounds to lose, those details to recontruct, old habits to break, killer-vehicles to dodge, monuments to circumvent, directions to look in. Almost not worth it. The Place de la Concorde radiates outward for centuries. Centuries of cobblestones, of parts—it is made of so many parts. Concrete-islands * Fountain-islands * The central chalky **"MORNING PATCHY FOG AND BOYYY *IS IT* BAD OUT**

**THERE!"** obelisque with golden totem-markings that who would ever really see except from this angle? * **"I JUST TOOK A LOOK WHILE RUNNING DOWN TO GRAB SOME H TWO O IN A CUP AND BOY IT IS UNBELIVABLE OUT THERE!—YCAN HARDLY SEE A FEW FEET IN FRONT OF YOU SO DRIVE CAREFULLY DRIVE SLOWLY ON YOUR WAY TO WORK AND UH USE YOUR UH,"** Relentless invasions of crossings * Proud Hôtel Crillon * Stately American Embassy * Complicated combinations of walkway/street/walkway * A hint of the Madeleine down the Rue Royale * A hint of Maxime's down the Rue Royale if the timing is right and another appearance by Sacré Coeur may we point out staring from the far north down a split-second glimpse of rooftop * Constantly shifting heights of structures—gorgeous green gold-engraved marble columns, squat white stone stumps demarcating parking, ugly iron posts stringing chains * Constantly **"WELL, I GUESS IT DOESN'T REALLY MATTER *WHAT* BEAMS YOU USE RIGHT NOW BECAUSE IT'S BEGINNING TO SEVERELY ILLUMINATE OUT THERE BUT IT'S *VERY* TOUGH GOIN OUT THERE—LOOK FOR DEER LOOK FORUH PEOPLE LOOK FRANYTHING THAT'S IN FRONT OF YIF YCAN FIND IT! HIGH NEAR SIXTY."** shifting shapes of paved patches for people. As opposed to for monuments and cars.

The Place de la Concorde is everything that can be seen from the Place de la Concorde.
Tour buses are unloading onto islands already.
Postcard hawkers are loading their guns already.
Concession trucks are jockeying up to the graceful black wrought-iron gate. **"TONIGHT CLEAR AND LOW IN THE LOW FIFTIES. PRESENTLYYYUHUHUHUH........"**
Cars are parking at the extremities.
City buses are cruising the outer circle.
The trees of the Champs-Elysées are growing due west ahead.
The commerce of the Champs is crawling beyond the trees.
The Arc de Triomphe is topping the commerce.
The Grande Arche and the huddled towers of La Défense are dominating the Arc.
The longest urban axis in the world is explaining its perspective.
The river is repeating its call.

The trees are shadowing the river.
The barges are slicing the river.
The bridges are striping the Seine.
The Assemblée Nationale is being guarded.
The traffic patterns "………UHUHAANNNDD I HAVEN'T CHECKED ARTHUR IN AWHILE—THAT'S OF COURSE ARTHUR-MOMETER ON THE WALL HERE—BUT LAST TIME I LOOKED—AT ABOUT SIX THIRTY—HE TOLD ME IT WAS FOURTY-SEVEN DEGREES. AND RISING." are defying science.
The grand gray buildings on both banks are making rumbling noises and swelling.
The Invalides is shining brilliantly below the Tour Eiffel.

The Tour Eiffel—the Tour Eiffel hovers off to Leslie's 11 o'clock in the space and time beyond the riverbanks, and across everything that is the Place de la Concorde to the riverbank is where she has to get. She has to go on a diet and lose a hundred fourty-five pounds by next Thursday.

In little chunks, around the periphery, she takes it day by day, meal by meal, street-and-pavement-patch by street-and-pavement-patch. She could be running in the basement of the Town Hall in White Pidgeon, Michigan—she looks at nothing. Just keeps finding places to put her feet, putting them there, hearing a grandmotherly voice on top of lute music: **"PORTIONS OF TODAY'S PROGRAMMING HAVE BEEN MADE POSSIBLE IN PART THROUGH FUNDS PROVIDED BY THE FLOWER LADY OF BALLSTON, PENNSYLVANIA. SPECIALIZING IN THE CULTIVATION AND SALE OF EXOTIC AND TRADITIONAL FLOWERS, AS WELL AS PLANTS AND SHRUBS, THE FLOWER LADY OF BALLSTON IS LOCATED AT FOURTY-SIX O TWO LANCASTER BOULEVARD. HER PHONE NUMBER IS TWO ONE FIVE-SIX EIGHT THREE-FOUR SIX ONE O. THE FLOWER LADY OF BALLSTON, ANOTHER FINE NEIGHBOR HELPING WDVQ OFFER YOU COMMUNITY RADIO AT ITS BEST."**

Then all that's left is geometry. **"ANND,"** Too tired to receive anything through other than the most primitive filter, Leslie sees Paris as a play of primary forms along this first leg of this last angle home. **"THERE'S SOMEONE NEW AND WE DO THANK HER FOR COMIN ABOARD HERE AT DVQ AND HELPIN US *KEEP ON GO IN* . WORKIN OUR WAY UP TOWARDS THE"** Every shape checks in. Street-level above the Seine, following parallel between a stone chest-high riverside wall and wide grassy oblongs outlined with trees and benches, the pavement from the Place de la Concorde to the Pont d'Alma dips then rises in a chain of three Vs spaced by two intersecting busy bridges. The Eiffel Tower is in charge of verticality from **"FRIDAY-MORNING"** its **"OPINION WITH ROB GREENBAUM IN ABOUT TWENTY-ONE MINUTES ."** inland command post ahead on the opposite bank. Led by Napoléon's dome-tomb, the semicircle delegation blazes at the end of the splendid Esplanade des Invalides straight left from the midpoint of the Pont Alexandre III. **"GEORGE GERSHWIN AND HIS BROTHER IRA AT SEVEN FOURTEEN THIS FRIDAY APRIL TWO-FOUR. NOW THAT EASTER'S BEHIND USSS... CAN THISS BE TOO FARRR AWAY? SSSSSUMMERTIIIIIMMMME...............PORGY ........ANBESSSSSSSS."** Old red and old green wooden houseboats moored at the banks below have round port-holes in their diamond-shaped topdecks. On the sidewalk benches facing the water, young artist-vendors display little square scenes of just what Leslie is looking at. Triangular people walk oval dogs on the grassy oblongs.

Between the Pont des Invalides and the Pont d'Alma the path narrows, cooled and darkened under the trees, breached halfway in by twin red-metal stair structures waiting to transit tourists to and from the elaborate bridge-to-bridge Bateau Mouche headquarters down at river level. The perverse thrill of watching the now tightly guarded and closely cordoned Bateau Mouche complex in its own kitchen is Leslie's last landmark kick of the run, as underclass overalled men delivering mineral water on forklifts and washing down concession stands make their final showing before being removed from camera range.

Squatting on his short stone ledge at the grass, the Jamaican kid who paints dozens of Eiffel Towerscapes a day in primary colors with no nuance whatsoever asks Leslie if she's still being bothered by dogs.

Paris smells of leaves. "I've ordered a spray from the United States!" she screams back over her right shoulder, wondering how someone with such an aggressive aesthetic sense can be so caring. She knows that when it finally happens between the grassy-oblong-stalking leashless ownerless doberman-pitbull hybrid and herself, the Jamaican kid will do the scene justice in blue (leg), yellow (teeth) and red (you guessed it). Meanwhile, she thinks it's fun to have a pal along the route and veers left—checks her watch—onto the Pont d'Alma. At the instant-flash when all traffic has just spontaneously combusted into one inert mound. And is now waiting for the giant helicopter-magnet airlift. Which will wrench it from the bridge. And deliver it in the same wretched configuration. To wherever it thought it was going to get by using its wheels.

On the crest of the bridge's steep arc she looks left, far up the river toward Notre Dame—Leslie looks toward Notre Dame whenever and wherever she crosses the Seine. Kilometer Zero. Then ahead, slightly right, to the immediate Eiffel Tower. And especially she looks at the river itself because by the time she arrives at the middle of the Pont d'Alma, it is a different river from the one she crossed at the Cathedral's doorway almost an hour before, and different from the one she watched play from the Pont Neuf five or ten minutes after that. Time of day is not the only alchemist at work here. There is where the Seine is headed, from where it's come, how fast, through how much murk. There is the weather of course and the number of fire- and policeboats and barges and houseboats mixing in its affairs. There is the latest hemline-length. News from Palestine, rice futures. The *plat du jour* at Fouquet's. Who'll win the Monaco Grand Prix. Everything affects the Seine. Everything changes the river.

The key to its persona residing in its relationship to the sky.

Over the peak of any *pont*, no matter what state the river is in, the sky will be defying it. Wanting to watch a different channel, to go to exactly the restaurant where it doesn't want to eat. No matter what state the river is in. Like a couple married too masochistically long. Like two spiteful, rivalrous kids. When the water is calm and prismatic the sky is nervous and opaque. Threateningly opaque. With clouds violently mutating and swimming from one end of the horizon to the other as if in a demonstration of computer animation or time-lapse videography on a giant overhead screen. But when the sky is still and bright the river stirs under the bridge in somber little spreading eddies—pockmarks on the vengeful child's face.

Final performance from the waterfront before Leslie heads inland and home.

She lumbers down the bridge to the light, pushes her headband back up on her forehead, knows exactly how many cars will pass before she can spring "YEAAHH!!...FRANCIS ALBERT-IN-THE-MORNING FOR A FRIDAY MORNING ON THE DANNEY-THE GREAT-BRITTAIN SHOW! DANNEY ON THE RAY-DEE-OH *WITH* YUH, AND WOULDN'T BE A BETTER WAY TGET US THROUGH A FRIDAY MORNING THAN WITH A LITTLE BIT OF FRAN-CIS AL-BERT SINATRA. AND UH, FROM SWINGIN SESSIONS, NIGHT N DAY, OUT" off again, across straight onto the Avenue Bosquet, and it's all local stuff from here. Preparation for the shower from here. "OCOURSE TO *MAH* SWEEETIEE DENISE, AND PRIOR TO THAT OCOURSE THE GLYNDEBOURNE FESTIVAL OPERA PRODUCTION OF PORGY! SSUMMMER*TAHMMM* .....DANNEY KEEPIN YUH COMPANY AND PROVIDING YOU WITH YOUR REGULAR MUSICAL EDUCATION RIGHT HERE ON WDVQ EIGHTY-EIGHT SIX FM. SEVEN TWENTY-TWO IN THE MORNING! THE OPINION UP IN THIRTEEN." Some guys are jackhammering at the corner of Bosquet and the Rue Cognac-Jay, digging around. A young blond in a dusty Michael Jordan t-shirt breaks away and runs for a couple of mocking yards. Leslie pretends she has absolutely no knowledge whatsoever that the jerk is breathing on the planet. "You are a piece of human wasteproduct," "FOURTY-EIGHT DEGREES." she says in English, staring so straight ahead, seeming so disconnected from the act of expression, that the spell of denying him remains unbroken. "TRYING HARD TO BE FOURTY-NINE BUT NOT MAKIN IT HAPPEN. YOUR DETAILED ACCURATE LOCAL AREA WEATHER COMIN UP! *EVERYTHING'S* COMIN UP! WHATR WE DOIN RIGHT NOW?" She looks at her watch. "OH—WE'RE TRYING TO

**PRETEND I'M ORGANIZED HERE—OK—ALL TOGETHER WITH ME—LET'S PRE"**

She looks at the Ecole ("Hello, Soldier!") Militaire, six long **"TEND!"** blocks up the avenue. Before reaching it, Leslie will be asked to consider whether **"REGISTERING FOR THE SELECTIVE SERVICE—"** is **"ANOTHER FORM OF BUROCRACY, RIGHT? BUT THINK OF IT THIS WAY—IT ONLY"**

Paris will smell like food. There will be more people not getting out of the way, **"TAKES A COUPLE MINUTES FROM WHAT YOU'RE DOING NOW. BUT IT'LL HELP GUARANTEE THAT YOU STILL HAVE A COUNTRY TO DO IT IN!"** nuns from the daycare center in the Rue St-Dominique, heading for the same piece of sidewalk **"CALL"** at one-tenth the speed. **"TWO ONE FIVE-THREE SEVEN SEVEN-FOUR THOUSAND. DO IT TODAY."** There will be lethargic boys in red bib-aprons stacking fruitcrates and toiletpaper cartons in front of the supermarket in the Rue de Grenelle. A black Peugeot 405 chasing the redlights through the sunstreaks of the avenue. Roving clumps of schoolkids looking like they're almost ready to begin thinking of getting serious about finding a bus to climb into. Crowded, coughy cafes that weren't open when she headed out ninety minutes before, ("ThankyouH Hh Danh hhH!") and with that, no more purple velvet in the sky. *Yout!.....Gotta Good Reason....For Takin The Easy Way Yout! She Was A DAYY-Y-Y TRIP-PER, Sun-day Dri* For today. *ver Yea-a-ahhh.....It Took Me Soh-oh-oh Long...To Find Out...AnIfoundout! DZZZZZ-DZZ-DZZ-DZZ* ("DZZ-DZZ-DZZ-DZZ-DZZ-") ***DZZ-DZZ-***

# VIII

# A ẘAILING, HOWLING ẞELCH ẞEGGING FOR ⓇELIEF IÑ ṪHE ÌCE-WHITE ÌNSULATED ĐEATH-$ILENT ĐAWN

Blocking his breath at the end of an inhale, Thierry opens the door for his guests. He offers the joint up to Jacques, who slaps it away and heads straight to the stereo to turn off a Van Halen CD. The kid "Whowh-wh-wh-wh-wh-wh-wh-wh-whhhhgood shit, old man. Good move. More for me." turns it on again and crosses the all-purpose room into the kitchen to pour Marcel a Jack Daniels.

Jacques sets up his watch at the floor-to-ceiling window. His hands in his brown suitpants pockets, he spies down onto the Boulevard Raspail where a young man in tight black jeans is changing the posters in the glass display cases on the Alliance Française gate. Thierry moves a pile of computer magazines "Xavier'll be here in twenty minutes. He called." and pornographic comic books "Asked if the new guy was here yet." so Marcel can set his drink on a little glass-top green wrought-iron table near the sofa.

"What's he, with her?" Jacques wants to know, still facing the window.

"She's at the opera tonight."

"What's her seat number?" Marcel wheezes, looking to show off Thierry's showing off.

"Orchestra T twenty-three, old man."

Jacques twists his body stiffly around toward the kid, turns back to his poster prince.

On his second try "I Gotta Go" Marcel billows up from the low navy canvas sofa "Piss!".

"You know where it is. And twenty four. She bought em by e-mail. When's your tunnel-guy gettin here, old man? By e-mail on Thursday March twelve."

"What'sis name?" Jacques asks.

"Aaaaaat....." The kid runs over to a pile of printouts and flips

some pages. "three minutes after noon."
"What color fuckin bra was she wearin at the time?" Jacques sneers. He lights a cigarette and flicks the match out the window with his middle finger and thumb.
"Doesn wear a bra, old man!" Thierry says smugly. "Or she pays for em with cash."
Marcel comes back into the room and tells them "At nine. Officer's name is Palletier. Claude Palletier. Comin at nine. That's no bra *I* see joggin past in the mornin." He stands in front of the sofa

"Do I know him?"

contemplating his strategy for descent.

"Do I know the jerk?" Jacques repeats.

"How the fugckh," Marcel grunts "do I knugnh," lowering his right flank into a macaroni-shaped cushion then rolling gingerly onto his buttocks. He marks his successful landing with a gut-generated snort that sounds like a dying horse in the final thrusts of orgasm.
The three men hang out in their own worlds waiting for Marcel's tunnel expert and Roque to arrive. Secure in the knowledge that Marcel knows where to go when he has to piss, Thierry makes no effort to entertain. In the middle of the large sparsely furnished room he sits on an old red wood-slat folding chair at a long raw folding table with plywood top and metal legs—the kind whose simple ugliness is always disappointing when its white cloth is removed after a banquet and it's no longer masquerading as the dessert corner. Working two screens at the same time, the kid is playing a multilevel calculus-based tactical game on one and, on the other, building a diagram comparing the effects of atmospheric humidity on tertiary limestone for every quarter hour of every day of the year. A third machine, across from him and facing the other way, features little colorful fishes cruising the black ocean floor in the company of graceful green seaplants and winged toasters in happy flight, while its neighboring system drably monitors Leslie's electronic-mail activity with plain white letters on a black bed. The kid starts asking Marcel if he wants to come over and see the one with the dancing cones and pyramids again but doesn't feel like waiting for the sofa scene to happen so "Nothing—forget it, old man!" drops it.
As neglected and shabby and empty as the rest of the echoey stu-

dio is, the work station—centered on the scratched parquet floor like an altar is centered between two columns of pews, like a butcher-block is centered in the head chef's kitchen or a featured sculpture in a gallery hall—is dense with detail, arranged with reverential attention to order. Each of the screen/keyboard sets has its own personality, defined by the accessories in its surrounding space. A trio of flat orange aluminum ashtrays tells of the interdependence between video game and weed, between chain-statistics and tobacco, surveillance and abstinence. Each litter of healthy printouts nestles close to the mother machine that bore it and that nourishes it with fresh harvests of analyzed relationships and balanced portions of charts. The virgin disks and loaded disks are obsessively color-coded and color-stacked according to their turf, like so many gang members sporting the threads of their block, while a tall aerosol can of official hardware-cleaner and a fat roll of deputized papertowels stand guard in the center of the neighborhood. This is dustless, serious country, across the frontier from the Jimi Henrix poster and the unmade bed in the far corner and the newspapers by the sofa that haven't been thrown away in a month.

Down on the street, the solid-packed black jeans shamelessly rubbing the display cases with Windex have become a desiccated lavender-gray cardigan waiting in a self-negating ball on the bus-shelter bench. But Jacques keeps watching anyway, where has his poster prince gone? In her way, the cardigan queen is more engaging, richer for the hard, passion-crushing work of her formative years and the lifetime accomplishment of continuing to incarnate the standards fixed in those first twenty-four months. Where is he? Getting rammed by the president of Alliance Française in the closet where he keeps his giant spray-bottles. Knock-knock. Knock-knock. "*Monsieur le président*, your wife is on the phone." "TELL HER I'LL BE RIGHT THERE! ONE MINUTE!" Where the fuck's the bus?

Marcel is leafing through a German mail-order electronics catalogue not knowing what he's looking at, turning pages to the rhythm of his settled breathing, remembering a conversation with Claude Palletier. His head tilted onto the navy canvas backrest, he closes his eyes, sealing off his center from external stimuli. From threats to the purity with which he will once again deliver his scenario, this time to a sold-out crowd. He goes back to the page with the funny-shaped headsets, then back to his repose, asks Thierry if he has any Brahms. The kid puts on the Second Symphony, slipping Eddie Van Halen back into its case as he walks over to the window and taps Jacques on the shoulder. When Jacques turns around, Thierry drops the CD into his partner's jacketpocket. Jacques sneers but leaves it there and stays at the window while his cock flies down six flights to the giant-spray-bottle closet and stuffs the disc in a dark hot compact. "Xavier's here," he hisses. Roque gets out of his car behind the bus stop.

Grabbing one of two cordless phones from a holster on the back of his chair, the kid leans against the table and "I'm not gonna ask what you old men want because it'll just turn into a fucking domestic scene here." punches a single number. "They'll have to send a squad car over. Whatever you don't like you'll scrape off and take back for a refund. I have beer."

"I don't like fuckin mushrooms!" Marcel tells him. "I want wine."

"I have wine, old man."

Jacques opens the door "New guy's not here yet." and moves back to his window. Roque walks over to the work table and puts down a bottle of wine, which Thierry immediately scoops off as being unauthorized personnel in a badge zone. The kid nods his thanks and "just across from the Alliance Française.....yeah—you have a great voice! Yeah!" continues his quality time with the pizza operator of his dreams. Roque goes to the sofa to shake Marcel's hand. Marcel is turning pages in time to the first movement. Everyone seems to be somewhere else, waiting for the real evening to begin. If no one wants to play he'll walk around the apartment...stroll...just.....stroll around the apartment until the........until the new guy..........until the new......................the fuzzy new surroundings begin to come into focus. Roque steps and stops.....steps.....and stops.....steps.....he cannot believe what he sees.....stops...............................cannot. ..........believe.....what........he................................................. ...............................................................................sees....................... ................................................................................................
...............................On the same side of the room as the sofa, above the cot-like bed in the corner near the window, there is a giant white metal calendar with black characters and numbers in bold modern typeface. A fat red magnetic ring encircles the current date, May 29, and a green ring frames June 26. Except for this area, and that draped in war-weary Hendrix—a huge yellowy replica of the Electric Ladyland album near the calendar and a blurry black-and-white blow-up of a sweaty concert shot next to the john in the hall—the entire perimeter of what Roque can see as Thierry's entire living space is covered with photographs of Leslie. Leslie mostly in motion.

Big—giant—grainy black-and-whites glued onto stiff backing, smaller black-and-whites thumbtacked at eyelevel and sometimes up toward the seam with the ceiling, color Polaroids slapped with silver duct-tape and wide red plastic adhesive-band to the corners of the bigger photos, to spaces in between the other shots, to closet doors and frames and a lampshade and off the edges of the little wrought-iron table where they sway in the wake of nearby movement. The progression of the run. Starting to the right of the kid's front door and advancing around on God help anything in it's way every available surface up to the left of the kid's front door.

Leslie running through the richness of each defining stage—the place de l'Ecole Militaire in the purple, Invalides in the gold, Leslie running, the Montparnasse Tower and the intersection and cafes and *cinémas*, straightening her earphones, Luxembourg at all its angles and when the lights go off, in shorts, in sweatpants, the Panthéon, pictures taken from the inside of a car, looking in motion at a window display, the St-Michel green-men sweeping some daylight in, Mickey Mouse sweatshirt, the Place St-Michel at the ignition of the sun, throwing her head back, looking at her watch, Sunday-desert streets, taken through the window of a car, adjusting her headband, the river at Notre Dame, adjusting her headband, Police HQ at the Quai des Orfèvres—the hugest picture: saluting the cops in the lot—unsettling close-ups, the Place Dauphine, sometimes taken across the hood of a car, the river at the Pont Neuf, the Samaritaine department store, waiting for a light, a baseball cap in the rain, smiling, glaring back at a glarer, the open dullness of the Rue St-Honoré, the Comédie Française and the pillars, the Avenue de l'Opéra, cursing to a driver, waving to a runner, the *Opéra* coming, the *Opéra* going—twisting her hips and head to look back—an ace-bandage anklet, no ace-bandage anklet, Monoprix, the hood of a black car, the arcades up to the Place des Pyramides and the Rue de Rivoli, four different shots in the Tuileries alone, concentrated coordination from her feet, coordinated concentration from her eyes, crunching up her face, running with her hands on her waist, leaping over puddles, six separate realities of the Place de la Concorde, shaking out her arms at a wait for a light, afraid of the dog, the dogs and trees and boats and buildingtops that travel with the river at the *quais*, stomping into puddles, the Jamaican artist waving hello, traffic tips from the Pont d'Alma, more light more cars more people more invasion in each succeeding shot, Leslie walking down the *passage*, Mr. Darotto and his scallion shock-troops falling out the window of the *loge*. Even a dripping Leslie kissing Mrs. D.

on the cheek inside the dark corridor in front of the mailboxes ..............................then.............ten francs for nougat from the Luxembourg candy-lady..............sports page chez Georges.....hood of a black car............. Leslie...and...Patrick...at...the...gourmet...take-out ...place...on...the...Avenue...de...la...M...............................................
................Aware that Marcel is closely watching him take the voyage, Roque throws off a careless laugh and says, "Hnh you fuckers aren't kidding, are you?" so that Marcel will count that as a comment and an attitude and go back to his symphonic toggle switches. But each knows the other is smarter than that. Even Marcel, when he first saw "the exhibit," as he calls it, questioned whether Jacques and his spooks had gone too far, whether they'd ever contemplated the fine line between he can't remember now what he said, now as he monitors Roque's eyes and his shoulders and hands and crotch, but he knows he said it and it was something like between attention to detail and attention to pussy but he knows he put it better. Something like between thorough work and cheap thrills but he knows he put it better. And he remembers what Jacques answered, though, he remembers, while Roque gets up close and runs his fingertips across the biggest grainiest shot—the HQ lot—that Jacques answered that in this business, Marcel knows more than anyone, there's "no fuckin line at all—No Fuckin Line At All!.....More Than Anyone!"

Jacques remembers that chat too, because he is standing stiffly at his window with his hands in his jacketpocket and his back to any possibility of a poster-prince reunion and he is watching Roque's eyes and shoulders and hands and crotch.

"Under thirty minutes!" Thierry announces triumphantly into the tension, lowering the phone antenna with quick jerky stabs of his palm. "Thanks for the wine, old man! See you found the eyes." He winks at a wall. "Want a tour othe brains?"

"Wait'll Palletier Gets Here!" Marcel waves his hand at the kid.

"I ever see this guy?" Roque asks Marcel.
"How the fuck do I know!"
The kid offers an *apéritif*.

"Wait'll PWHAT THE F "
"Sh-sh-sh!" Thierry runs over and punches the amplifier up "Sh-sh Listen!" on one of the phones at the work station. "Listen!"

"UNPROTECTED ANAL SEX WITH A PROMISCUOUS BISEXUAL *NATIVE* AF-

Rican who just got back from a trip to Manhattan and San Francisco! Leslie! You heard me right! Now there's no reason to panic. I've an appointment Monday. Don't ask me why I did it! Don't call me, either. I'm planning to sleep all weekend. I'll call you. B—oh—and PS—my little reconciliation trip to Geneva? Was...why don't we say, indefinitely postponed. And guess by who. Hint—*not* yours truly! Don't call me—I'm Pl "

"Turn That The Fuck Off, For The Love OGod! Can't understand a fuckin" Marcel rocks himself out of the crack between two cushions into which he's been progressively sliding, and props himself in the corner of the sofa while.....Jacques begins to say something but kills it and stuffs a cigarette in his mouth while.....the kid patrols the border between the work station and the rest of the cosmos, straightening already straightened objects and papers and objects and papers while.....Roque grabs a folded red wood-slat chair from a little dining table near the bed and goes back to the parking-lot shot. The room is a slender airless elevator with four guys in it who sell insurance in the same company now for, what it is? years! Jeez! that long! and live in the same little cul de sac—which means asshole of the bag in French if you must know—and watch the game together every Sunday after lunch for, Christ, it must be what? goin on years now, right? and would covet each other's wives if each other's wives had kept themselves down to even *double* the weight they were when they went to each other's weddings do you believe it, it's been years already! nah! yeah! and ride in and from on the same train every eight o'clock and every five-thirty now for remember that time when you didn't show cause you had that emergency tooth extraction and cripes it took us guys half the rest othe day to get used to the idea that you were missing and into this elevator that already—it must be they must've changed somethin in these walls lately don'tcha think?—seems tighter than it did when they started riding it together four times a day years—right?—years ago now—oh, yeah, and eat lunch together, too—into this elevator with these four guys, Claude Palletier is supposed to be gettin on in—what? a couple minutes, no more, right? Claude Palletier this supposed expert in crawlin on your gut through Medieval tunnels that none of us guys has ever we don't even know if we've ever even *seen* the fucker in a goddamn hallway for all we know, right? That's what they put lighted floor-numbers in elevators for. So guys like Claude Palletier can come on and stare at em til we get used to his goddamn smell.

Thierry takes a hit from a new joint. He closes down the plodding game-screen and calls up a total-immersion war experience, within seconds risking his own harmonious galaxy in the interest of sound-enhanced bloodsplashed cosmological conquest.

In front of the parking-lot shot Roque opens the chair and installs himself, attending the photograph, legs crossed, hands folded in his lap, as one attends a play or a lecture or a film. His emotions—his pride excitement rage—interact with the photograph, participate with the photograph, as with a piece of music coming from a stage, float in and out of the photograph's borders at the cadence of the performance. A jumbo unprotected Leslie taken from where, where was the car? Running like on a poster advertising running. Running full. Past guys he kids every day about when the hell they're gonna get outa uniform and get a real job. Running through his own scenery. An asshole taking a picture two inches away how the fuck would she know? I pull out now.....stay in to protect her. from myself. there's a knock on the door.

There's a knock on the door that jolts Thierry out of the mystic concentration they taught him, obviously not well enough, in galactic-warrior school. His hand slips and he kills a valiant universe-knight by mistake. One of his own. Sad. Tragic even. He will surely have to answer to the Regional High Congress of the Inter-Beings for this. If not worse. If not to the OmniCongress itself. "PIIZZZZAAAAAAAA!" he beams, on his way out of his spacerig to grab a 200-franc bill from a jacket tossed over the bed.

"Could be Palletier!" Marcel growls as the kid turns the bolt.

"Pizza!" he confirms, nodding into the livingroom and then to the short, skinny, bird-faced, chicken-necked young lady in brown jeans standing before him, a pack of Marlboroughs stuffed into the breast pocket of her matching jacket. "WhatdI owe yuh?" He tilts his head to read the brand name on the motorcycle helmet wedged under her arm.

"Huh?"
"Where is it?"

"Where's what, man?"

"What the f—you lookin for someone, honey?"

"The commissioner," she answers, lifting her navy-and-red I ♥ Paris baseball cap and recentering it onto her boyish hair.

"It's Some There's Some Babe Has A Message For YHere, Old Man! Should I "

Marcel ceremoniously closes his catalogue and tosses it onto the floor near the wrought-iron table. "Let Er In!"

As the kids opens the door wider "You got a problem usin the phone, honey?" the young lady struts past him over to the sofa. "Hey, old man," he asks, "who else knows you're here tonight anyw "

"Don't get up," she says tenderly, placing her helmet on the seat cushion farthest from Marcel so that it won't roll down the slope he's created.

"I won't!" he wheezes and they shake hands. Jacques and Roque make no effort to do anything more than look in the direction of the sofa.

"You're just gettin ready to tell me who this...charming young.....person is! I can tell," Thierry says impatiently. "I can feel it....Here comes.......Aren't yuh? Old man. Old man?" He sticks the 200-franc bill into his jeans.

Marcel laughs as if reading—badly—a stage direction that says: MARCEL LAUGHS. "Oh I thought you guys knew each other." He nods around the room and recites the names for the young lady, after which she looks square into each new colleague's eyes and nods at him as well. "Thierry Batiste,,,,,,,,Xavier Roque,,,,,,,,Jacques Dupuy,,,,,,,,may I present "

" the pizza-delivery girl," Jacques jeers from his window, keeping his hands tight in his pockets. The pizza-delivery girl is standing near the sofa with her right hip thrust slightly higher than her left and her thumbs hooked into the beltless waist of her jeans. Her features look wirey and nervous. Pugnacious. Like turn-of-the-century New York schoolyard bullies in knickerbockers and tweed caps about to squawk "Ohh-ohh yeeeeah-eahhh? Ssseh-ehzz Whoo-oo?" But her presence is centered and calm.

"This here's Officer "

"Holy Mother Don't Say It!" Thierry shrieks, backing up, his arms in a Dracula-averting cross.

With a smile way beyond irony, softly, in answer to the kid's near-hysteria, Marcel says

"Claude Palletier."

"Why don't" Jacques pulls a wad of bills from his pants and starts walking toward Claude "you be a good girl and run down and get us a pizza?" with slow, measured, noisy steps that seem like they're not going to stop once they reach her.

As Claude suddenly becomes aware of the photos of Leslie on the walls, Roque stretches out of his chair and points both index fingers at her.

The doorbell rings. "*There's* my fuckin pizza!"

"Oh, whadyih know—must be Officer What'sisname," Jacques says. "What's his name?"

Thierry runs to the door and returns with a medium-size box stacked onto a larger one. "Claude!" he says, narrowing his eyes and nodding to himself. While with one forearm he sweeps the books and magazines and change and belt "Claude!" ashtray underwear *métro*-tickets from his small oak dining table onto the floor, he slides the boxes down off the other "Claude Palletier!", then shoots frenetically into the kitchen for plates utensils beer wine "It was Claude Palletier out there!", throwing them into approximations of place settings as if participating in a timed competition. "Out there delivering our pizza! Wouldn't stay, though! Asked him in! Nother time maybe! You gentlemen wanna come eat? Merde! I forgot glasses!"

"You're fuckin er, right, old man?" Jacques helps Marcel out of his sofa crater. "You're fI want you to tell me you're fuckin er because then at least I'll have some fundamental understanding of the "

"THE OLD MAN'S COCK," Thierry yells from deep inside a cupboard, "IS BIGGERN ER WHOLE BODY!"

"LAST TIME YOU CHECKED!" Roque yells back.

In monk-like serenity, the schoolyard bully looks around the room, seemingly totally aware of the positives and totally untouched by the negatives. A schoolyard bully monk. She mumbles something about "floorplan" and smiles peacefully at each of Marcel's independent eyes, as if telling him not to worry.

"Sorry I only have one mug you'll—" Thierry slams down three matching glass tumblers, an elegant heavy cut-rose-crystal goblet and a blue/white/red Albertville Olympics plastic stadium-mug with a white plastic bendable straw sticking out of a hole in its red lid. "what the hell you old men standin around for don't you wa—look—" The second round of timed competition—the Super Seating Challenge—begins, the kid taking a healthy lead thanks to his deft performance in most events, including: the Soggy Clothing & Bathtowel Shift (from the middle of the bed onto the pillow to make a place for Jacques and Roque), the Only Armchair Slide (over from near the sofa "Here, old man." for Marcel), the Roque's Photo-Seat Retrieval (handing it, folded, to Claude) and the Other Wood-Slat Chair Unfolding (for himself).

"Kid finally got y'into his bed, huh, old man?" Roque says to Jacques. Jacques looks toward the window. Marcel breaks the tape on the larger box and says "Officer Cl "

"Merde! I forg "

and when Thierry's back from the kitchen with the roll of paper towels says "Officer Claude Palletier is twenty-six years old. She was twice "

"Let me do it," Claude says softly, leaning over and putting her hand on Marcel's arm.

*"NON!"* He waves at her and swats her away. "She was twice silver medalist in national gymnastics, once national champion and went tSeoul with the French team. She's tiny, fast, agile, afraid onothin and the greediest little bitch I ever saw in my life. She got no family. No sick old mother she gives half her salary to who expects her every fuckin Sunday for lunch in a little room with not enough light. Been on her own since" He pauses, Claude nods. "well more or less since ten years old. Got so sick orunnin from the cops she figgered the only way to get em off her skinny ass was tbecome one of em!"

"And you're fuckin er," Jacques adds as the kid reaches over and pounds on Marcel's back. His wheeze has turned from a laugh to an assault.

The kid says "Go ahead." No one's looking at Claude.

"When I was thinkin about who would do this with me, in my—in my—I let my head go where it wanted. Guys I knew in other countries. Even thought of trainin a fuckin dog! Thought of" He raises his eyebrows to Thierry "a robot." and begins a wheeze which quickly subsides. "In weeks of doin nothin but rearrangin lists of people in my brain lists of people for weeks after forty years othis thing growin in my gut in weeks ochewin up guys' faces in my brain and spittin em right the fuck out again I never in my farthest imagination came up with anythin as perfeck as Palletier."

"And you're f "

Roque wants to know who came up "with her, old man?"

"I did. But only because she came up with me. She's a filthy cop. A great cop. But as dirty as they come. There's no fine lines between anythin with her, old man," he says straight to Jacques. There's none with her. She's a survivor. She survived on the streets as a kid, now she's survivin on the streets as a cop. No lines at all. But when it got to the point when even her division couldn't cover for her no more—they didn't want to let er ass go—but she was mixin up who was the bad guys and the good guys was supposed to be—they sent er to me. And there she was standin in front o me in my office this little rotten face in my face. What the fuck was I gonna do with er? I asked her what the fuck I was gonna do with er. I asked her what she thought gave her the right to different trea—rules—to different rules. She gave me the answer. And so I sent er the fuck outa my office. And I thought about nothin but her and the Cathedral for a week. And I called her back in at the end o eight days and we took a walk around the block. Tonight we're gonna lay it all out for her no one's eatin why ain't you sons obitches eatin gimme a piece othe one with the beef probly fuckin cold by this time!" He hands a corkscrew and Roque's bottle of wine to Jacques.

"I'll heat it what she tell you?" Thierry asks, like a child. No one *is* eating, no one is moving, the men are fixed on Marcel and Claude. Even Jacques's body has relaxed, become more boylike, as close to sitting crosslegged on the floor at the feet of the master storyteller as it's likely to get in this lifetime.

"I told him I have a tattoo," Claude answers in a raspy, smoke-scarred voice which would be sexy if she didn't look like such a little barnyard critter. Her manner is easy but she is deadly serious.

"I told him I have a tattoo," Jacques repeats flatly, making eyecontact with her for the first time.

Still in her Paris cap, Claude causally removes her jacket, like someone would do if they were feeling a bit too warm, and arranges it neatly over the back of her chair. She stands and turns, bunching her black t-shirt as far up as it will go, both elbows in the air, both hands laboring to uncover the back of her right shoulder. The men are hardly breathing. Marcel is delighted. "See? There." High up near her neck is an exquisite, elaborate little Cinderella coach in pinks and purples and pastel blues with regal white horses—almost mythical creatures—detailed down to the feathery strands of hair in their manes. The coach is lush, full, round, sprinkled with tinily-tooled aquamarines and amethysts, topazes and pearls. A soft miniature dream-vehicle that just checked its fittings and is off on a tour of Claude's angular, nearly emaciated, totally unfeminine frame. About to climb her shoulder and drive downhill to see what's doing across her flatland breasts. Maybe hit the peak of a hip or two, wander back up by her bony buttocks. Won't be long—be home before you miss us.

She tucks her t-shirt back into her jeans, sits down and starts on her dinner. Thierry relights his joint—Claude doesn't want any. Jacques and Roque are hungry but are having a hard time wading through the viscous surrealism of the scene into the actuality of picking up a piece of pizza with their hands and getting it into their stomachs by way of their mouths. "Yeah, heat it kid!" Marcel growls, waving his arm over both pizza boxes. Bibbidi-bobbidi-boo. . . . . . .
. . . . . . . . . . . . . . . . . . . . . . . . . . . . . . . . . . . . . . . . . . . . . . . . . . . . . .
. . . . . . . . . . . . . . . . . . . . . . . . . . . . . . . . . . . . . . . . . . . . . . . . . . . . . .
. . . . . . . . . . . . . . . . . . . . . . .After a good ten minutes where the only movement and sound in the apartment are made by Claude eating all the topping off first and then attacking the dough, and by Thierry playing the buttons of his microwave like a keyboard, after a good ten minutes of the kind of stillness that clicks in between the punchline of a disturbing joke and the listener's reaction and lasts a breath but this one has lasted a disturbing while, Marcel and Claude start asking each other if each other remembers the one about how she had to cover up the tattoo for the Olympics and—the kid comes back with the second pizza—the one about how he met a guy once with a tattoo "othe map oJapan that covered his whole fuckin ass" and—Marcel wheezes and serves himself—the one about how there's a bill before the legislature to have tattooing covered by national health insurance..........after a good ten minutes of held conversational breath followed by a spray of skin-pigmented salon-banter, Jacques, who has gotten up and started pacing around the apartment, his hands locked into his pockets, without anyone's even noticing he's left the table, comes skimming back across the floor and lands, like a musical comedy dancer, on one knee, eyelevel with Marcel at his chair.

He says "You're not asking you're not basing the success of this operation on a fairy tale, are you old man?" in the same tone of plaintive understatement that Nelson Eddy used to employ after he'd skimmed (scum?) across the floor and landed, on one knee, eyelevel with Jeanette MacDonald at her chair.

Marcel eats for awhile, keeping his eyes and hands in his plate. *"NON!"* He's constructing a beef-and-olive fort with the help of a burned-crust cement-mixer. "I'm basing it on you. Sit down. It's time to tell Claude a fairy tale of our own."

Roque and Thierry remind Marcel with their eyes what the deal was. Jacques reminds him with his twangy voice. Don't they get their say about her first? Claude swallows her last bite of naked dough. Serenely. As if she just came back from begging for her daily ration of rice outside the monastery—or bullying for her daily ration of recess money outside the schoolyard—and she is consuming the fruits of her labors. "Get this stuff off!" Marcel answers, waving his hand over the dinner remains. The kid clears the table. Once everyone is seated, Marcel finshes the story he began when he and Claude took their walk around the block. This is what he says:

Marcel had a sister. Skinny little ugly thing—he was the beauty of the family, if that gives you any idea, he says. Born after he'd been an only child for five and a half years in the same somber northern town from which shamefully numerous generations of ancestors had never had the curiosity or the courage to venture. Even though its factories came nearly a millennium after the stone ramparts and airlessly narrow streets, the town seemed more naturally an annex of its industry than the other way around, a convenient grouping of surfaces onto which the smokestacks could deposit their soot before spraying another coat up to the sun. Had there been more than the merely several other children of Marcel's age with whom to play, his interpersonal experiences would have been none the richer, since the physical coldness of the town's meteorology and the emotional coldness of its piety drove its inhabitants inward—to the insulated places of their own chambers and their own minds—even the girls and boys.

When Marcel's sister was born he was old enough to understand that life had just been created from life and young enough not to understand that it had not been created exclusively for him. That she wasn't a soccer ball or a schoolbook or a jacket to go to church in.

The baby girl was given the most sacred of names of course—a fate from which Marcel himself had narrowly escaped when on the eve of delivery his father was forced to promise his dying brother Marcel that Joseph and John would be bumped to second and third places respectively—and Mrs. Tronchet was no sooner off the diningroom table than little Marie-Madeleine's training for a life of emotional enfeeblement began.

Fortunately, however, for Double-M, as Marcel called her from the moment he mastered the alphabet, she belonged to Marcel. He owned her. Not in the restrictive controlling sense of ownership, not in the negative inegalitarian sense where there is an owner and an owned, but in the same way he owned his body parts and his thoughts and feeling and his future. In the very positive participatory intrinsic-element sense of ownership. Double-M had at the spark of her birth, as Marcel struggled in the next room against Aunt Béatrice's efforts to save him from the sight of that sullied canal, become a component of his existence.

Everything he needed to know and do to save his sister from her environment and help her get out alive Marcel learned from Double-M herself. He received it from her by watching her and gave it right back, looped it right around, in a continuous circulation of energy and life-affirmation. Through years' worth of hours on location at cradle and crib and garden and Christmas dinner and asphyxiating little street on the way to school. Marcel had patience for nothing else ever in his life but he had patience that lifted his time out of all time and his place out of all place when he entered the pull of Double-M's energy loop to pay attention to the freedom and joy with which her body and mind approached her world.

He learned from her that there was in fact an environment from which she—both of them but especially she—needed and deserved to be saved, a fact which the inhabitants of his town had kept from him less through active malevolence than through passive ignorance, terror and denial. Marcel sensed as soon as Double-M began breathing the grimy air which contained them that he'd been living in a world with no emotional oxygen.

So that was the plan: they were going to work from within—get growing up out of the way as expeditiously as possible and then pack up all their passions and take them on the road.

They'd thought in the very early years that the way they'd eventually make their run for it would be to head back up the birth canal. As it had been through that very passageway that Double-M had brought all the life into their lives, this move, at the time, seemed blessed. Besides, their having pieced together the knowledge that, although in a considerably less enlightened state, Marcel had transited along the same route, and was the only other being in what they now assumed to be a vast universe who had done so, the return trip took on a celebratory symbolism that demanded respect.

With the passing of time, however, they came to see that taking the train would be a better idea. Although they fixed neither a specific date for the escape nor an itinerary, they knew solidly that they'd know solidly when they were ready to move and where they were ready to go.

They were wrong.

They missed it by an immeasurably small unit of time. And the very lifeforce upon which Marcel had drawn to deliver his sister from the most frightful fate is the lifeforce which delivered her into the core of it's grip. Through his intense attempt to make her the perfect escapee, he had made her the perfect victim.

Their existence had been about passion. About the challenging newness and the radiant danger of passion. About recognizing passion, cultivating it, nurturing it in all they touched and did. Encouraging it to progress exponentially into subpassions and subpassions of those, like branches of branches of trees. They lived as the Russian doll which holds a series of progressively smaller, more precious dolls, concentrating their energy to open the next smaller doll and the next, finally to uncover the lucent purity of the most concentrated energy of all. They imagined a blackened room, a vault, under inestimable amounts of layers of earth—one layer, they would say, for every gray blunted resident of their gray anesthetized world—and in the middle of the vault, on a black monolith, a chunk of bluish mineral, spotlit by its own brilliance, sustained by its own supply of atmosphere, protected by its own force, its irregular edges peaking into the shape of a flame. The only source of light and air. Ever. This was original passion. They approached the room with relentless persistence, looking to get closer, to get closer, into the shrine, straining to see the bluish chunk, then to touch it, then to cleave it open and crawl into it, then to be consumed by it. In the convention-enslaved biophobic soot-strangled community where their age was holding them temporarily hostage, they scorned everybody and everything that did not lead them there.

They made a pact never to surrender to the atrophy of marriage or the suffocation of parenthood, to celebrate only holidays of their own creation and to change those creations from year to year, to worship human promise and human performance as the highest form of sanctity.

Then when Double-M was fifteen and being regularly reprimanded for drawing elaborate Eschereque sun-celebration scenes among math problems in her notebook, and Marcel was almost twenty-one, working at an eyeglass factory and watching Double-M grow like a flower, Double-M started getting restless. Started thinking about now being the time to take off for Paris, suggesting, asking, then entreating, and getting angry when Marcel told his stories about the importance of completing the school year which had just begun. She whined until Marcel said whining did not become her then she stopped speaking altogether until Marcel frightened her by doing the same. She told him she was feeling all these...all these...explosions—these little hot crackly explosions in her heart and vagina and her head and she needed a place to put them and hadn't they thought all along that Paris would be the place, wasn't that what all this had been for?

That's exactly what it had been for, Marcel told her. He took her outside one night. Introduced her to a star which had waited millions of years for its light to reach its destination. Introduced her really—"Double-M, this is Star. Star, this is Double-M."—and asked her if she wasn't prepared to wait another eight months for her light to reach its own. She told him again about the heat coming out of hiding inside every part of her, the heat telling her it was time, about the urgency of needing something bigger and even bigger than that to use it for, someplace higher and even higher than that to put it. About sometimes feeling the passion turn to rage. Marcel understood. That was all he did.

The other side said it happened because of a perfect confluence of time, place and person. Marcel's side said just the vehement opposite. Marie-Madeleine couldn't even understand the debate. She didn't really remember the one thing that did it or if there ever was one isolated thing, and when she thought about it—which was not very often because it wasn't really important—it wasn't actually a thing or an incident or a gesture that brought it on but a.....but a wave of warm feathery light, with a sharp electricbolt right in the middle of it, which drizzled down upon her—down, it seemed, upon only her—there where she sat in church one Sunday with her parents and her neighbors and Marcel. She remembered there was a new priest that day, a new young a very young priest there for the first time, and his robes seemed whiter than the robes the very old priest had worn all those years and he had a deep voice, deeper than you'd expect for a fair young man of his age—that's it I remember now it was I was looking following where he was in the prayer book and I read a word in my mind like I always did—before the priest got to the word—to get it out of the way—one less word in one less prayer book I'd ever have to worry about again—and I was already onto the next word maybe even the next line or paragraph and his deep voice rolled the word out of his stomach and through the air into every part of the church and the word landed right up inside me I could I think I remember I could hear it land I could feel it anyway and I looked up—no, I don't remember what the word was, I just don't—and I looked up and first I didn't see anyone—not even the priest—but then I saw everyone I know in the world—even people who weren't there that day—and they were all calling me toward them with their hands from the front of the church and saying something but I couldn't hear them and that's when the drizzle of warm light with the electricbolt floated in and found me and each droplet of light was like in a kid's drawing like a little silver sliver except the electricbolt which was gold and pierced down first into the top of my head and then each droplet fell individually onto me until all the light was on my body and it was me who was the light and the warm drizzle floated away.

At dinner that night, Marie-Madeleine told her parents she wanted to become a nun. Marcel guffawed into the pyramid of buttered carrots he was building in his plate. But there was a look in her eyes he'd never seen before. The following week she avoided him as much as she could. He thought she merely needed a while to adjust to the timetable they'd agreed upon. He understood her impatience and frustration and considered it a healthy sign, a sign confirming they were almost ready, almost there. But she was holding her body differently, her shoulders seemed smaller, softer. She looked...humble.

Marcel came home from work Thursday just in time to sit down at the table. Where's Double-M? His father told him she'd left that morning for Paris. She'd entered a convent, attached to Notre Dame, which worked with needy children. Mostly orphans, his mother said. Marcel asked where Double-M was and waved his hand in the direction of the bread. His mother passed him the basket, he lifted out a piece of *baguette*, his father said they'd just told him where his sister was.

Marcel lowered the bread to his plate in very slow motion, as if fighting a fierce wind, or moving unaided by gravitational pull, or using his arm after a severe accident or illness had immobilized it for a long while. With the same sluggish numbness he slid his chair back.... rose....worked his stuperous way out the door. In front of his house he stood motionless for an amount of time he would never be able to define because the time he was out there, in his cotton workshirt and cotton pants in the icy dark November air, his head locked upward toward Double-M's Star friend, his arms deadened at his sides, was time that for everyone else in any world never was. It was a dimension other than time, alongside of time, parallel to it, and for which no measurement or reference could be known. His parents, who took turns coming to the door and looking at his spellbound back and the back of his tilted head and gave up trying to talk him into consciousness, would say he was out there all night, but that was vocabulary which applied to the world Marcel had left back at the dinner table. Not the world which started where he stood in front of his house.

If he felt anything at all standing through that night, fixed upon that Star, he felt as if his body had been lain atop a screen of the finest mesh and pushed, pushed, crushed against it until he oozed through its minute openings like potatoes through a ricer, his skin and organs and bones breaking up into thousands of minuscule bits and passing through the holes, his blood and water and juices crowding into the metal pores and splashing sloppily out the other side. Once all the pieces and liquids of him had been thus processed, they each floated off on their own path through the universe. Some went up to be by Double-M's Star, some filtered to the floor of the farthest sea, some hovered just at the seam where the atmosphere is attached to the planet, some went to Paris, to Africa, to West Virginia, some circled the roof of the eyeglasses factory.

As Marcel watched the night's lifecycle drain to its end, its vibrant black strength gradually maturing into blurry gray softness, Double-M's Star-friend disappeared. Faded as if on a celestial dimmer until it was no more. Marcel's entire systemic functioning had by frost and shock slowed to near standstill—his heartbeat, his breathing, his ability to produce a thought, the reaction of the sensors in his skin, the time it took for a stimulus like a sight or a sound to be received by his brain and dispatched to the appropriate storehouse. But when the filmy light of the dawn was just reaching the far edge of the sky, nature's anesthesia wore off, and Marcel felt. Felt first the cold, then tingling in his arms, soreness in the muscles of his legs, felt the stiffness in the back of his neck. He felt that he must have been standing out there for a very long time. He remembered why he was doing all the standing. He felt the skin peel off his heart. He felt the pain.

Taking one step back, he slowly raised his arms toward the heavens in a stretched, wide V. Spread his fingers. Tilted his head up again and aimed his eyes into the marrow of the morning. With a long swell he drew all the foul oxygen of the town in through his nostrils to the depths of his chest. His lips parted, he held still for a second...and then a stunning scream, bred on the bottoms of his feet, pumped its way up his tremulous body like mercury climbing a thermometer, strangling then releasing every organ it passed, squeezing its way through his constricted throat, filling his mouth, then overflowing into the scenery on its way up and around to join his bodyparts and fluids which had passed through the screen.

The scream strengthened and weakened Marcel at the same time. Energized his soul as his rage rode out high on its crest, exhausted his body as all his systems labored to expel its purifying poison. Traveling through him it gathered, as if treated with a dust-attracting chemical, the bilious particles which had accumulated and festered throughout the night. By the time it escaped into sound, flushing him clean, it was more of a vomit than a scream. A vomit into the heavens. A wailing, howling belch begging for relief in the ice-white insulated death-silent dawn.

When he was finished, bent at the waist, his hands digging into his abdomen as if against physical pain, when his convulsing core could produce no more wind to propel the toxin upward and out, he straightened, turned, and entered the house. He walked past his father, who had been standing at the door, splashed his swollen face in the hallway washroom, picked up his workbag from where he'd dropped it near the diningroom table the evening before and, still with no covering against the cold, left for the station. He took a train to Paris and never saw his town or his parents again.

Of *course* you can't see your sister, they told him at the convent in the garden behind Notre Dame. For eight days in a row they told him he could not see his sister. They reasoned with him, watched him plead, they listened to him talk and they listened to him scream and insult them. They reminded him he was only insulting his sister. He offered them every little bit of money he had. He offered to work for them. He offered to murder them all. He came back every day at a different hour and stayed on the doorstep until he was too sick to stay any more. He brought them flowers. They thanked him and told him Sister Christine-Joseph did not want to see him. "Christine-Fuckin-Joseph?" On one of the days he even allowed himself to believe them. He had dreams of walking up a mountain in a sandstorm or a snowstorm and wanting to needing to cry for help but when he opened his mouth and tried to scream the sound died in his throat. Right before bursting out. A matter of seconds. And instead his mouth filled up with sand or snow and he was still walking up the mountain and he couldn't breathe or see and he awoke in his little hotel room every night for eight nights and saw the rage standing there—over there by the doorway—no! the washbasin—at the window, wearing his clothes. In the middle of the ninth day the Mother Superior called the police.

The officer who showed up, also in his early twenties, was moved by the agony on Marcel's face. He tipped his hat to the Mother Superior and asked Marcel if he'd like a beer. In his state of need and fatigue Marcel followed him to a cafe a block away, like he'd follow a pal with whom he'd weeks ago set a rendez-vous for the convent steps as a convenient meeting-point. The affinity was immediate and mutual and for an afternoon of beer and coffee during which Marcel excused himself many "I gotta go piss!" times, he spoke to the officer as if picking up the threads of a story interrupted the night before. That evening, after Gérard Aubart finished his shift, he went to Marcel's hotel near the St-Lazare train station, packed him up and brought him home to Montparnasse to share his flat with him. Within three weeks Marcel was walking a beat by the La Villette slaughterhouses in the northeast section of the city.

Because his rage made him tough, intolerant and cynical and the open wound in his heart made him exquisitely aware of the cries of those around him, he became an excellent cop, distinguishing himself in almost everything he undertook, rising quickly and continuously in rank. He was intensely hated or greatly loved—often at the same time—by everyone in the force, whether they'd ever met him in person or not. Eight months after he arrived in Paris he picked up a girl in a Montparnasse bar, made her pregnant and married her when she was in her fourth month. They had a son, whom he named Joseph and all but ignored if not disdained, after whose birth Marcel never touched his wife again, although his opportunities for sexual release did not diminish for the measure. He never told his wife about Double-M and why he had come to Paris and who he had been back there and who it was that the rage came to visit in the middle of every night. He never told anyone, except his best friend Gérard Aubart, who dedicated a good part of his energy to keeping Marcel from returning to the convent steps, threatening to arrest him if he ever did.

As Marcel walked through the door one evening just after Joseph turned five, his son proudly handed him a registered letter which had arrived that day. It was the first letter Marcel had from his parents since he'd left and he was sure it had not been sent to let him know Aunt Béatrice wore a new dress to church last Sunday. At dinner his wife asked him what the letter said and he told her he hadn't opened it yet. He hadn't opened it yet. He'd buried it in an armoire drawer. He spoke of it to Gérard, who suggested he bring it over and they open it together. Marcel waited more than three weeks, then in the middle of lunch one Sunday with his wife and Joseph and his in-laws he suddenly stood, unearthed the letter, took the *métro* to Montparnasse and banged on Gérard's door. At the kitchen table where he'd had his first real meal in Paris, Marcel opened the envelope. He looked at Gérard. Looked back to the envelope. Slid the letter out. Unfolded it. Read it. Nodded. He inhaled as deeply as he could and slowly released his breath, nodding all the while. He handed the letter to his best friend Gérard Aubart.

His parents thought he might be interested to know, the letter began, that his sister had committed suicide last evening by hanging herself in her little room. She had had what she described in the note she left as the most passionate of all love affairs, with the director of the orphanage where she taught. She became pregnant. She said in the note to tell Marcel that when she touched the blue mineral he was the only person in the vault with her. Whatever that means, the letter said.

Gérard immediately raised his eyes to Marcel. The two men sat in silence, Gérard not daring interrupt what Marcel seemed in a constant state of being on the verge of uttering. Marcel would take a deep breath followed by a quick intake of air and silently embrace the beginning of a word with his lips. As if putting the final mental touches on the declaration he was just about to make, he would nod and look off into the distance, lurch slightly forward in his chair, closer to his listener. Then he would reverse the process. Whatever Gérard longed to say to his best friend Marcel Tronchet he knew would have to wait until his friend first found the sound of his own voice. No matter how much time at the kitchen table that took.

When the noise of the traffic through the window became the sound of Parisians leaving their Sunday afternoons and entering their evenings, Marcel, in a faint distant monotone, said "They-found-the-body."

Gérard leaned forward and wrapped his hands around Marcel's forearms where they lay like lifeless logs on the table. "*Oui,*" he said softly.

"NON! That's not what" he meant, Marcel told him, his hand flapping toward the ceiling, his voice sharing space in his throat with bulky broken breaths. Now he could mourn her. He knew she was really gone. Here are the remains of the avalanche victim, closing the circuit of awareness. Opening the way out of the middle place between knowing and not knowing, believing and not believing, being sure the next knock on the door will not be her and never ever being able to go to sleep any night in complete certainly that it won't. That's what the past six and a half years had been for him, he said to Gérard. Now he could finish what he'd started on that freezing sickened November night in front of his house in the north.

Marcel cried the first tear he was able to produce since he'd lost Double-M. A scout tear which went ahead of the others and blazed the trail so that the thousands of millions that followed would find their way through. The thousands of millions of six and a half years of tears layered in a congested bulging bilge in the top of his chest and his throat, pressing, pushing, ever pushing to flood out, always backing up into his skull, bringing death-by-drowning to the cells in his heart. Sliding his chair closer, Gérard put his arms around his friend. He held him and rocked him for hours as Marcel laid his eyes on the body. When in the middle of the night Marcel was ready to leave, Gérard flicked him on the shoulder with the back of his hand "Let's go!" and tilted his head toward the door. Together they walked across Paris.

At Les Halles, near Marcel's apartment, Gérard bought them a beer in a bar that was open very late for the taxi drivers and cops and whores and very early for the butchers and vegetable merchants. Although the day Joseph was born Martine Tronchet ceased all pretense of waiting up for her husband—certainly not lacking for occasions on which to reverse her policy—even she must have felt the weight of the moment, for at three fifty-five when the boys walked in she was in the livingroom in her bathrobe, smoking a cigarette and listening to a recording. As she jumped toward them from her chair, Gérard shook his head and waved her back and she took any questions she might have asked and stocked them away with all the other dead issues in her life. Marcel went to sleep that night knowing for the first time there would be no knock at the door.

If Double-M's first death had thrust Marcel into the middle place with a jolt, her second death launched him out of it with an explosion. As thoroughly as the first had asphyxiated and paralyzed him, so the second unclogged his body, liberated his brain, unsealed his heart. He recognized and accepted that he had a five-year old son. He rediscovered fine food and drink, allowed himself to let life in through his senses. He began to read again. He began to read again. He read, principally, about Notre Dame.

Consuming anything available about the Cathedral, Marcel circulated among the words of architects, historians, theologians of course, alchemists, educators, linguists, even mathematicians, economists, psychologists, sociologists, politicians, cartographers. He read about Notre Dame as business, Notre Dame as art, as magic. He learned about once-secret tunnels, rituals, lives. Priestly initiations in the crypt under the altar. Holy fornications in hidden cells. He joined international societies dedicated to the study of the sacred site, went to meetings and lectures, subscribed to magazines. He collected lithographs of the Cathedral and old maps of its realm; he even brought home a set of antique dessert plates with sketches of its different facades for Martine. There was not an antiques store, library, bookshop, art dealer, museum, university, religious-gear supplier, trafficker in the occult anywhere in France and most of Europe or the world for that matter who did not know to call Marcel as soon as something came in.

In one of his magazines "Wait—I gotta go piss!........And then I'm goin!"

"But wh—but old man wh " The others want to say exactly what Thierry is saying but can't manage it at all. They are so immobilized, it is as if were they to move back, the shapes of their bodies and faces would remain molded into the air, like plastic Halloween character-masks, just where they left them, just where they'd been sitting through Marcel's cathartic tale. Jacques is most mask-like of all because he's known Marcel the longest, and except for noticing that the old man has alot of old maps on the walls of his apartment, and being aware that there's a particular map buried in the bowels of the Cathedral that they've all come not to be able to live without, Jacques, as the others, has known none of this. Nor did Marcel have any intention whatsoever of telling them. He has no idea what that all just was, what well it all just pumped out of. Yes he does. But he doesn't really know why. Yes he does. But he doesn't know which why to choose from....or whether he couldn't find an easier excuse to talk about it again without having to blow up the....................................
................The others hear him speaking either softly to them or loudly to the toilet. In either case they can't make out what he's saying. And they still haven't gotten it all. The ultimate connection is still floating around somewhere inside Marcel, between the north of France and the kid's john. But they're too frazzled to go on, certainly on with the kind of brutal detail they came tonight to discuss in the first place. Marcel is emptied. The others are saturated. Everyone wants everyone else to get up and leave.

"Monday!" Marcel decrees as he clomps back into the room, much more out of breath than a trip down the hall should have made even him. At the work station a fax pours out of the machine that's programmed to receive what Leslie receives.

Thierry catches the fax, "I'll get" glances at it "Chinese food." and stuffs it into Jacque's outstretched hand.

"*I'll* bring Chinese food."

"The Fairy Godmother'll bring Chinese food!" Jacques twangs.

Claude lifts and recenters her baseball cap, dipping it toward her forehead.

"You seein her this weekend?" Marcel growls, more as an order than a question.

Roque points both index fingers.

Marcel nods to Thierry who grabs a giftwrapped box about nine inches long and six inches wide from his equipment table and hands it to Roque.

"Eight O'Clock! I Don't Like Anythin With Fuckin Soybeans In It!......................Thanks, kid!" Marcel says on his way to the front door. He looks back into the room "And tha " and leaves.

# IX
# ℒITTLE ⒸRYSTAL ØLD ℒADIES ẂITH ǤIFT-ẂRAPPED ÞASTRIES ÌN ŦHEIR HANDS

"Welcome to International Relations! Please leave a message after the tone or fax or email us at"**beeeeeeeeeeeeeeeeee**............
................................................................................
................................................................................
................................................................................
................................................................................
................................................................................
................................................................................
.............................................................."Welcome to International Relations! Please l"**beeeeeeeeeeeeeeeee**................
................................................................................
................................................................................
................................................................................
................................................................................
................................................................................
..............."Welcome to In"**beeeeeeeeeeeeeeeeee**..........................
................................................................................
................................................................................
................................................................................
................."W" "FOR THE LOVE OF"**beeeeeeeeeeeeeeeeeee**
"GOD!" Roque socks down the receiver with such fury that one of the five empty cans of Kronenbourg on the nighttable hurdles up over the two butt-choked ashtrays and joins the scraps of the first six-pack on the floor. Squinting through his smoke, he secures his magazine under a leg yanked free from the blanket then reaches over to grab a highlighter from his denim jacket tossed across the frayed brocaded armchair next to the bed.

> Sophisticated, beautiful, sassy SW Dutch F, late-20s, living in Neuilly-sur-Seine, wishes to be placed over the knee of a gentleman who will lift her little skirt, lower her panties and seriously spank the arrogance out of her naughty behind. Write with note, photo, phone number: code 7631.

He grabs the phone without looking at it.

"Vice. Senaqui."

"X."

"Hey, X! What's your ass doin up?"

"How's business?"

"We're watchin videos—that answer your question?"

"There were alot of em, weren't there? Ngan told me th "

"You know, X, you know how like when you eat a big bowl of....of... "

"- - - - -" Roque hears someone squawk something in the background and then a collage of laughter.
"WHO ASKED YOUR ASSES? I ASK YOUR ASSES?" he hears Senaqui shout away from the phone. " when you eat a big bowl of like ice cream or pasta and after awhile it—there's so much othe shit that it don't like look ice cream or pasta no more but just this...this big bowl of "
"- - - - -" Roque hears someone squawk something in the background and then a collage of laughter.
"WHO ASKED YOUR ASSES?" he hears Senaqui shout away from the phone. " this big like...blob? Well—I mean like how much othis shit can you watch before it all starts to "

"School teacher, right?"

"It ain't the *shit* we can't figure out how he afforded. It ain't the shit. That shit you come by. You trade for. You fuckin get it for Christmas. Plus the shit he shot on his own—in his in his little—like—private-tutor office. It ain't the shit. It's the fuckin furniture he bought to keep it in! You should—it's fuckin—you should—must've—inlaid with these—like—jewwwwels like—must've brought it back from his trips to Bang-your-kok. I'm tellin ya, X, if I was him I'd miss the fuckin armoires while I was rottin my ass inside, more n the "

"I need a phone number."

"Which mag? HEY MARZAC GET YOUR ASS IN HERE!"

"Paris Contacts."

"Paris Contacts," Senaqui tells Marzac.

"Gimme Marzac."

"He's already at the machine. What issue."

"This week. Tell him no more cigars for awhile—my guy's all out."
"THIS WEEK. X SAYS HIS CIGAR SPIC WOULDN'T SUPPLY YOUR ASS IF HIS LIFE DEPENDED ON IT........Marzac gives you the finger. Whatsa code?"
"Se—hold it—" Roque shifts his position in bed, parking "hold it—" the receiver across his open belt and unzipped fly while he forages through the crevices of the yellowed cotton covers. He points both index fingers at the cap of a Bic when he sees it peeking out next to the left knee of his jeans, plucks up the pen, then cradles "Seven" the phone between his shoulder and ear "six three one."
"SEVEN SIX THREE ONE," Senaqui yells across the office........................................"You ready?" he asks, knowing when there's no reply that Roque is pointing his index fingers. "Forty-six......forty-one......thirty-five......o one..........Evelyne...............real name's.......... Frederika...van Lagen."

"And?"

"Cool your ass, X, Marzac's ass can't go no f...............and she's big on Charlemagne."

Roque takes a last drag. "On Ch "

"See yX! Hey—what's your ass doin up? Wanna come down and watch v"BEEEEEEEEEEEEEE

He reaches over to the nighttable, dials the first four digits of Leslie's number, hangs up with a careful—almost technical—arc of his arm, as if he were a repairman making sure the connection works. Pinching the corners of the page where he's written the girl's info next to her ad, he forms a little ashtray into which he sluggishly crushes his almost-extinct butt. He dials the first four digits of Leslie's number. Hangs up. Takes the receiver off the hook and tosses it onto his pillow behind him as he kicks the blanket away and gets out of bed. He dials. "WELCOME TO INTERNATIONAL RELATIONS! PLEASE LEAVE A MESSAGE AFTER THE TONE OR FAX OR EMAIL US AT THE FOLLOWING COORDINATES: FAX—THIRTY-THREE ONE FORTY-THREE NINETEEN FIFTY-TWO O TWO. E-MAIL—I R I AT MAIL DOT F R." BEEEEEEEEEeeeee

When he's totally naked he gets back under the covers, arranging them so that the entire left side of his body and his right thigh are wrapped. He dials half of Leslie's number, hangs up, lights a cigarette which he leaves in the ashtray after the first drag, dials Leslie, hangs up after WELCOME, swills the last can of the second sixpack, crushes the can, tosses it toward his feet and seizes his cock.

*"Wellll....ckommmeh,"* he breathes in unfamiliar sounds, working the back of his cock with his thumb as he pumps *"touou"* as he pumps as *"international"* Leslie is here in his head at his head at his crotch *"relations"* quickens the tick Leslie is here in his boosts the beat boosts the beast Leslie is here in his *"pleeezz leeeef"* squeezes and twists at the core at the core of his *"ah messahgge ahftehr zee"* here with her *"Leslie!"* humming with the rhythm of his cock with her "bare ass in the air Leslie!" humming with the running with the running with the rhythm of his cock he sculpts molds the torso of his "please leave a messAGE AFTER LESLIE'S ASS!" forges "BARED EXPOSED BARE TAKE YOUR PANTS DOWN" with his fist of fingers his cock into the column that's "RAMMING THE MEAT OF YOUR NAUGHTY YOUR NAUGHTY YOUR NAUGHTY YOUR NAUGHTY YOUR ASS LESLIE YOUR TAKE IT LESLIE LESLIE TAke it take it take take taketaketaketaketake taket t t t t t t t t t t t t t t t t tt t t t t t t t t t t t t t t t t t t t t t t t t t t t t t t t t t t t t t t t t t t t t t t t t t ttttttt tttttttt
t...................................................................................................................................................
...............................................................................................................................................He dials. "WELCOME TO INTERNATIONAL RELATIONS! PLEASE LEAVE A MESSAGE AFTER THE TONE OR FAX OR EMAIL US AT THE FOLLOWING COORDINATES: FAX—THIRTY-THREE ONE FORTY-THREE NINETEEN FIFTY-TWO O TWO. E-MAIL—I R I AT MAIL DOT F R." BEEEEEEEEEeeeee

He dials.

*"Oui allo."*

Takes the cigarette from the ashtray on the nighttable..........drags slow and deep..........leaves it in his mouth..........squints into his

*"Allo"*
smoke..........
*"A "*

"Only naughty little girls are up at this hour..........don't you think?"

"Depends on who wants to know."

"Don't you think?"

"This is Sébastien, right?"

With his thumb and index finger Roque pulls his cigarette out of his mouth. Looks at it. Puts it back, drags, sets it in the ashtray.

"Right?"

Kicks the blanket away from his sweaty body and starts lightly stroking himself

"Hey! who *i* "

as he glides out of his misty whisper into an impatient command.

"I'll be over in forty minutes."

"Who gave you my number?"

"D'you think that's really his crown and sword?"

"Who g "

"In the Saint-Denis Basilica. In the—that...display case there?"

"Of course not..........OK—so you got it from Dr. Kolkhaz."

"I'll be over in forty minutes."

"And anyway, anyone would *know* they're not his—*he* never had a C all over his stuff—*he* never "

"The only thing is, Doctor Kolkhaz didn't give me your address."

"*He* never called *himself* Charlemagne—that's a dead g—that's what *other people* called him—that's a dead give-away."

"The professor didn't give me your address."

"I'm w—it's........two-thirty I'm working in the morning."

"I want you in something frilly. White—or pink....frilly. Innocent... "

"It's too late. I'm wor "

"You'll call in. I'll pay you for the day."

"Sixty-four Boulevard Victor Hugo—Neuilly. Ring next to V L."

Roque points his index fingers "V L, Evelyne?"

"That's the...the former tenant's name I never got around to changing it."

and puts his whisper back on. "I'm not going to ring next to anyone's name, Evelyne........You're going to leave the doors open........Both doors........The big door......." He lights a new smoke, "that leads to the street........" leaves the old one in the ashtray, "Boulevard Victor Hugo,........" drags. "isn't it?................Isn't it, Evelyne?"

"Yes," the girl whimpers, as if someone is physically coercing her to respond.

"And the door to your apartment........which is on which floor, Evelyne?"

"S-sixth."

"Good girl. And the reason you're going to leave the doors open........is that you'll be in no position to answer them........when I show up,........Evelyne........Which is when?........When am I showing up at sixty-four Boulevard Victor Hugo—Neuilly?"

While the girl mewls something into her mouthpiece, Roque cradles the phone on his shoulder and wraps both hands around his himself, fist-to-fist, like two totems on a pole, one bearing deep into the base, the other tugging lightly toward the bulb, then reversing their routes and their rhythms, their independent mechanisms—as if on two separate organs—forming a harmony of purpose and design.

"Because," he breathes, looking straight at his grip, "where you'll be, Evelyne........when I walk into your home........" kneading now in unison, "is standing at the far end of the room........facing the wall........with your nose in the corner........and your little panties........with your little panties........" trying to sound unfazed, kneading thick, absorbing "down around your knees.........." into the hypnosis of his pulse, "and your........" kneading "skirt hiked up around you waist..........leaving thoroughly exposed........and on display, Evelyne........" pounding "to my view........to my examination........to my........insssspecc-tionnn........" working with his thumbs, trying to sound unfazed, breathing "that arrogant, naughty little behind of yours........" slowing breathing slowing to a save slowing "Will you do that for me?........Will you do that for me,........" to a "Leslie?" stop.

"Leslie?"

"I'll be there in forty minutes."

Roque hangs up. He dials. "Welcome to International Relations! Please leave a message after the tone or fax or email us at the following coordinates: fax—thirty-three one forty-three nineteen fifty-two 0 two. E-mail—I R I at mail dot f r." Beeeeeeeeeeeeee Stands in the shower for as long as it takes to finish his thirteenth Kronenbourg. Gets into his denim and into his car. Takes the Avenue de la Grande Armée toward Neuilly.

At this hour the only place open is a *tabac* at the Place de la Porte Maillot. He buys a carton of Marlboros, orders a double-espresso, coming up from the john tells the barman the phone isn't working. From a booth next to his car he dials the first four digits of Leslie's number then picks up Victor Hugo past the Palais des Congrès and cruises with his lights off to the end of the block.

Before he goes up—just as he eases his door closed as noiselessly as possible—he looks around in all directions—up and down the dark deadness of the residential street, behind him toward to the private, patrician woods, across to the little crystal shelter where the municipal shuttle picks up little crystal old ladies with gift-wrapped pastries in their hands. He lifts a smoke from the pack in his shirtpocket and goes to sit on Evelyne's steps. Looks around again—as if trying to get his bearings, or figuring out which road to take. As if thinking he's heard someone approach but knowing no one's really there. His elbows resting on his open knees, his hands dangling down past his crotch, he drops the cigarette on the ground and whispers *"Welckomeh tou international relations"* to the sky. *"Welckomeh tou international relations Welckomeh tou international relations Welckomeh tou international relations Welckomeh tou Welckomeh Welckomeh Welckomeh"* He stands. Evelyne has left the door open. "Good girl."

"AYEEIOOHH!" the girl squeals when she

"Don't turn around!"

feels a wide hot palm pressed flat against her chubby left buttock. "Don't turn around," Roque repeats, this time close into her right ear, his hand squeezing now and probing, his heated breath strengthening the scent of her piquant perfume permeating the apartment.

"I didn't hear you come in."

"You weren't supposed to. Stay there." He runs his thumb along the crack between her cheeks—gently, as if they've just finished rather than not yet begun. Her home is large, and lushly furnished, with woods and fibers and artwork too costly and valuable to reflect the income of a girl of her age, and too old and venerable to reflect her taste. A livingroom lit less to defeat the heavy darkness of bulky possessions passed through the genes than to ennoble the light itself, by affording it worthy surfaces upon which to repose. A Daddy apartment. Daddy absent. For business travel. Or death. "White.....frilly..." Or walking away. "white....." Roque says to himself as he walks away.....

.....through open grand sculpted-rosewood

double doors into the diningroom, as if reminding himself of what he needs to be focusing on, or reciting all he knows about the girl whose face he has yet to see.

On his return with a massive mahogany straightbacked chair he looks around as he did on the sidewalk—for a clue, for an answer, a reason, landmark, *"Le "*—moving slowly and quickly at the same time. Working to delay his penance. "Pull em up!" And to get it out of the way. With distraction and deliberateness. As someone who "Skirt back in place!" takes a course in pottery-making to forget about a problem at the office. And someone who confronts their fear of cats by holding one. "Turn around."

The girl's straight blonde hair whisks at her shoulder blades as she tugs at the pink-gingham panties by their layers of white ruffled lace. Her nose still pressed into the corner, "I'm watching you, Evelyne" she inches the hem of her white-eyelet halter-dress over her fleshy hips to the middle of her thighs. When she turns toward Roque, enthroned on the chair's thick silk-tapestry seat directly before her, they both flinch for the flash of an instant—as if she had not expected to see someone so solidly handsome, and he had not expected to see someone so plain. His

lips and knees part.

She kneels at his feet, anticipating the command.

He shakes his head coolly.

Flicks the fingers of his right hand toward the ceiling.

She stands.

He lowers his eyes to the carpet.

She kneels at his feet, heeding the command.

"Ask!"

She reaches to touch his kn

He "Ask!" blocks her arm mid-course and deposits it back at her side.

"I'm—I've—"

"I can't hear you, Evelyne. You'll have to speak up."

"I"

"And look into my eyes when you address me."

He points his index fingers.

The girl is wearing no mascara and very little lipstick—a glossy frothing to her pouty mouth which makes her look younger than she is, and "I" softer. "I've been.....naughty." Softer.

Roque nods.
"I n-need a—d—deserve a—to....."
                He's everywhere but here. He's playing every role, thinking every thought, passing every moment, occupying every space, interacting with every being but in this
                                "be"
                                ponderous apartment with this girl.
                          "s-spanked."
But with "Yes, Leslie."

"Leslie?"

He stands, fishes a wad of bills from his jeans, slides it into the girl's folded hands resting against her thighs, points his index fingers and leaves.

The phone across the street has been ripped out of the booth. Probably by a little crystal old lady whose municipal shuttle didn't show. He retraces Grande Armée, waits until he's on the other side of the Arc, pulls over at Le Drugstore Champs-Elysées. "WELCOME TO INTERNATIONAL RELATIONS! PLEASE LEAVE A MESSAGE AFTER THE TONE OR FAX OR EMAIL US AT THE FOLLOWING COORDINATES: FAX—THIRTY-THREE ONE FORTY-THREE NINETEEN FIFTY-TWO O TWO. E-MAIL—I R I AT MAIL DOT F R." BEEEEEEEEEEEEE

And at Foquet's three hundred yards away. "WELCOME TO INTERNATIONA"BEEEEEEEEEEEEE Rue Pierre Charron. "WELCOME

TO"BEEEEEEEEEeeeee At Rue Marbeuf both booths are occupied. He lights another smoke. After a minute he opens his wallet and shows his badge to the more North African of the two jabberers. "WELCOME T"BEEEEEEEEEEEEE Rue de Marignan. "W"BEEEEEEEEEeeeee At Avenue Montaigne, just before running out of Champs-Elysées cross-streets, he dials. "W"BEEEEEEEEEeeeee He dials.

"Vice. Senaqui."

"X."

"Hey, X! What's your ass doin up? Wanna come down and watch videos?"

"YI'll be right there." Roque points both index fingers.

# X
## THE TOASTER-ØVEN

"Oooh-oohooh! Lookin good, Roque!"

"You haven't opened it yet."

"Who does your giftwrapping? There a central counter you can go to at HQ once you've picked up a few things you need in the confiscated guns department? Scuse me, ma'am, I'd like to get this half-kilo of cocaine wrapped up nice for my son's twenty-first birthday? You know, somethin real festive-like.—or is there a little corner on each floor?—Prostitutes' underwear, sir? Right over there past the grenades. There's a special today on red lace crotchless panties left behind in the wagon. And don't forget to take advantage of our giftwrapping booth near the elevator."

"Leslie, open it, for the love of God "

"All proceeds go to the Inspectors' Widders' Fund, ma'am. A very *un*worthy cause, cause *they* knew their fiancés were Inspectors—they shoulda known widderhood was a screaming possibility when they married the sons obitches and if they can't fend for themselves and their hyperactive progeny then that's *their* prob "

*"Leslie!"*

Her mock-orgasmic breathing intensifying, at each stage, into a Boleroesque crescendo, "h" Leslie inches the gold ribbon "hh-hh" and its lush-looped bow "hhh-hhh-hhh" off the box. "hhhh-hhhh-hhhh-hhhh" She painstakingly peels each piece of tape away, "hhhhh-hhhhh-hhhhh-hhhhh-hhhhh" corner "hhhhhh-hhhhhh-hhhhhh-hhhhhh-hhhhhh-hhhhhh" by "hhhhhhh-hhhhhhh-hhhhhhh-hhhhhhh-hhhhhhh-hhhhhhh-hhhhhhh" corner, so as not to disturb a grain of the gold-flecked shiny white paper. Slowly she turns the package over "hhhhhhhh-hhhhhhhh-hhhhhhhh-hhhhhhhh-hhhhhhhh-hhhhhhhh-hhhhhhhh-hhhhhhhh" and starts picking at the tape across the bottom. "hhh "

"I could've sworn," Roque tells her, stopping for a light, "you'd be the kind of person who'd rip into that thing with such savagery we'd be lucky if "

"Oh........Gee........I really wanted a toaster-oven," she says with a disappointed whine.  Roque looks at her blankly and accelerates.  "Oooh-oohooh!  I Love It!  I LOVE it!  Ay-yy Nooo-ooo Walkbeing!  God this is a great one it has these great headphones that don't fall outa your ears when you run that I wanted Roque thanks, pal!  What Ay-yy Treat!"  She leans across the gearshift well to kiss him on the cheek "Yellow!  They'll see me coming in Versailles!" then turns and kneels on her bucket seat.  "It's especially for sports I know this kind it's I've wanted one for a long time howdj know?"  As she reaches to the backseat to get a tape from the satchel, Roque slides his hand up under her skirt.  She traps him between her thighs before turning back around, "This is the kind you can sweat on it like a farm animal and it doesn't do weird things to it," then leans closer, ".....a farm animal in Nikes," closer, ".....with a little terrycloth headband just above its snout," trying to get a reaction.  ".....and a little t-shirt with a picture of Old MacdAHH-AHH"  Staring straight ahead as if hearing nothing, Roque suddenly pushes on her shoulder, sending her tilting toward her door.  "You Don't Even Know Who Old MacDonald Is And Don't Gimme Any Smartass Shit About Left-over Hamburger Frchrissake!"

"I wanted to get you one with a radio.  But they didn't have it in.  And there was no way they could get it for me right away.  I didn't want to wait.  I wanted you to have it for this week-end."

"The customer is never right, Roque!  You did good you did good!  I don't listen to the radio when I run."  Leslie gathers all the wrappings and tosses them over her shoulder into the back.  "I only listen to my brother's" Pops a tape in.  "tapes."  Puts the headphones on.  "ING ABOUT THIS EAGLES TU-UNE.....THAT I ADORE.....AND I THINK IT'SSS.....THAT ESSSSENTIAL BEATTTT.....THAT JUSSST.....WORKS WITH THE RHYTHMMM.....OF MY BODY PROPERLY-YYY.....AND THE RHYTHM OF THE EARTH.....AND THE UNIVERSSSSSSSSE.....DANNEY-THE GREAT-BRITTAIN *WITH* YOU.....SEVEN THIRTY-SEVEN—BOEING STANDARD TIME.....WORKIN OUR WAY TOWARD CHRIS ETON AND THE RECORD RACK RADIO EXPERIENCE AT NAH-AHN O'CLOCK HERE ON DVQ FM.  GOOD MORNIN *TOO-OO* YUHH-UHH.....REMINDING YOU BEFORE I SHUT UP N LET YLISTEN TO THE REST OF THIS EAGLES S"

"It's great.  Thanks, sweetie," she says, stopping the cassette.

"Can't wait to use it! Especially since my old one just broke." Removing the headphones, she carefully bends and unbends their metal arc before laying them in her lap with the Walkman. "Is that not unbelievable or what!"

"No kidding."

"It's broken—just—didn't you see me messing with it when I packed it this morning?—Look!................................................
...........Shit!"

"What?" Roque wants to know as she emerges from her satchel, shaking her head.

"You don't love me anymore."

"What?"

"You didn't put your hand under my skirt that time. Don't worry, it's safe—I'm not wearing panties."

"I almost lost it last time I did that."

"Can you think of a better place to lose it?" She transfers the cassette from the new machine to the old. "Or maybe you can come up with a better bodypart to lose up there."

"Does it actually have to be a loss-type situation?" Although there is almost no traffic, Roque has not taken his eyes off the road.

"A new one'll grow back. Each time. Like whiskers or fingernails. Bigger! Better! Stronger! More resistant against...." she rubs deep into the denim between his legs "abuse. Not that we're not already talkin superior quhey! now this thing won't turn on at all! Weirdest fucking th—it worked on the run a couple hours ago frchrissake! How the fuck didjyuh know it was gonna stop working? There are no coincidences in this world, there's only cosmic synchronicity they teach you fortune-telling at cop school?"

"Maybe you did something to it—did you drop it while you were running?"

"No! I went into the bathroom that's all—well you were h—just when you walked in, remem?—I came outa the bathroom and there it was! Lying there on the table making little Boris Karloffian death rales like.....like Boris Karloff...like the guy who all he has is his fingertip showing and pretty soon that'll sink into the quicksand too and then there'll be no guy at all....like a walkperson whose on-button is stuck on off—well didn't you hear it frchrissake?—I must've done something" Leslie pokes at the buttons and peers into the little plastic window. "when I took the tape out but it worked just a—maybe when I was in the bathroom mascara particles floated over to the table and infiltrated the delicate mechanism of this! the only walkperson manufactured that day whose mascara-proofing inspector looked away for two seconds as it was riding past on the conveyor belt. Maybe it sensed the vibrations of the new one approaching—walking through the door...hello to the Darottos...past the mailboxes...telling Monsieur Fontaine what day it is...up the steps...down the hall... KNOCKKK....KNOCKKK....KNOCKKK—and got jealous and" She puts her hands around her throat, sticks out her tongue and makes strangled choking sounds as she reels and swoons in her seat. "KHCHKHCH-KHCHKH-KHCHKHCH. Stereophonic suicide. Well it wasn't really suicide it was more like stereophonic tent-folding. Stereophonic fate-ceding-to. Stereophonic up-giving. Stereophonic not-taking-your-future-into-your-own-hands-godamnit!'ness—like them Inspector-widders. They say walkhumanoids take on either exactly the characteristics of the household in which they're raised or exactly the opposite." She holds the broken player up to her face "We know what side othat equation *you* were on, sports fan!" then reaches with it back between the seats "dbe ASHAMED oyourself!".

"Let me hear some of your brother's show," Roque says, stopping her arm and taking the old machine from her before she can get it into her satchel."

"Ahh, gee, Roque, I wish I'd'a known. I brought tapes of the only two shows of his career where he wasn't broadcasting in French."

"Let me hear it."

While Leslie puts the cassette into the car's tape player Roque stuffs the broken Walkman under his seat. "I'll see if I can have one of the guys fix it for you."

"Thanks, swee " "ONG THAT MY SISTER LESLIE WILL BE HERE ON JUNE TWENTY-SIXTH EXPRESSLY TO DO LESLIE-AND-DANNEY-ON-THE-RAY-DEE-OH, FLYING IN DI-RECT FROM PARIS FRANCE FOR THE DOUBLY-GREAT-BRITTAINS-IN-THE-MORNING RADIO EXTRAH-HVAHHGAHHNNNNNZAHH RIGHT HERE ON WDVQ EIGHTY-EIGHT POINT SIX ERMEDE NOOO JER-ZEEE.

**JUNE TWENTY-SIXTH. LISTEN TO ME.....WHEN I TELL YOU.....NOTTT.....TOO-OOO.....MISSSSS.....ITTTTT.....** "

"What Was That He Said?" Roque snaps.

"What."

"What did he say—play that back—or—what did he just say?" He pounds his knuckles on the button to shut off the tape.

"nott tooo misss itt"

"Whatddeesay!"

"That I'm going over to do the show with him in June. I know you'll miss me terribly. It's good for you. Sometimes it's healthy in a relationship for people to be sep "

"WheninJune?"

"Not til the end of June. It's great—we'll have a hysterical goodbye scene at the airp "

"WHEN?"

"June twenty-sixth, Roque. It's OK. Maybe you'll find someone else to tie up while I'm gone. A stand-in debauchee. They have a service for that I think. You can look it up. In any case it's gonna be done in as little turn-around time as possible. A matter of hours if I can help it. I don't do family. And my friends have all become multiple-maternity-victims since I've been here—no connection—or maybe alotta connection—some of them even mega-multiple-maternity-victims, poor things—rendering them thereby incapable of participating in any conversation that does not have something to do with the contents of the supermarket. Hi, Leslie, how's Paris, Brussels, Monte Carlo, fucking your brains out, running under the Eiffel Tower, terrorist-dodging and working for billionaires? Oh! Before you get into it, let me just tell you—do you know I had new cabinets delivered from Kitchens Unlimited last week and do you know there was a scratch on one of the doors and they had to send them all back and now I won't have my new cabinets before the end of the summer at least and I where does that leave me for Bryan's birthday party and all those three-year-olds coming? Gee, Laura, I really couldn't tell you where that leaves you but it sure is something you and that homeless guy with no legs in front of your building should sicken yourselves worrying about."

"So you don't know when you'll be back."

"My Mistake! I thought I just said while you were getting outa your spaceship that it'd be a matter of a couple days at the most but now I guess I didn't say that at all are we there yet?"

"Where?"

"Normandy frchrissake! The farm house! The isolation where I can scream without Umberto running up the stairs to ask after my wellbeing, without you having to put your hand over my mouth like in a Japanese lithograph."

"Couple hours."

"Shit! Let's eat before we get there you know *why* the guy in the Japanese lithographs always has his hand over the woman's mouth? It's those rice-paper walls and supposedly Japanese women do their share of screaming. Indian women too. The whole Orient joining together in one erotic refrain. Believe in it. Healthy part of the sexual experience......Then again if you saw a dong comin at you the size of some othose in those prints, you'd be makin noises too! Wanna stop and eat? Are we there yet?"

"You wouldn't make noise. Yes you would. You'd scream for more."

"For bigger. The kind you have to strap to your thigh when you go swimming. Are there woods?"
"There are some beautiful old towns in a half-hour. Good traditional food."
"Better be traditional, Roque. I don't eat it if it ain't traditional are there woods?"
"Woods."

"Nearthe" Leslie imitates Roque's inflection. "beautiful old towns with good traditional food."

"Well of course isn't that why we "

"Good! Then we'll have a picnic!"

"I don't think so, Leslie. I want to eat lunch."

"You know what a picnic is, Roque, don't you? Peequeneeque. It's like marketeeng, babyseeteeng, parkeeng, shoppeeng, joggeeng—all those English words the Académie Française sits around and tries to hold at bay because they don't dare hold what they'd really like to be holding don't let them kid you for a minute. Whadya think ydo at a peequeneeque?"

"It's not "

"Don't get French on me, Roque—Look!" She turns-kneels-burrows once more in the satchel. "I brought Verlaine to read to you. Roque! You can't I have Verlaine's poetry for when you lay your head in my lap on the blanket we can't do that in a restaurant if Napoleon didn't do that in a restaurant we certainly can't and we know he didn't that's the first thing you learn as a schoolkid what Napoleon didn't do you should know that!"

"We don't have anything to—" Roque finally breaks his crash-dummy concentration and glances at the backseat "we don't have what would you have at your picnic?"

"Frchrissake, Roque, what dyuh have at a goddamn picnic, Roque, I dunno some bread cheese strawberries Perrier-n-orange juice, guy off in the corner in an apron with some asshole thing like World's Greatest Chef on it barbecuing a couple pieces ochicken, naked women with long blond hair and exquisite breasts and red mouths riding by, sidesaddle, on huge white horses with enormous erections—the horses, not the women—satyrs strolling past surveying their turf—talk about huge erections—the satyrs, not the turf—cherubs with gorgeous little pink heart-shaped bottoms flitting head-level dropping rose petals and gardenias, the park police making sure everyone's got" Her voice deepens "both hands on top othe blanket, ma'am". then resumes its normal tone. "string quartet in tuxedos and long black dresses—I'll leave it to you to divide the threads as gender-appropriately as you see fit—playing Borodin, with Mick Jagger in a turquoise leather jewel-encrusted jumpsuit, hunched over, strutting back and forth with the mike. I dunno, Roque, what do you have at a picnic."

Roque takes a cigarette from the pocket of his denim shirt and rolls it around between his lips.

"Baseball game in prog—adults, not kids—in progress on the same side of the field as the chicken barbecuer but a ways down—outa the way of rebellious sauce-particles—"..................................................
..........................................................................................................
...........................They silently watch a couple kilometers of scenery.......................................................................................
..................................................................." raging frisbees— I hate fucking frisbees—but they're at every picnic—ycan't keep em out—they're like bugs—the worst is dogs—big sloppy copper-colored dogs playing frisbee with human beings—jumping up to catch them in their germ-infested jowls—the dogs catching the frisbees, not the human beings catching the frisbees—or the dogs catching the human beings.....actually, I can think of a couple human b..."

He lights up.

"...some great-aunt-type in pastel-flowered polyester bermuda shorts that don't match her striped four-sizes-too-small stretch shell-top with bony knees peeking out under layers of licensed-to-kill thigh-cellulite sitting on a beachchair crocheting a baptismal dress for a great-niece-type reminding her sister-in-law about how much it rained at last year's peequeneeque and everyone had to go home before the band showed up. Mick gets annoyed at a kid walking past with a ghetto-blaster." Roque looks at Leslie. She opens her hands as if measuring something wide. "Biii-iiig radio—I'll explain—one day when we're not in the middle of such a ponderous discussion. Statu-esque women in evening gowns and tanned men in white dinner-jack-ets hovering over a baccarat table under a green-and-yellow-striped gazebo.....bold stripes. You're I know you're not serious here, right? You knew this all along, right? You just asked the question to make idle conversation til we get to the picnic site, right?"

Roque abruptly pulls off the road. He drives along the shoulder for several hundred yards "What'sa matter, sweetie?" then suddenly veers deep in among the trees, making his own path as he goes. At a small, flat clearing well into the richly wooded land he slams on the breaks, jolting Leslie forward against her "HEY-EE!" seatbelt. Then cuts the engine.

"Get out of the car!"

"You're a sweetie" Leslie says, pantomiming an effort to catch her breath. She leans over to kiss him but he turns his back to her and gets out. "Might be a better idea though if we picked up a few things before we" His door slams shut. "stopped. Donchya think?" She's talking to an empty car. Roque is rummaging urgently in the trunk. Stretching to her feet, Leslie watches him hide something in the waistband of his jeans, behind the front of his lightweight denim jacket.

"Comon!" he says, kicking her door closed and locking his arm around her waist. He hurries her across the clearing to a cluster of trees where the woods start again, her white Keds looking like little mechanized doll-feet fitting three or four scampery steps into the space of one of his strides. She is loving the mystery. She is being

fueled by his smell, by the heat filtering up from his skin through his denim and turning her t-shirt transparent with perfumed perspiration, by his sense of mission. Through the broad quickness of his movement she is absorbing his passion that rumbles, rumbles, never explodes until the flash of the instant of the end, but turns and churns under the surface like the guts of a race car, humming, whirring higher and faster when it kicks higher and faster, grinding sometimes grating its gears, working hard within its casing. His passion that you feel before you see it, that makes you look up and over at him because you smell it because you think you smell his passion and you want to check it out and be sure. His passion that anticipates, that breathes of what is about to happen next, not of what is happening here and now.

Leslie has that feeling again. Leslie has that feeling again that drives her whenever she hears the gearbox working. The powerful powerlessness through which she must pass when approaching that place she enters with him. She breaks the beam as she moves under the electric eye of the passageway to the place. She sees herself gliding through the passageway, she is sitting up there watching—up there, peeking down over from a ledge atop her vagina.

At the head of the cluster of trees across the clearing, aligned almost as a set of bowling pins, is the kingpin tree, a handsome huge oak stretching in the soft wind, presenting itself as both protector to the oaklings huddling and giggling behind it and doorkeeper to the infinite woods, inviting you in, bidding you to watch your step, asking if it can take your coat or show you where the restroom is. Roque stops ten yards in front of it and releases Leslie's waist. She looks at him. "Lift up your skirt...................................................

.........................Lift. Up. Your. Skirt."

"WhyshouldIliftupmyskirtfrchrissakeswhatifIdon'twannaliftupmyskirt andanywaythat's*your*jobtoliftupmyskirtwhyaren't*you*liftingupmyskirt frchrissakes," she says in her head. Then lifts up her skirt.

He slightly thrusts his chin in the direction of the tree. She asks with her squint what he means. He slightly thrusts his chin in the direction of the tree. Moving only her eyes, Leslie looks left to the oak then straight ahead to Roque. He puts his left hand on his hip, deliberately brushing the hem of his jacket away from the top of his jeans. She nods slowly, bites into her bottom lip. Widens, brightens her eyes. "OK," she whispers to herself. "OK OK OK" Bare from where her white-denim miniskirt is bunched at her waist down to the tops of her lacy white anklets, she approaches the tree and embraces it.

Roque goes around to the other side of the stout trunk and takes the length of rope from his waistband. He loops Leslie's right wrist, draws across the bark, catches her left wrist, then knots the end of the rope to the mid-point of the cross-cord. Before walking back to her, he checks the knot with two quick jerks toward his chest.

Her big curls pop free and tumble over her shoulders as he unties the skinny gold bow at the nape of her neck, "I'm "

"Aeechchchchch"

breathing deep into her ear while she jumps and shudders, fluffing her hair as if preparing her for a portrait shoot. " ready to tell you just now what I'm going to do to you." He holds his mouth flush against her head, gives her a minute to imagine what he is about to say. Leslie bucks back to try to touch his body but he moves away. She hugs tighter around the tree and contracts her labia, squeezing her wetness out as through an eye-dropper.

"I'm going.............I'm going........first........Leslie—you with me, Leslie?"

Leslie heaves, says nothing, Roque reaches around and pinches her nippl"yESS!..........................Roque." through her white t-shirt. Her mouth opens wide to host her deep breathing. "Yes."

"I'm going, first........out here........outside here in the woods......" He takes a cigarette from his shirtpocket. Lights up. Enjoys it awhile.

In her sneakers and anklets, with her hair half-way down her back, Leslie looks like a little girl who has to make pee-pee and is trying to hold it in by bouncing her pelvis against the tree. "....to step back and look at you........I'm going to look..." Roque continues, blowing smoke out of the side of his mouth, "........Leslie...my Leslie.....at how bare you'll be from the tops of those lacy little socks of yours.....up your calves........the tender part of the backs of your thighs—" Leslie is whimpering and grinding, pulling her hands out against the ropes, purposely making them cut into her wrists as Roque stands just far enough away to keep her from brushing against him in her range of movement. The ring of his voice is tender, almost soothing, but its tone is matter-of-fact and detached. "you know just what part I mean. Don't you? Leslie."

"nn nnnnnnnnnnnnnn nn n n"

"That charming little seam with the bottom of your buttocks. With" He leans over to her ear but does not touch her, "the fleshy part of your buttocks....." drags on his cigarette for awhile, tosses it down behind him. "Then I'll look at your bare bottom, Leslie. All by itself. I'll study how exposed and helpless and.....naughty it will be out here...naughty for presenting itself in this way.......for offering itself up to my............examination. What's the matter, Leslie?"
She's bending her knees and straightening them, crossing her legs, rubbing herself against the tree, whinnying whining through explosive moany crackly coughs, she's coming in every part but her pussy she's coming in her anus and her thighs in her knees she's coming in her head but her pussy she's there, there she is in her pussy she needs him to touch her and she'll come in her p"touch" she needs him to "touchmetouchmeRoque—t—yougottayougottatouchmeee-eee-eee-eeeeeeeeeyougottagottagottagottayougottAYOUGOTTAAYOU GOTaayougottaayouGOTTAAyougottAAA" she "Y" slams "Y" herself "Y" into "Y" the "Y" tree "Y" until "Y" she "Y" figures "y" out "y" that "y" she's "y" only "y" prolonging "y" the "y" agony.

"Next I'll take my hand, and with my open palm I will caress the exposed flesh of your buttocks. I will.....pre-pare.....the exposed flesh of your buttocks..........for what you want, Leslie.......for what you" Roque's words are reaching Leslie from a distance, filtering up from a far-away fund of reverie, from under her brain, from under the blankets, under her crib. Like whisper-down-the-lane words, mutated phoneme by phoneme, meaning by meaning, passed along the snaking string of minds and mouths of everyone who ever stimulated her senses and her mind and her mouth by any means. By the time they sear from her ear down between her legs, each individual sound-component of each individual letter has broken off and drifted away from the others, played at new—or very old—configurations, decided they like the one they just came from and recombined into exactly what Roque is saying, just in time for her to hear "need........for what you know you really.....need..."

—a breeze smears the sweat across Leslie's skin and she pushes her chest closer into the bark to share its warmth—

"....for what you can avoid no longer......for what you are going to get today............Leslie. For what I am going to give you today."

First Roque gives Leslie

silence. Standing peacefully behind her, a bit to the right, he makes masterful use of the passing of silent time while he thinks about the fact that he was never called to think about it before He takes another cirgarette, rolls it around unlit between his lips. only to perform it  observe it  as a holiday  as a rite  as a religion  that it is nothing short of that  that the substance of fantasy is ritual  that fantasy and religion share the same genetic material  He watches Leslie's shoulders rise and settle with her uneven breathing and thinks about the fact that he's wondered since the train to Brussels if he's falling in love with her. If he fell in love with her at the first flash of eye contact. No!  When he got up to lock the door. No! Well—yeah. He went in there knowing nothing, she could've been anybody. When he was a kid he kept having this dream about being at the mouth of a narrow overgrown path in a forest and each time in the dream he went in and each time the path became a labyrinth of different shape and complexity and shading and length, with different types of rocks and branches he'd have to move out of the way or work around so he could get farther in farther in to discover something no one else had ever seen before and nothing—nothing—nothing ever fascinated impassioned energized him more than penetrating the mystery and perpetual freshness of the labyrinth. That's why Marcel's

—he raises his eyes to the pastel-blue and white sky looks—

project fascinated him. He said yes right away and not for the money. He didn't tell Marcel about the labyrinth—the old man obviously has a labyrinth of his own—he doesn't need mine.  And if I'm falling in love with her what—I don't—would they kill me   if they knew   would they kill her  Dupuy would   if they knew  don't they know already for the love of God  do I know  she's like the dream  if I dropped out

—at Leslie again points both index fingers—

they'd do us worse   maybe not   maybe they'd do us better   they'd swear I told her either way   I know what the solution is   don't fuckin know yeah I do    maybe I don't love er    I don't love er.  She's like the dream. Look at er! She's begging for it to almost happen. Hanging

in the sweet sphere that hovers just above the image and just below the experience. Where the business of the approaching reality is the perpetuation of the approach, the perpetuation of the approach right up to that sharp point of demarcation whose tight air vibrates at its shrillest peak right here at this doorway and grips your head and dents your skull and you're gonna hafta either walk in and go through with it or put that book away, pull your pants up and go back out to your desk! It is here that everything starts and it is here that everything stops.  Once you're in you've already left.  The show's over. There's a little guy with a twitchy mustache pushing a long dustbroom through the litter of the day. Leslie has no memory of any time at any age when she has not been approaching wanting to approach it. She feels the nerves of her moist skin reach out and interknot with the soft soaked fibers of her t-shirt and the prickly threads of the wind. She hears Roque light a match. She begins flicking her pelvis against the tree again. Now she wants it to start and now she wants it to stop.  She wants to live in this endless exquisite state of being about to go in. She ("can't stand out here forever how long does he expeGod da Roque frchrissakes Roque where the fuck I don't wannaaaa")"aaaAAAH-AAAGHCHCH!"

Squatting onto his heels, the cigarette in the corner of his mouth,

Roque squints into his smoke as his hand hovers in the slim slice of space just above Leslie's buttocks. He glides from nerve-ending tip to nerve-ending tip, touching nothing below the outermost veneer of flesh, touching with no more than the solid heat projecting from his palm. After each passing he stops, reviews the results of his blending of air and flesh, contemplates his next stroke like the Japanese artist who spends years studying the tree he is about to paint and then years studying it again once its likeness has been rendered. Every pause gives the surface of Leslie's skin some seconds to sense its new vulnerability, and the kernel of her psyche some inches to absorb the new stage of sensing. To absorb Roque's smell which, by increments, at each caress, becomes the smell of the tree then the clearing then the supply of life-sustaining air on Earth inside Leslie's head. Inside Leslie's head she feels herself hugging her legs up around the trunk, locking it into her crotch, she feels herself fucking the thick oak in generous slow sweeping thrusts while she squeezes it harder into her arms, and her body and voice begin to vibrate in a lowgrade steady whirr as if connected to a motor.

Roque amuses himself by pulling her bunched-up skirt halfway down then shimmying it back to barely above the beginning of her hips—she needs to turn to look at him—a mischievous new covering magnifying her urgency to be uncovered—she dares not turn to look. He holds still. Tosses his cigarette. Watches her droplets dangle like diamond pendants from the points of her pubic hair. Starting on the right, he slowly grazes the tip of his tongue along the crease under her cheeks, following the contour, leaving his track in the silky sweat, flicking his tongue in and out in and out at the center of her universe where her two buttocks and her two thighs make a little box to put things "ooh.ooh.ooh.ooh." in, following the contour, finishing with a quick kiss on her left side.

Squatting still he slides the skirt by shades and bunches it below her waist then grasps her hips Leslie "AHaH—AH-ah" thrusts back by reflex and back farther "AH-AH" and up when her pursuit produces no contact she jiggles her legs bounces her feet against the ground in a springy whiney tantrum rolls the front of her body across the bark like a finger on an inkpad, pressing her breasts into the tree until they hurt.

In the middle of her right buttock Roque plants his half-open lips. He sucks wet on her wet flesh while he whips it with his tongue. She has stopped jittering because in her head she's seen her legs give out. She concentrates on her breathing. He moves to her left buttock and moistens it with flat, wide, full-tongued swirling licks as jagged howly sounds leak from a throat she can't recognize as her own. Roque stands up and back. Leslie breathes. He bends forward and pats lightly on the insides of her calves, bouncing from one to the other until she spreads farther apart. He stands up and back. Checks the angle. Hooks his left arm around her middle, pulls her as far from the trunk as her bonds and the length of her arms allow.

With the gold safety pin plucked from the front of her t-shirt he pins the back of her hem to her waistband.

Roque reviews Leslie for a minute. She is pink naked in the blue-tinged sun, sketched for him within the lines of her little white clothing.

On his way to the other side of the tree he caresses her round ass without looking at it. When he slides the rope—and with it her hands—down along the bark, she is forced to bend forward and tilt her hindquarters up. Leslie is in her crib with the blanket wadded up under her tummy and her little bottom in the air, creating receiving reacting to the original call, the primal invitation to relinquish control—the First and Ultimate Deal........where are you? I'll do it—OK I'll do it myself for now maybe you'll come "ah." by "ah." later. "ah.ah.ah.ah.ah.ah.ah." Leslie is about to come by later and Roque hasn't even begun. She can smell the swellings in her vagina while she tries to bend farther over, straining her muscles, stoking her submission, she thinks her ears are melting onto her t-shirt she bobs up and down against the resistance of the rope cuts her wrists into its fibers Roque is behind her she's exhausting herself his hand is on his buckle he opens his belt she hears it he snaps it out of his pants she shrieks he doubles it "NonoRoque. Roque. Roquenono don't give it to me don't do it don't. don't." and slashes it down against her right buttock "don'tgiveittome. giveittomegiveittomdon'tgi.do.m" then against her left then her right then left "nnnyehehssssuhhhh" right "giveittomegiveittomegiveitt" her labia and thighs are dripping with a viscous solid-liquid web left Roque has found his rhythm she looks behind her "aeeeeeiiiiiiuhuHUHUHUHUhuhhh hh-uhhhhh-uh" and comes right left right "uhhhhh.uhhhh. uhhh." left "hhh-hhh" right left he flings the belt away opens his pants seizes her hips packs into her rams with three dazing thrusts blasts up through her heat, along the oak trunk, out into the clouds above the clearing.........

.................................................................................................
.................................................................................................
.................................................................................................
..................................Once Roque has caught his breath he goes around to cut Leslie free with his pocketknife, embracing her when

he comes back, pulling her down with him onto the warm grass. His upper body sloped against the trunk, he cradles her on his shoulder, strokes her hair, blows little blasts of cooling breath into her sweat-streaked face as she dozes. *"Tu es belle, Leslie. Tu es très belle. Tu es ma très belle Leslie,"* he says as if reciting a poem. He has never been so tender with her. He has never, he realizes, been so tender with any woman.

While Leslie's dreams translate the spicy scent of his skin and damp denim into slow Peter Maxian images, Roque wonders whether having just reached the back door of the labyrinth is a good thing or not. He beats back questions about Marcel's project, coming at him from every corner of his brain, like a comicbook character deflecting bullets with metallic forearms. Minutes later when Leslie wakens he shifts her onto her stomach and reaches to rub her reddened bottom, making her hum with soft little sounds, soft little

sounds, she slithers down his body..................takes him in her mouth..................slithers up..................straddles him. Touching palms above his chest, they make love very slowly and warmly, as if giving each other a long, sensuous kiss.

"You got somethin against eating lunch, or what here?" she asks, still astride him, when they've finished, massaging his cock with brisk contractions of her vaginal muscles.

"Leslie.....there's something we have to...talk about."

"It won't wor "

"WHAT WON'T WORK?"

"Whatryall excited about frchrissake?" She gets up and yanks her skirt down. "Ythink one othese trees has an iron I can borrow see I told you you shoulda given me a household appliance see I knew what I was talking about didn't I? Gee, I wonder how *that* got there!" Roque stoops for his belt. "Actually with you, what I need is my own portable drycleaning establishment complete with Harvard-attending owner's-son sent there by the good offices of my soiled raiments— will you look at th—great thinking wearing all white, huh? when they were giving out brains I musta been out pickin up my clothes from the drycleaner's across the street from the Who concert what the fuck did I expect? Now you see this is a problem professional wives do not have—and we're not talking wives who work here, we're talking individuals whose job it is to be someone's wife—who that's what they put on their income-tax returns—Profession: Being Someone's Wife—oh, sure, their flannel nightgowns might get a little mussed once a month when MYY HUSBAND'S mistress takes the night off—from the same people who gave you MYY HUSBAND'S job and MYY HUSBAND'S transfer to Paris and MYY HUSBAND'S life—but basically their wardrobes remain unaffected by th "

"*What* won't work, Leslie?"

"Godyuh let a guy brutalize you and all of a sudden he wants you to answer all his questions frchrissakes!" Leslie turns to walk back to where they parked. Roque grabs her upper arm. "What the f—will you tell me what's gotten into you all of a—yknow, it's a little late tstart gettin nuts about what went on back th "

"You want it again?"

"You Know Goddamn Well I Don't Want It Again *That* Way Because Then It Wouldn't Be A Game Anymore Number One And Number Two I Don't Think You Could Take It Twice In The Same Day." She crosses the clearing and gets into the car.

Roque follows, steering out of the woods as brusquely as he'd cut in. When they're on the main road he asks "What won't work?"

"Falling in love won't work!" He flinches and stares at Leslie until the horn from the car behind them snaps his attention back to the wheel. "Well that's what you were getting at, weren't you? I mean it won't work with me. I mean love is a manufactured emotion. Made in a *fucktory*!........You don't get it, do you? See, the w—forget it. I don't have the energy. I'll tell you some day when we have nothing else to talk about. When we're married, for instance. And we've gotten all the mileage we're gonna get outa telling each other what we need at the supermarket." His eyes fixed straight ahead, Roque looks like he's either clogged with too many thoughts or occupied by none. "Which is just my point, Roque, jeez! maybe when we're finished our sessions your cock could send a little up to your brain."

"Leslie, "

"The ancient Gr—we eating soon?"

"Fifteen minutes."

"Sold! The ancient Greeks treated it as a malady—you lose your appetite over some broad in a pink flannel toga with poodles all over it and it was straight to Hippocrates for you, sports fNO! Not Again!" Roque is pulling onto the shoulder of the road. He hints at a smile and lifts a Guide Michelin from the net pocket on his door.

"Next exit," he tells Leslie while she strains to see what he's reading. "I don't remember your t-shirt being so dirty when I picked you up this morning."

"Nobody likes a smartass cop, cop. If anybody wants to know what happened we'll tell them you tied me to a tree and savaged me. They'll never believe us. Like The Purloined Letter.....Edgar Allen Poe?...Well there was this letter the police were looking for—you know about the police, don'tchyuh, Roque?—and this guy keeps it right in the middle of the table—right in the middle of his room—in full fucking view—while the cops are tearing the shit outa his place and who would suspect that what they're looking for is right there under their n "

"A smart cop, that's who."

"Just what I said! Who would suspect "

"There's always a first time, Leslie."

"For smart cops or for falling in love? You want me to tell you which othe two has a better chance omakin it to the finish line? You know, there's always a first time is a grandmother expression. It's a schoolteacher expression. It has no known meaning it might as well be pronounced hrumphtlisk. It has no known—hey!—it's a cop expression too, isn't it?" Leslie takes the Guide Michelin from Roque's lap, holds it in front of her face and jabs her finger into its chest. In a voice which she thinks is a good imitation of Joe Friday but which in reality is a bad imitation of Peter Lorre she says "You thugs are all alike, aren'tcha! You think you're always gonna get away with it, don'tcha! You think you can always stay one step ahead o us dumb cops, can'tcha? Wehhhhhhllllllllll—" She shakes the book with both hands and taps Roque on the shoulder "here comes—listen up!—", turning immediately back to her suspect and threatening, "THTHTHAYRRRSAWWWLLLWAYYYYSAHHHFFFIRRRSSSTTTTTAAY YYYMMMMeh-heh-heh!"

Roque whistles.

"Do I get the part? Or do I have to perform sodomous acts for you and your secretaries?"

"And your *secretaries*?"
"Talking about thugs, what's playin with your pals—the ones who are trying to blow up the city busstop by busstop?"

"Secretarie*sss*?"

"So what's happening with em?"

"We're working on it."

"Gee, Roque, you sure you really wanna tell me all that about the case? I don't know if I can be trusted with such a wealth of information is that why you went to Brussels that day?"

"No."

"Oh. OK. Well,,,,, Roque,,,,, whydjya go to Brussels that day? You do know which day I'm referring to, don'tchya, sweetie? By the way—it was fifteen minutes five minutes ago."
"There it is." They drive through a tall iron gate. A massive stone-and-wood inn several hundred yards ahead seems to be slurping up the narrow, tree-thick approach as if it were a string of spaghetti.
"Ooh-ooh it's gorgeous! It looks like a manor house! It looks like an *English* manor house look at those gorgeous yellow lights in the windows Roque I love it! Sure glad I decided to wear the filthy white outfit insteada the filthy blue one. So whydjya go to Brussels that day?" As they get out of the car, Leslie grabs Roque's arm and points to the side of the walkway.

"What."

"Oak Tree. You know—it's like when you own a Rolls Royce. You start noticing Rolls Royces on the street you never saw there before whydjya go to Brussels?"

"*Vous avez une résérvation?*" the *maître d'* asks Roque.

"*Non.*"

"Walk this way," Leslie says under her breath. "*Monsieur?*"

"*Madame?*"

"I wear a little metal bracelet here that says I have to be placed in a corner table at all times."

"*Oui, madame.*"

"I love corners!" Leslie announces as they follow from one rustic diningroom to another. "Can't get far enough in! Reminds me of those easy days and carefree nights splashing around in amniotic fluid." She points to the *maître d'* 's back. "I think he likes my outfit. You could tell! This is absolutely perfecto!"

"Nice, huh?"

"You did good, Roque! You did real good! You almost always do real good!"

"*Vous désirez un apéritif?*"

"Half-Perrier half-orange juice," Leslie tells the *maître d'*. "This is almost as good as a peequeneeque what are we celebrating?"
"*Une bouteille de champagne*," Roque says. "What do you mean *almost* alw " The *sommelier* hands him the wine list...................."*Une bouteille de Ruinart, s'il vous plaît.*"

"*Merci, monsieur.*"

"My trip to Brussels."

"Yeah, wh "

"*Which* I took to visit an old school friend. On my day off."

"I thought you told me you were on business."

"I wanted to impress you."

"Boy that sure did it right away! All the way to Belgium! By train! All by yourself! Like a big boy! Can't get much more impressive than that, can it Roque!"

"I wasn't all by myself. You were with me."

"So to speak. Hey I thought it wasn't macho to travel first class."

"Is that why *you* travel first class? To avoid being macho?"

"I travel first class because "

"*Merci!*" The *sommelier* pours for Roque. He tastes, nods, Leslie's glass is filled, then his own.
"To Roque's Trip To Brussels Which He Took All By Himself Like A Big Boy And Wasn't Alone On!" Leslie declares in English, waving her glass in an arc as if to include the entire diningroom in her toast before bringing it back to clink against Roque's. " because you're not gonna meet the kind of people I want for clients—or lovers—by traveling second class, shopping in Monoprix or standing in line to pay your electric bill. Why did *you* travel first class?"

"Because of the promotion."

"What promotion?"

"First-class ticket for the price of second-class every Monday in May. It was blasted all over television. To get people to extend their weekends, I guess. It was blasted all over "

"You know I don't have a television frchissakes, that little scum!"

"Wh "

"My travel agent! The creep charged me full price! 'Oh *Leslieee*, my deaearrr, my fayyyvorite cusstommerr!' I bet I am! Creep! And I call him a magician—Moe-the-Magician—he sure is! Wanna see *Leslieee*'s money disappear, boys and girls? You want it, Moe find it for you—one for the price of two! No wonder he always has a goddamn suntan! *Leslieee* sends him around the goddamn world! From the same people who gave you Trust No Dog!, we'll pay any bill stuck in front of our n........You think I can get my money back?" she asks Roque. The *maître d'* comes over with the menus. "You think I can get my money back?" she asks the *maître d'*.

*"Madame?"*

"You don't even trust me, Leslie?" Roque asks after they order.

"Gimme a break, Roque, how can you ask a question like that? Gimme a little credit here, willyuh? Of *course* I don't trust you. I'd like to know how many times the little—and I *do* mean little—sleaze has pulled this off before!"

Roque pushes his chair back. "I have to make a call".

"So do I," Leslie tells him, imitating his suddenly serious tone.

Leaning across the table, touching her forearms, he says "There's only one phone, Leslie." in the gooey lilts of someone pretending to be pretending to be indulgent. "Why don't you just go ahead."
"I-can't-right-now," she answers in a monotone. She's staring at something across the diningroom. "You-go-first."

"Why?"

"I'll-go-second." She's staring at something across the diningroom.
"Why?" Roque turns around to try to see what she's looking at. "What's the "
"I'll-tell-you-when-you-come-back," Leslie's mouth says, as if not on the same face as her paralyzed eyes. "Don't-you-have-to-make-a-call-Roque?"

Roque gets Marcel's machine, doesn't want to leave a message.

"Yo!" the kid answers before it rings. Roque can hear a keyboard crackling on a bed of rock music.

"Xa "

"I know, old man! Hey how's nature? What the fuck you wastin your time on the phone with me for you're supposed to be in the middle of gettin it regular."

"I tried the old man."

"Tget it regular? Not home."

"Good work, kid! Look—we gotta move the green circle on your calendar. Twenty-sixth she's in the States."

"Got it. He's gonna b "

"I know. We'll take care of it Monday night."

"Ygive it to er?"

"She loves it."

"Don't flatter yourself! Get me the old one?"

"Yeah. Damn thing, though, the fuckin on-button's stuck."

"Bravo, old man. When they let us out we'll go break Walkmen together—although by that time everyone'll have little receivers implanted into their ears at bir "

"Walkpeople."

"Watch that—you start soundin too much like the natives, we'll have to transfer you out to another Embassy."
"See you Monday night." Roque points his index fingers at the phone box.

"Hi! Find any mistakes yet? how's the apartment? who called? I miss you terribly! any faxes?"

"M-Ms. Br-Brittain?"

"Who else could it be, Patrick?"

"I—well—d-didn't exp—well—y-you to...a-are you—Imean.....OK? OK? M-Ms. Brittain."

"Of course I'm OK, Patrick, how sweet of you to be concerned. What page are you on?"

"I—dyou m—th-think—Imean—th-this—well...dyou m—p-print's a l-little.....s-small. Small. F-for an—Imean—annual annual r-report. Actually. Imean—those c-corporate—well—g-guys are........old. Old. A-aren't they? Ms. Br-Brittain."

"Patrick, Good Work! Where would I be without you! Probably selling t-shirts to tourists on the Rue de Rivoli. It's decided—we're enlarging the type! Which'll make it longer and more expensive but fuck it Jack Kote could afford to send the Encyclopedia Brittanica to every stockholder! Just keep reading. Anything I need to deal with right away? Then take a walk and come back and read it again. Anything I need to deal with right away?"

"No. Imean—n-no, Ms. Br-Brittain......Th-the—well—u-usual—well—M-Mrs. Daley s-says y-you don't have to do her resume after all because she found out Americans can't work in Geneva after all," From the distracted smoothness of his discourse Leslie knows Patrick must be reading from his notes. "a m-man n-named M-Martin F-Finger called to—well.....s-say he h-hopes the only reason you haven't been in touch is that you're watching television or else he's mad at you, and the o-only f-fax was—Imean—f-from some some m-magazine on the—well—R-Riviera that w-wants to.....i-interview you about how overseas Americans register to vote c-called the........R-R-Riv "

"Us."

"....."

"We're a package deal, Patrick. The magazine—they want me, they get both of us or nothing. Two for the price of two! Which is just why I called. You gotta call Moe and tell him he's a cocksucking crook and I want "

"M-M-Ms. "

"I know you can't say that, Patrick. Some day. It is my greatest hope that some day under my diligent tutelage you will attain such level of communicative finesse. For now you tell him I want my money back from the Brussels train ticket and he'll know what you're talking about and I'll tell you about it when I get back. CASH! It's too easy to just credit my account! Tell him I want it in bills with pictures of poets and statespeople on them or by Monday morning he won't have one American client left anywhere in the world and he knows I can do it!"

"W-*we* can d-do it. Actually."

"Don't get carried away, Patrick."

"Is he—dyou m—tr—is he tr-treating y-you.....Imean—OK? OK? M-Ms. Br "

"Who? Mr. Roque? Patrick, you're a sweetheart. As a matter of fact he just got finished tying me to a tree and beating me. Don't work too hard it's Saturday. But finish the fucking proofreading. Thanks for everything. Then take a walk and come back and read it again. See you Monday! Did you eat?"

"Yeah."


When Leslie reappears she marches right past Roque to the far end of the diningroom, scanning the area, finally doubling back to their table.

"Forget where we were sitting? I know a good traffic cop."

"No." Her head is locked straight on as her body maneuvers to take its seat. "No..........I was looking for Priscilla."

"Who's Priscilla?"

"I was looking for Priscilla."

"Who's Priscilla?"

"Priscilla is—Priscilla—" She finally looks at Roque. "Priscilla is the star. She's the star of the show. She's been with me for—for a good—" Squinting, Leslie nods to the beat of the calculations running in her head. "for a good at least twenty years. First she was a little flash of an image, scampering across my brain looking for lodging. I took her in, nurtured her and she grew into a strong, healthy..."

She switches to English and says to the young waiter serving their first course "stinging demand in my pussy...*Merci* and finally.........." then continues in French once he's left. "reached her prime as an exquisitely evolved this is champion goat cheese, Roque, you should've ordered it! creature, with a meticulously detailed story, the very *thought* of whose existence—even without evoking the endless minutiae of each exhaustive scene—is enough to....hh..hh...." Leslie starts grinding in her chair "make meeeeehh......hh......hh....", wrapping her open mouth around deep, wide shudders of breath.

"Leslie!"

"Oooh-oooh!   WHA-ATT was THA-ATT?" she says, pantomiming prissily brushing herself off and straightening her clothes. "Aa-and..........Aa-and....."

"For the love of God, Leslie, *what?*"

"And before? Just before when you were about to make your call?" She raises her eyebrows and leans across the table, whispering with surprise and reverence. "I saw her. Over there. Peeking out of the kitchen. *My* Priscilla." Twisting in his chair, Roque stares into the empty corner of the diningroom. "The impertinent little trollop works in the scullery of the Auberge des Deux Rivières in Normandy and I never knew it! Well!" Leslie spits indignantly in a British accent which brings Roque's eyes immediately back, "Uncle Roland will see that she's dealt with appropriately for THAT! Won't He!"
"For the—" Roque's attention shuttles between the far corner behind him and his grasp on Leslie's forearms. "you're kidding, right?" He points his index fingers. Leslie looks across the diningroom to the kitchen door.
"Roque I saw her after all these y—look! If someone would've said Here! we're gonna put you in a room for the next two decades and we'll do your laundry and feed you—in that order—and all you have to do is come up with the most precise possible description of Priscilla "

"What's her last name?"

"She doesn't *have* a fucking last name frchri—that's a cop question! She's never *needed* a last name!" Leslie shrieks to the assembled patrons as she flails into a passing waiter's hip. " with the most precise possible description of Priscilla, then that—that.....*being* who poked her head out of the kitchen is what I'd've come up with..........I guess her last name could be Bloomswell cause that's her uncle's last name and he's the one who takes care of her. I mean she lives in his house he's her guardian." She says "Priscilla Bloomswell" to herself several times then squints toward the kitchen. "I wonder if she's properly naked under that frock like she was told to be."

"Well let me have it."

"What?"

"Priscilla's story."

"Can't."

"Why not?"

"Because the only way I could get through even the introduction would be if you were standing by with a monster erection ready to whisk me right off into the john and fuck me into unconsciousness the second I finished the last word. You saw what happened when I just brought the subject up that wasn't playacting, Roque!"

"You got it."

"Really?"

Roque nods.

"Really."

Roque nods.

"Because otherwise I'll just have to take care of it myself."

"OK. Go ahead."

"Right here."

"All right, Leslie, I said OK."

"At the table."

"LESL "

"It's Victorian London. There's a men's club. Very exclusive, very small. Thirty members or so here comes the fucking waiter again let's wait until he deals with this!"

"Maybe you want to invite him to sit in on the story."

"Maybe I want to invite him to take care of me after I've finished............................................................Usually no more than twenty there at any given time. The men arrive late in the evening—around ten—after they've eaten a proper silent dinner at home with their musty wives. 'I'm going to the club.' And stay until well after midnight drinking brandy with each other in dark rich leather armchairs arranged in intimate groupings on intricate oriental carpets of burgundies and golds and rusts. Bankers, businessmen and industrialists, ranging in age from forty to eighty, they always wear fine dark elegant suits with waistcoats and pocketwatches and look as if each just bought a new pair of shoes before walking through the door. They smell of sweet cigars and expensive imported colognes. Some of them have full mustaches. Some are very handsome. All are removed from their central storehouse of lust by the thinnest veneer of social propriety and circumstantial convention, their appearance of restraint being nourished by external rather than internal imperatives.

"Sir Roland Bloomswell. In his mid-fifties, Sir Roland Bloomswell is a tall, thin bachelor with a firm body, thick silver hair and a face whose ugliness is exotic and attractive. His ugliness is mysterious and draws you in and gives him authority. You wonder what he's hiding inside the irregular angles of his pock-marked jaw, and you know you'll never find out unless he wants you to. His outrageous wealth is equaled in degree only by his faultless discretion; nobody knows how much money he has or certainly where it comes from. In fact, he owns the men's club. But nobody knows that either.

"Sir Roland's brother and sister-in-law sailed to America for what was to be a relatively short trip, having left their twelve-year-old daughter Priscilla, an only child, under her uncle's care in his vast mansion in Hempstead. Priscilla had of course spent time in Uncle Roland's presence before—at Christmas dinners, or when he came to the house to discuss business with her father—but their interactions were limited to a vague awareness that they were occupying the same general space, and when one of them got up and left, the other of them immediately ceased to exist. Neither Priscilla nor even her mother had ever been to Uncle Roland's house before. The day her parents went on their trip it was her father who dropped Priscilla off at dawn.

"If when she stood in Uncle Roland's entrance hall for the first time Priscilla sensed a strange and exciting tension in the air, then she felt that strange and exciting tension filter through her pores and absorb into her bloodstream when Uncle Roland called her into his study four days later and informed her that her parents had drowned in a dreadful collision at sea and that he was to become her legal guardian. He would be arranging, he announced, for a tutor to come give her lessons in the classics and training in etiquette, while he occupied himself with the rest, and most important part, of her education. He then dismissed his niece, who went to bed without shedding a tear and awoke the next morning as if she'd been an orphan all her life.

"For three months after that evening in his study, Priscilla saw very little of Uncle Roland, her practical needs being met by Mrs. Collright, the housekeeper, and her lifeline to the world of ideas and style being tendered by Sir Geoffrey Lycombe, a close friend of Uncle Roland's who had recently retired from service at the bar as a Queen's Counsel. Priscilla left the mansion infrequently during that time and when she did it was always to accompany Mrs. Collright on a household errand.

"This did not mean, however, that Priscilla was unaware of Uncle Roland's constant nearness. Like the blind with a sharpened sense of smell, her lack of physical contact with him heightened her receptivity to the strange and exciting tension which, she came to realize, was generated by and emanated from Uncle Roland himself. She was able to sense his relative location by the level the strange exciting tension reached. As if there were a homing device implanted in him and a tracker in her. When she was in her sitting room, for instance, learning about Ulysses and the Sirens from Sir Geoffrey 'those nawwwwwtteee Sirens!' and Uncle Roland was reading his newspaper in the library two floors down, the strange exciting tension was like a layer of lotion on her skin, caressing it, clinging to it, smelling sweet, but otherwise subdued. If next Uncle Roland moved to his bedroom, directly below hers, the strange exciting tension intensified and Priscilla's whole body felt wrapped in a tight elastic stocking. Should circumstances then bring Uncle Roland past the door of her suite, the strange exciting tension clamped onto Priscilla's temples like forceps, pressing, pressing, squeezing in and pulling up until the blood in her head began to whirlpool and crash into the backs of her eyes. No matter where Uncle Roland was in relation to her in his huge house, Priscilla heard the hum of the strange exciting tension. It could not be separated from the air. Or the lining of her brain. Like the white-sound background buzz in a reading hall, it was there to drown out all distraction, and to let in only those stimuli which were needed at the moment.

"Uncle Roland wielded his absence with mastery: he was always almost there. He had always just left the room Priscilla was entering. She could smell him; she knew they'd just missed. It was always his footsteps she heard coming down the hallway out of which she'd just turned. Mrs. Collright was always just clearing his place setting when Priscilla was sitting down to be served. She could always hear his voice next door to wherever she was, see the last streamer of smoke swirling up from his cigar in an ashtray in the library when she wandered in for a book. With his absence, with his almost presence, Uncle Roland teased and frustrated Priscilla, lured and tricked her. He engaged her in battle. He conquered her. He always won. With his almost presence he excited her, with his almost presence he seduced her. With his almost presence he controlled her. By the time Uncle Roland was ready to receive her for their first meeting since his announcement of her parents' death ninety days before, Priscilla had already become his.

"On the eve of her thirteenth birthday, as she was finishing dinner, Priscilla was informed by Mrs. Collright that the master of the house expected her in his study forthwith. Priscilla stood and said she would go first to her suite to wash, and Mrs. Collright wondered whether she'd made herself clear when she'd said forthwith.

"Her fair freckled skin flushing, and little pearls of perspiration threading from her forehead down the waist-length thick red ringlets framing her face, Priscilla knocked on the study door. There was no answer. For ten seconds she browsed through the pictures in her brain: Priscilla opening the door unsummoned, Priscilla fleeing into the streets of London and beyond, Priscilla as a grown-up elegant lady coming to spend the evening with Sir Roland, Priscilla as a little baby in a cradle of flowers rocked by Uncle Roland's hand. As she lifted her arm to knock a second time, 'Enter!' she heard Uncle Roland's voice.

"He was sitting in a burgundy leather armchair in the middle of the darkened room, the brass-and-green-glass desk-lamp behind his left shoulder seeming to be spitefully fighting back the dim light as it seeped from the fireplace before him.

" 'I say! Don't just stand there, young lady! Close the door and come let us have a look at you!'

"Priscilla approached the chair. Uncle Roland nodded at the spot where he wanted her to stand. While he smoothed a wrinkle from her plaid wool skirt and fluffed a puffed starched sleeve of her white blouse, he told her to sit on her heels at his feet.

"Out of awe and curiosity, Priscilla obeyed. Though dreadfully frightened by this mysterious man, and the countless resounding corners of his immense house, and his power so compelling and complete it gave off a sound of its own even when he was nowhere to be seen, she was also uncontrollably attracted by him. Attracted to him, but more accurately by him. He was the fiend in the cheap horror movie calling his hypnotized victim from a phonebooth and giving her the one-syllable code-word which would make her eyes go luminescent and lead her to walk off the cliff. Priscilla knew he'd been pulling her in from the beginning, constantly pulling her in, in the containment of his mansion, on the wave of his smell, by the presence of his absence, knew he was pulling her in at this instant with the suction of his inhales, on the line of his eyes, along the current of his brain. But she lacked both the maturity to measure how deep she was going and the courage to ask. So she just hung up the phone and walked off the cliff. 'Perfect,' said Uncle Roland.

" 'Pardon, sir?'

"Sir Roland asked Priscilla how she found her new life in his home. She answered that it was fine. He asked about her relationship with Mrs. Collright and with Sir Geoffrey. She said Mrs. Collright was allright, then smiled and spoke more quickly, saying Sir Geoffrey always had a story to tell and that she liked him alot and that he promised that when he came tomorrow he would bring a rare old book which once belonged to Queen Victoria herself with beautiful pictures painted in gold. Sir Roland said this pleased him and that Sir Geoffrey had told him she was a delightful student. And so it was, he informed his niece, that 'you are now ready for the next...dimension...of your education. This is a dimension, Priscilla,' he said in a soft, paced voice, fixing into her eyes in the faint light as she looked up at him from the floor, 'which I must personally supervise. And which will commence this evening.' You OK with this Roque so far or you wanna take a break? You haven't even picked up your fork frchrissakes."

"Leslie did you read this somewhere?"

"I haven't even gotten into the story yet. I mean the part that—that matters. The part I'll need my little waiter standing by for. I'm just giving you a little background so you know wh—you know, unity of time, place, action—like the classics. Like the classics Sir Geoffrey and Priscilla are reading together. So you know it doesn't take place in Japan next week or on the Space Shuttle in Biblical times."

"Did you read this somewhere?"

"I'm going to the bathroom. Why don't you eat a little, it's a shame. Kids are starving in the penthouse of the Ritz." Leslie gets up and starts walking away from the table.

"If You Touch Yourself In There" Roque yells, jumping half out of his seat "So Help Me God", pointing at her "I'LL NEVER LAY A HAND ON YOU AGAIN!", suddenly realizing every eye in the dining room is on him......................He sits down and starts eating.

"There's Nothing To Touch About," she yells back, almost out of sight. "We Haven't Even Gotten To The Table Of Contents Yet...............................................................................................
........................................................................................................
........................

...Is it good? Must be freezing cold. Maybe you can ask them to reheat it. It's a shame...Mine's delicious."

"I don't know how you can eat and talk at the same time. I can't even eat and listen."

"I've seen this movie before. And besides, this is all giftwrapping. There's really only one paragraph in this whole enterprise that matters. I'm just stalling." Leslie crooks her neck toward the door to the kitchen. "She's gotta come out again sooner or later........And then we'll kidnap her and take her with us!" she snaps in a Wicked Witch voice, her eyes spitting fire at Roque.

"What'll we do with her?"

"Ifygotta ask where it is yshouldn't be there in the first place. Sir Roland slipped his hand into the pocket of his jacket and produced an exquisitely wrapped box—a small cube covered in lush black velvet tied with magnificent white antique French lace. He held it out to Priscilla, who was so stunned by its beauty she was afraid to reach for it. Sir Roland told her with his eyes, however, that he would be displeased if she did not take it from him immediately, so she picked at the lace with her chubby fingers until the wrappings gave way. On a wide black velvet ribbon, inside a box of intricately carved ivory from the Orient, Priscilla found a breathtaking cameo wearing a tiny diamond at her neck. She stared at the cameo, then at Uncle Roland, then back at the gift, then again up into Uncle Roland's tranquil face. He nodded. Her hands fumbled with the treasure, carefully removing it, resting its box on the floor beside her. As she lifted the ribbon toward her neck, Uncle Roland reached out, stayed her hand, and, to her bewilderment, took the object from her.

" 'This cameo, Priscilla,' he explained in a near-whisper, 'represents the power that binds you to me. You will wear it every time we are together. And only when we are together. You will put it on just before we meet and remove it once our time in each other's presence has ended. You will wear it whether we are to share our space at a given moment with others or whether we are to be alone. But it is never to be on your body when I am not with you. As it is always to be when I am. Will you obey me, Priscilla?'

"The strange exciting tension had become so acute against Priscilla's skin, the pressure of the forceps so tight onto her temples—there in the sealed space of Uncle Roland's firelit study which smelled of his cigars and the fabric of his suit, there on the floor at the pinpoint of his feet, in the ownership of his eyes, where what she'd never had the knowledge to name but always wanted was now not only possible but required—the strange exciting tension had turned to such a strident siren in her skull that her voice could not compete with it and died inside her throat. But Uncle Roland knew that she meant yes.

"Holding the cameo, and in the tenderest of tones, Uncle Roland asked, 'Do you see that chair over there at the desk, Priscilla?' Priscilla nodded. 'When you disrobe for me just now you are to remove an article of clothing, here, in front of me, neatly fold it, and cross the room to drape it over the back of the chair. Then you are to return to me to do the same with the next. And so forth.' Priscilla rose and began undressing as naturally and unabashedly as if Uncle Roland had asked her to please hand him the ashtray, or as if it were Mrs. Collright who was wanting her to step out of her frock in the privacy of her chamber so that it could be ironed before the party. Uncle Roland watched her with quiet concentration, his legs crossed, his chin on the back of his hand, his elbow on the armrest, like when in his box at Covent Garden enjoying a opera. Once she returned to the center of the room, totally naked, from her last trip to the desk, he handed the cameo back to her.

" 'We are together now, aren't we, Priscilla?'

" 'Yes, sir.'

" 'Then put the cameo around your neck.'

"The drapes in Sir Roland's study were wine-red velvet and when drawn, as now, they billowed across the entire wall to his left. 'Stand over there, Priscilla.' His voice relaxed, almost tuneful, he turned his body imperceptibly and nodded to the angle formed by this wall and that dominated by the massive Italian-marble fireplace-mantle before him. As long as she was moving, with a little task to accomplish—undressing, tying the cameo around her neck, padding over to the corner—Priscilla was all business and preoccupation, no more self-conscious than a child doing her lessons alone in her room. 'Turn to face me.' Now stopped between the dark velvet and the velvet light, she became aware not necessarily of the fact of her nakedness or the morality of her nakedness before her Uncle Roland, but of the potency of her nakedness, the significance of her nakedness in his study, the way the study was absorbing her nakedness and nourishing itself with its perfection. She became aware of this but because she could not understand or even define it, she fidgeted in her corner, looking to her Uncle Roland for direction. For her next assignment.

"Sir Roland was back at Covent Garden, or maybe listening to someone speak, contemplating the presentation, slowly nodding from time to time, breathing evenly, slowly nodding, receiving the data. Analyzing it. Priscilla was on her own. Priscilla was thirteen tomorrow, a shade shorter than average, pink and a little chubby. Just a little. More soft than chubby. The artist had taken the strain of pink in her skin and mixed it deep and fiery for her long curls which were so thick as to be all but unruly, and for her pubic hair which was just as red and dense and fighting for its womanly space between her fleshy adolescent tummy and thighs. Priscilla fidgeted. 'Turn to face me, Priscilla.' The round wide outlines of her breasts were drawn and waiting to be further filled. They looked as if they would be heavy breasts whose undersides would dip, then cup upward. She tried to talk to Uncle Roland with her eyes. She didn't think to cover herself; she just wanted to know what to do next. At one point, when her restless hand brushed against the front of her vagina, with the black ribbon around her neck and the strokes of pinks and reds and golds spraying from her skin and her hair and the fire, she looked like a little

English-schoolgirl version of Botticelli's Venus.

" 'That will be enough for this evening, Priscilla.'

"For the next year Mrs. Collright and Priscilla did errands. With Sir Geoffrey she visited the cultural and historic milestones of Western Civilization from the table in her sitting room, and once Uncle Roland even allowed Sir Geoffrey take her to see the Sistine Ceiling. She continued to see little of Uncle Roland during the day but, after the initial torturesome week following the first session in his study, during which he did not summon her once and paid no attention to her whatsoever, she was expected at his door every evening at eight. She would finish dinner, bathe, soften and sweeten her skin with lotions and perfumes of Uncle Roland's choosing, tie the cameo around her neck and dress in a frock no different from that which she would wear at most other moments. 'Enter!' She neither spoke to anyone of her time spent in the study nor even gave it a thought of her own during the day; the being which Uncle Roland was cultivating within its privacy had little to do with the child who left her neatly folded napkin on the dinner table at seven-fifteen each evening, and the event for which he was preparing her was too monumental to have to share her attention with the names of England's most famous battlesites. I bet you wanna know what went on in there, you pervert, right?"

"*ME*, pervert? *ME*, pervert?"

"You're raising your voice again, Roque! You're gonna give French tourists a bad name, sweetie."

"*ME*, pervert?"

"Where's my emergency-back-up waiter?" Leslie looks around the diningroom.

"Hey wait a minute!"

"No it's OK I just want dessert."

"I think he gave up last time you waved him away."

"He'll come back. They all do."

"What went on in there?"

"There he is! See, I told you."

"What went " The waiter hands dessert menus to Leslie and Roque.

*"Merci."*

"Was monsieur not satisfied with his meal?"

"It's a Scheherazade thing," Leslie answers for *monsieur*. Listen—what time's your shift over?"

*"Madame?"*

*"LESlie!"*

"Mousse au chocolat. Just don't leave town, OK?"

*"Madame?"*

*"Lesl Une tarte tatin, s'il vous plâit."*

*"Merci, monsieurdame."*

"By the way," Leslie says to the waiter as he leaves the table.

*"Madame?"*

She reels in the young man's head with her crooking finger "In the kitchen....." and squints close up to his face "your...kitchen there?........", her voice lowering into a complicitous question mark.

"Lessss-Liee-Eee."

*"Oui, madame?"*

" there's a little—a...young lady who seems to be part of your fine team here...a.....young, uhhh....well we were just wonderi—we would just like to thank her personally for all the fi "

"But Since We Know This Would Not Be Possible," Roque interrupts, glaring at Leslie, "we were wondering if you could do it f'"

" if you could let her know we'd like to See Her, Please," Leslie interrupts back, smiling at Roque.

*"Merci, monsieurdame,"* the waiter lilts in the inflection of his trade, and slips away.

"COULD YOU JUST TELL US HER NAME?" Leslie calls after him.

"What went on in there?"

"In where, Roque?"

"YOU KNOW VERY W "

"OK OK. God knows we wouldn't wanna get you agitated, huh? Actually we're a couple sentences away from the good part if we don't spend a whole helluva lotta time on what went on in there so to make a long fantasy short Uncle Roland basically taught Priscilla—evening by evening, session after session—about her body, and to appreciate the aesthetic and scientific wonderwork that it was. Although during that year she remained a virgin in the strictest sense of the term, she learned much about the male body as well and of course about the ultimately sensual purposes to which all this bounty could be put. Guided by his instincts and his sense of perfection, Sir Roland proved the most creative and patient of pedagogues, skillfully manipulating a variety of tutorial tools to the degree that Priscilla's attention span and level of sophistication could accommodate them.

"As did Socrates on his interactive walks under the trees with his students, Uncle Roland transformed discussion into instruction, helping Priscilla find the answers to his questions or hers through the reach and power of her own intellect. As did the ancient Hebrew scholars with their young disciples, Uncle Roland read to Priscilla as she sat before him on the floor following the words upsidedown. No subject was forbidden and the only human act considered obscene was war. They read from the Kama Sutra and from the Song of Songs. They read from the precious little secret pamphlets of erotica in which Victorian England hid its sublimated passion.

"Together they explored their senses, spent entire evenings in experiments with smells and tastes and sounds. Sometimes Priscilla was blindfolded with a black silk scarf to heighten her sensitivity to non-visual stimuli, especially the stimulus of touch—the tenderest of touch and the most severe—until Uncle Roland deemed it time for Priscilla to see that which she was touching, or that with which she was being touched, and then the blindfold would come off. Objects and foods and fabrics from the most exotic to the most commonplace, from the bazaars of Arabia and the shelves of the local ironmongery, walked through Uncle Roland's study during Priscilla's training year. There were musical instruments. A white Persian cat.

"Uncle Roland and Priscilla progressed through blocks of evenings where no two sessions were alike, and spans where they locked into a theme and played it to its exhaustion. Once in the middle of the year Priscilla put on a grown-up-lady hat that Uncle Roland had had made for her in Paris, and they were suddenly off on a month-long project of draping her body in every type of apparel imaginable, dressing her as a ballerina, as a boy, as a tart, as a rani, a soldier, a baby, undressing her totally except for any number of different hats and pair of shoes or ankle-hugging boots and her cameo of course. Priscilla was caressed in fur and whipped in satin. She painted her lips, she washed her face. Sir Roland reddened her nipples with rouge, wrapped her mummy-like in white organza. She was Cleopatra, Annie Oakley, Joan of Arc, Salome, Queen Victoria, George Washington, Sitting Bull, Spartacus, Robin Hood, both Othello and Desdemona. Do you think they went to Wisconsin to get the apples to make your tart where the Fuck Is Our Dessert!"

"I think the kid's afraid to come back. I think he must be at the border by now."

"So Let Em Send Priscilla!" Leslie's voice sweetens. "Priscilla would.....serve us...OK OK Roque OK! So the goal of this whole thing and there's obviously so much more I mean I could do days on just the Paris-hat scene alone but—and *have*—but y—or on just the air inside the study and how Uncle Roland manipulated the purity of silence and alternated it with overwhelming sound, or the feelings which bred there and made everything right once she entered its familiar insulation—but you gotta be back writing parking tickets Monday morning so I'll have mercy and keep it to the basics so the goal of this whole year for Priscilla was to first have her love and appreciate and have fun with her own body and then—well, first-first learn *about* her body—her physicality and physicality in general—and then "

"Will monsieurdame be "

"OOHHH!"

" having coffee afterwards?" the waiter asks as he serves dessert.

"HOH-LEE-SHITT you scared me!.......Only if your little scullery maid brings it in to us while we're in the bathroom."

"*Madame?*"

"Bout ten minutes max—I'm almost there—don't start without me."

"Non, merci! We won't be having coffee. Non, merci!" Roque shoos the waiter away.

" and then ultimately to know that her body—actually her whole self—her whole selfness—was her key to whatever she'd want in the world. It was like a stamp collection. Uncle Roland was giving this to her—eventually leaving thiss...thiss.....knowledge and power—commodity—with her—as if it were a rare stamp collection which she could tuck away in the bank vault and get out when she needed to trade it against something. Or wanted to trade it against something. With the right people of course and under the right circumstances, which was the whole point of the exercise and what it all was leading up to. Or musical talent—it was as if he'd seen early on that she could play the piano and had brought in all manner of internationally acclaimed vituosi to teach her. Well Uncle Roland saw the talent the instant he looked into her eyes in his study when he told her about her parents and he watched her for awhile without her even knowing he was watching....And then he set about teaching her to play the most musical instrument of all. So here it comes.....So here it comes...Someday I'll tell you more about the rest. So here it comes. Yready?"

"If I said no?"

"I'd talk about something else I've seen this movie before. You asked me who Priscilla was I'm telling you."

"I'm ready."

"We're back at the men's club. It's the eve of Priscilla's fourteenth birthday it's exactly one year after the cameo evening. Mid-December, raw raw cold outside. Inside, as in Sir Roland's house and especially his study, the gilded warmth cracks outward from the fireplaces and slithers through the lush threads of the fabrics and the rich grains of the woods, harvesting their noble comfort along the way before spreading into the spaces of the rooms. The twenty-five men in the main parlor are sitting as usual in their Venetian red armchairs grouped for discussion or angled for semi-privacy. Their conversation is a smooth blanket of quiet politesse, rippled with a random rolling laugh, or an occasional controlled expletive offered in courteous disagreement to an opinion slightly steeped in spirits.

"Between ten-thirty and eleven—closer to eleven—several of the men hear the parlor door open and turn to see who has arrived. There is a gasp and other men look up, then more gasps, and exclamations of shock. Soon all awareness in the room is driven to the entranceway. The voices settle, subdue, disappear into breathless silence. Stinging breathless silence.

"In an impeccably cut suit of a gray so dark as to be almost black, Sir Roland stands framed by the thick mahogany doorway. His chin is lifted a degree, as if he were playing to the balcony while still looking his leading lady in the eyes. The long proud line running from his gleaming shoes to his silver hair seems to have become the central vertical axis of the parlor itself. Resting in the pocket of his vest, his right hand has swept the front of his jacket aside. His left arm is around Priscilla who, except for her cameo, is totally naked.

"Both Sir Roland and Priscilla appear exceedingly serene, presenting themselves with repose nearing indifference. As if this were not the first time ever that a woman has penetrated the sanctity of the club. Especially a fourteen-year-old woman with mother-of-pearl skin and an uncontainable fire in the hair licking her shoulders and thighs. Whose rounded heavy breasts dip soft, then cup upward into nipples crimsoned with a hint of rouge much lighter than the shade on her full lips. A fourteen year old woman putting a parlor of patrician millionaires to shame in the ease with which she defiantly exhibits her bareness before their agitated self-conscious lust. Ah, Uncle Roland taught her well! I think I want tea after all."

"Keep going."

"Ah, she proved a fine pupil, our Priscilla! I'm ordering tea you want coffee?"

"Keep going, For The Love OGod!"

"HAH! You're gonna need a quick-fix trip to the bathroom sooner n I will! HAH! HAH HAH HAH! I Love Itt! Never thought I'd live to see the day, mister hardened impassive seen-it-all-and-then-some

Poh-leece-In-Spec-Tawr! Well, I think that's all for today, you know what they say about too much of a good thing, don'tchya Roque? Maybe we can pick up riiiiight where we left off on another one of our little weekends away from the big city where you've supposedly seen it all so nothing phases yAAHHCH! "

Roque takes half the tablecloth with him as he lurches forward and grabs Leslie's forearms. "Will yFor The L "

"WheeeeeeeWHWH! My-y Goh-od!" Leslie says, staring at Roque's crotch while she waves the waiter over. "Un thé au lait—two teabags—and I think monsieur wants a good "

"*CAFE!*" Roque snaps. He settles back into his seat as Leslie reaches over to try to touch his jeans.

"Damn!—too late. Yknow if the sultan woulda treated Sheherazade this way she'da been packed and outa there on the next magic carpet.....After poisoning him in his sl—after cutting off his balls and then poisoning him in his sleep!"

"Sheherazade wasn't calling the shots!"

"Don't be so sure, sports fans!......BUTT!—Priscilla is *not* serene and certainly not indifferent. She is merely doing—supremely—as Uncle Roland has taught her: establishing her majesty through appearing unaffected by the emotional excesses of others. Until such time as it profits her to be, or at least to seem, affected thereby. Kinda like you, Roque.....maybe she's really a Police Inspector, the little...dyever see a little English girl with red hair runnin around the Quai des Orfèvres?...Never mind!...With a cigar in her mouth?...Never mind!...Barkin orders at some OK OK OK! Priscilla at this moment, standing in the parlor doorway, is in fact so" Leslie leans forward and whispers "you know this scullery business could be a front."

"Good. OK. Fine," Roque says,

"And a damn good one too! All the way up here. Must have operatives all over the place reporting back to her from the capital."

smacking the table top. "Right You Are! No More For Today! Ah, here comes our coffee—just what I need before getting right up and out and hitting the road! Merci!"

"Great! We're even! Priscilla at this moment, standing tranquilly in the parlor doorway, is in fact so fiercely excited, that little prisms of wetness are sparkling on her vulva and trickling in delicate tracks down the inside of her right thigh. The thigh that's touching Uncle Roland's thigh. Forced up against it—for even though he knows she is prepared for this evening, Sir Roland feels compelled, out of prudence or possessiveness or excitement of his own, to keep his arm fast over her right shoulder and diagonally down her back. To pull her, his fingers fanned wide across her left side, almost too tightly to him. As if she were trying to get away. Although she isn't. Pinching one last particle of pepper into the spectacle at the doorway. Blending one last nuance into Priscilla's awareness of the moment. And the men's appreciation of the scene.

"Is that why she was excited?"

"You're a goner, Roque—once the sultan starts asking questions you know he's "

"Why was Priscilla excited?"

"Hey is this like a police investigation? Huh? I love it!" She crinkles her brow. "Ma'am, could you in the best of your recollection please tell us why on the evening of she's excited....." Leslie continues, giving her pal Joe Friday his voice back, "she's excited...not because she's on display. Being on display has become Priscilla's natural state and destiny. It's not so much the fact that she's naked before twenty-five men of Uncle Roland's club that's making the little prisms drip down, as much as the fact that they're clothed. It's the sublime contrast for her between the crisp authority of their perfect suits and the soft vulnerability of her skin. It's the exquisite incessant exchange of roles, their secure state of dress mastering her in her unprotected nakedness which masters them in their dark desire.

" 'Good evening, gentlemen,' Sir Roland says, smoothly and slowly, with a quick nod. 'I present to you....my niece. Priscilla.' He pauses a moment, his grip around her body no less strong, and then in the tender melodic voice with which he's addressed her in his study, bids 'Priscilla, enter and greet my colleagues.'

"He releases her, taps her on her bottom, and Priscilla goes into the parlor."

# XI

# THE SHIITAKE MUSHROOMS

"What are they then, if they ain't fuckin soybeans!"

"I don't know, Marcel. I just know I told them no soybeans. Does it matter as long as they're not soybeans? I know these guys. They're pals. They wouldn't give me soybeans if I said no soybeans." Marcel pokes into his plate with precision, working the tips of his fork and knife as if dissecting a frog in chemistry class.

"Don't get much bettern that, does it, Fairy Godmother in bed with the Vietnamese-restaurant mafia! Don't get much bettern "

"They're Greeks," Claude tells Jacques.

"Egg foo moussaka!" he sneers, glancing around the table for a reaction.

"Tell us your undercover work's better than your nightclub act, old man."

"Why don't you ask your girlfriend, old man?" Jacques kicks Roque's chair.

"Then it wouldn't be undercover work, would it?" Claude says calmly. She offers the platter of curried shrimp to Marcel, who waves her away.

"Tell us she has brains in a" Jacques grabs a couple shrimp "ddition to all that beauty!" as the platter floats past him.

Claude says "Thanks, Dupuy."

"I was talkin about "

"the shrimp," Thierry finishes for Jacques.

Holding his fork up to his face, Marcel looks like he's about to have a conversation with the slimy brown disk on the tines.

"Shiitake mushrooms," the kid tells him with his mouth full.

Marcel drops his shiitake mushroom back onto his plate and waves his hand over the table. "Gimme some more rice!"

"Sounds like a fuckin disease," Jacques says.

"Moren that!" Marcel shouts at Roque. "So in one o my magazines there was this article about this old guy in Singapore who—he's half I think his mother was a chink from Singapore and his father was British somethin like that—who collects religious art. Not just on the Cathedral. Everythin—from all over—Europe, the Orient, America,"

"What's religious art in America," Jacques asks, "the Golden Arches?"

"Why don't I call my girlfriend, old man, and get back to you on that one?"

"Don't have to bother," the kid tells Roque. "She'll be callin *you* in about an hour."

Roque looks over at the equipment in the middle of the room. "She called you just before you got here—left a message on your machine. Said she'd catch yagain about nine-thirty. After some kinda meeting.......Don't worry ol man, I only listen to the good parts."

"Yeah he turns it off just after she starts talkin about chokin on it!" Jacques twangs. "Kid never could stomach anyone gettin sick."

Roque glances at Claude, Claude looks at the blow-up of Leslie running past Brentano's.

" even Aztec and Incan pieces, Brahmanism, Shinto, and not just what's in museums he collects sculptures and paintings and objects na—icons—naturally but whole pieces ochurches like walls of churches and tiles from the floors of mosques. Guy got pieces oheadstones. Got a whole tombstone from a fuckin animal cemetery in Wales Lord knows how he gimme some more rice willyuh? Has robes come from priests and American Indian healers some ancient ancient pieces crucifixes rosaries sacred beads. From North Africa I think, the beads. And books—scrolls, Egyptian stuff, you can't imagine—it was all—Hebrew texts—it was all in this article. Tried to get his hands on the Shroud oTurin, for the love oGod! Offered millions for it if—if that gives yany—still offerin still won't give it a rest. Says it'd be safer with him and yknow what, the fucker's probly rhhhc hh" Marcel holds up his hand to stop Thierry from coming around to pound on his back. "...............Has this mouth organ from a slave church in the State of Virginia. And voodoo dolls, black magic shit. Witches. Stuff they use in witch rituals. Ycan't you just can't take it all in it was all in this interview get back here kid, where ygoin?

"So I was readin—couple years ago this was a couple years ago—and the interviewer wants tknow if the Shroud's the only piece he really wants but can't get his hands on and he says no. Interviewer wants to know what else, The Dead Sea Scrc hh chc...................
........................................chHe says there's somechhc somethin else. Getta—get this—getta Loada Th—Get Your Ass In Here, Kid!"

"You know we all know what it is, old man," Thierry whines, back from the kitchen with fresh bottles of beer, "even Claude here knows wh "

Claude looks up peacefully from her plate and adjusts her baseball cap. "If these guys know all this already "

"These Guys Know These Guys Know What I Fuckin Need Em T—the other treasure, he says, is a miniature copy othe original floorplan for Notre Dame de Paris that was when the—in eleven sixty-three when the Pope laid the—Alexander Three—laid the first stone with Louis the Seventh, they—and Maurice de Sully—they—the Bishop of Paris—they put under the stone this miniature copy othe floorplan with this secret message on it about salvation this secret message a missionary just come back from China brought to the Pope, some—somethin about bein visited by the Lord and salvation. Pope transcribes the message onto the back othe floorplan just before they place the stone. Almost a century later this Cl—twelve fifty—this Clerk of Works, Jehan de Chelles, starts rebuildin the Cathedral before it's even finished—new facade on the transept, the nave—redoes the nave. Has the miniature removed from under the cornerstone. Hides it in this underground tunnel. Thinks it's the safest place around since he's the only one knows it's there since he poisoned all the poor fuckers who dug it since "

" since he didn't want em rattin to the Pope," the kid says, "since the whole reason he built the tunnel in the first place was to accom "

" was so the priests could get laid without havin to leave town," Jacques says, using Marcel's empty rice-carton as an ashtray. "Fuckin guy thought of everything. His *true* contribution to Gallic culture. Man of priorities. There was this convent about five hundred meters away." His hands in his pockets, he gets up and starts over to the window. "Center of sacred geography on one end of the tunnel, center of sacred pussy on the other."

"De Chelles planned to come back one day nclean up," Marcel continues. "But he dies first. And this guy in Singapore—name's Blyster—Tai Yang Blyster but that's not his real name it's like an alias, guy's a real—it's the name he uses doin his collectin—guy's a real he's a recluse-type. Like that American fucker—who was that

Amer" He waves his hand at Thierry.

"Howard Hughes."

"Yeah good work, kid. De Chelles's diaries—heat this for me, willyuh kid, I gotta go piss!— show up a half-dozen years ago in some Goddamn Cellar In THE LOUVRE WHEN" Marcel's voice gets louder the deeper down the hallway he disappears. "THEY MOVE THE FINANCE MINISTRY OUTA THAT WING TO RENOVATE. DIARIES TALK ABOUT HIDIN THE MINIATURE FLOORPLAN, ABOUT There's No Rush TGo back nget it. Give the location."

"More or fuckin less," Jacques snivels.

"MORE LESS THAN MORE," Thierry yells on his way out of the kitchen.
"He gives the fuckin location! Gives exact coordinates in all directions."
"Here, ol man. The mushrooms reproduced in the microwave. Ygot a whole new generation to match wits with."
"Fairy Godmother here wants to know why this joker in Singapore never went in and ripped the fuckin thing off before."

"No I don't, Dupuy," Claude says with seraphic composure.

"The man" Roque serves Marcel another heap of rice before being waved at. "was busy looking at his guilt about raping Western Civilization.

"In a train," Jacques adds.

"Who Gives A Shit What Belongs To Western Civilization?" Marcel barks, making a steamy little rice-fort in the northeastern sector of his plate. "A thought like that don't enter Tai Yang Blyster's mind long enough to be chased out. Fuckin Dead Sea Scrolls belong to *God* and you better believe if he could—in Blyster's mind he *is* Western Civilization because he's bought half of it and the other half's on lay-away. No, bec—Eastern Civilization too, for that matter—no because when de Chelles stashed the miniature the whole known world consisted of a couple underground tunnels, his piss pot and the half-built Cathedral which since then there's three-quarters of a millennium it's spent bein mutilated, destroyed, bein put back together—above ground under ground sometimes more under than above, over and over, you know what the fuckers di—in the eighteenth century, you know wh—in the eighteenth century the canons complained there wasn't enough light and the f—remember this, kid?—the fuckers smashed the stained glass windows, for the love o " Everyone braces for another wheeze but Marcel seems fine.

"Fuckers in the full sense of the word," Jacques says, back from his window.

"Yeah I remember," the kid answers. "No one caught us, though—we were too fast for them dumb cops."

"Eighteen forty-four it's in ruins. Viollet-le-Duc restores it again. Eighteen seventy-one the fuckin Communards almost burn it down—burrrnnn it dowwwnnn—" Marcel leans over and peers into the faces around the table one by one, intoning like a preacher at a healing session. "can you—for the love oGod in the meantime the city's buildin buildins and sewage systems, Police Headquarters five hundred meters down the r "

"Excuse me. Excuse me," Jacques says, like someone's priggish old aunt asking a passerby for directions. "Is that a building or a sewage system?"

" reinforcin the river walls twelve times, diggin up for electrical switchin stations and fillin the holes and openin em up for gas mains and fillin em and goin down for twenty subway lines and fuckin cable TV and Christ knows what else. De Chelles's secret ain't alone down there no more." Marcel marks the on-schedule completion of his fort by holding his glass up with one hand and waving at Thierry with the other. "Ain't as easy to get to as it was seven hundred and forty two years ago. From what Tai Yang Blyster figgered you'd have to blow up the whole fuckin neighborhood includin Notre Dame to get to it now and since he's countin on *ownin* Notre Dame one day he ain't lookin to damage his goods."

"Or fuck around with" Roque fills Marcel's glass. "the kid's cable TV reception."

The old aunt wants to know if we can have "a vote on what represents the greater of the two losses to humanity."

"So that was that. Nice interview. Blyster wants the floorplan, can't get at the floorplan, I want a vineyard in Bordeaux. Everyone goes on livin. I put the magazine away and went annn, I dnknow "

"Took a piss!"

"No I think the old man was takin a piss *while* he was putting the magazine away," the kid tells Claude.

"Incredible how things work sometimes sometimes I think there ain't no coincidence." Roque snaps out of a thought and looks at Marcel. "Bout a year ago—bout this time a year ago—it's—I read the article in nineteennn—I dnknow, it's about a year and a half after I read this thing—one week—in one week—these four things happen the same week that it was like it was sleepin in me, this whole thing was sleepin in me for years but I had to wait until—it woulda never woke up cept for "

"It's me, Leslie. I'll try Later. Kiss it for me, baby! *BeeeeeeeeeeeeeP* ****BeeeeeeeeeeeeeP*****

"Turn That Thing Down, Willyuh, Kid!"

"Kiss it for me, baby? Isn't that—doesn't someone say that? Who always says that?" Thierry looks at Claude, she shrugs her shoulders. "Shit I can't think of "

"Just turn the fuckin thing down, willyuh, kid—cept for—in one week....." Marcel is silent for a moment. "There ain't no coincidence someti "

"There's just *cohzmihk sihnnncrohnihsssihtty,*" Thierry says into Roque's face, mocking Leslie's accent and fluttering his eyelashes.

"What four th "

Marcel flaps his hand at Claude. "Bout a year ago—good couple years after I read about this guy—the Arab kids start trashin the city. Gets so bad the fuckers are bein blamed even for shit they ain't doin, which makes their little dicks feel even bigger, kinda publicity they're eatn up mixed in with their cous-cous. You know it—every time a lightbulb burns out in someone's crapper it gotta be a.....whadid that paper s "

"act of urban terrorism," the kid says while he reads a fax that just rolled from the machine programmed to receive what Leslie receives.

"Someone gets a cold it's the Arab kids, someone—not even talkin the real hits goin down twice three times a week. So this week was when they do the Dylan concert that Monday night at Bercy. So that was number one. Number two is next day we gotta evacuate tmake room for the fuckin reporters lookin for the dirty cop! Nothin new there, happens every time don't it? they move in with their goddamn furniture, wife, kids and the fuckin dog! Who lets these cannibals in? I been sayin all along you wanna know who's plantin the bombs, go interrogate a reporter—guaranteed income—I swear they're makin the stories then writin about em couple hours later. Number two was we all know the gangs have someone livin inside our house. We know it, the press knows it, the public knows it, no one even makes a big deal about it no more cept the company sellin tape recorders to the reporters. The—whadyuh call em, kid?"

"Howard Hughes?"

"You listenin to me?"

"Act of urban terrorism."

"What do *you* call em?"

"Do you know what he's " Thierry looks to Jacques for help.

"Internal Fuckin Affairs For The Love OGod!" Marcel snarls.

"Oh-hoh. Cro-Magnons."

"Yeah good work, kid. The kid's Cro-Magnons at Internal Affairs—who's probly the contact in the first place—they fit their investigation in with everythin else they gotta get done in their two-hour work day. So number two is every time a lightbulb burns out in a crapper at headquarters it's gotta be the cop workin for the Arabs. Everyone's a suspect and no one's a suspect and since no one includin the government wants to g—specially the government—wants to go near it, gives every one of us free reign to trash the place. Long as we keep the trash inside the buildin which already has it piled up so high who'd notice another bag or two? So there's number two.

"Here's number three: couple days later—same week—gotta go downstairs and ask this dealer they run in the night before a couple questions about his employer. Gotta wait for his lawyer so I'm waitin for the lawyer in my office so we can go down and see this jerk and in walks this babe about twenty-five years old—tall, real long legs, fucked up a gorgeous face with these little—these little.....glasses." Marcel makes little glasses with his fat index fingers and thumbs, squinting through them at his colleagues around the table. "This was supposed to be the fuckin lawyer! So OK so we head out so we're in the elevator and yknow where they're keepin this clown—those cells as far down as you can get. The ones under the floor that ythink this gotta be the last floor, we're already hittin the center othe earth here, but no there's that last basement level. Yget off ydon't know whether you're up or down. Good place for these clowns they weren't dumb when they built the place. So we're in the elevator and this lawyer asks me where they're keepin her cli-yent and I tell er and then don't she start tellin me the history othe fuckin buildin. I say what ryou, an architect, too? She starts talkin bout why they built it like they did with all the floors under the floors and all the interrogations that went on there durin the war and before and after and the whole—the whole...psychology, is how she says, othe place. Wise-ass little thing, the shit she knew......Wondered why I didn't know about my own...place of employment, is how she said. So we're almost there and I'm bein polite and sayin well isn't that interestin, mademoiselle, and she's fixin up her little gray suit and rattlin some shit around in her little briefcase before goin in to see her cli-yent and then she says not half as interestin as what's *under* the buildin and she starts talkin bout this tunnel that leads from right under the floor just where we were standin, straight up to Notre Dame itself, she says, cause, she says, in the Middle Ages, she says, there was this..............convent.........THIS FUCKIN CON-VENT—" Marcel looks like his entire bloated body is about to rise out of his chair, eyes-first. "right where we are now. RIGHT, she says, WHERE, she says, WE, she says, ARE, she says, NOW, she says." His chest sprawls across the table into its faith-healer posture again. "Forrr the lo "

"Come on, old man, she didn't actually say this *fuckin* convent, did she?" the kid asks.

"And isn't that fascinatin, she says, an underground tunnel from door to door. I grab her arm an say you bet your fuckin ass it's fascinatin I tell her!"

"Come on, old man, you didn't actually say *you bet your fuckin ass* it's fascinating, did you?" the kid asks.

"You bet your fuckin ass I did! So there's number three. But you gotta realize none othis—wait—wait—I gotta tell yuh—yknow how she knows all this? Yknow how she knows? I grab her arm and ask er how she "

"I thought her arm was already grabbed," Jacques says.

"Did you guys hear all this before?" Claude asks, softly but firmly.

" knows about the tunnel. You wanna know howkkh " Marcel starts wheezing and waving his hands and Thierry tells Claude to pound on his back while he runs into the kitchen to get water. "kkhkh khhkhGE-O-LO-khhhGYkhkGEOLOGY CLASS for the love okkh the babe studied about the particular kind oEARTH that's supposed to be thanks, kid......................................................be in *our* tunnel in fuckin high schoolkkhkhh-hhkhgeology class for the love oGod! "

"The old man—you discover something new each time," Roque answers Claude. "Like seeing Gone With The Wind ag "

"hourly," Jacques twangs.

"And then she gets real interested in this convent-express shit and then starts readin shit and then about the buildins that came after.....But you gotta realize none othis—all this was—until next mornin all this is separate, not even in my head no more. Nothin to do with each other. Until next mornin. It's Friday. I remember. I'm in real early they're transferrin my dealer out to Rennes about six and I wanna refresh his memory about the tea-time chat we had yesterday. So bout half past six I'm back up in my office lookin out the window decidin whether I'm goin across to Le Palais for a coffee or not, tryin to wake up, and I see a buncha uniformed men standin down there in the lot. Hangin around the electric arm. There's I don't know there's maybe four of em at first and a couple minutes later there's two more, three more, and then I see this broad come runnin right the hell into the lot come runnin east to west right through the lot. Dressed like one othem joggers, you know, carryin a radio, earplugs and the works in her ears. Gets up to the electric arm, could easily run around the fuckin thing *I* fit around it easy for the love oGod there's nothin but curb on the other side. But no! Don't we have six or eight Christ knows how the fuck many jerks in uniform down there wishin this broad good mornin, wavin, tippin their hats like they're on the streets ogoddamn London, she's blowin kisses with one hand, holdin onto that radio like it's a gold fuckin ingot with the other, then these clowns *liiiffft* up the barrier—together—like they're all chained to each other on a goddamn work crew for the love oGod which is where they belong—so Mademoiselle Ben Johnson don't have to move three centimeters to the left to get her ass around the fuckin thing.....They make a big deal about it, too, like they're hoistin a block ogranite to go build the fuckin Pyramids you'd think she'd be sick otheir routine by now! Then she turns around nwaves good-by to her officer pals—still runnin, yunderstand—and they wave good-by to her and everyone's all smilin and hootin and some othe jerks are doin a pantomime runnin-routine in place like uhhhh "

"Marcel Marceau," Thierry says, thinking he's making a joke.

"Yeah good work, kid. In Their Fuckin Uniforms For The Love OGod. Some othese guys it's the first time I ever seen em smile. Then she goes on up the road up toward the Pont Neuf and they get ready tgo jerk-off in the john. Jeee-*zuss* what a sickenin sight! But before they get their dicks all the way out I'm down there in the parkin lot—you shoulda seen em when they see me come outKKKHHhh-hhkh—askin what the fuck that was all about. They tell me the broad runs by there every mornin. Tell me the broad runs by there every mornin—every mornin six-thirty. Give or take four-fifth of a second one of em says. Been doin it for years. Pourin rain, any season. Ice—ice is the only time she ain't there they tell me—when there's fuckin ice on the ground. So after a while they're married to er. She's like the...what's th " Marcel waves his hand.

"Mascot."

"—yeah good work, kid—othe Quai des Orfèvres for the love oGod. They know anythin else about er I ask em. No they tell me but we'd sure like to," Marcel says in a breathy voice, miming masturbation. "Fuckin animals! FUCKIN ANIMALS, I scream at em! Any oyou clowns hear chivalry's dead, I ask em! Since when they gettin paid tspend their mornins jerkin off in the lot with some jogger broad, I scream! Christ what's she doing runnin through our lot in the first place, I scream! Government Fuckin Property, for the love oGod! The Mayor can't even drive his vehicle onto that lot without special clearance, I scream! The fuckin *President* couldn't drive onto that lot without special clearance, I scream! And here's this total stranger no one knows anythin about, violatin our property every mornin and gettin a goddamn police escort to do it, I scream! And *those* assholes—I point—I point to the idiots guardin the yard entrance—are so used tseein er they don't see er no more, I scream! She could run by one mornin and throw a fuckin bomb into the courtyard, no one'd even know she'd been th.................................................................
........................................I stop..........I stop...........Shut up. Wish the clowns a very good mornin and tell em when they lift the arm up for their jogger friend from now on they should be careful not to hurt themselves and I g—or her—specially her—and I go across to Le Palais for a coffee. Poor fuckers! kkKHhkhProbly kkkhkhthought my brain went tokkhprobly thought my brain went to mush, the pohkhth "

"They thinking wrong, old man?"

"So that's number four," Marcel says, looking at Claude and waving Roque's question away. "I stay at Le Palais a long time drinkin coffee and thinkin. Yves Cruchot and François Taquet walk in and start sittin down at my table and I tell em not now I'll get back to em. Can't stop the thoughts. It's like my brain's.....boilin like someone's shootin boilin liquid in there with a needle. With a fuckin cannon. Get back over about eight and think all mornin and at lunch. The hot liquid keeps sloshin around in there. Eat lunch alone. Go back to Le Palais no one goes there for lunch. It's not I don't wanna talk to them fuckers—just.......words just won't come. Words havin anythin to do with anythin else. About four-thirty can't stand it no more. I find the broad that did the article on Blyster. She was a big fuckin help! Afraid of her own goddamn shadow could hardly even hear her fuckin voice over the phone. Kep havin to tell er to speak up. SPEAEAK UUP! Felt like tellin er tgo out and get herself porked ncome back ncall me! Maybe she'd find her voice at the end osomeone's big dick!"

"Shoulda sent Xavier to tickle her vocal chords," Jacques says, back at his window, then, turning toward the table, adds "But you did say *big* dick, didn't you?"

Roque nods, "Last time you looked." pointing both index fingers.

"Only thing the bitch had to say to me is she thought he's queer, only she couldn't bring herself to say queer she had to say homosexual. Hoh-moh-secks-yoo-al." Marcel tightens his lips and raises his eyebrows. "Hoh-moh-secks-yoo-al. Hoh-Moh-Secks-Yoo-Al. Hoh-Moh-Secks- "

Thierry and Jacques pick up Marcel's chant "yoo-al", with the kid prancing "hoh-moh-secks-yoo-al" over to the window, putting his hands on the back of Jacques's shoulders "hoh-moh-secks-yoo-al" and the two of them snaking train-like through the apartment "hoh-moh-secks-yoo-al", flapping their right hands in the air, then their left, then their right, warbling "hoh-moh-secks-yoo-al", flapping, smiling to the crowd "hoh-moh-secks-yoo-al", snaking, warbling, flapping "hoh-moh-secks-yoo-al", smiling, snaking "hoh-moh-secks-yoo-al", finally slinking off toward the john blowing big-lipped flirty kisses like a combination of Marilyn Monroe and Jimmy Durante attached to the back of a combination of Mick Jagger and Jackie Gleason exiting the stage after knockin em dead.

"Big fuckin help," Marcel presses on as Roque and Claude applaud and whistle and Marilyn, Jimmy, Mick and Jackie take their pre-spectacle places. "Fuck it—didn matter—broad even makes me even more "

"obsessed," Jacques says.

" determined. I tell the best detective on the force he looks like he needs someone to buy im dinner."
"But he wasn't available so the old man read through the phonebook and came up with Dupuy here," Roque tells Claude. "Or was it a bathroom wall?"
"I thought that's what the old man brought *you* in for, Xavier." Jacques looks at Marcel and points both index fingers at Roque. "Isnhe the bathroom-wall specialist in this family?"

"You obviously found him—Blyster," Claude says.

"Six hours!" Jacques hisses out of the side of his mouth not holding the cigarette.
"Wo-ow. Good work, Dupuy," she tells him soothingly, as if blessing his soul. Thierry clears his throat. "What did you do, have to go to " Thierry clears his throat.
"A good man knows he can't do it all himself," Jacques says to Claude. "A good man doesn't try to do it all himself that'd be dumb, wouldn't it, and we don't do dumb, do we?" Thierry clears his throat a little louder. "What makes a good man good," His hands in his jacketpockets, his cigarette dangling from the corner of his lips, Jacques paces in a tight circle in front of his window. "is not how fast he can fuck things up by doing it all himself, but knowing who to go to for the help he needs to fuck things up." Thierry clears his throat in three thick individual gravelly barks. "Like the old man here, perfect example, right, old man? Look at th " Thierry leaps up, kicking his chair out of the way, lands on spread legs and beats his chest in time to piercing jungle-howls. "You got somethin go down the wrong pipe, kid?" Jacques asks.
"Your mother, old man!" The kid seizes Claude and drags her out of her seat over to the big table in the middle of the room "THIS is what delivered our art fag!", pointing to one computer, jerking her with him as he moves to another "THIS is what delivered Leslie Brittain!", locking his elbow into her arm, running around to the guts of a Walkman on the other side of the table "THIS is what's gonna deliver the Pope's lovenote and THIS", finally waving both hands

Marcel-style over the whole set of work stations "is what's gonna deliver enough soybeans to keep us sick to our stomachs for the rest of our lives!..........Once we break out."

"I Hate Fuckin Soybeans Bring Er Back We're Not Ready For That Yet!"

"Shiitake mushrooms. I meant shiitake mushrooms, old man."

"I get Dupuy to find this guy for me," Marcel says, continuing where he left off as if no one's said a word in the meantime. "Don't tell him why. He don't ask. Is There Dessert For The Love OGod? Just find im, is all. He been usin the kid here for years on his shit so he gets the kid on it I swear you could find someone who ain't been born yet on those fuckin machines don't think you can't don't think" The kid goes into the kitchen "they don't know every time you and your grandmother go jerk off!" and comes back with a huge apricot tart. "Good work, kid! Get me some wine, willyuh!"

"Tarte aux soybeans!" Thierry beams, handing "Monsieur?" Marcel a knife.

Roque pokes his fork into the crust. "But what's the rest of us going to eat?"

Takes em not half a day and they have a contact for this supposedly uncontactable art fag," Marcel says in what he thinks sounds like the voice of an uncontactable art fag, "for the love oGod! Guy who represents him cause Blyster doesn't—he's like that "

"Ho-ward-Hughes," the kid tells him in a patient monotone.

"Once I know this guy's for real—gimme another piece, willyuh?—and not just some fantasy omy magazine babe I figger it's time to look at it nsee what we got. I call Jacques and tell im I'm takin im out to dinner."

"Dupuy's sure gettin his share ofree dinners outa this deal," Thierry says.

"The kid's sure gettin his share ofree toys outa this deal," Jaques says.

"My toys are your toys, old man."

"Ywant my dinner?"

"How much of this do you guys know already?"

"We didn't know the part about Jacques offering the kid his dinner," Roque tells Claude. "That part's new as of tonight."

"I tell im who Tai Yang Blyster is, what gets im off. Everything I know about im. I tell im there's a particular relic gets im particularly off specially because he can't supposably get to the thing. I tell im whoever *could* get to it and deliver it to Blyster wouldn't ever have to look at a price tag again. I tell im it's buried in a tunnel leadin out from under Notre Dame and I have an idea the other end othe tunnel's somewhere under our buildin. I tell im if it is, it might be a simple question of blowin out a wall or a piece othe floor and takin a little walk. I say if someone was ever gonna set a bomb off at headquarters for that particular purpose, now couldn't be a better time what with the gangs makin life real easy for us, and everyone's favorite subject—the cop on the inside—or maybe its the whole fuckin force for the love oGod—makin life real easy for them. I finally I tell im I found someone tpush the button. Someone from the outside. Someone who'd leave us clean and could be trusted beyond question since we could work it so she don't ever know she even did it and I tell im about my little chat with them fine, chivalrous officers in the lot that mornin. Whatdya think o*that!*, I ask im. Dupuy here "

"sat there and stared at the old man." Jacques says. "Fuckin smiling and all proud of himself like he just found a worm on the way home from school and brought it in to show his goddamn mother! Like he just got laid for the first time." He lights a cigarette and jams it into the corner of his mouth. "I don't know—what do you say to a guy who comes out with something like that? I just fuckin stared at the old man."

"Then he "

"Leslie, you lucky girl! Guess who's calling you from Orly! My, the last time I saw you you w "

Marcel pounds on the table and starts out of his chair and the kid runs over to turn the amplifier down.

"got up and left," Jacques says.

"Leaves me to eat dinner by myself I *hate* that!" Marcel waves his hand at Jacques's window. "....Cept when I gotta think........Weekend comes. Try not to think about it. Think about it all the time. Saturday and Sunday go see for myself. There she is, six fuckin thirty straight down. Different assholes out there playin in the lot but they're all her long lost cousins when she shows up! Appeaearrrs outa the misstss" Each bulging eye orbiting in its own course "of the St-Michelll Briiidgdge", both hands waving above his head, Marcel's faith healer is now telling a ghost story. "Conquerin hero—whatsisname—comin home from the wars!" He looks at Thierry.

"Norman Schwartzkopf?"

"I play games with myself, make deals with myself, I'll trade yuh an hour of not thinkin about it now for two hours othinkin about it after lunch, try to convince myself I'll wind up dead—or worse—in the same fuckin cell in the basement where the lawyer babe gave me the geology lesson. Try thinkin about ballin Monique Derichebourg from Community Relations. Try "

Jacques sends retching sounds over from his window.

Marcel flaps at him. " thinkin about retirement and that makes me think about it even more. Fuckin—what dthey call em?" Thierry shrugs his shoulders. ".....*wanin* years! Monday mornin there she is again it was too fuckin perfeck. In the rain like the man said. I spend most othe day outa the place. Walk around. Know where I went? Know where I went?" Marcel doesn't want an answer and doesn't wait for one. "Went all the way the hell up to La Villette and back! Went to where I—Clear This Shit Away, Willyuh, Kid?—so I'm puttin my jacket on about quarter past seven tget the fuck outa there and I look over at the door and yknow who's standin there? Yknow who's standin in my doorway?"

"Monique Derichebourg," Roque says.

"Dupuy for the love oGod! Come to take me out to dinner he tells me! We go for a drink first, he don't say much about it neither do I. Fac I don't think we bring nothin up at all about it that first place we go. Fac I can't remember what the fuck we talk about, I just figger it's his way of makin it up tme for leavin me eatin dinner alone. I *hate* that! Then about an hour later we get in his car, drive to this little place—this place the fuck out in St-Gratien this restaurant he has reservations made reservations like he knows for months I'm eatin with im that night! They all know im there, big celebrity, Oui, tout de suite, Monsieur Dupuy! I didn't know better I'd say he that's where he takes his "

"mother," Roque says. "See that's where he *would* take his.....friends if his mo " Jacques rips his cigarette out of his teeth and hurls it out the window like a hand grenade.

"So this Oui, tout de suite, Monsieur Dupuy fag shows us to our table and who's sittin there but the kid!" Thierry produces a glittering show-biz smile-and-wave, as if he's just been acknowledged by Ed Sullivan as the guest celebrity in the audience. "Never met the kid before. Heard about im from Jacques. Heard about im from the fuckin Chief, for the love o—no one should be that smart that young."

"No one should be that smart that *poor* that young," Thierry says.

"No one should be that smart that goddamn *lazy* that young," Marcel tells him, swatting at his head. "If you weren't so goddamn lazy we'd be havin this meetn tonight in your villa in Monte Carlo. We'd be haKkhKHh—at the Hhkkheadquarters-fortress:" Marcel holds his hands before his ruddy face then spreads them with reverence across the huge imaginary horizon before him. "Batiste Enterprises."

"If we were having this meeting tonight in my headquarters-fortress in Monte Carlo I wouldn't be hungry or dumb enough to be having this meeting! But we *would* be enjoying a superior grade of take-out Chinese—" The kid turns to Claude. "all due respects. What I Been Doin For The Past Eight Months Here, Ol Man, Jerkin Off?"

"YEAH!" Jacques answers for Marcel.

"YEAH!" Thierry yells, mimicking Jacques's laugh. "And in the middle of while I'm waitin for it to get hard again I pound a couple keys here, right, old man?"

"Doin a lotta poundin, huh, kid?" Jacques asks.

"..........nnnnnNYEAH!" Thierry yells.

"When I see him I realize I've seen him around. Never knew he was the kid, though. So Jacques tells me he does it with the kid or not at all and I should tell the kid everything I told him at dinner."

"That answer your question?" Jacques says to Claude, squeezing the words out through a small space between his lips. "Way last year, we're already twice in the first seventy-two hours."

"Just like that. Just like he didn't walk the fuck out on me last time we're eatin dinner—I *h*—gave me got me real—figgered if a cynical sonofabitch like Dupuy's comin back for more we gotta look at what we got. We decide that night nothin moves until we make sure we're all talkin about the same tunnel. We give the kid a week."

"We give the kid.....Substances," the kid declares, getting out of his chair, "to keep the kid as brilliantly alert in the middle of the night as he is known region-wide for being during the day don't mind him get your ass over here!" At his window, Jacques is working on a more ballistic version of his Monique Derichebourg retch. "We give the kid........SOFTWARE!" the kid exclaims triumphantly "SOFTWARE! Like big-boy architects use!", pulling Claude into a chair in front of the flying-toaster screen "And bigger boy doctors!" while he stands behind her "It lets you turn around the object you're looking at—" and reaches over her shoulders "let's you see the other side of what you're looking at without having to go in there and actually turn it around physically—" to frantically work the keyboard in pace with his excited speech. "moves it electronically or constructs it from raw data or lets you see it from other vantage points. Like you tell it there's a tree so many meters away from this house and then it draws the tree for you and then you say no I want to see the tree like I'm looking out the window of a helicopter hovering just above the house and it redraws the same tree like that and you say no I want to see it like I'm a slug crawling in the rosebed next to the house and it redraws the tree again or you say I want to see what this brain tumor would look like on the opposite lobe three months from now only the lobe belongs to a baby instead of a seventy-year-old man or I want to see where de Chelles's tunnel would be in relation to the convent if the earth in the past seven centuries shifted a given amount of degrees per year in a given direction at a given progressively accelerated rate allowing for the influence of modern technology on the stability of the bedrock of the city as studied by the old man's geology lawyer and while it was doin all that shifting how much dirt accumulated in the thoroughfare so Claude Palletier can get her ass through it n back and the old man can get his Rolls!"

"Vineyard!"

"Hey baby," Roque asks Claude, "wanna come up to my place and see my dirt graphs?"

"They got lash marks on em?" Jacques asks Roque.

Thierry lights a joint and holds it out to Claude, who takes it. "I suggested to the old man we just let the computer *create* a *new* old floorplan for Blyster."

Claude looks at Marcel.

"Kid was kidding," Marcel tells her.

"No-ho I wasn't."

"How long you think it'd take Blyster's army to carbon-date your ass, kid?"

"Be fastern Internal Affairs," the kid tells Jacques, getting the joint back from Claude and offering it to him because he knows he doesn't want any. "And cleaner. They'd get it right the first time."

"Once we know we got the tunnel," Marcel continues, "we go for the girl and to go for the girl we gotta get a "

"pre-vert." Jacques points both index fingers at what looks like no one in particular.

" but before we get a "

"pre-vert," Jacques points both index fingers at what looks like no one in particular.

" we gotta know what kiFOR THE LOVE OGOD I *HATE* THAT!" Marcel jumps as a phone on the equipment table rings. The kid nods to Roque and points to the one he should pick up. The others look at Roque looking toward the phone. The phone rings again.

"Better get it, old man, your machine takes it on four," Thierry says, jabbing the amplifier button with a quick-wristed twist. The phone rings again and the kid dives for it, lifts the receiver and holds it out on a straight arm to Roque.

"Hello? Hey, Rock N Roller!" the room hears Leslie say. Roque springs up and over to grab it.

"Leslie! How was your meeting?"
"What the fuck was that?"

Roque turns his back to his audience. "I dropped the

receiver.....How was your meeting?"

"That was just the question I was about to ask you, Roque!"

"I didn't" He twists quickly around and back. "say anything about a meeting tonight."
"I'm Not Talking About Tonight! I'm Not Talking About Tonight! Cop!"

"Leslie are you "

"I'm talking, cop," Jacques moves slowly back to the table and sits down. Marcel looks terrified. "about the little rendez-vous you and your four pals had in Brussels.....copp!"

"In Brussels?" Leslie is silent. "In Br "

"Yeah, you remember, don'tchya, Roque? May eleven. You remember. You were in Brussels. Took the train back. Remember? The train? Remember the train, Roque? Only you weren't in the compartment alone, were you? No, you weren't there alone. You weren't even there alone with me, Roque. Were you? There were four other guys in the compartment with us, weren't there, cop, and I unfortunately ain't talkin about the Dream Team. Four other guys there with us all the way to the Gare du Nord, all three and a half hours of it, and can you beat this, Roque, can you beat this, they all of em talk about cosmic synchronicity had the same name and they all of em" Roque turns around again and his eyes hit Marcel's and stay there. "if you wanna really deal with cosmolissimo synchronicitoid here had guess what name, Roque. HUH? You just pull a guess out of your asshole and see what the fuck name you come up with!"

"Just go on, Leslie."

"As incredibleness will have it, Xavier Roque," Roque flinches at hearing her use his first name. "all four of our fellow passengers on the eleventh of May were named Xavier Roque, Roque. And, hey! Wait a minute! Just wait one little—YOUR name is Xavier Roque, as well, isn't it, Xavier Roque? That means there were *five* of you! And here I was all along saying there's no such thing as coincidence! Maybe I should have that particular aphorism struck from my vocabulary! Maybe I was in the wrong car! Maybe I shoulda looked for the car with four other Leslie Brittains in it and ONE Xavier Cop Roque!"

"Leslie how did you come up with "

"Leslie how did you come up with? Leslie how did you come up with? Leslie's about to tell you how Leslie came up with! Remember Moe the Magician travel agent and the train-ticket deal he didn't tell me about?.....Well Do You Remember What I'm Talking About Here Or Not Frchrissakes?"

"I remember, Leslie," Roque says softly. As he half-sits on the table, Thierry motions to him to keep away from the equipment.

"Well at the restaurant Saturday when I went to make a call I called Patrick to tell him to try to get my money back. I told him to tell Moe he's a cocksucking crook but of course my little snow-angel Patrick couldn't do that so he did the next best thing, the sweetheart ARE YOU THERE ARE YOU WITH ME ARE YOU FOLLOWING ME HERE?"

"I'm here, Leslie." The louder and more strident Leslie's voice becomes, the more Roque softens and sweetens his.

"The little saint took half his Saturday and went right down to the train station itself, hardly even speaks French, the diamond!, and marched right up to a window and didn't he make himself understood enough that the kid behind the window said he'd look right into it. So the kid asks Patrick my name and punches me up on his computer and then the kid looks at the screen and shakes his head and punches up something else then he shakes his head and punches up something else then he puts up his This Window's Closed Please Step To The Next Window sign and of course Patrick being the terrified little follower that he is—God! his parents shoulda been jailed!—though he's improving exponentially under my assiduous supervision—thinks the kid means him and starts walking away. The kid screams Hey! No! Not you! Come back here! and keeps punching keys and pulling up new screens and closing down old ones and comparing screens and finally my Patrick gets up enough courage, which'd probably even be overwhelming for him in English, to ask the kid—who was about Patrick's age using a computer so there was this bonding thing there— what was going on and the kid says he's getting the strangest thing he ever saw and then tells Patrick sure enough his boss's ticket was sold to her at the non-promotional price and of course there was nothing they could do about it because of course the customer in France is

NEVER right—my words, not his—his concept, not mine—" Claude rolls her eyes. "but that what meanwhile he's getting is that the five other seats in the compartment were all purchased—I repeat, Roque, in case your inverse-proportion-to-your-cock-sized brain isn't absorbing all this—" Jacques gives the thumbs-up sign. "were ALL PURCHASED BY THE SAME PERSON! AND YOU DON'T HAVE TO BE A FRENCH POLICE IN-SPEC-TEUR OR EVEN A FRENCH SEWER-FLUSHER TO FIGURE OUT WHO THAT SAME PERSON WAS, DO YOU? COPP! In Brussels to see an old school friend my fucking rear end, Roque! What were you after? Huh? HUH? WHAT WERE YOU "

"Leslie, "

"What were you after who put you up to this? Jack Kote? WAS IT JACK? That goddamn sleaze if he wants to know something why the fuck doesn't he just ask me himself Who PWhat Were You "

"Leslie, I can "

"Looking For?" Marcel is gray and transfixed.

"Leslie, let me "

"Drugs? Guns? Whadjya think, I was hiding an Arab terrorist up my pussy well you didn't show me no search warrant! No! The French Police wouldn't be smart enough to go after a terrorist with such a complicated scheme! You're still using butterfly nets! That's why the fuckers are still out there! Do I Look Like A Danger To Soci "

"LESLIE!" Roque shouts and for a moment there's silence......... .........."I tell you I can—it was my friend. It was the friend I went to visit. He bought me the tickets and did it as sort of as a—a gift. For a luxurious ride, he said. He said it was the only compartment with almost every seat available. That there was only one other person. Otherwise he would've bought me the whole compartment!"

"Well you sure had your luxurious ride there, You Fuck, didn't you? Nice and smooth and silky and satiny and wet and YOU'RE A FUCKING LIAR!" Leslie hangs up...................................................
........................................................................................................
........................................................................................................

...........................................................................Roque leans against the table with his head down and the receiver dangling from his crossed hands in front of his crotch, the off-the-hook BEEP....BEEP ....BEEP....BEEP.... the only sound in the apartment for the next five minutes. Except for Jacques, who goes back to his window, everyone is inanimately still............................................................................................
..........................................................................................................
..........................................................................................................
...........................................................................................
..................................................................................."So once we know who she is," Marcel resumes, looking to make it all go away by pretending it never came, "the kid goes snoopin through her whadjyuh call "

Thierry answers "El-ec-tron-ic-his-tor-y" in a numbed, nearly inaudible monotone.

"Look—" Roque says with a voice not much more alive than the kid's, "I gotta get over there." But he is unable to move. Finally the kid gets up and takes the receiver from him, the gesture somehow setting Roque in motion as if a key has been turned. Roque nods to Marcel and grabs his jacket from the sofa.

"You think she'll let you in?" Claude asks. Her near-meditative placidity contrasts sharply with the surrounding nervousness.

"For once I gotta agree with him." Crossing the room "He gotta get over there.", Jacques is talking to Marcel but looking at Roque, who is taller than Jacques and whose denim shirt and jacket next to Jacques's shapeless brown suit make his upper body look even broader than it is. "I don't personally care how you do it, old man." Jacques clasps the tops of Roque's arms, opens his hands wide, clasps again, "Just," opens, clasps, opens, clasps "neaten it up." He is speaking softly and calmly. "Get her back, old man. Fuck her back, buy her back you want money you got money. Neaten it up, old man." He lets go and starts circling Thierry's equipment table./././././"It's not that I give a fuck about the old man's piece of paper because I don't."./././././lights a cigarette./././././shoves it into his mouth./././././buries his hands in his jacketpockets./././././walks./././././"It's not that I give a fuck about the money because I don't."./././././. The slow./.sharp./.rhythm./.of his shoes./.on the wooden./.floor./.telegraphs his message, makes his words superfluous ././././.   ././././.   ././././.   ././././.   ././././.   ././././."It's just not neat this way," he twangs, walking back to his window where the light from the Boulevard Raspail picks up the shiny veneer of sweat forming on his face. "And I like things neat." From exactly where he was leaning before the call came, he points both index fingers at Roque. "It's just not neat this way. And I like things neat."

On his way to the door Roque stops in front of a photo of Leslie running across the Place de la Concorde. He tries to brush what he thinks is a speck of dust from its surface, near her hip, but sees that it's a mark in the paper. One foot in the hallway, he turns and comes back in. "Give me the keys to her apartment." The kid goes around to the metal-box department of his work table, unlocks a small container, then tosses Roque a strip of white lacy garter-belt elastic with a stocking clasp on one end and two keys knotted onto the other. Jacques darts over, hunches down and stares at the back of Thierry's leg, moving as Thierry moves so as to keep his target in view, following the kid's thigh clear across the room.

"What—what the FUCK" The kid kicks him away. "you want down there, old man?"

"Wanted to see if you could still keep em up with only three left. Or what did you do, replace it with one of your black ones?"

"Why white?" Roque asks from the doorway.

"For luck!" Thierry tells him. "It's Tibetan. In Tibet when you go to the temple to pray for success if you wear all white you up your chances by tons of percentage points."

"Tibetan broads wear garter belts?" Jacques wants to know.

"I thought it was yellow," Claude says gently.

"It's monks. Monks wear yellow," the kids tells her.

"Tibetan monks wear yellow garter belts?" Jacques squawks, putting his hand over his mouth to mime a giggle.

"Xavier!"

"Yeah, old man?"

"Call me in the morning!"
Roque points both index fingers at Marcel and lets himself out.

"Where did he come from?"

"I gotta go piss!"
Claude recenters her baseball cap and tries again. "Where did he c"

"Was married to my wife's cousin. I put in a good Word When He Was Up For PROMOTION TO INSPECTOR. SHE THREW IM OUT YEARS AGO. SAID SHE KEP FINDIN THESE MAGAZINES AROUND ABOUT—WHAT SHE TELL MY WIFE?—*QUESTIONABLE* SEXUAL PRACTICES ONLY I Don't Think That's What she said it was more like "

"perverted."

"Yeah somethin like that," Marcel tells Jacques.

## XII

## $CREAMING-©HARTREUSE-MATTHEW JUNE

"ust a t-shirt," Roque hears Leslie say as he inches the door closed behind him. The only light in the apartment coming from a candle in the bedroom-alcove, he stands in the dark entranceway trying to determine if she's on the phone or if someone is there with her.

"Nothing."

"_ _ _ _ _"

"Well maybe I could put the t-shirt on the bottom and then have nothing on on top. I can stick my legs through the armholes so the bunched-up fabric rubs against my pussy while I "

"_ _ _ _ _"

"Holding the phone, frchrissakes!"

"_ _ _ _ _"

"Well why don't you tell me what *you're* doing with *your* other hand first."

"_ _ _ _ _"

"Oooh-oooh! Well I have something big and black in mine, too. Oh wait! That's the phone, isn't it! Never could keep track of my hands and feet. Yknow when I was a little girl in dance class they used to have to tie a red ribbon around my ankle and then say Leslie, lift the ribbon leg, or Leslie, lift the no-ribbon leg, cause they wouldn't've made any headway with right n left. Maybe we can tie a red ribbon around what *you're* holding in *your* other hand so "

"_ _ _ _ _"

"No you're right. I don't think there's much chance of me missing it. Or mistaking it for someone else's!"

"- - - -"

"It's in something.....thightt..........and wett..............and hott."

"- - - -"

"Good thinking, Tulipe. That's just where it is! If you slug as good as you deduce you'll have no trouble Saturday night."

"- - - -"

"Deduce. Means...figure out."

"- - - -"

"No, it's not an English word, it's a Fr—well, it's an English word, too, Tulipe, it's just the particular word I just pronounced was the French version. Don't try to don't worry about it, sweetheart. You got other things tworry about."

"- - - -"

"No I won't be there and you know it!"

"- - - -"

"Lemme tell you about where my hand is."

"- - - -"

"Because I will not go like some Damon Runyon figure to sit there ringside getting absorbed into the scenery in a white mink and heavy-artillery diamond earrings and blood-red lipstick with a bookend broad on the *other* side oyour manager in a white mink and heavy-artillery diamond earrings and blood-red lipstick going Ooh-Ooh, isn't Tulipe the best, Ooh-Ooh, give it to im, Tulipe, knock his ass out, Tulipe, yeah, yeah, you can do it, Tulipe, yay Tulipe!.....I prefer my circuses in more intimate surrou—and besides—I don't have anything on on the bottom—I can't go like this!"

"- - - -"

"An author. A book writer. Wrote stories about gangsters and— Here! I want you to do something for me. I want you to put your hand up to your mouth....OK? OK is it there?"

"- - - - -"

"Good. Now. Spit on your fingers....OK? Get em all wet n gooey with spit stick em in your mouth and get em all wet......OK?"

"- - - - -"

"Now, I want you to slowly—slowwwww-lyyyyy—bring your hand down and just touch juuuuussssst the tiipp—just the beginning of the top of the tip.......of your..........khohckh.....Tulipe?" Roque strains to hear as Leslie lowers her voice. "Are you touchin it, baby?"

"- - - - -"

"Good. That's what I want you to do. Touch it for me, baby. You just get that big ball all slippery and shiny for your Leslie, Tulipe. Where are we, Tulipe? You know where we are? You know where we are?" The words are riding out on Leslie's lungs rather than her vocal cords.

"- - - - -"

"We're in the fields. Yeah, in the fields in your village we're back in the high grass and it's midnight and the only light there is is comin outa our eyes and you're standing with your legs spread wide and your hands on your hips and your huge cock pointing outa your pants and why don't you move your hand a little farther down now, sweetheart, just a little farther down and then back up again but not all the way and I'm on my knees in front of you on the cool ground yeahhhh-hhh yeahhhh-hhh oohhhh-hhhh" Leslie starts breathing in grainy deep gulps and whimpering and Roque can hear her moving around on her bed. "and both my hands are wrapped hhuuhh uuhhuuhh hoooh around your majestic cock move your hand down all the way now, Tulipe, and DO it for yourself! go for it baby doitdoitdoit doitdoitdoitdoitdoit! and I take your black masterpiece coHHOHHwhahhhah WHAH! WHAHTTT THUHH-UHH FFFF "

"_ _ _ _ _"

"NO I'M NOT COMING WHAT THE FUCK ARE YOU DOING HERE!"

"_ _ _ _ _"

"No Not *You* Tulipe FrcrisWWHHAATTT "

Roque snatches the receiver from Leslie "She got another call, Tulipe, bye!" and slams it down on its cradle.
"DO YOU KNOW WHO YOU JUST HUNG UP ON YOU CRUD?"

"Tulipe a boy or a girl?"

Her hand curled up by her ear as if still holding the phone, Leslie stays immobilized on her back for a moment before suddenly "THAT'S FOR YOU TO FIG—DEDUCE!" lurching to her knees on her way off the bed. Roque blocks her with his hips and grabs her arms she struggles against his attempt "THOUGH IT'S PRETTY OBVIOUS YOU MISSED THE PART ABOUT THE HEAVYWEIGHT FIGHT AND THE COCK!" to pin them back he holds both her wrists behind her with one hand and drops to his knees
"YEAH I CAUGHT SOMETHING ABOUT BIG AND BLACK AND MAJESTIC!" in front of her on the edge of the mattress. Leslie screams butts her knees against his one after the other
"BUT YOU THOUGHT IT COULD BE A GIRL WITH A STRAP-ON!" tries to bite his shoulder but he
"LESLIE YOU'RE DISGUSTING-" shoves her with his free hand and his chest "-A DOUBLE-TIPPED STRAP-ON?"
"ROQUE YOU'REAAAH-IEIEIE" and she falls onto her back "DISGUSTING!" with Roque on top of her....................
.........................."And now, Xavier Roque," she says in a sweet tranquil tone, looking up into his eyes and feeling his breathing subside, you and Xavier Roque, Xavier Roque, Xavier Roque and Xavier Roque can go break into someone else's bedroom and be disgusting there cause you're about to get outa here."

Roque smiles, more with his eyes than his mouth, and asks "What's your favorite food?"

"OK," Leslie says slowly, nodding, her eyes and mind and voice a bit distant, as if she's contemplating a new philosophical tenet which has just been proposed. Still on top of her, Roque relaxes, drawing himself up onto his elbows. She glides her eyes back into his, locks her lips into an oversized synthetic smile, flutters her lashes, and knees him in the balls. With a martial-arts cry.

Roque grunts.

Leslie howls.

Roque bends in two like a prodded amoeba and rolls half off Leslie.

Leslie slides over like a shell-game walnut and rolls half out from under Roque.

Roque yelps "OOHH-HHH!"

Leslie shrieks "HAH!"

Roque raises his arm to slap Leslie across the face.

Leslie seizes Roque's arm with both hands and digs her nails beyond the denim into his flesh.

"LESLIE!" Roque shouts.

"ROQUE!" Leslie shouts.

"I GOTTA TALK TO YOU!"

"ROQUE!" Leslie shouts.

"LESLIE!" Roque shouts.

"I DON'T GOTTA TALK TO YOU!" Leslie breaks free and bounds off the bed. "I don't gotta talk to you."
"You know you still have marks on your ass," Roque says, lying serenely on his back with his hands under his head, waiting for the poolside barman to return with his drink. Leslie stomps over to the dinette table. Snatches a pair of sweatpants from the back of a chair. Plunges into them, each gesture shouting a profanity.

"What's your favorite food?"

Stomps back. Stands over Roque. "Get your filthy cop-shoes off my bed!"

Roque's shoes drop to the floor. "What's your favorite food."

"Leave your filthy cop-shoes on and get your ass outa my apartment."

"I asked you a question, Leslie," Roque says tenderly. He rolls onto his side and reaches under the back of his jacket.

"I did better than that. I gave you an " Leslie stops dead—silenced by the crossfire shooting out from her brain and heart and pussy in reaction to what Roque's just pulled from the waistband of his jeans. He holds it up to her in the palm of his hand as if offering a tray of hors d'oeuvres.

"Take it," he says, sounding kind and friendly.

"I don't give a shit!" Her brain is speeding, trying to analyze whether or not she gives a shit, zapping through flashcard scenarios of what she'll do next. Her

Roque doesn't move. Just keeps on smiling with his eyes and presenting his hors d'oeuvres.

"Doesn't scare me!" heart is keeping up with her brain, then straining to break away and overtake it, to beat its best time. Her

Roque nods to his hand and waits patiently for Leslie to accept his offer.

"Doesn't impress me!" pussy is pacing ahead of them all, pulsing its wetness onto her sweatpants seam.
"Take the gun, Leslie. It's.......collateral. Toward the purchase of your.....trust. It's your insurance policy. If I pull anything you can shoot me." Leslie takes the gun and opens it to see if it's loaded. "What's your favorite food?"

"Where are the other ones?"
"The other what?"

"The other guns. The four other guns. For the four other Xavier Roques."

"No you don't understand, Leslie. There are six bullets in *one* gun. You don't need five separate guns."

"Oh."

"Plus, you then even have one bullet left over for the travel agent."

"Lobster."

"What?"

"And ice cream."

"Oh. Where do you get a flavor like that?"

"Not lobster ice cream, dick-brain! Lobster. Now I'm gonna pause to let the cop take that one in. I'm pausing now. Pauauausiiinnngg. Pauauausiiinnngg. Now that I've paused I'm gonna say the next word, which is the following word: and. Now here comes another pause but this one's a bit shorter since *and* is a shorter word than *lobster*. Pauausiinng. OK, that pause is accomplished. Now the next word here it comes but wait! This word is a compound word so we wanna make sure the cop is ready to take this one in. Although if he has any trouble with it he can always call upon his four colleagues who happen to have the same name as he does to help him. OK. Word one of the compound word which is the last word of the entire phrase under discussion at the present time: ice. Everybody comfortable with that so far? Fine. Fine. Moving right along, here goes word two: cream.".........................

.........................Roque stares up at Leslie, expecting her to keep going, finally realizing she's finished.

"All right," he says, getting up. "Then we're going to Le Duc." Leslie springs into the air, does a half turn and lands on bended spread legs facing away from the bed, the gun held by both hands at the end of rigidly outstretched arms, her head vigilantly focused on her imaginary target. Roque waits for a response. Leslie looks like she hasn't even heard him. She repeats the maneuver, this time landing a quarter turn facing the livingroom, her special-forces concentration shrinking Earth to the relationship between the framed New York City Ballet program on the far wall and the barrel of her new toy. "They don't have ice cream," she says, seeming to move nothing but her vocal cords, then, with another quarter-turn bound, Leslie the Commando has just jumped out of a helicopter on a mission to fill her courtyard window full o lead.

Roque puts on his shoes and moves toward her. "They have the best shellfish in Par—the world."

Like a battery-operated armed bunny, Leslie springs and turns in the air once more, whipping her head around before her body arrives, touching down in position, legs light and supple, ready to take off again when duty calls, arms straight and stiff, aiming the gun point blank at Roque's cock. "Weh-hell, that's where you're wrong, mister! That's where you're dead—you should excuse the expression—wrong!" Roque isn't completely certain Leslie's just amusing herself. He waits for her next move before making his. "Just not on the money at all with that one, sports fan!" she says, squinting to check the accuracy of her aim. She's silent for a moment and Roque stands motionless. Then "**CAP-TAIN STARNES!**" she blares, startling Roque into reflexively covering his crotch with his right hand. "Now *That's* A Useless Move If I Ever Saw One! If my inverse-proportion theory is correct—which we know it is—that's muuuuch too big an area to protect with just five fingers. Your Brain! Now your brain, now that's a different story!" Leslie's gun and eyes are still locked onto their mark. "You could hide two of them behind that hand of yours and be safe for life! Like I was saying, Captain Starnes has the best seafood in Paris. Only it's in Atlantic City." She suddenly drops her arms to her sides and says to herself "Or did it close after the casinos opened?" As Roque takes a step toward her "HAVE TO" her right arm stiffens again, training the gun on him while she dials the phone "call Danney and ask him."

"Leslie, this is getting "

"Hey! Who's this? Tom? Tom Michaels? The famous Tom Michaels of the North Jersey-renowned Dance Party Oldies?"

"_ _ _ _ _"

She puts on a heavy French accent. "Vell, ahee emm cahllink fchrom Pahreese Fchrahhnce veess ah dedicatiawnn. Your Lyin' Eyes," she goes on in her natural voice, "from Leslie to" her gaze rising from Roque's cock to his face. His blank expression tells her he doesn't understand a word. "Your Deaf Ears, forget it, Mike! This is Leslie Brittain. Is Danney there?"

"- - - -"

"Shit!"

"- - - -"

"No it's OK I won't be here. I just had a question to ask him."

"- - - -"

"OK you probably do. A big famous radio personality like y "

"- - - -"

"OK OK! Is Captain Starnes still open?"

"- - - -"

"What Kind Of American Citizen Are You Frchrissakes didn't you spend your summers gettin it under the boardwalk on a bed of used ru "

"- - - -"

"Well then how can you not know if Ca "

"- - - -"

"One thing has *everything* to do with the other! All right. My Danney'll know. Tell him to e-mail it."

"- - - -"

"Yeah, June twenty-sixth."

"- - - -"

"OK! Sure! Seeyuh then. Thanks!

"He doesn't know," Leslie tells Roque, the gun still relentlessly in place. "They'll get back to me. Meanwhile," She walks over to the coat-rack at the entranceway and drops the gun into her handbag. "my people and I—we've decided to let your cock live. For now. Consider it a reprieve. A stay of sentence. For now. Might come in handy." She yanks her sweatpants off, opens her closet "Be able to be of service in some bath house somewhere." and puts on a pair of white jeans. "If they have no alternative that day." Looking in the mirror, she takes a skinny navy satin ribbon from the top of her dresser and ties her hair back. "Sorry my t-shirt's so clean. You'll get used to it. Wonder if they'll let me in the restaurant though. Come on!" she yelps, smacking Roque on his ass. "We don't want our lobster ice cream to melt!"

"Yon a diet?" Leslie asks Roque once the waiter takes their order. "You know they have the best seafood in Paris."

"This is my second dinner tonight. I'm glad your favorite food isn't shiitake mushrooms."

"No that's my favorite ice cream. I lied about lobster."

"Isn't it yours?"

"Isn't it my what?"

"Your second dinner."

"We sound like a goddamn married couple frchrissake! What do we need at the supermarket and what did you eat today, what do we need at the supermarket and what are you going to eat today, what do we need at the supermarket and what would you have eaten today if you hadn't been out at the supermarket shopping for something to make to eat today! Go ahead."

"Go ahead what?"

"So this friend oyours has nothing better to do with his money than buy five times the amount of train tickets necessary to get your lying ass to Brussels."

"Yeah. Let me set the record straight about this friend of mine," Roque says. And does. He sets the record straight about his friend while Leslie eats progressively more slowly and less of what would under other circumstances be one of the most tasty dinners in Par— the world. He sets the record straight about his friend as he deposits Leslie's soundless body into his car and drives to the Haagen-Däzs at the Place Victor-Hugo to find it closed. "Whadyexpect?" she wants to say but can't bring herself to break the beat of Roque's entrancing verbal tapdance. "This isn't the neighborhood for all-night Haagen-Däzses!" she would remind him if she weren't so invested in his getting on with his folk tale. "This isn't the neighborhood for all-night *anything* frchrissake!" she almost yells but is afraid Roque's insult to her intelligence would lose its momentum and she wants to see how far he's planning on taking it. "Except maybe the flannel-nightgown vendors—the flannel-nightgown vendors in these parts gotta take advantage othese post-Haagen-Däzs hours to get their inventories ready for the renewed wifal-onslaught tomorrow morning!—although wife-types in these parts don't slaught on, do they?" are the words Leslie saves for maybe another time, realizing they're no match for the vaudeville act Roque is trying to pawn off as a performance at the Old Vic. He sets the record straight about his friend as he does a car-chase turn around the Victor-Hugo fountains and heads out across the river for the Haagen-Däzs off the Place St-Michel. "This is where we shoulda come in the first place frchrissake!" Leslie sees herself telling him on any evening other than this. He sets the record straight about his friend as he undresses and installs himself atop Leslie's comforter with the pint of Chocolate Chocolate Chip and the pint of Pralines and Cream under heavy guard in his possession while Leslie forces herself to concentrate on getting spoons and napkins and water and forgets the water, tosses the spoons and napkins onto the bed, takes her clothes off, goes back to the kitchenette for the water and settles in opposite Roque, grabbing the pint of Chocolate Chocolate Chip from behind his pillow-fortress and digging a moat for it in the covers between her legs.

For three and a quarter hours, across eight *arrondissements*, through five courses—including dessert at the restaurant—and the ice cream picnic on her bed which doesn't count as a second dessert and therefore as a course but as an ice cream picnic on her bed, Leslie has listened, mute and rapt, to Roque's trying to talk his way back into some semblance of believability. If Roque has just said more in one evening than he has in the three weeks he's known Leslie, Leslie has just listened more in one evening than she has in her whole life. Over her amazement at his absurdities, her indignation at his inanities, her ire at his irrationalities, over her disbelief, wonder, her impatience and her systemic need to shower the crowd with a spray of smart-ass retorts, Leslie's generosity and sense of justice have triumphed: Roque came tonight asking to communicate and communicate she has selflessly allowed him to do. Now, after he has talked and explained and clarified the evening and most of his energy away, Leslie, with a mouth full of Chocolate Chocolate Chip, says

"Go ahead."

"Go ahead what?"

"Hand me a napkin, willyuh, Roque?........Thanks." She swallows, reaches over and stabs into his Pralines and Cream, hauling her booty up to her mouth just in time to fill the void. Suddenly a spoonful of "Cee Cubed!" circles his face for a landing. "Trade?"

"Go ahead what?"

"Cee to the third power—chocolate chocolate chip......For-get-it-Roque," she warbles, and snaps at the spoon herself. "Works in English. Doesn't work in French. Doesn't need to. They had other things to talk about in the court at Versailles besides what flavor was stashed in the Royal Freezer. Like what Royal Cock was stashed in what riff-raff pussy. So tell me, Roque. How come you bought up all the seats in my compartment on the train to Brussels?"

Roque's left foot, which is resting on his right knee, starts flapping up and down at the ankle, the lower-extremity equivalent of drumming your fingers on the table. He inhales deeply and looks at the ceiling, where Patrick's phosphorescent planets and stars are lying dormant, frugally storing light from the bedside lamp. When he finally releases his breath, little whispered words "Merde!" ride out on its wave "Putain!", like pieces of litter on the sea. "I knew you wouldn't believe me," he says, no longer avoiding Leslie's eyes. "I know it seems "

"Roque.......Roque....Listen to me, Roque." She puts her hand gently on his thigh. "Listen to me sweetheart, OK? Here—wait—you really gotta taste this............tsgood, isn't it? Roque sweetheart, there are good lies. Real masterful museum-quality lies. Lies that people sit around on New Years Eve and talk about for years. Lies that are so historically significant that civilization shudders at the thought of what this world would have become had the truth been told in their place. There are lies that have inspired and embellished great works of literature. There are lies that have been ingenious enough to launch brilliant careers and reputations, and powerful enough to dash them. Lies that have proven themselves invaluable, indeed crucial, to missions of mercy and love, and vital to the security of the world itself. There are lies crafted by gifted women and men whose artful minds have allowed them to assimilate essential elements from the realms of psychology, diplomacy, economics, politics, and even science in order to emerge with that one perfectly synthesized and balanced fabrication to serve the purpose at hand. These are great noble lies, forged by great noble liars, which stand as ideals to which young dreamy potential noble liars aspire and toward which they work. Hard. Your lie, Roque, is unfortunately none of these. Your lie is not a great lie. Your lie isn't even a good lie. Your lie is bullshit, Roque. I am ashamed of your lie. And you should be too."

Leslie gets up and goes into the livingroom. She comes back and stands over the bed, Roque's clothes in one hand, her pint of Chocolate Chocolate Chip, with the spoon in it, in the other. Her voice has been quiet and soothing and patient, that of a loving parent taking pains to teach an important lesson to a receptive child. Roque feels reassured by her tranquillity. "I can't leave, Leslie," he says plaintively. "I can't leave until I make you believe me. Because it's true. Every word of it is true."

"ALL RIGHT, PAL, IT'S OUTSKY CITY, ARIZONA!" She dumps Roque's clothing onto to his head, hurls her carton onto the nighttable and swoops back into her sweatpants and t-shirt. He doesn't move, except to crawl out from under all the pieces of denim and throw them on the floor. "CUMAWN! UP N ATEM, ATOM ANT!" Grasping his shoulders, she tries to dislodge him from her bed "BLOWING UP A TUNNEL UNDER THE FUCKING CATHEDRAL OF NOTRE DAME DE PARIS, ROQUE? I DON'T KNOW IF YOU HEARD YOURSELF BUT THAT'S WHAT ACTUALLY STANDS TO DATE AS THE ONLY THING YOUR DUST-PARTICLE BRAIN COULD COME UP WITH!" then suddenly lets go of him and troops over to the dinette table. "GANG OF FRUSTRATED-GENIUS POLICEMEN, ROQUE?" Charges back and attaches herself to his shoulders. "CHANNELING ALL THAT FRUSTRATED-GENIUS ENERGY INTO THE CRIME OF THE MILLENNIUM?" Shuttles between pulling at Roque's anchored body and pacing under the archway between the bed and the table. "USING ME AS AN

IGNORANT-SLOB PAWN, ROQUE?" Leslie pulls. "THAT'S WHAT YOU JUST WASTED THE ONLY JUNE FIRST NINETEEN NINETY-TWO EVENING I'LL EVER HAVE IN MY LIFE TRYING TO GET ME TO INGEST, ROQUE?" Leslie paces. "DIDN'T THINK YOU HAD IT IN YOU, ROQUE!" She pulls. "I TAKE IT BACK—STORY LIKE THAT'S THE WORK OF A GREAT MIND, ROQUE—A *GREAT* MIND!" She paces. "DIDN'T THINK YOU HAD IT IN YOU!" Pulls. "BETWEEN DOUBLE-CHECKING WITH YOUR TRAVEL AGENT AND CRAMMING ALL THOSE HALLUCINOGENS DEEP DOWN INTO THE BACK CRYPTS OF YOUR MEDULLA OBLONGATA, ROQUE, WHERE THE FUCK DIDJYUH FIND TIME TO GIVE OUT ALL THOSE PARKING TICKETS?" Paces. Leaning against the dinette table, she asks, in a mock-pleasant tone, "What, honestly, Roque, kind of a zone-out do you take me for?"

Roque rocks slowly forward and gets off the bed. He stabs at the phone on the dresser. "What are you doing *now*?" Leslie whines, slapping the side of her thigh. The receiver cradled in his neck, he calls her over with one index finger and puts the other up to his mouth.

"Shshsh. This is the guy has you wired. He has *very* sensitive equipment. He'll hear you breathing." Leslie moves in close and stands on her toes so they can share the receiver. She rolls her eyes impatiently when Roque locks his arm around her waist.

"Former Soviet Union, may I help you?"

"Xavier," Roque whispers.

"Yo, ol man! You're still at her place. Been thinkin aboutchya. Where is she?" Leslie opens her eyes wide to Roque who shakes his head and puts his finger back to his lips.

"Taking a bath."

"Thanks, old man, you chose option number one—leaves more scratch in the crime fund to buy me equ "

"What the fuck are you "

"J—remember?" As Thierry slides into a sneer "Fuck her back or buy her back—" Roque lets go of Leslie's waist because she looks like she's about to shriek into the phone. "so we OK here?"

"Any more OK I'd be making this call from inside the tunnel. What time you guys finish tonight?"

"Jacques couldn't take anymore, he cut out right after y—hey!—hey!—you know who your babe's fuckin? Old man, you gotta—you gotta get me tickets! Do you know who she just picked the phone up and called after you left here like I call my Cousin Richard?"

Roque scowls down at Leslie. Leslie sparkles up at Roque.

"Come on kid she's not gonna be in the tub all night!"

"TULIPE BOKAFFE! Tul-ipe Bok-af-fe, old man—The Flower of the Ring! He—Kiss it for me, baby!—*that's* who says that *that's* who says it—she isn't goin to the fight so just tell her I'll go in her place. Hey—tell her I don't mind white mink one bit!

"And the old man?"

"He doesn't either. So the old man took Claude over to the Coupole and I put the leftover soybeans in my Tupperware. I told em to pretend he's a famous director with this muse he discovered in the gutter, they like that shit over there.

"They'd be too embarrassed to admit they can't quite place him. He's really pumped up—it's getting close."

"We scared im tonight. We fucked up. We shoulda bought all the tickets under different names. We fucked up.......This is the only thing he has, yknow."

"I know."

"And if you think it has anything to do with history or artwork...or religion........or money. Money least of all."

"I know I know.........." Roque tries to make eye-contact with Leslie while she moves her head mechanically from side to side. She's staring at her image in the dresser mirror without really seeing it. "......old man's settling his account with God."

"And if you think it's actually gonna work "

"Then w "

"I'll tell you why—we OK here on time?"

"She's in there singing some fuckin..........Doors song." She's out there flicking Roque's thigh with the back of her hand as he moves away with the receiver, pulling her down with him by the waistband of her sweatpants to sit on the edge of the bed.

"Jacques lives with his eighty-year old mother who he should thank God she's blind because then she doesn't have to get a load othe torture on her son's face. A fucking virgin closet queer. I mean, who could come up with a combination like that it's gotta be real! It's what makes him the best snoop there is, the old man's right on that one. He catches all that rage as it slowly seeps down inside his gut he catches it and wads it up into a big hard ball and throws it back out when he got a job to do. The old man's right on that one. But the thing is, he doesn't catch it all and what gets away is gonna eat through his gut so deep so bad one day it's gonna poison him, it's gonna kill him and he must know that, so what the fuck—this way he gets a shot at losin it good in prison or driving away in a Rolls and never coming back either way.

"Me I'll do anything—anything—I think that's been adequately proven to the panel of experts—to be able to play with what I'm playin with here. Free dope and equipment—no!—free unlimited best dope there is and free unlimited best equipment there is. I still—hey someone's trying to send her a fax."

"Someone's "

"Someone's tr—you'll see, a fax is gonna come in. I still wake up every day nthink it's all gonna be gone. Every day I swear old man! But there's always more where that came from. Jacques makes sure othat. I figure the anticlimax'll be so intense it won't be worth living in the real world anymore anyway. And besides—on the inside—well if you want shit you might as well be where the shit is. Wheredyuh think Jacques does his shopping for me anyway? This is instant gratification, old man. This is instant pharmaco-electronico-electronico-pharmaco gratification. And if we make it, well then I'll be able to put it on my resume, won't I? Masterminded, implemented and evaluated the Electronics Department of the Crime of the Millennium. Then maybe I can quit hangin around with you whores and get my ass one othem good middle-management jobs. In a bank or something. Information Services Manager, right, old man? Mr. Batiste, how would you define your career goals? Where is she?

"Hold on................" Roque takes the phone away from his mouth.

Leslie draws slow wind-it-down circles with her fist in the air above her right ear. "…………She's ritualistically massaging white creamy lotion all over her tits……..all over and around…..underneath. You got five minutes max." Leslie gives him the finger. Roque points two back at her.

"You, you just needed to get laid and Claude, well, she's the only— I don't think she realizes what we're really—I mean it's a game for all of us but when we're shaving or driving on the A4 or turning the key in our door it hits us it at least hits us on some level—even if it goes right out again—that…..it well it could be interpreted as not a game too. I don't think she ever got that far. I think she's still stealin oranges from the local greengrocer to test how fast and far she can run from the cops."

    "Maybe because she doesn't shave, kid."

"It's not her fault…..She idolizes the old man it's criminal using her that w "

    "I know I know."

"He's nursing a goddamn hangover……..Stuffin his sister back in his gut to get her the fuck outa there. And neither of em even know that's why he's—Claude just materialized in his office one day—you know she's not dumb—there *are* no coincidences—she's not dumb that American cunt of y "

"AhhheeeiiiiiEEE—NUU-UUFFFFF!" Leslie shrieks, shoving Roque backward on the bed with both hands.

                " of yours What The Fuck Was That?"

"She's comin out I gotta go kid!"

"Get us a new date ol man only you can do it! Get back to work! Call the old man in the morning—hey! get us a date that holds! We can only clear the guys outa the lot once before they start gettin their brains outa cold storage and using em! Ciao!" Thierry hangs up. Roque hangs up with the confident closure of a judge who has just brought the gavel down on a conclusive decision. Leslie prowls the apartment silently, looking for a place to put herself. - . - .into the kitchenette, turning on water for tea. - . - .out of the kitchenette, waving an empty mug at Roque sitting on the bed watching her prowl, no thanks, he doesn't want any. -. - .back into the kitchenette, lifting the top off the kettle, staring in at the water, putting the top back on. -. - .over to the nighttable, picking up the dead ice cream cartons and spoons. -. - .back into the kitchenette, putting the cartons and spoons in the sink. -. - . out to the livingroom, looking through the archway to the bed, taking a deep breath and holding it in Dizzy Gillespie cheeks for some seconds then spitting it out through a tiny hole between ant-eater lips. -. - .over to the phone on the dresser, lifting the receiver, looking at her watchless wrist, putting the receiver down. -. - .back into the kitchenette, pouring the tea. -. - .out of the kitchenette with the tea, sitting down at the computer at the dinette table, staring at an unilluminated screen. -. - . into the bedroom-alcove, picking up the fax that's just rolled onto the floor. -. - .back to the table, writing something on the fax. -. - . through to the dresser, faxing the message. -. - .over to the big manila envelope between the bookcase and the sofa, taking an old Danney-tape. -. - .across to the stereo on the partition between the livingroom and the kitchenette, snapping the tape in "TWO-CUBED—THAT'S SIX O NINE-FOUR TWO TWO-NINE TWO TWO TWO—IF ANYONE IS UNFORTUNATE ENOUGH TO BE UP THIS EARLY AND COHERENT ENOUGH TO DIAL A PHONE AND EXPLAIN TO ME THE DIFFERENCE BETWEEN PARTLY CLOUDY AND PATCHY CLOUDS! COME ON KEEP OUR FRIENDS AT THE NATIONAL WEATHER SERVICE ON THEIR TOES! NO MORE OF THIS ARBITRARY METEOROLOGICAL LEXICOGRAPHY, I'VE-HAD-*ITTT!* ENOUGH! FINITO! CURTAINS! WASHED UP!—ACTUALLY I *HAVE* SOME CURTAINS THAT NEED WASHING UP! MEANWH— AH! THERE'S THE PHONE—POOR SLOB UP AT THIS HOUR!— MEANWHILE HERE'S AN IMPORTANT MESSAGE YOU'LL WANNA CATCH FROM YOUR FIRST LADY—WELL, FROM SOMEONE'S FIRST LADY—AT LEAST FROM THE FIRST MAN'S FIRST LADY—I'M GONNA GO GET MY QUESTION ANSWERED AND IF YOU'RE LUCKY—IF YOU'RE JUUUUU-UUUUUSSSSST LUCKY ENOUGH...........................I'LL—YOU GUESSED IT—SEE Y'ON T'OTHER SAHAHDD!" . -. - .stopping the tape and cruising with her Picasso mug to the dinette-table chair closest to the alcove, turning it so she can sit and see Roque.

 Roque pats a spot on the bed beside him. She shakes her head and sips her tea, her eyes speeding to catch up with her thoughts. She seems to be working very hard behind her deceptively steady breathing and otherwise expressionless face and finally says "I don't wanna," filtering the dazed message through a realm nowhere remotely near the space of her apartment. As if capturing signals from another dimension and simultaneously translating them for Roque, she asks "How do I know you didn't just set it up with this kid so if you ever called in a pinch he'd know to say these things?"

"L"

"And you were on the train for a whole different reason."

"Leslie.....What can I do to—you can't make something like that up. You can't—that's a—that's a full-time career making something like—No!—the fax!—did you hear him say you had a fax coming in, or not?"

Leslie takes off again from the helm of her dinette-table chair. Roque doesn't dare move, afraid to abort what's beginning to look like a journey that's bringing her back to him. She sips at her tea and gets up to turn Danney back on.

### "Hello, I'm Barbara Bush."

Danney (from a distance): "I'm on the horn, Babs, catchya in a bit!"

Barbara Bush: "Do you know anyone with mental illness?"

Danney (in an echo-effect): "Hey hold on, man, willyuh, I got Bee-squared on the other line!"

Barbara Bush: "That used to be a dirty word, didn't it?"

Danney (up at the mike, softly): "Great! Got my answer! Gohead, Bee-Bee, back with yuh, babe!"

"Wish you could understand what he's saying." Leslie pops the tape out and sits down again. "Funny bit." She looks like her thoughts are far ahead of her words and that she's speaking merely out of convention. "Funny, funny bit. And it's a real public service announcement that's what makes it so—I mean, it's really supposed to be there. He gets away with some shit, man," she says with a little laugh. "When they wrote the First Amendment they were staring up at a portrait of Danney-The Great-Brittain in a powdered wig and lace jabot behind his console—checking off his log with a quill pen and "

"Who was the fax from?"

"This girl in Philadelphia I used to dance with. She had to fax me right away to tell me that in her estimation six—and by the turn of the century ten—billion people, of which two are her own doing, is not a sufficient number for the population of Earth and she and her social fucking worker husband are gonna personally see to it that the situation is rectified in short order."

"She's "

" pregnoid. Again. Tee Em Vee. Triple-Maternity-Victim. Hit three times. And coincidentally enough the only most-brilliant-most-good-looking kids in recorded knowledge always seem to drop out of the same womb. Hers. Her fat little womb just sitting there on Roosevelt Boulevard waiting to dilate. Howdyou suppose that is, Roque?"

"What did you write back?"

"My condolences."

"No you didn't! What did you write back?"

Raising her eyebrows and grinning one of her modeling-clay grins, Leslie holds her hand out toward the fax curled up on the machine. *"My condolences,"* Roque reads in a heavily accented approximation. "Aren't you afraid she'll take it the wrong way?"

"Yeaheaheah," Leslie says through a crunched up face. "Hey you're right, Roque! I never thought othat. She might think I'm kidding! Gimme that willyuh? Maybe I should write back—what time is it there?—" She looks at her watchless wrist "and tell her— How did you know I" then crumbles the fax into a ball and tosses it over her left shoulder into the middle of the dinette table. "was taking that train that day that seat that minute?"

"How did the kid know you had a fax coming in? Ask him! That's not my department."

"What *is* your department, Roque?"

"Did you make the reservation from this apartment? That's how he knew!"

"What *is* your department, Roque."

"Leslie work with me on this, OK, I'm working with you, we got alot to deal with here."
"Oh you sure are working with me," Leslie gets up and looks behind her livingroom drapes and

"OK?"

"You Sure Are Working With Me," under her sofa.

"OK, Leslie?"

"YOU SURE ARE WORKING WITH ME!" She grabs a dinette-table chair and slams it down at one corner of the apartment, "YOU" stands on it,

"Leslie?"

examines the ceiling, "SURE" jumps off,

"Leslie what are you doing?"

hauls the chair to another corner and slams it down, "ARE" stands on it,

"For The Love Of"

examines the ceiling, "WORKING" jumps off,

" God, Leslie!"

repeats the maneuver everywhere two walls come together, "WITH" becoming more agitated at each new location

"What Are You Looking For, Leslie Brittain?"
and totally ignoring the sound of Roque's voice "ME!"

The livingroom and kitchenette duly inspected, Leslie mobilizes her forces into the bedroom-alcove. She slaps her hands onto her hips and looks down at Roque from her survey-tower command-post in front of the window. "CAMERAS!"

Roque lets a laugh punch through the tension drawn like a drum-head across his throat. "Sorry to disappoint you," he says, reaching up to touch her leg. "But I can have some in here as early as tomorrow morning if you'd like."

She kicks his hand away, gets off the chair and "I see your department's filing a report!" drags it past the bed out to the table. As Roque looks down at his erection, she zips back over, shoving her new Walkman into his chest. "HERE! Show me where's the tracking device—No!—I don't give a shit about that—Yes!—I give a shit about that but show me where's the fucking boh-ohmb-detonator! Frchrissake!" Roque begins to say something and "And I want my old walkperson back! Danney gave it to me I want it back it's not even broken is it?.....I don't even care even if it *is* broken I want it back! It's mine!" He takes a quick breath and "And I don't know how you and your purchasing department choose your merchandise but this one doesn't even have a radio! Mine had a radio!"

"But you don't ever use the radio you only listen to your brother's t "

"Is That The Point Here? What's The Point Here? Is That The Point Here? Whatsa matter the frustrated-genius cops too poor to get me one with a fucking radio?"

"When you get where he needs you to be, the kid lowers the sound on the tape. When you go to turn it up, the volume knob sets off the bomb."

"How The Fuck Can He Be So Goddamn Cock-Sure I'll Turn The Fucking Thing Up?"

"Because he "

"Maybe I Like My Cassette Lower When I'm Running In Front Of Police Headquarters!"

"Because he "

"Maybe That's An American Fucking Tradition For All He Knows!"

"Because "

"Maybe It's In The Constitution—Little Kids Pledge It Every Morning In School With Their Hands Over Their Hearts Lookin At The Flag!"

" he "

"Maybe I Woulda Turned The Volume Down All By My*self* Like a Big Girl Just At That Very Mili-Inch Of Parking-Lot Space And Planned To Keep It Down Until I Hit At Least The Opera If Not God If Not The Pont d'Alma Frchrissakes!"

" he "

"If Your Whole Hookah-Smoking-Caterpillar Plan Depends On Whether I Turn The Volume Up When My Tape—How The Fuck Does *He* Know That's What I'll Do?"

"Because he tried it this morning."

"Oh."

"A lot of times."

"Oh........OK....Oh...OK....................But how "

"He didn't explain it all to me."

"Just like I'm sure *you* didn't explain to *him* all the technical nuances involved in *your* department either. Just like I'm sure you guys didn't sit around getting explained the difference between a throat blow-job and a throat-and-tongue blow-job. You just told them what they needed to know and let them get on with their tasks. I'm sure you guys didn't have whole weekend retreats dedicated to the study and anal-ysis, you should *not* excuse the expression, of the data generated by *your* department, with "
"No, we didn't. Leslie you gotta know that from the very beginning...." Roque reaches over to the side of the bed where Leslie is standing. She doesn't respond. "....from the very beginning, once I——once we—you and I—it wasn't the same for me—like for the others....once I........knew you. I'm not explaining this the right way."
" charts and graphs—no! what am I talking about?—with instructional fucking videotapes and you up there at the screen with an ar-

row-flashlight pointer!" Leslie looks at the corner of the ceiling again, "Or maybe you used an inflatable doll!" tilting her head and widening her eyes as if spotting something up there.

"Leslie this isn't easy for me.....And I can't get your old one back, by now it's "

"on its way down to a chop-shop in Mexico! I wonder if it's like Zen monks killing themselves—I mean me disintegrating on the Quai des Orfèvres. They say Japanese monks who jump off cliffs because they're upset they haven't reached enlightenment wind up reaching enlightenment on the way down but then of course—you guessed it, sports fans! Too Late City, Arkansas! Of course no one ever asked how anyone ever determines this I mean is there an anchorperson holding a microphone in a parachute following the little monk down— Hello, Rock n Rollers, I'm here today with" She whispers in an anchorperson voice into her fist. "—but then the monk'd be dropping at a faster rate than the anchorperson, wouldn't he? Maybe the anchorperson would be killing herself too—and her story would reach enlightenment on the way down. Anyway, as I'm eatin it there in the parking lot I wonder if I'll see a part of my whole life flashing before me that I'll really wanna deal with once I say hey to Umberto and get my shower outa the way but—you guessed it, sports fans!"

"You wouldn't get touched, Leslie. I told you that. You just don't want to hear it! It's less dramatic for you the way *I* told it—you prefer to think of yourself as some great sacrificed—look—the bomb, first of all, goes off way way the hell back and way way the hell down— the whole point—in the building. It'll rock the building that's for sure and probably wipe out the guys in the cells but it won't travel out to the lot. Number one. Number two, it doesn't go off the minute you touch the knob, you'd be—you'd be—what it does is set off a timer for five minutes later. Where are you five minutes after you pass us?" He reaches for her again.

"Other side of the Samaritaine." She flails his hand away. "Rue de Rivoli."

"Leslie, by then you could reach enlightenment ten times. Though if you miss it there you're almost sure to reach it by the time you hit the Place de la Concorde."

"Worked for Louis and Marie, why not for me, huh? Why can't it be detonated from inside?"

"Building's too tight now, with the gangs. Too many questions to answer to get the material in and out.....even with the blind mute collaborator corpses we have working security."

"Corpses'll do that, Roque, won't they—go be blind and mute on you when you least expect it. The bomb?"

"The material for the bomb's already there it's common stuff that's always around or the kid could bring in easily from the outside—he'd construct it on site. The detonator's more sophisticated. Problem getting it into the place and then they'd have to get it out."

"Why can't it be detonated from his apartment? Or anywhere? A cafe, Egypt, Jupiter? A bakery truck parked on a side street? If they can do it in the movies frchrissake they can do it in something as uncomplicated as real life you're looking at me like you're about to tell me it's not your department. Did it ever occur to your department" Leslie drops to her knees and crawls like a jungle cat across the bed into Roque's face "that it could be set off by any one of the six and by the turn of the century ten billion people in this world—six and by the turn of the century ten billion people and *one*, once Cheryl Braunstein squats in the field in seven months—but they're using me as a character in a human video game just for the fucking challenge of it just cause it's a Cool Idea That Someone Pulled Out Of Their ANAL PASSAGEWAY WHEN IT WASN'T OTHERWISE OCCUPAHHHH " Roque slams his palms against Leslie's shoulders and tackles her onto her back. "WHY DIDN'T ANYONE TRY TO TALK MARCEL OUT OF IT FRCHRISSAKE!" "YOU DON'T KNOW MARCEL!" He splats on top of her. "I FEEL LIKE HE'S MY BEST FRIEND AFTER TONIGHT WHY ARE *YOU* DOING IT?" She struggles to get up. "THE LABYRINTH!" He pins her wrists to the pillow with one hand. "THE WHAT? AND CLAUDE WON'T GET NABBED DIVING INTO THE TUNNEL? THE WHAT?" She tries to free her legs from under him. "IF ANYONE DOWN THERE LIVES THROUGH THE BLAST THEY'LL BE BUSY SAVING THEIR OWN ASS!" He tries to yank her sweatpants down. "HOW DOES THE THING GET TO THE GUY IN SINGAPORE? HOW MUCH IS HE COUGHING UP FOR THIS THING?" She bites into his shoulder. "OUUWW, LESLIE! THAT'S JACQUES'S DEPARTMENT. FIVE MILLION FRANCS EACH!" He shakes free from her teeth and tightens his grip on her wrists. "THAT'S A MILLION FUCKING DOLLARS EACH WHERE'S *MY* TAKE? AND I WANT MY OLD WALKPERSON BACK!" She bites into his other shoulder. "OWWWSHITT LESLIE! NOBODY'S GETTING A TAKE OBVIOUSLY NOW BECAUSE NOW" He backs off and lets her free. "it's not going to happen."

Leslie pulls up her sweatpants and goes out to the livingroom bookcase, returning with what looks like a rolled-up giant poster. "I knew this'd come in handy some day!" She unrolls it, "Always there when you need him, Umberto is," rolls it in the other direction so it will lie flat, "bless his sweet endive-purchasing soul—that's sweet soul, not sweet endive." then shakes it out like a blanket. "It's the times he's always there when you *don't* need him that represent one of life's great challenges. Covering the bed "Offensive sonofabitch, isn't it?" is a huge sheet of neon-yellow glossy paper bearing, in two vertical columns, one headed by January and a hot-orange John and one by July and an electric-pink Peter, a calendar for each month of the year printed into the chest of its own day-glo-robed apostle who seems to be gathering his little document in his arms like a pile of delicate—cold water—laundry ready to be transferred from the Holy Washing Machine to the Holy Dryer, the entire assemblage blessed by the Lord Himself—or, actually, twelve Lords Himselves—whose metallic benediction-delivering image flickers on or off at the right ear of each apostle, depending on how you hold the paper. If the Last Supper had taken place in San Francisco in nineteen sixty-six, this is what the souvenir guy in the stand outside the arena would have run out of even before the t-shirts were all gone.

"That this stationery-store equivalent of a guitar mass is still ours to consult is *not* a tribute to my kindness!" Leslie tells Roque, sitting on her heels at the foot of the calendar as if about to perform a Japanese tea ceremony. "It's a tribute to my laziness.....well it's a tribute to my kindness-inspired laziness in a way, when you think about it." Roque reaches to the floor to get something from his shirtpocket; Leslie lifts the cigarette pack out of his hand. "Can't smoke in my apartment. I don't want it in my hair. He walked all over Rome last fall looking for some "

"Who," Roque takes the cigarette pack back from her. "Leslie?"

"Umberto—didn't I say Umberto? I thought I said" Leslie takes the cigarette pack back from him, opens the bedroom window, drops the pack into the courtyard and closes the window. "Umberto—for something to bring me back and then walked all over Rome looking for a cardboard tube to carry it in when he finally found it. He tells me it was hanging on the wall in some exclusive men's clothing shop outside the Vatican and he had to pay hundreds of millions of lire and fuck the owner's wife to get them to part with it. I told him I believed every word and that I thought the owner's wife was one lucky owner's wife in the bargain! But since " Roque reaches down to his jacketpocket this time, pulls out a fresh pack and a small box of matches, gets up and goes totally naked into the hallway outside

Leslie's door to have a smoke. She sits in silence on the bed and when he returns resumes as if he's never left " he goes through not only our own trash downstairs but every can in the neighborhood, and someone in the building told me once they saw him doing a can way the hell over near where the Rue St-Dominique meets the Boulevard St-Germain, I couldn't ditch it safely anywhere on the Left Bank and Jesus—" She looks at the calendar and salutes. "to the twelfth power—I wasn't about to take a fucking metro to like....Belleville just to throw the thing away so—oh! and—and—when he asks me where it is I tell him I sent it to a special place in America to have it framed where all the movie stars get their shit framed, at which point he recoils in reverence, especially when I tell him the owner keeps faxing to tell me mine's next after Jane and Ted's wedding invitation and Arnold's Planet Hollywood menu. But the real reason I kept it was I must've known we'd need it this very evening. Pick a date. How was your smoke, by the way, Monsieur and Madame Favre come by on their way in from midnight confession?

"Yeah they did, as a matter of fact."

"Good. Good, Roque. Good Roque. Real good. Roque. Well it could've been worse. Could've been Tulipe out there.....Or better. Depending on your point of view. Actually it's probably the first cock she's laid eyes on in forty years they're probably up there screwing their seventy-five-year-old asses off as we plot. You two guys talk about how the Cubs are doing? don't ask, it's a baseball team. Pick a date."

"For what, for the love of God?"

"There's that word again!" Leslie jiggles the calendar to try to make all twelve Jesuses flicker on at the same time.............
................................................................................
.................................................................."So Anyway! Pick A Date!"

"Aren't you running in the morning?"

"God I wouldn't miss running in the morning now if my life depended on it—Hey! Wait! Guess what! It does! I forgot! And I ain't talkin cardiovascular health here!"

"Isn't it a little late for you to still b "

"Don't worry, you're not staying over so I just bought an extra couple hours' sleep right there.....And I had to make sure the Favres got in safely." She smoothes her hand over the calendar. "Now what we want to be concentrating on is this area right here—Screaming-Chartreuse-Matthew June, Assassin-Violet-Thaddeus July—isn't that a great name? I guess they just called him Thad around the Holy Little League Club. Thad.—and Rape-Artist-Red-James the Less August. For your information, James the Greater is here." Leslie points to February. "Wonder if Judas got December for any particular reason......why not, I guess. I'm guessing your sports fans wouldn't want it to drag on much later than that, right?"

"Why "

"Well if they were already counting on June twenty-sixth I can't see them accepting anything much past "

" aren't I staying over?"

" anything much past the beginning of August and even that's a stretch. Although frankly, with half the city away for vacation I'm surprised you guys didn't set an August date right from the get-go. Know what I mean?"
Roque grabs Leslie's arm with one hand and rips the calendar off the bed with the other. "I asked you a "

"I think you know the answer."

"Why aren't I staying over?"

"Can't you—frchrissake, Roque, you're an Inspector—Inspect! Dig down real deep, you'll find it. I'm beginning to think you really do give out parking tickets! Look—" She scoops the calendar from the floor and spreads it neatly back on the bed. "this uncharacteristic show of moderation might surprise you but the closet submissive in me stops short of giving myself over to someone who's been plotting to rub me out for the past six months. We all have our limits, Roque, and guess what—that's mine!" In her Annual-Meeting-Of-The-Stockholders voice she announces "Now, if there is no further discussion, our man Thaddeus and I have just come up with the perfect date!"

"Why are you doing this, Leslie?" Roque is sitting on the bed, leaning against the window-wall, smelling of smoke and cologne and skin,

"Well for one, "

his bruised-little-boy eyes fixed on his half-hard cock. "Why didn't you ever ask me about my.......background?"

"You mean what merit badges you made and that sort of th "

"You know what I "

"Actually, Roque, I do know what you mean. You are referring to a particular badge which demands the most meritorious achievement of them all. Even more meritorious than that demanded by the Swimming Badge, the Clean-Bandanna Badge and the Getting-Your-Algebra-Homework-Turned-In-At-Least-On-Time-If-Not-With-Right-Answers Badge. And that's the Marriage Badge. You mean why didn't I ever ask you if you're married."

"Yeah. If I'm married. Or "

"Well first of all I figured you didn't live with anyone or you wouldn't've left your home number on my machine when I got back from Brussels. See maybe because I don't use up all my energy worrying about whether you're married or not my powers of deduction are still intact enough to be able to make stunning assessments like that. And second of all I don't give a shit. No—I'll change that—in fact, I give an immeasurable shit—I would *hope* you're married. I'd want nothing more than your being married. It'd be a Christmas present for me if you were married. Cause then there'd be less chance you'd start beatin up on me to marry you. Or live with you. Or.....be within earshot of hearing you brush your teeth! Let the woman you don't live with or you wouldn't've given me your number hear you spitting your toothpaste out into the washbasin while she's on her way out to look for hemorrhoid cream. Anything else you want, chéri, while I'm at the pharmacie? Maybe some matching stemware for when Mother comes for lunch next Sunday? You're looking at me like I just left my spaceship in a loading zone." Leslie wipes her palm back and forth in the air in front of Roque's eyes.

"The Truth According to Leslie."

"Yeah pretty soon I'll have a calendar assigned to me. I'll move it if you want."

"Move what?"

"My spaceship frchrissake, you're the one with the book of tickets! SO! Yready to hear our new date?"

"Why are you doing this, Leslie?"

"Get this: GETT THISSSS: I can't stand it! When they were giving out brains *I*, on the other hand, was camped out the night before—like for a Who concert—why didn't—Marcel shoulda come to me himself, in the first place—he woulda had a solid team member and a bit more creativity to this thing frchrissake.....but then that's true, then I wouldn'ta had the opportunity to give you a blow-job in the train compartment, would I? You're right—better this way. Yready?" Roque, tired, impatient, about to grab his smokes and make another spectacle of himself in the corridor, is squinting at Leslie as if waiting to see what excuse she comes up with *this* time for getting home late from a date. "Yready?" She looks at the calendar, runs her palm across it, flickers the Jesus on and off near Bartholomew's ear. Glances at Roque. Glances at the calendar. Looks at Roque............."**JULY FOURTH!**" she finally blares, smacking her right fist into her left palm. JOOO-OOO-LAHH-EEE FOURRRTHTH! July fourth, Roque! The Fucking Fourth Of July!"

Another punch to the palm and the jungle cat's springing off the bed, prowling the apartment, taking some quiet-time to iron out the kinks in its prey-swallowing strategy. Roque sluggishly picks his cigarettes and matches off his pile of clothes on the floor. "DON'T.....go anywhere—here—" Leslie bounds back into the bedroom. "Just," she says as she opens the window, "open the window—and dangle out. This date—this date—was put into the calendar by Julius Caesar just for Marcel's mission. It was *borrowed* by the American colonists in seventeen seventy-six because they considered it an *honor* to sign the Declaration of Independence on the same date that I was gonna set a bomb off under the venerable Notre Dame de Paris two hundred years hence—probably consulted General Lafayette himself, him being the most familiar with the terrain and all. Look—we all know the twenty-sixth is out—this is so close after the twenty-sixth it's almost the same day—hey! why the twenty-sixth in the first place?

don't throw the match into the courtyard, sweetie—here—give it to me here."

"The kid's limestone study, it's at its optimum—soft enough to open up with the minimum amount of explosives, hard enough to stay on the walls and ceiling of the tunnel and not come crashing down on Claude."

"Thoughtful."

"Actually, the kid had it down to ten-something—in the morning—ten like...twelve, or something like that—but we voted against asking you to change your schedule."

"Thoughtful. Bet they counted on your getting me to fall so in love with you I'd cancel my trip—avoid a hysterical good-bye scene at the airport. Well tell em it's me, not you. Someone else'd be out buying hemorrhoid cream by now. But then the mission'd *really* be in the shit. So you see, there're no coincidences—there's only cosmic synchronicity. I'll be back a good couple days before the fourth—I'm only going over to do Danney's show and if Aunt Helen wants me to stay longer so we can go shopping at the Cherry Hill Mall, why I'll just inform her I have a Police Headquarters to blow up. She'll understand. So I can rest up, maybe train a little by running around the neighborhood and turning the volume up and down on my walkperson a couple hundred times. But the don't throw the butt into the courtyard, sweetie, put it in your pantspocket or something."

As Leslie performs the tea ceremony again for her apostles, Roque settles back onto the bed and tries to turn her toward him.

"But the majesty of this date," she continues, arm-wrestling him with her shoulder, "is, of course, its symbolism. I mean, the minute—the mihihihih-nuhuhuhuht—you guys found out I was American the date should've been automatically changed without having to wait til *I* made the suggestion. This'll put those jackasses at Max Akron Playground and their award-winning annual fireworks display in their places—at least match em bang for bang! If you guys really had class you'd set up a little barbecue in the tunnel—some hamburgers, hot dogs, maybe stage a little baseball game off in one corner, red-white-n-blue crepe paper—no frisbees!—I HATE fucking frisbees!—make it look—and certainly no dogs!—make it—and raffle off a crocheted afghan, give the proceeds to the upkeep of the local church—HAH!—which in this case just happens to be the Cathedral of Notre Dame de Paris, that way they could repair the damage to their end of the tunnel, hey, Roque?—make it look like the Fourth oJuly frchrissake! I mean, just a bunch of firecrackers does not a July Fourth make. Charles de Gaulle said that, didn't he? Though it's a good start. Didn't he?" Leslie peers into Roque's weary face. "And a high school band."

"I wouldn't know, Leslie."

"All right so forget the band. Too short notice anyway."

"I mean about General de Gaulle." Roque looks at his watch and inhales deeply, "Look," releasing his breath in a long bumpy blend of confusion, frustration and fear while he reaches down to his clothing. "if I'm not staying over, "
"Hey you think Thierry's still up?" Leslie asks, grabbing his arm and taking her turn looking at his watch. He picks up his shirt and starts putting it on. "Well do you?" Ignores her and goes after his jeans. "We could call him and tell him about the new date!" Finishes buckling his belt and bends for his jacket. "Well isn't that—didn't he—get back to work old man! get us a date old man! only you can do it old man!"

He takes her hands and pulls her to her feet off the bed, hugging her to him in a tender gesture without much tenderness. "I'll let you know when I come up with how to get out of this. I'll call you in the m "
"Roque You Can't Be Serious!" She shoves him away with a flail. "We just spent all night pouring over neon apostles, coming up with a championship date, a date that's gonna go down in history. Again. I coulda sworn you were right here in this very apartment with me while all that was going on!"
"No, *you* can't be serious, Leslie! It's not always easy for me to know when you're kidding and it's never easy for you to know when to stop but this time *I'm* telling *you*," Roque points both index fingers and pauses a beat "You're Not Serious!" then moves to kiss Leslie good-bye on her forehead.

She turns her "Listen to me!" back to him.

"No Leslie!"

"Listen To Me!"

"No!" Half-way to the door,

"LISTEN TO ME!"

"No!" he hears her pick up the phone and start punching numbers. "What The Fuck Are You Doing?" he shouts as he opens the bolt.

"I'm Calling You," she yells back. "Leaving A Long, Detailed Message On Your Machine Thanking You For Telling Me All About The Plot And For Suggesting I Call My Pals At Interpol In The Morning To Tell Them All About It Too.......It's Rinnnginnng......Onnnnne......Rinnnginnng......Twooooo......Whadyuh Have It Set For, Four As I RemAACHCH!"

Roque grabs the receiver and slams it down. "Whatryouafuckinmaniac? That call goes right to the kid! We'll both be dead before you finish the first sentence!"

Leslie strolls into the livingroom and pulls two chairs out from under the dinette table. In the sweetest, most subdued near-whisper she says "Come." then floats into the kitchenette to get a Batman mug for an ashtray. Roque sits down and shakes a cigarette up from his pack, grabbing it directly with his mouth. Taking her seat, she puts her hands on his thighs, and with a tranquillity in inverse proportion to the urgency and agitation banging against her body from the inside, purrs "That, Roque, is my point." She pauses a minute.....Strokes his legs.....Gives him time to enjoy the effects of his smoke....."You see," She is speaking so softly he has to lean forward to hear her "you let them know I know....we're dead.", so sweetly she sounds like a newly crowned Miss America thanking her Mother and Minister. "You drop out and tell them I know nothing....we're dead. You drop out and tell them I know everything....we're dead. You tell them I know all about it but" Confident that she has Roque's attention, Leslie slides into her normal voice. "that I think it's cool and am here to please and that I've suggested maybe after we hit Notre Dame we can think about other national monuments and even other national monuments in other countries....we're dead. You tell them you've decided I'm not the right human-video-game-blip for the job but that you've told me nothing....they don't believe you, we're dead. You tell them that as staggering coincidence will have it, just this very night I realized that routine was slowing me down so I decided to change my route forever and nevermore run anything remotely resembling the old route, especially the part that took me past Police Headquarters....they don't believe you and we're dead. You beginning to get my drift here?" she asks affectionately, caressing Roque's shoulder through his denim jacket. "You want anything, you need anything? Glass of water maybe? You OK here? Cup of tea? Nother smoke?"

"You don't have anything to drink, do you?" Roque asks on his way to the john.

"No but wh " Leslie lops off her smartass answer in its early developmental stage, afraid to break the mood she's worked so diligently to establish "No.", but then realizes that the contrast with her normal personality might do more harm in that direction than good, so she shouts in after him "But When We're Married We'll Buy An Extra-Big New Liquor Cabinet At Comforama And Spend Romantic Saturday Afternoons At Carrefour Stocking Up.....OK, Dear?", adding, when he comes back to the table, "Unless of course the children need shoes, at which point we'll spend that particular romantic Saturday afternoon dragging them screaming through you see, as I see it, we have basically two options. Three. But I'll get to that in a minute. No tea, right?"

Roque shakes his head.

"Option Number One involves the following two possibilities: we live; we die, each possibility bringing with it a series of sub-possibilities as follows: Live: we continue to live the same pitifully common existence we do now, incessantly and torturously ruminating about the meaning of life and our place in the pulsating amorphia of humanity...or...we get rich overnight and never have to see the inside of a metro car again. Die: we die immediately...or...we die a couple days later...or...we rot in prison and then die—in prison. Option Number Two involves the following one possibility: we die immediately. No sub-options—well, there are, but they're not important for the discussion at hand—they'll be part of your homework assignment and can be found on page one hundred fifty-four of your textbook. Option Number Three I'll get to in a minute. Now that we have explored the features of the various Options, let us move on to a look at their particular scenarios: Option Number One is we go along as if everything's the way it was before Patrick, the Jewel, made his little discovery at the Gare du Nord. On July Fourth I turn the volume of my walkperson up, Claude retrieves the ancient document, Jacques gets it to whatisname in Thailand, "

"Singapore."

"What, the guy move?—you get your million dollars, you give me half, and we never see each other again." Roque's eyes widen and mouth opens as if being worked by a puppeteer.

"Kidding." Leslie caresses "Roque." his chin "Kidding." and smiles. "What I really meant to say was: you give me *all* of your mil—no no no. Kidding. Kidding. No one'll ever know we had this discussion tonight, they'll think you came in here, waved your cock at me, I took a bath, you called Thierry, and we fell asleep in each other's arms which of course is not going to happen. Now there *is* the chance this guy in Malaysia'll fuck "

"Sing "

"you guys and not come through with your allowance or have you all wasted or that your pals'll waste you and keep your share, or that Thierry gets it severely wrong and the entrance to the tunnel remains intact but the entire Ile de la Cité blows, or that they catch our asses—including mine—and put us away, but there's also the chance you'll step off the curb during your next parking-ticket round and become a human cobblestone. The important thing is that if we shut up and play dumber than even *we* have the capacity to play, we might run head-on into the sub-microscopic chance that all goes as hoped and planned. HAH! Or at least graze it. Option Number Two is we do anything other than precisely that and Jacques and his blind invalid mother come calling with automatic weapons—Do you take your tea with one round or two, Leslie, dear? a.a.a.a.a  a.a.a.a.a.a. a.a.a.a.  a.a.a.a.a." Leslie spits a round of bullets from the magazine in the back of her throat. "And by the way no one's a virgin here."

"What's option number three?"

"Thierry's speedo'd-up stor—whadhe say?—a virgin closet queer or a closet virgin queer? Jacques. For-get-it! Virginity doesn't exist. It's a myth. Researched, developed, produced and marketed by that big corporation in Rome with branch offices around the planet bearing the company logo." She makes a cross with her index fingers.

"What's option number three?"

"First thing tomorrow morning we get entire-face-and-body plastic surgery and new passports and move to New Guinea."

"Sub-options?"
"Endless, Roque, come on! You know how *big* New Guinea is?

OK, it's not Russia, but God we'd have to choose where to live, where to send the children to school, where to buy wood to build the extension on the house for when Mother comes to live with uaAAHHH!" Roque puts his hands loosely around Leslie's neck and shakes her back and forth. "UGHGH JAAACQUES! Where Are You? Get-your-ass-outa-that-closet-and-Helllllpppp! Sayyyvve Meeeee!" She Wizard of Oz-witch-melts in her chair.

"I vote for option three!" Roque announces. "I want to look like James Dean."

"James Dean is dead, Roque. That's just my point. You won't need no back-alley nose-bobber for that—you'll've been to the Main Man. Death. Death is the Ultimate Plastic Surgeon. You listen to me or you n James'll be rollin cigarette packs up in each other's t-shirt sleeves for the rest of eternity."

Roque stands up, stares at Leslie and nods. "OK," he mumbles, chucking his cigarette butt into Batman, "OK." then slowly pushes his chair back under the table. "OK."

"REALLY?" she beams proudly. "Really? Just like that?"

"Well, just like that, Leslie, I don't know, it's almost three in the morning."

"How bout me giving you a note for your boss so you can sleep late?"

"How bout you making me sleep even later?"

"See yuh, Roque." Leslie goes to the entranceway and opens the door. "Howsit feel to be out there with clothes on? Bet if the Favres walked by now they wouldn't even recognize you. They'd think you were the second shift. The only way they could be absolutely sure would be if old Madame Favre got down on her knees and did some comparative investigating. Or Monsieur Favre for that matter but I bet he wasn't as riveted as she was tonight on the potential object of investigation."

"Good night, Leslie." Roque starts walking down the corridor toward the staircase.

"Or the object of potential investigation. After all it wasn't the first cock *he'd* seen in thirty years."

"I thought you said forty," he says, still walking.

"I'll check it out and go out to a phone booth and call myself so Thierry can give you the message. Oh!—just so no one has a heart attack when they don't see me run past tomorrow, *I'm* gonna sleep late and then go run at the gym." Her feet inside the entranceway, her hands gripping the doorframe, the bulk of Leslie's body is bulging into the hall in a huge graceful arc. "Well, Roque! How nice it is to see you again," she croons as he spins around just before the turn down the stairs and heads back toward the apartment.

"For a smart woman," he tells her, pointing both index fingers, "you can be really dumb!"

"Luca Brazzi sleeps with the fishes, huh? You're right...I'll run the route at six.......gettin outa hand here......" She looks at her watchless wrist as he spins around and heads back toward the stairs. "Hey! Get this one!—I take a bus—in my running clothes with the Walkperson That Ate Paris—to a block before Headquarters, I get off, run past like I'm not about to pass out from having stayed up all sexless night—which is fine with me, I mean, if you don't wanna stay over, who am I to force you?—get on another bus once I'm outa sight, come home, nap, and when Patrick shows up at ten, go to the gym! Talk about bril—when they were giving out brains "

"Hey! Get this one!" Roque says from halfway down the hall, imitating Leslie's accent and flail. "Jacques has check-points manned by guys who know your route better than you do!"

"Every Fucking Day? Don't these guys have work to do? Who follows the real live criminals around frchrissake?" She glances over her shoulder to the entranceway ceiling. "I *told* you there were cameras!"

"There are no cameras, Leslie. I know you wish I could tell you there were but...there was no need."

"Yeah, they had all the camera they needed on the end oyour dick! A walking fibre-optic!"

She crosses her arms in front of her chest and looks away then back at Roque. "And by the way, those fibre-optic fibres are reaeaeal reaeaeal skinny!" He points both index fingers at her and goes for the stairs.

"Wait!" she yelps, skipping into the apartment for a second........ ....................."Here! Lose it!"

Roque disappears down the staircase with the apostle calendar under his arm.

# XIII

# THE BELLE ÉPOQUE
# ©URLICUE METAL METRO $IGN

Patrick and Leslie are walking late morning through the ninth *arrondissement*'s insurance and banking district whose imposing sobriety turns what would in any other *quartier* be a silver drizzle into a shower of tin. It is as if the buildings themselves are wearing business suits—uniform insurance-broker brown, somber banker gray, pinstriped with perfectly wiped windows ("You wouldn't want your savings looked after in a place with dirty windows, would you Patrick? If they let the windows go, imagine what they'd do to your cash!")—standing solidly together, conferring with each other in clipped whispers, setting the rules for the old ordered streets of the neighborhood.

Patrick has something to tell Ms. Brittain but first he wants to know, if she didn't get any sleep last night and ran in the morning ("at the ssaamme exxaacct hour, Patrick!") nonetheless and has three urgent faxes, a frantic message from Mrs. Daley and an overdue Embassy-reception guest-list waiting for them back on the dinette table, and everyone else is scattering into cafes for shelter from the rain, "wh-which, if y-you don't m—which—well—i-isn't exactly exactly—Imean.....w-warm. Warm. M-Ms. Brittain. Actually. I've......noticed. F-for this t-time of.....well.....y-year" why they are loping along the Rue de la Victoire like "w-well f-fed t-tourists out for—Imean—a s-summer...stroll. Stroll."

Leslie compliments Patrick on the increasing expressiveness of his language—though she suggests that well fed is besides the point and that what he probably wanted to say is well rested—noting his progress, in that area among others, in the time since they made each other's acquaintance at Jim Morrison's house and realizing she's actually glad he said well-fed because that reminds her that she owes Georges for a basket of croissants she accidentally knocked off the table this morning in her stupor ("I'm sure he put them right the fuck back and fed them to the next poor slob who walked in but he can use the money to buy Maude combs for her hair while she's out getting him a watch chain."). It's like jet lag, she tells Patrick, if she ("or a new apron") gives into it she'll sleep through the summer; she has to convince her body it had a normal night like all its fellow bodies. Patrick has something to tell Ms. Brittain but first he wants to know whether she spent the night with Mr. Roque. She says that she and Mr. Roque had a small gathering with four of his business associates.

She also tells him there's a "time to ingest paper and a time to just be" and that the reason they are just being in this and not any other neighborhood this morning is precisely *because* it is raining. That if it were not raining, this *quartier* would be the *last* place she would have brought him because this is a rain *quartier*, it has to be experienced in the rain. ("Chilly spring rain optimally, or very late-fall/very early-winter rain. Summer rain is useless for this *quartier* because if it's summer rain it means it's summer which means the entire neighborhood is on vacation. Walking through this part of the ninth is like walking through the model heart at the Franklin Institute—it has to be fully turned on and beating or you might as well've gone to the movies.") It's an urgent *quartier*, she explains to Patrick, where people scurry—to meet someone, to eat something, to deliver somewhere—and Western Civilization scurries most and best in the chilly spring or the very late fall/very early winter. ("People in the, in the—for instance—sixteenth don't scurry. They glide—out of bed, into their baths—not showers, Patrick, baths—into their Chanel suits, into their fur coats with huge shoulder pads, into their automobiles—not cars, Patrick, automobiles—into the awninged entranceway where the porter opens the door so they can glide into the vestibule where the coat-check girl busies herself with their wrap and the *maître d'* shows them in which direction to glide to join their luncheon date—not lunch, Patrick, luncheon. And the sixteenth is a sun *arrondissement*. Rain is not kind to fur.")

Patrick has something to tell Ms. Brittain.

("The buildings in the ninth must've all been built in the rain, designed even in the rain. In early nineteenth-century rain. The architects and contractors and the laborers in their blue workclothes must've waited around for the rain to be right like so many movie directors with a scene to shoot. The same way they don't put you totally to sleep when they redo your nose because your face has to be more or less during the operation the way it'll be when you're walking around with your new nose on it going to pick up your dry-cleaning. Otherwise, Patrick, you walk out of the operating room with an asleep nose on an awake face, a nose that only ever really looks right when your face is doped up the way it was when they gave it to you. Well these are rain-conceived buildings, and they only ever really look right on a day like today, or at least a day when it's just about to rain or it's just stopped and whatever metallic threads of sunlight are dangling from the horizon are there expressly to let you know that fact. The discrete nobility of these structures turns self-conscious in the shameless sun. Like in those nightmares where all of a sudden you're sitting at the opera with no clothes on.")

Patrick has something to t

("See how the pavement and walls match the rain? Receive it, absorb it? Alchemize it and send it back out to energize the air of the neighborhood, to slice down upon its movement like little individual razor blades, and dispatch its agents indoors, inside? For despite the buzzy eddies of bodies before every cafe and stationery store, at every busstop, struggling past each other up and down every steep skinny side-street, this is also a *quartier* of inside. Inside bank vaults and filing cabinets. Inside meetingrooms with mahogany on their inside walls. Inside clauses inside paragraphs inside pages of documents. Inside eyes and inside brains behind desks inside these weighty spaces. All due respect to its cool basketball players, Patrick, we could not have permitted ourselves to go to the Luxembourg Gardens on a day like today.")

Patrick has something to tell Ms. Brittain but first he worries about the people expecting answers to the faxes on the dinette table. Leslie pushes them on to the Place d'Estienne d'Orves where streets straggle out around the solidly centered Trinité Church like the frazzled random strands of a ball of yarn the cat left behind. Tight little streets, leading away from the Rue de Chateaudun and the Rue de Provence whose prudent advisors work to make sure you keep your money, out to the St-Lazare train station and up to the Place and Avenue de Clichy whose garish hucksters work to make sure you don't. He asks if they'll be angry at Leslie or if they'll just send second faxes, more urgent than the first. Leslie leads around the church, and on their way up the Rue de Clichy tells him that's why these are streets that must be returned to. ("You'll keep coming back, too, Patrick, you'll see. They try to take you inside with them, aspirate you into their mystery. It's like going to the same film fifteen times, always hoping the ending will be different this time, this time the ending will be different. This time you'll see what happened all those other times after the screen went black. You sit in a different seat, you go at a different hour, and sometimes you think maybe you *did* make the dead guy get up and walk away.

"Nana walked these streets, Patrick, Zola's Nana and her lesbian friend Satin walked them in fiction and even more important Henry Miller walked them in fact. One time when you come back you'll see Nana and Satin sweeping along the Rue des Martyrs and then they'll be invited into the Nouvelle Athènes for an absinthe and you won't see them anymore. But if you wouldn't have come back you wouldn't have seen them. One time when you come back you'll see the buildings ripple along the Rue Blanche, do deep-knee-bends in their spare time in the rain.")

Patrick says that he thinks he saw a building do just that back there when they crossed the Rue Moncey and Leslie tells him good try but not to let himself be taken in by buildings which pawn themselves off as authentic ripplers but which are only out after his life. Or worse—his money. The farther north we go, she tells him, the more he should be concerned about buildings with thin mustaches and snug striped sailor t-shirts, scarves around their necks and magnetic dark darty eyes, hiding knives in their boots, keeping all the money their girlfriend-buildings bring in from their neighborhood nights, promising him it's an authentic Rolex then taking his last hundred-franc note. Patrick suggests that if they sit down for awhile she'll feel better. He says that happens to him, too, when he doesn't get enough sleep.

And besides, if they sit down, he c—well—he has something to tell her.

At the end of the street they surround a woman with a baby carriage ("Quick! Patrick! Positions!")—Leslie flank-right, Patrick flank-left—and the four of them cross the rain-crazed Place de Clichy *en famille*, once again proving Leslie's double-jeopardy theory of traffic confrontation, whereby a woman with visible evidence of having been victimized by maternity is not permitted to then go on and be victimized by the operator of a motor vehicle and is therefore the safest traveling companion between two sidewalks. ("Unfortunately, for some reason I haven't been able to figure out yet but I'm working on it, it doesn't hold in the other direction, thereby eliminating a history of pedestrian mishap as an effective form of contraception.") She tells Patrick she feels great. They open the door to the Café Weppler.

"I have to make a call."

"Are-are you—well—g-going to c-call the people who...Imean—s-sent you the f-faxes? Faxes? I h-have—dyou m—well...s-something to t—well........t-t-tell you you. Actually. M-Ms. Brittain."

"Order me *un thé au lait et un sandwich au chèvre*—without butter—and anything you want. Will you still be here when I get back?"

Leslie does not head for the phones but walks Patrick to a booth and sits on the ribbed burgundy-velvet *banquette* across from him. She leans forward and puts her hands on the table, just far enough across the middle to be in his space without scaring him into unfocus. Patrick immediately grabs the green plastic stackable ashtray, whose washed-out gold letters are trying to still spell Heineken, and inspects the hole engineered into its underside. "Patrick. Patrick. Patrick,,," Leslie says very quietly, "Henry Mi—this is whe—this cafe is where Henry Miller did alot of his coffee drinking. And while he sat here and drank his coffee—maybe even in your very seat—he looked liiiike..." she scans the room "...that guy over there!"

Patrick turns around cautiously, as if Leslie had rasped "don't look now" between clenched teeth instead of having sprung up and boldly pointed to a table behind him. "Frayed collar up, posture that must be grinding his organs into a terrible mess. The kind of almost-shaven face, the kind of preoccupied stare where you don't know whether he's extremely wise or extremely stupid, whether he's in his own world metabolizing the scene—like those Steinberg maps of New York: the coffee, the cup, the table, the Weppler, the Place de Clichy, the ninth *arrondissement*, Paris, France, the Galaxy—and is already on the third rewrite and doesn't even own a pencil, or whether he's in his own world gazing down at his coffee and out the plateglass window at the arrow pointing towards the Montmartre Cemetery and, well, seeing his coffee and the arrow pointing towards the Montmartre Cemetery. You can turn back and look at me now, Patrick."

Patrick turns back and looks at his ashtray. "Well what I'm trying to say is—*Attendez Un Instant, Monsieur, S'il Vous Plaît!* damnit whatdyou want Patrick?" The long-white-aproned waiter who materialized while Leslie and Henry were migrating from France to the Galaxy is walking away from the table. "*Un thé au lait, un sandwich au chèvre sans beurre et.....*" Leslie glares at Patrick. Patrick's entire cognition is penetrating the plateglass window and counting the number of movietheaters ringing the *place*. "Forget it! We'll get back to you for the rest!" The waiter bursts away, squalling Leslie's order to a hearing-challenged food preparer in Newfoundland. "We just lost him forever, Patrick, you'll never eat again. Right at this very moment he's throwing a couple things into a backpack and stuffing his apron into the microwave: frozen-*escargot* setting. By the time one of his colleagues brings my sandwich and I send it back cause they put butter on it and they bring it back having substituted the butter with low-cholesterol rat-feces, he'll have the Incan treasure half-way dug out of the cavern.....Selling it to a guy in Si "

"I h-have to—well—g-go g-go g-go...Imean........h-home. Home. Actually. M-Ms. Br-Brittain," Patrick says, neatly putting back into his bag a notebook in which he has just recorded the results of his cinema census.

"I acknowledge, Patrick, that we are living in the two-and-a-halfth, i.e., bordering on third, world here, but I'm sure there's some kinda hole in the floor downstairs you can aim into."

"No! Imean—M-Ms. Br-Brittain, n........H- "

"Or squat over."

" home. Actually. M-Ms. Br- "

"As the case may be."

L-last—well—m-my m-m-mother c-called l-last n-night and s-said—well—i-it's—well—s-said........i-it's en—well—en-enough. Enough. Actually. M-may I h-have—well—o-orange j-juice? And a—well—h-ham and ch-cheese? S-sandwich? M-Ms. Br-Brittain. Please," Patrick asks a gash named Ms. Brittain in the woodgrain tabletop near the salt/pepper/mustard caddy.

"Whatr yasking *me* for do I look like I'm wearing an apron? The guy might get back from his expedition yet—they always do!—so given the sacred nature of this shrine—due, by the way, less to the rodent droppings than to Henry Miller's vibrations throbbing inside the air molecules—it is crucial to our spiritual survival, to say nothing of thrival, that we set aside our admirable concern about the people who faxed us this morning, in favor of the more lofty occupation of zealotic reverence. I have to go down and make a call. When I get back up we'll go out to the magazine stand on the corner and together we will choose the postcard on which we will tell your mother—on which we will politely tell your mother—what we think of her sense of humor—send my tea back if it's not scalding—and parenting."

On her way to the stairs Leslie stops in the doorway to peer out at the primary colors of the Place de Clichy. No pastels for this neighborhood. It doesn't seem to merit the pinks blushing over the Avenue Montaigne from Dior's Spring windows or the apple greens splashing from the Place des Vosges onto the Italian Renaissance arcades bordering its little square park. It's being at a baseball game, the Place de Clichy, being at a baseball game, sweeping the bleachers in a huge visual arc and always seeing the reds first—starting at the seats to the left of where you are, letting your eyes drift right, from point to point, full around, up and down aisles, across rows, until you're back where you began, wherever your eyes want to go, and where they wind up wanting to go is wherever the red is—caps, banners, halter tops, lipstick, shorts, programs, sneakers, lettering on popcorn boxes, t-shirts, sunglass frames, an empty seat. Then the yellows bleed in, the blues bubble up to the surface, but pastels are on the bench at the ballgame, it's always the reds up at bat.

As Leslie blurs her eyes, the Place de Clichy secretes its red, smears it around, lipstick on the Place de Clichy. A Moulin Rouge dancer carrying a red workout bag flits from rehearsal, past a street vendor's red plastic table, into a *tabac* whose red neon sign and red awning are partly blocked by a bus-borne ad for the laundry detergent which got the model-baby's overalls back to their original, pre-mud-pie red. Only then does the yellow on the street vendor's jacket filter through, and the blue in the fast-food place lettering next to the *tabac*. And only after that the tarnished-copper green of the Belle Epoque curlicue metal *métro* sign.

"Mr. Kote's phone, Charlotte Nyle."

"Hi it's me."

"Leslie! How good to hear from you."

"Is he somewhere on the face of the Earth as it's currently being defined?"

"En route from Singapore."

"Again?"

"En route from Singapore."

"You can be honest with me, Charlotte, it'll go no further, he has a wife and four war-orphans in Singapore, doesn't he, and he goes there every night for dinner on his way home from the office in Brussels so they won't think he's the kind oguy who lets his work get more important than his family, right?"

"En route from Singapore."

"Shit, Charlotte! I need to talk to him. When he checks in tell him I need to talk to him when's he checking in?"

"Are you calling from your phonebooth?"

"Yeah. Well—no. Not from Georges's I owe him for a basket of croissants he won't let me back in til I get honest I'm out with Patrick when can I talk to him?"

"It can't wait until tonight?"

"I guess....when's he checking in? I'll call you back after that and you'll tell me what time he can call me at Georges's."

"How many other faxes didn't you read this morning, Leslie?"

"Oh shit Charlotte talk to me here!"

"The cover page had urgent—yoo arr gee ee en tee—in forty-point characters with a double-shadow frame around it."

"I *told* Patrick not to come pick me up so early! What if some forty-point double-shadow-framed urgent fax comes in and we miss it! Yoo arr gee ee en tee. From Jack no less! I warned him! Buh-uht, you know how insistent kids of that age—uhhhh.....had I read the fbeen there when the fax came in, what would we be speaking about right now, Charlotte?"

"I'd be telling you that there's no change in plans."

"Oh! Good! Well! That's sure a relief! Whew! While Patrick and I were walking past the Moulin Rouge just now I was saying that very thing to him—gee, Patrick, sure hope there's no change in plans for WHAT PLANS, CHARLOTTE, FRCHRISSAKE STOP JERKING ME! Excuse me."

"He's landing in Paris this evening. You will b "

"With Pascal?"

"Pascal is no longer with us. Mr. Kote found out he took the plane for personal use one weekend when Mr. Kote wasn't flying and he "

" had him taken to the junk-car compressing plant and turned into a little square-foot block of "

" almost. Why don't we just say he'll never fly a *paper* airplane again."

"So it's that other one that slob, what's his "

"Erik. I don't know how much time, Leslie, you're prepared to devote to a discussion of Mr. Kote's personnel given the kind of schedule you don't know you're on."

"OK OK. Shame about Pascal though. He had the most intense "

"You will be picked up at nine o'clock. Dinner "

"Shit!"

"Leslie?"

"I slept about four seconds last night, two fucking nights in a row staying up late like a big girl, Charlotte, I don't know."
"Dinner is at Le Divellec at "

"Ooh-ooh! Goo-ood!"

" nine-eighteen."

"Sure that's not twenty-two, Charlotte? Or nine-twelve? Better check your notes. How seriously does he really take this shit?"
"Your dress, shoes and make-up will be del—they're probably there already."
"Oh-ho, weh-hell, then this was a totally unnecessary conversation! If that's the case then all I had to do was walk out onto the Place de Clichy and buy a newspaper! Not even *buy* a newspaper— just *saunter* past a kiosk and let my eyes *graze* the front pages of all the newspapers that are there waiting for *other* people to buy them."

"How's your "

"The dress and make-up arrive. I'm not there. I'm here. Talking to you. About the dress and make-up arriving. Mrs. Darotto gets the package. Opens it with the kind of lust she knows only when opening a package that comes for me. No! Opens it with the kind of lust she knows only when opening a package that comes for me having first sent Il Duce on an errand to an address that doesn't exist—in this city anyway. She checks out the contents then calls the horoscope hotline—*Madame Soleil*—can you dig it?—to make sure there's no astral injunction against what she knows she now must do—and then sets out on her appointed rounds, systematically, like a fucking meter reader, meting out word of the delivery to all the *concierges* in her *concierge*-network according to the amount of details of which they've proven themselves worthy. To those, for instance, who have withheld news from her, she might show the box, allude to its international importance, but not open it. Those who've been forthcoming with their own morsels, but whose honesty she questions, get to see but not touch the dress, and hear a summary of the particulars of previous packages of the same nature. For her pals, she'll have them run and get their hygiene-deficient daughters so they can try the fucking thing on! Time I get it it's a rag and she thinks I don't know. Right to their sex organs, all this secret peeking goes right up into their destitute little pussies, much cleaner n prettier than their husbands' sloppy drippy dicks hidden in those folds of flab. Usually "

"Oh, my. I hope she leaves the lipstick sealed."

"Usually stashes make-up and accessories in her *loge* and picks them up on the way back in—on the way up to my apartment with the package that *just* arrived—which not only minimizes risk of damage but also allows a certain freedom of description of those items according to who her listener is. With all the concierges otherwise occupied, *quartier* business stops dead. The neighborhood becomes a ghosttown. Mail and papers don't get dis—read first then distributed. Messages don't get delivered. Rumors don't get passed on—except about the dress. Real meter-readers don't get let into apartments and vandals enter unnoticed. Vacationers don't get their plants walked and their dogs watered. Steps don't get scrubbed. Eventually this has repercussions on adjacent *quartiers* and on *quartiers* adjacent to those and soon the whole city starts to wither, to the point where the editors of the undis—un-read-first-then-distributed papers send their investigative reporters out and all of a sudden you see: "MAN WHO OWNS EVERY BUILDING ON EARTH SENDS DRESS TO PARIS FOR DINNER DATE".

"How's your hair?"
"Fine thanks, how's yours?"

"You have an appointment at Carita at four o'clock. He wants it in a French knot. To go with the dress. You'll see."

"Shit I'll have to get the dress drycleaned how am I gonna do it all Charlotte I can't do it all what if I'da had somethin else goin down today then what? When am I gonna take a fucking nap?"

"Leslie, you surprise me."

"I don't have time for this, Charlotte."

"What happened to who the "

" fuck does he think he is? Telling me what to wear and how to do my PATRICK! hold on a second, willyuh, Charlotte? How Long Have You Been Standing There?"
"Y-you've been—dyou mind—well—g-gone a.....while. While. M-Ms. Br-Brittain. I d-didn't—Imean—kn-know what........I was g-getting.....w-worried. Actually."
"Hold on, Charlotte, willya second? You coulda had them announce over the PA system Attention Weppler Coffee-Drinkers, There's A Little Boy Who Lost His Internship Supervisor. Listen Charlotte, that's cause I need him immense-time to answer some questions for me. I'd go wearing a clown suit if he asked me this time."
"You'd go wearing a clown suit anyway, Leslie, you have no shame."
"Big floppy shoes, red nose. Pity—Mrs. D. would leave the shoes and nose back in the *loge* cause they're basically accessories but they're the best part. The girls'd miss the best part. To say nothing of the press corps. I'll check in with you later. If eh-nee-ee-thi-ing changes by a breath, fax me! Patrick's gonna be velcroed to the machine we're on our way did he say anything about nails?"

"Red. Like the lipstick. It was sent to the salon."

"OK just—when he checks in tell him he was right it was brilliant it all went like he said Roque's back on track and it was brilliant! Bye!" Leslie hurls the receiver onto its hook and swats at Patrick's "CUMAWN PATRICK UP N ATEM ATOM ANT!" bottom. "Get your backpack we're in a taxi!"

"D-day af-after—well—t-t-tom.....Is-is w-when I—well—h-have to—well—Imean—b-be—well.......h-h-h-h........or sh-sh-she s-said n-not t-to b-bother. Actually. H-home. E-e-ever. Actually. D-day after after t-t-tomorrow. Actually. M-Ms. Br-Brittain."

"HERE!" As she sprints past him up the steps she takes a hundred-franc bill from her purse and stuffs it into his hand like a relay-race baton. "Throw this on the table we'll buy the postcard tomorrow what oxygen-brain had the idea to just stand there watching faxes roll out onto my floor and not give a flying fongoola what the fuck they s " She realizes he's not with her and, hearing the door to the men's room close, darts back down, bursts in and plants herself at the urinal next to his.

"M-MS BR-BRITTAIN!"

"Real lucky you can type, Patrick, what oxygen-brain had the idea to just stand there watching faxes roll out onto my floor and not give a flying fongoola what the fuck they said ARE YOU FINISHED PATRICK FRCHRISSAKE Shake It Off And Let's Get—OK OK" Patrick is down on his hands and knees following the adventures of a fearless urine droplet as it fights its way along the crevice between two floor tiles in the name of urine droplets everywhere. Leslie smacks both palms against the swinging door and bolts up the steps.

"A-are we—dyou m—are we th-through w-with our—Imean—M-Ms. Brittain—a-are we thr-though with our—well......f-fanatic r-reverence?" Patrick wants to know as he trots after her, kneading the hundred-franc bill like an arthritic working out on a rubber ball.

"That's zealotic reverence there's a time to hang out and a time to ingest paper don't you have an Embassy list to work on, Mr. Trucock?"

The cab lets them off on the Avenue Bosquet behind a black Peugeot 405 trying to pull into a small space. As they march and trot down the *passage* they see Mrs. D. coming toward them. She is carrying a pie plate covered with a bonnet of aluminum foil. "Where Is It?" Leslie demands, flailing, marching.

Mrs. Darotto chuckles self-consciously and smiles at Patrick. "Listen Umberto made a leek pie for Madame Charthellère, the baker's wife. She's sick. I'm takin it to her. She's a week late—horoscope said she shoulda started throwin up last Wednesday morning."

"Little culinary activity between Mensa meetings, huh?" Leslie and Patrick have stopped moving forward but Leslie is shifting impatiently from foot to foot. "Madame Charthellère doesn't get the chance to come in contact with too many baked goods in the course of her life. She'll be real obliged. Why doesn't he take it to her himself where is it?"

"Listen she can't stand the sight of im."

"I've always had alot of respect for Madame C. tell her I hope she feels better Where Is It?" Patrick is crouching under Mrs. Darotto's outstretched hands studying the method by which the aluminum foil is folded onto the bottom of the plate.

"Listen it's ravishing," Mrs. D. assures Leslie.

"WH "

"Laid out on yr bed. There were alotta of faxes on the floor. I put them with the others—on the table—with the—there's a real urgent fax on the table, yknow? And some messages."
Leslie crouches eye-level with Patrick and in a gravel-voice out of the corner of her mouth asks "Cn yoozguyz tink "
"Listen one fax was a weddin invitation," Mrs. Darotto continues, as if Leslie is still participating in the conversation with her. "Don't they just up nsend weddin invitations by that thing now! Listen are yallowed to do that?.....Or is it just the people *you* know?"
"You can go in my place!" Leslie snaps from under the pie plate, "I don't go to weddings or their more joyous counterpart—funerals." then resumes her question to Patrick. "Cn yoozguyz tink of any reesn why crouchin heyuh in da *pah-ssahge* unduh a leek pie fra vomitn bakuh'z wife—dat's a vomitn wife of a bakuh, not a wife of a vomitn bakuh—is maw impawtant dan da shit dat's waitin frusguyz upstayuhz?" Mrs. D. stands motionless, loath to disrupt the conference taking place under her makeshift roof.
Focusing deep into Leslie's eyes, Patrick produces a little sound which she realizes must be a giggle. "C-Cumawn Patrick.....R-right?...Ms. Br-Brittain?" he whispers, as if he's just found the secret password.
She flicks him on the kneecap with the back of her hand "Man, get you under a pie plate, Patrick," and darts out from their huddle "and you sure start gettin aggressive!" toward her building. Patrick whoops like a self-effacing rodeo-rider and follows.

"Listen What Time YGetting Dressed Tonight?" Mrs. Darotto shouts after her. "I'll send him teat at my niece's without me."

"It's not tonight it's not tonight tonight is the absolute last night it could possibly be I'll let you know in a couple days as soon as I find out I wouldn't disappoint your niece on my behalf nope nothin movin tonight with *this* baby actually from your niece's maybe you guys could continue on to Rome and ask His Holiness whether you're allowed to send wedding invitations by fa " Leslie spins around in front of the mailboxes and runs back out to the *passage*. "IF MRS. PORTASILVA'S SLUT DAUGHTER GOT ONE DROP OF SWEAT FROM HER HANGY UNSHAVED ARMPITS ON MY DRESS I'LL HAVE THEM DELIVERED FROM NOW ON IN SEALED CONTAINERS WITH COMBINATION LOCKS!"

"Ahhh-ahhh, petita colomba, Umberto wanna "

"Ignore him Patrick hurry up!"

# XIV

# Ŧhe Ëunuch-$orcerer

A Suzy Wong dress. A sleeveless high-collared sliver of black raw nubbly silk sewn "from the sap of sacred silkworms," Leslie said as she knelt over it on her bed, ran her palm across it. Caressed it for the first time. Raw nubbly black silk, soft and strong, obviously poured out to the milimetered measurement of her uninterrupted body by "a eunuch-sorcerer resurrected from dynastic days, beaten and kept in a closet and let out only to make my dress, who went blind just as he looped the last knot in the last thread and whose massive stone likeness now blesses and guards the portals of tailor shops from Beijing to Ninety-third and Broadway."

She was in awe of it. She felt its force field. "Like Dorothy's slippers." She told Patrick it was the best one Jack ever came up with. "Ever." Better than the filmy white muslin djelaba sprinkled with hundreds of little hearts woven in with real gold thread, sent, the day of his arrival from Marrakech, with fresh jasmine flowers dripping from gold wire to be braided into her hair and twined around her ankles, and face powder laced with diamond dust—all of which she refused to wear to dinner. She canceled the appointment at Carita and gave Mr. Darotto the flowers, gold wire and all, to put in his soup. ("Couple months later I cut the djelaba up and made pillows for some wedding present. The present I'd originally wanted to get them—the best wedding present of all—the top divorce lawyer in town—was outa town so these were the next best thing because they smelled of the wicked mysterious cinnamon-and-sweat-washed marketplaces where imperious older men with bulbous bellies—kinda like Jack when you think of it—hold court in secret dope-smokey chambers, their gleamy-bare-skinned little boys sitting at their feet and draped over pillows—kinda like the ones I made when you think of it—scattered throughout the room, waiting to be chosen and used. I wanted my pillows to be there when this couple returned from an exhaustingly lusty day riding up to the Factory Outlet Mall on the autoroute to exchange their vacuum cleaner and maybe pick up a couple rolls otrashcan liners on sale.")

Better than the sterling-silver-studded black leather micro-miniskirt, corselet and thigh-high pirate-cuffed boots, courriered, on his way in from London, with one of the original tubes of copper lipstick manufactured by Mary Quant and kept in a refrigerator since the sixties—all of which she refused to wear to dinner. She wore her navy business suit instead. He'd left orders that her hair be frizzed like that of a cartoon character who'd just stuck her hand in an electric socket. When she called the salon to cancel she told them that he must be losing it; that she was disappointed he didn't want it streaked violet and shaved off altogether at the sides; that then she would've kept the appointment. ("It's intact in storage with my winter clothes. I usually wear the pieces separately not only because of the resultant creative challenge posed by appropriate accessorization, but you get on a *métro* with the whole deal on at the same time and you look like one of those subway-stalking caricatures of urban evil who have over the years brought much *raison* to Charles Bronson's *être*. I don't always feel like dealing with Charles. I also wear the boots when I whip my administrative interns....................................................................I said, Patrick, I Also Wear The Boots When I Whip My.........forgetit!")

Better than the wine velvet Katherine the Great tzarina gown with a multi-jeweled brocaded bodice inspired by the Fabergé eggs in the Hermitage and by the teal blue/forest green/topazine/vermilion unicorn tapestries in the Musée de Cluny, delivered, for his return from Leningrad ("they kept the brocader in a closet, too; same closet, different continent"), with wine velvet slippers discreetly trimmed in sable ("as oxymoronic as that sounds") and an emerald-satin-lined sable muff—all of which she refused to wear to dinner but she kept the appointment at Carita so they could set the diamond tiara into her thick curls, then showed up in jeans and an Alice Cooper t-shirt and was denied admittance to the restaurant. Jack remained and dined and had Raoul drive her to the McDonalds on the Champs-Elysées. ("If it'd been Pascal...he had the most intense......Katherine the Great, Patrick, was huge. The dress I'm talking here, not the woman, although from what her courtiers and horse-hoisters said, the woman packed a bit obulk herself. I woulda hadda get a new apartment. Or turn it into a sofa. I mean.....it was a real big dress. The diamond tiara went of course right to the safe deposit box, the muff and slippers are in my mother's basement in Philadelphia and I ripped the brocaded bodice off with the jewels—I'll make a pillow some day—and threw the dress away. Mrs. D. cried for days. She said her horoscope had warned the week before about a problem blowing in from the East and she knew this was what it meant. For days, Patrick, every time she saw me she stopped, stared into my face, held her breath, then ran away crying.")

Better than the oyster satin Jean Harlow nightgown trimmed in almost imperceptibly fine pearl-gray Venetian lace and microscopic seed-pearls, with matching high-heeled mules, flown in, hours before his own landing, from Hollywood—with strict orders to have her hair died platinum blond—that she was so dying to wear to dinner, she actually got as far as the door of the hair stylist's before listening to her gut tell her she'd live to regret giving him the satisfaction and that if she loved it so much she was better off just wearing it around the apartment, which she did for weeks, mules and all, sending and receiving faxes, washing out her sweat-sopped running clothes, talking to Roz on the phone, as if William Powell were about to stick his head out of the kitchenette any minute and announce that he'd just put the finishing touches on their plans for the next twelve months. (When Patrick asked where Jean was now, Leslie put her index finger up to her lips and silently, solemnly, opened a top dresser-drawer. With the care of someone transporting an unpinned hand-grenade she removed a small silver-lidded cut-crystal box—almost an inkwell—containing oyster-colored satin confetti shining delicately in broken angles of light through the facades. She raised her other hand shoulder-level and set the receptacle onto her open palm.

"Ssshhh..........she's in here."

"W-what's she d-doing...I mean.....th-there? M-Ms. Brittain."

"Ssshhh..........it's like this.....Right after Jean showed up, Jack got me this real great job organizing an international symposium on the economics of environmentalism—you know, are business and government in it to preserve the green you have picnic food *on* or the green you buy picnic food *with*? I was the absolute wrong person for the job since I kept suggesting we get all these speakers who are for limiting the number of children per family to zero, letting the human species go into extinction and giving the planet a chance to shake itself off, take a good shower, slip into something more comfortable—like my Jean Harlow nightgown—and let out a well deserved gut-wrenching scream of relief at finally having rid itself of the cosmic practical joke that stayed just a couple millennia too long: Whew! Glad *that's* over! Thought they'd nev-er leave! Look at this mess, will you! Remind me never to invite *them* again!

"The conference was gonna be in London but the organizational meetings were held all over, rotated to the home countries of the corporate sponsors. I couldn't make the one in Frankfurt so what I did was I went to the Samaritaine and bought the most enormous stuffed Snoopy I could find, but the girl Snoopy—what'ser name—Belle, I think, isn't it?—something like that. Anyway I spent an entire Sunday dying her hair platinum blond and I dressed her in my Jean Harlow—even sewed the shoes on with transparent plastic thread—and shipped her to the executive assistant of the guy who was hosting the meeting, with a note saying to sit her at the table in my spot. I also said in the note that this wouldn't cause the assistant any problems and put in a bottle of perfume for her, which I'm sure she wears every day in her new position as convenience-store checkout girl.

"Turns out the sense-of-humor quotient around that table wasn't breakin any records and this host guy then shipped the doll—a real frequent flyer all of a sudden—to Jack—he wasn't at the meeting either—with a note asking him what kind of deviate he'd brought in to this job. As always—as alllll-ways—with two words, Jack was able to turn the whole thing around to make this guy feel like an idiot for not having seen the ingenious far-reaching symbolism in the move, adding that he knew *exactly* what kind of deviate I was and that that was why they were so lucky to have me on their team! But in reality Jack wasn't any more impressed with my powers of judgment than he'd been in all the years he'd been throwing jobs my way, and he put my Jean Harlow nightgown from Hollywood through his fucking shredding machine and sent it to me in this box. Which could be worse, box musta cost a fortune. He gave Belle to Charlotte's daughter—who's a grown woman by the way—and I never asked him what he did with the shoes isn't that funny?—couldn'ta shredded em, yuh think?" Leslie carefully lifted the crystal box from her palm and held it close to her eyes, twisting her wrist so as to see the oyster satin confetti from all angles, then raised it above her head to examine the contents from below. "Probably kept them on the naked doll, that wouldn't certainly surprise me about Jack!")

"W-were there—well—any.....Imean—dyou m—well........m-more? Any more. Ms. Br-Br "

"Any more what?"

"C-costumes. Were th-there "

"These aren't *costumes*, Patrick! They're...states of existence. Externalizations of realities. Expressions of consciousnesses."

"W-were there?"

"Aren't those enough? It doesn't matter. Suzy Wong is the best. It gives off energy and light, the others absorbed it. The others confiscated it, for themselves; this is providing energy and light for the planet."

"B-but it's—M-Ms. Brittain—dyou m—it's—I mean—all....well......b-black. Black. Actually."

"My point exactly, Patrick. Inviolate in the purity of its blackness and therefore free and unafraid to give. Come........Touch it."

Patrick couldn't. He'd get near it, up close to the bed, Leslie would warmly take his wrist and guide it forward and downward, and smile, and then Dorothy's slippers would let out a shock-blast and he wouldn't be able to break through. As he focused into its fibres from far back in the livingroom, he seemed less afraid of the dress itself than of Leslie's lack of fear of it.

Now Leslie is standing still and silent and naked—except for the high-heeled black silk ankle-strapped sandals and the Far East-red lips and nails which flew in with the dress—at eight fifty-five in her bedroom, in front of the phone, waiting for the call from Raoul telling her he's downstairs with the car. At eight twenty-four she got rid of Roz who called to say she's decided to go back to school to learn furniture repair. She hung up on Martin at eight thirty-seven when he wanted to let her know there was a bomb discovered in a cloakroom at the Théâtre National de Paris seconds before it was supposed to go off and to compliment the kids on their new upscale target and especially on their choice of program, as it would have been one of his all-time favorites—Maurice Béjart's La Crucifixion—blown to high heaven. She let the machine run when Roque checked in the minute Martin checked out, and then in a Russian accent she told a man who had attended her time-management seminar at the American University last year and lost the handouts and was calling to ask for copies that she was subletting the apartment from someone who just went to prison for relic theft, and she had no idea what the guy was talking about.

Raoul will call in three minutes and take five seconds to say he's arrived. She'll have forty seconds to slip into the dress, which Patrick—crouching in terror on the sofa while turning pages of old American Business Club magazines, as opposed to playing with the computer which is what he really wants to do but which would put him in direct line of vision with Leslie—will zip, for which anticipated service he was treated earlier to the pizza-without-anchovies that Leslie owed him anyway and was, despite the devastation the dilemma is obviously visiting upon him, refused a discussion of his mother's marching orders since "it was decided this afternoon you're never going home again—postcard or not!".....twenty seconds to say goodbye to Patrick and remind him to lock up.....five seconds to look in the mirror at her hair, pulled severely back and up, to the point where her eyes are the slightest bit slanted and her scalp is strained and tingling.....twenty-five seconds to get downstairs.....and a healthy probably too generous twenty-five seconds to stand in front of the mailboxes and draw her circle around herself before stepping out into the *passage* and the car. She will take nothing with her. Raoul will have duplicates of her keys, make-up and identification in the glove box.

She hasn't turned on music because she doesn't want to eat up seconds dealing with making sure it gets turned off. She hasn't said a word to Patrick since way before Roz's call because she sees no reason why they have to scream to each other from one room to the next instead of having a normal conversation with eye contact like everyone else the only difference being that she's naked. Looking at the surface of the dresser mirror without seeing her reflection, she thinks about the questions she has to ask Jack..........................
................................................................................................................
................"Throw water on it," she tells Patrick from the entranceway when the phone rings again. "Maybe it'll melt. Ahhhh-ahhh-ahh-ah........"

Jack is of course not in the car.

"Good evening, Ms. Brittain."

He is at the restaurant. Sitting at his private table. In his private room.

"Good evening, Raoul. Thanks. You didn't have to open the door, Raoul. Thanks. But you didn't have to. You know they say prisoners who've been in for awhile—even prisoners who've been in for not awhile—get so used to having everything done for them and everything decided for them that when they get out they stand in front of doors waiting for them to open electronically—doors, Raoul, I'm not talking air terminals or emergency rooms I'm talking Mr.

Beecham's Hardware Store and the bathroom—and they just don't know what to do when they don't open, they just stand there."

Waiting for Leslie.

"You look very beautiful this evening, Ma'am."

To be delivered to him.

"Thank you, Raoul. You look very beautiful too. Say, Raoul—what's playin with Pascal?"

As is his wont.

"He's no longer with us, Ma'am."

Even when they were really hanging out together and they would be leaving from the same hotel suite or the same livingroom or cafe, Jack would have Raoul drive him to the restaurant alone, and then he would send him back for Leslie.

"Shame. Hope it wasn't anything serious. You know I don't know if you ever noticed—being a guy and all, Raoul—but Pascal had the most inten—maybe someone he flew in might've mentioned it to you when you picked them up but he had really intense "

Even when he would spend all afternoon in a massive white terrycloth bathrobe, on his knees on misty black-and-white Italian tiles, bending over a big deep ivory-lacquered footed tub bathing Leslie in water swirled sweet with white bubbles and red rosepetals, and then rest her atop drifts of pink silk pillows and shave her pubic hair and drip spicy Arabian essential oils onto her body with an eyedropper then work them with his thumbtips into the strata of her skin, and she would tell him he should be ashamed of himself, using his big fat tycoon time playing Fatatateeta, what would the walking dead on his boards of directors think if they saw him now, even the evenings of those days, he would be taken to the restaurant first. And have Leslie brought to him straight away.

"We'll be arriving in one minute, Ma'am."

Thus reclaiming his control—as if with a ticket at a hat-check counter. A control Leslie has loved and hated at the same time. Which is why she has loved it so much. Resented and required. Which is why she requires it so thoroughly.

" thighs. The most intense thighs. Thanks, Raoul. I'll get it. Great job. See y'in a bit."

When Leslie enters the restaurant she is greeted by the *maître d'* and taken to Jack without having to say a word. In a secondary but spacious dining room all the furniture has been removed except for a small table and two mint-green velvet-upholstered chairs in the far right corner. The *maître d'* silently points his upturned palm in Jack's direction, nods to Leslie—who smiles and nods back—and walks gracefully away in time to string music being piped in so softly and subtlely it is sensed more as a hue or a perfume than a sound. Seated facing away from the door, Jack is scrawling numbers with a skinny gold pen onto a financial page of *Le Figaro*. Leslie crosses the pastel-flowered carpet to the table. Jack does not look up. She stands by his left shoulder and stares at him. He adds a column of figures, turns to the next page, follows an article down with his finger, turns back to where he was, crosses out a number, replaces it with another, readds the column and underlines, circles and puts an exclamation mark next to his answer. Leslie moves slowly to her end of the table. She pulls the chair out and starts to sit as Jack lifts a wafer-thin calculator from his inside jacketpocket "Keep standing." and punches some keys. Catching herself just before her bottom hits the seat, she straightens her legs. Jack notes his results next to the other scribbling "I want to see what kind of job they did." and puts the calculator back.

"The tailors?" Leslie asks, sidling back to her station at his shoulder. "Or the dispatch team in the gene pool?"

Jack still has not looked at her. He rips his jottings out of the page and tucks them into his pocket as well, "The silkworms." keeping his eyes on the newspaper as he folds it in crisp wrist-flicks "So for once your smartass mouth is not too far off base." and places it on the floor between the wall and his chair. "I had them bred specially but don't flatter yourself, not for you." He now turns to Leslie and smoothes his hand from her gold safety pin on her collar  down the right side of her body, "The fiber is more durable than anything that's come before," lingering under her buttock "more durable, so more" before giving it a ringing "functional." whack. "Sit down. We're patenting it. Five twenty-five a.m. October one: production begins under contract for the military."

"All-purpose-silk smart bombs—or is that all-purpose-smart silk bombs?—damnit, Jack, why do *you* get all the great ideas in this family! Whose *Merci* military? You know I know a coupla barracks of lance corporals who'd look luscious is a dress like this." As soon as Leslie is seated, a white-gloved waiter appears, serving her a tall iced glass of half-orange juice half-Perrier from a silver tray and setting a martini in front of Jack. "Much much better than they looked in their old, disappointingly *less* form-fitting Suzy Wong dresses. Good newsday for our boys Over There, huh?—or—I guess that'd be Over Here now, wouldn't it? Amazing how everything's relative, Jack, isn't it?"

"The word is *battalions*, Leslie. When you are referring to sizable numbers of lance corporals you say battalions."

"No that's football players, Jack, and the word is *teams*—when you are referring to numbers of sizable football players you say teams. Of lance corporals I so far unfortunately know only a couple barracksfull.....and not very well at that. Hello, Soldier."

"Sorry to hear that."

"You should be. I guess you're wondering why I'm being so.....cooperative...I mean about the dress and all. It's gorgeous by the way, Jack, thanks. It's really the best ever. Cept you always forget tpack the matching underwear with these things. But otherwise it's really the best. But aren't you wondering why I'm b "

"Not really. Well? I was right, wasn't I?"

"Jeezzuss, Jack, talk about right! Talk about Jeezzuss, Jack, Siggy Freud City, New Mexico! Bra-vo! You know it coulda gone either way, your Singaporian packrat coulda wound up with them calling the whole thing—including my life—off cause I started asking my rock n roller a couple too many questions—instead othem sending him over tconvince me not to worry my pretty little head about all those silly extra train tickets—instead othem then fucking *believing* that's just what he did! And then fucking believing that I fucking *believed* him! And now everything's back to normal, everyone loves each other, on the same track, business as usual, and I even got to choose the new date for the crime I know nothing about! The heist of the millennium depends on what my week's lookin like. Weh-hellll, lettt meee jussst seeeee heeere—no-o, can't bomb Police Headquarters the-enn, promised Roz I'd sit with her at the chiropodist's—I'll check my calendar, dear, and have my boy get back to you with a new d "

"Which is?"

"When they were giving out brains I—and creativity—I was hawking coffee n donuts to the ones in line cause the Who'd done a private preview show for me the night before! July fourth."

"That was when you had your private preview show?"

"You can be a real dorkface sometimes, Jack, I know you know that. That's the date. That's THE date. THAT's the date.......... ...symbolism a little too abstract for you, Jack, why aren't you telling me it's right up there with fire and the wheel? Jumping u—and the fax machine—jumping up n down and saying Holyshit, Leslie, that's the most br "

"I don't do jumping up and down."

"You would if you could."

"And I've known it since eight twenty-eight this morning. Paris time. Your boyfriend "

"Don't call him my boyfriend, Jack, OK?"

"Your boyfriend "

"Don't let your vocabulary be influenced by the use I make of his sex organ, Jack, OK?"
" called Keystone Kop Central with the date, and Jacques relayed it to Blyster through me."
"You.....then why the fuck dya have to ask me what the date is, memory problems settin insooner nthem guys at the clinic predicted, huh? How'd he sound? Roque, I mean. I mean—does he sound—he's with us, right?"
"Jacques, I said, talked to Charlotte. No one talked to Roque. *You* talked to Roque."
"Well you better believe if he wasn't committed Jacques'd pick it up right away especially now and the date he'd be callin in with would be for when you should go buy the *Herald Tribune*: American Public

Relations Tzaress "

"The word is *tzarina*."

"American Public Relations Tzaress And French Policeperson Finally Identified Through Dental Records After Weeks of Remains Anal-ysis. Christ you took a risk! It was like giving yourself tuberculosis to immunize yourself against tuberculosis only you gotta really be sure othat dosage, man, don't you? Here's a guy whose commitment to this thing is falling away in chunks and you get him—in slabs—and you get him right back with a dose of the very poison that got him uncommitted in the first place—his....................I choke on the word "

"affection."

"That's better. That thing that sets us apart from the lower forms of life—forms even lower than humans—the only thing fabricated in more countries than Coca-Cola. Love. When I called you last week and told you I had my doubts that Roque wasn't gonna blow the whole thing—including my life—by letting his cock—or worse—his heart!—get in the way between Blyster and the floorplan, you didn't even know what you were dealing with, you didn't know these guys, I mean any more than you know any othe other full-length-animated-feature characters who buy your airplane fuel. All you knew was they basically existed and in two seconds you're pullin this poor joker's strings: you got doubts about goin through with it, buddy?—I'll show you doubts!—I'll show you what doubts really are! Open wide—lemme cram a little more doubts in! You're the only person I know who can make it better by making it worse—in any category—not just crimes of millennia—how did you know my phonecall about the tickets wouldn't take us right up to the edge and leave us hanging there—or push us over!—instead of getting us right back on track, instead of bringin him running over with the Keystone Kock Seal Of Approval? To tell me the truth! You're scum, Jack, but you're smart scum."

Jack laughs the eruptive, aggressive laugh of a man who is right all the time—who is truly right all the time and who is unquestionably and sincerely acknowledged as being right all the time by the people around him—but whose personal experience of consistent rightness is never complete until his eruptive, aggressive laugh has put the period on each sentence proclaiming him right yet again. "No it couldn't have gone either w "

"You have no idea, Jack."

"Of course I have an idea."

"It was brilliant."

"Of course it was brilliant. I could tell you knew it was brilliant when you told me three different times during three different briefing sessions that you weren't going to do it. I could hear it in your voice. You knew the brilliance outweighed the risk. You counted on my proven knowledge of the human psyche to pull us through."

"I counted on my proven knowledge of the human cock to pull us through."

"You said it, I didn't."

"We did almost lose him, you know, Jack—no. No. We *had* lost him. It was lost. Finished. Curtains-for-us-baby. Washed up. The more I realize it—well he told me himself even, he told me himself—it was lost with him almost before it began—in the fucking train frchrissakes. Before I even knew about it—before you told me You're not going to believe this coincidence, but a client of mine is sponsoring the crime of the millennium and guess who's the star of the show? Spon-sor-ing—like it was a fucking soap opera.....which actually, when you think of it.......or a charity event....which actually, when you *really* think of it.....That was even before *you* knew it was me—Hey, Leslie! Did you scare up any action on the train back from Brussels? Like when you're at the movies and *you* know what's going on cause you've been watching all along but the asshole on the screen—nothing personal, Jack—doesn't, cause he was out rustling cattle when you were back there watching the scene he wasn't in, and you wanna scream No! No! He's not half-way to the border by now attt allll! Look in the closet—the clohhh-settt. Here it was Yeah! Yeah! She scared up action on the train but it's even better than that—it was with *your* guy! Actually when Jacques told you about this girl, this runner, you shoulda known it was me immediately."

"Are you the only runner in Paris, Leslie?"

"I'm the only one that fits that description."

"What description?"

"Whatever description he gave you! You don't see anyone else out there looks like me at that spot at that hour every morning, do you?

"I wouldn't know, Leslie. Would I?"

"Well then don't complain to me about not being able to jump up n down. Hey, Jack!" Leslie lowers her voice and leans slightly into the center of the table.
"What do you want, Leslie?" Jack lowers his and approaches at a similar angle.
"I want to know three things, Jack." Leslie drops another register and moves closer in.
"Which three things do you want to know, Leslie?" Jack sees her on both counts and raises her a bit, at which point she springs back against her chair and in her normal roar asks

"Why haven't they brought us anything to eat yet a *canapé* with the drinks something anything an olive I thought Charlotte always calls the meal in what's the waiter, out jerking off into the *amuse-gueules* are we eating dinner between now and the end of our life or what here?"

"Is that one question or all three at a volume discount?"

"It's one *category* of question, Jack. The alimentary category. Under which the number of admissible sub-categories has been assigned no limit."..................................................................
..........................................................................Leslie and Jack stare silently for some seconds, each thinking the other is about to speak.
"Why don't we do this, Leslie: why don't you give me all the ques—all the categories of questions first and then I'll do my best to answer them all at the same time."
Leslie reflects for a moment, half playacting, half serious, studying Jack's face and "If you wish, Jack." releasing a long, loud breathy sigh. "My attorney and I see no reason not to concede on that point. Provided the answers are distinct and appropriately coordinated. By that we mean, you answer question A with answer A, question B with answer B and so forth."

"Well why don't we say that if I don't, if I start mixing up the answers, you'll le—you and your attorney will let me know right away. OK, Leslie?"

"OK Jack. The other two questions are am I gonna die in the bombing after all and" Like the Escher drawings where the column of black geese or fish on the left fly or swim straight across the page, migrating and mutating by imperceptible degrees, melting into and finally becoming their white counterparts on the right, the detached lightness of Leslie's words and posture glides incrementally, as her sentence progresses, "this is" into an increasingly concentrated solemnity that sucks the sparkle out of her face "not", draws her forward into Jack's space "about", and unmistakably marks the border crossing between diversion "a floorplan" and danger. "is it?" "This is not about a floorplan is it?"

"Well, I counted three in all, all right!" Jack declares cheerily. "Am I right? Was that them?" He smiles big as if posing for a political poster.

Still leaning rigidly forward, Leslie says nothing and glares through frosty eyes.

"Three *categories*, that is," he hastens to add.

She isn't moving. Her breathing is slow and soundless.

"OK!" Jack jumps in. "OK here goes! Your answers are: no, probably, and not totally. What do I win?"

Leslie stays where she is for a while, waiting to see if there's more, then straightens in her chair, looks off to the doorway. Nods, as if having a conversation with herself behind her squinting eyes. Giving him one more chance, she peers into Jack's face again, but he's posing for another picture so she rises slowly and gracefully, turns her back to him, reaches around and starts pulling down the zipper of her dress. His arms crossed in front of his chest, he watches as her neck, upper back, lower back, waist peek in turn through the slit the zipper leaves in its path. When she reaches the top of her buttocks he calmly asks "What are you doing, Leslie?"

"I'm giving you your dress back and going home!" she snaps, still facing the wall and now inching the zipper tooth by tooth. "We're not eating dinner and I'm keeling over from starvation!" A bit more of her buttocks come into view. "You won't answer questions about life and death—mine!" The zipper hits the bottom of its track and she holds her hand there before "And I have a big rehearsal tomorrow between six thirty-one and six thirty-two and a half." slipping her right arm out, "We're working on the particular scene where, according to a couple words Thierry glissaded over in his phonecon with Roque last night and which for some reason you refuse to enlighten me on—because you're too busy refusing to feed me—instead of blowing up the tunnel it's actually the parking lot that's gonna go" then her left arm, "and they want me to do the scene so that the least amount of bodyparts—mine!—wind up strewn all the hell over the Ile de la Cité," finally baring her back and gathering the fabric about her waist. "thereby allowing them to get away with spending as little taxpayer money as possible on cleaning me up!" The dress slides down her lower body toward the ground, "Which when you think of it is something I'm real grateful for, cause you know what?" caught hip-level by its shoulder seams "Cause *I'm* a taxpayer here, too, frchrissake, and I wouldn't want to have to pay any more than what's reasonable to clean me up either!" between just the very tips of her thumbs and just the very tips of her index fingers. Her other fingers are daintily raised. "Being as I'm a foreigner and all." As at tea-time.

"Gee Jack, whatr you feeding your silkworms these days, *steak*? This fabric sure is heavy! I'm even having trouble holding it uuuwwwooopsAACHCH" As she pops her right hand open, leaving her hip exposed and the dress dangling diagonally across her buttocks, Jack's palm smmmackkks against her other side, securing what's left of her grip on the silk. "It's time like these make you wish ydidn't forget tpack the matching underwear, huh, Jack?" He slides the dress back up her body, threads her arms through "Hope I won't be late for school. Yknow all the other kids get tdress themselves in the morning." and closes the zipper.

"I'm afraid all the other kids," he says, grabbing her by the shoulders and plopping her back into her seat, "make people proud to be with them by acting like the mature five-year-olds that they are."

"Don't be afraid, Jack. Makes you look older than your age." Her arm propped vertically on the edge of the table, her chin on the back of her hand, she smiles her candy smile while Jack sits and finishes his drink. "That and lack of sex."

"The medium-range-expanded versions of your answers are: no, but that doesn't mean we're not going to eat at all; probably, the way things stand now, but we're not going to leave them that way for too long, and, not totally, though it all begins there."

"I guess to get the full-count-tactical-arsenal version I have to ride through the Place de la Concorde on the back of a horse. Eating chocolates. Meeeee—eating chocolates. Jack. Not the horse. The horse doesn't like chocolates. Well actually, that's not completely accurate. The horse used to like chocolates very much. In fact, a little too much, which is where all his troubles started. He used to put chocolate on everything—hay, grass, other-horse urine droppings. Steak—when the silkworms weren't hogging it all, that is. Then one day he had a severe allergic reaction and now he doesn't touch the stuff. You know what they say about too much of a g "

"Dinner will be in two stages. On the plane we'll have a series of little snackies while I brief you on y "

"You *do* get the reference, dontchya, Jack? It's Barracini! Lady Barracini! Rode through the crowd without her Suzy Wong on to celebrate that her chocolate company was showing a strong end-of-year curve......Or was it *she* who was showing the strong end-of-year curve? I always get those conf "

"On the plane we'll have a series of little snackies while I brief you on your meeting—substantial but not heavy.

"The snackies or the meeting?"

"Don't worry—I have all your funny food in—although to be brutally honest, "

"**HAH!**.....Excuse me, Jack."

" when Raoul couldn't find ricecakes with corn at the first place he went, he just got plain, old, unimproved ricecakes with..... with.....with rice, I guess."

"Salted or unsalted."

Jack clucks his tongue and "Got me on that one." shakes his head. "Couldn't tell you. How much does it matter? Which one do you "

"Depends on what the spread is. Unsalted's OK if you have yogurt-chive dip—or any dairy-based vegetable topping really. But the true inner meaning of fruit preserves can be actualized only on salted. And honey goes great on either one! So does peanut butter. Or a combination of the two. And then you get into the more esoteric spreads like tahini and guava butter but I'd be surprised if Raoul had any luck pickin up any othose. I mean, the first rule of healthfood store management is you see someone gettin out of an RR and you run and hide the tahini."

"And there's more than enough Earl Gray to get us to Singapore. The second stage will of course be a real dinner once we're there, before we turn right around and come back—though you realize it'll be the day after tomorrow before our next dinner-time on the ground."

"You're not kidding are you?"

"About what? Meanwhile there's always the food stalls—they're just....on second thought, I may never get you back—they're just you're k—you've never been there before, have you?"
"Where?"
"Singapore."
"You're not kidding. Are you?"
"About what?"
"We're really not eating dinner here."
"No."
"You took a whole room outa commission in one of the best restaurants in Paris to sit ntell me we're not eating dinner there."
"Yes."

Leslie holds her empty glass up to the light and examines it from all angles. "Onnne helluvan expensive glass of orange juice we have here, wouldn't ythink? Geez if I'da known that, I woulda poured some in my napkin and taken it home for later. Wonder how much that comes to per ounce. Wait!—look!—there's a little drop left in there—look—right here near my thumb. See it? I wonder how much that little drop is worth." She brings the glass to within an inch of her eyes "Do you know how much you're worth, little drop?" then looks over at Jack. "You think we should get it insured? Think of all the walkperson batteries I could buy with what it just cost you to tell me all I get tonight is the most expensive glass of half-Perrier half orange-juice in the world. Although that's a dumb example isn't it because I'm sure I could get all the batteries I'd ever want from Thierry. Whydjya do this for?"

"I felt like having a drink before dinner."
"But We're Not Eating Dinner. Jack."

"Blyster wants to see you."
Leslie puts her little drop on the table, patting the side of its glass

to let it know she's still there. "See me like that's why God invented polaroids or see me like pass the salt?"

"Pass the salt."

"Say please, Jack. Well how bout if I pass it to you and you get it to him?"

"That's what we've been doing up until now, isn't it?"

"And it's been working like a charm! I agree!" Leslie declares, slapping both palms on the table and rising. "Well, Jack!" She hams a fake-nervous giggle, "Big busy day tomorrow!" pushes her chair out of the way with the backs of her legs, "Big good healthy run in the morning! Huge international trade event at the Embassy to finalize with Patrick!" and starts walking away from the table. "May even fit in a little ess el ee ee pee, the good Lord willing, huh Jack?" When she gets to the door Jack reaches inside his jacket and pulls out a passport. "Have a good trip, Jack!" He waves it next to his head, then, smiling, "Thanks for a great meal! Really! See yat my cremation!" flips through a few pages. "I'll call you from Georges's in the morning like usual and you can answer my other two concerns—especially that little nagging one about my life." Leslie turns around once to remind Jack to "take care of our little drop, poor thing—give it the kind of upbringing only you can.....And make sure you get it's nose fixed for its sixteenth birthday." and she's gone.

"BRITTAIN....LESLIE....MARSHA," he reads, loudly enough for her to hear in the corridor.

SEX: OFTEN—NO! NO! I MEAN, FEMALE. BIRTHPLACE: PENNSYLVANIA, USA. BIRTH*DATE*: OCTOBER FOURTH NINEteen fifty-nine."

"You like it? Keep it! Keep it!" she says as she takes her seat again. "I can always get another one."

"Why go to all the trouble when you have one already?" Jack turns some more pages. "And a damn nice one, at tha—My Lord!" He jabs his index finger against a stamp, raising his eyebrows and the register of his voice. "I never knew you went to Russia. Why you little"

"This is why I think the plan's gotten a little off track here and I'm gonna get blown to bits and die, by Leslie Marsha Brittain," Leslie singsongs in a schoolgirl screech, swaying from side to side in her seat, her hands folded on her knees. In her normal voice she adds "From the same people who gave you This is what I did on my summer vacation, of which my last on Earth is likely to have taken place ten months ago!"

Jack puts the passport back in his pocket and looks at his Rolex.

"We take off at zero hours thirty from Le Bourget."

"When Roque called Thierry from my apartment last night to prooo-ooove to me that he wasn't making it up—though God knows you'd have to be a combination of Walt Disney, Rod Serling, Stephen Hawking and Timothy Leary to churn out somethin as rich as this—when they just before they were hanging up Thierry said—well, they were talking about me not being able to make outlaw history on June twenty-sixth so Thierry just before he hung up he reminded Roque to sodomize a new date out of me which is not exactly how he put it but that's the whisper-down-the-lane rendition—so *then* he said, and here it comes, Jack, here it goes—*then* he said that Roque better get a date that sticks this time because they can only clear the guys outa the lot once before they get suspicious are you with me on this, Jack?"

Jack glances at his watch and starts to say someth

"Which can only mean one all-encompassing sub-categoryless thing: I'm dead. You can see, Jack, how unnecessary subcategories are to the point at hand. Meaning something's gonna happen in that lot when I run by that's a threat to their fellow policepeople other than one less Bateau Mouche going past to take their minds off their meaningless little existences I mean Thierry didn't say We gotta clear the guys outa the sub-basement dope-cells where Jacques cops my speed—where we all had a vague understanding of that being where my new career as a poor-slob ignorant-victim perpetrator was gonna be launched, we're talkin what's playin up there in the parking lot and guess who'll be in the parking lot that they're worried about something playing up there in, coincidentally, Jack, guess who? Time's up—I'll tell you! ME!"

"Maybe you misunderstood what Thierry said," Jack offers calmly, as if discussing a lecture they just attended.

"But worse—and this, Jack, is, well, worse, that's all, this is—worse. Worse is that I could tell from Roque's reaction that he did not get it at all. I mean, he didd. nott. gett. itt. att. allll. What I mean by that is the following thing: he did not get it. At all. He did not react as if he had a terrestrial idea that the plan involved anything other than my total safety and a bomb buried deep in the basement of the building where he goes every day to get a fresh book of parking tickets. Which means one or a combination of a real lotta things, all of em bad news: either he never understood the plan from the get-go but pretends he does and doesn't ask a fucking question—bad news. Or his partners switched a few details on him and aren't telling him and he's too dumb to pick it up, even with Thierry's glissaded-in remark—bad news. Or he's too in love to allow himself to hear and/or believe what his partners *are* telling him—bad news. Or he knows exactly what his partners are telling him and instead of being in love with me and out to save me he's in love with me and out to kill me—the kind of bad news they make Oscar-winning movies about."

"No possibility he could be *not* in love with you and out to kill you."

"None."

"Just checking."

"But he agreed we go ahead biz-as-usual. So that narrows it down to either he doesn't know what the real scoop is and he's an idiot and I die, or he does know and he's a sociopathological maniac and I die. But that's certainly why you've called us all together here tonight, Jack, around this sumptuous dinner, because if anyone knows what the real scoop is, Jack, *you* know what the real scoop is. Jack."

"Maybe you misunderstood what Thierry said. He was speaking French, wasn't he?"

"Yeah? so? what difference does that make? And anyway, even a first-year French student'd understand what he said. It was a classic line—in all the textbooks—especially beginners'. There's always this little sketch of a coupla big-ass tourists wearing jogging suits made outa guidebook pages asking this little sketch of a beret-wearing, *baguette*-carrying guy-with-a-mustache *Où...est...la...Tour...Ei...ffel?*—or I guess in this case they would be more appropriately asking *Où...est...No...tre...Dame?*, and the beret-carrying, *baguette*-wearing guy-with-a-mustache always answers the same two things: *Là-bas*, while he's thinking You're standing right in front of it, you gringo dork-heads, and Get us a date that holds because we can't clear them guys outa the parkin lot too many times without them startin tget suspicious about us murderin Leslie Brittain. And then off in the corner there's a little sketch of this runner and her semi-automatic walkperson floating out over the Seine in a thousand forty-five pieces, each piece wearing a little headband and looking at its sportswatch. It's in all the textbooks, Jack, so I really don't think I misunderstood him.....And he wasn't speaking entirely French."

"Well I don't think *Ciao* really counts."

"Well wh " Leslie stops the new pitch even before the wind-up begins. She slumps back in her chair as if she's been struck by the ball and looks at Jack, shaking her head. At the "Frchrissake Jack!" call, she brings the game inside, slinging her words between the back of her darting eyes and the rubber walls of her brain. After a time-out to get the debris off the field, she asks "Where do you get it fed from? My phone or Thierry's?"

"Both."

"I'll be glad when this is over," she says in the detached, matter-of-fact tone she'd use if speaking about an uninteresting television program.

"No you won't."

"I'll rip all the communication devices out of the walls and take in laundry for a living."

"How will your customers contact you?"

"That's why God invented knuckles." She knocks on the table three times.

"How will your lovers contact you?"

"That's why God invented cocks." She knocks on the table three times. "Only difference'll be, my customers'll be standing in the hallway. My lovers'll be out on the Avenue Bosquet."

"Maybe if you combined them—did your lovers' laundry—you could save yourself some time running back and forth to answer the door."

"Maybe I could. Yknow, Jack, I've had this dream, this dream—I've had it a couple times now—where I come into the apartment and it's just a mass of wires—that is, the air, the space, of the apartment is no longer air or space that you can walk through, it's a thick, knotted, matted solidity of wires—skinny different-colored plastic-covered wires like you see when they open a central phone-station box. In the dream they're hanging down from the ceiling and sticking out in all directions from the walls and growing up from the floor, but more than that, they just *are*—they just are there, in front of me as I walk—

it's real hard to explain with waking vocabulary—but it's like....the air—that you breathe and move through—is not made up of invisible odorless colorless air molecules, it's made up of this presence of matted phone wires that you have to breathe and move through.

Jack studies the rhythm and span of Leslie's flails, trying to read whether her sharp staccato edge has momentarily rounded into soft sincerity, or whether she's closing in for the verbal kill. "Well now I'm just gonna hafta move into a bigger apartment in my dream, Jack, tmake room for all *your* wires too, now, aren't I?" A little of both. In between the two. "I shoulda known—hey!—maybe *you* got cameras in there maybe there's hope after all!—and howdjyknow where I keep my fucking passport?"

"Different union."

"Well how the fuck did Raoul kn—how many people have keys to my apartment, anyway? You know what would disappoint me, Jack? Even more than realizing I broke Chocolate Chocolate Chip Haagen-Däzs with an inversely cock-brain proportionate sociopath who's part of an international plot to have me internationally killed? Even more than the only food I've had even remote contact with since last night is a goatcheese sandwich I didn't get to eat because while it was being ordered I had the misfortune to call Charlotte and learn you were coming in—to take me to dinner, Jack—and a croissant I didn't get to eat because I knocked over the basket and Georges threw me hysterically out of the place and here I am sitting here watching waiters prance by for the past hour with some of the most reputed food in Europe and I feel like the peasants in Doctor Zhivago who were crunching their frozen noses up against the restaurant window while the besabled elite dined and drank inside—even more than that, Jack, dyaknow what would disappoint me even more than those two things?"

Jack takes a folded piece of paper out of his passport pocket.

"If the reason you're not feeding me is you know I'm history on July fourth. And why use up good *saumon fumé* on a future corpse. And instead of doing anything to try to save *me*, you're concentrating all your energy on saving the *saumon* from being wasted on someone who won't be able to sit around in five years—shit! what? five weeks!—and say Hey Jack, remember that great chunk o old *saumon fumé* we had at Le Divellec that night you saved my life? That would disappoint me the most, Jack." He unfolds it and clears his throat. "I mean, that you're a sleaze, no one's questioning here, but there's a difference betw what's that?"

"It's something I'm going to read to you just before we head out to the airport."

"Didn't I j "
"It's a list of reasons I don't want to hear from you as to why you're not taking off for Singapore with me at twelve-thirty."
"Ja "

"And their answers. Ready?"

"No!"

"Good! Hee-eere we-ee go-oh!" Jack sounds like a nursing-home-activities director who's being paid to look like he loves his job. "Reason one: I don't have my passport. Answer one:" he pats his pocket and smiles.

"Reason two: It'll interfere with my running. Answer two: there's a treadmill on my plane and in my apartment. I wouldn't advise running outside because apart from the heat and humidity and the fact that a sidewalk there bears no resemblance to anything you've come to know by that term, they drive on the left, and if you're going to be killed I'd rather save it for your friends in Paris, not because you looked the wrong way at a crossing.
"Plus, if there's no planetarily renowned monument to blow up, why waste good air-sole cushioning running outside, right, Jack?"

"Right. Reason three: I don't have my toothbrush" Jack reaches into his side jacketpocket, produces a transparent hot-pink toothbrush with glitter, swimming in the handle, that you can stir up by shaking the brush the way you could make it snow in those little glass-enclosed Santa Clause scenes, and slams it onto the table. "or my other things, es "

"Yeah especially m "

" especially my running clothes. Answer three: you don't need a briefing from me to know that everything you need is either on the plane, in the apartment or will be purchased, and we're only going to be there thirty-six hours."

"Somehow Singaporean hours seem to span anthropological eras.....dyathink that has anything to do with driving on the left side of the street?"

"Reason four: Don't yneed some kinda visa or something, Jack," he imitates Leslie, "to hang out in Singapore? Answer four: "

"Uhh, Mr. Ko-ote.....you...you in the corner there—" Leslie wags her index finger and lifts her chin. "yes—you almost had it that time. Once again, with feeling. And, uh, you have the voice down pretty well, son, but that world-famous trade-mark intellectual sparkle, well, it still needs some w "

"Answer four: No. Not if we're going to be in and out in thirty-six Pleistocenian hours. Reason five: "

"Reason five:" Leslie interrupts, "I just remembered I have a husband and I wouldn't wanna disappoint the guy and not be there to refuse to let him stick it in when he gets home from those increasingly tardy hours at the office."

"Reason five:" Jack continues, "I don't have any pocket-money on me. Answer five: You don't have any pockets." He turns the paper over as his eyes flash playfully at Leslie and his portly body ripples in a kid-like giggle.

"You're a crud, Jack."

Then he quickly grows back up. "Reason six: This is not about a floorplan, is it? Answer six: Blyster wants to see you."
"Hey wait a minute I asked that question *after* you made out your list how the f "

"Reason seven: what about all my faxes and phonecalls from my laundry clients? Answer seven: fuck em. Reason eight: what will happen when Mr. Sennett and the "

"Keystone Kocks"

" realize I've gone away? Answer eight: fuck em."

"What about Patrick?" Leslie asks.

"We're taking him with us," Jack answers.

## XV

## THE BOAT-GHOSTS

The Oriental woman greeting Leslie and Jack at the top of the boarding steps is strikingly beautiful. Reed-thin, she is about six inches taller than Leslie and about ten years younger. Her mini-skirt and Pullman-porter jacket are made from the same black silk as Leslie's dress and the buttons on the jacket's bodice and sleeves look like they are real gold.

Leslie nods to the woman without actually acknowledging her and starts into the plane but then turns back in an almost slapstick double-take, pulled by a presence of docility and strength. As if two separate countries divided by a guarded border, the softness of all that is above the woman's waist—her long satiny-black hair and translucent skin and submissive eyes—lives in tense co-existence with the severity of all that is below—her bony hips and the stark whiteness of her bare thighs and legs as they shoot from the hem of her skirt to the tips of her black leather spike-heeled shoes.

"This is Sun," Jack says, as Leslie stares and studies, seeking to define what she is sensing. "She'll show you to your cabin."

"I'm sure she will." Leslie shakes Sun's hand and the scent of patchouli suddenly flutters across their space like the wings of dozens of doves all released from captivity at once.

Sun covers the handshake with her left palm while she says "*Come. With me, wont you?*" in a British accent sweetened with a hint of Oriental song. Keeping her grip on her guest's hand a single second longer than would be expected, she smiles with her torso while her pelvis sets out to take care of business.

"Sun." The women pass through a crack in a forest-green velvet curtain and cross a contemporary wood-paneled sitting area furnished and carpeted in greens and browns. "Is that as in The Also Rises, or Yat Sen?" As Sun leads the way, Leslie follows little Hansel and Gretel patchouli-crumbs in the air.

"*Youve never been in Mr. Kotes plane before, have you?*"

"Well I can see we're sure not gonna have any trouble communicating, Sun! Have you?"

"*Have I what?*"

"Been in Mr. Kote's plane before?"

"*You'll find everything you need in here,*" Sun says, stopping at a door, of wood matching that of the sitting-area walls, whose engraved brass plaque says

### Ms. Leslie Marsha Brittain

The patchouli stops as well. Sun looks at Leslie as if expecting her to say something. Leslie stands with her hand on the round brass doorknob and her eyes on Sun, waiting for the question for which Sun seems to be waiting for the answer. Sun's strong thighs walk away and the rest of her floats close behind in a spicy mist.

Glancing in all directions, Leslie turns the knob.....the knob...notices that one of the two wooden doors across the corridor bears a brass plaque as well.....as well...starts walking cautiously over to see if it says what she thinks it says.....it says...approaches it with controlled uncontrollable ("Hoh...Leee...Shittt") feet, knowing that even from way across here she'd be fooling herself ("Hoh") if she thought she couldn't read it—she'd figured Jack ("Leee") was kidding—it doesn't seem to be getting any less clear the closer she ("Shittt") goes, OK that's what it ("wrong last name") says, so that's what it ("fucking") says ("frchrissake certainly didn't waste any time gettin the engraver outa bed!")—figured they'd get word to him somehow and everything would be ("but there it is") but there it is

### Mr. Patrick Ryan Trucore

For the first time since, a couple days after the train from Brussels, Jack's courriered note told her to call him immediately from a pay phone, Leslie is frightened. The other times—the scenes with Roque and Jack about eating it out there on the Quai des Orfèvres—had been a recreational mix of melodrama and existentialism, with part of her being grateful for such a beguiling conversational alternative to the ever-menacing supermarket list and part of her truly believing that whether there were six billion or five billion nine hundred ninety-nine million nine hundred ninety-nine thousand nine hundred ninety-nine wretches-who-shouldn't've-been-born-in-the-first-place wandering—or running—aimlessly around the aimless Earth didn't matter a hoot to the dinosaurs and surely would matter even less of a hoot to the technoids a couple millennia down the line. Or even next Tuesday.

She'd agreed to get on this plane more out of curiosity than self-protection. She'd agreed to get on this plane because it was the only place left in town at this hour to get a decent ricecake and certainly not because she thought they were holding Patrick hostage or because she believed that the intricacies of this floorplan business had gotten to the convoluted point where two or God knows how many men who wielded such power and controlled such wealth actually needed the services of a terrified little emotionally battered nerd-innocent from the Midwest who can't look you in the eye when you say have a nice day but who can focus the hell out of the hole in the bottom of an ashtray.

With Patrick involved now it isn't fun any more. This Crime-of-the-Millennium biz is no longer a little side-job that Leslie can tend to when she isn't calling the caterer about the USO fund-raiser. A way to meet interesting people and learn a bit about history at the same time. With Patrick on the other side of this door now it's not fun anymore. It's chilling. Even if they do have his last name wrong. Or maybe especially.

**MR. PATRICK RYAN TRUCORE**   Leslie's first impulse is to thrust the door open and barge into the room. Force her way if necessary. Take the guards by surprise all the while shouting orders to Patrick to stay calm and trust her. She takes a step back. There's no lock or keyhole or card slot on the outside. Maybe it's locked from within. She not worried. She's strong. She lunges forward. She stops. No. Wrong approach. That's exactly what they'd expect her to do. Give them all the justification in the world for retaliation. And you remember what happened in those James Bond movies when a gun went off in the plane—sucked half the airline company out the bullet hole, stockholders and all. To say nothing of passengers and beautiful Norwegian stewardesses—fat passengers even, right out that bullet hole as if they were a piece of linguini left over from lunch. They're still floating around up there from Christmas nineteen sixty-five—you can sometimes see them passing over in the summer when it's clear, making grotesque gestures with their Nehru-suited limbs. Leslie looks up and down the corridor. She's still alone. Just she and her baby Patrick, incoherent with terror on the other side of this door, his every movement monitored by a small army of goons on Jack's—no—Blyster's payroll. No. This calls for a more discrete approach.

She places her hand on the knob and turns it by increments. When it can go no further she pushes against the door with her left hand while pulling back at the knob with her right so as to keep the crack as minute as possible. By crushing her right cheek into the doorframe she is able, with the far corner of her left eye, to see into Patrick's cabin. It is handsomely appointed as a sitting room/office/bedroom in the color scheme and mood of the main salon, through which she and Sun had passed. She hears little beeping and explosion noises. Must be some kind of surveillance system—like those work-release bracelets they hook prisoners up to. Widening the door crack from a fissure to a sliver, she can see a little farther in to the left now. A huge-screen VCR, a beautiful full-length mirror on a stand of the same light, polished wood as its frame—tilted upward—there's the ceiling...and the top of an Impressionist *tableau* from the opposite wall. Everything seems calm. Patrick's backpack on the beige carpet at the base of the mirror. The system noises come and go. Ah wait! Patrick's voice! An exclamation of some sort! She dares to inch the door enough to clear the field for both eyes.........detects movement.........pushes-pulls the crack again......... ......... ......... ......... ......... ......... ......... ......... ......... ......... ......... ......... ......... ......... ......... ......... ......... ......... .........At a spotless wood-and-brass work station in the left corner, one of two computer screens is divided into hundreds of vibrant organic cells, each cell an existence in and of itself, each containing a life-form from a fantastic futuristic forest—multi-appendaged soil-creatures, anthropomorphised flower-giants, percolating micro-organisms—transmogrifying and evolving, enriching their own shapes and positions at a military cadence then slowing and oozing into shared space then suddenly speedily spinning all together and becoming an utterly other unit of animate reality. Changing color and texture and echoey sound with each mutational stage. Freezing just long enough—slices of seconds—to rebreed their original states. What were their original states? The back of Patrick's little blond head follows the metamorphosis—zipping from one edge of the screen to another, Sssssweeeeping. Bbobb-bbing. J ER K I NG.

Waa / aal / tzing. Waa / aal / tzing. Waa / aal / tzing— while his hands, anchored in gloves projecting from the front of the machine, reach into the scene itself and move a little computerized Patrick-figure, as if he were a chess piece or a sylvan GI Joe, through the intercellular vegetation in an intensely focused effort to find his proper place among his new digital pals.

Close by, at the real Patrick's (though who's to say—though we're not going to get into that right now) left elbow, a royal-blue screen flashes bright yellow data that Leslie assumes is related to the flight. Keeping a sixteenth of an eye on the data screen, Patrick punctuates his electronic field-trip with yelps of glee that even the Harley Davidson never elicited. Leslie shakes her head. ("Poor dear.") She opens the door further. ("Misses his internship supervisor so.") Puts a foot in. ("He's worried sick.") Finally outright enters the cabin. ("You can tell.....You can just...tell.") His trance-like concentration is so consuming, his participation so complete, that even without the software-sourced sounds of fanciful flora and fauna crashing into his own elated exclamations, Patrick stands no chance of having heard her come in.

Which is just as well. For at this very moment the virtual-reality Patrick is hanging by his feet from a sunflower—with Richard Nixon's face and Brigitte Bardot's body (the young BB and the more mature RN)—trying to swing himself up and over to form a bridge by grabbing onto a nearby satyr—with the face of Kirk Douglas and the body of a Ford Mustang—thereby allowing a Tinkerbellesque figure—whose barbell wings are too heavy for flight—to tip-toe across his back. And this before all parties involved except the virtual-reality Patrick completely transooze themselves out of their current locations, shapes, hues and configurations. This is a delicate maneuver. The real-reality Patrick is with his on-screen counterpart all the way, rocking and lifting his own torso, launching strained, explosive grunts and snorts, dancing like a boxer watching a fight on TV.

Leslie moves closer.

("Shit he's") gotta ("make it!")

Tinkerbel is standing on Nixon's nose—ready to slide right down and across the instant Patrick's in place—all jittery like she's about to miss an important appointment.

Hurry, Patrick, Hurry the flower's beginning to shrink!

Both-realities Patrick are arching their backs and sweating and heaving. Leslie hopes the perspiration doesn't short out the whole adventure—on either side of the action.

She takes another step and

folds her arms in front of her chest and

watches without breathing.

Just as the satyr changes from reds

and

yellows

to

purples

and

greens on its way to becoming a Leonardo da Vinci pyramid in the opposite corner of the screen, Patrick tries onemorereach and

"Aahhuugghhcchh!"     hooksontoKirk's                    neck.

    Tink skittles right across.the computer warbles.*Patrick is ecstatic!*

    He yanks his hands out of the gloves, wipes his face, smoothes his hair. He sighs, giggles. Applauds. The well-equipped Ford is now a camel-headed rainbow-fish. The little Patrick-figure is resting on a huge diamond.
    "Yaahh-HEEE!" Patrick shrieks, still totally unaware of Leslie's presence, "YAHhee!" and pounds the table between the two computers and punches the air. She knows that he must know that the reality on this side of the screen is distinct from that on the "Yah-hee!" other, but she champions the fact that he doesn't seem to ("Why") care ("should he?"). He applauds. "YAH-AHH-HEE!"
    Into the sound and stir of Patrick's personal celebration "yaHEE", Leslie leans, her arms still folded, a hip thrust "yaHEEyaHEEyaHEE!" out, so startling him with her snide monotonal

                                  "My-he-ro.", that he lurches forward in his seat and crashes his head into the screen.

    "M-MS. BR-BR-BRITTAIN? M-MS. BR-BRITTAIN!" he cries, whipping his tan leather swivel-chair around and ejecting himself into her arms. "MS BRITTAIN! MS. BRITTAIN! MS BRITTAIN! MS.

BRITTAIN!"

"Yes, Patrick?" she croons tranquilly, like this is yet another of the most normal situations in the world.

"Y-Y-YOU'RE A......L-LIVE ALIVE! ACTUALLY!"

She looks around the cabin in all directions—the best she can with Patrick hanging from her shoulders like an over-affectionate performing monkey—as if trying to see who he's talking to.

"Y-You're A-M-Ms. Br-Brittain You're A-M-Ms. Y-You're You're Al-Alive!"

"Now, Patrick, what have I always told you about coming to unresearched conclusions? That's a perfect example of the kind of throw-away remark that can get you into significant trouble if you don't have all your facts together." She clears her throat and in her Board of Directors baritone hurrumphs "I don't think this company is prepared to release a statement to that effect at this particular time. Thank you. Good night."

"M-Ms. Br-Brittain Ms. th-thank G-God y-you're..." Patrick is creasing the bodice of the Suzy Wong beyond recognition. "h-how.....well—how *a-are* you? M-Ms. Brittain." Leslie tries to pry him loose.

"Fine thank you, Patrick. How nice of you to ask. How are *you*? How, Patrick, are the wife and kids? Would you pass me another scone, darling?"

"M-Ms. Br—wh-when that m-man c-came kn-knocked on my c-came to my to-tonight wh and t-told me you w-were in—well—t-trouble and—well—I didn't.....Imean at f—well—I......didn't...b-be-lieve—Imean—him. At f-first. Actually. And wh—and wh—he—well—he s-said he started t-telling me th-things about about y-you to—well—p-prove he r-really.....Imean—" Patrick's eyes are like those white triple-beam used-car-lot searchlights that always criss-cross each other at some point in their otherwise independent sweeps across the sky: beaming at an object on one side of Leslie, on its way to an object on the other, his focus scans her face for a privileged instant of contact then renews its erratic rhythm for the return sweep. "well—I th-thought I h-h-had n-no ch-choice b-but—Imean—to I h.....wh-what did I—well....M-Ms.Brittainhetoldmeto ......make sureIhadmypassportIwas............w-worried. Actually."

"You sure looked sick with worry, Patrick, when I walked in. For a minute there I wasn't sure the little dragonfly would make it to the bathroom."

They both look over at the Nixon Forest, just, according to most unidentified sources, successfully completing its transition to an Italian Renaissance court, where the virtual-reality Patrick, sitting on his diamond, which is now a monster mandolin, is waiting for some action. "I th-they I didn't th-they......didn't...t-tell me when—well—you'd b-be they didn't "

"You were spectacular," Leslie says, approaching the computers. "Especially since Kirk Douglas sure didn't break his ass makin it any easier for you!" She gently pokes the screen where the peak of a tall mauve-gauze-draped princess-hat is calmly enjoying a live-calimari sandwich on a chess-board floor of grass-and-ocean squares.

"M-Ms "

"He could've at least pulled up a little closer frchrissakes, what's this? Hey look at this! In Singapore it's already time to get up and remove your husband's filthy socks from where he chucked them last night over the shower stall. Whatr all these other numbers what's this?"

"M-Ms. Br-Brittain?"

"Is this how high we're flying, or how fast?"

"C-can I—dyou mind.....well—what...a-ask you wh-what's going-going—Imean..........on?"

Leslie takes a long breath. She hooks into Patrick's elbow and walks him over to his swivel chair's matching leather sofa opposite the cabin door. "I mind if you ask if I mind if you ask," she says as they both slowly sink into the hissing oversized seat-cushions. "But you already know that...............Patrick,,,,, believe it or not,,,,, I don't know. Well—I know part of what's going on—I know part of one level of what's going on—part of one level of what went on up to this very instant here. But what I thought was going on—even the one part of the one level that I was sure I knew was going on—even that has all of a sudden become a variation of itself—though not all of a sudden for the people who've turned it into a variation—though certainly all of a sudden for me—and even more all of a sudden for you. But what's going on from now til the end of our lives—or even til we land—or even til we take off for that matter......Patrick, believe it or not, I don't know. Am I making sense? Did anybody tell *you* some mildly basic approximation of what's going on?"

"You l-look—dyou m—well.......t-tired. Actually. Ms. Br-Brittain."

"I look embalmed. It's been a long life since last night." Leslie's voice is weak. "I'll tell you what I know, sweetie," She caresses Patrick's head and brings her hand down to rest on his shoulder. "but it's gonna hafta wait til whatever version of internationally-datelined-defined morning we come in contact with. Meanwhile, don't trust anyone—even me—and try not to be too frYE-ES?" She and Patrick look at the door. Someone has knocked.
"Well I See You Two Have Found Each Other!" Having just abandoned nursing-home-activities directing for the heady world of children's-party MCing, Jack bursts into the cabin, his hey-you-lucky-people-here-I-am, bow tie-y, big-faced smile more of an assault than a greeting. "Didn't believe me," He winks at Leslie, "did you, pal?" throwing his chin in Patrick's direction. "My Lord, Leslie, you look tired. She looks tired, doesn't she, son?"
"That's because I'm tired. You two know each other, don't you? You use the same chauffeur—you know, Jack, you should lighten up a bit on Raoul. All this running around foraging into people's passport drawers and kidnapping their interns is gonna take its toll on him some day. Patrick, you remember our host—the gentleman in whose air you are a guest—even though he got your name wrong on the door plaque," Leslie adds out of the side of her mouth. "The gentleman around whose table we have broken brochure. The gentleman whose factories have probably made an article or two of the clothing you are wearing tonight—the gentleman whose factories have certainly made the particular article of clothing I happen to be wearing tonight. The gentleman in whose apartment buildings some of your relatives have most likely dwelled. The gentleman "

"He gets the drift, Leslie."

" to whose radio stations you have no doubt listened and whose newspapers you have no doubt "

"Like I said, Leslie, our boy here ge "

" read. The gentleman, Patrick," Leslie stands up, shuffles to the door, turns to face the sofa. "who has" She raises her eyebrows. Looks at Jack. At Patrick. Jack. Patrick. "the answer—" Pushes onto Jack's stomach to move him out of the way. "scuse me Jack, willyuh, I gotta go get into my drop-bottom pajamas—" Looks over at Patrick again "to the question" as she backs through the doorway "of what", holds still for a second in the corridor, then starts taking little Japanese-lady reverse-steps "is going", mincing almost out of Patrick's line of vision before Jack reaches out! grabs her arm! and pulls her back in "on."

"Pleased To See You Again, Son!" Jack shouts, glowering at Leslie and squeezing her wrist. "We have a tradition on board here! And that is that we do not take off until everyone is gathered in the main salon for a good-luck take-off champagne toast! And if my calculations are correct—You Wanna Check That Screen For Me, Son?" Jacks eyes are still on Leslie, who, too tired to shake his grasp, is making grotesque faces at him.

Bounding off the sofa, Patrick trots over to the work station. "Wh-what—well—wh-what—well—w-would—Imean.....y-you would y-you l-like t—w-want to.....kn-know? Know? Sir."

"You Can Let Up On The *Sir* Shit, Patrick," Leslie yells into the cabin past Jack's shoulder. She rises onto her toes even though she's taller than he is. "What Have I Always Told You About Not Being Impressed By Outward Signs Of"

"How Many Minutes To Take-Off, Son?"

"T-twelve min-minutes and th-thirty-seven seven s-seconds," Patrick announces with pride and terror, as if just having been named Director of NASA. "Actually."

Leslie says, "thirty-six, thirty-five, thirty-four, thirty-three, thirty-"

"Thanks, Skipper!" Jack releases her arm. "See you guys at the launch site," he trills, and walks away just as merrily as he came, on to the children's party down the hall.

"two, thirty-one, I haven't even seen the inside of my fucking cabin yet, thirty," Strutting across to her door in rhythm with her "twen-tee-nine, twen-tee-eight," countdown, "twen-tee-seven," Leslie steps and dips left on each first syllable "*twen*-tee-" and right on each third, "*six*," left on each first, "*twen*-tee-" right on each third, "*five*," left on each first, "*twen*-tee-*four*, *twen*-tee-....." Patrick checks the computers before heading out. "*three*, *twen*-tee-" The

Italian Renaissance is now the Civil War. The virtual-reality Patrick is sitting on a gigantic gold mustache waiting for some action.

"Fasten your seatbelts," Jack tells Leslie and Patrick once they've settled into the milk-chocolate leather sofa to the right of his matching armchair. "We'll be taking off during our "

"Where are they?" Leslie asks. She hands Patrick her glass and pokes around in the cushions. "Being held against their wills in some private plane en route to Si "

" toast."

Sun stores her silver tray in a teakwood breakfront near the entrance to the corridor. At the wall opposite Leslie she takes her seat on a sofa which completes the set.

"Dyou m—h-how c-can—dyou m—M-Ms. Br-Brittian...h-how we c-can t-take—well.....off if—Imean" Patrick whispers, pointing across the room with his head while his eyes stay focused on a strand of hair Leslie's too tired to brush from her face.

"That's Because He's The *Co*-Pilot Son, Not The Pilot!" Jack startles a splat of champagne out of Leslie's glass—in Patrick's hand—while the blond young man in a navy-blue-silk uniform sitting to Sun's right smiles and smoothly salutes around the salon. "Kjell Targensen!" Jack announces, as if calling roll.

"Kjell will be taking over," Leslie informs Patrick in her progressively withering voice, "when one of us makes the startling discovery in the middle of the night that the pilot's really one of those cardboard figures they used to prop up in a window in Mission Impossible so the tubercular goon in the Buick down on the street wouldn't know the real guy was crouching with an atomic bomb in the fake Abe's Appliances truck two cars away." Patrick immediately focuses on a teak-and-brass-framed digital wall-clock above Kjell's head.

"*Reach behind you,*" Sun sings to Leslie in her Sino-British chords. She demonstrates and emerges *They're here.* with a seatbelt end in each hand.

"Although it's the middle of the night *now*, isn't it?" Leslie continues, following Sun's instructions. "It's been the middle of the night for the past two days hey Rock n Rollers guess what *I* just found!—thanks, Sun!"

"We have a tradition on board here! And that is that" Jack waves his glass and scans the room for inspiration. "..................! the youngest person present gives the toast!"

Everyone looks at Patrick, waiting for him to take it from there. Leslie worries that Jack's gone too far with him, that this will unfocus him all the way to Asia. She glances at the clock, noticing on the way that Sun is staring at her, then "Uhh, maybe, Jack," takes her glass back from Patrick. "someone el "

"Th-th-this—well—is twhooppp! heh" Patrick starts to his feet and another drop springs from his glass like a flying fish as the seatbelt breaks his movement. Jack and Kjell toss him a supportive chuckle. He does what he thinks is pretend to clear his throat. Leslie and Sun are looking at each other.

"Th-this "

"Ystart Again, Son! Maybe Su—Start Again, Son!" When he looks over and senses the concentrated force looping between Sun and Leslie, Jack decides not to tell Patrick that maybe Sun can do something about replacing those bubbles he spilled.

"Th-this is—well—t-to......M-Ms....L—Br-Brittain," Patrick does what he thinks is hold his glass triumphantly high. He cringes with his eyes and smiles with the tops of his cheeks, waiting for a sign that he's making Ms. Brittain happy. Jack and Kjell wait for a sign that Patrick is making Ms. Brittain happy. Leslie's breathing is very slow and very deep. Her face is the kind of relaxed blank which signals activity beneath the surface rather than no activity at all, which means contemplation rather than reverie. You're stopped at a bookstore window trying to trace back through all the people you leant it to, to see who has it now, because you really want to read it again. You're listening to a colleague tell you who's going to be lieing about what at the meeting this afternoon. Leslie is listening to the part of Sun's white thighs which she hadn't seen until the woman sat down.

"wh-who—Imean—wh-who........t-to M-Ms. Brittain, who....."

Sun's lacquered lips have slightly parted. Though not even moving, her whole body seems to be pulsating. Beating with in-bound rhythms shock-absorbed by her organs. She uncrosses her legs, opens a rush of patchouli, keeps her eyes on Leslie, crosses her legs the other way.

"t-to Ms. Br-Brittain.........." The plane begins to taxi. Looking at Jack in panic, Patrick pulls his glass down to his chest. Jack smiles patiently and nods for him to continue. " 's l-long—well—l....h-health and l-li........longlife." Leslie is leaning forward. Sun is rubbing her thighs together. Lightly. Rubbing her thighs. Together. Leslie plants her glass on the floor and jams her hands deep into the crack between the cushions and the back of the sofa. Thighs. "Actually." She raises her chin and opens her lips as well, breathes in the spice, lifts her torso toward Sun's space, breathes in the

"Sköl!" Kjell gets up and goes to work.

Patrick looks at Leslie.

Jack says "Good, Son! Drink Your Champagne!"

Patrick focuses on the breakfront but looks at Leslie.

The plane is off the ground.

"M-Ms. Brittain dyou m—d-don't you—you don't—don't—d-don't you w-want y-your ch—well "

"Drink Your Champagne, Son! Don't know as that we want to wish that on her or not right now, son. Doesn't look all that alive to me, She Look That Alive To You?"
Leslie is looking at Sun and ringing all her fingers around her seatbelt at its base caressing it across the back of her waist past her hips onto her belly where she spreads her open palms Sun is looking at Leslie and unhooking her seatbelt with a jerk throwing it off as if it's been a terrible constraint Patrick opens his seatbelt and leans over to "M-Ms. Brittain dyou m—is e-everything" Leslie releases the clasp with her right hand and lets the metal tongue tumble out not removing her eyes from Sun's eyes not breaking the beam between
"Your Young Man Here Just Toasted To Your Life, Leslie, How Do You Feel About That, Leslie?" Patrick holds his glass up and looks at its underside.

"Leslie, your young man here "

"Jack why don't you take Patrick up with Erik and Kjell to see the plane," Leslie says straight into Sun's eyes. "Sun and I have some business we have to take care of."

"Why don't you and Sun use your brains first and go conduct your business in your cabin, or were you counting on their giving us an extended course in aeronautics?"

Still locked onto their steel streak of vision, Leslie flicks her head toward the hallway. Sun starts breathing to the tempo of Leslie's breathing and begins to stand. She looks like a length of black silk scented ribbon being gently picked and uncoiled from a leather treasure-box. "That was a great toast, sweetie, you did good you did good!" Leslie says, not turning to Patrick until Sun is out of her chair. "I'm gonna be just fine—hey!—" She puts her hand on his shoulder "that's what you're here for, right? To protect me, right?" and feels the flavored air change shape as Sun moves toward the sleeping quarters.

Patrick looks over at Sun for the first time since she siphoned Leslie's attention. He focuses on the fine gold band ringing the seam where the leather heel-tip is affixed to the spike on her right shoe. "Y-you don't w-we don't—Imean—y-you d-didn't you s—d-don't know wh-what.....we're h-here for. M-Ms. Brittain. Actually," he whispers, his sober eyes following the heel, seeing it as if, in its independent act of walking away, it were courageously carrying Sun with it. As if it were an ant dragging half a Clark Bar home to the hill.

Tightening her grip on Patrick, Leslie snaps her head toward the hallway. She knows that Sun's leaving the room is only bringing them closer to what they want, that Sun is merely doing what she has to do to get from here to there. And yet Leslie is a little girl in a supermarket cart watching her mother walk away from the frozen vegetables aisle and being sure she'll never see her again for the rest of her life.

"How Bout Coming Up And Giving Us A Hand Flying the Plane, Son!" Jack orders more than invites.

They all rock out of their respective bulging cushions onto their respective feet. "Better get it while you can, Patrick," Leslie says. "I got a feeling tomorrow's gonna be a real mortuary on this plane." Her speech is slowed. She salutes and walks to the mouth of the corridor then leans against the wall. "You know, like those pirate ships that arrive in port draped in gossamer tatters which turn into ghosts and float away while the trembling townsfolk look on in wonder." Swaying and waving in a little ghost-like float, she points herself in the direction of her cabin.

"Did you ever think of offering yourself as a subject for sleep-deprivation studies?" Jack wants to know as she ghost-floats down the hall. "You Girls Start Without Me—I'll Be In To Give You Some

Pointers On That Project Of Yours."

"Youououou'rrre" Her warble grows fainter as she hurries toward her door "scumm", puts her hand on the brass knob "mmm", turns it with more force than she thinks she has at this moment and "Jaaa" closes the door behind her. "ackck," she whispers in awe as she sees Sun standing in the far corner by an antique washstand and basin.

Leslie pretends to collapse in a pantomime of Jjeezz! Finally got rid of them! And the rest of the world! And even elements we don't at this very moment know we got rid of we jjeezz! finally got rid of too! Sun leads with her hip bones, the black silk scented ribbon being extracted, extruded straight across the line of air toward Leslie. With a step. a box of powdered flowered spice spills into the cabin, with a step. the spice begins to eddy at the ground, with a step. the scent crackles and explodes within the eddies Leslie's shoulder blades and wide-open palms and buttocks are pressing tight onto the door with a step. the explosion pops patchouli-buds and piles them in a waist-high perfumed field Leslie pushes even farther back against the wood not to get away but to make another milimolecule of space for Sun's approach for the receiving of Sun's approach with a step. Sun brings her field of perfumed lips to the space before Leslie's lips...

Leslieimmediatelyopensthedoorandrunsout.

In her dignity and grace, Sun sits on the edge of the bed with her legs crossed and waits for Leslie to return.

LESLIE BLASTS IN SEConds later and quick-shuts the door with both hands and a shoulder as if she's being chased and if she doesn't shut it this very second trans-Asian hallway-monsters will slip in and terrorize her and Sun, and Mom n Dad'll find out they're staying up late looking up body parts in the encyclopedia with a flashlight in the dark. She has a champagne bottle and two glasses in her hands.

"*Jack told me you don't drink,*" Sun hums to her.

It's not speaking that she does, Leslie knows it's not speaking that Sun does, and it probably shouldn't even be called humming, either; she knows she'll put her finger on what it is one day but not right now. It's more like calligraphy—spoken calligraphy. And storytelling. But storytelling within every word. She starts at the beginning of a word, even a tiny word, even a word where the beginning and the end are the same, like I or a, and by the time she reaches the end of the word, the last letter of the word, she's already provided you with a preface, taken you through an introduction, set a motif, sprinkled several leitmotifs, developed multiple characters, thickened the plot, layered the subplots, discovered a deus ex machina, crafted a *dénouement*, furnished an ending, added an epilogue and drawn a little symbol like an asterisk or a crosshatch or something in the middle of the bottom of the last page to make it look final. This on a word-by-word basis. Once Sun's individual word-stories have fusioned into a sentence-story and heaven knows into a paragraph-story even going as far as becoming a story-story, you have discovered the core sensation which verbal communication was invented to produce. What they were aiming at when messages like "Do you have a phone I can use" or "Hello" or "Jack told me you don't drink" were brought onto the scene, let alone treasures like "Once upon a time" and "Stay tuned for more".

"I don't," Leslie answers, finally determining it's safe to unwedge her shoulder from the doorframe. "It's for you.....I brought an extra glass for ." She grins and shrugs her shoulders like a teen-ager and holds the glasses up in an awkward jerky gesture, moving slightly away from the entrance toward the bed in the middle of the room.

*"Pardon me?"*

"N-nothing," Leslie says, feeling self-conscious and rough next to Sun's composure and delicacy. She wants to say something but knows that whatever it is will come out too.....too.....muscular. Her voice will be muscular next to the harp-strings that vibrate from Sun, her words will be muscular. *Pardon me? Pardon me?* Whoever says *Pardon me??* In books they say Pardon me?, and in old black-and-white movies so old that the words are never in synch with the lips but the ladies always have these long long necks equaled in longness only by the cigarettes they're holding while they're saying Pardon me? to a guy in a tuxedo. Sun says Pardon me?. That's who says Pardon me?. Leslie feels bulky. She does not feel like a black silk scented ribbon. She feels like a bolt of loden-green corduroy who's been up for too many hours. She walks to where Sun is sitting and hands her the bottle and glasses.

Sun uncoils. She carries Leslie's provisions to the nighttable and fits back into her spot on the edge of the bed as if it were a straight-backed chair. *Its both,* she says.

"Frchissakes!" Leslie asks "What's both?" tautly.

*"My name."* Sun answers *"Like you said."* smoothly.

Leslie crosses the cabin to a bureau in the dressing area and brings back a heavy antique sculpted-silver hairbrush with white sable bristles. "So which parent was what?" she wants to know as she kneels on the bed behind Sun

*"My mother,"* "was?" and starts brushing her hair. "Nowait lemme guess! Chinese!"

*"British."*

"Shit"

*"She was running the Byron Institute in mmmmnnnn"* With her right hand, Leslie draws the brush from the top of Sun's scalp to her waist, then follows with her left palm, smoothing close to Sun's head neck torso *in Amsterdam, where my father was Ambassador.*

"But Byron didn't write The Also Rises." She pulls at Sun's shoulders and flips her backwards and

*"Oh!"* over onto her stomach, straddling her hips, continuing to stroke and smooth, to scoop Sun's perfume into the bristles and up through her own arm out to the air. *That's not where it comes from,* Sun sings with girlish amusement. *You'll never guess.*

Taking her task seriously, Leslie is studying every stroke, seeing that she treats each shiny strand with equal devotion. "Well," she says softly, bending forward and placing her hands on the bed by Sun's shoulders "you'll" and her lips at her ear, "just have to tell me" kissing her, "where it *does* come from," lightly at first, all around, little crisp kisses "won't you," from one side of her neck to the other. Delicate kisses. Like Sun. "Sun?" And then more intensely, deep into the top of her spine and under her ears, sucking Sun's skin into her open mouth and teeth. Rough kisses. Like Leslie.

Sun rolls onto her back between Leslie's legs and Leslie's wetness whitens the skirt of the black silk suit. Leslie stretches her body onto Sun's body and the women get caught in the clasp of each other's eyes, almost unable to break free, stopping all but their breathing so as to fortify the bond. On straightened arms with her back arched, coated in her own black silk, Leslie is a serpent atop Sun. Sun is a rock and a flower and a brook. She is nowhere to be found. She is rippling away and giggling in hiding then gushing back and Leslie is chasing her. She has never left her anchored banks. It is all taking place in their gaze.

Leslie no longer feels weighted and graceless, she feels as if all her skin has been removed and replaced with Sun's skin, she feels as if their skin is layered lamb on a huge vertical Greek-restaurant brochette, turning on its axis while a knife so sharp and fast you don't see it cut, flicks down in angled slices and lifts a strip of them, exposing the next strip, lifting the next, exposing the next, lifting the next Sun is lifting her pelvis her hip-bony pelvis to try to be touched by Leslie Leslie sits back on her heels over Sun and opens the bottom gold button of the Pullman jacket.

When Sun moves to help her, brings her arms down from the pillow around her head to join in the unbuttoning, Leslie very gently collects her wrists and returns them to where they were. She lingers around Sun's face, caressing her chin and lips and geometric cheekbones with the palms and backs of both hands before moving down to open the second button from the bottom.

Then Leslie rises. Walks to the door and turns off the cabin light, lights the dusty-rose candle in the crystal goblet on the nighttable. Sun hums with her breath and lifts her pelvis as Leslie once more sits across her hips. Leslie opens the third button and gets off the bed.

She steps out of her shoes and reaches around for her zipper, draping the Suzy Wong over the treadmill on her way to the dressing area. When, totally naked, she straddles Sun again, Leslie has a thin white satin ribbon and a thicker black satin ribbon in her hand. Holding onto the white she lays the black on the bed at Sun's left, smoothing and extending it from its center to its ends in ritualistic preoccupation, twisting her torso to give it full attention. She opens button number four, then with a satin loop traces the side of Sun's face from the top of her ear to the bottom of her neck.

Leslie's breasts lift as she raises her arms to her hair. Sun reaches up to her. Leslie smiles softly and stops Sun's hand before the touch. Sun allows Leslie to guide her wrist gently back to the bed. One at a time Leslie pulls out the six small tortoise-shell hairpins holding her French knot, dropping each to the floor before uprooting the next, shaking her head and fluffing her big curls when they spring free. The last two hairpins hit the others with quick sweet clinks where they fall. Like Sun would sound if she were a tortoise-shell hairpin. Leslie ties her hair back with the white ribbon. She opens the fifth button.

Sun looks down at the button remaining. She and Leslie are particles of solid suspended in a receptacle of gel, two tight little beads centered and focused into their own distinct compact cores, separated from each other by the same semi-fluidity which is holding them together, which they are sharing. In this viscous atmosphere of Leslie's cabin they cannot run to each other—the gel is just this side of too thick, the emotional circulation just this side of too sluggish. But the surface of the solid sphere of each of them is in contact with the viscous atmosphere in which they are contained and thus they are in contact with each other. Their independent orbits roam the close folds of the same universe inside this room and so they roam together. They are observers participating in the thickness and the slowness of their scene; they are participating mutually observed. Sun and Leslie both know that with a little extra heat the gel will liquefy and the particles that they are will first flow and then effervesce and then crazily collide with each other, aggressively break up upon each other. Each knows that the other will know when they want that.

What they want now is a visit. An artistic experience. A walk through a museum. The patchouli is enough for Leslie at this moment, the way it exhales from Sun's skin every time Leslie touches it, like wind from a fireplace bellows, as if Sun were an elongated patchouli-filled pillow whose contents are displaced, forced to flutter out, when sat upon by Leslie. The patchouli and the time and quiet space. Knowing that she's going to learn about Sun's name. Knowing that she's going to sleep with Sun, to fall asleep with Sun..................................................

...........knowing that she's
going to fall asleep with Leslie. That her Chinese body and British mind are a unity for Leslie's pleasure and are extensions of each other's power for herself.

Leslie gets up and pours a glass of champagne at the nighttable. She hands it to Sun and lies across the bed, her torso stretched sideways upon "Gohead." Sun's legs.

*"Just direct your feet,"* Sun begins in a declarative sculpture, propping herself on an elbow, *to the*

*"sssu-nnny?"*

"*side of the street.*" She gracefully raises the glass toward Leslie's face in a silent toast.

"Gyiimmeeabrea-eakk!" Leslie screeches, pushing onto Sun's shoulder with the heel of her hand. "Your parents didn't—I mean—that's a real nice song and all but that's not—tell me—don't do this to me, Sun, OK?" She leaps off the bed while Sun quietly sips her champagne, her white abdomen and the insides of her breasts peeking through the opening in the front of the jacket when she lifts her glass to her lips. "That's not what ambassadors and fucking English teachers are supposed to base their reality on!  A name is a sacred—frchrissakes a song like th—*janitors* whistle that song while they're changing pipe elbows frchrissakes cellulitic ladies in mint-green polyester pants-suits who sell thread and dress-shields in fucking Woolworth's hum it up while they're waiting for their goddamn bus to take them home to make lamb chops and canned mixed vegetables for their husbands who work in check-cashing agencies. It's from an Oriental game, right? You were named after an intricate cryptic millennia-old Oriental game of strategy passed down in secret ceremonies through the ancestral houses—invented by the women but played only by the men—that your parents used to sit up playing well into the sunrise—kind of in a combination of the chess scene in The Thomas Crown Affair and the food scene in Tom Jones. And one dawn, in a flash of psycho-erotico-mystico-strategic inspiration and enlightenment, they and the spirits of the ancestors decided to conceive a girl right there on the ivory-and-onyx gameboard."

Having roved and flailed herself as far against the dressing-area wall as she can go, Leslie walks back to the bed "And to name her", to where she was lying, fitting her waist and underarm over Sun's legs like puzzle pieces "Sun.", her voice and face dreamy with self-congratulatory enchantment at her substitute reality. "In honor of the game. Which," she wonders, leaning forward and looking into Sun's eyes, "in Chinese means...?"

"*She liked the song.*" Sun hums an imploding giggle at Leslie's seriousness.

"Well Then Why The Fuck Didn't She Name You Sunny, Frchrissakes! Or—or I have a better one—Str—no—even better than that—Feet!" Leslie cackles. "That'd sure be appealing, wouldn't it," She readjusts her position, locking Sun tighter under her side. "sitting out there across the salon flashing me your little pussy, me knowing your name was.....FEET! Least then your little story wouldn't break the mood there'd be no mood left to break!"

*Now, Leslie, that's not exactly an appropriate name for the daughter of an ambassador and a scholar, is it?*

"OH-OH! KAY-EE!" Leslie grabs the glass from Sun and stabs it down onto the nighttable like a murder weapon. She crawls to the middle of the bed "Recess Is Over Rock n Rollers!" and resumes her perch, her buttock on her heels, her knees straddling Sun. Like twin fish frisking through fresh water, her hands roll back to front to back across Sun's forehead and forehead and cheeks and cheeks and neck, down to the top button, which she opens while seizing and holding Sun's eyes in her eyes.

In sustained application and care she peels away the fronts of the jacket, isolating one side then the other, working as if against a resistive force, as if mindful not to set off an alarm. As if exposing a creature to the light of the world for the first time. She lifts the half at her right, folding it slowly and neatly outward but keeping it in her hand, looking at Sun's small tight round breast, into Sun's eyes, Sun watches Leslie look, back to Sun's breast. Leslie nods, looks, looks like she's thinking, looks like she's looking, doesn't touch, rests the edge of the fabric onto Sun's shoulder. She lifts the half at her left with the same attention, while Sun watches her with the same attention, then removes the jacket and skirt, sending up such swells of patchouli, especially as the skirt grazes Sun's close-cropped pubis, she might as well be digging into the buds of the blossoms themselves. It's her skin, Leslie tells herself, it's not perfume *on* her skin, it's skin spun with the spice-fibres of the flower. There must be a little patchouli flower walking around somewhere—being undressed at this very moment by a flower of another species—with human-skin molecules laced through its cells, there must have been an exchange.

Leslie picks the black satin ribbon from the bed and sets Sun's suit in its place. Rising to her knees, she holds one end of the ribbon high above Sun's body and lets the other end dangle and dance, not exactly touching Sun but not exactly not, occasionally making contact between her breasts, in the hollows of her collarbone, across the lips and along the cleft of her vagina. Sun closes her eyes, buries her head back deep into the pillow. She reaches up behind her, weaves her spread fingers through the brass bars of the headboard, lifts her body in a fluid wave which follows the ribbon's route. Now Leslie is drawing the ribbon in huge looping tracks from one end of Sun to the other, streaming up the inside of one thigh, one wing of her pubic **V**, eddying around one breast and then around the other and back down. Like a magnet, the black satin strip passes over a section of Sun, pulls that part up, carries it along for a breath-held instant until the force flows forward and the present part subsides and breathes and cedes its seat on the wave to the next part the ribbon pulls.

Sun starts "*Aaaaaachchch*" rolling from side to side. Squeezes her fingers around the headboard bars then releases and brushes her hands down to her face weaves them up through the bars again. Leslie raises the ribbon just high enough that it stops almost-touching Sun Sun whimpers bounces her buttocks against the bed closes her eyes even tighter Leslie drips the ribbon onto Sun's pussy and shoots her other hand into her own, jerking her pelvis forward and back, stirring the ribbon with progressively bigger sweeps of her arm until she is whipping Sun with big black satin strokes and looks like a lasso-swinging cowgirl holding onto the saddle of her unruly mount.

The women find and match each other's breathing, steal each other's cries. Leslie's gravel-grunts grow melodic, the sweet song in Sun's throat moves all the way down to her gut. They draw each other in to the rhythm of their bucks and waves and rolls then push each other back readjust the tension of the lightwave linking them readjust again Leslie whips and whoops and pounds her pelvis Sun tries to spread and kick her legs Leslie's knees brace them in Sun senses that Leslie is going to come she wants to come with her she fires a hand down toward her pussy Leslie slaps it away mid-course like a missile deflector fires a hand down toward her pussy Leslie slaps it away Sun tilts her pelvis deep into the bed and rubs and breathes squeezes her labia sucks her labia up into herself Leslie is quick-whipping onto Sun's face Sun lifts into the blows smiles Leslie smiles Sun pre-shudders Leslie stops. Sun stops.

"You didn't come." Leslie wants confirmation.

Sun doesn't know whether Leslie needs a yes or a no. "*No.*"

"Good. Girl." She takes her hand from between her legs "Neither did I." and offers it to Sun.

When Sun has licked and sucked along and between each finger, treating each finger as a new encounter not to be licked and sucked like its neighbor but according to its own stature and needs, Leslie gives her the black satin ribbon and tells her to go over to the dressing-area mirror and tie it around her neck. Shaking her head back,

Sun sits up and starts tying the ribbon. Leslie stays Sun's hands. She moves off her body onto the bed and nods toward the dressing area. Sun slowly rises.

"Leave them on!" Leslie orders as Sun bends to remove her shoes. Like a model on a runway "I want to see you walk." Sun begins to walk, "From behind." holding one end of the ribbon and dragging the other coolly after her along the carpet, as if it were her matching evening wrap....leading with her hips, swinging her arms in shoulder-to-wrist ripples, allowing nothing to distract her arrogant head in its aim....transporting herself not by cutting through the air particles but by camouflaging herself as one of them.

The farther Sun gets from the bed, the more narrowly Leslie focuses on her structures and textures until she winds up squeezing all peripheral vision out of the scene. The long stark stalk of white skin growing out of Sun's black high heels and blossoming into her head of black hair becomes a white streak between two black slivers becomes the line that molds itself to the back of her calves and flows up over her bottom to her shoulder blades becomes the part of her thighs that softens just before they become her buttocks and the part of her trunk that strengthens as her buttocks become her back becomes the outline of her buttocks becomes the flat flesh of her buttocks as they walk to the other end of the cabin, one advancing, the other ready to go, the other advancing, the other ready to "Stop there. That's fine."

In the dressing area the full-length mirror is the same as in Patrick's cabin but its frame and base are of a lighter-toned, more feminine wood which blends with the beige of the carpet and the dusty-rose - beige - gray of the bedclothes, walls and drapes. Angled slightly to her right toward the bed, Sun stands facing the mirror. She ties the ribbon in a bow at the nape of her neck and starts walking "Knot it." back toward Leslie,

"I want a knot."

sending the black satin streaming down behind her almost to the ends of her hair. While Sun advances, Leslie slithers on her stomach. Meets her at the edge of the bed. Ssllaapppps her hands onto Sun's hips. Stops her from climbing in.

"That's what I want," she says softly, straight into Sun's pussy, then shimmies forward, pulling herself along against the strength of Sun's stance. "A knot." Extending her tongue. Although Sun is certainly within reach, Leslie takes great pains not to reach her, hanging off the mountain while her tongue tries to connect with the life-saving rock inches away.

Sun's fingers lace through Leslie's curls, scoop her hair and scalp into two tight fists, lock her head in place. Leslie wraps her hands wider around Sun's flanks, her red nails digging into her buttocks and hips, her thumbs pressing toward each other on either side of Sun's pubis, forcing the top of her labia forward and up, massaging the sticky-wet labia one against the other, one thumb up the other down up down up down upushing Sun's pussy apart, pushing Sun's pussy apart, pushing her head against Sun's fists and her tongue through the thicket of her thighs cutting up into the inside of Sun's inside Sun stands still and straight slightly tilting to Leslie's mouth Leslie braces again against Sun's hold shoots her knees up to her chest on the bed and arches and bobs onto her back pulling Sun down on top of her"rrraahheee!".

The women roll as an uncontained unit, across the bed—howling and grappling like a couple of urchins resolving a problem in the playground dirt—and back—yelping and pawing like a pair of puppies fighting over a toy—across—laughing and chirring like teenagers exploring each other's body—and back—laughing and chirring like women exploring each other's body.

Their mouths and hands and legs catch and keep whatever comes into their path.

Suddenly Sun is on her back.

Leslie's mouth is between Sun's legs.

Sun's hands are on Leslie's head.

Leslie's hands are on Sun's hips.

Sun's feet are flat on the bed.

Leslie is stretched on her stomach between Sun's bent knees. Sun lifts and swings her pelvis into Leslie's face.

Leslie lowers her hands and cups and squeezes Sun's buttocks, boosts them even higher.

She serves herself Sun's pelvis.

Helps herself to Sun.

To tasting Sun.

To smelling Sun.

Sun is a handful of fresh water Leslie's ladled from a stream. From Sun's stream.

To lapping Sun.

To licking Sun.

An ice cream cone.

A bowl of squishy noodles.

To slurping every one.

Sun inches little inhaley whimpers from her throat.

Leslie launches large rolling roars from her gut

and licks.

Leslie licks.

The door opens.

Sun lurches to get up.

Leslie licks, and presses onto Sun's hips to keep her there.

 Sun fights against the pressure Leslie presses harder thrusts her tongue up into Sun  *uhachch"*  and her teeth up into Sun and hops onto to her knees for better fit,  *ah-h-h ah-h-h ah-h-h"*  making Sun come with her better fit,  *ah"*  looking like she has not heard the door,  *h-h"*  acknowledging the presence of no one  *h"*  but Sunnnnnnnnnnnnnnnnnnnnnnnnnnnnnnnnnnnnnnnnnnnnnnnnnnnnnnnnnnnnnn nnnnnnnnnnnnnnnnnnnnnnnnnnnnnnnnnnnnnnnnnnnnnnnnnnnnnnnnnnnn.............

...................................................................................Stretching out her legs,

Leslie props herself on one elbow while she strokes Sun's stomach with her free hand. She watches Sun look to see who came in, watches her nod, but does not look herself. As it shifts and settles, she studies Sun's shape "You're scum, Jack", returning the quiet smile "But I'm sure you didn't come all the way across the aircraft to my little sleepy cabin for me to tell you that." which Sun beams up to her just before closing her eyes. When Sun reaches for her hand "I'm sure there's a reasonable chance you at least had the beginning rumblings of that piece of intelligence even before you set out down the hallway." Leslie offers it to her, never turning her head away, seeming to be talking to herself, gently folding the bedspread up around Sun's cooling skin.

"Remember when Juliet's nurse comes on the scene in a big flowing dress?" Leslie says to Jack on her way to the dressing-area closet. She "Oooh-oooh! How inappropriate!" chooses a short silk kimono hanging among several others, all of different lengths and floral patterns in the color-scheme of her cabin. "I was thinking more along the lines of, say, a serape. Or a grass skirt Hey does this thing automatically change color once I leave this room or do I have to stay in here for the rest of my life if I have it on? HEY LOOK!" Backed into the drapes, her arms and fingers spread, she glances down at her body "Do I look like just a mouth talking? Bet you can't find me, huh? Has my entire body disappeared into th—HEY! WAIT!" then turns to face the drapes. "Just wait one minute here!" Beats and pinches them. "Just wait one—" Pulls them out from the wall every several inches. "Do you have are you are we alone here?" Gives them a thorough shakedown. "Do you have—I bet you're harboring a whole band of floral-kimono-clad voyeur scum who've disappeared into these drapes and I didn't even—at least *you* had the decency" She joins Jack in the sitting nook past the foot of the bed, where he installed himself when he came in. "to walk in the front fucking door."

"As opposed to the back-fucking door."

"I don't remember which scene but Juliet's nurse comes in and Romeo shouts A sail! A sail! cause the woman—who's no *haricot vert* to begin with—is in this big white thiss thissss vestment and she looks like a fucking sail." Leslie hugs her knees to her chest in a large pearl-gray leather chair. "It's a great line—one of his best. Rivaled only by Lie thou there., which is of course Juliet having a little conversation with the knife.....You're staring at me like you're trying to remember the name of the asteroid I was just beamed on board from. Name That Asteroid!" she announces, surprised to find herself pointing both index fingers.

Jack flicks his ashes into a heavy crystal ashtray on his lap. As he gathers and builds them into a neat little pyramid with the tip of his cigar, Leslie leans forward and grabs the hem of his immense sparkling-white terrycloth bathrobe, lifting it away from his legs with one hand while pointing to it with perpetual-motion jabs of the other, as if that arm were on an electric spring. "A SAIL! A SAIL!" she mouths, offsetting the soundlessness of her words with exaggerated movements of her lips and eyes. She continues lifting the robe and leaning forward to peek under it, her head and arm growing farther apart along their axis in a slow, smooth balletic stretch, her children's-theater-pixie face pantomiming discovery.

"Do me a favor get that ashtray off your lap, willyuh, Jack, it's weighing down the robe and I can't see your cock." Like a kid demolishing a sand castle, Jack spears into the apex of his pyramid. The ashes scatter into a stratum of sloppy pools. "Oh I get it! Sorry, Jack. I didn't reali—sorry—you didn't have the ashtray there after all, didjyuh?" Leslie stands and gets out of her kimono "Feel free to stay as long as you like.", rolls it into a tight silken ball and "I'm gonna go kryogenically freeze myself" stuffs it into Jack's ashtray. "so when we land in Singapore in a couple years I'll be just as "

"revolting "

" as I am at this very moment. Feel free to stay as long as you like, Jack. Maybe you and the drape-goons can measure each other's ashtrays. Make the trip go faster. Are we there yet, Daddy?" As Leslie slips under the covers Sun turns onto her stomach and the bedspread falls away from her body. She still has her shoes on. Aware once more of the patchouli in the air, Leslie wonders whether she'd gotten used to it or whether it had been stockpiling under Sun. Jack makes no move to get out of his chair. Leslie blows him a long, desperate, hysterical-good-bye-at-the-train-station kiss, flutters her eyelashes and selects a wax-lips number from her extensive collection of smiles. Once she's covered Sun again she rolls around to blow out the candle on the nighttable.

"I hope you'll be able to sleep."

"Cause oyour fucking cigar?"

"Because you didn't come."

"Prove it. Funny. I had the same concern about you, Jack."

"Prove it."

"Wonder what Blyster wants with Patrick. Is he OK does he know what the scoop is? I guess this is his answer to his mother's criminally parental phonecall, huh, rock n rollers?" Leslie turns back to Sun, mumbling "I hope he makes it through this thing."

In the emergency-lit darkness Jack builds another pyramid. "Funny. He had the same concern about you, Leslie."

# XVI

# "THANK YOU, CHAN. THAT WILL BË ÅLL."

| "Is this gonna be like the Wizard of Oz?" |
|---|

At noon on the day after they arrive in Singapore, Saintjohn, Jack's driver, fetches Jack, Leslie and Patrick at Jack's apartments in the Raffles Hotel.

| "You remember the scene don't you?" |
|---|

While Leslie was spending the better part of the previous day commuting incommunicado between the treadmill and the imperatorial lacquered-pearl bathtub in her guest suite, Jack and Saintjohn took Patrick riding and walking all over the city. Saintjohn was a schoolboy at the time of the Japanese invasion in '42. Left to fend for himself when his British civil-servant parents were herded into Changi Prison with the rest of the European population of Singapore, he immediately discovered that what hooliganism and jack-of-all-tradery lacked in the type of security his home had provided, they more than made up for in the type of lawless excitement it had not. Saintjohn is what Patrick might have become had the Japanese invaded Nebraska and herded all the self-sacrificing housewives and righteous male authority figures into an internment camp. Or, as challenging to the imagination, Patrick is what Saintjohn might have remained had his parents stepped out for a refresher bird-watching course several seconds before the ravagers knocked on the door. On some level Patrick and Saintjohn knew this the instant they saw each other, the minute they read each other's body language as the Happy Travelers lumbered into the car at the airport at dawn.

> "It's been all these hours already and all these yellow bricks and songs and locking elbows into each other and the closeness that can only come from sharing the experience of fending off flying Witch-Monkeys together and all these plans and points of reference reinforcing the refreshing optimism of fantastical youthful celluloid-endangered hope."

So what with Jack's unflagging, self-stroking certainty at being the direct and exclusive catalyst for any positive connection which occurs in his presence, nothing could have been more gratifying all around than The Boys' taking off on a Singaporean adventure, in the mighty beige-gleam Bentley with cream leather seats and walnut dashboard, and leaving Leslie for dead in the bathtub.

> "And now here they are."

Patrick sat up front, close to Saintjohn, answering with almost imperious confidence Saintjohn's questions about whether he *minded* if they went here and there or *minded* if Saintjohn asked him about life in America. Jack busied himself in the back at taking full responsibility for both the electro-magnetic vibrations passing between the two and the apparent reversal of roles.

> "At the end of their long journey."

But it wasn't a role reversal at all. It wasn't a reversal of anything. It was an exchange. An exchange. Not the kind of sharp, tidy exchange as with objects, where one person is holding an object and another person is holding another object and then they hand each other their respective objects across an invisible line of demarcation. Not an exchange like that. Rather a blurred, borderless exchange as when the blood of one person's cut finger presses up against the blood of another person's cut finger. Where whatever is exchanged is also kept and whatever is kept is altered. Potentiated by the exchange. Like the mixture of two chemicals forming a third, more powerful chemical.

> ("But which of all of us crouching in front of our television sets on Easter weekend know is of course really the beginning of an even longer journey.")

In this way Patrick and Saintjohn exchanged their histories. Silently. In the bubbling, churning layer under the layer of their interaction. By what was playing in their eyes and thus their thought-flashes and their sense memories while they were talking about everything but themselves. About, for example, what they were seeing. Or at least what Saintjohn and occasionally Jack in the back there were attempting to get Patrick to see—because for all the psychodynamic promise this newfound soul-brotherhood held for him, it was preventing him from appreciating the sights of the city-state from either side of the window of the mighty beige-gleam Bentley. He would not take his eyes off Saintjohn.

> "Together—in if I remember correctly their classic sextuple-elbow-lock, allowing of course for the unattached state of the two end elbows and don't ask me whose cause no matter how many times I see it, and it's up there going for the record with Gone With the Wind, that's just one detail, albeit in a radically important scene, that I never retain—in the entrance to the Hall of the Wizard."

But finding himself exceptionally relaxed rather than unsettled by Patrick's pinpointed focus, Saintjohn was disposed to provide an even richer experience for them all. His tall lanky body streamlined by his black silk uniform, his scar-kissed asymmetrical face shaded under the matching cap, Saintjohn drove and strolled and described and explained, furnishing little follow-up comments like "Well, Pat, it's everything I told you it'd be and more, eh m'boy?", as if Patrick were goggling out the window of a car he'd come expressly to Singapore to hire for an afternoon of serious tourism, or marching with notepad in hand on a reconnaissance mission for his upcoming series of travel books.

> "In to see the big man."

And it *was* an afternoon of privileged serious tourism, whether or not for all Patrick knew he was riding in a *métro* car with the Shah of Iran and Saintjohn through the garment district of Havana.

> "And then as they stand there trembling in anticipation and awe of the life-altering moment when this symbol of potent magnanimity and omniscience will at last reveal himself, and thereby confirm his universal truth, to their suffering little souls..."

They drove north of the river to the Victorian architecture and gray stone structures of colonial Singapore, and further north for a look over the city from Fort Canning Hill (Patrick looked at Saintjohn). They swung south through the commercial district that borders on the harbor, then slipped into Chinatown to walk among fortune-tellers foodstalls outdoor-barbers temples calligraphers shrines effigy-makers keepers of shops of ancient realities like temple furniture crafted from ivory and wood and lion-dance masks made from paper and bamboo.

> "...they hear it. There it comes. Here it is. The line. THE line. Enlightenment. Life. Reinforced steel spoons clanging on immense cauldrons in your ear at the best part of your dream:"

In a rare moment of separation from Saintjohn, Patrick stopped in front of a shop window where a thin gold chain strung with pearls and coral beads snaked on a swatch of black velvet. Jack and Saintjohn watched Patrick suction all the energy and concentration from the world around him—as with a hypodermic needle—and inject it into the necklace on display. Watched for awhile, as Patrick kept being about to make a move, looking like he knew he desperately needed to do something but was having difficulty figuring out what. Jack approached him and put his arm around his shoulders. "Yes, I agree, son!"

> "PAYYY NOHOHOH ATTENNNTIONNN TOOOOO THE MANNNN BEHINNND THE CURTAINNNN!"

Saintjohn dropped Jack and Patrick off at the Ng Tiong Choon

Sembawang Fish Pond, a seafood restaurant built on stilts over the old Ng Tiong Choon Sembawang fish pond out past the zoo in an exquisite rural setting. Patrick did not understand why Saintjohn would not be lunching with them and why they didn't stay in Chinatown and eat radish cakes and prawn mee soup and fried bananas from the hawkers' stalls. But he was too afraid even to know that he was too afraid to ask. Asking didn't even make it to the status of being an option to reject. Jack recommended the fish-head curry or chili crabs, assuming that Patrick wasn't an eel man and that he could probably get all the abalone he'd ever want back in Paris. Or Nebraska. Especially after the Japanese invaded. It wasn't easy for Patrick but he finally focused long enough to, well, not exactly choose what he wanted, but at least eliminate what he didn't. He eliminated everything but the chili crabs, Jack ordered the fish-head curry and the owner's giggly balding little grandmotherly wife, who tells Jack every time he walks in that he and she were married, with many sons, in another life and that he is still the number-one favorite of all her karmic husbands, took care of everything else.

> "Is this gonna be like that?"

Then Jack went to work.

> "I mean I can't be the only one in this car who any second now expects to see straw-droppings lying all over the carpet....Can I?.......I mean—don't you guys?"

Thanking Patrick for having agreed to join him on his trip to Singapore, he told him why they had come. More accurately, he told him that the next day they were going to meet with someone who would be telling him and Leslie why they had come. And he briefed him on what had led them to this point.

> "I wonder who everyone is! Well I mean it's a little obvious who's Dorothy. Isn't it?"

With the personalized impersonal dexterity of an expert called in to talk someone down from a skyscraper ledge or negotiate with a hijacker, Jack constructed the balance between the hard and soft doses of truth needed to prepare Patrick's sturdy mind and precarious gut for tomorrow and July 4th and possibly the rest of his life.

> "The problem is there's only three of us."

Leslie had warned Jack.

> "Well if you don't count Saintjohn."

You expect Patrick to react to a normal situation—like ordering a sandwich in a cafe—like a normal human being and he speeds straight into unfocus, delivering the results of two and a half decades' of Midwestern guilt-inducing, personality-annihilating self-effacement in a sloppy little package you can do absolutely nothing with, taking long-gone refuge in the undersides of ashtrays or the microscopic striations of windowpane glass that no one can see but him. Then you do what virtually amounts to kidnapping him way the hell to the other end of the planet, you tell him—over a fish-head lunch in a restaurant on stilts where an endearingly grotesque gnome-queen greets you with eel meat and tales of nuptial reincarnation—that the life of his idolized best and only friend in the part of the world from which you've uprooted him—which isn't even his habitual part of the world but which may be the only part of the world where he has a friend at all—is if not in grave danger then at least experiencing significant changes in routine, and you feed him a fantasmagorical story to prepare him for an ominous meeting with a reputedly gay hermit relic-rustling billionaire who got everyone into this fix in the first place and who will be proposing an even more fantasmagorical plan to get them if not out then at least further along. And what does Patrick do?

> "Or Sun hey wait!"

He sits there calmly eating his chili crabs and his noodles that look like human hair. (Maybe they came from to the owner's wife.) Nods.

Makes firm eye-contact. Exhibits all the rest of the heedful, extrospective body language that people like social workers and interviewers spend fortunes on weekend retreats learning how to exhibit. Smiles warmly to the endearingly grotesque gnome-queen when she brings yet another alien addition to the feast. Asks excellent questions in a composed manner. Furnishes pertinent answers to those asked of him.

> "But damn! Then if you count them both then there's *five* of us."

Leslie later suggested to Jack that maybe Patrick's consciousness is a series of delayed reactions: by the time the grotesquery hits him it's sandwich-ordering time, so what looks like an inability to say ham and cheese is really a healthy response to last week's human-hair noodles and tales of treachery; and then when the next portion of perilous exotica comes his way he's just about ready to smile at the nice waiter and ask for lunch like you're supposed to.

> "So it's *still* one off. Well that doesn't matter that doesn't change anything as far as I'm concerned!"

Whatever the annotation, Jack took full credit for having brought the boy out of a lifetime of unfocus in an eighth of a day. He asked Patrick how he felt about what he'd just heard.

> "Or anything of any relevance anyway."

After waiting discretely for a break in their conversation, the owner came over to shake hands, wanting to know if everything was all right and thanking Jack for having sent some people to him the weekend before. Not To Worry! the owner informed them, The Imperial Wheel Of Color Was On Its Way! He hoped it would be of pleasure to Jack's grandson. Patrick shrugged and did what he thought was wink at Jack but what turned out to be more like squinting both eyes and his right cheek at the same time. The owner hopped off, snapping his fingers as a young

> "I wonder who's the Wizard. That's what *I* wonder!"

woman in a blue-and-green sea-scene sarong appeared with a round silver tray that almost matched the dimensions of the table top, leaving just enough room for the place settings. Shooting out from a large central whole pineapple were perfectly aligned spokes of partially overlapping trapezoidal slices, each spoke showcasing a different-colored fruit, each slice progressively larger the closer it sat to the rim of the tray. While the waitress—who had an Oriental face but an atmosphere-butchering New York accent about which Jack planned to speak to the owner—pointed and recited her way around the wheel for Patrick "rambutan / mangosteen / nangka / papaya / ", Jack noticed that he was losing him again "durian / starfruit" (or "sdahhhfrooottt" as the exchange student saw fit to articulate) " / zirzat / mango / ". Patrick had discovered a seed cluster in the middle of a piece of kiwi "kiwi / jambu / buah duku / strawberry / " and was voyaging farther and faster into its meaning-of-life with each new syllable "chiku / coconut / jeruks / banana / lychee." Jack threw a wad of bills onto the table and herded him out the door. "Aynd.....of caww-awwsse.....poy-nappuhhll."

> "Maybe it's Sun. Hee!"

At the foot of one of the stilts Saintjohn was waiting with the car doors already open, as if Jack and Patrick were Latin American dictators fleeing a coup or rock stars under flashbulb attack. Patrick resumed his Saintjohn-watch up front while Jack, having taken care of the business for which the day had been organized, opened a briefcase he'd asked Saintjohn to have ready for him after lunch. He remained in the Bentley and worked while Patrick watched Saintjohn tour the Jurong Bird Park and the Chinese and Japanese Gardens. Lulled by tales of the Cloud-Piercing Pagoda and the White Rainbow Bridge, Patrick dozed on the return to the Raffles where, in his guest suite on Jack's floor, he found his way for the rest of the day and night among several computers, an entertainment center in an atrium all its own, a room-service menu bound in an oil-on-silk painting of peacocks and dragons, and a beige silk suit in the closet for tomorrow.

> "Now that's dumb isn't it Blyster's the Wizard that's the whole point of this whole thing isn't it?"

He had not seen Leslie since they landed.

"Hey, rock n rollers!"

And now here they are.

"This is like the airplane!"

Patrick, up front, sparkling in his beige silk suit, focusing alternately on his custom-made Italian loafers and the visor of Saintjohn's cap. His cocoa silk shirt and wide flowered-silk tie, hand-painted in browns and tans and just a hint of lavender, turning him into a cross between a Mafia lieutenant and a kid being driven by his mother to his first date. A Mafia lieutenant being driven by his mother to his first date.

"We all match the interior of the car!"

Leslie, in the back with Jack, jittery in an off-white raw-silk suit with a very short skirt and a very long collarless jacket buttoned to her neck by small gold disks hidden behind a fold of fabric. Her hair gathered under an elaborately twisted matching turban. Fingers fiddling with her new coral-and-pearl necklace. Gold safety pin relegated to her camisole.

"All except Saintjohn."

Off to see.....well.....you know.

"Which wouldn't be the case if he had a brown suit.....or a black car........but then the rest of us wouldn't match anything at all, would we?"

No one seems especially interested in feeding Leslie lines right now. Holding the chain away from her neck with her thumbs, she uses her index fingers to swat and flick at a pearl and a coral bead, trying to get them to spin in opposite directions, as if the necklace were a miniature version of those colorful plastic sense-stimulators strung across Baby's crib.

"Well looks like I'm just gonna hafta do all the being color-aware for all ofWELL!" she blurts, lurching forward and startling Patrick into rampant unfocus. "You Sure Have Gotten Blasé In The Last Twenty-Four Hours, Haven't You, Mr. Trucock?"

Patrick shifts his weight and says "Wh-wh—M-Ms.—wh—" to the part of Saintjohn's cap where the visor starts widening out of the body.

"Might Stand You In Good Stead To Pay As Little Attention To The Man Behind The Curtain As You Can Get Away With, Son," Jack tells him, squeezing a wrist caught in mid-flail.

Leslie wriggles out of his grasp "Twenty-four hours ago" and stuffs his hand down between his legs. "you would've been hyperv— in addition to obsessing about your mother's cordial invitation to come right home or die of independence—you would've been hyperventilating M-Ms. Br-Brittain, we're at the airport we're back at the *airport* are we—" She is talking to her shoe in quite a respectable rendering of a Patrick voice. "are we going *home*? Wh-what's that is that h-helicopter waiting for *us*, M-Ms. Br-Brittain?" The car cruises through a security gate. "WHATDJYOU *DO* TO HIM?" she barks at Jack as she slams her hands onto Patrick's headrest, pulling herself over next to his ear. "This is like changing metro stops to you, isn't it, anymore? Outa the Bentley into the aircraft, Ho World-Class Industrial-Strength Hum!"

Jack puts his hand on Leslie's thigh. "I think you've made your "

She seizes his wrist "DON'T" and stuffs his hand down between his legs. "make yourself too at home, Patrick, the movie starts *and ends* in black n white. What goes on in the middle's only there to sell Coca-Cola and—" Patrick double-eye/one-cheek squints as he watches Saintjohn cut the motor then get out to "thank you— jujubees." open Leslie's door.

"My Lord, You Twiddle That Necklace Much More, Leslie, You're Going To Wear It Out," Jack says loudly enough for her to hear outside the car.

She rushes around to Jack's side, stooping to greet his tremendous stomach "Catch his bit about wearin out what ytwiddle, Patrick!" as Saintjohn helps him to his feet. "The man speaks from a number of nights' experience far too incalculable for at least *our* small brains to wrap themselves around."

Saintjohn closes Jack's door and opens Patrick's. The three passengers walk across the tarmac to a white helicopter with the navy-and-gold THE KOTE GROUP logo on both doors. Jack says something but the blades are whirring too loudly. Neither Leslie nor Patrick ask him to repeat. "Let him sit up with you," Leslie tells the pilot, a skinny aging Oriental man in navy trousers and a short-sleeved white silk shirt, as he helps her in. Patrick climbs in up front, looking as if he's either trying to camouflage his confusion with nonchalance or reacting to his nonchalance with confusion. Leslie slides over to make room for Jack. The pilot closes the door. Jack is still standing outside. Leslie looks at Jack. At Patrick. At the pilot. At Jack. The pilot gets in. He says "fasten your seatbelts" in a chimy Chinese accent that sounds like someone making fun of a chimy Chinese accent. Jack nods to Leslie. She shakes her head. Looks at the pilot. Looks at Jack. "Hey! Sports Fans! Wh " Hears the engine rev. Glances at the control panel. Back to Jack. Patrick is focusing, peering straight ahead, as if he's the one who's about to lift them off the ground. As if he's the chopper preparing itself for its job. The chopper vibrates. Wobbles. Lifts. Whirrs. Vibrates. Lifts and floats forward. Jack looks up and smiles broadly, waving with calm, wide, open-palmed arcs. A contented insurance-company-ad Gramps sending the grandchildren back home after a pleasant weekend visit with him, Gramma, the cats and his renewed confidence in the benefits of long-term-disability coverage. Leslie shrieks.

She twists in her seat to keep Grampa in sight as he miniaturizes below and behind her. She shrieks again, pressing her eyes shut, holding her fists in front of her chest, bouncing on the seat for as long as her breath will last.

"Mr. Kote," the pilot says, establishing the fact that her vocal ruby-slipper-heel-clicking was premature and did not make everything go away—or come back, "will meet you and Mr. Trucore at your destination." Patrick continues to fly the helicopter with his eyes.

Leaning forward, Leslie tries to speak softly and sweetly over the roar. "By destination I assume you mean where you're taking us—and it's Tru*cock*—now. Cause *everyone* will be meeting me at my *ultimate* destination, as I will be meeting everyone at theirs—we ain't gonna need a Jack Kote helicopter for that—unless of course the helicopter becomes the instrument of our arrival at that ultimate destination. Or they at theirs. If you get my drift. What is there about this particular helicopter that made Mr. Kote decide not to what-the-hell! just pile right on in with the rest of us?" She closes in on the pilot's ear and turns up the soft and sweet. "Not the driving. I'm sure. Mr. Kote surrounds himself with only the best people. Isn't that right, Patrick?"

"Mr. Kote," the pilot says, "will meet you and Mr. Trucore at your destination." The pilot's voice reminds Leslie of a black-and-white nineteen-forties film where, in a large livingroom with a piano, a built-in mirrored bar and little round pedestal-tables full of onyx knick-knacks and silver picture-frames, a tall thin blond elegant woman wearing satin man-cut pajamas and carrying a long cigarette-holder, and a tall thin dark elegant man wearing a smoking jacket and carrying a huge leather-bound volume are being served drinks by an obsequious Oriental servant whose English has been so heavily accented by the racist scriptwriters, and so unintelligibly fuzzied by the poor sound quality, as to be beyond caricature. "Thank you, Chan," the pajama-woman would say. "That will be all."

Leslie leans back into her seat and crosses her legs—the pajama-woman would do that too. "Hey Patrick! Where're we going?"

Sleeved in the virtual-reality membrane which fits on under his skin, Patrick's movements are mirroring the chopper's dips, floats and bucks.

"Hey Patrick! Where're we going?"

To Leslie and her tall thin elegant people back there, he looks like an old retired once-famous helicopter watching a helicopter match on TV, sticking with his prodigy helicopter jab for jab.

"Hey Patrick! Where're we going?"

The chopper and Patrick fly on over the water. They climb a bit then suddenly mount an aggressive campaign of dodges and fakes to outsmart the wind. On restricted leave from the movie set for this particular assignment, the pilot has left his drink tray on the mirrored bar and is tending to the technical aspects of the crossing, while Patrick's eyes and chin and shoulders continue burning forward into the sky to clear a path for the mission. "Hey Patrick! Where're we going?" Leslie looks down at some small islands. She tells herself she never thought he'd hear her to begin with. Tells herself it's not worth trying to bring him back from the aviational dead just to find out they're going someplace she doesn't want to go in the first place. That he doesn't know anyway. If *she* doesn't know then *he* certainly doesn't know. So what's she asking *him* for. And besides, we'll be there in the time it'd take him to reenter Earth's atmosphere and tell me. And besides, I don't wanna know any "T-to an i-island. Actually. Ms. Br-Brittain." way. Patrick continues to fly the helicopter with his eyes.

"Oh.....Oh..OK, Patrick.......Thanks, Patrick....Thanks........... That's..that's real good.......Patrick. Way to go. I've always said, haven't I, that being informed is to the Information Age what pickaxes were to the Stone Age. That knowledge is to the technological frontier what Colt fourty-fives were to the yknow—Mr. Kote doesn't have an heir to his empire—well, an heir he'd admit to anyway—well, he has a daughter but she's one othose you know how you either become exactly like your parents or exactly not, like if your mother's this clean-manioid and doesn't let you sit on the sofa or walk on the rug like she expects you to float like a Mary Poppins character in an antiseptic purgatory just between the two and then you grow up and either start every morning making sure the baseboards are dusted when you could be busy getting laid or at least eating a great *croissant chez* Georges or you spend your whole life fucking your literal and figurative ass off while boards throughout every house you ever live in fall away from their bases from the heaviness of their accumulated dust? Well that's what his daughter's like, all that money and she's off in some third-world country and I don't mean Paris-when-they-turn-the-water-off—which is two-and-a-halfth world—but some like South American I don't know where painting pictures of what's supposed to be flowers, in a goddamn hut—probably the only piece of real estate on Earth not owned by her father—not a baseboard in the fucking place—with this artist-derelict-dope-fiend lover who's twenty years younger than her who she picked up at some protest meeting in New York about letting the Haitian refu "

"Th-that's where M-Mr. T-Tai Yang B-Blyster lives. Lives. Actually. M-"

"In *Haiti*?........In New York. In South A "

"O-on the i-island. S-see d-down......over—well—there? There?"

"Yeah. So if Jack eats it steppin off a curb, she wouldn't walk into his office even with the express intention of running the company into the ground. In fact, I think the last time she was there she was like twelve years old and was so horrified that he had an ashtray on his desk that cost a thousand dollars—and this was thirty years ago—she left in disgust and had the chauffeur drive her home and never went to visit Daddy at work again. In fact, I think it's in his will she has nothing ever to do with the business. Except continue to hoard the checks it's allowed him to write her so when she abstract-paints herself to death in the probably not-too-distant future they'll come to this pitiful little hovel to pick at her remains like the scene in Zorba the Greek and discover four thousand times their national budget under the mattress didn't we just go past the island?.....DIDN'T, SHE ASKED THE EVER-RESPONSIVE CREW, WE JUST GO PAST THE ISLAND?"

"We await permission to land."

"Thank you, Chan," Leslie tells the pilot, in an upper-New York/lower-New England clip. "That will be all. So you see, Patrick, if you play your cards right, well I mean what with Jack giving you first crack at all this privileged intelligence and all that, well I mean even before his long-time pals like.....like well for instance me for instance, well who knows what he may be grooming you for, Patrick. Yknow? I mean.....yknow? Just remember, Patrick, through whose good offices you were introduced to Mr. Kote in the first place I have two questions are we landing and did you know Jack wasn't coming with us?"

Patrick turns around to Leslie but catches himself mid-way, as if he's forgotten it was really something else he'd wanted to do. His face looks like those children's books whose pages are divided in half so that, by flipping the eyes/nose pages and the mouth/chin pages independently of each other you can come up with combinations that range from interesting through funny to bizarre. Although tired from focusing the aircraft, crew and passengers all the way across the Straits of Singapore, Patrick's current eyes page comes from the face of a calm, confident man, in control of himself and of his environment and ready to help others take control of theirs. It is sitting uneasily above a mouth page modeled after a frightened little boy.

"And I hope the answer to at least the first one," Leslie continues, smiling and waving hello to the back of Patrick's head, "is no, don't worry, we're just losing fuel while our buddy here checks his map to see which island is the right one because while he was engaged back there in breakneck, mind-whipping repartee, he obviously made a wrong swoop since what we have down there at this given point is a bunch of blades of grass with water around it and unless our host is a slug—which he very well may be and most probably is but that's not the point of this particular discussion—he'd have a hard time, especially given his reputed financial state and appreciation for fine things, feeling comfortable about calling that home. Or even office."

As the chopper hovers over the middle of the small island, the pilot squawks numbers into his headset. Patrick is focusing on Saintjohn even though he's looking at Chan.

"Well, that explains it all, doesn't it now? Thanks. That actually answers *both* questions at once and precludes my having to even bother my pretty little head reasking either one. Anyway, we're obviously landing. Cause the ground is getting bigger. So you're already off the hook for that one. Unless of course we're hovering and the ground is coming up to meet us, at which point I'd have a whole *new* set of questions. So you better hope that isn't the ooh! look down there! wh—does theee uhhhh ground look like it's opening up to you or did I change depths too quickly yesterday in the bathtub?"

In the absence of the visor on Saintjohn's cap, Patrick focuses on the year numerals on Chan's wristwatch. His breathing shifts between settled and agitated, depending on which face page is prominent when which exhale is produced. He seems to be laboring at not

"interacting with me in any way, Patrick! I know you know what's going on! I know Jack *BRIEF*ed you," Leslie says in a deep, serious, Jack-In-The-Boardroom voice, stiffening her neck and narrowing her eyes. "Let me have your attention, son! I have to *BRIEF* you—I've got to *BRIEIEIEIEFFFF* you. About our *MMMISSSSSSIONNN*. I have to *br* Jack has this genetically transmitted need to *brieieff* people. Been in the family for generations. Makes em feel like they have a big dick. Even the women. I wouldn't be surprised if his daughter—much to her personal shame and despite all her efforts to overcome the impulse—wanders entranced around the sub-equatorial jungle *brieieff*ing the biota about the pictures she's gonna be painting of them—which in her case wouldn't be a bad idea since then when the final product emerges with its little pigment-pimples all over it there'd be some prexisting record of what she was aiming aFrchri Look At That Will You The Fucking Thing's Opening Up!—OK! OK! You know what we're gonna do, Patrick? This is what we're gonna do. We're gonna do the following thing: Ignore It. We're ignoring it. That's what we're—we're kicking into our Scarlett O'Hara mode right now except Scarl put it off till tomorrow we're never gonna deal with it ever for the rest of our Lives Ygot That PATRICK?"

Patrick does what he thinks is throw his chin in the direction of the pilot but what is more like the head-jerk maneuver the guy at the bar in Westerns used to employ to get the rot-gut down past his tongue and into his rotted gut as quickly and efficiently as possible.

"Because I already *know* that Mr. Kote will meet me and Mr.

Trucock at ourWHAT THE FUCK *IS* THAT BLACK HOLE DOWN THERE IS THAT SOMETHING WE'RE SUPPOSED TO BE *LANDING* IN?    CHCHCHCHCHAAAAAAAAAAAAA AAAAAAAAAAAAAAAAAAAAAAAAAAAAAAAAAAAAAAAAAAAAA AAAAAAAAAAAAAAAAAAAAAAAAAAAAAAAAAAAAAAAAAAAAA AAAAAAAAAAAAAAAAAAAAAAAAAAAAAAAAAAAAAAAAAAAA AAAAAAAAAAAAAAAAAAAAAAAAAAAAAAAAAAAAAAAAAAAAA AAAAAAAAAAAAAAAAAAAAAAAAAAAAAAAAAAAAAAAAAAAAA AAAAAAAAAAAAAAAAAAAAAAAAAAAAAAAAAAAAAAAAAAAAA AAAAAAAAAAAAAAAANNNNNNNNNNNNNNN!"

The pilot doesn't respond.

"Patrick frchrissake do you know what's g—What's This Guy's Name?"

Patrick's mouth page and eyes page are flipping furiously through every persona in the book.

The helicopter descends.

Hovers.

The patch of ground slides wider away.

The chopper drops through.

The patch slides back in place and becomes part of the grass again.

Leslie and Patrick have been swallowed up by an island off the coast of Singapore.

# XVII

# THE $EVEN DEADLY GOLDFISH

Its blades seeming silent in the absence of the wind, its navigation lights illuminating what looks like infinite empty space all around, the helicopter flutters slowly down a long dark shaft. Patrick half-twists in his seat again toward Leslie then they both turn to the pilot, more out of reflex than expectation of running commentary about the landmarks along the way.

"Damn!" Leslie says with the exasperation of someone who just broke a nail or ran a stocking.

Focusing past her, out the back window, Patrick marks the descent with quick little dips of his forehead, as if counting off the layers of invisibility through which they are falling, making sure they're all there, that no one's made off with one in the night.

"Well *this* sure changes everything, doesn't it!"

With the points of his eyes he slices off a fragment of black air and asks Leslie if she minds if he asks her what the matter is. The helicopter slows even further.

"Nnoww we have to start allll over again, don't we!........If I'd'a known this my whole approach woulda been different!" Back and forth across the seat Leslie scurries like a laboratory rat, looking down into the dark through one window, up into the dark through the other, up into the space being blended by the blades, down into the space still tranquil. "My whole perception of the experience!"

The chopper hovers.

"Yknow I know the way it works don't think I don't know the way it works! First they start switching metaphors on you. All innocent-like. Next thing you know they're sittin up there in your head on little fake-leather swivel-chairs workin your brain like a switchboard.....Ordering out for pizza.....Crumbling up scrap paper and missing the basket.....Putting little post-its on the back o your eyes with instructions for the night shift don't think I don't know how it works, Patrick."

The pilot spits a string of syllables into his headset. Patrick repeats, "M-Ms. Brittain, dyou m—i-is ev—dyou m—well—all.....right. Is ev-everything allright. Allright. M-Ms. B "

"Of Course I Mind Frchrissakes Patrick And Of Course Everything's Not All Right They Sw" Leslie grabs Patrick's headrest and yanks herself to the edge of her seat. She takes a long, dramatic deep breath to calm herself, which has the effect of making her look like she's taking a long, dramatic deep breath to calm herself, rather than of actually calming her. Squeezing into the headrest from both ends as with an accordion, she stretches her voice into a slow soprano singsong "They switched metaphors on us, Patrick. You know a switched metaphor when you see one, don't you?" then sits back and continues her flail-punctuated screed. "We had it all cast! All timed! No one even noticed I'd written Toto totally outa the script! Or if they did, they knew enough not tsay anything! We all knew who the Wizard was—well, we had it narrowed down, we knew we were about to find out, which is the whole point isn't it? Which Is The Whole Point."

"Ms. Br-Brittain, dyou m—we're—well..... "

"WHAT!"

"Here. We're.....h-here. Here. Actually." The pilot takes his headset off "L-landed. Ms. Br-Brittain." and opens his door.

"WAIT!" Leslie barks as she sees Patrick reach to open his. "We're in no hurry are we? I'm in no hurry, Patrick. Are you in any special hurry? You have an appointment or something? I mean, other than The Appointment Which Ate Reality As We Know It. Which is still gonna be there whether we open our own door now or wait for the White Rabbit to open it for us once he" She twists around and looks out. "gets finished letting the Black Queen know her next shipment of heads has arrived." Lit by only a razor-beam light from the back of the chopper, the pilot is standing still, speaking into a radio. "It's part of his job. So we might as well be good enough to let him do it. *His* job is to ensure that we experience a meaningful drop down the Rabbit Hole. And to open our door for us once we get there. *Our* job is not to interfere with his considerable responsibilities." Patrick is focusing to the northeast of the pilot's ear as if reading words in a cartoon bubble above his head.

Plopping "I don't think" suddenly onto her back, Leslie looks up through a window. "the Queen paid her electric bill last month, whatdyou think Patrick? I think she was busy doing other things with her money. Like receiving rare works of sacred stolen art, that's what *I* th—and trafficking in kidnapped administrative interns, that's what *I* think I think that's what this whole delay is all about, him being out there on the phone and all, I think he's crackin a deal with the power company to turn the lights back on just this once, being as we're on this...." She sits up and glances in all directions before mouthing "MISSION".

"M-maybe—well—he's—m-maybe he's t—Imean...t-talking to....Mr. K-Kote. Kote," Patrick says, obviously reaching for reassurance and stability by introducing a name from their pre-Rabbit Hole days.

Leslie announces over a loud-speaker in the back of her throat "Looking Glass Regulations Prohibit Descent From The Hallucinogen Until All Lights Have Been You-Should-(Not)-Excuse-The-Expression Turrrnnned Onnn By Our Hookah-Smoking Power-Company Decision-Makers. I think just to be on the safe side, Patrick, we should start choosing our bunks and decide who gets first dibs on the bathroom in the morning. I'll tayyyyyyyke....." As if surveying a vast campground, she scans the inside of the helicopter, looking beyond its dimensions, finally pointing to the pilot's seat. ".....THAT ONE! You think they deliver pizza to this neighborhood?" Her fingertips poke into the cushion.

"M-maybe he's t-Maybe he's...he's...t-talking t "

"You mean the Mr. Kote who will meet Mr. Trucock and me at our " Leslie's door opens. She steps out. " destination?" she says into the pilot's skeletal face, eliciting no reaction except a hand dutifully offered for leverage, which elicits no reaction except "Thank you, Chan. That will be all."

Waiting for Patrick to wait for his door to be opened, Leslie smoothes her suit and adjusts her turban. When Patrick emerges into the narrow triangle of dimmed landing-light beams, she turns to tell the pilot not to be late for his teapar..........."Wherethef...Hey! ......HEY!" She "Patrick." walks "Now" completely "cuhmmawawnnn," around "how" the "can" helicopter, "that...." bumping into "PAATRRIICKCK!" at the spot where the White Rabbit had the Queen on walkie-talkie.

"Ohhh-oh-oh Kayyy-yy-yy, Paa-trickck!" she warbles, her fists on her hips, her eyes straining to determine whether the space they're in is the size of a two-car garage or a shopping mall. "Whadjyuh do with h "

"M-Ms. Brittain, dyou m—well—wh-where—Imean—wh-where did the.....p-pilot g-go? M-Ms. "

"Ms. Buhhhrrrittaiainnnn wherrre didddd the piiilottt gohhh, Paatrickck?" On her knees now in the near-total darkness, sounding like a slow-speed recording of Sherlock Holmes at full interrogative storm, Leslie is tentatively patting the cold floor with her right hand while covering it in wide sweeping arcs with her left. "If I knew that, Patrick, I'd be a much more enlightened woman than I already Did Anyone Think To Look In The Chopper? Go See If He's In The Chopper!"

By the time Patrick bolts over and trots back, Leslie's crawled further out, just to the limit of the light beams, practicing the combined skills of looking for a contact lens and transplanting begonias to the bed in front of the house. "N-no. Actually. M-Ms. Br "

"Good!" She stands.

He stoops.

"GOOD!.....Frchrissake whatryuh doing down there?"

"G-good!...Imean—I w-wanted—well.....t-to—well—s-see...w-what are.....wh-what y "

Leslie reaches down and pulls Patrick up by the shoulder. "A trap Rabbit Hole. Service entrance. But we've just decided the best thing that's happened to us all day is this joker's finally wised up and decided to leave us alone." She takes a tentative step away from the helicopter. "We do much better on our own." Patrick follows. "Don't we, Patrick?" She steps again, placing her off-white silk heel lightly on the floor then rolling the rest of her foot down from that point, as if fingerprinting her shoe. Patrick stands still, looks back at the air layers northwest of the chopper, "Don't we? Patrick?" catches up.

"Yeah."

The process begins with the other shoe: heel, "The way I figure it, as long as we watch where we're going here," incrementally followed by instep, "which is no different from the way a person should move through life in general, right?," then "we'll be just fiiieeeOHHHH-HHH MYY YY-YYYYGOHHHH-HHHHD" toe. As if electric-shocked, Leslie springs back to where she started.

"H-h-how did y—M-Ms. Br-Brittain—h-how-h "

"Idon'tknowitjust........did it by itself." They hook onto each other's glance and hang there, Leslie crawling deep into the familiar safe-haven of Patrick's face, Patrick trying to focus on Leslie's newfound magical powers by inching along her optic nerve.

"N-no, y—Imean—Ms. Br-Brittain—dyou m—y—I th-think *y-you* did it. Actually," he says to one of the ganglia along the way. "G-go a—go a—go.....t-take a-another st "

"Shit, Patrick!" Leslie waves and shakes her hands up around her ears like a little girl who just saw a spider. She steps again "ahhhhhhhahhhshittPaaatrrRICKCK!" and again leaps instantly backward to the begonia bed from where she came. "Oh-oh Go-ohd Pah-ah-tri-ick, I'm not sure how satisfied I am with this arrangement. I think we shoulda followed our instincts in Paris when they told us it was totally up to us whether we came or not—or we could look through their numerous full-color brochures and feel free to chose a whole other entirely different vacation spot—I think we should not have let ourselves be seduced by the superficial attractions of saving my life. We shoulda just gone to Atlantic City instead, Patrick, and called it a summer."

"C-come b—M-Ms. Brittain come—d—qu-quick Ms. Br-Brittain c-come b—d-do it.....a-again. Again!" Patrick is excited to the point of jubilance, focusing on whatever piece of blackness meets his eyes in their wide, vaulted flight around the hangar, not even thinking to ask Leslie if she minds.

"Why don't *you* try it?" she whines.

"It was—Imean, Ms. Br-Brittain—well....*y-your*......n-name. Actually. M "

"Well then maybe *your* name'll come up what's th dif—OK OK........" She fires a mischievous smile. Lured back into the schoolyard. Doing what it takes. Taking the dare. At the boundary line where it all kicked in before, she raises her right leg, looks at Patrick, dangles her foot a couple inches out in front. "Yready?"

"G-GO!"

"TAAAHH-DAA-AAHH!!" Leslie trumpets into the black space, and as her foot touches the floor hundreds of yellow seedlights awaken along both sides of a pathway leading to a massive golden door about a city block ahead. In the middle of the midnight-blue-lacquered concrete walkway, between the parallel light-lines which seem to narrow and flow into the apex of an optical illusive triangle further on, written in what looks like paint made of electrified gold, are the words

### "Hello, Ms. Leslie Brittain. And welcome."

"There," she says quietly, as if having just put a baby down to sleep. "You happy?" Keeping her left leg behind the magic zone, she raises and poses her right shoe again, raises and poses several times, making the message and the seedlights alternately disappear and glow with the power of her pressure. "Well That Does It!" she declares, slapping her palm against the side of her thigh. "Numm-ber Three!"

Patrick, of course, is in his element. Flat on his stomach before the left-hand row, he is taking the first light head-on, meeting it at eye level like an enlightened kindergarten teacher stooping at the desks of her charges in an act of great non-threatening communicative equality.

"Hansel and Fucking Gretel. I *hate* Aitch n Gee! Always have! Fingernails against my literary blackboard! If any story was out havin a cup ocoffee when they were handing out class, it's Aitch n Gee! Have *you* ever seen a well drawn witch in Hansel and Gretel? They're always juusst a little bit off, just a little bit too ugly. Or too cute. Well, nice try, but we ain't buyin! Patrick Get Up Here Frchrissakes! We'll stick with Alice, thank you, and hope the Wizard makes a miraculous comeback but I'm sorry—and don't go startin any yellow-brick-road shit these are *crumbs*!" To emphasize her point in her conversation with the walkway, Leslie jabs her index finger into the air above what would be it's bloated belly if it had one. "PA-TRICK!"

Patrick hasn't budged, except to seep further and further into his seedlight's core. As Leslie walks slowly along the sparkling path toward the golden door, the magic message moves before her, remaining always just in front of her toes. At her fourth footstep it changes to

### "Continue, Ms. Leslie Brittain. You are doing fine."

and then suddenly to

### "Hello, Mr. Patrick Trucore. And welcome. We are glad you have decided to join Ms. Leslie Brittain."

Leslie whips around just as Patrick sets his other foot into the enchanted forest. "Th-they g-got my......name...wr-wrong. Actually. M-Ms. Brittain."

"You got a bigger message than me!"

They are both frozen in place, concentrating so intensely on keeping their feet fixed that they wind up moving them. When they set out again both messages precede their steps, first Leslie's, then Patrick's farther up. Not flicking off then reappearing right ahead, but flowing along the lacquered concrete as on a conveyor belt, to the rhythm of Leslie and Patrick, slowing when they slow, stopping when they stop, picking up the pace at their cue.

"You got three sentences!"

"Th-they g-got m "

"I only got two!"

"Ms-Ms. Br-Brittain they g-g "

"Is that cause you—whatdjyou give Jack Kote yesterday in exchange for a bigger message than mine, Patrick, huh?" Leslie stops. Patrick stops. They're about half-way there.

"They gL-LOOK! MS. BRITTAIN!"

**"Why stop now, Ms. Leslie Brittain and Mr. Patrick Trucore? You have already journeyed so far to reach the beginning of your journey."**

"No they didn't. Patrick. It's Patrick. Isn't it? Look. Looks enough like Patrick to me, Patrick. Eh? See—pee-ay-tee-ar—unless of course you've decided in the past several seconds to finally dispense with formalities and call yourself Pat. In which case I'd agree, they "

"Dyou m........do you kn-know wh-what—Imean—they-they—well—mean? Mean?"

"Oh it's just some Oriental bullshit it's an Oriental thing they're always talking about *journeys* and beginnings of *journeys* and first steps of *journeys* and ends of *journeys* and life is a *journey* everything's a *journey* to them. These are little sayings invented three thousand years ago just in time to be printed on posters and t-shirts in the nineteen-sixties."

### "How nice of you to have come, Ms. Leslie Brittain and Mr. Patrick Trucore. Please enter."

Focusing on the new message, at the threshold of the golden door, Patrick looks like he's about to dive into the center of one of the **os**—probably that of his wrongly spelled last name, although the one in **come** keeps vieing for his attention. "Is it....r-real? Imean........r-g-r-g-gold? Gold?"

"I don't know." Leslie goes to feel it. "If it isn't ysure could've fooled mOhMyGod!" The door begins to split, its heavy halves opening slowly away from the end of the walkway into a vast white hall. She snaps her arm back down to her side, raises her eyes to what are now the outermost edges of the moving panels, the parts which were touching each other when the door was closed. Hopping on for the ride, the receptors in her head register ("Ohhh myyy Goddd") at first only a flash of brilliant empty air. Then progressively capture the creation of the hall as if, like a conductor from a podium, the door itself is giving the time - space - sensory commands to the room. As if through its act of opening, the door is producing the depth and width and whiteness of an expanse which would otherwise be ever a darkened sliver. She does not hear Patrick calling her name or feel him tapping on her elbow. It is only when she turns to tell him to come stand beside her, to watch transparent infinity being rolled out in front of them, that she sees he wants her for something.

"What? You gotta see this Patrick come here. Wha..........Oh." Leslie sounds stunned, her voice is dulled. Patrick is pointing to the path just behind his heels.

### "You are invited no longer to face in this direction, Ms. Leslie Brittain and Mr. Patrick Trucore. Your reality is in front of you now."

"..........You gotta see this." Patrick has grown comfortable on the walkway. He seems to see no reason to go any further, to move to a new neighborhood and leave his seedlight friends and their message club behind and have to get used to a whole new standard of socially acceptable behavior. He is holding onto the clothesline pole in the yard while the moving truck heads out and his mother tries to drag him off into the car. Leslie has turned her vital attention away from the unwrapping of the room. The infinity is evolving from a vision to a feeling. To a nourishment. She has to get back to give it her bloodstream. But she has to take Patrick with her.

"L-look. M-Ms. Brittain."

"No, *you* look." She lifts Patrick's chin toward the helicopter.

"Yeah."

All its lights are now out and it is in fact invisible. Or not there at all, for all Leslie and Patrick know. They don't know. Maybe it's lifted off, emitting sounds unseizable by their ears. Maybe it's disintegrated or turned into something else. Or into nothing. Maybe it was never there to begin with. There is no longer light or life at the spot where they remember its having landed, from which they walked along the midnight-blue-lacquered concrete to the golden door. The seedlights are dead. The darkness in that direction is so dense that it looks like a solid block of once-liquid black, poured in to fit the space and then hardened. The void is so oppressive that it drains all energy reserves and Leslie and even Patrick feel compelled to turn toward the life-lit whiteness of the hall to replenish theirs. It's all in front of them now. Just like the message says.

"Just like the message says, Patrick."

"M-M-Ms. B....." Patrick is standing as Leslie stood when she first saw the hall. Looking up into it and out into it. Trying to define its dimensions. Trying to make his eyes catch up with the uncontainable space, to follow it as it endlessly expands. He is not actually focusing in the Patrick sense of the word. If anything, the room is focusing on him. And on Leslie. For the room is at first perceivable only as a whole. As a boundless bleached openness to which one's attention must pay respect before being permitted to stop and rest upon a detail. As a containment for itself, rather than for any fixtures or objects or architectural particularities—or people—which may be singled out as distinct entities within it.

Even though they are in there—all of them—the fixtures and the objects, the architectural particularities. The people. But they seem to appear one by one. Abruptly. Like. In. A. Film. Of. Overlaid. Frames. Made. By. Salvidor. Dali. Or. Andy. Warhol. Squinting. Into.

A. Stationary. Camera. At. The. Entrance. To. The. Hall. One by one once Leslie's and Patrick's awareness has adjusted to the stunning assault of the foundation frame, to the presence of the vast white square perpetually flooding with more light and more air.

Then comes the barely seen twitch in the picture.

And suddenly an alcove is in the room.

For a while they watch a room with an alcove in it.

The image jerks again.

A second alcove. Like someone had been filming, turned off the camera, brought in the architects and the contractor and the construction crew, built the second alcove, cleaned up, then started the camera rolling once more.

Another twitch.

Something straight ahead. Far ahead. A shrine. A kind of shrine. A vase in front of it. Several. Vases. Which pop. Into. A. Row. One after the other at the very far end of the space. Flowers. Back at the beginning of the row. Slowly waving crests of flowers. Click. Onto. The. Vases. In the same spasmodic cadence and order.

It is in this way that the hall begins to take shape for Leslie and Patrick. Frame by frame. Detail by detail. As if the images of its contents, standing in line at a door in their brains, are being granted admission one at a time to their optic nerves by a guard who gives each image a moment to walk around in there, to find its place and settle, before letting the next one enter. The longer and more intensely Leslie and Patrick peer into it from its white-marble threshold, the quicker and more completely the vacuous space turns into movement texture topography tone.

Now they need no electric-paint message to tell them which way to walk and not to walk. And there is none. And now no message could keep them out. They step into the hall, become part of its contents-images, and suddenly see the logic to the whiteness.

"If you've been to one Hilton you've been to them all," Leslie says out of the corner of her mouth as they cautiously advance, so close to each other's body that their hips collide. "Wait." She holds Patrick back by his arm, whispering as a tourist in a temple with a service going on, then slows to a stop "Just wait, will yuhOK?" and looks up. "I want this to be one of the scenes I image on when Sigmund and I are in the dentist chair trying not to have pain and pleasure at the same time."

Patrick tries to start walking again. Leslie squeezes his elbow. "Will you—will you focus on something frchrissake don't you have any idea what you're lookin at here do you—do you realize how many times you'll never see anything like this again—even if they *do* let us live—you look like you're heading for the cereal aisle with a shopping list from your mother LookAtThatFrchri—ohh!" She slaps her fingers onto her mouth as her raised voice rebounds throughout the whiteness.

"Is—dyou m—Imean—does—did—is......M-Mr. K-Kote here....y-yet? Yet?"

The room is in fact not square at all. It is a stratospherically ceilinged oblong whose far end looks like it's half a mile away. Something you'd have to give directions to by talking about traffic lights and maybe a gas station or two. Once you hit the convenience store you know you've—though you might go right past it if the light's not on. Anyway don't worry if the street sign's down—the kids did that a couple weeks ago—just keep countin blocks and you'll be fine.

Its width is about half that. Significant but still believable as interior space. As opposed to being the other end of the neighborhood. Like its length. Its length is basically out of town.

Underfoot, an enormous mosaic fiery sun is beheld as a mosaic and not as a floor—a mosaic that was put where your shoes happen to be and that you wind up having to walk across if you want to get anywhere in the room. In sharp tightly aligned spikes its flames sear out from its center to the seams of the white marble walls, each spike itself a unique, unduplicatable composition of tens of thousands of bits of everything that is rare and white—chips of ivory, fragments of pearl, flecks of alabaster, specks of opal, particles of albino lead, granules of marble, none of which were visible from outside the door, all of which receive and contain and emit the tens of thousands of shades of white that endow the room.

Your eye takes a flame-spike. You travel with it. Shoot out on its speed. Don't get off until you've ridden its precious pavement to its point. Reel your eye back to the source. Jump to the next. See how far you can stay aboard as it burns itself up to a sliver. You hypnotize yourself. Like watching a strobe-light. Forever. Or you do it in reverse and come crashing into the center on the sweep of a spike as it spreads and offers its rich bits up to the sun's face.

The sun's face is inset entirely with mother-of-pearl half-moons. The size of grapefruit sections. The second atop the midpoint of the first. The third atop the midpoint of the second. A taut sculpted skin of scallop-shaped scales. The fourth atop the midpoint of the third. Meticulously, laboriously, densely laid rows from forehead down to chin up to forehead down to chin, the nuanced reflections in the mother-of-pearl working to forge the features of the face. The face. A visage. With cheekbones and lips and eloquent eyes that you see—think you see—that you see move with the utterings of the light.

A Man In The Moon in the sun.

Fresh through a dome of textured-glass sky, a white electric sheet lights the hall. Electricity that seems attached to nothing, electricity that seems to hang from nowhere, to claim no relation to the principles of science. Self-generated, self-nourishing power, present beyond the glass. Like a blazing cloud. Functioning at two different speeds, in two different cultures, a perfectly balanced product of its own effort: Igniting in the fathomless sphere above the dome, where it rages in perpetual spontaneous combustion; then filtering down into the hall through the uncountable prism-panes seamed to each other by kilometers of fine gold wire, where it granulates, and sheathes each atom of oxygen individually.
You don't realize you're looking at trillions of particles of gilded air in the same way you don't realize your cells are regenerating or the aircraft is moving or the picture on the television screen is a cluster of minuscule dots. Even as the gilded air is everywhere. Except at the floor. Where you don't realize you're looking at air pinkened by the mother-of-pearl sun.
"Come on, sports fans." Leslie flicks Patrick on the arm with the back of her hand "Let's do it." and nods toward the far end of the hall.
"Wh-what are you—dyou m—wh-what are we—Imean.....wh-where"
"The cereal aisle." She starts slowly walking, looking up "I know it's here somewhere." and all around.
"M-Ms. Brittain a-are you—well...dyou m—c-can I.....Imean ........sure? Actually."
"Frankly? No. I've never been in this particular supermarket before. Although I gotta say they're all basically laid out the same I mean it's kinda like the perfume's always right there when you walk into a department store, right?, well, basically, if you follow the same logic, you're not gonna wander too far off the mark I mean if you want M & Ms" As they walk upon the mosaic sun, Patrick packs all his effort into trying to step only on the chunks of ivory—and only on

the medium-sized ones at that. "you can be pretty sure you're not gonna have to go on a search-n-destroy mission to unearth them they're gonna be comin out to the parking lot to help you outa your car—little M & M-beings with huge thick fake-tortoise-shell glasses, marching toward you in militaristically perfect ranks," They are moving at a slow, syncopated pace. "reducing for you—and, of course, the whole point of this exercise, for your hysterically screaming progeny mutilating each other in the back seat—to as great an extent possible, the turn-around time between getting up that morning and purchasing impulsively." As if in a museum. Or a graduation ceremony. Or a commercial about two people having a serious discussion about their stockbrokers. "It's a tribal thing, you know?"

They haven't even covered the first half-block of the room.

"Dyou m—th-that's not—M-Ms. Brittain.......I m-meant are y—sh-should we—Imean—w-w—j—" Patrick stops walking and puts his hand almost on Leslie's shoulder, to stop her as well. "just w-wait? H-here?......U-until s-someone—well....c-comes f-for us? Actually."

Leslie nods. "Maybe we should." And starts walking again. "Meanwhile, while we're waiting for someone to come for us, why don't we just walk awhile, OK?" Pointing just up ahead to the left side of the room, she whispers "Maybe take a peek around that wall over there and see what they're selling." as if trying to keep their big plans to themselves. "It'll................Ohhhh.............Myyyy........................ Gohhhhd Patrick..........Willll......Youu...........Lookk.........Att......... .....Thiss!"

Starting at about a block from the door, eight five-foot-thick white marble partitions, four on each side wall, protrude like matching crooked teeth, or cogs, a hundred feet diagonally toward the far end of the space. They stand six and a half feet tall—just high enough to hide whatever is behind them, just low enough to make you think you can find out what that might be. Placed twenty-five yards from each other, the slanted slabs of marble create three three-sided rooms anchored by the right of the gaping hall and three anchored by the left, each visible and accessible, if you are walking in the direction in which Leslie and Patrick are walking, only by going slightly past the first partition of the enclosure and then making a sharp turn back into it. In perspective with the hall, the areas have the feel of special-exhibit galleries that can be wandered into off a main art-museum floor.

These are the alcoves which, from the threshold, Leslie and Patrick thought they saw materialize as the warm white fluid light bent around and ricocheted off the cold white solid marble, creating pouches of measurable space in the immeasurable space.

"*Look* at him Patrick is he the most incredible thing you ever saw on the planet?" Now, in the absolute mathematical middle of the first alcove on the left,

"Is h-is he……..r-real? Real?"

near the narrowing tip of a mosaic sun-spear, what they know they are seeing is a two-foot square, five-foot high white marble monolith wearing a giant bulbous glass fishbowl like a hat. "Is he *armed* is what we should be wondering! He's huge! He's too huge to be real. He *has* to be real. Maybe he's battery-powered. You think he's real?"

"I-I don't…..wh-what dyou th-th "

A single fish, the color of a goldfish, the size of a flounder, is swimming serenely in water so brilliantly clear it looks like liquid diamonds. There is nothing else in the alcove. "Let's ask him!" Leslie approaches the monolith.

"Hi, sweetie!" she coos in a combination of Tweetie Bird and Mae West, "How's the wife n kinds? Gettin any lately?" nuzzling up to the part of the bowl where the fish's eyes and mouth seem hot to chat. "Hey are you reaooh! hey Patrick look at this! hey! come here what's this?" She turns to the alcove entrance, from which Patrick has not budged.

"Do you know what—wait!" Leslie rubs her finger on the side of the fishbowl. Takes a step around. Stops. Rubs her finger on the side. Takes another step around. Stops. Rubs. Steps. Stops. Rubs. "do you know what...." Steps. Stops. Is almost back to where she started, rubs. "what……....geran means?" Patrick joins her.

Engraved deep into the bulging midsection of the otherwise smooth, transparent bowl, at perfectly spaced intervals, are the letters **G** "Look!" She traces the shape. **E** "Come here look gimme your finger!" The glass where the letters are cut out has been left rough, a bit whitened, **R** like the curlicues etched into some Belle Epoque restaurant windows, **A** or like the glass equivalent of Florentine gold. **N** Leslie circles the bowl again, this time more frenetically, Patrick by her side, her index finger crooked around his, feeling the letters with him like a first-grade teacher trying to turn the alphabet into an exciting proposition.

"You think it's his name?" she asks.

"Anger."

"I bet it's Chinese."

"Anger."

"Sure doesn sound Chinese to me. Sounds German. Doesnit sound German to you? Or Norse or something. Sounds—you know what? Like a character from a Wagnerian opera—Ge-ran.....wasn't Geran someone's nephew or something on Valhalla?" She looks up at the seams where the partition tops meet the wall, hoping to make eye contact with the hidden cameras she knows must be there. "The architecture's super. Really big-league," she says with sincerity to the camera staff. "But why spoil the effect by giving a German name to a Chinese fish frchrissake?"
Patrick gently takes her arm and walks her several steps around the bowl, squaring her shoulders in front of the **A**.

"What?" she asks, following the letter with her finger. "What?"

"Anger. That's wh-what it.....s-says. Actually. M-Ms. Brittain."

Leslie stares at the bowl for a some seconds "Nohhh! Waitt!" then stalks the circumference again, pointing to each letter, mouthing its name "A.....N.....G.....E how did you know that? WELL? How Did You *Know* That Frchrissakes Patrick?" Patrick is focusing on a sliver of albino lead near Leslie's left heel.

"Wotan," he says without lifting his head.

"WHATT?"

"Is wh-who y-you're—well—th-thinking of"

Seizing his lapel, "Come on this is ridiculous! We have people waiting for us! Bye, fish!" she yanks him out of the alcove,

" i-in the opera. Opera. Actually."

the far end of the hall once again in her sights. "Curiouser and curiouser frchrissake!" she growls. Her pace quickens. Determined to give neither Patrick, the hidden cameras nor especially the fish the satisfaction of any interest in the contents of the other alcoves, "Alice was home *asleep* compared to *this* shit!" she locks her head onto the room's axis and kicks into a march, "Havin a black n white dream about goin t*church* compared t*this* shit!" then a trot, "Mutant attack-goldfish frchrissakes and they think their little psychodelium is gonna break us but what they *don't* know what they *don't* know, Patrick, is it takes more than a fat fish with" and finally a full run, "a Norwegian name to break Leslie Marsha Brittain and Patrick Ryan Trucock!" breathing her impatience out through her nostrils while Patrick gasps to keep up. "RIGHT, PATRICK?"

And then she comes to a full stop.

And then she turns around.

"M-Ms. Br "

"BACK!" Her voice shoots up to the gold-seamed glass panes, bounces around the hall like a stray bullet. Across the sun she troops toward the alcoves on the other wall, covering large patches of mental and physical ground between crisp sentences spit through tightened lips. "Back!........" Shoulders punching forward in cadence with opposite feet, forearms pumping up and down. "That's where we're going!........Back!........" Huffing and hrumphing like the Our Gang schoolmarm on her way to the boys' room to catch a couple of kids lighting up. "I'm in no hurry!........You in any hurry?........We're in no hurry!"
Out without his backpack for the first time in years, Patrick is hobbling as if it's still on his shoulders. Full of rocks.
"A little field trip!......We cut our nature study a little too short back there!......" Leslie progressively slows to her stockbroker-discussion saunter. "That wasn't decoration back there that wasn't cause the Wizard ran outa velvet paintings of Elvis so he stuck a fishbowl in there so it shouldn't look empty if you stop by for a drink Jack Kote doesn't work that way and if *he* doesn't you can be damn sure the Wizard doesn't everything has to have a meaning with Jack ehhhhhhverything has to have a goddamn hidden meaning knowledge is power, Patrick, and we're about to get real powerful here real fast.

Here! *Voilà!* Here! I *knew* it! Whaddoes *this* one say? Wait! Lemme guess!"

This alcove is identical to the one on the opposite side of the hall. Leslie circles the bowl as Patrick, hanging out by the **N E S**, watches her lips move and her head tick off its findings with sharp abbreviated nods. "Wait! Don't tell me!" She starts around again, tracing each letter with her finger...........**"V E T O!**" she announces triumphantly to Patrick, who has moved over to the **C O** in anticipation of "There's **V E T O** in it! Wait!" baby's first word.

Apparently enjoying this game, she traces the next letter and says its "**U**" name aloud, does likewise with the "**S**" beside it, then, positioning her finger for its neighbor, suddenly whips her hand down to her side. Drop-jawed, she gapes at the fishbowl .... at Patrick .... Fishbowl .... Patrick .... fishbShe looks horrified.

"Y-you—dyou m—y-you l—well—l—dyou m....l-look—Imean........h-horrified. M-Ms. Brittain. Actually."

"Ohhh-ohhh Myyy-yyy Gohhh-ohhhd Paaaaaa-triiiiiick" Her gaze distant, her voice and movements slowed "Hoh-Lee-Shitt!", she staggers over and props herself against a partition "holyshitholyshit", staring into the air of the alcove and muttering to herself in a numbed "holyshitholyshitholy shitholyshitholyshit" guttural entranced roll. As Patrick approaches, she grabs his "holyshitholyshitholy" wrist and pulls him close. "shitholyshitholy shit, Patrick."

"M-Ms. Brittain?"

"Holyshitholyshitholyshitholyshitholyshit" Patrick is sure she thinks she's having a coherent converation with him.

"Ms. Br "

"Pah-trick!"

"Ms. Br-Brittain, wh-wh "

"Pah-trick!" Leslie's anxious eyes shuttle for a long minute between the inside of her thoughts and the inside of Patrick's calm face. Her fingers are still wrapped around his wrist, holding it near her ear like a telephone receiver, unconsciously kneading its flesh. "This-thing-is-huge-Pat-rick," she says in a dim monotone, as if her words have been diluted en route from her brain to her mouth. "It has nothing to do with art collecting........or saving My Pitiful LitTLE

ASS.....OR YOURS." Each in its own trajectory, the letters of her words float up toward the dome on the heat of her "N O T H I N G!" increasingly raised voice. "YOU'RE LOOKING AT ME LIKE I JUST LANDED FROM ANOTHER SOLAR SYSTEM FRCHRISSAKE GO SEE FOR YOURSELF!"

Patrick shakes the blood back into his arm as Leslie in one movement loosens her grip and pushes him away. He walks around the fishbowl "Wh-what.", taking note of each letter. "M-Ms. Br-Brittain."

"Could you please tell me what these four letters say?" Like a switchblade her index finger pops out before her. She follows it over.

"V-veto. Veto. L-like y.....y-you s-s "

"Go on...What's after th whatr the next three after that?"

"U-usn"

"The *letters*, what are the *letters*?"

"Y-yoo E-ess E-enn. Actually."

"As in?"

"U-Uni—I don't kn—U-Uni—I don't—Imean....U-United St-States—well—N-Navy? M-Maybe?"

"Good, Patrick. You're thinking like me. And like *them*. Which may turn out to be more important in this particular case. Now do you see? Didn't I tell you there's always a hidden meaning? Life's one big Sunday-edition cryptogram for Jack. Aren't you glad I decided to turn around and check the action out in this particular alcove before we went on to meet them? Can you just imagine what we're gonna find in the other four? I can't. Can you? Can you just imagine showing up at our little rendez-vous down there at the other end of this marbleized moon-crater *unarmed* with this particular morsel of intelligence? Can you just imagine what a position that would put us in?"

Leslie is speaking calmly. Softly. Softly and calmly. Conversing, not sermonizing. Not flailing. Too softly and calmly, as far as Patrick's concerned. In inverse proportion to the explosion that must've been held up in traffic but'll be here any second now. Seeing that Patrick has no earthly idea of where she's going with this, she walks softly and calmly over to him and once again hooks his index finger into hers.

"They're going to **V E T O**," she singsongs as they trace the letters for all the boys and girls watching us at home, "the **U S N**avy, Patrick." Patrick snatches his hand away. "Veto, Patrick. As in say no to—stop from happening—put a big fat ex on top of—get rid of—destroy—wipe out—they eat it—washed up—curtainsfinitokaput. Blow every fucking battleship and beautiful young—Hi, sailor!—sailor outa the global aitch two oh." Through the bowl, Patrick is focusing on a little prism skimming the rim of the water. "You *still* don't—PATRICK!" Leslie grabs his lapels. Here it comes, he thinks. It must've made that green light after all.

"WE'RE INNOCENT PAWNS IN A PLOT TO OVER-THROW ONE-QUARTER OF THE ARMED SERVICES OF THE UNITED STATES OF AMERICA!"

"Covetousness."

"DOESN'T THAT HAVE ANY EFFECT ON YOU AT ALL?"

"Covetousness."

"TRUST NO GOLDFISH PATRICK HAVE I ALWAYS SAID THAT OR NOT?" Wadding even more of his lapels up into her fists, she tries to pull him out of the alcove. "Here! Come! We gotta go see what the other fish have to say to us! Quick!" He stands firm and pulls her back in.

Two letters to the left of where she got religion, he points with one hand "M-Ms. Brittain" **C** and gently takes her elbow **O** with the other. **V** They **E** stroll **T** around **O** the **U** bowl. **S**

"NESS!" Leslie liquidates the lesson in one syllable as she dashes out, leaving Patrick to his promenade. "I'll believe it when the next one says Oops, sorry, hadjya goin there for awhile, huh, honey!" she shouts, in full flight, up to the dome, figuring the sentence will find its way down to him on one of its bounces. Not until he turns around to tell her to come watch Covetousness doing a stunning series of *grands* clear-across-the-bowl almost-out-of-the-water *jetés* does he realize she's gone, at which point he sneaks out without the fish's noticing and trots to catch up. His non-existent backpack seems lighter now.

Once again they cross the immense sun-floor. Once again the

alcove and its monolith and its fish in its bowl are identical to the others.

"I *knew* it!" Leslie says, slapping her thigh as she stomps around the bowl.

"I *kn-knew* it!" Patrick says, doing what he thinks is snap his fingers as he stands in the entrance.

"You take the letters **E N V Y**. You first-off change the e to a. That's the first thing you do. You rearrange what's left. You'd think they could've at least been a little more *cryptic* about the deal frchrissakes what kinda dumb cryptologists are they anyway I'd hate to have them hangin out in *my* radio shack they'd blow the whole mission before it even got started what dthey think we are, so dumb we need it spoon-fed frchissa "

"C-Come On M-Ms. Brittain!" Patrick seems to have totally forgotten that he'd ever forgotten how to laugh. Joyously. "G L U T T O N Y!" he screams as a war-cry, grabbing Leslie's hand, dragging her out with him, back across the hall's gaping width, diagonally toward the next alcove, laughing from his gut, looking around the space and throwing his head back to take in the dome, squeezing Leslie's fingers so she won't get away, allowing himself to tell her "Ssh!" when she makes any kind of sound at all "Ssh! Oh, M-Ms. Brittain, Gluttony, The-The Next One's Going T-To Say...Gluttony! Ssh!", picking up speed with Leslie flapping along behind him like a paper doll in the wind, entering the **G** alcove **L**, taking **U** a **T** spin **T** around **O** the **N** bowl **Y**, leaving the alcove, zipping back through the white air to the opposite wall, "Ssh! Y-You Have Gr-Great Friends, Ms. Brittain! Ssh!", bursting upon the next alcove **L**, circling **U** the **S** bowl **T** at basic-training pace, still flying Leslie as a kite, blasting out of the alcove, flashing way over again to the other side of the hall, out of breath from running, from living in the here-and-now, "Ssh! Y-You Get It Now, M-Ms. Brittain, Right? Ssh!" charging into the last alcove, braking the **P** sprint **R** around **I** the **D** bowl **E** with a walk for the final few...hhhh .....steps....hhhh............hhhh..hhhh............. hhhh..................hhhh....hhhh.......hhhh.............hhhh ........hhhh........hhhhBent at the waist...hhhh...beside the final partition,..hhhh..his legs slightly spread, his hands..hhhh..pressing up into his stomach, Patrick lets his laugh finish out its course.....hhh...hhhh ..and gasps for air..hhhh.h.h.h.h.h.h.h.h.h.h.h........................
..........................................................................................
..........................................................................................
..........................................................................................
............................"You're one of em, aren't you?" Leslie

asks in a quiet, matter-of-fact voice. She is standing beside him, her arms folded across her chest, waiting for him to catch his breath. When he hears her words his body jerks a bit, as if he's about to straighten, but he seems suddenly to change his mind and stays where he is.

"I have a question for you, Patrick Trucore."

Now he pops up. "M-M-Ms. " Like a spring.

"What, Patrick," Leslie's tone is chokingly sweet. "led you all to the shamefully erroneous conclusion—and if I were you I'd focus on *zero* right now except the particular question I'm asking you at this time—that I was so dumb?"

"....."

"I mean, I'm a lotta things, Patrick. We all know I'm a lotta things." She sounds like the hostess at a church social making sure the new couple in the corner have helped themselves to cole slaw. "But one thing I'm not is the following: dumb."
Despite Leslie's suggestion, Patrick is losing himself in a grain of etched glass in the northeast curve of **P R I D E**'s **D**.
"Oh it was an admirable try. It *was* an admirable try. You actually even had me with you there for a bit Patrick *please* pretend to be listening to me. I'd say the earth moved at about the...the u of Lust—an appropriate place, *n'est-ce pas*, Patrick? It was just around there that I began to see the abject inanity of my suspicions back there, thanks to our little romp, it was just about there that I began to see that all we're really talking about here is the "

"S-Seven D-Deadly "

"Goldfish. The Seven Deadly Goldfish, Patrick. Hah. Hah hah. But that's just the point DON'T Unfocus On Me! that's just the point."

"M-Ms. Br-Brittain. Wh........wh "

"Sloth. That's what. Sloth."

Patrick's eyes look like they were suddenly turned on by a switch. He mutters something to himself, as if he just remembered on the way home that he forgot to pick up the dry-cleaning. With nervous little glances he scans the alcove then steps out and surveys his side of the hall. Turns. Counts the alcoves across the way. Turns. Recounts the alcoves over here. Leslie hasn't moved. "Wh-where...... where............'s "

"Your collective undoing, Patrick. Sloth. Just like it's been the undoing of the masses. Ever since the first good-for-nothing goldfish-on-the-dole decided no reason to swim on any further when staying put on a beach chair in the Nile Crescent with a little drink in its fin was just as easy."

" S-S-Sloth? M-Ms. Br-Brittain."

"I was just gonna ask you the same question, Patrick ("or was it the Garden of Eden? I always get those two confused."). So much for keeping up with your Bible studies, huh? I guess your buddies were too busy *buying* the Bible—original manuscript—limited edition of one—that miraculously doesn't show up on film when photographed—whitebeard droppings all over it—to have any time left for actually reading what was in it." Leslie throws her chin toward the far end of the hall and "They probably think there were nine little indians." heads slowly out of the alcove. "Two blind mice. Six dwarfs. The Four Satins. The Dirty Eleven. The "

"Th-they—Imean—c-could they—couldn't have—c-could th-they—c-couldn't have.......*f-forgotten* it. C-could they? M-Ms. Br-Brittain." Patrick trots.

"*They* could have forgotten anything *they* chose to forget, Patrick."

They're walking now as if they've been walking all along,

"Dyou—well—st-still—Imean—dyou m...th-think they're pl-planning on bl-blowing blowing up the—well—U-US.....N-Navy? Navy?"

at this

very pace.

"Why would they wanna do a thing like that frchrissakes? I mean what with Jack's c—I remembered this at about the n of Gluttony—an appropriate spot, *n'est-ce pas?*—Jack's contract to make silk panties—or uniforms—same thing—for the military, the man has a consumer base to maintain I mean no matter how much they'd pay him for that particular act of international terrorism and as attractive a career move as it'd be in terms of level of responsibility and the respect you get when you go home for Christmas, wasting the Hi, sailors!'d be a one-shot deal and if you do the math it's gotta be a better bet in the long run to keep em alive and wearin out their crotches and comin back for more. Uniforms that is."

As if their voyage to the other end of the great hall had not been interrupted by the Sev—by the Six Deadly Goldfish.

"Dyou st-still think I'm—well—one of—Imean.....th—dyour m—th-them? Ms. Br-Brittain."

"I wish I did Patrick. Well—what I mean by that is, I wish you had—you're working on it mind you, sweetie, you're on your way—but I wish you had the, well, the...the killer inst—the self-assurance that would make me worry that maybe you were. You'll be a good international terrorist one day." Leslie reaches around Patrick's neck and squeezes his shoulder. "You just need to read your Bible a bit more often that's all........................................Patrick?"

"Yeah."

"Who's gonna be there when we get there and whatr they gonna tell us?"

"H-how—dyou    m—Imean—M-Ms.    Br-Brittain    h-howamIsup......h-how "

"I just thought...well, I just thought maybe.....in case. You know? In case on the outside chance....I'm Giving You A Compliment Frchrissake!" She flails her right arm and punches at Patrick's shoulder with her left. "Like—what if you were the *mastermind* of this whole elaborate plot to blow up a tunnel under Notre Dame de Paris and steal its ancient parchments and kill me!" As if she's narrating an adventure film, her voice is a little hushed, a little awestruck, a little fevered. While Patrick focuses on a lightbeam, the slow metered click of Leslie's heels echoes off the mosaic...  ...and they walk... ...on...  ... to...  ...their...  ...meeting...  ...at...  ...the...  ...far...  ...end... ...of...  ...the...  ...vast...  ...white...  ...space......   ......   ......   ......   ......   ......   ......   ......   ......   ......   ......   ......

......   ......

......   ......

# XVIII

## 1193.66 KILOMETERS ÞER W̊ORD (OR 1074.30, ÐEPENDING ØÑ HOW ¥ØÜ ©OUNT)

...... ......

...... ......

...... ......

...... ......

...... At about the equivalent of two blocks from it, the shrine that Leslie and Patrick think they've been seeing in the far wall comes clearly into view and, more than that, seems to overtake their peripheral vision so that it becomes the only thing they are aware of in the hall and, more than that, seems to be generating a sound of some sort—a distant high-pitched hiss that each of them winds up figuring is just a freak ringing in their ears, and probably is—and, more than that, seems to be reeling them in toward itself, tapping into their magnetic fields, beckoning to them and locking them onto a cadence and a course through coded vibrations to which the muscles in their legs have been programmed to respond.

When they were back at the entrance they believed that what they were looking at down here was a kind of *toko-no-ma*, the sacred recessed area in a Japanese home where the beauty of one magnificent work of calligraphy, balanced by the perfection of a single flower set before it in a simple vase, reflects and defines the surrounding harmony. An integrated isolation which you ritualistically stand in front of and admire for the sake of admiring magnificence and simple perfection and balance and beauty.

But the closer they get the more they realize that the perspective of the hall had been playing with their perception of the shrine. Just as now the perspective of the shrine is playing with their perception of the hall. —Leslie thrusts her wrist up under her nose. She suddenly thinks she smells patchouli, sniffs her leather watchband where it must be coming from. Trapped in there, left over from touching Sun.— What they first saw as vases they know now are low, wide chairs—four white-upholstered gold-framed armchairs in a semi-circle facing the far end of the space. The imagined flowers are the backs of heads. Two men. Sitting one on each end of the semi-circle. Moving slightly now and again but not interacting across the two empty seats between them. And the artwork. The magnificent calligraphy hanging in the recess of the recess is a tall thin figure in off-white trousers with matching morning-coat and turban, tall and thin as if being pulled upon at both ends and continuously stretched, standing in strict stillness and silence on a small half-moon white marble stage flush against the white marble wall, his back to Leslie and Patrick. As they walk.

Between the figure and the wall is a monolith with a goldfish bowl. "S-seven. Actually," Patrick says, so softly that the dome doesn't even get to play with his sounds. Afraid that any movement more magnified will send a message of irreverence to his hosts, he points his index finger without lifting his hand from his side.

"Whew!" Leslie whispers back. "They must know there are five Satins after all." They're getting there... She sniffs her watchband again. "Don't they feed him frchrissakes?" ...about a block and a half to go...

"S-sloth? M-Ms. Br-Brittain." ...though they've slowed considerably...

"The Wizard!" ...without even realizing it... "Blyster! Look at im he's a *haricot vert*! Men with one-tenth his stash are being rushed to intensive care units every day with whole Thanksgiving turkeys wadded up in their arteries." ...to the point where they're little more than walking in place... "He hasn't figured it out he could hock an old prayer shawl or something and actually get himself something tput in his stomach maybe we could lend im a couple til he finds a free minute tget over to the temple and make a withdrawl." ...several hundred yards from the wall, from the shrine, from the backs of the chairs with the backs of the men's heads slightly moving now and again... "You got a spare prayer shawl on you, Patrick? No. Guess not. How could you? *He's* got em all. That's why we're here, isn't it? how quickly they forget!"

"Dyou—well—th-think—Imean—h-he's wh-why isn't—dyou th-think he's is he is he.....g-going to.......m-move? T-turn around? Around?"

"Pay no attention to the man behind the curtain, Patrick, huh? Huh? Did I tell you or what? HUH? Did you not believe me?—WORSE!" Leslie leaps into Patrick's path, pointing at his face. "Did you choose to ig-noooore me, sittin up there with your little servant-pal? HUH?" She moves back next to him. "Just—when the disembodied voice starts beatin up on us in a couple minutes about not paying any attention to the man standing up there being emaciated and not moving, don't come tellin me you weren't warned!" They are whispering at this point not so much out of reverence for the awe-inspiring site as out of comfort with a vocal level to which they've become unconsciously accustomed. "Look do you really *want* him to turn around? can you imagine the network of wrinkles we're talkin about on that face! Delayed gratification, Patrick. It's what medical school and life is all about. It'll come soon enough." Leslie smells her watchband.

Patrick and Leslie are at the point on the runway where, after moving frantically forward for several days—getting your tickets, packing your bags, stopping your newspapers, making arrangements for your plants and your dog, setting your light-timers at different intervals all over the house, saying your good-byes, getting your body to the airport, standing in line, going through security, standing in line, checking in, taking one of the new escalator-modules they built in when they renovated, standing in line, going through security, thinking about the hours ahead, buying a magazine and a cup of coffee and a bagel, walking around the boarding area, standing in line, boarding, stashing your bag, fastening your seatbelt, finding your pillow, checking the movie listing, ignoring the security film and your neighbor, thinking about the miles ahead, feeling the plane rumble then rouse then inch then pull out then glide into position for takeoff—you stop. The plane stops. It and you have to pass from preparatory forward through stopped in order for the most important forward to be able to work—the one that's going to get you there. Although you assume its a technical stop, it feels more like a symbolic stop. As if the plane is standing there looking up into the sky. Contemplating what it's gotta do. Crossing itself. Taking a deep breath. Reviewing its life to this point. Saying a couple words to its Aunt Edith to whom it promised on her deathbed always to say a couple words at challenging moments like this. And, when it and Aunt Edith are ready, nodding slightly, off into the distance, to tell the tower the time has come.

And then taxiing down a runway which doesn't look any more or less equipped to receive it than it did before the whole stopping business began.

This is where Leslie and Patrick are at the moment. Slowed finally to a technical and symbolic stop a hundred yards or so from where they've been enroute to for days now. For weeks now. The human figures in the shrine area, if not the goldfish with them, look like automatons in a creatively furnished display case, all made up, dressed and in their places, ready for action and awaiting only one last turn of the wind-up key, for which Leslie's and Patrick's company seems required.

There is no line of demarcation between the cavernous hall through which they've been walking and the concentrated arena just ahead, about to come alive. No door or window or threshold, no curtain or change in flooring—the points of the mighty mosaic sun stab out to touch all four walls. No switch from black-and-white to color, or sign that says: HARD HAT AREA or THE JOINT IS JUMPIN. Or place provided by the control tower where you and Aunt Edith can have a little private moment before taking to the skies. Where you can stop moving forward so you can start moving forward.

So Leslie and Patrick make one.

They stop walking, whispering and evoking the eternal spirits of Oz.

The engine doesn't cut but it's quieter than when they were gliding out here. If ever, it will not be quiet again like this until they've taken off, gotten there and come back to Kansas. They nod slightly, off into the distance—Leslie sniffs the air around and above and looks at her watchband—and they do the last hundred yards in silence and resolve.

"Hello, Jack."

"Hello, Leslie. Hello, son."

The man sitting at the other end of the semi-circle of chairs bounds out of his seat the instant Leslie's and Patrick's presence is acknowledged. His reaction is so synchronized, it is as if Jack's greeting and his rising are part of the same act—as if one could not happen without the other. He looks like he couldn't stand it anymore—like he'd stayed seated in that armchair as he'd been told to do, until they made it from one end of the hall to the other as he'd been told they would—and now that they're here goddamnit he can consider his duty done. He paces nervously away from his chair, paces impatiently back. Stuffs his hands into the pockets of his suitjacket and troops over to sit on the steps cut into the base of the stage. The figure facing the wall has not so much as breathed.

"Whadjya swim over, Jack?" Standing with her hands on her hips and her knees almost in Jack's barely discernible lap, Leslie crooks her neck and squints out into the vast whiteness through which she and Patrick have walked.

"Have a seat," Jack answers, nodding to the empty chairs. Patrick takes the one closest to him.

"No—" Leslie reaches down to rub her hand across Jack's thigh.

"too dry. I know what you did. I know what he did," she says to Patrick, who seems to be focusing on the other man through some strange combination of nodding and smiling. "When the helicopter took off, Chan—the pilot, Chan—Chan lowered a rope and you jumped up and held onto it like Sylvester Stallone all the way across to th "

Jack is shaking his head.

"No! You're right—not like Stallone! Uhhhh—uh—wait! gimme a second wait! lemme guessss—liii-iiike.....LON CHANEY—Got It I *Won*!" Leslie thrusts one hand up to her nose and the other out in front of her to complete her game of charades.

"Have a seat, Leslie" Jack says cheerily as if she just this instant walked in.

"Arnold Scwartzenegger? He does all his own stunts." She settles in between Patrick and the empty place on the end while Jack pretends to ignore her.

In silence the three of them watch the man at the steps chew on an unlit cigarette and stare off to the side of the hall. Jump up. Pace. Return to the steps. Jump up. Pace. Return to the steps. Jump up—on his way back to the armchair at Leslie's left he nods slowly to Patrick who immediately stops focusing on a diamond-like chunk in the floor, sits up taller, widens his eyes. The presence of the motionless being before them both dominates and melts into the atmosphere.

Although nothing has actually confirmed it, it is unquestionable that this is their host, the Wizard, the Man, Tai Yang Blyster, the supposedly recluse supposedly Sino-British supposed billionaire with supposedly rarefied taste in sacred art and profane men, choreographer of the successful kidnap of Leslie and Patrick and the impending pillage of the underbelly of Notre Dame. It's his party so he can stand up there without moving, facing the wall, guarding his goldfish, for as long as he wants. Pay no attention to the man behind the curtain. This tall skinny man, said to have been seen by almost no one all his life, is visible from every vantage point of the great hall. Of his great hall. He is the pinhole in the vacuum toward which all the air whooshes at once, the single point on the screen which the mass of animated laser-lines is racing to bombard as you ride them like a rocket through the software stars. He is a sudden siren in a hushed museum.

And yet, with his head tilted slightly back, his arms relaxed but straight at his sides, his palms spread wide toward the wall, he looks like a modern dancer in position on a darkened stage without a curtain. Waiting for the curtain to go up. Waiting for the signal telling him to begin, pretending that you as the audience can pretend he's still in the wings. Until it's time. Until the curtain that isn't there isn't there. Pay no attention to the man behind the curtain.

The four of them are seated now, facing the figure facing the wall, in the semi-circle of shining chairs whose seats and armrests and backs tell intricate sylvan-scene stories in hundreds of nuances of white silk brocade. Like the sun-floor. So many shades of clarity and light. There's Jack then Patrick then Leslie then the other man. Anybody who knows what we're waiting for raise your hand.

Leslie sees that Blyster's outfit and turban are made of raw silk. Almost the same off-white as her suit. Only, a little more yellow. A little more.....golden. But not gold. Off-white. ("Skinny sonuvabitch.") She tries to imagine what his face will look like "Leslie?" then imagines him with no face at all. Like a Magritte painting—a frame of a head filled with clouds, as cloud-like as clouds can be, filing across a southern-France sky like "Leslie, I think ev " ducks on a shooting-gallery belt. "Leslie, I think everyone LESLIE I'M TALKING TO YOU!" Jack leans across Patrick and claps his hands into her right ear. "Yes. You," he says softly when she revives and turns her head his way. "I think everyone knows each other here, with one exception." He sweeps his arm out toward the end of the semi-circle.

Leslie looks front again and imagines Blyster with the face of a goldfish. She thinks maybe it isn't Sloth in the bowl at all, but a mirror reflecting Blyster's goldfish face, and that if he doesn't stand there like that there will be no Seventh Deadly Goldfish. Holy Shit! Talk about controlling the treasures of Western civilization! She wants to tell this to Patrick—tell him she's figured it all out—but first she takes a deep breath and glances at the man on her left, then looks straight ahead at the goldfish man, crunches up her mouth like people do when they're thinking, turns to Patrick and instead says to him "You're one of em aren't you?" in a flat, calm voice.

Patrick has been focusing on the evolution of the diamond-like mosaic piece. He's watching it, and the chips of what it mutates into, creep along the floor and mutate into chips of something else. Like in those games where there's a word at the top of the page, a different word with the same number of letters at the bottom of the page, and, in between, a long column, each of whose numerous lines have the same number of blanks as there are letters in the top and bottom words, the instructions saying: "START WITH THE WORD **NEAT** AND, BY CHANGING ONE LETTER EACH TIME, END UP WITH THE WORD **ROCK**".

Patrick started with diamond near the man's shoe and is too busy ending up with mother-of-pearl near the stage to answer Leslie's question.

Jack continues "It's my pleasure to introduce you to one of m...one of *our* business partners, *Monsieur*"

So she asks him again—nudges him this time with her elbow—and he says

"M-Ms. Br "

"Jacques Dupuy."

"You *are* one of em."

"M-Ms. Br-Brittain I-I only only I-I o-only h-he—well—c-came t-to........t-take—well— "

"I knew it, Patrick." Leslie is speaking in the exquisitely serene, barely audible voice in which she speaks only when ragingly furious.

" m-me to the-to the—Imean..... "

"I knew it. You wanna hear *how* I knew it, Patrick?"

"Mr. Dupuy has come from "

"PARIS! I KNOW, JACK! CUT THE SPEECH TO THE NATIONAL LOBOTOMY SOCIETY, OK? you wanna know *how* I knew it, Patrick?"

" p-p-plane. Plane. Actually. M-Ms. "

" to join in our little meeting here today, which will be starting any" Jack glances at his watch.

"The Harley. That's how I knew. Don't think I didn't know. Because I knew. The Harley, Patrick. You can't drive a Harley the way you drive a Harley and be the kinda dorkface you've been pretending to" Leslie suddenly turns to Jacques. "You don't *look* gay."

"minute now."

Jacques looks at her blankly,

"Or virginal."

as if he doesn't hear, or understand, what she's saying. "Virginal you *certainly* don't look." As if she isn't even there and he's just happening to look in that direction. "But I might give you gay *and* virginal," she concedes, leaning in her chair as far to the right—as far away from him—as possible, so far that she's almost lying across Patrick's lap. Working out a good vantage point, she narrows her eyes and passes them up and down Jacques's body, a prospector surveying a piece of land from a neighboring farm, muttering farm-surveying "Yupp!......uhhh-hhuh!..." sounds to herself. "...yyyyuppers!"

Jacques's eyes look artificial—like the eyes of your stuffed rabbit watching you from atop the pile of pillows as you do your math homework there on the bed—them little glassy brown beadsr lookin right atchya, ain't they?—but you know damn well they ain't seein ya fra darn.

So Leslie skates a couple inches over to thinner ice.

"Not virginal and gay, mind you." One minute, "That's a whole different *gestalt*." the stuffed rabbit's just hangin out there near the headboard. "Definitely." The next minute, "Definitely gay and *then* virginaaAAAAAAAAAAHHHHHHHHH SHIT YOU MANIAC GET THE FUCK AWAY FR " he's bounding out of his chair, diving onto Leslie, going for her throat with his hands. "YOU FUCKING M " Leslie frantically pounds on him. "AAAAAAAAAA AAAHHHHHHHHHHHH" Patrick wildly leaps up and kicks at him. "AAAAAAAAAAAAAAAHHHHHHHHHHHHHHHHH" Jack calmly stands and guides him by his armpits back to his seat as Leslie catches her breath and screeches "WHO'S HOME TAPPING MY PHONE, YOU FUCK-FACE, IF YOU'RE HERE, HUH? HUH?

Standing behind Jacques's chair, Jack is digging his chubby fingers into the shoulders of the brown suitjacket, pushing down with all his weight. "That's enough, Leslie."

Leslie springs to her feet. "WHO'S BACK THERE INTERCEPTING MY E-MAIL IF YOU'RE HERE STRANGLING ME TO DEATH, YOU FUCKING SICKO CRUD, HUH?"

Patrick is almost crying.

"WHO'S KEEPIN TRACK OF "

"Leslie. That's enough."

She's bending into Jacques's face now as Jack keeps him pinned. " HOW MANY TIMES I SUCK YOUR DICK-FRIEND'S DICK? HUH? HUH, YOU ANIMAL, WHO?"

"Thierry."

Lesliepopsupandlooksattheceilingandallaroundlike someone who's just heard from God. She thinks a female voice has echoed through the white space she looks all around all around again hears nothing more looks at Patrick Patrick's focusing on her looking she looks at the two men the Wizard hasn't moved on the stage maybe she didn't hear a female voice after all no female voice for this baby. Maybe she didn't hear a voice at all. At all. She goes back to her seat.

"Thierry," the voice echoes again, as the figure on the stage starts turning from the wall toward the semi-circle of armch

"H!H!H!H!H!H!H!H!H!H!H!H!H!H!H!H!H!H!H!H!H!H!H!H!H!" Leslie smashes her hand onto Patrick's forearm   draws her breath up   holds it in   arches her body   doesn't breathe out   can't breathe out   can't breathe out   presses presses her back down into the chair. The figure, fully facing them now, /can't breathe out/ slowly, strongly crosses the stage to the steps /Leslie's head floods with heat and motion heat and heat and motion/ and begins to walk down "H!H!H!H! H!H!H!H!    H!H!H!h!    h!h!h!h!    h!O!h!H!    h!M!h!Y!h! hG!h!O!h!D!h!............h!P!h!A!h!T!h!R!h!I!h!C!h!K!h!................" toward her guests. "...........h!S!h!U!h!N!h! h!*I!h!S!h!*................h! T!h!H!h!E!h!h!W!h!I!h!Z!h!A!h!R!h!D!h!h!h!h!h!h!h!h!h!h!h!h!h!h!

!h!h!h!h!h!h!h!h!h!h!h!h!h!h!h!h!h!h!h!h!h!h!h!h!h!h!h!h!h!h!h!h!h!h!h
!h!h!h!h!h!h!h!h!h!h!h!h!h!h!h!h!h!h!h!h!h!h!h!h!h!h!h!h!h!h!h!h!h!h!h
!h!h!h!h!h!h!h!h!h!h!h!h!h!h!h!h!h!h!h!h!h!h!h!h!h!h!h!h!h!h!h!hh!h!h
!h!h!h!h!h!h!h!Because she has envisioned an emaciated wrinkled face for so long—for so many footsteps and minutes since she and Patrick checked out of the Goldfish exhibit at the beginning of the hall—and because each wrinkle in that vision has deepened, and the face has further shriveled, the longer the figure has insisted on standing there like a statue of itself facing the wall, and because, as in those clever riddles designed to trap racists and sexists, Leslie has left no unit of space in her consciousness for the fact the Blyster might not be a man—regardless that all reference has been by masculine pronoun—because of all this, Leslie is now having a difficult time making the switch—exchanging the old, imagined, unimaginable image, imprinted on her brain as on photographer's film, for any new image at all. Let alone the image of Sun. As Sun approaches, the wrinkles fade one by one. The mental photographer's trick.

Let alone the image of Sun.

Her long black hair hidden under the off-white silk turban, Sun's translucent skin itself looks like a thin membrane of silken threads covering a layer of light. A membrane that could be lifted away only with the help of tiny tweezes. Like a sheet of gold-leaf. She is standing before Leslie and Patrick with her legs apart, her pelvis thrust slightly forward, her fists on her hips.

"Wonder Woman," Leslie chokes out in a voice stripped by shock and lack of oxygen. She sniffs the patchouli in the air and shakes her head, glancing down at her watchband. Then, as if she's just run into her at the dorm cafeteria, she lilts "Hi, Sun!"

Patrick is comparing the degree of toe roundness of Jacques's half-shined half-scuffed mud-brown cop-shoes to that of Sun's off-white leather bucks, focusing from one's right shoe to the other's left in time with the changes in Leslie's breathing.

"It is my privilege and honor," Jack says, with authentic reverence of which Leslie didn't think him capable, "to present to you our honorable and generous host, Tai Yang Blyster."

"Hi, Sun!" This time Leslie gives her a little wave.

Without turning his head from Blyster, Jack asks "What does Tai Yang mean in Chinese, son?"

"S-sun, s-sir.......it m-means s-sun. Actua "

"SUN *SIR?*," Leslie blasts, twisting in her seat to place a hand on each of Patrick's armrests. "OR JUST SUN?" Stretched across his chair, her chest is pressing down against him while her eyes try to catch his.

"S-s—M-Ms. B "

"And we just happen to know this because that's the kinda thing we Nebraskans sit around on our pickle barrels after Bible-study class chewin on when we run outa news about the local alfalfa crop, RIGHT? RI "

Jack flicks at her shoulder as at a mosquito. "Let him up."

Leslie doesn't budge. In fact, she budges—she presses closer in. "And did the folks at Bible-study class say anything about how come we bargained for an old dried-up fart and wound up with a.....a "
"The real Mr. Blyster died two years ago," Patrick announces straight into Leslie's face, smoothly, as if reading from a script or singing—and seemingly unbothered by the fact that she's nearly smothering him. "This is his granddaughter." He sounds about thirty years older. "Since he was a hermit all his life anyway," Where's the real Patrick? Bound and gagged in some closet? "it doesn't matter if he's dead. In other words, no one misses him. In fact, it would be bad for business if...." He looks at Jack and loses thirty years, the script "....if a-anyone kn-knew—I mean—he was—well.....g-gone. Gone. Actually." and the lyrics.

"and wound up with" Leslie sits straight in her chair and glares up into Blyster's eyes. "a hired hand?.....Although they got the part about sexual preference right." She rocks back then forward in a move to get to her feet, a non-verbal declaration that she's tired of this game and wants to go see what's playin down the other end otown. Pushing out a haughty sigh, shaking her head, she looks at the floor and bears onto the silk brocade armrests to help herself up and when she raises her eyes she sees Blyster's arm flashing high above her head Blyster's open palm whooshing down toward her face she takes one instant too long to try to figure out if this is a joke before moving out of the way too late Blyster cuts her hand down through the air like a sabre slaps Leslie across the mouth

then turns to the wall.

Leslie rushes the back of her wrist up to her face.

Jack and Jacques stand.

Leslie spits something under her breath.

Patrick stands.

Blyster takes two steps forward.

A small crack, appearing in the center of the three steep steps leading to the stage, travels like a stocking run up the middle of the stage to the wall then up the wall all the way to the textured-glass dome.

Leslie stands.

Along their central axis, which is the central axis of the great hall, the steps and stage and entire towering marble wall begin to split in half in one massive rupture around and away from the goldfish-bowl monolith, whose base is revealed to be resting not on the surface of the stage, as had appeared, but at floor level where Blyster and her guests are gathered, and around whose centered solidity the monumental apparatus moving before them has been built.
  Into the chasm thus created, Blyster briskly leads the way. The others follow in the order in which they rose from their seats. Patrick slows and moves back to Leslie's right while she repeatedly jabs her knuckle into her stinging lips, as if they were a sheet of bubble-wrap and her knuckle had the responsibility of bursting every one of its tiny pockets of air. The procession files along in total darkness. Where are Patrick's Hansel and Gretel seedlight pals now? When, about a hundred feet in, they are the only ones who don't know exactly where to stop, Leslie and Patrick collide with Jacques's back like slapstick comedians.
  If the hall which they just left was an arena for the most elite light and the most elite air, vying, vying with each other in an ongoing competition between the forces of their flooding, then the space through which they are now being led is the absence which existed

before that light and that air were born, and the grave to which they will go when they die. There is no light at all and the air is heavy and hot and laced with a swampy smell of wet leaves and acrid perspiration and...and something else—powdery maybe, a substance—something that Leslie can define to herself only as ("dust"). And of course patchouli. And of course the sound.

From the minute the wall opened. The low-grade scratchy sound. ch-ch-ch Everywhere. It is not a sound that is *in* the space, or *a part of* the space, it is as if the space is in, or a part of, the sound. ch-ch-ch As if the space is existing to conduct the sound, as opposed to the sound's being there filling the space. It is all around. ch-ch-ch You want to brush it off your skin like a ch-ch-ch swarm of sea lice just come to attack you on your beach blanket. You feel the sound surround your ankles. You think at one point that it is coming from inside you ch-ch-ch and you hold your breath as tight and long as you can to smother the sound at its source. And yet it is very far away. Muted. It is coming from over in the next valley and must travel up the mountain and then down again to get to where you stand. ch-ch-ch It is made by hundreds of thousands of kindergartners sitting at the other end of the room rubbing together wooden blocks covered with sandpaper. ch-ch-ch  ch-ch-ch  It is generated by a conveyor belt which rolls out on a machine that never stops which itself rolls out on a yet bigger machine that never stops which churns the machine which churns the belt which churns the ch-ch-ch sound. It is an eternal sound, repelling all other sound as it absorbs all other sound. It is the dissonance of natural governing rhythms, of the air, of the inside of your ears ch-ch-ch of the inside of your brain. ch-ch-ch Of the earth rotating. ch-ch-ch  ch-ch-ch  ch-ch-ch  ch-ch-ch  ch-ch-ch  ch-ch-ch  ch-ch-ch  ch-ch-ch  ch-ch-ch  ch-ch-ch  ch-ch-ch  ch-ch-ch  ch-ch-ch  ch-ch-ch  ch-ch-ch  ch-ch-ch

A sound that could unsettle if you let it. A they're-coming-to-get-you sound. Coming from far away and in unison. ch-ch-ch Too many of them to count. ch-ch-ch Scratching along the ground at the other end of the world en route to your ability to keep the lights off in your bedroom. No. ch-ch-ch It's not. ch-ch-ch It's a they're-here sound. ch-ch-ch Patrick's hand r-reaches for contact......for Leslie's....hand—h-haltingly—as when he—well—r-reaches for his w-for his w-words. She is unsure this is not just another exquisitely conceived theatrical moment in his participation in Blyster's plot. She takes it. Grateful for the feel of his skin. Waiting. ch-ch-ch It's OK, I'll wait. ch-ch-ch Don't mind me. ch-ch-ch I'll stand here forever. ch-ch-ch Take your time. ch-ch-ch They're nowhere near here yet.

They're still in China—no! wait!—we're *near* China aren't we?—they're still in Connecticut. We have a ways to go yet. Why is no one moving? What do they ch-ch-ch know about the sound? Has there ever been light in this place? Has there ever been Patrick squeezes the blood from Leslie's hand. Why is no one moving? ch-ch-ch She smells a puff of patchouli. The air feels and smells like rancid grease. Like dust. ch-ch-ch Like a solution of individual particles of dust each coated separately and painstakingly with a lamina of rancid grease. ch-ch-ch Her hair is wet with sweat under her hat. She has to pee ch-ch-ch has to keep her rancid-grease-dust skin from being absorbed into her skull. ch-ch-ch ch-ch-ch ch-ch-ch ch-ch-ch ch-ch-ch ch-ch-ch ch-ch-ch ch-ch-ch ch-ch-ch ch-ch-ch ch-ch-ch ch-ch-ch Patrick is shaking violently she smells a puff of patchouli smells his horror he suddenly seems lifeless at the end of her arm a

dim light creeps slowly into the space. Creeps. Slowly. Like the sound. Light that's not here yet. It's still in Connecticut, too. Well, Texas. It's in Texas now. It starts in Leslie's and Patrick's head and leaks into the void in which they are standing. Like the golden light from the dome next door, it takes the time to work on every molecule of air separately. Dimly. With illumination so dim it looks dirty. Dirty light. As each individual air molecule receives the dim dirty light, Leslie's and Patrick's eyes acknowledge its presence. Lit air molecule after lit air molecule. Until an area again as vast as the white hall materializes before them and they realize, at the pace that their brains give their eyes give their brains the ability to realize, that this immense space is filled, across every millimeter of its unfathomable walls, from its dank floor to its invisible ceiling, with tiny cages crawling with ch-ch-ch silkworms. ch-ch-ch

Patrick makes a heavy grunting swallowing sound which is the shriek of horror he would hurl were he able to permit himself that freedom. His grasp on Leslie is at the same time so inert and so oppressive—like the greeting you get from one of those slimy rubber hands you buy at novelty stores—that she returns to serious doubt that he could ever be one of *them*. She instinctively moves him several steps further back from Jack and Jacques, for whom the existence of this and probably similar sites is certainly not news, but who are nonetheless scanning the cage-encrusted walls with steady sweeps of their heads in awe of the sheer enormity, if not concept, of the scene.

And thus instinctively several steps further back from Sun Blyster. As she slowly pivots, reviewing her troops. Counting the little dears to see if there have been any additions since the last time she came calling or if anyone has decided to slip out for a quick smoke without signing the register. Rapt in insulating concentration, Blyster looks like she's working an abacus without moving her fingers—or without having an abacus to work at all. As if her being itself is the abacus. As if she would be able to tell you not only if there were one less or more among what must be the millions of silkworms on the walls, but also in what cage and when the change in population took place.

Leslie crinkles her mouth, squints, strokes her chin. Not daring to remove herself from Patrick's lifelock, she keeps her eyes on the top row of cages, just under the ceiling she can't really see, and takes him with her as she does a slow, complete rotation. "You know what I think this place could use?" she says in a high-pitched voice drawled by mock contemplation. As if having forgotten that any being was capable of producing a sound other than ch-ch-ch, Jack and Jacques snap around to Leslie in surprise, while Blyster, her head crooked all the way back, continues flicking her abacus beads with her brain.

"Silkworms. I mean," No one's made a move but Leslie shoots her palm out like a traffic cop. "in my only in my humble opinion mind you. I mean I'm no interior decorator or anything. Although I did once help this Brazilian friend of mine choose carpeting for his poolhouse in Monte Carlo." In the old security of hearing her start in on something, Patrick begins to loosen his grip and relax his rigid neck. He focuses on the first family of silkworms he sees. "Although by the time they came and put it in and then came and ripped it all out again because of the problem with the fountain it was time for me to go back to Paris so I couldn't help him with the dressing rooms like I promised but *silkworms*—silkw—listen to Aunt Leslie she knows of what she speaks. *Silk*worrrmmsss..." Jacques lurches. "...*silk*worrmss..." Jack grabs his armpit and holds him back. "...silkworms are what—you know how you walk into some people's homes and you just *feel* there's something missing? A......aaaaaaa*warmth*, a sense of....*life*? Well I certainly think that—especially for those of us who cultivate large fields of mulberry leaves right out our back door— I mean—just close your eyes a minute and think what ohhhh, I dunno, sayyy, let's just pick a round figure—two, two and a half million silkworms'd do for this place. And you could give them each names from the Bible, like—wellll, let'sss seee-eee...the sins are already spoken forrr...what about the plagues—there were how many of them were there?—and then when you ran outa plagues you could do the reindeer—you know, Dasher, Dancer—well that's not really Bible-Bible but it's related enough for our purposes and then—who was it had all those wives? you could do wives—I think if you put your mind to it—yes! and the tribes of Israel—God there were a good number of them, right?—I think if you put your mind to it you could come up with two and a half million names easy and then all you'd need to d "

"Here's what you're going to do and when you're going to do it:" Leslie realizes that this is the first time she's heard Jacques's voice—the first time since she and Patrick arrived that Jacques has used his mouth for anything other than—or in addition to—chewing on an unlit cigarette. His accent is so thick, Leslie thinks he's kidding. He sounds like one of those comedians who—usually while playing a drunk—string together a bunch of nonsense syllables peppered every quasi-sentence or two with a real word so it kinda sounds like they're kinda gettin at something and you're towed along in their relative syntax only to suddenly lose a train of thought you never actually had in the first place.

"Pardon me?" Leslie says politely, casting a glance at Sun Blyster. Jack whispers something in Jacques's ear. Jacques takes a hand out of a pocket, pulls the unlit cigarette from his mouth, stuffs the hand, and the cigarette, back in his pocket. "My hero," Leslie warbles to Jack, easing away from Patrick's grasp. From the corner of her eye she sees Blyster slowly approaching.

"Here's what you're going to do and when you're going to do it: on June twenty-six you run your route as usual."

"Can't. In the States."

"Your trip's been canceled."

"The fuck it has!"

"The fuck it has."

"By who?"

"By us."

"It's Been Planned For A Year Danney's Been Announcing It For A Y "

"On June twenty-six you run your route as usual."

"............................................................................................Yeah?"

"That's it."

"Yeah?"

"That's it."

"Tell me something, Jacques. You uhh, you fly in from Paris for this little Class Trip?"
Jacques doesn't answer. Leslie is on the verge of suggesting that holding this conversation in French would be less punishing for the both of them but doesn't want to lose the only trace of home-team advantage she seems to have here. "Sorry," she continues, nodding to Sun Blyster who has just joined them, "it must be my English. Lemme put it tyuh this way, Jacques: You uhh, you fly in from Paris for this little Class Trip?" Jack begins to grumble something. Leslie hops over a couple feet and speaks in a Jack-imitation to the spot where she was just standing. "My Lord, Leslie, Mister Dupuy here is not necessarily the type of gay v—of gentleman" She looks at Jacques—looks back at the spot— "with whom being a smart-ass is necessarily going to get you anywhere. You know very well he came in from Paris." hops back to her original place and kicks into a "YES!" Basil Rathbone. Shooting an index finger up in front of her nose she exclaims "But do I know very well the number of kilometers from Paris to Singapore? HAH! NO! That is ONE QUESTION the answer to which I do not know v "

"T-ten th-thousand s-sevenhundredforty.....th-three. Actually. M-Ms. Brittain."

"AH-NOTHER COLONY HEARD FROM! *Thank* You, *Misss*-ter *Tru*-cock! Good work! Good work! Which means that Mister Trucock and I have traveled ten thousand s" She turns to Patrick.

"s-sevenhundredforty th-three. Actu "

"kilometers for the scoop of my lifetime—literally—which consists uhuhuhvv" She counts on her fingers, mouthing "ON JUNE TWENTY-SIX YOU RUN YOUR ROUTE AS USUAL", then counts and mouths once more to be sure before announcing "nine words! Ten if you count twenty-six as two words but I count it as one, given the hyphen and all, which comes out to how many kay ems per word, Mr. Trucock?" Though addressing Patrick, she's glaring into Jack's face.

"One thou "

"On the basis of nine, of course." She looks around the space and waves her hands at the cages like a game-show host asking for applause. "Everybody OK with that? Basis of nine? Basis of nine," she tells Patrick.

"O-one th-thousand one hundred ninety-three p-point s-sixty-six kilometers kilometers per word," he says to the belly of a silkworm, seeming straighter and taller than he did a couple minutes ago. "Actually."

"Thank you. Now, we could of course take this precept to the next higher level by basing our calculations on the fact that Mr. Trucock and I *both* in fact traveled ten thousannnnn—whatever—kilometers—in the same aircraft," She stares at Sun Blyster "but in different bodies...." —stares at her again, for several seconds longer, "....bringing our kilometer variable up to uhhh-hhhh....." tries to get Patrick's attention but he looks like he did when he was doing movie-theater calculations back at the Place de Clichy, only with silkworms. Pacing with her hands behind her back like an old-world philosopher, she makes a sudden stop in front of one of her pals whenever she comes to a particularly important point in her discourse. ".....all the while retaining the same amount of words as the formulitic base, unless of course your persp "

"When Mr. Dupuy initially contacted me through my representative, Mr. Kote, on behalf of Mr. Tronchet,"

Sun Blyster's unmistakable harp-string voice sounds deeper and harsher than Leslie remembers from the airplane—like a Victorian headmistress who's taken singing lessons.

"the discussions centered themselves upon a document whose possession has been of interest to me."

She pauses after each clause, waiting for her guests and especially Leslie to grow a bit more impatient before she continues.

"I was informed of the arrangements that were to be made"

Her vowels are old vowels, which have had centuries of superior wisdom and authority to mold themselves to the dimensions of her powerful mouth.

"in order for this document to come into my hands."

Leslie is spellbound and smells patchouli, wonders if her wetness will stain her skirt when she sits.

"That you, Ms. Brittain, were to be involved in those arrangements,"

Brilliant move, the airplane, Leslie thinks. ("Wonder whose i—hadda be Sun Blyster's—Jack's not that smart.")

"and that you happened, as well, to be an acquaintance of Mr. Kote's,"

("Was pure coincidence, I kn ")

"was a fortunate coincidence of which I felt it behooved us to take full advantage."

("Hi, Sun! Remember me?")

"I have sought to receive you in person in order to express my gratitude for your willing cooperation thus far,"

Leslie becomes aware of the sound of the silkworms again, of the heavy heat, she reaches for Patrick's hand, his very alert response surprises her, Jack is looking at him,

"and to emphasize the wisdom of your seeing to it that that cooperation continues,"

seeming to say something to him with his eyes.

"given the crucial theme of the document in question."

("Salvation") "Salvation?"

"Opium."

"Same th " Leslie suddenly realizes what she just heard. "OPIUM?"

Sun Blyster steps back from her little audience and begins strolling through the ch-ch-ch. The others follow. "You are correct, Ms. Brittain," she says as they file in the weak light past and under the cages. "It *is* the same thing. You see, encoded in the divinely inspired message which Eustache of Chartres brought from China to Pope Alexander the Third—and which the Pope in turn transcribed onto the back of the miniature floorplan of Notre Dame, to be buried under it's first stone—was a formula. For making an opium-like substance from the secretions of the silkworm. Opium-like, but infinitely more potent. And infinitely more...infinite. For the substance can be made from the substance itself—like the very worm which regenerates when cut in two."

"Like yogurt!"

"Seal it, Leslie," Jack says under his breath.

"Like yogurt," Sun Blyster confirms graciously. Leslie beams smugly at Jack. "To obtain the equivalent of one worm's potential output, you would need fields of poppies. Continents of fields of poppies."

"And Judy'd need a stuntperson to do all that sleeping."

"And that would be insufficient still. The Pope did not know this of course."
"Of course," Leslie mimics as she peers into a cage and waves to a worm. "Hey if this shit's so potent why haven't we seen Chinese guys walkin around with gold chains dripping from their necks for the past half-millennium and their shirts open to the waist riding around in big pink rickshas with fins?"
"The formula belonged to the Emperor. The young lady who took it upon herself to make a gift of it to Eustache "
"forgot to photocopy it before makin the drop well then why didn't Eustache cash in frchrissakes it *hadda* be bettern God-biz! why was everyone so hot to give this thing away, whadit have, plague germs all over it?"
"Eustache had learned much during his sojourn in the Orient. Especially the relatively insignificant place of Christianity in an otherwise very non-Christian world. He knew he could never share this blasphemous discovery with the Pope. And yet it fascinated him. The formula was thought to be a sacred gift offered to the Emperor

by a magician whose body took the form of a "

"Oh my God don't tell me."

" goldfish. The grand plans for Notre Dame de Paris called for the incorporation of the symbols of virtue and vice into the Cathedral's architectural details. The alchemists of the day saw in these same gargoyles and medallions the symbols of alchemic transmutation, centered of course on the four elements: Earth, Water, Air and Fire, and the two natures: Female and Male. By giving Alexander the formula for a very eastern form of euphoria—opium—disguised in a message about a very Western form of euphoria—salvation—so that he may bury it under an edifice which was to stand in glory to the ideals of theologian and alchemist, scientist and magician, Eustache was...cashing in, as you say, Ms. Brittain, as far as he was concerned. He was, in his way, sharing his discovery with the Pope."

"You can call me Leslie how dyou know all this?"

"Eustache kept a diary, Ms. Brittain."

"You can call me Leslie how dyou know what it says?"

"I own the diary, Ms. Brittain."

"You can call me Leslie all this shit's in there?"

"And most of the formula, Ms. Brittain."

Nowhere near the end of the first wall yet, they all continue strolling slowly and silently behind Sun Blyster—almost ceremoniously, as in a wedding, or funeral, procession—with Leslie giving Patrick a nudge whenever he stops to focus on an eyeball, or a drop of moisture in the middle of a mulberry leaf. "Pick It Up, Mr. Dupuy!" Sun Blyster suddenly orders, never having turned to see Jacques's saliva-sopped cigarette hit the floor. As the entourage approaches the corner, Leslie jogs back a couple yards to pry Patrick from alchemic communion with a silkworm.
"So Much For Silk Army-Uniforms, Huh, Jack?" she shouts up ahead, Patrick's sleeve trapped in her fist.

"My Lord, Leslie, one deal has nothing to do with the other!"

"Multi-purpose fauna ("or is it flora?—I always get those two confused")—maybe our girls n boys in the trenches can run a contest—top bunk to whoever's lucky enough to be wearin it and smokin it from the same critter. Just how much is *most* of the formula? why don't you just wing the rest? figure it out? make it up as you go along?"

"If we could do that, Ms. Brittain, we wouldn't have to blow up Notre Dame. Would we?" Sun Blyster is standing in her Wonder Woman pose again, her eyes fixed onto Leslie's.

"Oh. Well anyway you're not actually gonna blow up actual Notre Dame anyway." Leslie has struck the same stance in front of Sun Blyster. Their faces are inches apart. "SO—" She puts her arm around Patrick's shoulder. "what do you want us to do?"

"Mr. Dupuy has already informed you of your responsibility, Ms. Brittain."

"Yeah but I mean about the walkperson and the detonation device and then the bomb goes off and everyone runs for cover and Claude rushes in where angels fear to do gymnastics and you get your shit and by that time I'm already at the place de la Concorde I mean the Marcel plan you know what I mean I mean the "

"Mr. Tronchet and his plan have outlived their usefulness, Ms. Brittain. While Mr. Tronchet has been busy amusing himself with his little tattooed gymnasts and his railroad schedules, Mssrs. Dupuy and Batiste, Mr. Kote and myself "

"Thierry!" Leslie says, more as a breath than a word.

" have been preparing for the explosion under the Cathedral's altar which will afford us direct access to the ancient, buried crypt—where the document really is, not, as Jehan de Chelles's writings would have one believe, in the series of tunnels leading out to the Quai des Orfèvres. Notre Dame was constructed according to the human form. As with the genitals, the altar is the point toward which all converges. And the point from which all flows. Radiates. It is the most sacred site of the Temple. The point of contact with God."

"Don't tell me—you have de Chelles's diary too."

"The entry about moving the document from under the stone into the tunnel was written in a different hand. Radiometric tests confirmed it as dating after de Chelles's death. It was obviously added by an individual who intended to deter treasure-hunting rivals."

"Why the f—why didn't you start this years ago?"

"Good girl, Leslie," Jack says.

"Like I said, why the fuck didn't you start this years ago?"

"We did. My grandfather wanted the document of course, albeit for a different reason—he had purely his collection in mind. But he refused to be involved in any endeavour which would cause even the most minor damage to the Cathedral. The day of his death I arranged for the magazine interview which Mr. Tronchet read. And then I w "

"Helped you deal with your deep sense of loss."

"And then I waited. No realization of such a plan would be possible without frequent visits to the Cathedral, during hours and to sections outside the realm of public access. For such visits, the support and indeed collaboration of the police was a sine qua non. Mr. Tronchet's profound interest in Notre Dame was well known to individuals of like mind. The virtual free reign he enjoys in the use of law-enforcement resources was well known to myself."

"How did you know he'd contact you when he did?"

"I didn't."

"Well what if he w "

"He would have. I would have continued to wait. I am a young woman, Ms. Brittain. He would have." Sun Blyster turns and faces the wall. Without her seeming to have done anything to cause it to move, an entire section of cages swings outward, like a door on a hinge, creating an opening through which the helicopter is visible, its propellers just beginning to twirl.
  "CHAN! Gee I hope he wasn't bored. Maybe he hovered around the neighborhood for awhile, had a chance to smoke his suit. Although he coulda stayed and finished out the pack—we haven't even gotten to the part about saving my life yet, or anything!

*"I am sorry to disappoint you, Ms. Brittain. Your life was never in danger.* Sun Blyster is speaking in calligraphy strokes again, as she did on the plane. *We wanted you to be as...willing...as possible to accompany Mr. Kote on his visit to me today. And now we want you to be as willing as possible to leave. And to proceed with the daily details of your life as if none of this ever happened. When you peruse the newspaper on the twenty-sixth of June, you say tsk-tsk with the rest of the world. And then you put it out with the trash."*

"The world or the paper?"

*"Or your life will be in danger. Look at them,"* she hums, sweeping her hand out toward the infinite cages. *So eager to get to work.*

"Well that's sure a relief!"

*"Ms. Brittain?"*

"Well now I can go visit Danney after all. Seems like you guys have the Western-Civilization-Monuments-Destruction and Historical-Documents-Theft Departments all under control. Last thing you need is me hangin around pulling on the bottom oyour aprons telling you I gotta go potty."

The Victorian headmistress erases the calligraphy from the blackboard. "Your presence in Paris, until I have accomplished my objective, is something with which I would feel most comfortable, Ms. Brittain."

"And anyway. You'll have Patrick!" Leslie continues cheerily as Patrick, who has been focusing square at her, turns his head away. "He's better company than I am any day! And anyway y "

"Your name will be removed from the Foreign Ministry list as soon as our workday comes to an end," Jack says. "You'll be able to leave France again, no problem, after that." He takes Leslie's passport from his inside jacketpocket and hands it to her.

"Would that be a Pleistocenian or a Biblical day, Jack?"

"I won't be going back with you. I'll call yMy Lord, Leslie, What Are You Doing?" She doesn't answer, keeps on doing it. "Leslie wh "

"Boy are you dumb, Jack! Where you been for the past sixty Easters, huh?" Jack stares at her blankly as she continues to click her heels together. "Well if you don't get it you don't deserve to be told! Cmawn Patrick!" She starts walking to the chopper then looks back for Patrick. Standing between the two men, he seems very tall and much older. "Patrick Let's Go Frchrissakes It's Gonna Change T Black N White Any Second Now!"

Patrick doesn't budge. "Good-bye, Leslie," he says in a deep, confident voice.

# XIX

# THE WAISTBAND OF MARTIN'S UNDERSHORTS

*BeeeeeeeeeeP****BeeeeeeeeeeP****

"Hey Batgirl! What kinda fecal-matter message did you just leave on my machine? You're joking, right? Hah hah! Knee-Slapper City, Michigan? What kinda emergency meeting in Ukraine? Ukraine, Ikraine, we all kraine, ain't no mericans livin in Yookraine, what're ydoin, PR for the Red Army? stick with the LA Rams, girl! I'll see yon the twenty-sixth tdo the show! Nothin more important than Doubly-Great-Brittains-On-The-Ray-Dee-Oh!"*BeeeeeeeeeeP****BeeeeeeeeeeP****

"Leslie! Where ARE you?! This is the fifth message I've left! Have you been kidnapped? No! Worse! Have you run off and gotten MARRIED? Don't do this to me, Leslie! If I find out you've been there having sex and ordering in pizza with some...some.....airline pilot....listening to this the whole time I'll come over and cut the balls off both of you! You might've tried to call here I was—I've been—I might've been asleep. Leslie why didn't you tell me you were going on vacation I coulda come use your apartment with—did I tell you he's leaving Geneva for good—moving to JaKARta?—well, he's actually n—with his WIFE of all people?—well, he's not actually here at the present time.....but if I'd've known you were going away maybe I could've—although he'd probably wanna do it in that hotel on the Rue des Beaux-Arts, you know?—or the—next time you go away would you please let me " *BeeeeeeeeeeP****BeeeeeeeeeeP****

"Hello, Ms. Brittain? This is Sylvia? The Ambassador's secretary? We were wondering if maybe you might've it might've slipped your mind to get the guest list to us? Could you give me a call? Tha—as soon as you get this? Thanks."*BeeeeeeeeeeP****BeeeeeeeeeeP****

"LESLIE! IT FEELS LIKE IT'S BEEN WEEKS! I THOUGHT MAYBE YOU'D BE BACK BY N—WHY DID YOU LEAVE THE MESSAGE WITH JEAN-MARC, I WAS HERE ALL THE TIME. I HOPE IT WENT WELL. YOU NEVER MENTIONED A JOB IN VENEZUELA. I TOOK THE CALENDAR HOME WITH ME. IT'S ON MY KITCHEN WALL. LESLIE I MI—I'LL CALL AGAIN."*BeeeeeeeeeeP** **BeeeeeeeeeeP****

"LESLIE!...............I MISS YOU." *BeeeeeeeeeeP****BeeeeeeeeeeP****

"I'M TRYING TO REACH A MISS LESLIE MARSHA BRITTAIN. I'M WITH THE ORGANIZATION OF AMERICAN WIVES OF " *BeeeeeeeeeeP****BeeeeeeeeeeP****

"BONJOUR, PRINCESSE! I'M BACK FROM NICE—I'M SURE YOU TRIED TO GET ME THERE BUT I WASN'T IN THE ROOM MUCH. WELL I'VE DONE MY THINKING. I KNOW IT'S BORING FOR YOU WHEN WE DON'T SEE EACH OTHER. AND YOU MISS ME. BUT I NEEDED THE TIME. DO YOU THINK YOU CAN UNDERSTAND THAT? WELL ANYWAY, I'VE FINALLY DECIDED WHAT I HAVE TO DO—WHAT'S BEST FOR THE BOTH OF US. IN THE LONG RUN, I MEAN. WE HAVE TO THINK OF THE LONG RUN IF WE WANT TO GET THROUGH THIS THING. DO YOU THINK YOU CAN UNDERSTAND THAT? THE ONLY SOLUTION THAT MAKES SENSE IS THAT WE START SEEING EACH OTHER AGAIN. I'LL BE AT THE DEUX MAGOTS NEXT MONDAY NIGHT AT EIGHT. SEE YOU TH—UNLESS NATHALIE HAS AEROBICS—I ALWAYS FORGET WHICH NIGHT—AND THEN IF I'M NOT THERE I'LL BE THERE THE NEXT NIGHT. A BIENTÔT, PRINCESSE!" *BeeeeeeeeeeP****BeeeeeeeeeeP****

"THIS IS FOR LESLIE BRISTOL." *BeeeeeeeeeeP****BeeeeeeeeeeP****

"I FIGURED IT OUT! IT'S A CODED MESSAGE! YOUR KIDNAPPERS GAVE YOU ONE CALL! AND YOU KNEW IT HAD TO BE ME! BECAUSE IT'S JUST YOU AND ME KID! BECAUSE I'M THE ONLY ONE ON EARTH WHO'D VERSTEH THE HIDDEN MEANING! UKRAINE. UKRAIAIAINE........YYOOO-OOO-KRAIAIAINNNNNE....I'LL GET BACK TYA ON THAT ONE. SEE YAT THE AIRPORT!" *BeeeeeeeeeeP****BeeeeeeeeeeP****

"MRS. BRITTAIN, YOU DON'T KNOW ME. I HEARD YOU SPEAK LAST MARCH AT THE AM " *BeeeeeeeeeeP****BeeeeeeeeeeP****

"Leslie, dear. Your message says to leave my name. I don't have to leave my name. I'm your mother. Mothers don't have to identify themselves. If you don't want to call me back after all the messages I've left in the last two days, that's your prerogative. I know you're alive because the man on television said the woman killed in the supermarket wasn't you. And besides, you don't go to supermarkets. You don't buy food. You don't eat. But—you're a big girl now. And you're not exactly across the street. If you don't want to call me back, that's your choice. Just remember, when I'm " *BeeeeeeeeeeP****BeeeeeeeeeeP****

"*Leslie!* " *BeeeeeeeeeeP****BeeeeeeeeeeP****

"Hel " *BeeeeeeeeeeP****BeeeeeeeeeeP****

"Leslie? Martin! I'm calling all my friends who don't have televisions—all one of them—to tell them they've hit A*nother* supermarket—second in a week! Way To Go! See, supermarkets are much more challenging than rock concerts or bus terminals bec "

"YYES!" Leslie shrieks triumphantly as she slams her finger down to stop the tape. "YA-HOO! YAHOO-YAHOO-YAHOO!" She runs into the kitchenette, "YA-HOO!" where Mrs. Darotto is fishing "YA-HOO!" in the wastebasket, "YA-HOO!" throws her arms around the woman's neck and kisses the "YA-HOO!" back of her head. "Brrill-lliantt brrill-lliantt idea!" She kisses her again. Mrs. D. straightens and holds her catch up to the light of the little window.

"Listen what kinda idea, I didn't have no idea, whatryuh throwin away such a lovely suit for? This musta cost ya fortune wheredyuh get it? I ever see this before?"

Leslie pries the outfit from the woman's hands, stuffing it back into the trash, "No. And *I* never wanna see it *again*. And don't get any i—your girlfriends' daughters don't wanna see it either." then sprints to the phone and stabs at the auto-dial. "It has a curse on it. Whoever wears it is tied to a chair and forced to listen to—at close range—to a recorded message from the president of every Women's Auxiliary in thDAMN!" The receiver crashes down.

Mrs. Darotto once again lifts the jacket from the wastebasket. Leslie pounds on the redial button. "Listen horoscope didn't say nothin about a curse today.......isn't this the same kinda st "

"SH!"

"You have reached the world-renowned, luxuriously and expensively appointed showcase residence of Martin Finger, the envy of art collectors from Argentina to Zimbabwe, the antiquaire's dream. I can't come to the phone right now. In fact, I'm away from my burglar-alarmless penthouse—which was recently featured in Privileged Few—for several months to oversee the packing of the pharaonic artifacts I have just purchased from an excavation site in Luxor. The solid-gold front door is unlocked and all the valuables are laid out on the desk at which Robespierre sat when he plotted the Revolution. Please leave a note on your way out or, better yet, a message when you hear the beep. Oh—and by the way—there are cardboard tubes for the paintings in the lower drawer of the Oriental precious-stone-inlaid armoire, next to the Rodin statue, in the valet's wing." .BEEEEEEEEP.

"MARTIN GODDAMN IT PICK UP THIS PHONE I KNOW YOU'RE THERE IT WAS JUST FUCKING BUSY FOUR SECONDS AGO MARTIN CUMAWWWWWWNNNNN FRCHRISSAKES PUT IT BACK IN YOUR PANTS JUST THIS ONCE PUHLEAEAZZZE MARTIII-III-IIIN AND PICK UP THE— IT'LL STILL BE THERE WHEN WE'RE FI*Mar*tin! Hi! Got your— hey want me to wait til you go get some kleenex?"

"No it's OK—the dog's right here."

"Ooooh Martin you're re*vol*ting!"

"How's trix?"

"Got your message I'm dying to see you I need you desperately I can't live without you I think about you all the time I gotta see you uhhhhh—uhhh—Look—remember where we were that time when I talked you outa getting married to that flooze?"

"Yeah, the "

"DON'TSayIt! I know. You know. That's good enough for us, huh, Martin? And you remember what day of the week it was?"

"No."

"Oh. Uhhhhmmmmm"

"Leslie are you in some kind of trouble—I mean—more than usual?"

"Trouble? What gi—well frchriss for heaven's sake no, Martin, I just—ummmmmm—OK!—OK!—I've got it—Oh-oh Goh-ohd when they were giving out brains—remember what you told me your favorite TV program was as a kidDON'T Say It Out Loud!"

"Yeah. Excuse me one second while I occupy myself with not saying it out loud."

"Good. Good. Moving right along here. Well, on the day of the week that the main character's name reminds you of DON'T Say It Out Loud at ummmmm—God—whattime whattime.....at ummm—OK!—the time you shaved this morning."

"How the fuck do y "

"Deal with me with this, willyuh, Martin?"

"You *are* in trouble, aren't you?"

"If anyone stops you in the middle of the street or leans over to you at a cafe or breaks into your apartment at night and one guy holds you down while the other injects truth serum into your arm—the one not otherwise occupied "

"Get stuffed, Leslie."

"Don't you wish. —no matter what you do—no matter WHATTT YOUOUOU DOOO—DO NOT—repeat: DOO-OOO NOH-OHTTTTT—tell them what your favorite program was as a kid, what time you shaved today and where I talked you out of marrying that sleezoid."

"Well geez, Leslie, that doesn't leave me with much conversational leeway, does it?"

"Get stuffed, Martin."

"Don't you wish."

"Will you do this for me, Martin?"

"I gotta get to the office."

"MARTIN will you "

"I'll be carrying a copy of War and Peace so you'll recognize me."

"You're the best."

"Don't we collectively wish."

"Listen isn't this the same stuff that black dress was outa?" Leslie socks the receiver onto its cradle and plunges into the utility closet near the entranceway. "Well?" Mrs. D. follows close behind, the off-white silk suit dangling delicately from her fingertips. While the woman alternates between rubbing the fabric with her elbow—as in testing the water for baby's bath—and stroking it against her cheek—as in expressing affection for your stuffed animal (not the one with Jacques's eyes)—Leslie burrows deeper, vandalizing her way through the storage space, overturning everything in her line of attack, finally emerging with "Isn't it?" the yellow pages and

"WHAT! ISN'T IT WHGIMMETHAT!" rushing the suit back to the excavation site in the kitchenette before diving with the phonebook onto the bed.

"The stuff—isn't it the same as that black dress that was delivered?"

Her index finger turning blacker as she draws it down and across each successive page, Leslie frantically rips and flips through the "HAH! AHAH! A! HAH! AHAH! I knew it! Iiiiiiii knewww ittt! IknewitIknewitIknewIT!!" listings. "I Kn "

"Only difference is the color."

"WHATT Are You Still Doing Here don't you guys gotta go get parsley or something? I gotta go take a shower nget outa here!"

"Listen ydidn't give it to me yet...."

Leslie heads from the bedroom-alcove to the bathroom.

"....my present."

Leslie heads from the bathroom to the bedroom-alcove. "Oh-ho—your present! Of course! Your present. How stupid of mWHATT Present?"

"The one ytold me about. When you called. To tell me about the emergency meeting. You said you'd—don't yremember? you said..........................you know?" Mrs. Darotto squints into Leslie's face. "Listen you don't *look* like someone who's just been in Hawaii."

"The tan faded on the daily commute to Venezuela—*what* hal*lu*cinogen" Leslie bangs her fist against her thigh. "were these jokers on? if they ever drop outa silkworms they can write for the Haight-Ashbury Tribune. Look, I haven't even gotten my non-bags non-unpa—look—here." She opens her top dresser-drawer. "Sorry it's not wrapped—that's uhhh—that's the way they do it in—it's bad luck in Ve—in Hawaii to wrap presents—you know, evil eye and all that. There! You like it?...................Whatsamatter frchrissakes?"

Mrs. Darotto is grinning and nodding. Gurgling a quasi-chant in Italian and nodding. Nodding, rambling on, holding her present up to the heavens like Kunta Kinte's father, bringing it back down and pressing it against her breast. Nodding.

"Hey I gotta *real real* lotta work to do here, sports fans," Leslie says, locking her arm around the woman's shoulders and inching her mass toward the entrance. "Emergency meetings held simultaneously in Latin America and the Pacific atoll'll do that to yevery time, yknow? Gladjya like it. OK? Fine!" She pushes her out the door.

Through a little window in the corridor, Mrs. D. peers down into her geranium-rich courtyard. "Listen isn't this about the time that young man oyours should be gettin here?"

"I Bet If You Guys Hurry," Leslie shouts, giving the power-of-suggestive illusion that Mrs. Darotto is walking away, "There'll Still Be Some OThat Parsley Left They Decorate The Poultry Display With." She closes the door to within a sliver.

"Pisces."

"WHAT!"

Mrs. D. nods.

"This Is As Open As It's Gonna Get!"

"Horoscope said today was a special day fr Pisces."

Leslie makes the sliver disappear, "YOU'RE NOT A" turns the

bolt "PISCES!" and rushes back to her phonebook.

"Coral and pearl," Mrs. D. confirms to herself in Italian, rolling her present lightly between her fingers and nodding on the way to the staircase. "Comes from the sea."

"**Chick Corea, Miroslav Vitous and Roy Haynes,** *live* **trio-music,** *Live* **In Europe—good good stuff, the title of this track is something tha-tuhh escapes me at the moment cause I forgot to write it down, heh-heh. Cloudy outside. Still drizzling. Something like sixty degrees outside—frgotta check—as usual. I'll have the en-***tirety***—theee** *ennn* **tirety—of your accurate local weathercast in a sec or two just after thisssss.....DVQ.....**" At "**six-thirty.....**" on the following Monday "**in yrmorning.**" Leslie runs past police headquarters as always, hoping, as she has since she got back two days ago, that Roque doesn't see her and that Jacques and the others certainly do ("Hi, Jacques! Guess who? It's me! Here I am! Yup! Yrol pal from the ol country, huh Jacques! Just you n me, kid, right, Jacques? Yyyuppers!"). While she spent all weekend promising Roque that once she finishes the report on the Venezuela job she'll start running again, and he'll be the first person with whom she'll have a hysterical hello-scene at their favorite antique fountain, she's been relentlessly vigilant, for the sake of Jacques and the boys, t—and girls—to give at least the appearance of leading the kind of business-as-usual post-Singapore life she'd be in fact leading if she had any sense—or fear—or both.

She knows the call to Martin was a risk, and this meeting. But they'll never figure it out in a million years—and besides, if the guys come in the middle of the night with the truth serum she knows Martin'll have enough brains, once he closes up his pajamas, to tell them his favorite program was something with Tuesday Weld. Or Robinson Crusoe's administrative assistant. And besides, right at this very second she's where she's supposed to be when she's supposed to be there so that should be good enough for everyone. ("Shouldn't it? And ") besides........

........just out of direct eye-range of the police station, veering to the right onto the Pont Neuf, she pretends to trip and fall, allowing the Walkman to go flying from her hand and crash to the ground in the path of an on-coming petrol truck, the only sign of life in sight. She limps over, retrieves the mangled machine and throws it into the Seine—Notre Dame side—dangling it first by the little circuit-board which was squeezed out under the huge tires.

With it all, she hits the avenue de l'Opéra only a minute and forty-one seconds off. She does not cross it or run up the middle as she would on other mornings. Staying on the right-hand sidewalk, she turns, several side-streets up, into the Rue des Petits-Champs, en route to the sweeping noble breadth of the circular Place des Victoires, half a mile ahead. At this favored private hour, with forty-five minutes left to run, she can amuse herself doing laps along its large ring of pavement which strings together, like flowers on a garland, the handsome facades of the designer boutiques.

The Rue des Petits-Champs becomes the Rue La Feuillade just before it arrives at the *place*, one of six byways of varying widths which pierce the protective pavement-ring and blend beyond it into a broad hoop of street with a raised concrete circlet at its core. Here, wreathed by a fence of pointed iron posts, a bronze Louis XIV rides his bronze warhorse atop a white granite block engraved in front with Latin praises and inset with matching metal battle scenes on its sides.

The blind men and the elephant. The point at which you first-ever penetrate the Place des Victoires, that artery tip among the six on which you choose to enter its heart, determines forever your relationship with it, the reference to it in your mind. The color of the first flash of awning or facade becomes the color you see when someone years later asks "Have you ever been to the Place des Victoires?" The order in which the buildings define themselves as you finally finely focus from the border of the breathtaking expanse will ever govern your gait when you walk before them. This is a solid space, where the bankers from the Crédit du Nord and the Crédit Industriel et Commercial tolerate their leather-plated mannequin neighbors living in Thierry Mugler's window. This is a fluid space, where the flower-splash jackets hanging from Kenzo's puppet-string display seem to flutter slightly when the bankers file by.

Leslie starts around left from the Rue La Feuillade—Martin will be able to see her from wherever he enters—counts her steps—glad they hadn't been standing in the check-out line at Monoprix when she told him not to marry that rodent ("When they were giving out brains.....")—checks her pace—Crédit Industriel et Commercial-

Stéphane Kélian-HOM-Thierry Mugler-Victoire—Rue Vide Gousset—Blanc Bleu-Plein Sud-Enrico Coveri—Rue d'Aboukir—Esprit—Rue Etienne Marcel—Crédit du Nord-Chevignon Girl!-beautiful heavy dark wooden door-Cacherel-Kenzo-door-Laurent Mercadal—Rue Croix des Petits-Champs—Louis XIV Spécialités Lyonnaises-door-Mikihouse—Rue Catinat—Hugo Boss-door-door, each more beautiful, more heavy, more dark wooden than the last-Aridza Bross—Rue La Feuillade—she thinks of Patrick—HOM—rue Vide Gousset—misses Patrick—Rue d'Aboukir—Rue Etienne Marcel—the little shit—Cacherel-Kenzo—Rue Croix des Petits-Champs—door-Rue Catinat—has to ask Danney to replace the tape, it's probably washed up on the shores of Atlantic City by now—Rue La Feuillade—360 steps—Rue Vide Gousset—three steps a second—Rue d'Aboukir—two minutes around—Rue Etienne Marcel—Cacherel-Kenzo—Rue Croix des Petit-Champs—door—Rue Catinat—Rue La Feuillade—Rue Vide Gousset—Esprit—two minutes around—Rue d'Aboukir—Rue Etienne Marcel—Rue Croix des Petits-Champs—door—Rue Catinat—two minutes around two minutes around—Rue La Feuillade—Rue Vide Gousset—Rue d'Aboukir—Rue Etienne Marcel—Rue Croix des Petits-Champs—Rue Catinat—Rue La Feuillade—Rue Vide Gousset—Rue d'Aboukir—Rue Etienne Marcel—Rue Croix des Petits-Champs—Rue Catinat—Rue La Feuillade—Rue Vide Gousset—Rue d'Aboukir—Rue Etienne Marcel—Rue Croix des Petits-Champs—Rue Catinat—some people in the *place* now—Rue La Feuillade—Rue Vide Gousset—Rue d'Aboukir—cleaning ladies leaving their boutiques with buckets, bankers—Rue Etienne Marcel—Rue Croix des Petits-Champs—a couple cars—Rue Catinat—Rue La Feuillade- "Leslie!" -Rue Vide Gousset—d'Aboukir—Rue Etienne Marcel—Croix des Petits-Champs—Catinat—La Feuillade- "LESLIE" -Vide Gousset—d'Aboukir—Etienne Marcel—Crois des Petits-Champs—Catinat—Feuillade—Gousset—Aboukir—Marcel—Petits-Champs—Catinat—F—Gou—Ab—Etie—C—Ca—F- "LESSS-LIEEE!"

"Wait!" She looks at her watch, screams "Five More Times AroUND TEN MINUTES MARTIIIIIINNNNN" back over her shoulder, skims across the rue d'Aboukir..................................................................
..........................................................................."Four!" reaches out, flicks him on the stomach as she passes, trying for the brass ring. "It

Takes A Thief, huh? HUH? HUHUHUH? HUUH?!"......................

...................................................................................................

..............................................."AlexandER MUNDY," Martin affirms when she comes back around. "TAUGHT ME TO "...............

...................................................................................................

...................................."tape windows befORE YOU BREAK N ENTER EM. TWO MORE AND I'M ALL YOURS!"........................

...................................................................................................

.............................."DON'T YOU WISH!" Martin screams across the *place*, through Louis's horse's bronze legs.....................

...................................................................................................

...................................................................."How the fuck did you know ooh get away! don't touch me! you're all sweaty!"

"Oh yeah hhhh-hhhh I forgot hhhh-hhh you came in contact with your daily quotient of sweat this morning before the hhh-hhh guys got there with the truth serum hhh-hh-hh how the fuck did I know what?"

"What guys?"

Leslie starts walking around the sidewalk ring, in the opposite direction from her run. "How the fuck did I know *what*?"

Martin follows. "What guys?"

"I'll show you mine, Martin, if you show me yours. Did any suspicious stranger ask you anything suspicious since our phonecon? You know, other than the usual questions you get in the course of your given week, like Is that as hard as it gets?".

"No."

"No one wanted to know what your favorite TV program was or *anything*?"

"No."

"Shit! I'm insulted!"

Martin eyes follow a reedy Oriental woman in yellow leather shorts and a denim cowboy-jacket as she leaves one of the massive wooden doorways and slithers out of the *place*.

"How quickly they forget! I'm not even worthy of having my phone tapped any more! Ycan't depend on *any*one these days frchrissakes. And here I ruined a good walkperson for nothing. How the fuck did I know what?"

"What time I shaved last Saturday. When you called."

"Who knows what time you shave frchrissakes! I have no idea! HowmI supposed to know a thing like th*ouch!* Ooh!" Leslie flails into the shoulder of a passing policeman. *"Pardon!*—Hello, officer!— I just knew it hadda be after *I* got here.....I mean let's face it, Martin, by the time you get the videocassettes and magazines back into their brown wrappers, and change the sheets before the maid comes in to change the sheets, and burn your PJs it's gotta be half the morning's gotta be history."

"Can't we go sit down somewhere?"
"Walking's good for you. People who walk don't need as much sleep. Leaves you more time for "

"I'll buy ydon't you want a cup of tea, I'll buy ya c "

"Can't. Can't go anywhere we might be overheard."

"Will You Get Your Hands Off Me You're Dripping With Sweat!"
"You're not wearing a wire, are you?"

"What" He pushes her away and brushes at his suit. "kind of trouble you in, anyhow? Let's go sit in a cafe."
Leslie pouts as she opens her wrist-purse. "Not even worthy of being under electronic surveillance any more." She takes something out and zips the purse closed, not having removed it from her arm.
"Well." Martin clears his throat. "I might be wondering why you've called me all here today."
"Precisely, Martin. I uhhhhh..." Leslie clears her throat. "...well uhhh...uhhhmmm, welllluhh uhmmm....wellll, pshaw, Martin....." Her hands behind her back, she takes tiny, embarrassed, uneasy, shy-little-girl steps in place and when those calm down she keeps her hands where they are and her feet still and sways from side to side as if she's

singing a gospel song on stage with the entire cast as an encore except there's only her and when that runs out of steam she grabs Martin's arm and spurts along the sidewalk with him until they're well wedged into a gleamy green wooden doorway between the Rue Catinat and the Rue La Feuillade. Where she thrusts her open palm under his nose.

"Well, *Les*lie! How *nice* of you! Gee! Pshaw! You *shouldn*'t have! I'm glad you *did*! What *is* it?" Martin carefully extends his index finger and thumb as if about to pick up an atomic particle. From Leslie's hand he lifts a silver medallion about an inch in diameter, engraved with a Capricorn and the sign's dates, attached to a silver chain.

"Will you go steady with me, Martin?"

"Well gee, Leslie, I don't know. It's all so sudden," he swoons, the back of his wrist at his forehead like a character in a Sheridan play.

"Put it on."

Martin fumbles with the clasp. Leslie helps him. He fastens the chain around his neck, looks at the medallion's face and stuffs the whole business into his shirt. Gathering her hands tenderly into his, peering deep into her eyes, he exhales "Lheslhie!" in his best Cartlandian desperation.

"Yhes Mhart-hin!" She pushes up against him.

"hI'm nhot ha C-hapric-horn."

"Yeah but Jesus was, that's all that matters."

"And whadI do to deserve offerings from Jerusalem? Can we go sit down somewhere?"

"Nothing." She starts walking again, in the direction of her run. Martin doesn't move. After several steps she turns and says "Yet." and continues on her way.

"IIIYYYUHHH," he yells from the doorway, "THINK I'LLLUHHH BE GOING NOW, LESLIE! GOTTA GET TO THE ORIFICE!"

"YOU HAVE YOURSELF A NICE DAY, MARTIN, YHEAR?" she responds, waving above her head without breaking her gait or looking around.

"Awright awright awright awright." Seconds later he's hovering behind her right ear, trying to catch his breath. "Right after they dropped you on your head—while they were waiting for the team of experts to be flown in—what did you tell yourself you'd propose I do to deserve this?"

"They never dropped me on my head, Martin." Leslie is chatting sweetly on a stroll around the *place*. "Least not that I know of.....what a funny thought. Least not that I know of.....have to ask my mother next time she calls to tell me I wasn't killed in a bombing. Just to make sure, you never kn—I don't like the length of that skirt at all! Look—you like the length of that skirt? Wonder if that's what we're in for next Fall or if it's just Kenzo's way of "

"LESLIE!"

"Get-ar-res-ted," she says in a distracted monotone as she stoops to read a little framed price-list on the floor of the window case.

"Yeah, I agree. These hemlines don't do anything for me."

"Because I have to get a message to someone in the police department."

"I mean—they're nowhere."

"Headquarters, actually."

"They're not short."

"See, the back of your medallion slides away."

"They're not long."

"And there's a little space."

"They just..."

"I've put a note in."

"hang there."

"But DON'T try nbe clever and try nget the note out cause you'll never get it back in in a million years—the guy who made it for me—this guy in Chinatown I once heard of—does false passports and stuff like that—found him in the fucking phonebook of all things—he hadda—under Gift Shops of all things—he hadda have me write the note right there—in teeeeeny tiiiiiny little letters with this reaeaeaeaeal fine fine pen-point—looked like little insects by the time I was done—and put it in himself cause only he on the planet knows how to do it—and so if you start messin with it not only will you then have gotten arrested for nothing but the person I'm trying to get the message to—who'll let you go the instant he sees the note cause he'll get the drift—would never let you go if you didn't have the note cause then he'd think you just got arrested cause you're scum—not that you *are* scum, but that's what he'll think—and you'll wind up rotting with homosexual homocidal maniacal pimping dopefiends in the sub-basement of the Quai des Orfèvres for the rest of your life."

"Not sexy at all, if you ask me."

"The thing is, we have no time to lose so it's gotta unfortunately be today."

"And, frankly, what are hemlines for if not to be sexy?"

"I know Monday's your day for your chiropractor but she'll understand, one, and two, who knows—you might even be out in time for the appointment I mean you never know, you know?, I mean it's only eight o'clock in the morning frchrissakes."

"For that matter, what are skirts themselves for if not to be sexy?"

"Now, the guy you want to get to is called Tronchet. Marcel Tronchet. He's the Commissioner. Real important. Might not look it. But is."

"For that matter, what is anything for?"

"You just make sure you see him—alone—then you turn away from the camera in the cell—kinda hunch over like—yknow?—like you're tryin to light a cigarette in the wind, yknow?—slide open the back of the medallion, take out the note, give it to him and go home."

"Skirts,"

"It's as simple as that."

"blouses,"

"Now, the only thing left to do is figure out something to get you arrested for that merits being taken to HQ. I mean a parking ticket ain't gonna getyuh hauled into the Big House."

"sweaters,"

"Fifty tickets in a row would b—unpaid"

"shoes,"

"—but we don't have time for that."

"stockings,"

"Murder would, but then they'd probably keep ya little longer than we need you to be in there, and there'd be no *question* you'd miss your chiropractor appointment."

"garter belts,"

"Maybe even a couple of em."

"bras,"

"I thought of the perfect thing—"

"panties,"

"getting caught without your papers on you!"

"g-strings,"

"I go up to a cop, tell him I saw a suspicious character hangin out in front othe *Crédit Industriel et Commercial*, they come check your ID, you don't got it, and *voilà!*—you and Tronchet are as good as face-to-face."

"What makes you think all I have do is ask one of the ten gorillas pounding on my cranium if Maurice Tronchet wants to join me for tea, and they'll all drop their electric cattle-prods and ask me one lump or two?"

"Well! Welcome back from the haberdashery! Marcel."

"Martin. It's Martin."

"It's Marcel. Not Maurice. Marcel. Good question, Martin—I like a petty criminal who thinks. That's where this comes in." Leslie goes back into her wrist-purse, pulls out a small rectangular piece of cardboard "Here—put this in the waistband of your shorts." and hands it to Martin, who glances at it, then, about to throw it on the ground, suddenly realizes what he just saw and rushes it back up to his eyes.

"Tuli—The Flower—Monte C—July ninet—Lehhhhslieeee!"

"Now obviously we can't put it in your wallet cause they'll take all that shit from you when they run you in. But I don't think they'll have any reason to take your shorts off. At least not right away."

"Good God How Did You *Get* This?"

"Yknow, I knew all those *charlottes au chocolat* would come in handy some day—" She flicks his gut with her knuckles, "shoulda actually ordered you a few extra helpings at the Franklin lunch." then pulls at his waistband to see how far it gives. "Hope the thing stays in.....the ticket, I'm talking about."
"Did you take out insurance on this? Leslie! People would kill for a ticket to this fight!"
"Ringside," she gloats, posting a prefabricated plastic smile and holding out her hand.
Martin scans the ticket again, mouthing the seat number. "People would do any—Aristotle Onassis couldn't buy a ticket to this fight—people would do anything for a ticket to this fight do you rea "
"Even put the cattle prods down and go fetch the nice Commissioner?" She flutters her upturned fingers in front of Martin's face. "And leave you guys alone for a couple minutes?" Flutters them again. "Cmawn."
"Cumawn wha-huht?" Holding it under his nose with both hands,

Martin is reading the ticket as if it has the entire text of Lolita printed on the front. "Tulipe Bokaffe I cannot bel—Monte fucking Carlo what do you *want*, Leslie?"

"Givituhme I'm gonna help you put it in your pants.....come to think of it maybe that's been your trouble all along, Martin, it's supposed to be the other way around, isn't it?" Leslie grabs at the ticket. Martin snatches it away behind his back. Leslie grabs behind his back. Martin pushes it high above his head. Leslie grabs. Martin snatches. Leslie grabs. Martin snatches. You're *not* getting my peanut butter sandwich. Am too. Are not. Am too. Are not finally the ticket flies from Martin's hand Leslie swoops to pick it up Martin slams his foot down on it Leslie kicks Martin in the shin Martin grabs his leg up to his chest. "GOD DAMNITLESLIE I'M NOT GETTING GODDAMN ARRESTED SO GIVE IT A REST OK?" Leslie seizes the ticket. "I LIKE IT MARTIN I LIKE IT A REAL LOT GODDAMN IF YOU'RE NOT" Martin starts stomping away. "WHY IN GOD'S NAME DON'T YOU JUST PICK UP A PHONE? IF EVERY TIME SOMEONE WANTED TO TELL SOMEONE SOMETHING THEY GOT THEMSELVES ARRESTED THIS WORLD WOULD HAVE TO BE ONE BIG JAIL" Leslie stomps right behind him. "IT *IS* ONE BIG JAIL FRCHRISSAKES DO YOU THINK IF I COULD DO THIS BY TELEPHONE I'D BE WASTING MY VALUABLE TIME FISHING AROUND IN YOUR UNDERWEAR?" Martin suddenly pivots and changes direction. "THEY'D NEVER BUY YOUR SUSPICIOUS-CHARACTER LINE ANYWAY LOOK AT ME I'M WEARING A SUIT" Leslie pivots without missing a step. "THEY WOULD IF I USED THE MAGIC WORD" Martin walks faster. "*WHAT* MAGIC WORD?" Leslie walks as fast as Martin. "RAPE. *THAT* MAGIC WORD! RAPE......RAPE............**RAYYY-YYYAPE! RAYYY-YYYAPE!**" Martin keeps walking. Leslie keeps screaming. **"RAYYY-YYYAPE! RAYYY-YYYAPE!"**

Martin doesn't sense Leslie behind him anymore. He hears the sound of fabric ripping, looks over his shoulder. Leslie is slouched against the thick glass door of the Crédit Industriel et Commercial, her sweatshirt on the ground by her feet, her t-shirt ripped, an arm and a breast hanging out of her halter. A crowd is starting to form around her. She's panting, holding her stomach, pointing to Martin, looking like she's trying to scream but can't get the words out. Martin shrugs his shoulders and pumps his palms toward the sky. Smiling, he walks back toward her, appreciating the joke. More people join the crowd, seeming to have materialized from nowhere. Leslie tries to straighten up. One woman helps her while another fetches the sweatshirt and drapes it across Leslie's bare shoulder and breast. Martin gets closer. He's chuckling, saying something about really outdoing yourself and sitting down at a cafe. An old man grabs his arms. Martin curses at him and tries to pull away. Leslie finds her voice "YES! HIM! HIM! TAKE HIM AWAY! LOCK HIM UP! TAKE HIM AWAY FROM ME! ANIMAL! YOU'RE AN ANIMAL! AAA-NIHHH-MAHHHLLL!". Martin feels a pair of hands on his right shoulder. "YESSS! HIMMM!" A pair of hands on his left shoulder. The policemen thank the old man and say they'll take over from here. Martin begins to speak. One of the officers twists his arms up behind his back. Leslie pushes the crowd away and runs up into Martin's face. As her left hand punches and pounds at his stomach "ANIMAL! ANIMAL!", her right hand drops the ticket into his pants. He looks stunned. As if he's watching it all happen to someone else. To a guy on a wavy television screen that he's too tired to get up from the sofa to straighten out. Again he tries to say something and the officer twists farther.

"You'll have to come to headquarters and make a statement, Miss," the other policeman says.

"Take him! Take him!" Leslie groans, holding her stomach as if nauseated. "I have to—I have to be alone...for a little while.....I have to..........take him.....I'll be there...I'll be there." Her voice trails as she walks off. "I'll be there."

Confused and enraged—like *he's* the one who's just been raped—Martin is led away. His short shallow victimized breaths alternate with long deep arrogant inhales. Every time he forms the beginning of a word the officers tighten their grip and shake him. He keeps forming, they keep tightening and shaking.

As they head into the Rue Croix des Petits-Champs, Martin in the middle with a cop deadlocked around each arm "Wait! Wait, officers, wait!", they hear Leslie again. "Please! Come back wait!" She's half-limping half-jogging toward them, her index finger in the air as if bidding to have her question acknowledged at a lecture. *"Merci, messieurs,"* she says in a weak, whiney, self-pitying voice which Martin wouldn't have thought she could produce even in high drama such as this. "I want to get a good, last look at him. You know? So I can identify him, yknow?"

*"Oui oui, mademoiselle."*

"At the station. Later. You know?"

*"Bien sûr, mademoiselle."*

Standing inches away, she scans Martin's body and face. "ANIMAL!" she shouts again in French, launching the crowd in front of the bank into a chorus of cheers. "I HOPE THEY LOCK YOU AWAY FOREVER!" she shouts in French. Some people who've followed her over echo her words, like at a gospel meeting. "YOU DON'T EVEN DESERVE TO GO TO A CIVILIZED JAILHOUSE!" she shouts in French. *"ON DEVRAIT VOUS JETER DANS UN TROU!"* The officers stand there patiently, offering Martin up to her for as long as she needs him to be there. She is yelling so quickly and so angrily that no one except Martin catches the English sentences laced into her ravings. *"DES GENS COMME VOUS NE MERITENT* REMEMBER THE MEDALLION! *PAS LA LIBERTÉ!* AND THE TICKET! *VOUS ETES L'INCARNATION DE LA SALETÉ MEME!* AND THANKS FOR THIS! YOU'RE A PAL! *AH! LES HOMMES—ILS SONT TOUS PAREILS!* OH—AND—MIGHT NOT BE A BAD IDEA TO KEEP IN MIND THAT IF THIS FUCKS UP, *LES PLUS COCHONS DES COCHONS!* THE SAME PEOPLE WHO KILL ME *LES PLUS SALAUDS DES SALAUDS!* WILL the Rue d'Aboukir. ("Hey I know! Sitting down! What a great idea! Wonder why Martin didn't think othat!.........................June twenty-sixth. June. Twenty-sixth...........................................Junetwentysixth. June twenty-sixth....*June* twenty-sixth *June* twenty-sixth *June* twenty-sixth *June* twenty-sixth *June* twenty-sixth *June* twenty-June twenty-sixth *June* twenty-sixth *June* twenty-sixth *June* twenty-sixth *June* twenty-sixth June *twenty*-sixth June *twenty*-sixth June *twenty*-sixth June *twenty*-sixth June *twenty*-sixth June *twenty*-sixth June *twenty*-sixth June *twenty*-sixth June *twenty*-sixth June *twenty*-sixth June *twenty*-sixth June twenty-*sixth* June twenty-*sixth* June twenty-*sixth* June twenty-*sixth* June twenty-sixth June twenty-sixth June twenty-sixth June twenty-sixth June twenty-sixth June twenty-sixth June twenty-sixth June twenty-") *"Un thé au lait, s'il vous plaît."* ("sixth June twenty-sixth June twenty-sixth June twenty-sixth June twenty-sixth June twenty-sixth June twenty-sixth June twenty-sixth June twenty-sixth June twenty-sixth June twenty-sixth June twenty-sixth June twenty-sixth June twenty- sixth June twenty-sixth June twenty-sixth June twenty-sixth June twenty-sixth June twenty-sixth June twenty-sixth June twenty-sixth June twenty-sixth June twenty-sixth June twenty-sixth June twenty-sixth") *"Merci!"* ("June twenty-sixth June twenty-sixth June twenty-sixth June twenty-sixth June twenty-sixth June twenty-sixth June twenty-sixth June twenty-sixth June twenty-sixthJune twenty-sixth June twenty-sixth June twenty-sixth June twenty-sixth June twenty-sixth June twenty-sixth June twenty-sixth June twenty-sixth June twenty-June twenty-sixth June twenty-sixth June twenty-sixth June twenty-sixth June twenty-sixth June twenty-sixth June twenty-sixth June twenty-sixth June twenty-sixth June twenty-sixth June twenty-sixth June twenty-sixth June twenty-sixth June twenty-sixth June twenty-sixth June twenty-sixth June twenty-sixth June twenty-sixth June twenty-sixth June twenty-sixth June twenty-sixth June twenty-sixth June twenty-sixth June twenty-sixth June twenty-sixth June twenty-sixth June twenty-sixth June twenty-sixth June twenty-sixth June twenty-sixth June twenty-sixth June twenty-sixth June twenty-sixth June twenty-sixth June twenty-sixth June twenty-sixth June twenty-sixth June twenty-sixth June twenty-sixth June twenty-sixth June twenty-June twenty-sixth June twenty-sixth June twenty-sixth June twenty-sixth June twenty-sixth June twenty-sixth June twenty-sixth June twenty-sixth June twenty-sixth June twenty-sixth June twenty-sixth June twenty-sixth June twenty-sixth June twenty-sixth June twenty-sixth June twenty-sixth June twenty-sixth June twenty-sixth June twenty-sixth June twenty-sixth June twenty-sixth June twenty-sixth June twenty-sixth June twenty-sixth June twenty-sixth June twenty-sixth June twenty-sixth June twenty-sixth June twenty-sixth June twenty-sixth June twenty-sixth June twenty-sixth June twenty-sixth June twenty-sixth June twenty-sixth June twenty-sixth June twenty-sixth June twenty-sixth June twenty-sixth June twenty-sixth June twenty-sixth June twenty-sixth June twenty-sixth June twenty-sixth June twenty-sixth June twenty-sixth June twenty-sixth June twenty-sixth June twenty-sixth June twenty-sixth June twenty-sixth June twenty-sixth June twenty-sixth June twenty-sixth June twenty-sixth June twenty-sixth June twenty-sixth June twenty-sixth June twenty-sixth June twenty-sixth June twenty-sixth June twenty-sixth June twenty-sixth June twenty-sixth June twenty-sixth June twenty-sixth June twenty-sixth June twenty-sixth June twenty-sixth June twenty-sixth June twenty-sixth June twenty-sixth June twenty-sixth June twenty-sixth June twenty-sixth June twenty-sixth June twenty-sixth June twenty-sixth June twenty-sixth June twenty-sixth June twenty-sixth June twenty-sixth June twenty-sixth June twenty-sixth June twenty-sixth June twenty-sixth June twenty-sixth June twenty-sixth June twenty-sixth June twenty-sixth June twenty-sixth June twenty-sixth June twenty-sixth June twenty-sixth June twenty-sixth June twenty-sixth June twenty-sixth June twenty-sixth June twenty-sixth June twenty-sixth June twenty-sixth June twenty-

## XX

# "SSSSHHHH!"
# "SSHH!"
# "Sh!-sh!-sh!-sh!"

"OK would you tell me *now* why it hadda fuckin be in the goddamn *library* frchrissakes!"

"I felt like reading a book."

"BUT YOUR N "

"SSSSHHHH!"

"*Excusez-moi, madame.* But you're not reading a book are you reading a book is that what you call reading a book you're sittin here whispering to me how's that reading a book frchrissakes?"

"I might get a sudden urge."

"Yeah plus you might wanna read a book. Yknow I don't have time for this shit, stuff piles up when you're engrossed in the exigencies of being kidnapped to Backstairs at the James Bond House I got stuff to d "

"I have no idea what you're talking about. You wearing it?"

"Of *course* I'm wearing it didn't I wear Katherine the Great?"

"No."

"Oh. Yeah. You're right. How quickly they forget. Well of *course* I'm wearing it..........This one would be too good not to wear. In fact, I may never t "

"Lemme see."

"Right here?"

"Open your trenchcoat."

"Look frankly I couldn't care less. All I gotta do is *live* in this town. A little indictment for *decent* exposure would "

"Don't flatter yourself."

" only help biz but *you*, on the other hand, can ill afford to have your oozy little mug plastered all over the "

"Open your trenchcoat."

"I don't think you get it—I'm wearing *it*. As in: *it*. Meaning, like, that's what I'm wearing. Like, I'm not wearing anyth "

"You all of a sudden getting prudish on me?"

"*On* you? Prudish *on* you? To get anything *on* you I'd need a rappelling device."

"Lemme see it."

"YOU KNOW WHAT IT "

"SSHH!"

" looks like frchrissakes you bought the thing didn't you? Or maybe not—maybe you had it spun up by your vast collection of polyesterworms."

"I have no idea what you're talking about."

"No—not possible. You wouldn'ta had time to get to Rio, choose worms of the right vintage, let the seamsperson outa the closet, have her piece it together, beat her, throw her back in the closet and get your felonious ass to Paris."

"I have no idea what you're talking about. Lemme see the thong."

"Not from Singapore."

"I have no idea what you're talking about."

"I mean, if you'd've kidnapped me to, say, Florida, then Rio woulda been doable. But *I* just got back, and you left later than me.....at least that's what Chan said—while he wasn't otherwise dizzying me with his breathrobbing—there's that word again— "

"Breath?"

"Rob."

"I have no idea what you're talking about."

" chit-chat about art, truth, beauty and the meaning of religious artifacts."

"I have no idea what you're talking about. Open it."

"Yeah Heaven knows that nonagenarian over there could use a quick n dirty flash of my well oiled—thanks, by the way—brilliant idea to send it with coconut body oil—though "

"You're welcome."

" you'll now hafta put my drycleaner's *second* son through Harvard's post-nuclear-brain-surgery program cause we're gonna hafta get the coat lining world-class cleaned—buttocks. To say nothing of the matching, color-coordinated breastal units. BUTT— "

"Sh!-sh!-sh!-sh!"

"*Excusez-moi, monsieur.* But if I open the coat and get dragged away, I probably won't be available on the twenty-sixth to rhrhrhuhnn mahee rhrhrhououtte ahzzz yyuuzzyyuuelle as "

"I have no idea what you're talking about."

" Jacques's diction coach dutifully instructed."

"I have no idea what you're talking about."

"What happened to the bad old days when you reserved entire rooms in restaurants so we could eat a pre-abduction peanut why does it hafta be in the fucking LIBRARY FRCHI "

"SSSSHHHH!"

"SSHH!"
"Sh!-sh!-sh!-sh!"

"That's why. I have no idea what you're talking about."

"You're not kidding are you?"

"About what? Why don't you try flailing with the other arm for awhile? This one must be getting tired."

"About not letting up about saying you have no idea what I'm talking about about Singapore."

"I have no idea what you're talking about."

"And Notre Dame."

"I have no idea what you're talking about."

"And the silkworms."

"I have no idea what you're talking about."

"And all that."

"I have no idea what you're talking about."

"Where's Patrick, by the way?"

"How should I know? Did you try calling his apartment?"

## XXI

## The Moon Walk

("Children are going walkpersonless in China frchrissakes the") third in two months. This one has a radio. Leslie sets the dial to all-news-all-the-time and secures the headphones under her sweatband. Leaving her wrist-purse next to the computer, she plucks out the keys and ID and puts them with a 100-franc bill ("Shit! I still owe George for") into a khaki-colored leather pouch she's unhooked from the coat-rack and strapped around her ("although when you think of all the precious time I spend giving him advice") waist.

She unlocks the door.

Goes back to the dinette table.

Framed by all the office supplies and tea paraphernalia and incoming faxes which have been crunched into piles to make room for it, yesterday's *International Herald Tribune* is folded so that the top half of the front page is displayed. Leslie runs her hand over the date above the masthead

June 25, 1992

then over the large photograph of two security agents—one in a business suit and one in a hard-hat and work clothes—passing through a thin opening in the city-within-a-city of barricading structures. Partly covering the huge bold headline

**SURPRI**
**THE PO**
**SECURI**

she folds the paper lengthwise and leaves.

"Leslie? Martin! I'm calling all my friends who are raving maniacs—all one of them—to tell them they were right. I gotta give that to you. Big of me—and the Mormon Tabernacle choir—I

KNOW. YOU WERE RIGHT. IT'S GETTING BETTER. IT *IS* GETTING BETTER. EVERY DAY IN EVERY WAY. THE STORM OF ANGER IS SLOWLY DISSIPATING INTO A LIGHT DRIZZLY FOG OF UNCONTROLLABLE RAGE. CALL ME." *BeeeeeeeeeeeeeP*****BeeeeeeeeeeeeeP*****

Locks the door behind her.

"I'M HAVING A RING MADE FOR YOU, LESLIE! TO MATCH MY MEDALLION. IT'S GOING TO BE INSCRIBED IN A MIXTURE OF HEBREW, ARAMAIC AND UCHARITIC AND SAY I'M-MORE-READY-THAN-YESTERDAY-TO-ABANDON-MY-IDEA-OF-HAVING-LESLIE-BRITTAIN-AXE-MURDERED-WITH-HER-DIAPHRAGM-CREAM-APPLICATOR.....AND-LESS-THAN-TOMORROW. ROMANTIC, HUH? CALL ME." *BeeeeeeeeeeeeeP*****BeeeeeeeeeeeeeP*****

Drops the keys into the pouch and slowly zips it on her way along the hallway....

"HEY YOU THINK YOU CAN GET ME MY MONEY BACK FROM MY CHIROPRACTOR? IT'S THE LEAST YOU CAN DO, DON'T YOU THINK? I'LL MAKE A DEAL WITH YOU: I'LL TAKE A COUPLE YEARS OFF THE MOLTEN FURY IF YOU TRY TO GET ME MY MONEY BACK. SEE, YOU HAVE TO PAY IN ADVANCE FOR EACH OF YOUR SERIES OF TEN SESSIONS AND SINCE DUE TO BEING OTHERWISE INCARCERATED I MISSED A TOTAL OF FUCK! THERE'S SOMEONE AT THE DOOR I'LL CALL YOU BACK. CALL ME." *BeeeeeeeeeeeeeP*****BeeeeeeeeeeeeeP*****

....down the stairs....across Mrs. Darotto's courtyard to the heavy wine-wooden door and its windowless, dark corridor. At the other end, with the mailboxes on her left and the entrance of the building before her, she stops. Hits the timed-light button, looks at her watch—Mr. Fontaine, in pajamas, strays back into his doorway—the digital dial shows: 5:58:33

Almost imperceptibly nodding to the rhythm of each passing second, she raises her head at 5:59:12. At 5:59:30 with a soft *click* of the little silver button in the quiet she releases the latch. The front door groans as she pushes it open.

There are horns and motor moans that do not belong in the air at this hour. It is bright outside—as if it has been daylight all night long. She stands square facing the mouth of the *passage*, shifting her weight impatiently from foot to foot. 5:59:50 begins to walk. 5:59:55 ..56..57..58..59 pushes the on-button of the Walkman... **"..*France-Info. Six o'clock:*"** ...runs left onto the Avenue Bosquet, up half a block into the racketous tangle of the Place de l'Ecole Militaire. ("Hello,

Soldier! Hello, Soldier! Hello, Soldier!") *"d morning. Paris is still recovering from the shock announcement yesterday that Pope John Paul Two will honor the city with a surprise visit today. Security forces from both the Vatican and the City of Paris have been working round-the-clock since one AM Thursday when it was learned that His Holiness would be celebrating mass just thirty-five hours later at the Cathedral of Notre Dame de Paris. Reaction around the city to the news has been varied and intense as rerouted traffic has come to a standstill in most areas, flights into and out of Orly have been suspended and a steady flow of the faithful from every corner of France has left virtually no hotel room or restaurant table unoccupied. We go now to Dominique Brive who was able to speak earlier this morning with the man responsible for turning Paris overnight into an armed camp, Alain Guérimet, Chief of Security Operations for the City of Paris."*

*"The coffee is flowing this pre-dawn at the Quai des Orfèvres as thousands of police, security agents, construction workers and members of the religious and diplomatic communities attempt to do in a day and a half what usually takes weeks if not months of planning and preparation. Monsieur Alain Guérimet, Chief of Security Operations for the City of Paris. What do you think of being called the Miracle Worker?"*

*"No time to think!"*

*"Did the recent attempt on the Pope's life have any influence on the type of security measures you're putting in place now?"*

*"Our job is to protect the Holy Father during his visit."*

*"Monsieur Guérimet, any word as to why this visit was not announced until yesterday?"*

*"Non."*

*"No word from the Vatican, the Elysée Palace?"*

*"Non."*

*"Will Mr. Mitterand be returning from his trip to Romania in order to welcome John Paul Two?"*

*"Non."*

*"Can you tell us what the Holy Father's agenda will be once he lands on French soil?"*

*"He'll be spending an hour down the street."*

*"On a more personal note, Monsieur Guérimet, do you remember when was the last time you had a good night's sleep?"*

*"Excuse me. I have to go."*

*"Thank you, Monsieur Guérimet. Monsieur Alain Guérimet, Chief of Security Operations for the City of Paris, of course referring to the world-renowned Cathedral, down the street, if you will, from Police Headquarters on the Ile de la Cité, Notre Dame de Paris, where Pope John Paul Two will be celebrating mass at noon today. This is the first time in papal history th "*

Already the traffic is hardening in the arteries of the *quartier*. ("What *is* this frchissakes, what, the *Pope* comin or something frchrissakes?") By the time Leslie gets to Invalides a couple blocks away "Hey! *Mon Empereur!* Hear The News? Pope's Comin To Town!" she's already passed four tour buses filled with ("Ninety-nine Bottles of Beer all the way from") nuns ("Orléans!") and a street-vendor selling red-plastic-bound pocket-Bibles from a card table. At sunrise. "What, *Mon Empereur*, are we gonna be lookin at at noon?"

*"nding as close to the Cathedral as she can get. Marie-José? What's it like down there?"*

*"Thanks, Christiane. Close is a relative term in this case. The Luxembourg Gardens is as far as I've made it. All access is barred from there up to the Seine.* ("Shit!") *Even for the press.* ("Especially for the press, horseface!") *They've put up big screens here as they have all over the city and we'll have to watch the event from the outside like everybody else. Already a crowd is forming, some people have been here since the announcement yesterday morning. There seems to be a little of everything around me—young and old, Levis and Chanel suits, Parisians an "*

At the corner of the Boulevard des Invalides and the Boulevard du Montparnasse Leslie considers turning around and going home.

This is exactly why she runs at exactly this hour on all those other days of her life when the Pope isn't making a surprise visit to a Cathedral she used to be supposed to be blowing up but isn't anymore but I still wouldn't leave town if I were you—so she can be back at Georges's before the entire city's up pressing to catch the last plane outa Saigon. What, *Mon Empereur*, are we gonna be lookin at at noon?

*"lutely right, Christiane, those are the questions on everybody's lips. Why such short notice?"* ("Wha—don't these ray-dee-oh broads know *anything* frchrissakes hey! wonder if Martin's still mad at m ") *"nts to know just what is the purpose of the Pontiff's sudden appearance at the Cathedral?"* ("It's to—frchri—Yo! Marie-José! I got that one—wait til I get there I gohh-ohht thirteen minutes and forty-one secs I'll be carryin a copy of War n Peace so you recognize me.") *"that given the assassination attempt last month in Johannesburg, the inside of the Cathedral will be strictly off-limits to everyone but John Paul Two and his small camera-crew. A mass without the masses. Marie-José Delorme. France-Info. At the Luxembourg Gardens.*

But she does not turn around.

*"Thank you, Marie-José. Word's has it that security in and around Notre Dame is so tight even the Pope won't be allowed in!"*

Does not go home.

*"Franco-Info. Six-twelve. When we return after this we'll see what the crowd gathered at the big screen under the Eiffel Tower has to say to Francis Dony about this history-making visit by John Paul Two."*

("history-preventing visit frchrissakes") She presses on outa Saigon with the rest of em, through the rest of em. Pretending they're invisible. Climbing the pizza-place sidewalks at the Montparnasse station. And they are. The cafes the one-star hotels. Pretending she's invisible. Multi-movietheatres magazine kiosks. Hyperventilating the magic oxygen from the pores of the Select. And she is. Cat n mousing the cars across the Boulevard Raspail. On the block up to the Closeries, weaving in and out of the Pilgrims. They're never both invisible at the same time, Leslie and the Pilgrims. Leslie and the      . The Pilgrims and    . When Leslie is invisible the Pilgrims are pumping their way along the pavement, pumping, spurting, like thick blood from a sick struggling silent heart. When the Pilgrims are invisible Leslie sees clear to the distant northern Basilica of Sacré Coeur seeming to sit tight atop the Luxembourg Gardens' regnant Medici Palace.

*"all the way from Lavandou! How many hours did it t "* "I can't do this." But there comes a point when one of them breaks the rules—a point somewhere along the middle of the beginning of the Boulevard St-Michel where one or the other forgets to stay invisible until one or the other finishes their visibility shift, a point right around the first of the bookstores—not the one with the poster of the teenaged beauty—who won't be about to be ravaged in that window much longer, because her artist's show is over July 1st—the bookstore after that—with the travel agency attached—there comes a point where Leslie sees the Pilgrims seeing Leslie seeing the Pilgrims and people start bumping into each other and looking at each other like they don't got a right to run on a piece otheir own sidewalk even though *you* just got off a goddamn *tour* bus *"sprawled out on blankets, sharing croissants and thermoses of coffee—at least I can only guess it's coffee, Christiane—well, if it's love the Pontiff wants to spread like he says he does, it looks like his message is working even without today's midday m "* from somewhere *else* and it isn't fun anymore making a game out of going around and through the wads of bodies and now people look fatter and more pimply and their teeth are rotting faster in their mouths than they did back there in Montparnasse and the skinny guy on skates she sees coming at her every morning obviously has not made it through the crunch alive ("frchrissakes")—at that point Leslie says "I can't do this." and slows finally to a walk and walks over to the curb to a black Peugeot 405 which has been following her since before the buses with the ninety-nine bottles of nuns.

There are three men in the car. Two in front, one in back. All in dark suits. ("Hmmm-mmm. The ollld dark-suited men in a darrrk carrr scene, huhhhh, rrrock n rollers? Hmmm-mmm.") They all look like they just lost their mother. Well, the driver and the guy in the back look like they just lost their mother and are sad about it. The other guy in the front— the youngest of the three—looks like he just lost his mother and is happy about it. He's reading something, thumbing through pages. Leslie approaches with the relaxed relieved gait of a runner who's just finished running. The car has slowed. ("Hmmm-mmm, rock n rollers, has that car slohh-ohhed, or is it just our rock n roll imaginayy-shuh-uhn? Hmmm-mmm?") She looks at her watch and pushes the headband up on her forehead. She had just started to sweat. *"France info. Six-*

*twenty-four. In other news, President François Mitterand will meet today w"*

*"Salut, Jacques!"* she says to the man in the backseat as she keeps pace with the car. Without moving his head, the driver raises his eyes and looks at Jacques in the rear-view mirror. The guy next to the driver—the one who's appreciative of his mother's recent passing—keeps leafing through his pornographic comic book. Maybe they don't understand her accent. Maybe they think she's just asking for directions. To Notre Dame for example. "You n thboys come out twatch the big Pope-show?" Leslie and the car are strolling together through the crowd down the Boulevard Saint-Michel. "That's *big* Pope-show not *big-Pope* show.....I mean from what I understand he's not a remarkably large individual...I mean physically speaking, that is of cWHOOOP!" She leaps sideways as Jacques grabs at her through his open window. The driver says something to the younger guy who turns around and pumps his hand up and down in front of Jacques's nose like a pornographic-comic-book-reading choir director asking for pianissimo.

Having made way for a sprawling band of scraggly adolescents, all carrying red-plastic-bound pocket-Bibles, Leslie struts back to the car. Which has stopped. She sticks her head through the driver's window "Oh I see your p—Wait! Wait!" then pulls out, raising her index finger and the "Sports Roundup!" volume on the Walkman. Thirty seconds later she's in again. "NFL's coming to Europe in August for exhibitions I see your pal's been allowed to choose from the honors reading-list this semester." As the contented orphan continues to ignore her, she notices he's wearing running shoes. Somehow that makes her uneasy. "Could—could you move your left thumb a little, you're blocking a buttock."

The car begins to roll once more, Leslie seeming unaffected by the change. Her head well through the window, she walks along, bent at the waist, chatting the guys up as if she were a hunchback with a car for a head sauntering down the boulevard to the Pope party. The driver behind them begins to honk her horn. And the driver behind her. And then drivers in remote lanes in remote boulevards, their vehicles calling to each other in some primal automotive tongue that scientists with hidden microphones have been trying to decode for decades. Like a caustic chemical through a blocked drain, the traffic is eating, eroding its way through the street. Half a block up, at the Rue Soufflot intersection, it is being stopped in its trajectory toward the Seine and sent off left past the main Gardens-entrance, down the Rue Medici, to be caught in the tightwoven cobblestoned clog of the sixth *arrondissement* and never heard from again.

The guy driving Leslie's head fishes under his seat. "Here. Allow me," she offers, trying, before he shoves her away, to help him reach his magnetized blue police-light through the window and plant it on the roof. "Listennnuhhh, I thought you guys might like to know my itinerary from here on out." Back to strolling upright, a head where her car used to be. "Yknow? Take that stressful guesswork outa tailing me. Leave your minds empt—free to concentrate on the chase."

The guy up front puts his comic book in the well beside him.

"Anyone...anyone got a pencil"

He takes off his suitjacket.

" n paper?"

The car stops.

"I can draw ya m "

He opens his door.

"Ayyyyyuhhhhhh......a map."

Gets out,

"Running shoes, huh?" Leslie's eyes flash Jacques sneering driver waiting traffic dragging sidewalk crawling Gardens filling guy in "running.....shoes....."

stretching.

"Iyyyuhh happen tooouhhh prefer Nike 180s. Myself."

Like he just woke up and is about to go put the coffee on.

**"Archbishop de la Minglière, when was your office informed that Pope J"** She doesn't even realize Marie-José and her pals have been hanging out in her head this whole time. Now wouldn't be a bad moment to ditch the Walkman if only she were aware it was attached to various parts of her body. You see now wouldn't be a bad moment because right now is that pulse-beat time-taken-out-of-time where one and a half million numbing years of walking upright and cooking food and making tools and conjugating verbs fall away in great sheets, leaving only the keen-edged animal-instant of awareness that now wouldn't be a bad moment to ditch the walkperson annnnnddddrrrrrrrrrrrrrrrrrrrrrrrrrrrrrrrrrrrrrrrrRRRRRRRRRRRRRRR RRRRRRRRRRRRRRRRRRRRRRRRRRRRRRRRRRRRRRRUUUU UUUUUUUUUUUUUUUUUUUUUUUUUUUUUUUUU UNLeslie lunges sideward/cop takes off around back of car/Leslie slams into couple with stroller pushes mother out of way stroller rolls /cop breaks through couple holding hands/small side-gate of Garden blocked with bodies too many bodies/she turns mid-air heads for main entrance/he leap-frogs over litter can heads for main entrance/microphone clipboard Marie-José *"Hold on, Christiane, there—there seems to be a distur—there's a young woman just ran past me into the Gardens like she was being chased by the devil himself—she is being chased, Christiane, a man in a suit and running shoes just"* "GOOD WORK, M-J, REMIND ME WHEN I GET OUTA THIS TO—Here!" Leslie tears walkperson off/hands like relay baton to nun must be eighty years old  "CHILDREN ARE GOING WALKPERSONLESS IN CHINAAAAA!"/looks back/cop close/she gets off main open expanse into trees near bandstand at right/can't see cop/no! dumb! not trees!/back to main open expanse/can't see cop ("jerk can't run as fast as m ")/sees cop/she flies down royal stairway to fountain-flowers-statues looks for bodies bodies/looks for big bulking bodies leads cop into bodies/she runs left around fountain/he runs ("Holy Shit!") right around fountain/she pivots heads back other way/ he sees what she's done pivots heads back other way/huge TV-news crew in his path/"HAH!" she pivots resumes original plan flies up matching royal stairway on other side of fountain/he punches preening TV-announcer out of way/cameraman points to stairway/cop pivots heads for stairway/she has good lead crosses trees refreshment kiosks to basketball court crosses court in middle of game ("at seven o'cl ") catches ball makes basket crowd cheers she smiles sees cop screams runs/he crosses trees guardhouse to basketball court eight huge black guys block him two short white guys do nothing he pulls gun guys move/she's off to back gate passes tennis courts miniature Statue of Liberty apiary more refreshment kiosks playground no kids only basketball players pony rides no kids only basketball players more statues bumps—slams—into runner ("GOH-OHDAMNRUNNERS!") boccie players/cop runs through boccie lawn kicks ball away ruins game/she's out back gate/Rue Guynemer/there's Jacques's car waiting for her/*THERE'S JACQUES'S CAR WAITING FOR HER?*/she looks back /cop on way/blue light flashing on Jacques's car's roof no traffic no other cars motherfuckers cleared traffic from Rue Guynemer while she and pal playing in Gardens ("Hoh-oh Lee-ee ")/she looks back/ here comes cop/car or cop? car or cop? car or ("COP!")/runs back into Gardens/cop grabs her/she kicks misses balls bites arm/he lets go/she turns/back on Guynemer/runs in direction car not pointing/ cop dives back into car/door slams tires screech car spins/she hits corner/flies across Guynemer/car misses her by inexistent measure/ feels fender on leg/runs straight ahead down Rue Vavin narrow lotsa traffic/car stays at corner/cop charges outa car/cop charges outa car as woman on corner shrieks as other car comes plowin down Guynemer at two hundred ks per into Jacques's door Jacques and car are dust Jacques's driver through windshield/Roque gets outa other car tears down Vavin after cop tearin after Leslie/cop hears Roque behind him/turns/shoots/Leslie looks back sees Roque *"LESLIE!"* hit ground/headband soaked with sweat eyes burning with sweat tired she trips on curb crossing Rue Notre Dame des Champs falls slams down on side of right knee sits on curb dizzy rubs knee looks up cop comes into focus standing at her feet.

"Need help?........Leslie?"

"Creative imagery.........Thierry."

"I said, need help?"

"*I* said, creative imagery." Thierry's shirt is soaked, transparent. He and Leslie are both hacking out cracked breaths. He extends his arm to help her up. "You see, there are two ways I can deal with this knee problem of mine," she says as if speaking to a friend over tea, ignoring his offer, sopping up blood with her torn tights. "I can get all nuts about it and do the ambulance-doctor-dope scene," Moving very slowly, she begins to unzip the pouch strapped against her stomach "or I can just relax, close my eyes" then raises her right hand to her eyes and casually brings it down to rest upon the pouch. "and imagine myself well again." Thierry's breathing is subsiding. He puts his hands on his hips. "I can imagine that I'm not sitting here in this silly position on the sidewalk with a bloody knee, torn tights......hurt pride." As she gets to her feet she slips her fingers into the pouch by imperceptible increments. "I can imagine something completely different. Somethinnng....healthier....safer....much more to my liking."

Her voice is very soft and very sweet. She's clamped onto Thierry's eyes and won't let go. "Like, for instance, that I'm standing here on the sidewalk with a *fine* knee, *clean* tights, and my pride" Out of the pouch she pulls Roque's gun. "pointing right at your head." And cocks the trigger. "That's called creative imagery."

Calm, unfazed, almost contemplative, as if trying to decide which of these two options would be best for Leslie, Thierry nods and looks toward the rooftops across the Rue Vavin. Leslie keeps her eyes and the gun on him except for the second when she remembers whose gun it is and glances past his shoulder down the street to Roque lying on the sidewalk Thierry kicks at the gun goes for his own/Leslie panics turns runs as best she can with her slammed knee he's shooting she still has her gun in her hand can't turn around run shoot breathe at same time/intersection Vavin and Raspail/northbound crawl/southbound zip/which is worse?/she's gridlocked in northbound lane on Raspail/where is he she doesn't see him doesn't see Thierry/can't get across/opens a door *"Bonjour, Monsieur,"* slides along back seat "off to see His Holiness?" opens other door *"Au revoir, Monsieur!"* gets out looks around doesn't see him/opens a door *"Bonjour, Madame,"* slides along back seat, "gettin any lately?" opens other door *"Au revoir, Madame!"* gets out looks around doesn't s"UH!"..........her ankle a hand around her ankle he's under *Madame*'s car and his hand's around h*"AAAHHHMERDE PUTAIN!"* she batteringrams her other foot into his fingers he opens his hand/she opens a door *"Bonjour, Madame,"* slides along back seat, "door squeaks—oughta get it fixed." opens other door *"Au revoir, Madame!"* gets out/across grassy island across southbound lane to Boulevard Montparnasse/hears a shot hears a shriek/looks back sees him/does a block blindly/at the Select "I can't do this I can do this I" no more energy no more adrenaline no more adrenaline no more pain in her knee now. Now pain in all her body. She seeps past the Select. Pivots. Doubles ("that's brilliant why didn't *I* think othat?") back. She's in the revolving door he's in the revolving door ("dumb") she's out the revolving door. Down Montparnasse downhill....downhill....her route in reverse....downhill she can't do this......"I can't do this".......her whole body's a huge hurt knee thudding down the sidewalk like a bundle of blood-soaked laundry.........she feels him behind her..........she's limping, hardly moving............she doesn't even remember she has a gun in her hand.......................................................

..................................................

"Leslie!"

"Here's what hhhh I suggest hh." He's walking beside her now.

"hhh-hhObviously you're h-hhrefraining from making a spectaclehhh of yourself" She's attempting to sound strong through her pain and exhaustion.

"Leslie!"

"because this hhamount of eye witnesses nobody hh neehh h nobody needs."

"LESLIE!"

At the Eglise Sainte Mère des Champs "Comeere" she stops, takes Thierry's hand—the one without the gun—in her hand—the one without the gun—and leads him over to the front steps. "I gotta sit down. We got a minute, don't we?"

"LESSS-LIEE-EE!"

"So here's the deal." She sits facing the boulevard, her elbows resting on her open knees "You ready?.....Thierry?", the gun dangling from her fingers.

Thierry is breathing hard but doesn't appear as tired as she is. "I got all morning.....Leslie." He stands in front of her. His hair is dripping onto his dripping shirt. "Well—at least til noon—I'd kinda like to go to mass." Packed into his pants pocket, his gun is pointing straight ahead.

"LESLIE!"

"Well I don't think this should take too terribly long really. We'll see what we can do." Leslie seems to be staring straight out at the person trying to get her attention. But she does not react to the sound of her name. "The way I figure it—what'd be best for your career and all—"

"LLEESSLLIIEE!" Every time Thierry turns around to see where that's coming from, the person looks off into the distance, at his watch, up the street, down the street, like he's waiting for a very irresponsible date.

"would be if we pooled our respective resources, put our heads together, worked as a team—yknow—and found some"

"M-MS. BR-BRITTAIN FRCHRISSAKES!"

"secluded back alley or—or even better—warehouse—some, yknow, emptyyy.....empty warehouse somewhere" Leslie slowly starts to stand. "and finished me off there." Thierry smiles but does not move. "Yknow? I mean, obviously if you wanted to slaughter me right here where Hemingway found his real-life characters for The Sun Also Rises, you—you did know that, didn't you?—right there—look—comeere a minute." She takes his arm and leads him to the sidewalk. "Look—right there—right on that very terrasse where that fat bitch is trying to look sexy aaaat...seven-thirty in the morning—right even at that very *table* is where—you ever read it?"

"What?"

"The Sun Also Rises frchrissakes you got a problem with attention span or what here?"
Leslie is now at the curb with Thierry standing next to her, his gun on guard, his attention only partly on her gun because he figures it'll do more harm lunging for it than letting it hang from her pinkie.
"So whadyuh say?" She backs up ever so slightly "Ready to go finish me" and in one movement turns, jumps onto the Harley and "OFF?" they're off!
Thierry shoots. Leslie screams and ducks and presses against Patrick. Thierry shoots. Patrick pulls a U, finds a sliver between a bus and a pedestrian, streams back in front of the church. Thierry shoots. Patrick shoots and Thierry drops.
"Frchrissakes Patrick We Have Work To Do!" Leslie shouts into the wind. "Yknow, public relations isn't like selling shoes at the mall, you leave it alone for two days and it multiplies like mold, we got faxes back there, faxes like you wouldn't believe, and there's the fucking Embassy list and you won't guess who called and left a message the other day remember that woman who wanted us to organize a dinner for the fiftieth anniversary of her church gr............................................................

\*

"What Dyah Mean You Can't Find Her, For The Love OGod?—

hold on—turn th "

"_ _ _ _ _"

"—hold on a mi—Turn That Fuckin Th—No! Only underground."

"_ _ _ _ _"

"I Gave You Fuckers The Coordinates I don't have em any more accurate nthat Will You Turn Th—hold on willya a mi "

"_ _ _ _ _"

"Whatrya wastin your fuckin time askin me for my source for? WhatdI call here, Interpol or the local brasserie you know I ain't gonna tell you my source for the love oGod whatdI call here? Look she gotta be there it's huge you just don't *disappear* a set-up like that it'd take half a year to make a set-up like that—what was it you called it?"

"_ _ _ _ _"

"Yeah off the face othe Earth it'd take half a year, just find er, is all, I ain't buyin she evaporates off the face of thWill You I Can't Hear A Fuckin Th—hold on a minute willyuh!" Cradling the receiver between his shoulder and ear, Marcel flaps his hands at two men sitting on a decayed sofa in his office, one in streetclothes, one in uniform, watching a portable TV wedged into a bookshelf. The man in uniform slowly rises and walks as in a trance, standing fixed for a moment in front of a tight close-up of John Paul Two before lowering the volume and returning to his seat. Marcel slams the "For The Love OGod!" phone down and struggles out of his chair. "OK! Show's Over! Time TKiss Me Good Night N Get Back TFuckin" He waves his right arm as he lumbers to the television and pummels the off-button with his left fist. "Work!"

"Hey you can't do that, Commissioner, that's the Pope!"

"Yeahhe can," the guy in streetclothes says. "He just did."

"What, ynever seen the Pope before, this the first time yever seen the Pope, you need *my* fuckin TV to see the Pope frthe first time?"

The cops raise their hands to their heads in mock fear while Marcel bends over the sofa to swat at them. "Get the fuck outa here don't you losers got work to do *I* got work to do." As if pantomiming, he opens his door as wide as it will swing and makes a gallant sweep of his arm toward the hallway. "It ain't like the moon walk for the love oGod, you seen the Pope before!"

"You still believe that shit, don't you, old man?" the plainclothes cop asks as he walks out. "Everyone knows the moon walk was filmed in Hollywood. The old man still believes in Father Christmas, too!"

The guy in uniform follows. "All I know is I'm glad *I'm* goin home, and I'll be glad when the *Pope* goes home."

"Goes home from where?"

"Well from *here*, Commissioner, where else from?"

"Who said the Pope was ever here?" Marcel asks as he shuts the door and lopes across his office to the windows. Looking up the Seine toward the barricaded Cathedral, he selectively sees only the streaks of sun on the water and the stains of age on the stones. He pries his wallet from his back pocket and, working his bulky fingers with great care, pulls a minuscule pie-wedge of paper from a flap behind the bills, unfolding it then unfolding it again so that it becomes a disk, about an inch in diameter. As he has countless times before, he reads the message on it. A message written in letters so minute, with a pen point so fine, that its words look like little insects nibbling their way to the other side. He waves his free hand toward the window, as if talking to someone in the office, or maybe someone on the river. Or on the wind. Or in the sunlight. Then refolds the tiny disk, so he can put it back in his wallet for safe keeping, making sure, as always, to crease the paper in such a way as not to touch the signature:

*M.M*